TOURIST

BY *Gerald Green*

TOURIST

by

Gerald Green

DOUBLEDAY & COMPANY, INC.
GARDEN CITY, NEW YORK   1973

All of the characters in this book are fictitious, and any
resemblance to actual persons, living or dead, is purely
coincidental.

ISBN: 0-385-04284-1
Library of Congress Catalog Card Number 73–83592
Copyright © 1973 by Gerald Green
ALL RIGHTS RESERVED
PRINTED IN THE UNITED STATES OF AMERICA
FIRST EDITION

For *Scott Meredith*

For my part, I travel not to go anywhere,
but to go. I travel for travel's sake.
The great affair is to move.

—*Robert Louis Stevenson*

THREE WORLDS: 20 days, from $1,135 including jet fare.
LONDON   PARIS   BERLIN (EAST & WEST)   VIENNA
BUDAPEST   LENINGRAD   MOSCOW   ISTANBUL
JERUSALEM   ROME:

For diversity, excitement and beauty, nothing can match THREE WORLDS, PLANET TOURS brand new, all-class jet marvel!

This 20-day magic carpet affords PLANET clients a look at three fascinating worlds—the great cities of Western Europe, the mysteries of Eastern Europe, and the inspiration of the Holy Land! One glorious adventure combining all three!

Whether it be a champagne night at the naughty Lido in Paris, or *Tannhauser* at the Vienna Opera, or a stroll inside the Kremlin, or a moment of reflection in Jerusalem's Old City, THREE WORLDS offers something for every traveler. This wide-ranging tour is the result of PLANET's experts five years of careful planning—unique, varied, diverting, bridging centuries, brimming with entertainment, intellectual fulfillment, and the greatest shopping on earth!

—from the 1975 MASTER TOUR BOOK
OF PLANET TOURS, INC.

Day 1: Depart USA, from JFK Airport, non-stop overnight Jet Flight to Swinging London!

Dr. Wicker was debating whether to buy one or two air-flight insurance policies when a soft-voiced man in a gray suit appeared at his elbow.

"Take 'em both," he said. "They're a bargain. Rates were lowered last month."

"Humm." Wicker nodded. "It isn't much, is it? Should I take out policies on my wife also?"

"I'd advise it."

"But it's like making a bet I don't want to win." Wicker, an orthodontist, was staring at the man's teeth. When the fellow in the gray suit smiled Wicker perceived some protrusion of the maxillary incisors.

"Have you decided, sir?" the girl at the insurance counter asked.

"Both, please. Just in my name."

Addressing the envelopes, the dentist realized the man was still at his side—a blond crew-cut chap in his thirties. He had no sideburns and wore a blue insignia in his lapel.

"You with Planet Tours?" Wicker asked. He licked the stamp and affixed it to the envelope on which he had written:

> Arnold Wicker, DDS
> Old Logging Road,
> Riverford, Conn.

"Government."

"What'd I do?"

"Not a thing. Maybe there's something you can do for us."

"Us?"

"The United States Government."

"I'm on a pleasure trip. I'm leaving in less than an hour." Wicker peered into the man's frozen smile. "Say, that's a nasty problem you've got with your incisors. In three visits I'd fix you up."

"I'm sure you could, Dr. Wicker. And I know all about your trip. Leaving for London on BIA 776. Traveling with Mrs. Wicker."

"Who is waiting for me at the newsstand right now."

The man took out his wallet and showed Arnold Wicker a card encased in plastic. The orthodontist read JOHN T. LELAND, CENTRAL INTELLIGENCE AGENCY. The lettering was overprinted on an official seal.

"Oh, come on," Wicker said. "What is this, a Rotary Club gag? Just because I agreed to be fall guy at the Riverford Old Timers' Luncheon . . ."

With a firm assertion of power, Leland grasped the dentist's elbow, steering him away. "It's a small thing, Doctor. We do this often with reliable citizens. I'll buy coffee."

Wicker—he was a gangling man in his late thirties, with an innocent long-jawed face and tousled dark brown hair—allowed himself to be directed toward the coffee shop.

"My wife . . ."

"Wave to her when you pass the newsstand. Tell her you'll be back in ten minutes."

Arnold Wicker frowned. "I'm not sure I want to do this."

"You haven't heard what it is."

Wicker looked toward the coffee shop: no sign of Rose-Anne. No matter. They had lots of time until departure.

An elderly couple was standing in the doorway of the coffee shop, each carrying a purple Planet Tours bag. The man stood straight and stiff as if favoring an ancient pain in his body. He wore a black homburg and a black topcoat. His wife was very small. Her white hair was combed into coquettish waved bangs. She noticed Dr. Wicker's purple flight bag and grinned at him. The dentist frowned at two rows of nicotine-browned teeth.

"Three Worlds? Are you with us?" Her voice was deep. She wore lavender slacks and backless green bedroom slippers.

"Ah, yes."

Leland directed Wicker toward a rear table. When they had ordered coffee, he spoke quickly in a persuasive tone. "This is simple. We do this every day with people we consider reliable. We've checked you out. Leading citizen of Riverford. Orthodontist. Community work. PTA. Little League. Conservationist."

"How's my serve?"

"What?"

"My serve. My *tennis*. You seem to know everything else."

"Terrific. You play a steady game."

"Rose-Anne and I have won the husband-and-wife doubles trophy three years running at the Riverford Swim and Tennis Club."

Did the man look annoyed? Bothered by Wicker's attitude? He pulled out a small folder, which the dentist saw was an itinerary. "You'll be in Moscow on the twenty-ninth and thirtieth."

3

"Hey, I'm not sure I want to get into this. I've read about tourists being jugged."

"Doctor, take my word. This is absolutely routine."

"How do I know you're you?" Wicker laughed. His boyish face tried to minimize his doubts.

"Call the FBI office in New York. They have a man on duty. He'll vouch for me."

Dr. Wicker sipped his coffee. "I get it. You're from Internal Revenue. You don't like the idea I'm going to visit orthodontists in different countries and claim a partial tax deduction. Mr. Leland, I checked that out with my tax accountant, and it's kosher—"

"What's kosher? Where's da corned beef?"

An enormous fat man, trailed by five or six people, all rigged for travel, laden with cameras, totes, newspapers, and Planet Tours bags, lurched against the table where the dentist and the agent sat. Hot coffee danced from Leland's cup into his lap.

"Sorry, pal. I was doped."

Wicker laughed. The fat man wore a checked pork-pie on his jowled, beet-red face. He had a thick orange mustache, orange eyebrows, and shaggy orange sideburns. A mahogany cigar the size of a billy club sprouted from his mobile mouth. Ashes sprinkled over the CIA man.

"Watch it, goddammit," Leland said.

Wicker looked warily at him. The friendliness had gone, replaced with something hard and mean.

"Herbie, apologize, for Chrissake," a small pretty blonde woman cried.

"Sorry, pal. I *said* I was sorry. *Gottenu,* they don't make these coffee shoppes for size 54 portly."

The party surrounding huge Herbie made a tour of the shop, found no seats, and left.

"Tour mates," Leland said sourly. Wicker didn't like his tone. It connoted a shared secret, contempt for Herbie and his friends.

"I get along with people."

"That's why we're asking you to help us. We like people who get along with other folks."

Outside the glass doors of the coffee shop Herbie and his party—it seemed to have grown in number—had apprehended the old couple, the man in the black homburg and the woman wearing scuffs. As the door swung open, Wicker heard Herbie's bellow: "Hoo boy, do we have a swinging group! Lady, you sure you don't wanna cancel?"

"Read this," Leland said.

4

Wicker, resentful of the man's do-it-my-way briskness, took a letter from him. The letterhead was official. The eagle glared at the dentist.

> . . . perform a service for the United States Government of a confidential and important nature . . . no risk involved nor anything illegal and at all times . . . protection of your government and its consulates, embassies, and representatives abroad. . . .

Mr. Bettenhausen glowered at the wedge of grayish cheese. In the gloom of the elegant airport restaurant it appeared singularly ill favored.

"Waiter," he called.

"Yeah?"

"Yeah? *Yeah?* Are you not trained to say 'Yes, sir'?"

"Look, Mac. I'm a fireman. I do this in my spare time. You're lucky you got the cheese. Between seven and midnight only main courses."

"Send me the headwaiter."

"Now, Betts," Mrs. Bettenhausen said. "It's only cheese."

"He's havin' his dinner."

"The manager."

The young man's lip curled. Warren Bettenhausen raised a hand. "I beg you do as I bid, sir. Moonlighting is illegal and the fire commissioner is a personal friend."

Two tables away—Bettenhausen had a potent theatrical voice—a man turned to watch him. His head was hairless and gleaming.

"More is at stake than cheese," Bettenhausen said.

"I know. But maybe we'll find a decent waiter in London. Or Berlin. Or Istanbul."

Bettenhausen sniffed from a plastic nasal inhaler and gazed at the behemoth jets moving on the runway, shrouded in night lights, hiding their power in ponderous maneuverings. He sensed the mystery of the moment, the imminent wonders—and resented the bad cheese more than ever. Bettenhausen was a stout, white-thatched, white-bearded man, sharp-eyed, deft in his movements, flamboyant in his dress. For travel he favored a beige hacking coat and a hound's-tooth vest. Under his bristling whiskers a floppy white and black polka dot bow tie nested. Cornelia Bettenhausen was lean, with frizzy blue-rinsed hair. Like her husband, she had an alert knowing look about her. But it was softened with tolerance. Warren Bettenhausen's pouched eyes did not tolerate fools or knaves or rude waiters.

The bald man, two tables away, caught Bettenhausen's eye. "I heard that waiter," he called. He had a harsh voice. It seemed to issue from the top of his head. "It's Roosevelt's fault. I employ two hundred

5

and sixteen people, and they aren't worth a damn any more. Reuther was a Red and Meany isn't much better."

"Don't respond," Mrs. Bettenhausen said. A scarlet flush was rising in her husband's face, so fiery that it seemed to infuse his white beard with a roseate tinge.

"My own fault for talking so loud," Bettenhausen growled.

"Don't look now, but he has a Planet bag. A fellow member of Three Worlds."

"You say Three Worlds?" he called out in a voice that seemed to reach a high E over C. "Three Worlds? I'm on Three Worlds. Wattle's the name. Horace T. Wattle. You've heard of Wattle Rubber."

Cornelia Bettenhausen smiled. "I believe so . . ."

"Corny," Bettenhausen rumbled, "we are not even aboard the plane and I am having grave doubts about this venture. You are no madcap heiress and I am not a penniless reporter. We are the better side of sixty. How will it be, cooped up on buses, hotels, museums, with people we don't know, and most of whom I will hate?"

"We promised ourselves this. To celebrate your retirement."

"Hmph. Retirement. Fired by the conglomerate."

"Something wrong? The cheese?" The manager had materialized in the gloom. Bettenhausen squinted at a furtive face, a black mustache.

"In this gold vellum broadside of a menu, created at great expense by some posh advertising agency, I am promised imported Brie cheese. My good man, look at this blob. It is not Brie. It is not imported. I doubt that it is cheese."

"You don't like it, don't eat it."

"I shall not eat it, and I shall make sure that the world knows about your boorish treatment of customers. My wife and I are journalists and we shall sound the clarion." (This was not the case but Bettenhausen had found it effective.)

"You can do what the hell you want. I did you a favor letting Charlie serve you at all."

There was a rumbling noise, as if deep in Bettenhausen's 240-pound body lava was beginning to bubble. "Now, sir, listen carefully. You will not charge me. Not a penny. Not for this smear of library paste or the lukewarm tea or the stale coffee. If you dare to make an issue of this or present me with a bill, you will be reported at once to the Port of New York Authority, the Better Business Bureau, the American Restaurant Association, and the Dining Out editor of the New York *Times*, with whom I am on a first-name basis. I shall also write to the Consumer Protective Agency of New York, the Federal Bureau of Standards, and the Associated French Cheese Producers and Importers. If you dare to challenge me on this, you will regret it. Come along, Cornelia."

Several huffing attempts were needed before Bettenhausen got to his feet. The manager retreated a few paces. He and his fireman-waiter exchanged a few curses. The latter made a cuckoo gesture—wheeling a finger at the side of his head.

"Say, I heard that," Mr. Wattle cried as the Bettenhausens walked by. "I have a seven-million-dollar plant in Bay Landing, that's near Seattle, and I can't get a lick of work out of them, thanks to Truman. Are you people with me? Let's sit together. . . ."

Bettenhausen's pupils disappeared into his skull. His beard trembled. "Air. Air." He took his wife's arm, and they walked away.

The bald man was on his feet, a napkin tucked into his collar, waving a fork after the Bettenhausens. "People think I'm kidding, but it's the truth."

In queenly isolation, Louise (Lulu) Flemington sat on top of the tallest of her fourteen pieces of luggage. There was style to everything Lulu did. Marooned in the midst of a bustling air terminal, plaid coat draped on her spare shoulders, gray-gloved hands resting on the ivory umbrella handle, her fine-boned face (ravages hidden by artful cosmetics and outsized sunglasses) tilted high, she conveyed an air of bred-in-the-bone superiority. People tended to move around her, to stare, and to speculate.

From several yards distance she appeared astonishingly beautiful—a firm chin, a small nose, a serene forehead, the bouffant lacquered crown of ash-blonde hair. On closer inspection, brittleness was evident.

"Excuse me, but isn't that a Della Chiesa original?" a dainty young man in a yellow suit asked. Arm on hip, head tilting, he knew class when he saw it.

The manner in which Mrs. Flemington raised her head to reveal nostrils and the corded underside of an arrow-shaped chin had its effect. The young man retreated.

She crossed her legs atop the custom-made Gucci (it contained a separate compartment for dirty laundry) and gazed on the swarm of early autumn travelers. A minuscule oriental couple, chattering, both dressed in high mod fashion—Day-Gloed bells, cable-knit sweaters, leather sandals—skittered by. Both carried Planet bags. For a moment Lulu was not certain what to think. Were they on Three Worlds? If so, what would her attitude be? At the moment, she had no pigeon-hole for Chinese or Japanese, little people speaking slangy English and wearing expensive (if outlandish) clothing.

7

Crude people who could not hold a knife or fork properly. Perhaps . . . Negroes. Fear shivered her hard-corseted figure, the long white sheath that molded her sagging flesh into a hard continuous line. Why, why had she allowed Harry to talk her into this awful thing? And now . . . right at the start . . . this business with the luggage. . . .

She saw her husband approaching. Harry was calm. His dark face showed patience, understanding. His rugged figure was full of confidence. The clothes helped: a country gentleman in a blend of suede and tweed and cavalry twill. (The squire of Grosse Pointe they called him behind his back at the club.)

"Sweetheart, it's all straightened out," Harry Flemington said.

Lulu got up, balancing on her umbrella. She seemed to be hiding in a fortress of 24-inchers, valet bags, totes. "Harry, I wish to go home. It is not too late to cancel this."

"Jesus, get a load of them bags."

A bloated orange man in a comedian's pork-pie, blowing clouds of smoke into the terminal (it was Herbie) and trailed by a group chattering in harsh New York voices, strolled by. "Nothin' like travelin' light. Or else they're a vaudeville team."

"Herbie, shaddap," a woman snapped.

"I wish to go home," Lulu said.

A sweating young man, wearing a purple armband with the Planet insignia—a globe circled by lightning—was at Harry Flemington's elbow.

"Darling, this is Mr. Trapani from Planet," Flemington said. "It's all a misunderstanding. You can carry all the luggage you want on the tour."

"Why was I advised differently?"

"The girl at the check-in counter was misinformed, Mrs. Flemington," Trapani said. He mopped his forehead. He had just learned what Louise Flemington's maiden name was, what she meant to various corporations, board chairmen, stockholders. Trapani understood. The guy seemed decent enough, this Flemington in his tweedy coat and suede hat. But one look at Mrs. F. warned the Planet agent. *Trouble. Letters to the president.*

Trapani patted his lips. "The young lady was talkin' about on the other side, Mrs. Flemington. You can check anything you want on the plane, and pay the extra weight, like I explained to Mr. Flemington."

"That is no problem," Harry said.

"When you get to London, as the tour escort will explain, you are allowed one big bag, plus whatever else you can carry."

8

"I do not carry anything except a purse and an umbrella."

"Right, right, Mrs. Flemington. Now, the company *does* allow extra valises, at a cost of nine dollars per bag for handling. Usually we restrict these extras to three bags. I mean, as any tour man will tell you, luggage is our biggest worry, checking them in and out, planes, buses, hotels." Mr. Trapani seemed to sink a few inches. "However, seeing it's *you*, and seeing how important this is, I checked the New York office and it's perfectly all right for you to take *all* your bags along, provided the charge of nine dollars per bag is paid in London. Fair enough, Mr. Flemington?"

"Of course. Dear, I think Mr. Trapani has been very helpful, and I want to thank him. Can you get us a few porters?"

Lulu walked away in search of a seat.

"Hey, make room for a lady," Herbie shouted. "Give her a seat, Flo." He and his party had commandeered a half-dozen black naugahyde chairs. Lulu saw his looming figure, the foolish mustache, sniffed the cigar, and did a prompt about-face. Silently she cursed Harry, Dr. Crichton, her friends at the country club for insisting she take a tour "with other people."

"Looks like we ain't wanted," Herbie muttered.

Mrs. Flemington retired to a distant corner. A small gray priest, riveted to his breviary, was seated across from her. At least he would be silent and undemanding.

Flemington had just given Trapani twenty dollars.

"Really, sir, it isn't . . ."

"But it is. You were very helpful."

"Thank you, thank you. After all, it isn't every day that a member of the Deaver family goes with us. I mean, when I found out Mrs. Flemington's maiden name. Wow."

"I'm sure you'd be as courteous to anyone."

Trapani shrugged. "Of course. But knowing who she is, and so forth . . . Anything else, sir?"

Flemington shook his darkly handsome head. It was a face that would have been even better-looking were it not for the eroded lines around the mouth and chin. *Brothers,* he was thinking, he and Trapani, servitors to the queen.

Immediately on leaving Flemington, Trapani realized that the doll-sized oriental couple were on his tail.

"Yes, yes, in a minute, Mr. Yasuda," Trapani said. "As soon as I send this message."

Planet, a "specialized" tour organization, had no office of its own at the airport. Trapani went to the public cable desk and wrote a message.

9

PLANETTOUR LONDON
ATTENTION VIRGIL PLEASE GIVE VIP TREATMENT FLEMINGTONS AR-
RIVING FOR THREE WORLDS SHE IS FORMER LOUISE DEAVER DETROIT
HOLDS AUTOMOTIVE PATENTS WORTH MILLIONS ON TOP OF MILLIONS
PERSONAL CLOSE FRIEND BOARD CHAIRMAN THEY TRAVELING AT
LEAST FOURTEEN PIECES LUGGAGE MANDATORY THESE BE HANDLED
THROUGHOUT REGARDS

                                                        TRAPANI

Reading it over, Trapani nodded, approving his foresight. Virgil
was one of their best escorts.

"Hey, fellah," Murray Yasuda cried. "Just one question . . ."

"Yes, yes, Mr. Yasuda."

"How come me and Sandra never got a hotel list? We had to make
a special trip to get these crummy flite-paks, and mine's ripped
already."

"I am sorry, Mr. Yasuda. Perhaps your local travel agent made a
mistake."

"Baloney." Mr. Yasuda was an inch or so under five feet tall, but his
golden face and his snapping black eyes were full of authority. "You
guys blew it. I want a hotel list, or at least where we are staying in
London. I got business deals cooking and my partner has to reach me."

"Of course, Mr. Yasuda. I shall find out."

"I mean, nothing personal, guy, but the client's got rights also.
Here's my card. In case you ever get to California look us up. Me
and Sandra'll spring for the Ten Ingredient Soup."

Dialing the New York office, Trapani studied the card:

YASUDA'S IMPERIAL PALACE
Japanese, Chinese & Polynesian
Restaurant
Victorville, California   6780 East Lee Road

"I'm afraid I cannot get anyone," Trapani said weakly.

"That's a bummer," Mr. Yasuda sneered. Yet he did not look angry,
merely full of ancient wisdom, a tiny man who knew a great deal. "If
I ran my joint the way you guys run your tours I'd be on Bankruptcy
Street in a week."

"I'm sorry, Mr. Yasuda."

"No hotel list. No flite-paks. You sure we got plane seats?"

"I'll check you in personally, sir."

Murray Yasuda dug into the slashed pocket of his green denim bells.
He had seen the dude in the suede hat, the one rapping about the
luggage, hand Trapani a bill. Nobody topped Murray Yasuda. He

10

peeled a twenty from a gambler's roll and shoved it at Trapani. "You're faded, pal. Lead the way."

Father Konay pretended to be reading his breviary. Actually, folded on top of an appropriate evening prayer was a newspaper clipping from his home-town newspaper, the Ash Valley *Tribune*. The article had a hideous fascination for him, and he could not keep from returning to it.

OSPREY CHIEF DEMANDS KONAY BE OUSTED

Edward Marciniek, Exalted First Nester of the Ash Valley United Order of Ospreys, today demanded that the service organization's governing board, the Swoop, vote immediately to oust Father Stephen Konay as chaplain.

"I accuse Father Konay, whom I have always respected up to now," Marciniek said at a press conference at the UOO Nest, 1456 John F. Kennedy Plaza, "of conduct unbecoming a Brother Osprey. I speak for a majority of the members of the UOO in this demand, I am certain."

Mr. Marciniek, flanked by two members of the Swoop, Mr. Paul Kapuchinski, Second Exalted Nester, and Mr. Costic Radzovic, First Bird, accused Father Konay of "radicalism, agitation, and abuse of his post as chaplain." He said that the priest's statement at the last meeting of the Ash Valley Human Relations Commission, asking for open membership in the UOO and admission of Negroes, was "a violation of his trust as a loyal Osprey."

Father Konay, 64, is pastor of the Sacred Heart Church of Ash Valley, a post he has held for 27 years. . . .

The prayer book—Father Konay turned the article face down— offered no solace. Would there be balm for him in this twenty-day trip to distant places? He knew why he was going. The Laymen's Committee of Sacred Heart were getting him out of town until the angry Ospreys drew in their talons. "Conduct unbecoming a Brother Osprey . . ." With a wry grin, the priest wondered: Is there anything more sinful than to behave in a manner unbecoming an Osprey?

Sighing softly, and staring, perhaps a moment too long, at the legs of the attractive middle-aged woman opposite him, a woman wearing a coat that breathed money and status, he closed the prayer book, shut his eyes, and tried to imagine himself enjoying his junket. He would have to enjoy it. He had no choice. It was a gift from the Laymen's Committee, from the good people of the parish, a reward for the old shepherd.

Like fun it is, Father Konay told himself. It is a gift aimed at getting rid of me. And the irony of it was, he didn't care one way or the other whether the Ospreys, or the Volunteer Firemen, or the Little League Executive took in "colored." He'd never given it much thought. Ash Valley did not have many black folks. Most of them were silent and tractable. It was that darn Father Folker, fresh out of Fairfield University, with his beard and his beads who started it. *Folker.* Konay had to admit he was a brainy one. Folker had told him that the Osprey affair was the place to make a stand, to force the Marcinieks and the Kapuchinskis to prove they were truly obedient to the will of God and the Pope. . . .

"But why me?" Father Konay had asked as they sipped Four Roses in the drafty old chancery.

"Because, Steve, you are one of *them.* They hate my guts. Some of their members smashed my guitar. If I tell the Ospreys or Volunteer Firemen to take in blacks, they'll harden their hearts even more. But you, Steve, they trust you and they listen to you. . . ."

Like fun. Folker apologized after Marciniek's denunciation. But what good did it do? Father Stephen Konay was finished in Ash Valley. He had a shivery feeling that the Laymen's Committee would talk to the bishop while he was rattling around Europe and get him transferred.

Oh, but his thoughts were too much on his own selfish desires. He studied the pretty woman, trying to forget himself. A man approached her.

"Darling, it's arranged," Flemington said. "As many bags as we want."

"Isn't there an executive lounge?" Lulu asked. Father Konay was surprised by the whiskey hoarseness in her voice. He'd expected something finer. It was the kind of deep womanly voice he heard from the richer golfing members of Sacred Heart.

"There is, Lu, but it's all the way at the other end. If we were on TWA, we could go right to the Ambassador—"

"Why aren't we on TWA?"

"It's a package, darling, and we have to fly whatever the arrangements are. I'm told first class on British International is marvelous."

Father Konay suffered for the man. He heard the plaintive note in Flemington's voice. It was consoling to him that the rich had their problems. Was this, he wondered, why people took—or were sent on—long trips? To resolve worries? Baby their neuroses?

He returned to the breviary, looking for an appropriate reading. *Jesus, therefore, being wearied with his journey* . . . No, no. It was not right to compare his excursion with the Lord's suffering. Closing the book, he thought about Jerusalem and Rome, the last cities he would visit.

Under pressure Huggins was cool. If terror sometimes ravaged his bowels, he betrayed nothing. A Bronx Irishman, a handsome ruddy man with an impish grin and shrewd eyes, he manipulated the world in a casual way. Barbara, his wife, admired these qualities. Hence she was upset to see him edgy as they checked in at the BIA desk.

"Any hand luggage?" the girl asked.

"Two flight bags," James Patrick Huggins said. "My wife's got this big sort of a sack, and my camera bag. Okay?"

It was not like Jimmy to ask anyone if *anything* was okay. Barbara, who showed the world a beautiful pained white face, full of uncertainties and cosmetics, wondered what was eating him.

"You're supposed to have *one* piece of hand luggage but it's a rule that's never enforced. That's *some* camera bag. It's the kind of leather you want to stroke."

Huggins lifted the camera case, joining the girl in mutual admiration. "Had it made up. I'm a camera nut. It carries everything I need and lots of film."

"Pigskin?"

"Peccary. Wild pig. Off the hide of a busted cop."

"Oh, Mr. Huggins." The girl did not get the joke (nor did Barbara) but she smiled anyway. Huggins made people smile. His face was chiseled, a cleft jaw, a broad forehead, black curls suggesting an Easter Rebellion bhoyo. Street-smart intelligence glinted in his blue eyes. Bronx Irish traits of speech, *v*'s substituting for *r*'s (*Vegan's Bahv & Gvill makes a gveat Bloody Mavy* for *Reagan's Bar & Grill makes a great Bloody Mary*), endowed him with a roguish charm. But he was Fordham-educated, college and law school, and he could fake his way through a conversation on Vivaldi or James Joyce or Modigliani. An appealing tough guy, he always seemed at home, whether in a Pelham gin mill, or a P.E.N. Club cocktail party, or a board room.

"Why you so nervous?" Barbara asked him. They walked toward the waiting room. As usual, they were late, squabbling over what to wear, what to carry, racing from the six-room apartment on East Eighty-ninth Street, as their two baby girls shrieked and hurled themselves at the door, and Barbara sobbed over leaving them with her mother.

"My jockey shorts itch."

"Don't be fresh. I was honestly innarested."

"For a change. Instead of the kids or your relatives."

13

Barbara narrowed her thickly blued eyes, touched her beehive of lustrous black hair, folds and waves and cunning caves of darkness. It was not like Jimmy to indulge in self-pity.

"When you gonna cut your hair?" Huggins asked.

"I like it this way."

"Yeah. Great for a big night at Loew's Paradise."

Barbara wobbled on spike heels. Her projecting behind, wrapped in an iron girdle and black silk, attracted hungry stares. Huggins, for his part, was looking arrogantly at a tall woman—it was Rose-Anne Wicker, the orthodontist's wife—coming out of the newsstand. The woman had an angular athletic look about her. She wore low-heeled shoes, a severe gray suit, and had large features. Her lank blonde hair fell to her shoulders. There was not a trace of make-up on her face. Huggins found her unbearably provocative.

"You're staring," Barby whined.

"So? You take a good look also. Women don't wear those whorehouse spikes any more."

"I've had no complaints up to lately. You been going to too many parties at Kuraskin's with all those show business phonies and hippie bums. When I dress, I *dress*."

Huggins said nothing. He longed for something else, some freedom he could not define. His law partners, Dan Kuraskin and Manny Jabloner, went in for Cardin suits, long-haired mistresses, Pop Art, fag decorators. Manny and Dan had the handle on everything. Taking Barbara to their parties meant a night of polite snubs. She would be the only woman in a roomful of bell bottoms, palazzo pants, and plaid skirts wearing a two-hundred-dollar black dress from Saks and a double strand of pearls.

Barbara's enormous eyes looked at him appealingly, searching for common ground. They were on line at the check-in counter. A tiny Chinese or Japanese couple was in front of them. Barbara could see Jimmy smiling, admiring the oriental's camera gear, his freak clothing. Huggins, in his Tripler suits and Whitehouse & Hardy shoes, his Chipp ties and Custom Shop shirts, yearned to be clothed by a head shop. He never would. He was too much the poor boy who had made it. Successful lawyer, rich clients, an apartment on the Upper East Side.

"Nikon?" Huggins asked.

"Yeah. The new model."

"I like that lens." Huggins had no idea what it was.

"Gives me instantaneous focus. You look like a camera nut yourself. Some bag."

"A present from my wife," Huggins said, nodding at Barbara. She smiled weakly. "Peccary."

"Yow. That's my kind of thing. You see that, Sandra?"

The Japanese woman giggled.

Murray Yasuda introduced himself and his wife. J.P. and Barbara learned that the Japanese couple was also on the tour.

"I checked this deal out with a pal of mine in the tour business," Murray Yasuda said expansively. "He says it's a bargain. *Billig vie borscht.*"

Huggins, who knew a little Yiddish, and whose law partners were Jews, laughed. Barbara grinned, her lipstick widening into a clown's smear.

"Where'd you learn that?" Huggins asked.

"Hey, man, you run the best restaurant in town, you got to speak the customers' language. You dig?"

"I dig, Murray." Huggins was feeling better. It would be a demanding twenty days, but Murray Yasuda would be good for a few laughs.

From the rear of the line laughter exploded, the cackling of women, then one thunderous voice rising above the others.

"My pal Herbie," Murray said to Huggins. "Wait'll you meet Herbie."

"*Move it on!* We got two pregnant ladies here, and a man carrying a chicken!" Herbie's rufous head towered above his party.

"Keep it down, willya, Herb?" his wife said.

"All aboard for Mosholu Parkway!" Herbie bellowed. "It's your city, so keep it clean!"

Huggins stepped out of line to look at Herbie and his group. As he studied the fat man in the whiskey-colored leather coat, he thought he saw distantly, his brother-in-law Ralphie. A dark face, a white turtle-neck sweater, a tight-fitting black suit. No, it was not Ralphie. Just another *walyone* whose notions of style came from the same poolroom.

It bothered Huggins. When he thought he spied Ralphie his heart had done a few flutters. He adjusted the straps of the camera case, nestling it against his ribs.

"We bring enough traveler's checks, Jim?" Barbara was asking.

"Humm? Yeah, yeah. I can always cable Jabloner for more."

He was too unnerved to be annoyed with her tremulous nasalities. Was it Ralphie? Had his brother-in-law come to the airport, to remind Huggins of his mission? That they were watching him everywhere?

Shake it off, Huggins told himself. The way the football coach at Evander Childs used to tell him, when he was a 155-pound corner-back. But he could not shake it off. As he approached the clerk with their tickets—"Smoking section, please, an aisle seat"—he saw himself back in the basement of Ralphie's home in Pelham. Mario had been

15

there, and Vinnie, and a few cousins. The loot towered about them—
a fortune in swag, tape recorders, cameras, speakers, tuners . . .

"We're goddamn fed up with your lousy insults, J.P.," Mario, the
elder statesman, said. "If you wasn't Barb's husband, we'd of leaned
on you long ago. We never had no use for Irish shits anyway. . . ."

And Ralphie: "Jimmy, you deliver on this, or you ain't gonna have
many clients. You'll be marked lousy, you know?"

"You bring the bag?" Mario asked.

Huggins had brought the bag. He swallowed his hatred and showed
the custom-made case. Too good to let such animals handle it.

"Okay, Vinnie, go to work on it."

"I'm convinced. What am I supposed to do?"

Dr. Wicker finished his coffee. He could see Rose-Anne at the door.
Her arms were laden with magazines.

"Deliver this letter."

"There's no name on it."

Leland nodded. "You'll have to remember it. Don't write anything
down. You'll be in Moscow on the twenty-ninth. You spend two nights
there."

"You sure you aren't with Planet?"

The agent ignored him. "On your free time you'll be visiting the
orthodontistry clinic at the Lenin Institute for Applied Sciences. Is
that right?"

"How'd you know? You fellows put a tap on me?" Wicker was not
angry, merely curious.

"Now remember this name. Dr. Anatoly Borkin. He's a molecular
biologist. He has an office at the Lenin Institute. Give him the letter."

"That's all?"

The CIA man studied the check, picked it up. "I told you it was
painless."

"What's in the letter?"

"I don't know. And you shouldn't either. It's in Russian, anyway.
Just give it to Borkin and continue with your tour."

There was a pained grimace on Dr. Wicker's face. He was consulting
a black memorandum book. A methodical man, he kept track of every
appointment, every obligation, a meticulousness that enabled him to
work a strenuous nine-hour day and also support the Riverford
Ecology Movement, the East Side Community Center, and other
causes. "Golly, I have *two* appointments in Moscow. And they've
scheduled us for the ballet—"

"We'd like you to deliver this." Leland sounded firmer.

"But if I knew what it was . . ."

Leland made an impatient gesture. "Probably scientific data."

Rose-Anne was approaching. The dentist, with a hint of hesitation, put the envelope in his inner coat pocket.

"I don't want to get anyone in trouble."

"You won't. That's why we picked you. You'll be helping a fellow scientist."

"Maybe to Siberia."

"Most unlikely."

"Maybe I'll wind up there."

"No way. Dr. Wicker, this is done every day. It's a way of keeping lines open. You're clean, safe, and no one's interested in you. Who could be more innocent than a dentist on a package tour?"

Rose-Anne had been shortstopped by the old couple—the straight-backed man in the homburg and the tiny woman with the white bangs. As always, Wicker noticed, Rosie was polite. He caught a word here and there. . . . "retired for sixteen years . . . travel all the time . . . they say this is a great tour . . . good hotels . . . we live in Bisbee, Arizona because it costs less . . ."

Wicker felt vaguely complimented. No, they wouldn't entrust *anyone* with these errands. Certainly not those two quirky oldsters. The government had come to him, Arnold Wicker, D.D.S., of Riverford, Connecticut, the Lord of Face Bows (as the PTA musical had termed him, in a vigorously applauded number). There was no point in being selfish.

"Well, I guess I'm it."

"One final thing. If anyone tries to find anything out, don't tell him unless he gives you the name of a city where there's a major league baseball team. Like Chicago, or Kansas City. We know you're a sports nut. You respond with the name of the team. Suppose I said Oakland."

"Athletics."

"New York."

"Yankees. Or Mets."

"Either one is okay. But you're not finished. Give him the name of a pro football city and wait for his answer. You say Yankees. Pause, then say, oh, Cincinnati. What should he say?"

Wicker, a compulsive watcher of Sunday football, a man known to have two TV sets and a radio going at once, so as to catch every flare-out, every down-and-out pattern, every safety blitz, grinned. "Bengals."

"Try it once more," Leland said. "A man approaches you at Orly Field in Paris. He says Detroit."

"Tigers," said the dentist. "Cleveland."

17

"Browns."

"What about the Browns?" asked Rose-Anne Wicker. Silently on crepe-soled walkers—she was the kind of woman whose legs managed to look sexy in dull shoes—she had approached them.

Leland glanced at Wicker, indicating he expected him to cover for them. The dentist, pleased with the subterfuge got up, and drew his bags, magazines, and papers with him. "Browns. The old St. Louis Browns. They once played in a World Series. Rosie, this is Jack Langford. We were on the Columbia College Fund Drive last year."

"Hi. You a Three Worlder? A couple of old Light Blues on one tour?"

"Afraid not, Mrs. Wicker. Much as I'd love to be with you."

Leland walked toward the cashier with them. "I'm an attorney. I do work for the airlines. Just happened to see Arnold, and I offered to spring for coffee. To celebrate the new gym at Morningside."

"Good God, not *that* again," Mrs. Wicker said.

Wicker, trailing his wife—Leland had waved good-by—marveled at the way they had checked him out. Pros, absolute *pros*. They knew about his profession, his community work, his jockery, his tennis game, and even the funds he had raised for the Columbia gymnasium!

The Flemingtons were the only couple on Three Worlds traveling first class. By paying an extra sum, they had reserved two first-row seats. Harry had resisted Lulu's demands but eventually gave in. He was willing to indulge her. Just getting her to take the trip had been a triumph. That she had gotten on the plane at all—particularly after the crisis over the bags—was a source of gratification to him.

Now she dozed with noisy breathing, her delicate head outlined against the chunky white pillow. So soon had she dropped off that Harry was convinced she had popped libriums in the ladies' room. He tried to keep track of her pills, but it was a lost cause. With booze, he did somewhat better, simply because it was harder for her to hide fifths and pints.

Humming, cushioned, the mammoth 747 moved insolently through the night. Flemington began to relax. He allowed himself one scotch, refused the late supper—he and Lulu had dined at Le Cygne in New York—and began to luxuriate in the old unearned security of his career as parasite. Only a handful of seats in the first-class section were occupied, and the scattering of passengers had the look of wealth about them—corporate executives traveling at company expense, an elderly couple with the suspicious faces of old fortunes.

If they knew, Flemington thought. Occasionally a traveler, someone in a New York hotel lobby, at the theater, would recognize Lulu and

18

make the connection with the Deaver fortune. There would be whispers, nods, asides. Amazing, he thought, how money made its own rules. Try as he might, he could not conquer a sense of elevation thanks to his marriage. He tried to minimize it, to dismiss Lulu's greening millions, that unassailable hoard of tax-free municipals, blue chips, income-producing real estate, tax-sheltered oil wells. But it stuck to him. It was perhaps the ultimate truth in the world, more potent than religion, more lasting than art, more inspiring than the glories of the natural world. . . .

"But you say she's getting worse?" the doctor had asked him in the Birmingham clinic a month ago.

"It's not just the drinking," Flemington had said. "She's more . . . more closed into herself. Lulu's only fifty."

"Get her away. Away from that crowd of sycophants at the club."

Flemington nodded. It would not be easy. Lulu enjoyed the club, the simple lunch, followed by the long afternoon of drinking and gossip. And always four or five women surrounding her—damned near at her feet—listening, agreeing, watching her slowly drink herself into a jellied state, until Harry showed up at four o'clock, to lift her from her seat of honor and bear her away.

("What in hell does Flemington do for a living?" Harry once heard two golfers talking about him in the men's room. "Do? He used to be some kind of newspaperman," the other said. "Then they said he managed Lulu's money, but that's baloney. She's got five people in Detroit and ten in New York who do nothing but manage it." They chuckled. "Looks to me like all he does is manage *Lulu.*" And the other: "A full-time job.")

"She used to like to travel," Flemington said. "But it's been years."

"Robbie?" the physician asked.

"I suppose so. My God, that was twenty years ago. I guess that's when the drinking got out of hand. In and out of sanitariums. Lulu wasn't built to confront a Robbie."

"She doesn't see him any more?"

"I won't let her."

The doctor shrugged. He had always liked Flemington. Married into unfathomable wealth, a man with the reputation of a suave parasite, he nonetheless maintained dignity. The man was well read, polite, and devoted to his heiress.

"Travel seems a good idea," the doctor said.

"We used to rent a Jaguar with a chauffeur in London," Flemington said nostalgically. "Pack it full of suitcases, maps, books, and just take off. Lulu never cared for museums or churches but she seemed to enjoy the riding."

19

The physician was shaking his head. "All wrong. May I make a suggestion? Force her into association with *other* people. Make her get closer to some ordinary Americans. They tend to be polite and helpful. Your wife, Mr. Flemington, has to realize that there are other people in the world besides those millionaires and remittance men she drinks with. They sit in wonder at her fortune and secretly they're glad she's an alcoholic."

"It won't be easy."

"She's got to get out of that twenty-seven-room house and away from that club. Get her on a long tour, three or four weeks. With people she's never seen before. Don't go on one of those posh things, she'll just meet the same kind. Even if she never says a word to the insurance salesman from Brooklyn or the schoolteacher from Cleveland, it will do her good."

"Lulu won't like it."

"Her liver is turning to a yellow stone. Her mind won't stand up under all that drenching. Get her out of herself. Even if she gets annoyed, or angry, or upset at being thrown in with other human beings, it will be worth it."

But would it? Flemington wondered. He looked at his wife's porcelain profile, the lips parted, the hair slightly ruffled, resting against the blue-veined temple. Christ, Harry thought, I really loved her. No one at the club, no one in Grosse Pointe—or Palm Beach, or Newport, or Ocho Rios—would believe him any more. But he had loved her once. And now he was old Harry, a shabby Prince Consort, a run-down Albert. And Lulu was royalty, regnant over an empire of fuel pumps, ignition coils, thermostats, shims, and gaskets.

In the economy section, behind him, he heard laughing and voices. Orange-haired Herbie and his people.

"Holy Jeez, this guy runs a restaurant. Hey, Murray, you gonna cook us a moo goo gai pan? Or one of them Kobe steaks?"

"You better believe it, Herb."

"I hear the food stinks on these tours."

"We'll change that, buddy," the Japanese said. "Murray Yasuda eats first class, or somebody gets burned. You dig?"

"I dig, I dig, *boychik.*"

Flemington sighed. They were fellow tourists—the raucous Jew and the mod Japanese. Already they were pals—noisy, brash, insulting. And the doddering old couple. And other surprises. And Lulu was to travel with *them*, talk to *them*, be part of *their* lives for twenty days?

Mr. Horace T. Wattle, president of Wattle Rubber, Bay Landing, near Seattle, Washington, strolled up and down the aisle of the economy section, looking for fellow members of Three Worlds. Not counting Lulu Flemington, who was in a class by herself, he was the richest person on the tour, and could have afforded the extra money for a first-class seat. But he watched his pennies, and he looked for value. Widowed a half year ago, childless Mr. Wattle discovered he had no one to talk to.

Mr. Wattle moved in sprightly jerkings of arms and legs. At seventy-one, he was compact and energetic, needing little sleep and less food. "Say, I wonder how many are on our little party?" he asked Cornelia Bettenhausen. "The fellow from Planet said there's about thirty-six on his junket, which would mean about seven and one half per cent of the total load on the plane, since we are carrying about two hundred and seventy people, which I feel is too much, even on a 747."

"I think he's with *us*," the old lady in slacks said. She had nudged off her scuffs and was wiggling ten corded toes. "How do. I'm Mrs. Legrand. This is my husband, Weston. My name is Elizabeth."

"Horace T. Wattle, Bay Landing. State of Washington."

"We're from Bisbee, Arizona. We're retired."

"Rubber hoses, tubing, gaskets, and washers. Are you aware that forty-nine per cent of the retired people in America would do better working part time than accepting Social Security benefits?"

Mrs. Legrand waggled a finger at him. "Now, now, don't give me that bushwah. I know all about Social Security. Weston and I are on the review committee for the Retired Peoples Association and we know how important it is."

Mr. Wattle did a backward fox trot and adjusted his eyeglasses. "It's socialism. It leads to Communism and free love."

"Goody," said Mrs. Legrand in a throaty voice. "You hear that, sweetie?"

"Heard it. Don't believe a word of it."

"You want to work, there's always work," Mr. Wattle said. His voice rose into upper registers.

"It's the welfare is killing the country," Mr. Legrand said.

"Yes, and the media," the rubber czar said.

Warren Bettenhausen shifted his Falstaffian bulk, made a noise like Mauna Loa, and opened one eye, which he fixed on his smiling wife. "I shall never forgive you, madam, *never*, for getting me into this."

"Piffle, Betts. No man ever suffered for woman the way you suffered for me."

Mr. Wattle, hopping about in jerky steps, cocked an ear to their conversation. He had assumed the Bettenhausens—older, well dressed

—were his kind of people, especially after watching the fat man complain about the cheese.

"Hmmm. You're digging, Cornelia. No man ever suffered . . ." Bettenhausen's other eye opened. "Zita Johann to Boris Karloff in *The Mummy.*"

"A plus, Betts."

"Senility has not yet robbed me of my memory of the classics."

"Not senility, Betts. The golden years."

"Are you aware that seventy-three per cent of all welfare money spent in Washington goes to support unwed mothers and dependent children?" Mr. Wattle asked after making a circuit of the non-smoking section and returning to the Bettenhausens.

Warren Bettenhausen's eyes, like those of a saw-whet owl, blinked shut. Cornelia smiled at Mr. Wattle and took her husband's hand. The rubber millionaire spun away and turned on the Legrands. "I designed the factory also," he said in a rising voice. "Here's a photograph of it. Won a prize in 1936 as the best-designed plant costing less than $450,000 in the state of Washington."

In the darkness, Cornelia Bettenhausen opened the going-away gift Maury Fallsberg had sent to the airport. Maury still asked for Warren's advice on a property, a new novel, a play, and he paid his old aide handsomely for these services.

Bettenhausen, snoring, did not hear the paper crackling as Cornelia opened the package. A book. Of course. Just like Maury. Probably with a note, something on the order of *Will the Old Arbiter please read the enclosed and pass judgment?*

But not this time. It was one of Fallsberg's gags. The book was called *The Civilizing Mission.* It was about Mussolini's invasion of Ethiopia. Cornelia stifled a guffaw. The inscription inside read:

> To Warren B:
>   Who tried to bring civilization to Hollywood, and who taught us more in failure than if he had succeeded.
>
> —Maury
>
> P.S.: I don't think there's a movie in this, except maybe with Dean Martin as Badoglio and Sinatra as Graziani. Sammy Davis, Jr., as Haile Selassie?

Cornela whooped. *The Civilizing Mission!* All the years they had spent in Hollywood tumbled back, all the disappointments and good times and fakery, and the rare triumphs. "They keep Bettenhausen around at Fallsberg's studio," the writers used to say, "so someone can read the synopses from the William Morris office." Warren was an A.B. from Swarthmore, M.A. from Pennsylvania, editor, critic, essayist—the man Fallsberg brought to Hollywood to "upgrade" the industry.

Grown peevish in his years at the studio, Bettenhausen conceded it had been a good life: a thousand dollars a week, and the chance to sit in on meetings and chip in with a bit of Shakespeare, a quote from Joe Krutch, a citation from Bunny Wilson, while they argued front money and producer's nets. Fallsberg and his people rarely listened to Bettenhausen but they liked having him around. A condiment at the commissary lunches, something to go with the Nova Scotia salmon and whipped eggs. And meanwhile Warren could screen old films (he loved them) and make plans for his own monument—*Gargantua and Pantagruel* with Jackie Gleason and Orson Welles.

Bettenhausen's eyes popped open. "You looked at my present from Maury," he said accusingly.

"Couldn't help it, Betts."

Warren read the title and laughed. He laughed again at the inscription. "Good old Maury. In his dotage he is developing a style."

"You taught him everything, Betts."

"Not how to get money from bankers to finance actresses who couldn't fill the Thimble Theater."

"Oh, tush. It's an education just being near you. Look at me. An orphan girl from Iowa, and you made me what I am. I was just a little kid. My people were killed by the Indians."

Tufted white eyebrows rose on Bettenhausen's face. He looked at his wife with affection. "Good, good, my dear, but not great."

"Identify."

"Claire Trevor to John Wayne. *Stagecoach*."

"What was all that nonsense about the St. Louis Browns or something?" Rose-Anne Wicker asked.

"Don't interrupt, Rosie," the dentist said. "I want to get all these postcards off the second we hit London. Browns?"

"Mr. Langford. The shaved head and the beady eyes."

Wicker had all but forgotten about his meeting with the CIA agent. "He's a frustrated jock. I can't stand him. He was a pain on the Dean's Day Committee."

"I thought it was the Fund Drive."

"What? Maybe he was on both."

"Was he at our house for the Fairfield County regional meeting?"

"I don't think so. Rosie, could you please read or something? Go see who else is on our tour. There should be lots of nice folks on the plane."

"Geritol, Unlimited. We're the kids."

"Great, great. It'll gratify our egos, if that's what we need." In a large hand, the orthodontist wrote on a British International postcard:

> Dear Davey:
> As your mother has told you I will be away for almost three weeks.
> I am absolutely depending on you to wear your *face bow* every
> night. I will be angry if you let me down. The first thing I will do
> when I get back is look at your teeth, and you know your old friend
> Dr. Wicker. I can't be fooled . . .

Davey Greenfeld would have a sleepless night over that one, but he would wear the face bow and he would save his teeth. No child under Arnold Wicker's care was free of his gaze; they feared him and they loved him. He was more than an overseer of open bite and malocclusion, class I, he was a conscience, a presence. Frantic mothers called on him to improve their small fry's spelling; harried fathers asked his help in changing a boy's backhand.

> Dear Abrams Children, Mark & Donna & Debbie—
> All of you must brush your teeth twice a day, and I want a good
> report on the care and keeping of bite plates. They are part of your
> life, your person, and someone who loses a bite plate or lets it break
> is just as guilty as if he didn't bathe, or was careless and broke an
> arm. . . .

"Aren't you overdoing it?" Rose-Anne asked him. She sneaked a look from her *New Yorker*. "You'll give those kids a complex."

"They love it. Kids have to be afraid of something. It might as well be teeth."

"It mi-ight as we-ell be teeth," Rosie sang. "Oh, Arnold, you are a beaut."

Wicker, intent on good work, now wrote a card to the Riverford chief of police, Dominic Parioli.

> Dear Dom—
> If there is a new outbreak of drug abuse at Van Diemen Junior
> High, please put in effect our optional plan "B," the one calling for
> an immediate shakedown search, police guard in the adjacent
> shopping center parking lot (in civvies and preferably a new man,
> not known to the pushers) and I shall keep in touch. . . .

Rosie, catching the salutation, sighed and adjusted the lever that pushed her seat back. There was no stopping her husband. Clearly, he was the best-natured man in the world, a Good Samaritan, whose zeal in improving the misshapen teeth of children was readily transferred to dozens of causes.

"I hate to say it, Rosie," Wicker said, "but maybe this wasn't the greatest time of year to run off. I mean, with the school budget in trouble, and the fight over the Minnipack forest coming up. Not to mention the Columbia Fund Drives."

"College or School of Dentistry?"

"Both."

"Good old Jack Langdon can handle them in your absence."

For a moment the dentist had no idea what she was talking about. Then, recalling the agent, he touched the envelope inside his breast pocket. *Dr. Borkin at the Lenin Institute.* He said no more to his sleepy wife, turned off her reading light, and started making marginal notes in a catalogue from a manufacturer of dental equipment.

The stewardess—she was a beige-skinned West Indian—spied Father Konay clutching his beads.

"Jolly safe with you aboard, Father."

"My first flight. I'm not frightened. I just do this out of habit."

"Never flown? Never?"

"Hard to believe, isn't it? I'm sixty-four, and I've never been on a plane."

"Are you enjoying it?"

"I love it. Makes me start wondering about a lot of things I haven't done." He winked at the girl. What had gotten into him? The sense of freedom now that, after years of being stuck in the parish, he was out in the world?

"Oh, don't kid me, Father. I'm a Catholic myself. The Faith makes up for everything, isn't that what they say?"

"They say."

"Blanket or a pillow? A magazine?"

"No, thanks. I'll meditate."

A middle-aged couple, plain-looking people from New Jersey, nodded approvingly.

"Meditation is marvelous," the stewardess said. "And you're close to the Boss here."

The couple laughed. The man pointed an accusing finger at Konay, as if to say, "Watch your step, padre, you're being watched."

"Not much of a joke, I guess," the girl said, turning her ravishing head. "I use it all the time with rabbis and ministers also. Excuse me."

Her curved figure vanished. Father Konay, his eyes half shut with fatigue, watched her. He was human. He was a man. Terrible, terrible. At his age. Maybe the officers of the Ospreys were right; he not only behaved in a manner unbecoming a Brother Osprey, but he was unworthy of his calling. . . .

25

What was he doing, in God's name, on this flight to distant places, he, who hardly ever went to Pittsburgh, and had visited New York three times in his life? Self-pity brimmed in him, and he tried not to think mean thoughts about Mr. Marciniek and the others, and especially about Father Folker, who'd made him stand up at the scatter sites housing debate at the City Council and come out for low-income high-rises.

"Traitor!" they had shouted at him. Men and women he had baptized, confirmed, married. Listened to their confessions. Interceded for them. A wise old paraclete (when he used the word once in conversation with Harry Zawoluk, one of his enemies, the man looked blank, thinking he had said "parakeet"), a spiritual pastor, concerned only with mysteries of Faith.

No longer, he could have told him. Not when young wise guys like Bert Folker were coming out of the seminaries, in their beards and blue jeans and wild ideas about integrated housing and anti-war protests.

Guess I don't belong anywhere any more, Father Konay thought. Certainly not on a tour with strangers. He would spend the next three weeks worrying about what they would do to him back home. Normally an untroubled man, he now began to fantasize dread possibilities. A priest couldn't function in an atmosphere of enmity. Let young Folker, that radical smarty-pants, try to run the place.

"I bet you're looking forward to Jerusalem," the woman at his right said. "And Rome. I bet it's like a dream to you."

"Oh, it surely is." What good were all the rituals when everything came apart? When people you helped bring into the world, educate, marry, bless, when these people hated you?

As he always did on flights—he traveled a great deal, pushing his products, visiting customers, attending conferences—Horace T. Wattle spent much time in the galley assisting the stewardesses.

"I have never seen a mon move so fast around a kitchen," the Jamaican girl said. "You are a treasure, Mr. Wattle."

"The wife thought so," he said. He was stuffing empty juice cans into a paper sack. "Say, that's well made. Seamless. You know, until these synthetics came along, forty-six per cent of the bag business in the United States was in the hands of small manufacturers. But the big chemical and oil boys are taking over. That's why I'm lucky. I'm not big and I'm not small. I got them where I want them."

"And where is that?" an exquisite blonde girl asked him. Mr. Wattle had taken his coat off. He was stacking soiled trays.

26

"Right smack dab where I can make my own sales, manage my own product, outdo the next feller, and know every minute what's going on in my factory."

The Jamaican and the blonde exchanged looks. "If you run your factory the way you stack garbage, you must do marvelously," the blonde said.

The black girl shook her ebony hair and turned away.

"How do they manage without you?" the blonde asked.

"They don't really. I sort of reached the point where I had to get out of it all."

The blonde nodded—mechanical sympathy. It was an old story from rich Americans. Lonely. Wife gone. Children away.

"But they know that Horace T. Wattle is watching. I took care of the manager and the shop steward and the police, and mighty generously. Say, that's an ingenious oven. Never seen one so compact. Does it perform well? Who makes it?"

A call buzzer sounded and the Jamaican girl walked lithely down the aisle, brushing by a paunchy man with a long uncooked steak of a face and great muscular arms. He eyed her wonderingly. "Dang. Ain't that a pot o' squirrel stew. All dark meat an' sweeter 'n' blackstrap molasses."

Mr. Wattle, helping the blonde tidy up, noticed that a hinge was loose on the aluminum cupboard door. He extracted a multipurpose tool from his $1.90 shirt and bent to fix it. "Secure this in a jiffy."

The big red-faced man ambled on splay feet into the kitchen area.

"You want something?" the hostess asked.

"Yeah, but it don' come in a bottle."

"Oh, really."

The newcomer bent low, inspecting Mr. Wattle's work. "Need he'p? Ah got me one of them fix-it gadgets also. Own the biggest hay, grain, feed, seed, coal, and coke store in North Memphis. Got a nice line o' hardware, too."

"I don't need help," the bald man said. "And I probably supply half your wholesalers with rubber goods. You're in my light."

Unchastised, the corpulent man straightened up. He seemed to be addressing the entire plane, not just the Washington man. "Gunthorpe is the name. Abel Tutt Gunthorpe. Ole A.T. Got me two hunnert acres of rice and a mess o' mallards. Dang if I know whut Ah'm doin' on a trip when the mallards is due home."

"Travel is broadening, Mr. Gunthorpe," the blonde girl said.

"Yeah, so mah family says." He bent again, conspiratorial, whispering in Mr. Wattle's ear. "Hey, buddy, you with Planet? Ah seen

yoah bag. Single lak me? You reckon we can git us some o' that fur-
rin poontang? Frenchy? Eye-talian? They say them gals cry for hit."

"Didn't hear a word you said," Mr. Wattle replied.

James Patrick Huggins was giving himself a dry run with his lenses
—trying to see how fast he could switch from the normal lens to the
wide-angle to the telephoto—when Murray and Sandra Yasuda
walked by. The Japanese had two Nikons slung about his neck. They
looked as if they belonged there, whereas Huggins betrayed a clumsy
unfamiliarity with his gear.

"Hold the case, Barb," J.P. said. "That's it. Upright. I'll drop the
wide-angle in, then you hand me the other. Jesus, not that way."

"Since when did you become a camera freak?"

"Since I learned I was a lousy lawyer."

Yasuda grinned. "No way, man. You look like a heavy cat. Anybody got a custom-made bag like that, he comes by his bread honestly,
and he goes first class."

Huggins had always admired originals. He studied the doll-sized
man in the mod shirt, the clanking medallion on his chest, the hip-
ster's bells and wide belt. Sandra Yasuda was broad-nosed, as small as
a fourth-grader, but she too knew how to dress: body suit, green bells,
rings clustered on her babyish hand.

"We all on this Three Worlds bash?" Yasuda asked. "I'm Murray
Yasuda, and this is Sandra. A coupla cats out of Victorville." He gave
J.P. his card. Huggins obliged with one of his and introduced Barbara.
"I can tell from the card, man," the Japanese said. "You *are* a heavy
cat. Ever handle negligence? Some joker hit me with a lawsuit for
MSG poisoning. I never use the stuff."

"I'm afraid not," J.P. said. "I do corporate work."

"Groovy. All that Wall Street bread."

"My wife's relatives." He darted a mocking glance at Barbara.
"They're in import-export. Ever heard of Malfi Associated? They're all
over the East."

"Not my turf. Born and raised in California."

"Crazy, Murray."

"Lemme see that bag, Jimmy," Yasuda said.

Huggins found he was clutching the camera case as if reluctant to
surrender it. Then he laughed, let go, and Yasuda took it. "Yeah, I dig
this," Yasuda said. "Designed it yourself, I bet." Huggins nodded.

Barbara, uncomfortable with strangers, watched their diminutive
figures vanish down the aisle. In an offended voice she asked: "Are
they in first class?"

"How do I know?"

"I think they are." She was annoyed over the possibility that two small Chinks or Japs should be up front, while she, a resident of East Eighty-ninth Street with a lawyer husband, should be in economy. "We could've gone first class. It wasn't that much."

"I'm a man of the people, Barbs. Mingle with other folks. Like Murray and Sandra."

"Chink restaurant owner."

"Japanese. And he's got style. So has that four-foot wife. They know where it's at. Not like *walyones*."

"I swear you better cut that out, Jimmy, those cracks about my family."

She could have been beautiful, were her cheeks less rounded, her chin more defined. There was a hint of pampered fat in her face, suggesting a slugabed, a secret eater of cakes and candies. "Those snotty comments about Mario and Ralphie. You know what I mean. After all they done for you."

It appalled Huggins (who could often speak ungrammatically for comic effect) that his wife, thirty-one, attractive, a graduate of St. Ursula's with a year at Manhattanville, could still butcher the language. What bothered Huggins was that Barbara knew better. She seemed to use gutter solecisms as an obeisance to her family, a concession that she was truly one of *them* even though she had married an Irish-American lawyer who wore Ivy League clothes. (At times, in her family's presence, she lapsed into "deses" and "doses.")

"They done me no good at all," Huggins said, fastening the last two buckles on the case but keeping it on his lap.

Cameras, like Ralphie had said, as they crouched in the basement, a congress of looters, swagmen, fences. "Like they never look in a camera bag, I been advised." And Mario nodding sleepily. "And, like, this tour you're gonna go on, with a lotta people, they never bother openin' bags, 'cause like everyone is so regular. . . ."

"You and Jabloner and Kuraskin got plenny of business from them, don't deny it," Barbara said.

"They're giving me the business all right."

"Legal fees. Clients they referred to you. You think you would've got Colosseum Olive Oil without Mario putting in a good word for you?"

"I guess not. I sure appreciate that free case of tomato paste every Christmas."

Barbara Huggins, youngest child of the family, was marginally aware of her brothers' dealings. Her parents were lower middle class, concerned with food and possessions. They lived modestly, bothered no one, and were silent about Mario's and Ralphie's line of work. Old man Malfi had owned a fruit store in the South Bronx but had long ago sold out to "a nice smart Spic with a gun under the cash register."

"I heard you yelling on the phone to Mario a few days ago," she said craftily. "What was all that about?"

"I didn't like him coming to my office in a white turtle-neck sweater and a black suit."

"It was not."

"On my honor, Barb."

"I heard what you said. You said you didn't wanna be a lousy errand boy. As a matter of fact, you said you wouldn't be an errand boy for a mob of *greasers*."

"A friendly argument."

"You know, it's a good thing Mario is my brother and respects me. He don't take insults like that from no one."

Huggins looked at his wife with slack-jawed contempt. "When do we get the refund from the nuns at St. Ursula's? Listen carefully. He *doesn't* take insults from *anyone*. Shall we try again?"

"Drop dead."

Huggins grabbed at her bosom. She moved an arm between them. Abruptly, as often happened when he was most distressed with her, he lusted for her.

"Later, Jimmy," she said. She smiled—for the first time since they had left their apartment. "When we get to the hotel."

Huggins, a cool man, found that his heart was pumping. For all his criticism of his wife—spike heels, tight black dresses, piled hair, and butchered English—he was in thrall to her flesh. Fair enough, Huggins thought. Life was a series of deals, trades, arrangements. You looked for an edge. More often than not you settled. He had been a lucky man. His law partners made no great demands on him. His appearance alone—handsome, terribly Irish—counted for a good deal. So did his contacts with the Malfis and their friends.

Barbara dozed. Huggins, drawn to the camera case, picked it up again. He had stowed magazines in the side compartment. (They were class magazines—book reviews, essays, political matters. Huggins liked to be aware of what was being talked about at Jabloner's parties.) As he fondled the bag, the leather came to life in his hands. When he was a kid his mother used to take him and his brother Brian to the "Irish Alps" in the Catskills for two weeks. They did not own a valise. Mrs. Huggins would stuff their clothing and toilet articles into cardboard boxes bound with clothesline.

Day 2: London, England! Your Tour Escort greets you at Heath-row Airport. En route to the hotel, a memorable tour of London's landmarks—monuments, churches, famed streets. Then some free morning time, for getting organized, perhaps a bit of shopping (cashmeres and tartans!), and a lunch, with our first taste of those great English beers—mild, bitter, lager.

On to an afternoon of sight-seeing, Westminster Abbey, Big Ben, Parliament, St. Paul's, the Old Curiosity Shop, Hyde Park, and other historic sites. At night, dinner at a typical Elizabethan pub, with lusty serving wenches, the roast beef of Olde England, tankards of ale, and madrigal singers!

Pepi Virgil, lighting a fresh Gitane with the burning butt of its predecessor, let the smoke drift into his black eyes and read the cable from Trapani. It did not upset him. He accepted his clients with neutrality. He was grateful to them for choosing Planet, to Planet for hiring him, to the executives for giving him, two years running, its "Tour Escort of the Year" award—a bonus and an engraved plaque.

"Ready for a new load of mischief, Mr. Virgil?" the cockney girl at the message desk at Heathrow Airport asked him.

"Ready as ever, Vanessa." Once again he read the message about the Flemingtons and their fourteen pieces of luggage. Years of con-finement behind bars, barbed wire, electrified fences, had taught him the importance of written orders.

"Don't you ever get cheesed off at Americans?"

Virgil tucked the cable into the pocket of his dark blue raincoat. "I am fond of them."

"But a steady diet?"

"A much better diet than I had in other places in Europe, my dear."

The girl looked archly at him. A handsome bloke, this Virgil. And what manners! Just the way he tapped those Gitanes on the cigarette case. The way he let the match flame light up his face! What was he? Vanessa had once seen his British passport. But the accent? What was it? German? French? Italian? Some of the girls thought he was a Greek—stocky, black hair, dark skin, dreamy eyes, the low voice and soft manners. "Dresses conservative, like a rich Greek bloke," a waitress confided to an insurance girl. "Always white shirts, black tie, dark blue suit, dark blue coat."

31

Pepi Virgil, who had no Greek blood (as far as he knew), would have enjoyed the gossip. Polite English girls, they did not ask personal questions. Virgil, a company man to the soles of his oxfords, revealed little.

"You've got a lovely September day to start," Vanessa said.

"Indeed we do. I have never had a tour begin in London that was not a success."

"Oh, please. With our bloody weather?"

"Ah, but the people. You are such splendid hosts. You set my Americans at ease and the rest of the journey is bound to be pleasant."

"Well, it's a tribute to you also. You're one of us, aren't you? British passport and all?"

Virgil studied the smoldering end of the Gitane. The pungent odor invigorated him. Two packs a day was a bit much. "By adoption."

The loudspeaker announced the arrival of British International 776. Cocking an ear, he had an excuse not to pursue the line of conversation. It got complicated.

From another pocket he extracted the tourist list for Three Worlds. There were thirty-six people, a large party for late in the season. He suspected it was the gimmick of the East-West-Holy Land combination that got them. The tour, a new one, had done well since its inception that spring. (So well, in fact, that the $8,000 which the company allocated for a mere two pages in the Master Tour Book had been recouped after the third junket.)

He was anticipating thirty-three people on the arriving plane. Three members were already in London and would join the others that afternoon. It seemed a manageable group, except for the Flemingtons and their luggage. He hoped Trapani had told them of the nine-dollar charge.

"Have a smashing three weeks," the girl said. Virgil glanced once more at the list of names and started toward the arrival area.

"I always do, my dear."

At the large doorway from which travelers emerged after a thorough, polite inspection by British customs, Virgil unfurled a purple flag and held it aloft. What he lost in dignity, he told other escorts, he gained in efficiency.

A handsome man in a banker's gray suit, with flushed cheeks and curly black hair, approached him.

"Three Worlds?" Huggins asked.

"Yes, please. I am your tour escort. My name is Pepi."

"Huggins. Mrs. Huggins."

32

Virgil managed to suggest a bow, a smile, and an air of welcome, yet he hardly moved his body. His eyes remained fixed on the gate, where a small Japanese couple and a fat man blowing clouds of cigar smoke emerged.

"Welcome. The bus is outside. You may wait aboard it, or here in the waiting room."

"Newsstand?" Huggins asked.

"To your left, sir. Mr. Yasuda? Mrs. Yasuda?"

"Howdja know it was us? Don't tell me, buddy. We're the only Norwegians on the trip."

Murray Yasuda, trailed by a dutiful Sandra laden with bags, coats, and magazines, showed no sign of weariness.

"Quite so, Mr. Yasuda."

"Hey, Planet Tours?" It was Herbie, sailing in a cloud of smoke, dangling a coat belt. His wife Flo threaded it through a loop.

"I am your tour escort," Virgil said.

"Hiya, pal. Herbie Shackman. My wife Flo. And the rest of the *mishpocheh.*" Herbie, flicking ashes, dropping newspapers, receipts, losing his belt again, began calling out the names of his friends. There were three other couples, all from Westbury, Long Island, all related, neighbors, or close friends. "Si . . . and Sid . . ."

Virgil smiled, keeping an eye fixed on the doorway for the Flemingtons.

A stout man in white space shoes, sporting a plaid tam-o'-shanter, was next.

"Bettenhausen," the man said.

"Welcome, sir. Mrs. Bettenhausen?"

"That's us." She had a reliable look. Virgil made a quick estimate of them. The kind who would go to museums on their own and not be concerned with bargains in perfume.

"Haven't been in London for fifteen years," Bettenhausen huffed. "Is it still true that when a man is tired of London he is tired of life?"

Virgil nodded. " 'For there is in London all that life can afford.' Dr. Samuel Johnson was right, sir."

Bettenhausen's eyes tried to free themselves from the pouches. His beard was charged with electricity. "Dammit, you are the first man I have met in thirty years who knew the rest of that."

"I have had occasion to read a good deal."

Father Konay, wandering in bemused fashion, emerged.

"Three Worlds, Father?"

"Ah, why, yes. You're from Planet? Oh, the flag, of course."

"This way, Father. You may board our bus outside, or wash your hands, or wait with me. Please."

What was a priest doing on an expensive tour like Three Worlds? And he did not seem the adventurous type, this hesitant man with pendulous ears and crinkled eyes. Clergy, notably Roman Catholics, did their traveling in homogeneous cut-rate groups. A heavy emphasis on Lourdes, Rome, Jerusalem.

"I'll use the men's room, if I may."

"Of course, Father." Virgil liked priests. Years ago the first man he met on being released from a camp (Gross Rosen? Sobibor?) was a young Italian priest, also newly liberated. They had talked in Latin.

"This way, please, to the bus, Three Worlds, Planet Tours," Virgil called.

A well-dressed couple, vigorous-looking people, walked up to him. "I'm Dr. Wicker," the man said.

"Welcome," said Virgil. He tabbed them at once—bright, quick. People one could depend on.

Another related group emerged, gray-haired men, older women, plainly dressed, smiling, eager, ready for twenty days of adventure. They had a solid Midwestern look about them. They saw his flag. He identified himself, then directed them to the waiting bus.

"Pleasant flight?" Virgil asked one of the gray-haired men.

"The booze helped."

The others around him guffawed. A woman dug him in the side.

The tour escort smiled. "It usually does."

"Boy, can that character Ed put it away," another man said.

Again there was laughter. Virgil managed a smile. Was there, anywhere in the world, a people as appealingly puritanical as Americans? The mere *mention* of alcohol, the faintest hint at liquor, the slightest reference to inebriation—and hilarity followed. They discussed their drinking the way other people discussed sex or crime.

"Hollow legs, that's your name, Maude."

"Look who's talking. The original sponge."

The party moved off, reminiscing about the drinking on BIA 776. It confounded Virgil. Statistics showed that Swedes, French, and Russians drank more than Americans. Americans were not drunkards. They seemed to have worked out a reasonable pattern of alcoholic consumption. Yet they acted, first, as if they were the most intemperate boozers in the world, and secondly, as if their criminal habits were cause for mirth. Why? Was it because deep down they were moralists?

"I've got to send a cable. Right away."

Horace T. Wattle, at the trailing edge of the party of middle Americans, was standing under Virgil's nose. His words floated into the escort's nostrils, a demanding voice that almost had an odor.

34

"Of course, sir. But perhaps you can wait until we reach the hotel? Just about everyone is aboard the bus."

"How long before we get to the hotel?"

"About an hour and a half. We make a tour of London."

"Can't wait. Delays are a curse. Why were we held up in customs? Do I look like a smuggler? I run my own business. We grossed over seven million dollars last year and were cited by *Business Week* for quality control."

"British customs tend to be strict. The cable desk is over to your right."

Mr. Wattle pirouetted, danced off in a series of ballroom steps. One could almost hear the fox-trot music as he moved.

Sedately, moving in stingy steps, Mrs. Flemington came out of the customs area. At last, Virgil thought. She would be a challenge. But that was what made for excitement in his work. Behind Mrs. Flemington—Virgil, a judge of breeding, liked her slender lines, the tilt of the head, the fragile neck—came three British porters, handling the fourteen valises, and with them, a good-looking man in a brown suede hat. Patience and tolerance were scored in his tanned face. It had to be Harry Flemington.

As they approached the purple flag, an elderly couple, moving with alarming speed, the woman gliding on bedroom slippers, charged by. Mrs. Flemington was jostled, tottered, righted herself. "Oh, I'm sorry," Mrs. Legrand said loudly. "Dear me, are you hurt?"

"Harry, please," Lulu called.

Flemington, darting from the porters, was at her side. "You all right, Lu?"

The old lady was all muscle and fiber. Lulu's bones took a few seconds to recover. As Flemington supported her, he realized he had help. Virgil was holding her other arm.

"Ah," Flemington said. "The man from Planet Tours?"

"Yes, sir. You are Mr. Flemington?"

"Right. You recognized us from the bags, I gather? Mr. Trapani said he'd notify you."

"He did, sir. All is in order."

A few paces removed, Horace T. Wattle, catching a glimpse of the Flemingtons, pivoted on agile feet. Mr. Wattle never forgot an important face. His rubber business had taken him in and out of Detroit for years. The leaders of automotive society were known to him—through some contact at a golf course, or a restaurant, or through the pages of the magazines he studied.

"Why, I'll be darned," he said. "That's Louise Deaver."

"Harry, I wish to sit down," Lulu pleaded.

"I shall take Mrs. Flemington to the bus," Virgil said.

Lulu managed a smile. There was something so solicitous about the escort's manner that she was reassured.

"Say, say, excuse me," Wattle cried. "Aren't you Melton Deaver's daughter? I met you at the Grosse Pointe Inner Circle about six years ago. Knew your daddy well. There was a man. Controlled sixty-two per cent of the laminated shim market through sheer initiative. Am I right?"

"Harry, tell him to go away."

The egg-bald man was not deterred. He danced alongside the Flemingtons and Virgil. "Melton Deaver was a giant. I never knew a man who understood the spare parts business the way he did."

As they approached the bus, a convulsed group was watching Herbie Shackman trying to entice his wife to board. Flo was protecting her behind with one hand, shrieking. "He'll goose me!" she wailed. "He always gooses me!"

"You're lucky I don't bite it," Herbie boomed.

Herbie's retinue—Si, Sid, Shirl, and Sylvia—hooted and applauded. Murray Yasuda unlimbered his Nikon and was taking photos. Inside the bus other members of the tour—the Midwesterners, the old couple—laughed.

"Go on, Flo, run up. I'll hold Herbie back!"

"Go up backwards."

"Two hands."

"Hold it, Herbie," Yasuda shouted. "That's great. Make like you're grabbing for Flo. Flo, start up again."

Lulu and Harry approached the group. It was as if a principal had walked into a rambunctious class. Sighting Lulu's face, Herbie retreated, stumbling on his feet. Flo flew into the bus. The others—Herbie's friends, the Yasudas—parted, forming two lanes of servitors. Lulu boarded.

Inside, Lulu turned to Virgil. "Till what time are the silver vaults open?" she asked. He was surprised by the deep beery timbre of her voice.

"Till five, madame. If Madame wishes, I can arrange an appointment."

Flemington smiled approvingly. Virgil understood; Virgil would be a help.

Hotels, particularly the neglected places that accepted tours, hated hordes of tourists descending upon them too early in the day. There was an understanding with Planet Tours that the groups would be

36

busied for the morning so that beds could be made, rooms cleaned, bills straightened out, before the new batch of travelers descended.

("We don't need you people that badly," a hotel official had informed Virgil a few months ago. "If you insist on barging in on us at 10 or 11 A.M., we'll think twice about your tours. I'm afraid that's the way it is." Virgil was tempted to reply that the sort of hotel that took large tour groups did so precisely because they *needed* the business. Brown's, or the Savoy, or Claridge's, or the Ritz did not solicit large groups of Americans.)

In any event it was necessary for Pepi to keep his charges occupied for several hours before checking in. Actually this was not a severe problem. The roundabout ride through London—midmorning was a good time—would eat up more than an hour, and the business of introductions would devour the rest of the time. The sedulous consumption of time, Virgil understood, was crucial to tours. Time had to be nibbled slowly, not devoured gluttonously. People had to feel they were getting their money's worth and a bit more—but not being suffocated.

"Ladies and gentlemen," Virgil began, in his unpeggable accent. "For those who have not had a chance to meet me formally, I am your tour escort. For the next twenty days we shall get to know one another, and I am certain this will be a good experience. My name is Joseph Francis Virgil, but my friends call me Pepi and I hope you will call me Pepi."

Halfway down the bus, Herbie Shackman and two of his friends had lit up monstrous greenish cigars. One of the retinue, Sid, had given Murray Yasuda a cigar, and he too lit up, the cigar so long and thick that it appeared to be smoking the man. Ancient Mr. Legrand was puffing on a gnarled black pipe. Cigarettes made their appearance. A thick blue haze filmed the interior.

"Ladies and gentlemen," Pepi said, "we shall be close together for almost three weeks, and it is a good idea to be on a first-name basis, the way Americans like to be, and to know a little about one another. So we shall go around the bus and let the man of the family introduce himself and his wife. Give first names, please, and home towns."

Lulu Flemington covered her face. "Harry. The cigars."

"I'm sorry, dearest. Let's change seats." They got up, Lulu navigating the narrow seat, the tricky step into the aisle. They moved back five rows.

"Murray and Sandra Yasuda, Victorville, California."

"Weston and Elizabeth Legrand, Bisbee, Arizona, although we're originally from Omaha."

"Vernon and Maude Simmons, Ames, Iowa."

"Herbie and Flo Shackman, Westbury, New York, and Miami Beach, Florida, when I can afford it."

"Sid and Sylvia Lushak, Westbury . . ."

"Si and Shirley Shapiro, Westbury . . ."

One of the small Midwestern men, seated in front of the Flemingtons, lit a pipe. Lulu coughed violently. He kept puffing.

"Harry, let's move. I am strangling."

They got up again. Virgil noticed them. He said nothing.

"This is an outrage," Lulu whispered as they settled into the rear seats. "Make them stop, Harry."

Flemington realized how far removed from problems of a day-to-day nature he was. In a way, he was as badly off as Lulu. A parasite, a freeloader, he'd been cocooned into country clubs, $150,000 homes, luxury hotels. He had forgotten the routines involved in getting along with ordinary humans. "Honey, I can't. I'll talk to the guide."

"Bud and Marge Hunt, Hastings, Nebraska."

"I'm, ah, Father Stephen Konay, of Ash Valley, Pennsylvania."

"Hiya, padre!" Herbie yelled. "Boy, are we safe! We got insurance on this trip!"

"Herbie," Flo squeaked. "Shut up."

"We're the Wickers, Arnold and Rose-Anne, Riverford, Connecticut."

"Warren and Cornelia Bettenhausen, Sherman Oaks, California."

"Horace T. Wattle, Bay Landing, state of Washington."

"Al and Lorraine Force, Aurora, Illinois."

The bus was now dense with blue-gray haze. The air stank of cheap tobacco, saliva-moistened cigars. Warren Bettenhausen, who suffered bouts of fibrillation, realized he was suffocating. He had noticed the Flemingtons moving to the rear and now he understood why. He began to cough.

"Betts? You catching cold?" Cornelia was a secret cigarette smoker—three a day, morning, noon, and night—and she was ruggedly healthy, unbothered by odors, noise, pollution.

"I am being stifled. This must stop."

"Walter and Jean Zuflacht, Hot Springs, Arkansas."

"Ed and Mavis Hutzler, Vandalia, Illinois."

The tall potbellied man lumbered to his feet. "A. T. Gunthorpe, North Memphis, Tennessee. Travelin' alone, and available, gals."

There was a shriek of laughter from the women. All turned to look at Gunthorpe, who winked lasciviously.

"Hey, Gunthorpe," Herbie shouted. "Ya can have mine, but there's a small service charge."

"Ah'll talk to yew later, Herbie."

"You ain't man enough, Gunthorpe. She could kill three like you."

The Midwestern ladies screamed with delight, dug their husbands in the ribs, craned necks to get a better look at Herbie.

"One on every trip," Ed said to Al.

"Ole Herbie," A. T. Gunthorpe said admiringly. "Ole Herbie a pistol, ain't he?"

"Clyde and Cecelia Kuchtenberg, Defiance, Ohio."

"Jim and Barbara Huggins, New York."

"Hiya, New York!" Herbie yelled. "You look to me like a Giant fan."

"Ah, Louise and Harry Flemington. Detroit." He wondered why he had not said Grosse Pointe.

Huggins grinned at Herbie Shackman. Herbie and his friends would be good for a few laughs. He had known a dozen Herbies in his Castle Hill Avenue days. The funny fat guy in the candy store.

"Sir!" Bettenhausen called. The last of the tour members had risen and identified themselves. "Sir! Can we not set a policy on cigars? And pipes? There is a stinking miasma in this bus. A choking cloud of poison. Can we survive three weeks of this?"

Lulu Flemington glared at Harry, as if to say, "Someone is man enough to say what must be said."

"Mr. Bettenhausen, I intended to mention that." Virgil looked directly at Herbie and the Japanese. "Company rules forbid the smoking of cigars and pipes aboard the bus. Cigarettes are permitted. I am sorry, but that is a rule. Gentlemen who wish to smoke cigars and pipes will have to avail themselves of the coffee breaks and other stops."

"Whah?" Herbie yelled. "What? You mean I gotta put out my Double Corona?"

"I am afraid so, Mr. Shackman."

"Hey, that's a bummer," Murray Yasuda protested. "That's a bad scene, man. Like if I can't light up my drinkless Kaywoodie, I'm dead. Or at least a coupla Flor de Mexicos. Come on, Pepi. How about a smoker's lounge in back?"

"Mr. Yasuda, that will not work. We are all introduced. We know the rules on smoking. We shall now proceed to London, look at some of the sights, then to our hotel for a rest." Virgil settled into the guide's seat.

"What time are the stores open?" a woman yelled.

"Almost all day, madame. When we finish our tour this afternoon you shall have an hour until closing at six. And you have a free morning tomorrow."

"Not enough," another woman sang.

"We need a whole day to shop," a third called.

"You shall have sufficient time to spend your dollars." He loved

Americans! How willing they were to part with their money, to spread their shrinking dollars, to buy, to bargain, to take, to be taken!

The bus made its way through airport traffic and onto the M-4 toward London. Midmorning clouds, battleship gray, thick with rain, obscured the sun. The ride to the city was rather dull—rows of one-family homes, connected like children's toys, tiny gardens, an inexplicable field of cabbage or turnips, factories manifesting a dreary postwar modernism.

"Say, guide!" Mr. Wattle cried. "What's growing in those fields out there?"

"Cabbage, sir."

"I hate cabbage."

"So do many English people, but they eat it anyway, sir."

"Worse for them."

Cornelia Bettenhausen reacted to Mr. Wattle's pronunciamento on cabbage. She caught Rose-Anne's eye and they grinned. The Bettenhausens were seated across from the dentist and his wife. "You think we'll get the opinions of Mr. Wattle on statues and churches also?" she asked.

"I hope not," Rose-Anne whispered. "If we can keep him on cabbage and cauliflower, we're safe."

One of the Westbury tourists—Sid's wife, Syl, a stunning brunette—called to Pepi. She had a warm intimate voice. "Hey, Pepi. We all told you about ourselves. What about you? What's your home town?"

"London, of course, dear lady."

"He's cute," Flo said.

"Love to take him home," Sylvia added.

"For your daughter Wendy? The one at Ohio State?"

"Wendy can plotz. For *me*."

"He'd kill you. At your age?"

Syl persisted. "So, London? But you're not English. What are you?"

"A little bit of everything," Virgil said.

"They get pretty personal, don't they?" Cornelia asked her husband. "No holds barred."

Bettenhausen, happier now that he had only to sniff an occasional wisp of cigarette smoke, waggled a finger. "He doesn't mind. Virgil likes the attention. Those sensual ladies from Westbury are safe temptresses. An eroticism predicated on smoked salmon and toasted bagels, like the sexiness of producers' wives."

"Oh, Betts. You must be feeling better."

"No secrets, Pepi," Sylvia teased.

"I am a British subject," Virgil said. "But I am of mixed Serbian,

40

Croatian, Italian, Austrian, and Hungarian ancestry, with a sprinkling of a few others."

"A whole United Nations," Mr. Kuchtenberg said to Mr. Zuflacht.

"And how many languages do you speak?" Rose-Anne Wicker asked. "Nine."

There were gasps, squeals of wonder. Herbie Shackman threw his hands up. "*Gottenu.* I got enough trouble with English."

"What nine?" Cornelia Bettenhausen asked.

"English, French, Spanish, Italian, Portuguese, German, Serbo-Croat, Russian, and Hungarian."

"You had me worried for a minute," Herbie bellowed. "For a minute I thought they gave us a dope for a guide."

From the others there was a respectful silence. They knew they were in the presence of some mysterious European knowledge. Virgil, who had to strike a balance between the role of servitor and disciplinarian, was glad that his credentials had been established early on.

"Revised itinerary, ladies and gentlemen," Virgil said. He walked down the aisle handing out leaflets. "Only a few changes. Please don't read about those few mornings when you must rise at 5 A.M. It may make you unhappy for the rest of the day. I insist on happy tourists."

"Hey, Pepi," Huggins said airily, "what's with the English tavern bit tonight?"

"Oh, it is delightful, sir. You are Mr. Huggins, right?"

"Yep."

Virgil had not been able to peg the good-looking man in the expensive gray suit or, indeed, match him with the pretty girl with the mountainous black hair. "All the beer and cider you can drink."

"Nothing stronger? In the home of gin and scotch?"

The guide smiled. There it was again. American obsession with alcohol.

Bettenhausen, overhearing, narrowed his eyes and looked menacingly at his wife. "I hate drunks," he muttered.

"Oh, God," Cornelia moaned. "Burt Lancaster. *Gunfight at the O.K. Corral.*"

The routing took them through Hyde Park, then along Knightsbridge, past Buckingham Palace, then into Whitehall, and back around Piccadilly. The handsome city, a *man's* city, Bettenhausen thought, revealed itself to them slowly and forcefully.

"This, ladies and gentlemen, is Piccadilly Circus, with the hideous statue of Eros, the god of love, in the middle," Virgil said. "If you look at the steps around the statue, you will see some of his worshipers."

A gaggle of young people, some sleeping, others lounging, one idly

41

strumming a guitar, loafed on the stone stairs. They were in the student mold: long hair, scruffy clothing, knapsacks.

Arnold Wicker opened a sliding window and with his telephoto lens took a picture of a lean bearded boy sitting beneath the statue. The elongated, hairy face might have been that of his oldest son Alan. (Wicker was neutral on beards.)

Herbie Shackman and Murray Yasuda also pointed cameras. Herbie's was a cheap model. Yasuda's, on the other hand, was a black Nikon. Two extra lenses dangled from his neck.

"I watch every move Murray makes," Herbie said. The dead cigar was locked in his mouth, giving off odors more vile than when it was burning.

"Just clock 'em off, Herbie baby," Yasuda said. He worked feverishly. "They call me Hypo Yasuda back home."

Shackman lurched against one of the Midwestern men. Mr. Hutzler laughed good-naturedly. "Watch it, brother. You hit me with that belly, I'll be flatter 'n' a squashed hen."

"Pardon, pardon," Herbie said. "You shoulda seen me when I was fat."

The man and his wife laughed. Shackman had an explosive self-mocking way of speaking. People laughed at him but also with him.

"I was here in the war," Herbie said, leaning over Murray's shoulder, trying to duplicate the restaurant owner's shots. "We used to call it Commando Corner. That meant hookers. Get it? Piccadilly Commandos. Or the Gonorrhea Race Track."

"Not long enough, not long enough!" Yasuda shouted. "Holy smoke, we whizzed by. Can't we stop?"

"We shall return tomorrow, sir," Virgil said. An endless headache: insatiable photographers. They never had enough time, enough stops, enough sunlight.

"The Nelson column, ladies and gentlemen, in Trafalgar Square," Virgil said. "Who is the scholar in our midst? What was Trafalgar?"

"A sea battle," Rose-Anne Wicker called out. "Off Spain."

Several heads turned to admire the dentist's wife. Sylvia dug Sid in the ribs: "Brains, huh? And good looks."

Bettenhausen cleared his throat with a thunderous noise. "Near Cadiz, Spain. Victory of the British fleet under Nelson over the French and Spanish."

"I admire education," Horace T. Wattle cried out. "But it should be useful. Why clutter your head with useless dates and names?"

Outside the National Gallery, an ebony African in a golden robe walked arm in arm with an alabaster-blonde girl. She wore tight faded blue shorts, and her legs were smooth and hairless.

42

Father Konay, huddled by himself, stared at the couple. So, it was happening all over. We are all God's children. But what would the Ash Valley Ospreys have to say if they saw those two sashaying around London?

Mr. Wattle noticed the couple and his eyebrows arched. "A lot of that went on at Kent State," he said. His high voice had a persuasive quality. "It's the media that did it."

"Hot damn," Gunthorpe exclaimed jealously. "Ole Buck got hisself somethin'."

"That's right," one of the gray-haired ladies said. "It's the media. They ruined the children."

"See it on television and you go out and want to do it."

Herbie Shackman gasped. "Get a load of that blonde. You see her, Murray?"

"Do I ever, Herbie. And with a *schvartzeh*. Well, change your color . . ."

The rage to buy was generating in Lulu. Harry could see it and he was glad. Purchases, the spending of money, the hard bargain, the visible bought object, these sustained her, made her forget about Robbie, about lost chances, a life of wasted hours, aimless days, alcoholic hazes, flatterers.

As soon as the group left the bus—creaking, moving slowly, craning necks to look at the severe gray buildings of Great Russell Street— Lulu walked toward an antique shop next to the St. David's Hotel. Harry was gratified. Attracted by a lamp or tray or screen, she would be less prone to complain about the second-class hotel.

"Will you want all the bags, sir?" Virgil asked him.

"I think so. Perhaps after a while we can work out a system. Which go to the room and which can stay. I'm sorry about this."

"It is perfectly all right, Mr. Flemington. You are paying the extra nine dollars per bag and are within your rights."

"I know. But the bother for you."

"No problem, sir." Virgil shepherded a few Midwestern couples toward the elevator, advising them to be in the lobby punctually at 2 P.M. for their tour. Flemington admired his ease of manner, his patience. There was also a touch of mystery about Virgil—his multinational background, his mastery of languages. Harry was an old newspaperman. The offbeat intrigued him.

In a coffee shop off the lobby Flemington thought he saw a woman look at him—a familiar-looking woman. She was seated with a black couple. Disturbed, he went to the newsstand and bought some postcards. Lulu would be awhile in the antique shop. He sat in a purple

43

chair, his feet on a flowered mauve carpet—*British taste!*—and in large print wrote:

> Dear Robbie:
> Mommy and I are in England, on a big trip. We are thinking about you. Ask your teacher to help you read this. Maybe you can read it yourself. That would be good. We will bring you a prize when we come back. I will take you fishing. Love.
>
> —Daddy and Mommy

In the same careful copy editor's hand, he addressed the card:

> Mr. Robert Flemington
> Burlington Park School
> Petoskey, Michigan

Flemington was grimly amused by the elegant name for an institution for brain-damaged children. Gangly, vacant-eyed Robbie materialized in front of him. He was wearing the blue football helmet, a precaution against increasing convulsions. He has passed his twentieth birthday, Flemington thought.

The rooms were small and narrow, rather like ships' cabins. The London hotels were inferior to the continental hotels, Virgil knew, and they tended to undo the good mood engendered by the friendly city. Décor had something to do with it. The British favored toxic green drapes, emetic yellow walls, funereal gray upholstering. Turner and Constable would have been appalled.

J. P. Huggins did not notice. Kicking his shoes off, loosening his tie, he sprawled on the double bed and read newspapers—the *Financial Times*, the *Financial Review*. He understood little. Exchange rates? Price of gold? Arbitrage? One thing he did know: the big decisions were not made by underpaid financial editors.

"Get me somethin' to read?" Barbara asked. She was in a black lace slip, teetering in spike heels. Her soft flesh bulged above the bust line. The long hard girdle beneath struggled. Slothful, Barbara refused to exercise, play tennis, ride a bicycle.

"They didn't have any movie magazines."

"I don't even hear your dumb insults any more." She was unpacking for both of them, intent on a simple chore. Away from home and children, she needed reminders of her importance to the family.

"What's been goin' on between you and Mario?" she asked.

"Ask him. He's your brother."

"You know they don't let me in on their business dealings."

"Business dealings," Huggins mocked. "How did I fall in with thieves?"

"You watch it, Jimmy. You aren't supposed to go around talking about that."

Huggins groaned. Truly, he was a man in bondage. He dared not refuse Mario and Ralphie. They could hurt. Pull the business out of his law firm. Threaten Jabloner and Kuraskin, make them get rid of J.P. Their techniques were ingenious. And he was in servitude to their sister. Huggins, an attractive man who had had his share of what the boys at Fordham (ah, the memory of his old buddy, the immortal Buck Sweeney!) used to call "quang and quiff," knew that he craved his wife's body more than any in the world. Strange captivity! He lusted for her the way other men lusted for movie stars.

He could bear watching her no longer. Leaping from the bed, he seized her from behind, hands locking on her breasts, mouth nuzzling her neck. "Stop. Cut it out." Her voice, feigning disinterest, made him erupt. He struggled with her to the bed. In seconds, after ripping off her armored underclothing, they were making noisy love.

"It's better in hotel rooms," Huggins gasped.

"That's only for people who don't properly fulfill their marriage vows at home."

Father Konay's black valise—a going-away gift from the sisters at Sacred Heart School—was giving him trouble. Trying to unlock it, he jammed the hasp. His roommate Mr. Wattle went to his assistance at once. From Mr. Wattle's inner coat pocket there appeared the multi-purpose tool—screwdriver, hammer, cockscrew, file, scissors. The industrialist went to work on the lock.

"Say, I'm lucky to get you as a roommate," the priest said. "You look like a man who can fix anything."

"Ran my own machine shop for years. I can fix any kind of motor, driller and shaper, high-speed bit, name it."

Both men had been unwilling to pay the eighty-five-dollar "single room supplement" for the tour. Father Konay's benefactors had offered to give him the benefits of solitude, but he had been so embarrassed by their kindness that he refused. For Mr. Wattle, it was part of his code. "Why pay for what I don't need? I can sleep anywhere. With anyone. I don't use the toilet that much. Why give them eighty-five dollars for nothing?"

"I see your point," the priest said. "I'm sure we'll get along with each other."

Mr. Wattle worked on the lock. There was a click, and it popped open. He shut it again, then opened it, satisfied that it was in order.

"It's the flanged doo-hickey," he said. "They never articulate right even on a good valise like that."

"You're very kind."

"We were put on earth to help each other. I tithe ten per cent to the Missouri Synod."

"Ah, Lutheran."

"Not by choice, actually." Mr. Wattle, to Father Konay's distress, began to undress, whipping off his drip-dry shirt—he wore one and packed another—and then removing his drip-dry gray slacks. He bounced around the room in drip-dry nylon socks and pointed black shoes. "It was Mrs. Wattle's religion, and there was nothing I wouldn't do to please that woman. My own people were River Brethren. I can sing any man's hymn so long as he lets me run my business the way I want."

"When did Mrs. Wattle pass away?"

"Oh, half year ago. I'm in the factory every day. I call on customers personally. I designed our display units. I set up the billing procedures—foolproof, fast. I might even copyright them and market the system. That isn't bad for a man of seventy-one."

"I'd never think you that age. You look fifteen years younger."

"Work does it. Notice how I pepper the guide with questions? I'll get my money's worth out of Planet. Don't give him a minute's rest."

"Mr. Virgil seems very nice."

"I never trust anyone who speaks too many languages."

Father Konay opened his valise. Much too elegant, he felt, much too elaborate with its red lining and compartments. And his simple possessions! They looked shabby in the interior—washed-out underwear, an aged razor, folded black socks, a pair of old bedroom slippers. The sisters should not have wasted the money on him.

Mr. Wattle was exercising, bouncing sideways, clapping his hands over his head, counting breathily. He was trimly constructed, and his green boxer shorts flapped from his stringy thighs.

"You stay in shape," the priest said.

"I invented these exercises myself. They're based on a careful study of anatomical charts. Ran 'em through the computer and came up with the perfect print-out for a man my size, age, and weight."

And ego? wondered Father Konay. But he said nothing. He was in awe of the Washington man. Besides, jogging energetically around the room (in his *gotkes,* as Sam Kesman, the department store owner in Ash Valley, would say), Mr. Wattle jogged into the bathroom.

To Father Konay's consternation, his roommate did not close the door. There followed a series of windy noises, grunts, other sounds. Having lived alone so long, isolated, confined, the priest was distressed. Still, he was a shepherd and a pastor, and he knew that men were born and died with a release of waste matter. There was purpose in everything natural.

"I can't offhand think of anything specific I have against the Roman Catholic Church," Mr. Wattle called from the open bathroom door.

Father Konay turned his back, but from the corner of his eye he could swear he almost saw the man's face peeking out, at john level. "I tend to be a tolerant man myself."

There was a grunt, another windy noise, and a long sigh from the bathroom. The priest shook his head, not so much in disgust but in distress with his inadequacy. Mr. Wattle's virtuoso performance in the hotel room—from fixing the lock to moving his bowels more or less publicly, with interim revelations about his creativity, energy, and resourcefulness—made Stephen Konay aware of how little he had done in his own life.

The toilet flushed, the faucets gushed. Over the running water, the high voice issued forth. "You have colored in your church, padre?"

"A few." He would not talk about the scatter sites housing problem and his behavior "unbecoming a Brother Osprey."

"Keep it that way."

"We're an ethnic town, you know. Poles, Croats, Hungarians."

"Good. They sure can work. Broad backs, weak minds."

"Oh, that's a generalization. The children go to college now."

Mr. Wattle did not hear him. He was doing jump-ups, rattling the bed lamps and the water colors on the wall.

A quintessential European, Pepi Virgil took his major meal at midday. Luckily tours were sold on a breakfast-dinner basis. Clients took their lunch as they wished. Some skipped it. Others snacked. Not Virgil—or most of the guides. "It has to do with our ancient insecurities," Virgil once explained to a curious American who had observed him, seated in the rear of a Parisian restaurant, eating through six courses.

"Insecurities? For this you have to stuff your stomach at one o'clock every day? I couldn't dictate a letter with all that in my gut."

"If we have come this far, we feel obliged to eat while we can. Who knows? By nightfall we may be in jail, out of work, deported, deprived of our food. So we eat fully as early as possible. We regard the rest of the day as a bonus."

Meat, potatoes or rice, a vegetable or two, wine, cheese, dessert, coffee. Virgil, who had spent years in prisons, liked his food well salted and well cooked. Too many pails of watery broth with a bone or fishtail haunted him. Naturally it was difficult for Americans, the blessed of the earth, to understand. They could afford to race from snack bars to stand-up counters to hamburger joints. There would always be more.

Sated, the smoke of his Gitane drifting into his hooded black eyes, Virgil, from his corner table, tried to spot the three members of the tour who had chosen to join Three Worlds in London.

He saw the nice-looking Negro couple. They were traveling with a tall woman, who Virgil suspected was a widow or a divorcee. The three were seated in a corner of the lobby. They seemed to be intelligent people, good tourists. The single woman—Virgil admired her excellent carriage, full hips, and long legs—was named Mrs. Carrell. She was a schoolteacher from Minneapolis, a colleague of the black woman, Mrs. Grant. They taught in the same high school and were on extended leave. The Negro man, who seemed a bit tense—he was lighter-skinned than his wife and tended to frown—was a physician. "Not a brain surgeon," he had said softly to Virgil, "no big deal, no Sidney Poitier. Just a plain doctor."

Approaching the three people, Virgil saw others of his group—the Midwesterners, smiling, buying postcards, the enormous Herbie, shouting at his wife, following Yasuda like an elephant behind his mahout, the dentist and his pretty wife—and he was pleased with his wards. They seemed manageable. Mr. Wattle might be a burden, and Herbie with his cigars and jokes might rub a few people the wrong way, but there seemed to be no insurmountable problems. Indeed, the black couple were a positive advantage. Refined, educated, they were the kind of Negroes who endowed other tourists with a sense of virtue.

"Dr. and Mrs. Grant, you are very punctual. And so is Mrs. Carrell."

"Teachers, Pepi," Theresa Carrell said. "Always on time."

Virgil liked her face. A high forehead, a long nose, suggesting French ancestry, a wide mouth. Her features were not conventionally beautiful, but the effect was one of serenity and intelligence. Virgil wondered how long she had been widowed, or divorced, or separated. She seemed a desirable woman, even in her early forties. Why was she unwed? If widowed, he ruminated, she must have been bereaved some years ago. Otherwise she would not be gaily touring the world. Or would she? Virgil had met odd types in his career. Sometimes they shed their widow's weeds immediately for a thirty-two-day jaunt. Without a twinge of guilt. Once he had had a client, a doddering old man barely able to mount the bus, die in transit between Vienna and Budapest. The new widow, a perky Californian with a pug-dog profile and woolly lavender hair, informed Virgil, "Ship the bones back home, Pep, so's I can get on with the fun."

"You have had lunch?" Virgil asked.

Mrs. Grant—her first name was Ibith—replied, "Just a bite. We're saving our appetites for that wild Elizabethan wingding tonight."

Virgil was tempted to warn them—"Eat while you can." The Elizabethan feast, featuring suckling pig or suckling lamb, was not all it was advertised to be. British cooks managed to wreck the finest meats. But the company had a long-term contract with The Nag and Dragon.

"Did your people arrive in good condition this morning?" Mrs. Carrell asked.

"They are splendid in every way," Pepi said.

With a skip and a hop, Mr. Wattle approached the black couple and the teacher. "I stand foursquare in back of the Supreme Court decision on school desegregation," the rubber manufacturer fluted, "but I draw the line at forced busing."

Virgil introduced him to Dr. Grant and his wife and to Theresa Carrell.

"You'll be undergoing forced busing for three weeks," Ibith Grant said easily. Her husband's frown grew deeper.

"That's different. People like you and the doctor are different."

There was a pause. Virgil saw it was a good moment to start herding his tour to the bus. "London awaits, ladies and gentlemen. This way."

Bodies shifted, girdles were tugged, undershorts yanked down.

"Did you have lunch?" Rose-Anne Wicker asked Bettenhausen.

"On the steps of the British Museum."

"Oh? An outdoor café?"

"No, a picnic. I bought a wedge of double Gloucester and some water biscuits, and Cornelia and I shared a bottle of Bass ale."

The dentist's wife's eyes widened in awe of the bearded man. Clearly Bettenhausen possessed a flair for the original.

Arm in arm, Mr. and Mrs. Legrand approached the bus door. It was a mild day, but his black topcoat was buttoned to the throat. She, on the other hand, shuffled along in scuffs. She wore no stockings.

"Who are we waiting for?" Wattle piped from the doorway. "Why the delay? Time is money."

"So's chopped liver," Herbie shouted. He hefted his bulk up the steps and tottered as if about to fall on Murray Yasuda. Herbie lumbered down the aisle, crushing feet, pressing his weight against shoulders, heads. "*Gottenu,* they don't build these like they used to."

"Back of the bus, Herbie," Murray ordered. "We'll set up a command post."

Virgil was missing the Flemingtons. They came out of the hotel, both of them looking too patrician for a Planet Tour.

"Our hotel room is a disgrace," Mrs. Flemington said to Virgil. "I demand it be changed."

"We'll pay the extra charge for a bigger room," her husband said.

"Really, madame? What is wrong?" Virgil gestured to the bus steps.

"It is narrow and poorly furnished," Lulu said.

"I shall take care of it when we return, madame. Of course, we are only in London one night . . ."

"See that you do," she said.

Virgil noticed that Flemington was carrying an elongated bag, full of hinges and straps. It was not one he had noticed among their fourteen pieces and he had an infallible memory for luggage.

"Expandable," Flemington said. "It looks like a flat briefcase, until you open it."

"Incredible," the guide said. He stroked it—light blue canvas. He realized he had to contend not only with the fourteen pieces the Flemingtons had paid for, but bags within bags.

Inside the bus, smoky fumes obscured their vision. Herbie and Murray were puffing cigars again, in blithe disregard of Virgil's rules.

"Gentlemen, the cigars," Virgil said.

There were mumbled curses in back, a loud "Jesus Christ, what a chicken outfit," from Yasuda. But the cigars were extinguished.

It was odd, Virgil mused, how minorities in America, alleged to be oppressed, seemed quite able to take care of themselves. He would never cease to be amazed by Americans, even when they ran him ragged.

Harry Flemington settled into his seat, giving Lulu the window, and relaxed. They were off to a good start. He would have to give Lulu shopping time, let her bargain, price things, beat down merchants, spend money. He had seen her studying the cashmere sweaters in the shop in the St. David's lobby. The sweater shop would occupy her during the free hour after the tour. And tomorrow morning —the silver vaults! Approvingly, he patted the canvas of the tricky bag. He had bought six from a New York store specializing in safari equipment.

"And so, London, ladies and gentlemen," Virgil said. "I shall now introduce your guide for the day, Mr. Derek Bell."

A pale young man with red splotches on his cheeks and waved yellow hair took the microphone. "Howdyewdew, and welcome to London."

At once everyone—including Herbie, who had been badgering Murray for camera tips—fell quiet. Virgil smiled. It was remarkable what an upper-class British accent could accomplish. Derek Bell's constricted vowels and slurred consonants, distilled through a fine Anglo-Saxon nose, shamed them all.

"Does he wake up at 3 A.M. and talk like that?" Herbie asked Flo.

"Shaddap. You might learn something. He's gawgeous. Like to take him home, Shirl?"

"You. I'll take Pepi."

Something was disturbing Harry Flemington. He tried concentrating on the guide's Oxonian cadences and flourishes (". . . of Roman London, veddy, veddy little remains . . .") but a vague unease was eating him. Suddenly he recalled the woman he had thought he recognized in the coffee shop of the hotel. Was she now on the bus? And had she smiled at him when he and Lulu took their seats?

Flemington turned. There was a moment of terror, of a thousand memories crammed into a second of shock. It was Theresa Carrell, seated in the rear of the bus, looking at him from behind sunglasses. Flemington felt an involuntary convulsion in his gut. Could he have been wrong? He turned away, tried to settle himself, then looked again.

"Is anything wrong, Harry?" Lulu asked.

"No, dear."

Unmistakable. The corona of dark brown hair, curling a bit wildly, the high forehead, the assertive nose. He recalled Virgil mentioning that people were joining the tour in London. What were the odds on this? Flemington wondered. Of all the people in the world, of all the people going on tours this year—how did it happen to him? He shuddered.

"The efficient Romans laid out London as a grid, with two crossing main streets and a rectangular wall. . . ."

Some lying was in order. He wished he had been able to see Theresa before she boarded the bus—alone, without Lulu around. They might have co-ordinated stories. Perhaps the truth would be best. They had last seen each other four years ago, just after Wade Carrell was killed in an auto accident in St. Paul. Full of fear and loneliness, Theresa had come to Detroit, called him from a motel.

He would keep it vague—"goodness, how long is it, Terry? Seventeen, eighteen?" Lulu had never met her and had heard about her only in brief bits of conversation, occasional reminiscences by Harry. Sometimes someone who had known Harry and Theresa in Minnesota would come by. "Still looks great, Harry, teaching, keeps busy. . . ." Lulu would pretend not to hear.

"St. Paul's is the most important of Sir Christopher Wren's work," the guide intoned. "The dome is a copy of the dome of St. Peter's in Rome. Now then, do we have any students of architecture? Who designed St. Peter's dome?"

"Michelangelo," Rose-Anne Wicker replied.

Lulu Flemington looked at the dentist's wife with vague envy. She had spotted the Wicker woman as someone with whom she might be willing to dine.

"Who? Who?" Herbie bellowed. "Oh, Charlton Heston. Get the angle, Murray."

As the bus parked outside Westminster Abbey, Flemington was trying frantically to work out a scenario. Perhaps Theresa would refuse to recognize him. That would not work. Lulu, while she had never seen Theresa, or even a photo of her, surely knew her by her married name. There was no way of escaping. They would have to greet one another. Harry would let Terry do the reminiscing, the recollections—"How long is it? How long ago was it?"—and he would feign indifference. Just a girl out of his past. Old now. All over, Lu. Haven't seen her in fifteen, sixteen years. Minneapolis. Widowed. Too bad. First marriage went sour. (But he would not add: I ruined it.)

"We call this architectural style Early English, or more properly Gothic," the guide was saying. The members of Three Worlds gathered around him. Harry, waiting with Lulu—she leaned on his arm, resting also on the umbrella with the ivory handle—saw Theresa smiling at him.

"Harry?" And the voice—musical, soft.

"For goodness' sake. Theresa."

They shook hands. An eternal woman, a woman who did not run to fat. "Terry, this is my wife, Louise. I don't think you've ever met. Lu, you remember me talking about Theresa. Let's see. Your name is Carrell, right? With an *e* instead of an *o*."

Louise Flemington's eyes were like rock candy—crystalline, jagged. The lines at the sides of her mouth lengthened down the sides of her jaw. "How do."

"I couldn't believe it when I saw you," Theresa said. She did not seem embarrassed or upset by the meeting, or the knowledge that for three weeks she and the man she had shared a bed with so long would be in close quarters. "I said to my friends, 'I *know* that man,' and I certainly did. Imagine."

The black couple, listening to the guide's nasal peroration . . . "rebuilt in 1245 by Henry III . . . and finally completed in the sixteenth century" . . . drifted back a few steps. Ibith Grant was looking at Mrs. Flemington.

"These are the people I'm traveling with," Theresa said. "Mr. and Mrs. Flemington. Dr. Grant and Mrs. Grant. From Minneapolis. Neighbors and friends."

Lulu barely nodded.

Flemington addressed the black couple. "Department of old flames. We used to date, oh, twenty years ago."

"I know," Ibith Grant said. "You were a newspaperman. . . . On the *Register*. Terry told me about you." She stopped abruptly. Lulu, guiding herself with the umbrella, suggesting a blind person, had strolled away, pretending to study the spires.

"We've got lots of ground to cover," Flemington said. "You still teaching, Terry?"

"Same old grind. Back to work after Wade was killed."

"Five years ago?"

"Yes. I'd been subbing up to then, then decided to try it full time." Theresa Carrell directed her head toward Lulu, who was moving away from the group.

"We'll talk tonight," Flemington said. He hurried after his wife.

"What was that all about?" Ibith Grant asked.

"Long story, Ibbie. Lord, what I've gotten myself into."

Ibith Grant faked a shiver. "Mrs. Flemington ought to invest in a few smiles."

"I've never seen her before." Theresa Carrell looked at the Flemingtons. They were walking into the church.

Inside, the cold tombs of statesmen, poets, and royalty impelled Mrs. Legrand, in an assertive voice, to inform Mavis Hutzler: "Twenty-five years ago they told my sweetie that he would die of ulcers unless he was operated on." Chubby little Mavis drew away, but Mrs. Legrand grabbed her arm, forcing her to listen. "They gave him six months to live. Look at him." She belted her husband in the small of the back. He laughed silently. "Look at him. Going strong, age eighty-five and on sedation every minute."

Flemington too was agitated with thoughts of death in the interior of the mausoleum-church. He was thinking of Wade Carrell, hardly the man for a woman like Theresa. Some dreadful accident—an unbraked concrete mixer or earth mover rolling downhill, crushing Carrell's European car. Hearing about it third hand, in the paneled den of his Grosse Pointe home, Flemington had felt the old fires spark. He had to suppress a nasty sense of exaltation. He could marry Theresa now. There had been times, getting the Minneapolis papers occasionally from newspaper friends, he would scan the obits to see if Wade Carrell had died. Now he was dead. Moodily he had examined his options. He would divorce Lulu. He would marry Theresa.

53

Finally, after all those years of fumbling, gasping meetings in motel rooms, friends' homes, they would be able to make love as man and wife—leisurely, with no worries about discovery. These fantasies came to nothing. Apart from a single meeting with Theresa, a final semi-clothed bout of coupling, he inadequate, she unaroused, and the question put to him bluntly: "Now or never, Harry . . ."

"When did you see her last?" Lulu asked. They had paused in front of the tomb of Lady Margaret Beaufort.

"Oh, gosh, sixteen, seventeen years ago. Maybe less. Ran into her on a trip back to Minneapolis."

"She wasn't married then."

"No, I don't think so. She and Carrell were married, ah, maybe nine years when he was killed."

The silence from Lulu was an accusation.

"She's aged terribly," Flemington blurted. "Her face is lined. She hasn't had an easy life."

"Heah is the grave of David Livingstone, the medical missionary," the guide said. "He died in Africa in 1873 and was buried heah a yeah later. You know, of course, the story of his two African servants burying his heart under a tree in Africa and then carrying his body for miles so it could go back to England."

"How could I forget?" asked Herbie. "I'm all choked up."

"Dat's love, massah," Ibith Grant said to her husband.

Dr. Grant's impassive face, always in a faint frown, crinkled with humor. "I'm torn between medical loyalties and black power."

"Where you folks from?" Herbie boomed. He towered over the black couple.

"Minneapolis," Dr. Grant said.

"Herbie Shackman, Westbury, Lawn Guyland. I'm a tax man. What line of work you in?"

"I'm a physician."

Herbie's orange eyebrows and mustache waggled in approval. "It's about time this mob got a little class, hey, Ma?" He directed his remarks to Mrs. Legrand. "A doctor, you hear, Ma? No charge for hustling patients, Doc. But I can help ya with your deductions."

For a moment the frown left Dr. Grant's beige face. Herbie Shackman was a relief from the pirouetting of so many whites when they learned he was an M.D. It was invigorating to confront someone crude and loud.

"Now, Harvey, you're teasing," Mrs. Legrand said.

"Harvey is my middle name. My name is Herbie. Actually, Herbie Harvey Shackman."

"Livingstone and Stanley," Bettenhausen said. "Hardwicke was bril-

54

liant. He played Livingstone like a choirmaster. Eighty minutes of Zulus singing 'Onward, Christian Soldiers.' When Spencer Tracy said good-by, Hardwicke barely noticed. He was looking for a second baritone."

Flemington had taken his wife's arm and was guiding her through the dim interior of the Abbey. For some reason, he was feeling a bottomless sorrow for her. A great deal of what they saw would be lost on Lulu. She was attracted only by what she could buy. The Abbey, with its marvels of the past, a cultural fruitcake too rich for one eating, would be valueless to her. As they approached the Kent memorial to Shakespeare, Flemington reflected that Lulu rarely read a newspaper or a magazine. Of course she had never been much of an intellect—boarding schools, a junior college in Pasadena that specialized in dumb rich girls.

Harry saw Theresa Carrell reading from a Blue guide. She was studying the monument to Handel. Her dark eyes were lively behind horn-rimmed glasses, and he envied her, envied the years Carrell had enjoyed as her husband. Theresa had always had this capacity to absorb new sensations, to encounter the past and make it part of herself. She was jotting something in the book.

"Ah, Disraeli," Bettenhausen said to a small circle of attendants. "Played by . . ."

"George Arliss, in the picture of the same name," his wife said.

In late afternoon, after some serious shopping, the results of which Flemington was transferring from paper sacks to the collapsible valise, Lulu rested on the hotel bed. She was sated with buying. But her silence told him that she was in an unsettled mood.

"That woman should leave the tour," Lulu said. Resting, in a peach silk and lace gown, a black eye-shield on her face to induce sleep, she seemed to have shriveled.

"Why, Lu? Because of a crazy coincidence?"

"She should disqualify herself."

"Lu, Theresa is a poor schoolteacher. She's probably been planning on this tour for years, counting pennies."

"Offer to reimburse her for everything she has spent."

"Ridiculous. You don't know Theresa."

"Not as well as some people."

"Listen, Lu. That business with Theresa was dead and buried when I married you. Over. Finished." Like a trained clerk, he folded cashmere cardigans.

"I'm not so sure. You were flustered when you saw her today."

"Shock of recognition. God, Lu, she's a middle-aged widow with a

55

grown son, and she's got a lined face and a lot of trouble." Flemington detested himself as he spoke. Theresa was forty-four and looked ten years younger.

"Harry, get me a small scotch."

"So early, Lu?"

"A halfie. I won't discuss that woman again. Not if I can help it. What a nerve. And traveling with colored people."

"They seem decent enough." He returned to his work. Flemington, the orderly, packing the general's PX loot for shipment to the States.

"A small scotch, Harry. I won't discuss her."

In the upper dining room of The Nag and Dragon the tour was greeted by a long oaken table set with tankards (plastic) and trenchers (aluminum). A half dozen busty "serving wenches" stood by. Three University of London students in doublet and hose wandered about singing madrigals.

"The fakery, methinks, doth give me a sinus headache," Rosie Wicker said to her husband.

"Oh, get with it, Rosie," the dentist said. "It's for laughs." The man was a born joiner, incapable of hurting anyone's feelings. When Cub Scouts demurred, Arnold would lead the singing of "I've Got That Old Scout Feeling Down in my Shoes."

Huggins registered approval of the beer and was informed by Mr. Bettenhausen that it was Barclay's, with a drawing of Dr. Samuel Johnson on the label. Possibly, the Hollywood man theorized, because the brewery was a descendant of Thrale's brewery. Johnson had been a friend of Mrs. Thrale.

"Learn something new every day," Huggins added.

"Hey, Jimmy," Murray Yasuda called. "You didn't take a single picture today. With all that gear?"

Careful there. J. P. Huggins pretended not to hear. He would have to start clicking them off the way Murray and Herbie did. His photos always stunk—out of focus, too dark. But the case, the case. It attracted attention. He would have to start using the cameras.

Horace T. Wattle, ensconced like a monarch amid a group of the gray-haired men and blue-rinsed women (they were impressed with his opinions), ignored the left breast of the serving wench (which was about to dip into an earthen ramekin of jellied clams) and fluted: "What is that garbage? Why does it smell like that?"

"Beggin' your pardon, sir," the girl said, "it's seafood appetizers—clams, shrimp, winkles—"

56

"Ye gods!" Mr. Wattle sang. "It's poison! Bring me a bowl of chicken consommé!"

Mr. and Mrs. Legrand were waving their arms. "For us also! Chicken consommé!"

The notion ignited, flared, and consumed half of the Three Worlds table. There were shouts of "Consommé!" "Chicken soup!" "No fish!"

"Just a bleedin' minute," the girl said. "Put up yer 'ands. Let's count all the perishin' chickens."

"Oh, dear God," Rose-Anne Wicker moaned. "They're ordering chicken soup."

"It was that guy Wattle," Arnie said. "He downgraded the seafood."

"Chicken soup!"

"Consommé!"

Flemington watched Bettenhausen with amusement. A man worth knowing, full of odd bits of information. He'd overheard someone say that he had worked in Hollywood, a director or something.

Barbara Huggins listened to the banter. It bothered her. "What are they yakking about? That fat guy and the dentist."

"Education, Barbs. Something ginzos hate."

She took Jimmy's abuse unemotionally. "You should talk. Graduated from Fordham by cheating. You hid the books in the toilet and got the answers there. And two fake exam papers in law school."

"Knock it off." Huggins stared at the waitress' breasts. He was ready for some escape from the bondage in which the Malfi family held him—their daughter's body, their sons' power. A free-style ladies' man before marriage, he had, despite his good looks, remained faithful to Barbara. Was the time now? Were there possibilities in this junket of Geritol drinkers and truss wearers?

"Trifle, sir? Tart? Flummery?" the waitress asked.

Huggins fixed his eyes on her breasts. "One of each."

Huggins stared at the gooey substances on his plate. He needed a few laughs, a bender. If he could find Buck Sweeney somewhere in Europe. Was he in Rome? Paris? Ah, the laughs they had. Like the old guy in *The Iceman Cometh* (there was a great harp for you, old O'Neill) kept saying: "There's no life in the booze."

At the distant end of the table, Mr. Wattle, having delivered an attack on welfare, glared at Dr. Grant and his wife. "Absolutely nothing personal in what I say," he told the black couple. "People like you are decent Americans."

"Thank you, sir," Dr. Grant said softly. "We regard you, too, as a patriot."

The compliment astonished Mr. Wattle. His bald head bobbed

57

back, as if avoiding a left jab. "I like to think I am. You spend a lifetime battling radicals like John L. Lewis, it gives you a perspective."

Virgil moved toward them. "Gentlemen, and Mrs. Grant," he said jokingly, "we usually put a limit on political discussions. We are on this trip to enjoy ourselves, to buy things, to educate ourselves."

"Good point," Mr. Wattle said. "An education never ends." He leveled a finger at Theresa Carrell. "Our charming schoolteacher friend there, Mrs.—ah . . . ?"

"Carrell," Virgil said.

"I saw Mrs. Carrell making notes in her guidebook today," the rubber manufacturer said. "I approve. But I'd sure like to know what she was writing."

Several heads turned toward Theresa.

"There's no mystery. I make notes of my impressions, or anything unusual. Sometimes I use them with my classes."

"She could keep me after school any day," Herbie chuckled to Murray. "Some teacher."

"But what were you writing at Buckingham Palace?" Mr. Wattle pursued.

Theresa explained. When the guard was changed, the band played Mozart, something from *The Marriage of Figaro*, and it seemed strange to hear Mozart at a military ceremony. She intended to ask why.

"Some people are too goddamn smart for their own good," Lulu Flemington said loudly. No one looked at her.

Pepi Virgil explained: Figaro is taunting Cherubino, who is going off to be a soldier—he will no longer be a ladies' man, but a soldier. "It's the one that begins, '*Non più andrai*,'" the escort said. "So, in a sense, it is a military air, but a mocking one."

Flemington was staring at Theresa Carrell with pained longing. She was not a beautiful woman when one analyzed the features individually—nose too long, mouth too wide. But there was a warmth in her face, a generosity that was a reflection of the woman's spirit. This bloody obsession of his! How long? *Twenty-five years?* Since they were at the University of Minnesota? In the dim light—amid a clanging of dishes—he heard the madrigal singers plunking lutes.

"Take your eyes off that goddamn woman," Lulu said.

"Lu, please."

"I am getting the hell out of here."

The people at the Flemingtons' end of the table tried to look away, studied their flummery and trifle. Barbara Huggins shoved her husband in the ribs. "She's drunk. Look, Jimmy, she's trying to get up."

58

"Snootful," Huggins said.

Lulu was swiveling on the wooden bench, trying to get her legs around. But she was trapped between her husband and Mr. Wattle.

"Goddamn smart bitch," Lulu muttered. She wrenched herself free of her husband's arm, spun her legs around, kicking Mr. Wattle in the groin with a heel, and then pitched face forward on the sawdust-strewn floor.

"Oh, the poor thing," Rosie Wicker cried.

At the far end of the table, Theresa pretended not to have noticed. The Grants did a fair job of helping her. They were adept at feigning ignorance of slights.

As Flemington tried to lift his wife from the floor, Pepi Virgil was at their side, helping. "It is so stuffy in here," he said. "Mrs. Flemington is understandably ill."

Harry braced an arm around his wife's waist and guided her to the door.

"I shall help you find a taxi," Pepi said. The couple left the tavern. Virgil was a step behind.

"Something was going on," Mavis Hutzler, one of the Midwestern ladies said. "She was sore about something, maybe the service."

Herbie Shackman stroked his orange mustache. "*Oi*, what a mouth."

Mr. Wattle adjusted his glasses. "Are you people aware who that woman is? Do you know she's a Deaver? I had them as customers some years back. Stock once sold at 16½, and it's up to 103¼ now, and just try to get some. She's the biggest single shareholder. Her father was one of the pioneers. He controlled eighty-two per cent of the gasket market."

"If she's so rich, she shouldn't waste herself on alcohol," Mrs. Legrand said. "Especially if she can't handle it."

"I choose to think," Mr. Wattle said, "that she suffered a spell of food poisoning."

"You hear, Moishe?" Herbie asked Murray Yasuda.

"Herbie, quiet down," Flo warned.

"You hear, Moishe? You get that rich, you do what you want, and he'll make excuses for you."

"They don't scare me," Yasuda said. "When I get ready to tie one on, I'll do it."

"Trifle? Who ordered the trifle?" the serving wench asked. "I have three trifles, two flummeries, two treacle pies, and someone asked for jello with no cream?"

"Me!" Mr. Wattle cried. "I won't touch any of that garbage!"

In the taxi Lulu passed out. Flemington practically had to carry her to the hotel room. There he undressed her, engulfed in pity by the sight of the flimsy undergarments, silk, lace, elastic, hanging on her meager frame. The tracery of blue veins on her shrunken hips frightened him.

In his silk Sulka pajamas, a gift from Lulu on his last birthday, he sat in the bathroom, engorged with guilt, puffing the pipe he had owned since his college days. (He could recall smoking it with undergraduate pride in front of Theresa, the first time they dated. "It's called Rum and Maple," he informed her proudly. "It smells good enough to spread on pancakes," she said.)

Flemington began reading the Planet Tours *Tips 'n' Hints* book— how to shop, what to buy, what to see, what to eat. It seemed sterile. When you traveled you had to bring your own magic to the places you visited. He envied people like the Bettenhausens and the Wickers —and Theresa—who seemed to draw so much fun, so much enrichment out of new places. Like Theresa making notations on Mozart in her guidebook. Once he had had that capacity—to see, to feel, to hear. What was that quote from Thoreau? Something about his youth, before he lost control of his senses and was able to see the light of common day?

Huggins and his wife, invariably late, had missed breakfast. The doors to the St. David's Hotel dining room closed behind the Bettenhausens.

"We blow anything?" J.P. asked the stout man.

"Kippers, sausage, eggs, tomato, bacon, toast, marmalade made of exquisite Seville oranges, and several pots of English breakfast tea."

Barbara pouted. She was starving. But she needed a long time to work on her face, her pile of hair. "Jesus, what a lousy way to start the day," she whined.

"You can get something in the milk bar next door," Cornelia Bettenhausen said. She felt sorry for the Huggins woman. Everyone seemed to have found friends, formed a group. The poor thing, stumbling on her spikes, forever touching her black beehive, seemed adrift.

"Care to join us?" Bettenhausen asked. He was studying a map. The Wickers and Mrs. Carrell came by, awaiting his word. "I'm leading a tour of the National Gallery and the Tate. And the Courtauld and Wallace collections, if there's time."

Across the lobby Herbie Shackman and his party were planning a shopping tour. Murray Yasuda was trying to interest them in a private car and chauffeur, but Sid and Si suggested the underground.

Huggins rejected offers from both groups, Bettenhausen's party and the Westbury shoppers. As he guided Barbara toward the door, a heavy-set man in a clay-colored suit approached. He was not, as far as the lawyer could recall, on the tour.

"Mr. Huggins?"

"James Patrick." So fast? Ah, those bastards Mario and Ralphie. Making him the patsy! The only one in the family with a law degree. Was it a trap? Their revenge on him?

"Do you know a Mr. John Leland?"

"Nope. No Leland." Barbara walked out of the hotel.

"You're sure?"

Huggins studied the stranger—a jaw wider than the top of his head, a bagging suit. J.P. knew what the man was: *fuzz.* "Let's see it, pal."

"What?"

"The potsy."

"Hmmm?"

"You know what I mean. The potsy. The *badge.* I'm a lawyer, you know?"

"I know, Mr. Huggins. Are you sure a man named Leland didn't approach you in the past few days?"

"In my line of work I meet a lot of Liebowitzes and Ledermans, but no Lelands. Excuse me."

"All right, sir. My mistake."

"No sweat, friend."

The wide-jawed man walked through the lobby. Once he stared at the gangling figure of Dr. Arnold Wicker entering a cab, and once he stopped to study Mr. Legrand, posted stiffly at the doorway. Then he walked to a black Austin parked beyond the hotel façade.

"No use," he said to the driver. "There's too many of them, and they move them too fast on these tours. Get after Paris and have them take it."

Virgil took a seat near the elevator and waited for the Flemingtons. He was disturbed by the events of the previous night. But he told himself that Mrs. Flemington, the heiress to the Deaver fortune (whatever that was), had been drunk. Doubtless she would get drunk again and create difficult moments. But at least he was forewarned—she was a bad drinker with a nasty tongue.

He wondered why she had chosen to pick on the teacher. After all, they were seated some distance from each other. Mrs. Carrell's comments had been anything but insulting. And he had seen no flirtation, no glances, arch winks. He decided that Mrs. Flemington was hallucinating. She was imagining that the teacher was after her husband. It was not a new experience for Virgil. Menopausal and alcoholic ladies frequently saw rivals in the course of a tour. Once an oil baroness had accused six women of sleeping with her semiparalyzed husband! Her assaults on innocent women had forced Virgil to dismiss her from "European Roundelay."

Flemington emerged from the elevator and held the door open for his wife. He was sporting another of those expandable valises, in the same navy and gray style. What happened to the one he had yesterday? Virgil could guess—crammed with cashmeres. Another nine dollars, he noted mentally.

"We'd like to visit the silver vaults," Flemington said.

"Of course, sir. I can accompany you if you wish. Or recommend some merchants."

"Never mind," Lulu said. "I know how to buy."

"I am certain Madame does."

"I'm on to you people. The business of kickbacks and favoring certain stores."

Virgil was not offended. He listened to these accusations on every tour. The world was convinced that every escort got rich on baksheesh from cheating rug merchants and cunning antique dealers. "They are located in Chancery Lane. I shall help you find a taxi."

There was crispness in Mrs. Flemington's voice, vigor in her stride. It was the thrill of the chase. He had seen this before in clients. They would brave storms, sprained ankles, dysentery, to hunt down a bargain. Their health improved, their limbs revived, their spirits soared at the hint of something for sale.

As the Flemingtons stood outside the building on Chancery Lane, Lulu took his hand coyly. "I was naughty last night, Harry. I promise you, not again. That woman set my teeth on edge."

"Lu, ignore her."

"I'll try."

The uniformed guard all but tugged at his forelock as Lulu swept by. Forever, Flemington would be stunned by her regal manner—the angle of the chin, the way she handled the umbrella, the raising of a hand.

The vaults were a series of individual shops, ranging from monkish cells to good-sized rooms. The merchants seemed to be uniformly Jewish, while the guards had the beefsteak faces of Saxon yeomanry. Two ancient types, he concluded, joined in commerce.

They made a tour of the exteriors of the shops, reading the names on the doors. There were Pearlsteins, and Hacohens, and Messelmans. Across the floor, Flemington, to his amusement, saw Herbie and Flo Shackman and his party, bustling noisily in and out of the shops.

"Whaddya got here?" he heard Herbie bellow. "*Shalom, shalom, chaverim.*"

"Herbie, quiet down."

63

Si Shapiro lingered outside. He was a quiet man, Herbie's brother-in-law. "Hello there," he said to the Flemingtons.

Lulu did not acknowledge his existence. Harry asked him how he had learned about the vaults.

"Flo's cousin works here," Si said. "He's got a place specializing in antique silver. Lovely people. If you want to meet him . . ."

Lulu marched by, ignoring him.

"*Oi vay!* Ten thousand for that little *drehdel?*" Herbie's voice exploded around the vaults.

"*Hondle* with him, *hondle* with him, Herbie."

Si shook his head, smiling tolerantly. "No stopping Herbie." He looked for tolerance in Flemington, who offered him a smile. "Although sometimes I wish I could."

"He's a lot of laughs," Flemington said.

Lulu continued her parade. For shrewd reasons—her husband never was able to understand her feints and parries—she now walked into a fair-sized establishment. I. KLEINERMAN & SONS was imprinted on the door.

A stout silken-faced man wearing a black suit and a skullcap was behind the counter. "Ah, good morning, good morning, madam."

The silver merchant also knew royalty. Harry did not mind being excluded. He was fascinated with the Yiddo-English accent. Or was it Anglo-Yiddish? It amused him: full of strange gutturals, Oxonian vowels. He had heard it often in London's kosher restaurants during the war.

"What is Madam's pleasure?" I. Kleinerman asked.

Lulu scanned the items in the counter—trays, bowls, services. She found nothing that appealed to her. Removing her dark glasses, her eyes riveted themselves on the breakfront behind Mr. Kleinerman.

"That one."

"Which, madam?"

"The coffee and tea service. On the middle shelf."

An appreciative smile turned the merchant's mouth. "Madam knows quality. She has gone directly to my pride and joy."

"Show it to me."

Mr. Kleinerman called to an inner office. A pudgy dark man emerged, possibly Kleinerman, Jr. "Madam wishes to see the Flaxman." Junior took a key from a chain tied to his belt and opened the breakfront. Gently he took out the set and placed it on a blue velvet cloth.

"A Flaxman, madam," the proprietor said. "Handle it gently, Sonny. Not many people ask to see the Flaxman."

Outside one of the guards had drifted by. Flemington laughed to

64

himself. Did he and Lulu, with their tweedy duds, suggest genteel crooks? A Terry Thomas couple about to pull a heist?

The silver gleamed with unearthly glory on the blue cloth. Flemington knew nothing about silver, but these had a rare quality about them. Whatever a Flaxman was, Lulu had, with a pointer's nose, gone right to it.

There was five pieces—a tray with a raised edge, a coffeepot, a shorter teapot, a creamer, and a sugar bowl. The lines were simple and severe and each piece had a raised design. Lulu picked up the coffeepot. "What does this represent?"

"Scenes from Greek mythology, madam," Mr. Kleinerman said. "On the piece you are holding, Artemis and Orion. The teapot is Castor and Pollux."

"The sons of Zeus," Harry said.

Kleinerman turned a flattering eye toward him: *brotherhood of culture, opposed to the brotherhood of cash.* "Yes indeed, sir. On the tray, Baucis and Philemon. On the sugar bowl, Pluto and Persephone. On the creamer—Sonny, what is this again?"

"Leda and the swan, Papa."

Lulu turned each piece in her hands. It saddened Harry that she knew nothing of mythology but understood the price of each item. In his mind he saw his father's ragged Bulfinch. Passages were underlined. Some were annotated. Like the notes Theresa made.

"Excuse my ignorance," Harry said. "But who was Flaxman?"

Mr. Kleinerman patted his yarmulke. "Late eighteenth and early nineteenth century. Sculptor and designer. He has work in Westminster Abbey and St. Paul's."

"And this is one of his designs?" Harry asked.

Mr. Kleinerman waggled his head. "It is proper to call it a Flaxman, although the history of the set and the appraisals refer to it as School of Flaxman."

"Not a real Flaxman?" Lulu asked.

"A student. There is an imprint of George III on the underside of each piece, madam, and the date 1822. That confirms that it is the work of the Worshipful Company of Goldsmiths and Silversmiths."

Young Kleinerman fetched a green cloth envelope bound with a string. His father untied it. Inside were yellowing papers, frail documentation. "Its history, madam. All previous owners including the Duchess of Wentford. Appraisals from the assay offices of London, Sheffield, and Chester."

"How much are you asking?"

"You are interested in a purchase?"

"I came in here, didn't I?" She was in pursuit. The fox had been sighted. Harry saw her eyes glistening, her mouth slightly parted, the lips moist. Years ago, when they made love, locking bodies and devouring each other's mouths . . .

"Madam realizes she went to the most valuable piece. I assume she knows something of the price of these items."

"I know all about them."

"Of course." I. Kleinerman's hands came to rest on the glass counter. "With the history, appraisals, packaging and shipping, insurance"—he gulped once—"the price is sixty-two hundred pounds, or roughly fifteen thousand dollars."

Lulu's eyes opened wide. The blue pupils froze. "That is an outrage."

"Madam—"

"I know about silver. I own a great deal. I own two Martinez sets I got in Spain six years ago, and they were real Martinezes, no Schools of."

"A Martinez is not a Flaxman."

Flemington had to move back a pace. It was a *mano a mano*, two old pros circling for the opening. He had to admire Lulu's strategies; he had equal respect for I. Kleinerman's defense.

"I did not pay anything approaching fifteen thousand for them."

"But that is not an excessive figure for this beautiful set."

"It is not a fair price and you know it." The tightly strapped minibreasts under her pink cashmere seemed to tremble with anger. It seemed outlandish to Flemington, but the creases around her neck vanished; there was ruddy color in her cheeks.

"I suggest Madam make a counteroffer."

"I shall offer you seven thousand dollars."

There was a new metallic timbre to her voice. Flemington thought of the sycophants at the country club, the *arrivistes* at the Detroit A.C., who lived in fear of that voice. And with it all—a sweet smile, something to melt the heart of I. Kleinerman. It was, Harry thought, like that superb scene in *Cavalleria Rusticana*, when the two Sicilian bravos, before battling with daggers, embrace to acknowledge one another's courage.

Kleinerman noticed a speck on Castor's figure and flicked it off with a handkerchief. "A set such as this will do justice to Madam's dining room."

"Do me justice with a better price."

"It is yours for eleven thousand dollars."

"You're way out of line. That isn't an authentic Flaxman."

"Make me a counteroffer, dear lady."

"I'll give you eight thousand dollars."

66

"Nine, madam. Nine thousand, and you may pay me in any manner you desire—personal draft, bank check, whatever. I include polishing, packaging, shipping, and insurance in the price."

Lulu had him. Either Kleinerman had not noticed the soft canvas bag Harry carried or he could not imagine its purpose.

"I have no need of shipping or insurance," she said. "We always take our purchases with us. It's safer and surer."

"We had some bad experiences once with a Moroccan rug," Harry added. Neither looked at him.

"Very well," Kleinerman said. "In that case . . ."

"In that case, eight thousand dollars. My houseman will do the polishing."

"Madam intends to carry these treasures around with her? In that bag?"

"Provided you wrap them properly in wool batting."

"Hmmm. Eight thousand?"

"Final offer."

"Eight five?" But there was terror in the merchant's voice. Once Flemington had heard a sports writer quote an opponent of Joe Louis. "You had a kind of warning, that this was it, just before he landed the big one. It was like something in the air, some look on Louis' face. And then it came." Looking at Mr. Kleinerman's quivering cheeks, Harry realized what the boxer meant.

"Eight thousand. We will pay in traveler's checks, here and now."

I. Kleinerman bowed his head. Impulsively, he seized Lulu's hands. "Done, madam. And a marvelous woman you are, an artist at bargaining, and an expert on silver."

Flemington saw a warm smile spread on Lulu's face. She was enjoying I. Kleinerman's flirtation.

"I doubt, madam, that in the United States there are three sets of a quality equal to this, and that includes the Sheffields in the White House."

Young Kleinerman ushered Harry to a desk in the rear. From an inner zippered pocket he took booklets of traveler's checks. The $500 denominations came in handy for major purchases. He carried $25,000 with him, and if he needed more, the bank on whose board Lulu sat (a post invariably going to a Deaver) would oblige.

Mr. Kleinerman, joking with Lulu outside, called in:

"Sonny, turn on the fan for the gentleman. Have Mischa start on Madam's purchases. Tea, Mrs. Flemington?"

"I would adore some."

Returning to the hotel in a taxi, Flemington gazed in silence at London. Had they passed Fleet Street, where Samuel Johnson had labored? In his study—*what in heaven's name did he study any more?*—was a steel engraving of Dr. Johnson, scowling and slovenly, reading Goldsmith's manuscript of *The Vicar of Wakefield.* Landlady and constable loom in the doorway. He had known the story since high school—Johnson proclaiming it a masterpiece and saving Goldsmith from eviction. There were giants in the earth in those days.

"I hate Harrods and those other big places," Lulu said. "You can't Jew them down. It's one price and you take it or leave it."

"You did very well with the silver, dear."

"I know I did. It may not have been an actual Flaxman, but I looked carefully at the imprint. It was cast by Storr."

"Storr?"

Lulu chuckled with satisfaction. His ignorance required no response.

Customs clearance went swiftly at Orly Field. Virgil knew the inspectors, and the French, except for stopping an occasional long-haired boy, were eager to move tourists along.

"No wonder all that dope gets smuggled out of Marseilles," Mr. Wattle shouted. "These people don't care. They want to corrupt us."

They moved through the gate, the French guards nodding sleepily. Huggins, swinging the camera bag, was grateful. Mario and Ralphie were dumb, but not that dumb. There was something to be said for tours—no one bothered to search you or harbored suspicions about a crowd of Americans.

Virgil took the party on a brief tour of Paris before stopping at the hotel. It was dusk, and the city was bathed in unearthly lavender light. It was cool, as Paris often is in mid-September, and the air had a mysterious charged quality.

"Too dark for pictures, Murray?" Herbie yawned at his Japanese friend. They had established squatter's rights on the rear seats. Here, without benefit of wives, they piled cameras, magazines, bags, coats, sneaking cigars and pipes whenever Virgil was not looking.

"Yeah, these tours screw you every which way," Yasuda said. "I got lotsa high-speed film, but it won't look like doodly."

As the bus wheeled into the Place de la Concorde, the sky slowly turned from lavender to purple-blue. It was the kind of half-light that had driven generations of artists into ecstasies. Suddenly the globes of light surrounding the enormous plaza were turned on, bright balls of silver, marking the limits of the traffic-jammed square. Everyone gasped.

"Oh, what a sight!" Theresa cried. "Ibith, look at it!"

Flemington, holding Lulu's hand, heard her voice. His skin tingled and he wanted to touch Theresa.

68

"Fantastic," Dr. Grant said. "Just fantastic."

"Say, look at that traffic," Mr. Wattle said. "I'd give a dollar and a half to learn how they control it. And the way they stop and start. Have you any idea what that does to brakes and clutches? I'd like to have the concession for repairing 'em. Forty-seven per cent of all car breakdowns are related to the transmission."

Lights burned brighter on the Champs Élysées. In the purpling haze, crowds of shoppers and home-bound office workers swarmed on the sidewalks.

"Do not be deceived by the Arch of Triumph," Pepi said, sounding more French with every sentence. "The scale is so grand that it looks closer to you than it is. If you try to walk the length of the Champs with your eyes fixed on it, you will see what I mean. Good shoes and a good wind are needed."

"I'm enchanted. I'm in love. I'm lost," Rosie Wicker said. "It's too beautiful to exist."

"The late great Robert Benchley," Bettenhausen said, "once claimed there was no such city as Budapest, that it was an optical illusion caused by the refraction of light waves on the retina of the eye."

"We'll find out when we get to Budapest," Cornelia Bettenhausen said. "Iron Curtain and so on."

The expression "Iron Curtain" pinged in Dr. Wicker's mind. He had given no thought to the letter he was to deliver to Professor Borkin. Suddenly he was eager to tell someone. *Hot dog!* He, Arnold Wicker, D.D.S., a courier! Wouldn't the kids who sat in his dentist's chair back in Riverford fall apart if they knew! He had a desire to buy a trench coat and a beret, start smoking those French cigarettes that Pepi fancied.

"Oh, my goodness, the Eiffel Tower," Mrs. Legrand said breathily. "Look, Weston, it's the Eiffel Tower."

Weston Legrand, drugged, slept against the window.

"We will not sit in the back of the bus," Ibith Grant said. "Not you, Terry, nor me, nor Henderson." She had come to Theresa Carrell's hotel room to borrow a needle and thread. At school, she was the teacher the others in the history department leaned on—for books, notes, guidance, teaching techniques.

"Oh, *you're* okay," Theresa laughed. "She won't raise a fuss about you. It's me."

"Honey, you imagine it."

"She was darting those glares at me all day. I didn't say a word to Harry. Or even look at him."

Theresa, in a light blue robe, sat on the edge of the hard, sloping bed. A widow's bed, she thought. Appropriately gray, in a room with streaked yellow walls and a cracked ceiling.

"Where's all the French elegance?" Ibith said, studying the heavy brown drapes, the feeble lamplight. "Ours isn't much better. Henderson and me decided to spend as little time as possible in it."

"It's an all-category tour, Ibith. A fancy way of saying economy. God, I wish I knew what to do."

"He was *número uno* once, is that it?" Ibith asked.

Theresa leaned back on the coarse coverlet. "Oh, so far back, Ibith. College. Then the war. I wanted to get married before Harry enlisted. But he didn't have a cent—neither of us did—and I was only a sophomore. So off he went, and when he came back—well, we thought it wasn't the same. At least that's what *he* said."

"He *said?*"

Theresa looked grave, lost in a twenty-five-year-old reminiscence. The past was no bucket of ashes, the way the poet said. It was with you all the time.

"Harry is a sweet man," Theresa said, "and one of the smartest I've ever known. But he's always had his eye on the main chance. When he got out of service he wanted to make it big—the New York *Times*, *Time*. So he started modestly—forty dollars a week—on the *Register*. I was teaching. We could have made a go of it. But he kept hedging. He said as soon as he went to New York and was on his way up we'd get married. Pretty soon it dawned on me. He was *never* going to New York. He was perfect on the night desk."

"I gather you lived as man and wife?"

"On and off. I'd have these bouts of puritanism. We slept together a lot. It was good, but it should have been better."

"Ahead of your time, Terry."

"It didn't appeal to me after a few years. I left Minneapolis. He begged me to stay, but he still was waiting for that big job so we could have a decent married life."

"Hate to say it, Terry. Sounds like a cop-out."

"I guess it was. I got tired of waiting. Did you know I was married before Wade?"

Ibith shook her head. It was hard to conceive of her friend as having had not one but two unhappy marriages, and a doomed affair. Theresa always appeared the best adjusted of women.

"Harry dawdled, and complained that he had no security, and that he didn't want kids brought up on a night editor's salary, and we slept around a lot, and when I went to Chicago, I married . . . well, let it go. It lasted five years, and it didn't work. Nothing did after I broke with Harry."

"And then he latched onto all that money?"

"More than he ever dreamed of."

"Sounds like he was waiting for it."

"I guess he was. Harry's got charm and style and he's the kindest man in the world, but there was something missing." Theresa stretched back on the bed and covered her face. "But oh, the good times we had. It was never the same with any other man. Ibith, forgive me."

"Let it all hang out, baby."

"Would you believe I'd never seen her?" Theresa asked. "Got to admit I was curious."

Ibith shook her head. "She must have been a beauty once. But the booze takes its toll."

There was a knock at the door. Dr. Henderson Grant, dapper in a navy-blue suit, blue shirt, and black tie, stood at the doorway. "Evening, ladies. Girl talk?"

"Back-yard gossip, Hen. We've cut up just about everyone on this tour. Seems as if we're the only ones we like."

"Thought we take a little stroll around the neighborhood before the rent party at the Lido."

Theresa shook her head. "I think I'll take it easy. I have to meditate before those confrontations with the heiress. I'm schizzing a little. You go ahead."

In the dim corridor, Ibith Grant tossed her head and looked concerned. "Bad scene, Hen. The Dragon Lady's getting to her. Wish there was some single dude on this trip for Terry."

Lulu Flemington, within hearing range of eight or nine tour members, halted Virgil outside the bus and was leveling a finger at him.

"There are brown stains around the sink," she was saying. "The room has not been properly cleaned. There is an odor of disinfectant. There are not enough towels. I am angry and I intend to write to your New York office."

"I am sorry, madame," Pepi said. "Yes, good evening, Mr. Legrand, did you enjoy your nap? I was saying this is an all-category tour, which means we must select a middle-type hotel, between first and second class, as it were—"

"This is a third-class hotel," Lulu said.

Harry, approaching, wished there was something she could buy, some store he could steer her to.

"Good evening, Mr. Shackman, Mrs. Shackman, Mrs. Shapiro, Mr. Shapiro." Virgil did not miss a face.

"I want my room changed," Lulu said.

Virgil bowed slightly. "I shall arrange it, madame."

71

Herbie Shackman's voice thundered from the bus. "What is it with that broad? With all her millions, she goes on a cheap tour with *shnorrers* like us? How come?"

"That's why she's got all the dough," Si said. "They know about bargains."

Herbie, weathering a furious glare from Flo, lowered his voice. "I gotta kibitz that husband of hers. Harry in the suede hat. There's a story there."

"Maybe he won't like to be kibitzed," Flo said.

"Anybody can be kibitzed."

Naked as herrings, the girls on the Lido stage raised their pale arms in a salute. The band played the last chords of "The Poor People of Paree." The selection was always a source of wonder to Virgil, who knew that the poor people of the city barely survived. The richest country in Europe with the worst housing. Open drains; tin-shack villages; meat on the table once a week; cold rooms and bad diets and constipated anger.

"Small boobies," Herbie shouted across the table to Si and Sid. "I like 'em big."

"You brag a lot," Flo said.

"How come small boobies, Pepi?"

"Mr. Shackman, they are mostly English girls. It is a matter of diet and breeding. Perhaps Dr. Grant can enlighten us."

But Henderson Grant kept his own counsel. He would not offer an exegesis on white breasts to an audience of elderly Midwestern folk. Not cautious Dr. Grant.

"The champagne wasn't bad," Mr. Wattle piped to the Hugginses as they made their way out of the Lido, "but the food was awful. We grow better produce on the West Coast. Did you know that California produces eighty-seven per cent of the apricots in the States?"

"You're kidding," J.P. said. "Is it true the state of Washington leads in horse manure?"

Mr. Wattle heard nothing. Helpful as always, he was supporting Mr. Legrand, directing him between the tables, the applauding diners. Mrs. Legrand was full of life, puffing a cigarette, nodding at everyone.

"That old broad reminds me of someone," Herbie said to Arnold Wicker when they reached the lobby. "She'll drive me nuts before I figure it out. Who is she? Someone I saw once in the movies? Nah."

"She sure's got moxie," the dentist said. "Up this late."

"Yeah. And I'm ready to be wrapped up. I shouldna eaten Flo's dessert. With that whipped cream."

People dozed on the bus, yawned, hummed snatches of French tunes, let themselves succumb to the lighted monuments.

"A magic city built by an alien race," Bettenhausen mused. "Surely not the French. A people incapable of fixing an electrical outlet could not have created such majesty. Strangers came, built the city, and vanished."

"Tell 'em, Professor," Herbie yawned.

Virgil, in his seat next to the driver, listened to the bantering voices. It was going well. He had even enjoyed the show at the Lido. It reminded him of the musicals they had staged in Theresienstadt, the concentration camp near Prague where he had spent part of his boyhood. He could recall the comedians, the singers, the skits. Best of all was the camp orchestra. And with good reason. Three fourths of the Czech Philharmonic were in Theresienstadt.

"Tell us a funny story, Pepi," Mavis Hutzler called out.

"Oh, dear Mrs. Hutzler, it is much too late for funny stories." Late at night, he thought too much of the camps, and those millions un-luckier than he. It was the nearest he came to spiritual meditation.

Day 4: Paris! Surrender to the City of Light! An entire day given over to the most beautiful city in the world. We visit the Opéra, the Madeleine, the Louvre, the Eiffel Tower, Napoleon's Tomb, Notre Dame, the Conciergerie and the Sainte Chapelle, and then up to Montmartre, the old artists' quarter. If you desire, lunch at an elegant restaurant or a modest brasserie. (But wherever, it will be delicious.) The afternoon is free for shopping. Ask Planet's tour escort for shops that give discounts.

At night, a moonlit cruise along the Seine on one of the Bateaux Mouches, with dinner aboard and all of the grand city as your dining room!

Virgil, in his command post near the elevator, was surprised to see Mr. Huggins the first one down. He had tagged the young couple as incorrigible late-comers. The peevish Italian-American girl was the kind who spent hours fussing with her face.

"A lovely day," Virgil said. "Rare for Paris this time of year. Sunlight on the sycamores and chestnut trees."

"Yeah. Great." Huggins looked around.

"Mrs. Huggins is all right?"

"Beautiful. Look, we're skipping the sight-seeing this morning. She wants to rest. I got some errands."

"Ah, what a shame. Who knows when you will get to Paris again?"

"Who knows?"

Virgil was sipping coffee and inhaling a Gitane. He said: "I can give you an itinerary that you and Mrs. Huggins can do by yourself if you desire."

"How do your insides stand that acid?" J.P. asked—as if relieved to be diverted from his own gloom. "And those butts. Like chopped-up GI blankets."

"Mr. Huggins, do not underestimate GI blankets. They kept me alive when I was freed from Buchenwald."

"Hunh?"

"As for the coffee, it is better than what I drank in Auschwitz."

"You got around. Didn't know you were Jewish."

Upward went Virgil's shoulders, sideways turned his head—a Gal-

74

lic shrug. "One eighth. What did it matter? There were reasons enough to arrest and murder people."

"I see what you mean." Huggins shifted his camera case. "Look, Pepi, where's the stamp market?"

"Stamp market?"

"A friend told me they have a big outdoor market in Paris. I'm not a collector, but I know some people back home who are. Thought I might pick up some bargains."

"It is off the Rond Point. We passed it yesterday."

"Thanks. If you see the frau, tell her I'll be back in a few hours."

After the stop at the Eiffel Tower, Virgil had to adjudicate the first battle over seats. As a result he had to put into operation his reserve plan for seating. It was not popular, but it helped prevent conflict.

When the party came down from the top of the tower an altercation developed at the front right seats. One of Herbie's friends, the brother-in-law, Si, a bespectacled, gentle man, had been in the seat, with his wife alongside him. They had left some purchases and a topcoat there. On returning, they found their possessions placed in the overhead rack. Two of the Midwesterners, Mr. and Mrs. Clyde Kuchtenberg, were sitting in the front seat.

"Beg pardon, I believe those are my seats," Si said.

"Is your name on them?" Mrs. Kuchtenberg asked.

"No, but we left a coat on them."

"Si, we'll sit somewhere else."

"No, hon, these are our seats. When you start in certain seats, you keep them."

"But these are the best seats for taking pictures. You've had them two days in a row."

"No, just this morning. That was my friend Sid who was here yesterday."

"We think we should have them for a while."

Mrs. Kuchtenberg whispered in her husband's ear. "It's all right, Clyde, we'll get out . . ."

"I won't let this bus go until I get my seat back," Si said.

The others had taken their seats by now. Herbie, seeing his friend in trouble, shouted: "Everybody back to their seats! Seats on a first-come, first-served basis."

Mr. Kuchtenberg folded his arms. He would not budge.

"Throw the bum out!" Murray Yasuda yelled.

"Let's go, let's go! Where the hell is Pepi?"

"Hey, Pepi, you're needed."

Virgil, cigarette dangling from his lips, entered the bus.

"He took my seat," Si complained. "Fair is fair. I want it back."

"Well, ladies and gentlemen," Virgil said softly, "this can be overcome. We shall have to adopt a rotating system. For the time being, Mr. Shapiro, let Mr. Kuchtenberg stay there. It is only for this afternoon. But"—he picked up the microphone—"from now on we will rotate, two seats forward, in a clockwise direction, around the bus, mornings and afternoons. That will give everyone a share of the best seats or what they imagine are the best seats."

"Hey, that's a lousy deal!" Yasuda shouted.

"*Shah, shah, boychik,*" Herbie said, patting his friend's hand. "We got us a headquarters here. Who'll wanna sit here with the cigar stink?"

There was confusion over Virgil's edict. Which way was clockwise? *Two* seats ahead? Why not *one?* Patiently Virgil explained again—after every major halt, everyone would move two seats in a clockwise direction, backward if he or she were on the right-hand side of the bus, forward on the left-hand side, and then around the front again.

Mr. Wattle was counting seats, standing in the middle of the bus. "Let me see. I'll be up front on Tuesday and then again on the following Sunday. That's two chances to get the front seat in a twenty-day period. It doesn't seem right. I could work out something better with my slide rule."

"Please do," Bettenhausen growled at him. "Something that would keep you far away from me."

The bald man did not hear him. He was bouncing up and down the aisle, counting off seats, intrigued with Pepi's arrangement.

"When everyone else moves, Moishe, you and me stay here. Have a cigar."

"You better believe it, Herbie baby."

They lit up and smoked, bad boys defying the teacher. By this time Virgil and the tourists had surrendered. Some coughed, others choked, most ignored the foul stench in the back of the bus. Bettenhausen swore exotic revenge on Shackman and Yasuda.

"Ladies and gentlemen, your Paris guide, whom you have already met, will take over, please, Mademoiselle Dunand . . ."

"Polly-voo fronsay?" yelled Herbie. "What about all that money you people owe us?"

Outside the Church of the Madeleine, Theresa Carrell read aloud from her guidebook. The French girl proved to be sullen, ignoring questions, exhibiting a superiority that intimidated most of the tourists. Bettenhausen was enraged.

"*France ne peut pas être France sans le gloire,*" Bettenhausen muttered to his wife. "One might add, without good manners."

"Quiet down, Betts, and listen to Theresa."

"It says," Theresa Carrell read, "that this is an important monument of the Classical Revival, started in 1764, but a lot of architects do not appreciate its imitative lines."

"It's a beautiful location, anyway," Dr. Wicker said. Around the Place de la Madeleine, traffic hummed and whirled.

As the party descended the steps, the Flemingtons found themselves alongside the Grants and Theresa. Others followed, listening to the teacher reading from the book. Flemington had heard that voice so often—breathless in secret meetings. Moments of lost love, of dishonored commitments, choked him. He saw the city blurred, wavering. Lulu had her eyes on a leather shop across the Boulevard de la Madeleine. She had been studying coats in the window, and her nose seemed to quiver, like a pointer's, toward the Château de Cuire.

"I can't seem to get my bearings," Harry said to no one in particular. "So long since I've been here. Let's see. Which way is the opera?"

"Thataway, to the left," Theresa said. "That's our next stop."

Lulu disengaged her arm from Harry's and took a step toward Theresa. "You will not address my husband," she said.

"Now, Lu," Flemington said.

"I mean that. I shall have you thrown off this trip. You are not to speak to my husband."

The Wickers and the Bettenhausens found it obligatory to cross to the Cook's office to cash traveler's checks. Dr. Grant and Ibith discovered that a pushcart selling jewelry was worth a second look.

Theresa shut the guidebook and walked to the bus.

"There are a few minutes to look in the stores, Mrs. Carrell," Virgil said.

"No, thanks. I'll rest."

It was going to be worse, much worse, than she had anticipated. Maybe the sensible thing to do would be to leave the tour.

Huggins, delighting in the sunny day, wandered amid the stamp stalls in the park off the Rond Point. He had walked from the hotel, down great boulevards, through tree-lined avenues, moved by the charm and accessibility of the great city. Fantasizing—something he rarely did—he imagined himself the sales rep for some corporation, living out his days in Paris, speaking flawless French, socializing with artists and writers. And no more threats from Mario and Ralphie.

Paris would be easy to take. Huggins possessed a sense of textures, of fineness. His favorite expressions were "class" and "no class." Poor Barbara would never have class. Nor did many people on the tour. Maybe that long-legged Rosie, the dentist's wife. You could see the class in the unadorned face, the high breasts, the gold clip in the side of the straight hair. That was class. And Paris had it. Wrought-iron balconies, mansard roofs, sidewalk cafés, where half the city seemed to be lazying away the morning sipping coffee.

Looking at the stalls loaded with albums, bins with mounds of cheap stamps, glassine envelopes of sets, air mails, colonials, he realized why stamp collecting had never been his bag. He'd been a hustler, and there was no money to be made in collecting bits of colored paper. Age eleven, Jimmy Huggins had shot craps with four-teen-year-olds. Later he booked bets. Twice he fixed punchball games. Faking his way through St. Nicholas of Tolentine, copying answers, buying papers, charming the brothers. But never earning their respect. Father O'Dea had laid it on the line a few days before graduation. "You are bright, Huggins, very bright, and not without charm." Jimmy smiled raggedly. Not bad, considering he'd damn near been suspended for phonying up a geometry final. "But you are something of a sneak and sneaks get found out."

Father O'Dea, meet Mario Malfi. For all J.P.'s glib tongue, two-hundred-dollar suits, and fifty-dollar shoes, something was missing. Mario knew it. Mario knew he could bend him. "You got no choice in this here matter, Jimmy. You do what you are told, unnerstan'?"

He understood. On a scrap of paper, Ralphie, in his retarded scrawl, had written a name: *Moussac, stamp market Paris.* Some expert in wrong turns and bad news whom the brothers had dealt with. "Tell him 'Hong Kong transistors,' he'll know," Mario said. "Then ask him for help. He owes us a couple."

The stamp market was charming in the checkered shade of live green trees. It hardly seemed the kind of arena that Moussac, what-ever his trade was, would frequent. Huggins wondered. Maybe there was illegal money in stamps. There had to be. There was in every-thing else. Mario and Ralphie would sit around and moan that there was nothing as good as a legitimate business, but they were so hard to find! Everything, it turned out, was crooked.

In his gray Tripler suit, short-brimmed hat, wing-tipped cordovan oxfords, Huggins looked as startling as a deep-sea diver. Elderly French gents in blue raincoats and stained berets crowded around the stalls. With rheumy eyes they studied new issues from République Malgache and Côte d'Ivoire. J.P. stopped one of them. "Mr. Moussac? You know Moussac?"

The old fellow nodded. "*Là-bas. Vous êtes spécialiste en Indo-Chine?*"

"No. Just a relative."

Moussac ran a stall at the edge of the mart. Adjoining it, on a plot of earth, was a children's playground, filled with nurses, mothers, and preschool tots. Huggins thought for a moment of the two howling kids they had left with Barbara's mother. It was good to be able to admit to himself that he did not miss them.

Moussac, a man of indeterminate age, seemed to be a character in a puppet show. A marionette constable with a truncheon should have appeared, Huggins imagined, and clouted him on his head. And what a head it was! The stamp merchant resembled an albino frog. His mouth seemed to begin at the sides of his neck. The nose was spatulate, the eyes spaced too far apart. I heard of walleyes, J.P. thought, but this cat has them on his temples.

"Mr. Moussac?"

"*Oui.*"

"Speak English?"

"What ees eet you weesh?"

"You mean you speak English for some things but don't for others?"

The mouth moved. Was it a smile? "I speak enough. You are interested in *Indo-Chine?* Per'aps the 1967 air-mail watermarked?"

"Mario Malfi sent me."

"Mario? I know no such person."

"The transistors. From Hong Kong."

"Ah, yes. Of course. You are in business?"

"Sort of. You got a minute to talk to me? On the bench over there?"

Moussac put his catalogue down and called to a gray-haired woman to mind the stall. Two kids started to sift through a grab-bag assortment: *10 assorti, un franc.*

They sat on the bench. Moussac waited for Huggins to speak. It took J.P. a moment to disengage the camera case from his aching shoulders. "Whew. That's better."

"Well?"

"I have, ah, dollars."

The Frenchman grinned. "So 'as everyone. Dollars are cheap these days."

"I got a whole lot of dollars. *Beaucoup.*"

Moussac's walleye worked its way over Huggins' dapper figure. "You are a *passeur.* I congratulate you. You do not look like any *passeur* I 'ave met."

"What's a *passeur?*"

"Money courier."

"I'm a lot more than that, Mr. Moussac. I'm a—" Insulted, he wanted to say he was a lawyer.

"No matter. You are a gentleman. Now, for my friend in America who 'elp me with transistors, what can I do?"

"I want to get rid of a lot of dollars. Make the best deal I can. Keep it secret, somewhere outside the States. Should be a familiar problem to you."

Moussac pursed his mouth. He had gone from frog to lizard. The ruffles around his neck suggested one of those reptiles Huggins had seen at the Bronx Zoo in his boyhood. "Very bad time, very bad. The dollar will be devalue' for a long time."

"That's why we want to change these."

"You Americans 'ave not wake up yet. You are no longer number one. You exchange for Swiss francs, Deutsche marks, you will take a big loss."

"We're prepared to."

"I understand. Money you friends 'ave not report? Cash? Money on which no tax is pay?"

"Never mind the details. We want to exchange it or deposit it."

"'Ow much?"

"Quite a bit, Moussac."

"Tell me. Eef you wish my 'elp—"

"Two hundred thousand."

A gargling noise, which Huggins assumed was laughter, issued from the dealer's throat. "*Fantastique.* So much, and you do not even ask for my 'alf of the dollar."

"Half of what dollar?"

Moussac pulled a half of a dollar bill from his vest pocket. "When contact is made, the *passeur* always show this and then I show the other 'alf, so he knows I am the *cambiste.*"

"I'd believe you, Moussac. You're a *cambiste* if ever I saw one. What do I do with my money?"

The Frenchman's eyes drifted to the camera case. "There?"

"Yeah, yeah."

"You will 'ave trouble selling that much in Western Europe. They will ask big commission, offer a low rate. In Eastern Europe you will do well. Provided you wish to take the chance of going to jail for long, long time."

"Back to Western Europe, pal."

"*Eh bien.* Forget Paris. You will be squeezed like a *citron.* Go to Switzerland. Eef that is a problem, try Beirut."

Huggins, whose forte was not geography, had a vague idea where Beirut was. Switzerland he understood, but it was not on his itinerary.

80

Ah, the stupidity of those *walyones*, those airport thieves! He had discussed the tour with them, showed them the alternate trips, and they had approved his choice. *And no Switzerland!* Huggins recalled a "Golden Mountains" tour—Alps, Apennines, Pyrenees—which spent five days in Switzerland.

"What do I do in Switzerland?"

"You must ask a Swiss bank."

"If I ask a bank, I'll get honest information and it may cost me. From you I can get the kind of answer I want."

"Buy gold."

"Gold?"

"*C'est ça.* The best thing to buy with your stack of bills. By the way, een what denomination?"

"None of your business." Huggins was feeling more sure of himself. So this was the way currency operators did it! How easy it was! How satisfyingly dishonest!

"I walk in off the street and buy gold?"

"Any Swiss bank will sell. But . . . with such a sum . . . I would suggest you do not spend eet all in one place."

"Naturally. I hate showy people."

"About ten t'ousand dollars at each bank. You will need twenty banks."

The conversation had assumed a logical madness that exhilarated Huggins. "That's a lotta banks, Moussac."

"Zurich will provide you with twenty, and twenty more, and twenty after that, m'sieu."

Switzerland. Zurich. It meant a detour. Leaving Barbara. People getting suspicious. Was someone on to him already, lugging that bag around and never taking pictures except when someone reminded him? The American cop in the London hotel lobby?

Moussac was grinning, not at Huggins, but at the camera case. "Two 'undred thousan', eh? How? I am curious."

"I'll tell you after I change it. Gold, huh? Suppose I can't get to Switzerland."

"Beirut. In Lebanon."

"I don't like Arabs. Where else?"

The Frenchman sucked at his teeth. "West Berlin. Vienna. Of course, eef you are daring and wish to pyramid your money, you will buy gold bars in Switzerland and carry them into Eastern Europe—Hungary, Romania, Russia. Then you can sell them for five times what you pay."

"And get stuck with a pile of rubles? And maybe get shot?"

"You are in a risky business, m'sieu. You run a risk carrying so much cash with you."

"I like to flash a big roll."

"I doubt that. You are not a *passeur*. From your ignorance, I see this is your first run. Go to Switzerland. Go to the Bahnhofstrasse and buy gold. For that much money they will give eet. Money involves neither patriotism nor morality. Eet makes eets own rules."

Huggins got up, slinging the case over his shoulder. "Moussac, you've been a big help. I'll tell Mario."

The Frenchman rose. His raincoat was grease-spotted and dirt-streaked. Huggins doubted that the Rothschilds started this way.

They shook hands. "Good luck," the stamp dealer said. "Good cover, my friend. But do not count forever on it. Go to Switzerland as soon as you can."

On the Champs Huggins bought a *Herald Tribune* and sipped coffee. The ignorance of his brothers-in-law had always astounded him. Given their stupidity, how did they get so rich so fast? They'd sent him into the unknown—no instructions, no plan, nothing. They had panicked. The Internal Revenue Service had been after them—receipts, books, returns. The past year, when Huggins estimated that they had cleared over three hundred thousand dollars in swag, they had reported a *loss* from their front—a fuel oil company in the South Bronx. It was imperative that they unload. People might talk. Some of the "boogies"—as Mario called them—who worked the freight terminals were getting suspicious, grumbling that they wanted to be cut in. Understandably they did not like being segregated from the thieving. It was upsetting to them to see whites only, and Italians at that, controlling the weekly haul of radios, hi-fis, tape recorders, cameras.

Huggins thought of the basement in Mario's red brick house in Pelham. There was barely room to sit. It was crammed with walls, stacks, random formations of cardboard cartons, most of them from Japan, Taiwan, Hong Kong, Western Europe. Name it, you got it from them. Or they'd get it on order. Tape deck with extra speakers? Six-band portable? Spotmatic reflex camera with matching lenses? Zoom lens projector for 8 and super-8 millimeter? The orders were transmitted verbally from bars and restaurants around New York, most of them in the garment district. No records were kept. There was never anything in writing. Mario transmitted them to Ralphie, or Sal, or Dom, or Vinnie. As for the oil company, it worked out of a storefront on Webster Avenue and was represented, unfathomably, by the Wall Street firm of Jabloner & Kuraskin, in which J. P. Huggins was a partner.

Huggins shivered. He detested the Malfis, not for what they had achieved through brutality, guile, and criminal insights into human greed, but for their damned dumbness where everything else was concerned. They were the dullest, most non-reactive people in the world. Like snails, slugs, invertebrates of ancient lineage, they crawled their way through the world, surviving, reproducing. J.P. had a yeasty admiration for a colorful cheater. He liked cleverness, people quick on their feet, sharp-tongued, elusive people. (How else had he managed to get through Fordham and law school?) But the Malfis filled him with dread.

"You'll do this," Mario croaked.

"I don't like it. I'm the patsy."

"No, you ain't. You get rid of this stuff, we buy you a new Continental."

"You'll steal it, you mean. I risk my neck, my career, and you *walyones* fix me up with a hot car. Know something? You greasers aren't funny any more. I don't get any laughs out of you."

"If it wasn't for Barb," Mario said, "we'd lose you altogether. You stop makin' those cracks."

"It's all I got left," Huggins said. "You want me to carry two hundred grand of mob money around Europe? You'll put up with me, jokes and all."

Mario's eyebrows met in a black cable over his nose. His eyes seemed to cross slightly. "We got rid of a smart nigger at Newark last week. Wanna hear what happened to him?"

"You breathed on him and he suffocated."

But they had not threatened him again. Finally he talked them out of the pay-off. He did not want a stolen car. He wanted ten thousand dollars—"a loser's fee." Mario agreed. He and Ralphie smiled at one another and the deal was made. They had known all the time he would not refuse.

After paying for his coffee, Huggins wandered about the city, mulling a trip to Switzerland. Better not to take Barbara. The other tourists would gossip, but to hell with them. He'd rejoin them in Berlin or Vienna. A better plan jogged his mind. He'd toss their loot into the Seine. Load the hundred-dollar case with rocks and throw it over a bridge! A cable to Mario—it was stolen. Reported to police. Someone took it from a café chair.

The tour lingered in the Salle Mollien of the Louvre, stunned by the giant Delacroix paintings. Virgil had seen it happen over and over. The Mona Lisa got a cursory look—too small, too dark. But Delacroix, with his gigantism, reached Americans.

"Zey call him ze Byron of painting," the Parisian guide said.

Theresa Carrell, glasses on the end of her nose, studied her guide. Ibith Grant had the feeling Terry sometimes spent more time reading her books than looking at the works of art.

"*Death of Sardanapalus*," Warren Bettenhausen read. "Delacroix was ahead of his time. He should have worked for De Mille. I once told C.B. he was influenced by Delacroix, and he walked on air for days."

"He talks too much," Lulu said to Harry. She looked unsteady. The thrill of the silver purchase in London was wearing off. She needed buying highs periodically. Flemington wondered if they would let her haggle for a Delacroix. *Women of Algiers?* It would not fit in their luggage. Lulu refused to buy anything she could not carry.

"Ingres is ze nineteenth-century master of ze portrait," the girl said. "Ze great reclining odalisque is one of ze most famous." They were in the Salle Denon.

"Man, that's a lotta woman," Murray Yasuda said, staring at the sleek body.

"Heh-heh," Herbie grunted. "You'd get lost."

"What a way to go."

"Murray, lower your voice," Sandra whispered.

"Can't help it, Sandy. I'm aroused. Boy, that's all woman."

"Almost too much," Rose-Anne Wicker said. She was trying to recall her art appreciation course at Silvermine. What was she supposed to know about Ingres? And what was a *violon d'Ingres?*

"Madame is correct," the French girl said to Rosie. "Ze body is too long. Ingres had ze habit of adding an extra vertebrate."

"Vertebra," Bettenhausen corrected her.

"Yes. Zis." The girl reached behind her back and fingered her backbone.

Flemington found himself hypnotized by the odalisque. The serene face, the sense of female power, stunned him. Glancing from Theresa's bespectacled face, reading aloud from her book to the Grants, he saw her naked—harem courtesan and teacher united in one woman. His knees seemed to come unhinged and he had to blink to force back tears of memory.

"For God's sake, stop crying, Terry," he had said to her five years ago in the motel room at the Detroit airport. "We made love. It was good. If this is so hard for you to take why did you call me? Why did you open up the wounds?"

She wept with discretion, ashamed of her weakness. "I'm still in love with you."

"Dammit, you know I can't leave Lulu. Without me, she'd die."

Through the rainy afternoon, they made love, reduced at last to

84

gasping, helpless embraces, dry kisses. Middle age had damned little honor, Flemington decided, and too much toil.

Harry studied the odalisque and cursed his memory.

In front of Filippo Lippi's *Annunciation*, Lulu told Harry she had to go to the ladies' room. All that Perrier he had forced on her that morning, she suspected. (Flemington regarded mineral waters as good antidotes for overindulgence.) As soon as she had left, he saw Theresa coming toward him.

"Hi, sport," she said.

"Hello, grand odalisque."

"I caught those stares when we were in front of the Ingres. You remember a line from Henry IV, Part I? The Death of Hotspur?"

Flemington laughed. "You've used it before, Terry. And it hurts every time. 'Oh, Harry, thou hast robbed me of my youth.' It's not true, Terry. You look marvelous."

"Getting long in the tooth."

"But clear of eye, and more damned involved than anyone I ever knew. No sulks, no pouts, no fits of temper."

"Tears, once."

No longer able to stifle his feelings, he seized her hand. She was a woman with strong hands, stronger than his own, Flemington felt.

"This is what it's all about!" Herbie Shackman boomed. "This is great! Who wantsa go shoppng and shlepping all day? Look—Bellini! Uccello! If only I knew what they were all about!"

Flemington, with a glance over his shoulder, released Terry's hand. It was as if they had just committed adultery again, two sinners in a scarlet bed. "I figured something out," he said. "That long line of your back. It's the extra vertebra. You must have one."

"No. The usual number."

"What was wrong with me?" His voice was choking. "How could I lose you?"

"Your choice, Harry. Now you're the man with the heiress wife and twenty suitcases. What in God's name did you lug back from the silver vaults? Those women from Westbury are going crazy trying to find out."

"Flaxman," Harry said. "We have Mr. Flaxman in there. Eight thousand dollars' worth."

Theresa's eyes widened. "You . . . ? She makes you carry this stuff around Europe? For twenty days?"

"It goes with the job." He took her hand again. "Theresa . . . still time . . . let's figure something out. . . . Dammit, when I saw you, the whole thing was replayed. What an idiot I've been."

"I don't believe you, Harry. How? Between hotels? Harry, they

85

should make it mandatory that the passenger lists are checked for old romances."

Flemington wanted to seize her. As always, she was dressed conservatively, beiges and browns, a woolen suit, low-heeled shoes.

"Not just a one-shot," he said. "I mean it. We don't live forever." An old Saroyan short story came to Flemington's mind: "What We Want Is Love and Money." There was a parlay. Theresa's love, Lulu's money.

She shook her head, turned, and left him.

"Of course, Mantegna," Bettenhausen was saying to Virgil. "*Minerva Triumphing over Venus*. There's a master for you."

Flemington had followed Theresa, like a teen-age boy trailing a favored teacher, to Veronese's *Susannah Bathing*. The Louvre was no place to try to arouse old love—not with those sumptuous nudes of antiquity around. Theresa had always appeared thus to him—a classic artist's model, somewhat aloof and austere of face.

Lulu walked unsteadily across the gallery toward her husband. With her sunglasses on, it was difficult to tell if she had seen Flemington with Mrs. Carrell.

"Hey, Terry," Ibith called. "You'll miss Professor Bettenhausen's lecture. Move it, gal."

Harry saw his wife. Flushing with nervousness, feeling a prickling on his neck, he went to her and took her coat, guiding her toward the group.

Friendless, Barbara Huggins teetered at the edge of the party. Huggins had roused her from the room and from a morning sulk. "Get out and try to learn something," he had snarled over the hotel phone. "Boy, what a grouch," Barbara yawned back at him. "You didn't sound like that last night, Mr. Hot Hands."

Her feet shrieking, Barbara was unmoved by the *quattrocento* and *cinquecento* glories produced by her ancestors. Her antecedents, impoverished farmers of stony slopes in Sicily, were not part of the Renaissance magnificence around her. To Barbara, these were "creepy and scary"—reproductions of which she would never hang in her decorator-smart apartment on East Eighty-ninth Street.

Herbie, swaying, his trench coat flapping, pockets bulging, approached Bettenhausen. They confronted one another—whale and giant squid meeting in the ocean depths.

"I tip the O'Connor to you, Mr. Bettenhausen," Herbie said. He lifted a yellow golf hat. "I never enjoyed hearing a person talk about art the way you did. I mean it. From now on, I call you the Professor. Okay, Professor?"

"As you will, Herbie." Bettenhausen chuckled. Shackman reminded

Bettenhausen of certain second-rank producers in the old days, coarse comical men, getting by on nerve and energy.

Mrs. Legrand, her eyes studying Herbie as if he were a hairy mammoth chipped from pack ice, simpered. "Harvey, you are a scream."

"Thanks, lady. Whatever I said goes double for you."

"He's joking, Mrs. Legrand," Flo said.

"I know he is, dear. Isn't it wonderful to have a funny fat man like that along?"

They walked down the steps, most of them suffering acute cases of museum feet. Lulu leaned on Harry's arm. "Was that woman trying to approach you when I went to spend a penny?"

"No, dear."

"I won't tolerate it."

On the bus ride to the hotel Flemington decided that an extended shopping trip for Lulu was indicated. But what reward for him? How manage the torment of looking at Theresa Carrell for seventeen days? A headache germinated over his eyebrows. Had he remembered to carry a supply of BC powders? Years ago—ages, it seemed—he had started using them on the advice of Mr. Armstrong, the overnight Western Union operator at the newspaper in Minneapolis. Old Armstrong, erudite, witty, a sage in sleeve garters and leather vest, always with a supply of BC powders, ready to minister to the young editor.

Flemington saw Paris in a blur. He loved the city, but it looked unfocused, affording him no joy. BC powders and the overnight. Forty dollars a week, and he and Terry sharing an apartment in an old Victorian house off Tenth Street near the university. She was getting her master's and her classes were at odd hours. He spent the long night writing leads, phoning the police and fire departments, checking the wire services, gloating over the morning to come, the slow dawn over the river, the girl waiting for him.

He would arrive to find her showered, powdered, in brassiere, slip, and a dressing gown. She would protest: she would be late for her classes. The long night of rewriting cables, changing leads, scanning AP and UP copy, far from leaving Flemington exhausted, filled him with excesses of passion.

"You're a lunatic," Terry would whisper, "you're crazy. Don't you even want some coffee?"

And he would be at her—a man with a dozen hands and four heads, exploring, kissing, hugging, stroking, now gentle, now rough, dragging her to the enormous creaking bed they shared. Giggling, they would make love, trying to find an area that did not betray them to Mrs. Olavsen, the humorless landlady. ("Day ain't married," Theresa heard

87

her telling someone on the phone one morning. "I know day ain't, and I don't like dat.")

The memories were colored and outlined in Flemington's mind as he opened the hotel door for Lulu. He was sweating. He could remember the shade of a slip Theresa wore twenty-five years ago; the distinctive scent of her perfumed soap clinging to her neck; embracing her from behind, pressing himself against the half-clothed body. Her protests never lasted long. She accepted him with a grin, arms and legs opened, a smug possessiveness lighting her face. Shivering, he remembered how she would refuse to release him after they had come to climax, pressing his nude back to her in a strong embrace. "No fair," Harry would gasp. "I've been up all night, I'm dead. . . ." "Big shot," she taunted. "All cave man before you bed me down and then what? Sending me off to school. When I want more." And he would roll away. "When you come home, sweetheart. Wake me."

Before lunch, Dr. Wicker and Rose-Anne sat in the lobby and wrote postcards. The orthodontist also sent a night letter.

BOBBY ALDERMAN
MALLARD CIRCLE
RIVERFORD, CONN.
GREETINGS FROM PARIS ARE YOU USING FACE BOW EVERY NIGHT
THIS VERY IMPORTANT REGARDS

DR. WICKER

Wicker then tipped the concierge and with the aid of a map of Paris had him locate the Université de Paris medical school, in the École Pratique of the Sorbonne. Wicker had a contact there who would show him the school's edition of Pierre Fauchard's *Chirurgien dentiste*, published in 1728—a pioneer work in corrective dentistry. That alone would make the tour worth while! He sent one more night letter, admonishing Nancy Simmenthaler to use the Water Pik nightly, then bought a Paris *Tribune*.

Rosie was seated at a desk in the lobby. She looked at her husband. "Happiness exudes from me. Arnie, this is grand."

"Glad you like it, Rosie. Not tired?"

"Gad, no. I'm full of ginger. Those paintings. I want to go back again, and again, and again. I wish we had two weeks here."

Wicker patted her knee. One of the things that had drawn him to Rosie was her enthusiasm. She could teach the kids a few things about "digging" the world. Before the jargon was popular, Rosie knew what it was to appreciate a statue, a sunset, a poem. She would come out of the twenty-day tour enriched, full of memories, colors, sensations.

He wished he were less the do-gooding nice guy, organizer of picnics for retarded children, fund co-ordinator for the volunteer fire department. About all he had time to do—what with his hordes of clients —was applaud her.

"Warren Bettenhausen is organizing something for the afternoon," she said brightly. "You don't mind?"

"Heck, no. Whatever you want, Rosie."

The dentist had a pang of longing for the old New York *Herald Tribune*. The overseas edition he held in his hands reminded him of what a fine paper it had been—Walter Lippmann, Al Laney, Joe Palmer, John Hutchens. They were rare men—gentlemen, wits, scholars. Dr. Wicker missed them as much as he missed old college friends who had moved away.

Away from the United States only two days, Wicker also missed the familiar routines. Last night, to Rosie's distress, he had longed for Walter Cronkite. He read the baseball scores, scanned the market report, and was pained by an article about the growing defeats of school budgets in American suburbs.

On the back page, above the classified ads—hotels, apartments, choice offerings in wine—he saw an article that drew his attention:

SOVIET PRESS MOUNTING NEW ATTACKS
ON LIBERTARIAN INTELLECTUALS

Moscow, Sept 18—(AP)—New intensified attacks on the Humanist Society, a group of dissident Russian intellectuals who are pressing for more freedom in the Soviet Union, appeared in *Pravda* and *Izvestia* today.

The Society, whose existence came to light last August with the publication of the Lomatov Papers, was denounced in a *Pravda* editorial as a "pack of cosmopolitan degenerates, toadies to Western materialism and bourgeois decadence."

It was by far the strongest recent attack on the Humanists, whose ranks include some of the USSR's most eminent scientists, writers, and intellectuals. The group, in a manifesto accompanying the Lomatov Papers, declared itself dedicated to "the furtherance of intellectual and personal freedom in the Soviet Union." The papers, named for Professor Gyorgy Lomatov, a founder of the Humanist Society who died in a Moscow mental institution under mysterious circumstances last year, consisted of the minutes of meetings held by the group, and an exchange of letters between Lomatov and his accusers.

The society called for freer issuance of passports and travel permits, an end to the persecution of Jews and other minorities, a wider range of studies at Soviet universities, a free press, and an atmosphere in which different political concepts can be debated.

Izvestia, in an article signed by F. M. Kucharsky, a member of the Soviet Writers' Union, attacked the Humanist Society as a "nest of toothless vipers, still capable of spitting venom, but not for any great distance."

Wicker touched the yellow envelope in his jacket. Dr. Borkin? Was it possible . . . ? Hardly. Leland had said he was a biologist, a man at Moscow University who wanted scientific data.

A man who always thought the best of people, Wicker dismissed notions of danger. Had not John Leland assured him that this was a routine mission? Did he not emphasize that citizens were enlisted to run errands for their government? In any case, who would ever bother with an orthodontist rubbernecking around Europe on a packaged tour?

The head of the Humanist Society is Professor Lev Marmaladov, an internationally famous plant pathologist, who has twice served prison terms for "acts against the state," and has been threatened with confinement in a mental hospital. A holder of the Order of Lenin, and a scientific luminary in the Soviet Union, Marmaladov has made no secret of his group's activities and has led demonstrations in Red Square.

As Dr. Wicker concluded the article, his apprehensions gave way to indignation. It was inconceivable to him that society could function in that manner. He was outraged by the suppression of such matters as the right to opinions or a free press. How did people keep their sanity under such circumstances?

"You look pensive, Arn," Rosie said.

"I'm fine. It's this business about school budgets in the *Trib.* They're shooting them down all over the country."

"Well, you can't fight for every one."

Dr. Wicker agreed. Somehow there seemed a distant connection between people who would not support the education of their children and a society that sent its intellectuals into sanitariums.

"Architecturally, I suppose the eggheads will tell us it is magnificent," Mr. Wattle said. "From a practical standpoint, I think it's dreadful."

The industrialist was talking about the cathedral of Notre Dame. Aboard a Bateau Mouche, Virgil's party relaxed after dinner. Cigars and cigarettes glowed in the Paris night. Disturbing odors rose from the muddy river, but the city and its monuments were forever beautiful.

"I guess when they built it," Father Konay said cautiously, "they weren't concerned with comfort."

"But they should have been," Mr. Wattle said. "No heat. Not enough light. Structural defects."

People drifted from the deck to the saloon, listening to the drone of the loudspeaker describing sights along the Seine. When Father Konay was the only one remaining in the bow, Mr. Wattle cocked his head at him. "You people believe in the afterlife, don't you?"

"Of course," the priest said. "This life is only a temporary stage. We're just passing through, in preparation for the kingdom of God."

Mr. Wattle studied the façade of Notre Dame, letting it know that he had its number. "When Mrs. Wattle was alive, we did a lot of churchgoing," he said. "I went along with it. Religion is all right with me. It keeps people in their place."

"Out of trouble?" Father Konay asked.

"In a manner of speaking. Mrs. Wattle was looking for that dead-certain guarantee that she'd live again in the great hereafter. She went from the Missouri Synod of the Lutherans to Christian Science, back to the Baptists for a spell, a short term with the Methodists, and back to the Lutherans. She had us into everything except the Romans and the snake handlers."

The priest was not offended. He did not mind the pairing.

"Still and all," Mr. Wattle said, "Mrs. Wattle cried a great deal when she was dying. She certainly did not want to die. For all those assurances, she wanted to hang on. Kept her alive with transfusions and intravenous feeding, and everything else known to medical science."

"But her faith must have been a comfort to her."

"No way, padre. I tried to comfort her, but it was no use. She was so drugged she barely knew me." He leaned over and tapped the priest's knee. "I've concluded that when I die I'll be buried and I'll rot. Back to the earth from which I sprang. I won't like the idea, but I won't kid myself."

Father Konay, distressed, had no idea what his roommate was talking about. The bald man, sighting Virgil, decided he had settled religion matters for the evening. He hopped to the guide.

"Does the service include female companionship?" he asked.

"I am afraid not, sir."

"How about asking that pretty schoolteacher, the widow, to come out here with a couple of geezers?"

"Mr. Wattle, you must ask her yourself. I cannot play Cyrano de Bergerac."

"Who in blazes was he?"

91

"An intercessor for a romantic gentleman. Mrs. Carrell is inside. I am sure you'd be welcome if you joined them."

"I was hoping to get her out here just with me—and the padre as chaperone."

"You must develop your own stratagems." He looked for an escape route, and found it in Mr. and Mrs. Huggins, emerging from the saloon. They paused, transfixed by the illumined tracery of the Eiffel Tower.

The truth was, Mr. Wattle was lonely for feminine companionship. A self-contained, self-made, self-propelling man, he would never admit this to anyone. But to be starved so long for a soft hand! The smell of perfume on a woman's neck! The curve of thigh and hip! Mrs. Wattle had been ill for twelve years. A long series of operations, cuttings, scrapings, stitchings. Cancer devoured her slowly, destroyed her appearance, her strength, finally her mind. She had been in and out of hospitals, clinging to life with a determination she had never shown in anything else. All that time, Mr. Wattle had been faithful to her. He continued to be continent after her death. Why? There was vigor and juice in him.

"Say, have you noticed how safe the streets are at night in this city?" Mr. Wattle said, bursting into the midst of a group that included the Bettenhausens, the Wickers, the Grants, and Theresa. "No one dares run around mugging and raping in this town. Those French cops would shoot 'em dead as soon as look at 'em."

Bettenhausen had been in the midst of a reminiscence about a Hollywood star who could not remember his lines, and Wattle intruded before the punch line. Sputtering, Bettenhausen refused to resume the story. All of them looked at Wattle, and he barged on. "They have the right idea here. No mercy. If I had my way there'd be a whipping post on every street in Seattle."

There was a nervous shifting. The people seated around Bettenhausen looked at one another, unable to formulate answers. No one looked at Dr. Grant and his wife.

"You know what I mean," Wattle plunged ahead—shooting a finger at Henderson Grant. "It must be the same in Minneapolis."

Ibith Grant shut her eyes. Her husband responded in an unnaturally loud voice. "I carry a gun," he said. "I won't give any hoodlum the chance to mug me. Our house has been broken into four times. When I make my calls that gun is in the outside coat pocket, ready for business."

"That's the ticket," Mr. Wattle said.

"A 7.56 Magnum with a double clip," Dr. Grant said, spacing each

92

word. "God help the mugger who tries to lift my wallet. Ever see what a few rounds of those do at close range?"

"Right," the rubber manufacturer crowed. "An eye for an eye."

"How about a little social conscience?" Theresa Carrell asked. "Shoot everybody, and there'll be no one left to go to school. We'd have less muggers if we had more schools and homes and jobs."

"Socialistic nonsense," Mr. Wattle sang. "I'm not against equal opportunities, but only for those who merit them."

"I'm with you," Dr. Grant said. Did a self-mocking note color his voice? "First come, first served. No handouts for welfare chiselers."

"Man after my own heart." The industrialist excused himself, saying he did not want to miss the view of the Pont Neuf.

"You lost that round, Theresa," Ibith said. "Thanks to Two-Gun Grant."

From the deck came the gargling voice of Herbie Shackman, serenading his party.

> "We were sailing along,
> On moonlight bay.
> You could hear the darkies singing—"

"Herbie, that *word*," Flo Shackman said. "The Grants may be listening."

"Whah? Doc Grant? Me and him are buddies already. I made a date to get a checkup next time I'm in Minneapolis."

Herbie's words boomed inside the saloon. "I'll check him up," Dr. Grant said. "Make him lose forty pounds before I even put a stethoscope to him. Consommé and grapefruit for Herbie."

Shackman bulged in the doorway. The boat glided effortlessly under the Pont Neuf. "Changed the lyrics for you, Doc."

"Sing, Herbie," Dr. Grant said.

> "We were sailing along
> The riverbanks.
> You could hear the hookers singing,
> 'Two hundred francs!' "

There was an explosion of laughter. Virgil applauded.

"What's a hooker, Harvey?" Mrs. Legrand asked, neatly spacing her words. Mr. Legrand was dozing in a corner, his homburg clamped tightly on his head.

"*Gevald!* Someone else explain," Herbie boomed.

Yasuda approached the table where the Bettenhausens, the Wickers, and the others were seated. "Brandy, anyone? I'm springing for brandy. Hey, *garçon!* The Courvoisier, dig?"

93

The cognac arrived. Voices waxed louder, the laughter was more sustained. Outside, his arm around Lulu, Flemington watched but did not join them. Lulu seemed at peace, resting her head on his shoulder. Less booze and more buying would be the prescription. At the end of Three Worlds she might be in good shape.

Day 5: Paris–Berlin. The morning is free. Further sight-seeing might be in order—a trip to Chartres, or Versailles, or Fontainebleau can be arranged. Or if you wish to stay in Paris, feast your eyes in one of the city's smaller museums, like the Jeu de Paume with its dazzling Impressionists, or the Cluny with its medieval treasures. Plenty of time, too, for more shopping, always a delight in France, and then a lavish lunch— cheese, wine, fruit!

Then, on to Berlin, into the heart of another Europe!

Flemington, shaving with care, sloshing Dunhill's cologne on his face, glanced at Lulu's frail figure, deep in a nembutal-aided sleep. She seemed tranquil, and he attributed her state to the red Bordeaux served aboard the boat. A man who valued serviceable information, he was touched with nostalgia for a Parisian landlady—a quarter of a century back, when he was working for the Armed Forces Network— who advised him, "*Quand vous êtes en doute, choisez un Bordeaux rouge.*" Sound advice, and not without a certain cachet. Externals were important to Flemington. He enjoyed handing the wine list back to the sommelier with the request: "They all look rather routine, so why don't you just select a reliable red Bordeaux?" And then to the guests at his table: "Advice from a Paris landlady, smartest woman in the 5th arrondissement. When in doubt go with a red Bordeaux." Their friends admired this quality in Harry. It went well with Lulu's money.

The money was splendid, Flemington had to concede. Euphoria, he had the notion that he was about to work out some ideal arrangement regarding his life. Other men had mistresses. Why not pursue Theresa? She was a widow, an old love, someone who had stirred him the way no woman ever had. But he had his duties to Lulu. Part of the unspoken agreement, when he had married her, over strenuous opposition from her mother (Melton Deaver, the erratic inventor of the self-sealing valve and the renewable gasket, had died when Lulu was in her teens, leaving her a fortune), was that Harry would "look after" Lulu.

In her twenties Louise Deaver was already a drunkard, a subject for gossip at the clubs, a patient at secret clinics, rest homes in forests. No one understood why she drank. "A chemical imbalance," one physician said. "An effort to find her dead father," a psychiatrist

95

opined. Harry believed that boredom made Lulu hit the bottle. He had hoped it would change after Robbie was born. But poor Robbie with his unfocused eyes and flapping arms and drooling speech made everything worse. Where once alcohol had been a weekly escape, Lulu now became insatiable. Soon she required less to render her glazed of eye, thick of speech, sensitive to imagined insults. At the club Harry bribed bartenders to water the gin. It did little good. Sometimes, it seemed to him, the mere sight of a bar, a liquor advertisement, the aroma of an opened fifth, could produce that unsteady gaze in her eyes.

Leaving Lulu in a snoring sleep, Harry went to the lobby. There would be more shopping this morning. A little guidance from Pepi was indicated.

At a coffee table, Herbie and Flo and their friends were handling a variety of glittery objects spread on a blue cloth. A French merchant was displaying costume jewelry.

"Good morning, brother," Herbie shouted. "Sleep okay? The missus feeling good?"

"Fine," Harry said.

"Two of these for the same price," little Flo said. "Got it? I said two. *Deux.* Who speaks French?"

"Nah, nah, two of these, and one of them," Shirl said, picking up a salt cellar. "Whaddya say?" She held up three pudgy fingers.

"Impossible, madame," the vendor said.

"Come on, all three, *trois,* get it?"

Herbie lumbered to his feet, moving Harry to one side. "You get what you were lookin' for in London? I saw you and the missus lookin' at some stuff. I know a little bit about silver. Used to do the tax returns for some shleppers on West Forty-seventh Street."

"Two hundred?" Flo asked. "You're nuts. A hundred and twenny-five. And throw in this pin. And the cuff links."

The Frenchman was sweating. "*Impossible, c'est trop. . . .*"

"Wait, wait," Shirl said eagerly. "Do it this way. The brooch and the green cuff links and the two necklaces. Right? Two hundred, okay?"

The jewelry salesman clutched at his collar. "*Madame, c'est beaucoup . . .*"

"But it's all junk anyway," Shirl said. "One more, one less."

Herbie nodded. "They know how to *hondle,* right? You know what it is to *hondle?*"

"Bargain."

Herbie studied Harry Flemington's face with admiration. "So how come you knew? With that hat and the vest, Grosse Pointe, all that?"

"I was a newspaperman in Minneapolis for a long time. You eat in delicatessens and go to bar mitzvahs."

96

"Oi, *a landsman*. You're okay, Mr. . . . ah . . ."

"Harry. Call me Harry."

"Throw in the cigarette box," Flo said.

"And the whole thing for a hundred seventy-five."

Shackman turned on them, feigning anger. "Hey, girls, hold it down, willya? Whaddya think this is? The pushcart market on Belmont Avenue?" He looked at Flemington. "I guess you and the missus don't do it this way, huh, Harry?"

"But we do, Herbie. Exactly that way."

"You're kiddin'. With all your moola?"

"That's why we have all that moola. My wife can *hondle* with the best of *hondlers*."

Herbie nudged his bulging belly against Flemington. "Whadja spend? Whadja buy? The girls are bustin' to know."

"We ordered a few things."

"Between us, Harry, how much?"

Flemington hated talking about money. Nor did he want to demean Herbie Shackman's modest purchases, Flo's haggling. It seemed wrong to dwarf their harmless fun with details about Lulu's blockbusting. Still, if Herbie insisted . . .

"We went for eight thousand dollars, Herbie," he said. "Tea and coffee service."

The orange mustache fluttered. "Great kidder, Harry. I get it. You didn't buy *nothin'*. *Garnicht*. Right?"

"Right."

Across the lobby, he could see Warren Bettenhausen studying a map on a coffee table. His wife and the Wickers were with them, planning an excursion. Bettenhausen knew his way around museums and art galleries and churches and restaurants. He'd become the leader of the elitists, a group that now included the Negro couple and Theresa. It would be pleasant, Flemington mused, if he were single, found Theresa, and they could then pair up for the tour. The notion summoned up joyful images. They would hold hands in the Champs de Mars; sip Tokay while boating down the Danube; walk through the Blue Mosque. And always, at the end of the tiring day, a shared bed. Flemington began to sweat. Why had he missed it all?

Theresa came into the lobby with the Grants. He could not control a pounding in his chest. Impossible. He would not be able to look at her for eighteen days. Maybe Lulu would get ill, tire of the trip, become gorged with purchases. They would cut it short and fly home.

Ibith Grant greeted him. "Mr. Bettenhausen is leading the culture vultures this morning. Impressionists and so forth. Want to join us?"

"Please," Dr. Grant said. "Come along."

"We've got some errands. My wife knows some people in Paris

we're supposed to look up." He could not get himself to say they were going shopping again.

"You used to be big on museums, Harry," Theresa said. "Weren't you on the Detroit Fine Arts Commission?"

"Lulu was."

"Then she'd love this tour of Mr. Bettenhausen's," Henderson Grant persisted, halting only when his wife's elbow found his forearm, then led him away.

Theresa, alone with Flemington, looked intently at him a moment. In the yellow-gray morning light of Paris he appeared weary.

"Wife all right?" she asked.

"Not you too, Terry. I'm fed up with these solicitations about Lu. If you must know, she wasn't too drunk. We even made love."

"I'm glad."

"You're not, and I'm lying."

"Is it true you have separate bedrooms in that castle in Grosse Pointe?"

"You've been spying."

"I have friends in Detroit. I'm sorry, Harry, but you get talked about a great deal. It isn't easy being the husband of a Deaver."

"Are you trying to hurt me?"

"You know me better, Harry. We're equally culpable. How did we ruin it all?"

"Me, *me*, dammit. Christ, you're good to look at. I'm standing here trying to be calm, and I'm in agony." He inhaled, as if needing oxygen to sustain himself. "I'm staring at your legs, and your thighs and your hips, and I want them. Bury my head in you. I never was good at self-control when we were alone."

"Funny. I always thought I was the pursuer. You managed to make enough excuses to avoid me. At least when it counted."

"Stop, Terry. If I could laugh about this lunatic relationship of ours, I would. What are the odds, do you think, of you and me showing up on the same tour?"

She touched his hand. "Maybe not as big as you think, Harry."

"And the odds on our making love again?"

"Much greater."

Ibith Grant called her. Bettenhausen was ready to lead them to the Jeu de Paume.

Savoring the flaky oiliness of the croissant, Huggins broke the news about his trip to Zurich.

"Switzerland? Why?" Barbara moaned. She had eaten voraciously, toast, a brioche, two croissants, a second cup of coffee. Give her five years, Huggins thought morosely, and she'll be popping her girdles, a waistless wonder.

"Business," he said. His eyes felt weighted, his neck stiff. He was a poor traveler, a man unhappy in hotel rooms and on strange sidewalks. His world was limited, reassuring—an East Side apartment, the New York Athletic Club, the Giants, some select restaurants, the Wall Street office.

"What kinda business?"

"Some client. Papers to sign."

"You didn't mention it."

"I didn't think I'd have to. It occurred to me this was a good chance."

She knew he was up to something. Barbara was a sad case. Not quite into anything. She was happiest in the bosom of her Sicilian family—babies, supermarket prices, relatives, deaths, horrid illnesses. As a lawyer's wife, she knew she was supposed to rise above it—yet could not. He had heard her spend an hour—a goddamn *hour!*—on the phone with her mother Serafina, comparing beef prices at A & P, Grand Union, and Shopwell. On and on it went, a litany of cuts, weights, bone in and bone out . . . There were times when Huggins was grateful for his poor Irish heritage; they were people blessedly free of enslavement to food.

"I'll be lonely," Barbara whimpered. "No one to talk to. Buncha phonies on this tour."

"Try Dr. Grant and his wife. Your brothers are always hollering about niggers. You can tell Mario you met a coon physician with ten times as much education as the two of them together."

"You're not funny."

"Neither are your brothers. Latch onto the schoolteacher, Mrs. Carrell. She's got a lot of class. And quite a behind."

"You would notice that. You really going?"

"Two days. I'll pick you up in Berlin or Vienna. Stop sniffling."

Mrs. Legrand, trailed by her husband, glided toward them. She seemed never to lift the slippers from the floor. "Something in your eye, Barbara?" she asked. Already Mrs. Legrand knew everyone's first name, although she insisted that Herbie was Harvey.

"Yes, but I got it out," Barbara said.

"Your wife is so lovely, Jimmy. That wonderful white skin and the black, black hair. Like the old song, 'Black Is the Color of My True Love's Hair.'"

Singing, the old lady bent close to Huggins. J.P. recoiled. The Legrands walked toward the lobby.

"Holy Horror," J.P. said. "She parted my hair."

99

"Hunh?"

"Parted my hair right down the middle. With her breath. I was wondering about the old broad's vigor. She skates around in those slippers, never loses a step, never misses a thing. No wonder. She's full of bourbon. I just got a blast of one hundred proof."

Seven or eight of the Midwestern people had surrounded Virgil in the lobby. Huggins waited until the guide had gotten them off for their free morning. Overhearing the conversations, J.P. noted that they all wanted to shop. Virgil's suggestions—a trip to Versailles, or Chantilly, or Vincennes—were curtly dismissed. Where were the department stores? Did you get a discount on perfumes in that place on Avenue de l'Opéra? Where did you go for nice ties?

It depressed Huggins. He didn't kid himself. He was materialistic as the next man. But after a brief period of indulgence in ties, suits, socks, expensive bathrobes, and luxurious leather, he lost interest. There *had* to be something else.

"Got a minute, Pepi?" the lawyer asked.

Virgil had sent the last of his petitioners on their way. "Of course, Mr. Huggins."

"Can you help me get a flight to Zurich? One economy seat. And a hotel room."

"When?"

"Today."

"So you will join us . . . ?"

"Coupla days. This thing came up." Huggins grinned at the guide. "The fellow at the stamp market was no help. I was after a rare Nicaraguan air mail, 1932 issue, with an upside-down watermark."

"And you think you will find it in Zurich?"

"I didn't say that."

Virgil saw something admirable in Huggins. The man would have been a good friend to have in the camps.

"Actually it's a business trip for my partner, signing papers, checking investments."

They moved toward the concierge's desk. Virgil took the phone and in flawless French requested the Swissair office. "You say investments?" he asked.

"Small change."

"So. Do you have a bank, or would you like me to recommend one?"

Huggins wondered: Does this guy know? Does he suspect? Suppose these guides had an agreement with the police? Did they get paid for tips on wrongos—money smugglers, dope handlers, black market impresarios? What had Moussac called him? A *passeur*.

"No, no bank, Pepi. But I might need a urinalysis. Know any medical laboratories?"

"In Switzerland, sir, everything is available."

"'Cheese complements a good meal and supplements a bad one,'" Bettenhausen pronounced.

"Ah . . . Dr. Johnson?" Cornelia asked.

"Briffault."

Arnold and Rose-Anne Wicker, seated opposite them in a booth at Androuet's, the Parisian restaurant serving over three hundred varieties of cheese, regarded him with reverence.

"You've got to go easy on a couple of Connecticut yokels like us," the dentist said.

"Now *stop*," Cornelia Bettenhausen said. "Nobody in the world can keep up with old Total Recall here. Don't be intimidated."

"Waiter, are you sure there is no Amou?" Bettenhausen asked.

The waiter displayed a wooden wheel dotted with dozens of redolent specimens—red, gold, gray, white, brown, orange, blue. It was the palette of some mad artist, a masterpiece in Brie and Chèvre.

"No, m'sieu. One eats Amou only from October."

"You sure you weren't an actor?" Dr. Wicker asked. "I haven't gotten straight what you did in Hollywood. I think you're kidding us. You acted."

"Only in college. The Swarthmore Players were the beginning and end of my acting career."

Rose-Anne's tongue recoiled from a bit of Chèvre. The goat seemed to have survived in the cheese. "I don't get it, Warren," she said. "What *exactly* did you do in Hollywood? Producer? Director?"

Cornelia and Warren shared a glance that was at once comical and rueful. Rosie was sorry she had asked the question.

"That would be hard to describe," Bettenhausen said.

"Cultural attaché," Cornelia said, her voice growing more nasal.

"I was an impecunious teacher of twentieth-century culture, one of the first such courses ever given at Central Michigan State College. I had written an article for the *Discoverist Review,* in which I compared the films of Von Stroheim to the novels of Conrad. It was a bravura performance, and in a way I anticipated a lot of the junk being put out now. In any case, Maury Fallsberg, about to take over his father's empire, read it, and hired me. And there I stayed for twenty-five years."

"But what did you *do?*" Rosie persisted.

"Attended meetings. Wrote memos. Screened foreign films. Tried to add meaning and style and taste to our films. I succeeded to a

101

limited extent. But for the most part I failed to convince the powers that the audience consisted not entirely of people with low foreheads. Still, it was fun."

"Fascinating," Dr. Wicker said. "And you knew all those famous actors and actresses and directors."

"Yes, famous people," the fat man huffed. "Directors are the worst. Now that all this *auteur* nonsense is current they have become insufferable."

"You wanted to be one," his wife taunted.

"I might have been different. But the writers! I liked them. Jumpy, bespectacled, shivering beside their pools, homes smelling like the hotel kitchens of Miami Beach, their children old before their time, their lives a sun-painted frenzy, all deep in left-wing politics, gambling, or art collecting. I liked writers."

"Gosh, like everyone else, I'm a frustrated writer," Rosie said. "How . . . what . . . who would you use, if you were doing a movie about the people on this tour? Herbie and Murray? The old people? Us?"

Bettenhausen scratched his neck, fluffed his beard. "Good question. Waiter, may we see the board again? I crave a bit of Cachat."

"*Tout de suite, m'sieu.*"

"Our fellow travelers? The widow, Mrs. Carrell, is an obvious choice. She's much too good-looking. She has that remarkable quality I've noted in certain straight-backed, well-rumped types. She gets better-looking as she gets older. I'll wager she was just a pretty girl when she was in her twenties. How old is she now? Forty-four? She's beautiful."

Rosie said: "You wonder how someone like Terry is single. She told me she was married twice. Divorced once, widowed once."

They were bursting to gossip. Cornelia made the first move. "Has anyone figured out why the Dragon Lady is after her?"

Rose-Anne raised her hand. "Terry says she knew Harry Flemington a long time ago. We had girl talk in the Tuileries this morning."

"How long ago?" Bettenhausen asked.

"She didn't say. She's never even met old Lulu. Just that she knew Harry once in Minneapolis. The heiress doesn't like anyone around who ever *knew* her precious mate."

Cornelia's pale blue eyes were narrow with shrewdness. "It ain't that simple, kids. That Flemington is a spiffy dude."

"But he's nice," Rosie said. "Elegant."

"Hmmm." Bettenhausen blinked his eyes. "I suspect that's his profession. Being elegant."

Cornelia made a wry face. "Gad, a triangle. Right here on old Three Worlds. But when? How? In whose room?"

Bettenhausen chewed pensively on a morsel of Pont l'Evêque. "Creamy. Just the right amount of salt. They'll manage. They do, on these tours, you know."

Wicker's long-jawed face was aghast. "Gosh, people on our tour?"

"I had a chat with Virgil," Bettenhausen said. "He claims it can happen on *any* tour. He once shepherded a party of Baptist Sunday school teachers from Iowa. One white-haired widow worked her way through every man on the tour, including two members of the cloth, one eighty-two-year-old organist, and the president of the State Society Against the Teaching of Evolution."

"He's speaking German now," Barbara Huggins said to Father Konay and Mr. Wattle. She sounded suspicious.

"Bitte schön, noch fünf Stücke," Virgil was saying to the porter at Tempelhof Airdrome in West Berlin. The party was delayed again. The Flemingtons' luggage had become a burden. The porter, a sway-backed old-timer, waved a hand and walked off.

"That's a nerve they have," Barbara said. "That Mrs. Flemington with all her stuff." Jimmy had left for Zurich from Paris late that afternoon. The priest and Mr. Wattle had come to her side.

"He deserves a lot of credit," Father Konay said. "To master all those languages."

"English does me fine," Mr. Wattle said. "They understand me, no matter where. So your husband went to Zurich, eh?"

"A business trip."

"Good idea. Make the tour a deduction. It can be done. Let Uncle Sam pay." The terminal lights winked on his bald head. He patted Barbara's soft hand. "The father and I will look after you, young lady."

Barbara shivered. Not that she would ever—*ever!*—dare dream of cheating. But what a joke! A bald-headed old jerk and a priest. Across the terminal two black soldiers looked her over with flat eyes. They wore high-peaked overseas caps, tight olive drab trousers, burnished boots. Their broad chests were garlanded with ribbons, braids, medals. One of them, over six feet, mustachioed, leered at her bosom, his eyes traveling to her hips, resting there, then turning his back. Jimmy would have made some joke. Mario and Ralphie would have known how to handle the spade. "One thing about our family," Barbara had announced proudly one night to a party at the Jabloners', "we all hate niggers and hippies."

"What the hell is this?" Herbie Shackman shouted. "Every time we stop, it takes an hour to unload that broad's valises."

"Right on, Herbie baby," Murray Yasuda added. "Hey, know what happened when the elephant had diarrhea?"

Shackman danced around the Japanese. "No, Father, tell me, what happened when the elephant had diarrhea?"

"It . . . it . . . it . . . was *all over town!*"

"The blue and gray bag is still missing," Lulu Flemington said. "You know the one, Mr. Virgil?"

"I do, madame."

Flemington felt the sweat forming in his armpits. The blue and gray one. With the Flaxman wrapped in felt coverlets and cotton batting. Eight thousand dollars' worth of eighteenth-century silver. The mountain of luggage grew on the hand cart alongside them, Virgil checking each item. Flemington had the sensation that he and Lulu had come on the tour for the benefit of their valises, those zippered, pocketed cases purchased in stores with names like Safari, Ltd., Kilimanjaro, and Expandables, Inc.

"There it is," Flemington said with relief.

Virgil tipped the porters, doing so in front of Flemington, who made a mental note to reimburse the guide. The group moved to the bus.

Virgil reminded the party to move in a clockwise direction. There was some confusion. "Except us," Murray Yasuda called from the rear. "We stay put, right, Herb?"

"Whatever you say, *ketzeleh.*"

"Say, what's that tower there?" Mr. Wattle piped. "That crazy-looking thing?"

"The Luftbrücken Denkmal," Virgil said. "A memorial to the Berlin Airlift." He spoke in German to the driver.

"Eisenhower sold us out!" Wattle cried. "That whole thing wouldn't have been necessary if Patton had been turned loose!"

"Listen to Pepi," Rosie Wicker said. "Perfect German. It's not that he talks all the languages, he *becomes* one of them."

"Come on, Rosie."

"Its true, Arn. In England he was stiff-upper-lip."

"Well, he's a British subject."

"By adoption. He's some kind of Croat, or Serb, or Austrian. But the point is he acted like an Englishman. In Paris he was all shrugs and raised eyebrows. Like a Frenchman. Look at him now—stiff, patronizing, like a German burgher."

They left the airport and turned on to the autobahn to Berlin. Flemington remembered the airlift well. At that time he was on the night cable desk and edited wire service reports. The names haunted him—General Clay, General Howley. Wasn't the British commander named Ian Robertson? Sir Ian Robertson. It was a long time ago. With a deep breath, Flemington tried to summon up images of 1948, 1949. He had been living with Theresa. Underpaid, miserable, full of self-pity, he had refused to marry her. Vivaldi and Corelli on his old record player . . . Chianti bottles . . . a set of Modern Library classics, secondhand from the U. of M. bookstore . . .

"I rewrote all those airlift stories on the cable desk," he said suddenly.

"You did?" Lulu asked. "When?"

"When I was with the paper." He left out the year. Lulu detested references to the years when he knew Theresa. The world began for her in 1952 when they were married.

"So, ladies and gentlemen," Virgil said, "this is the Kurfürstendamm, a street of endless opportunities."

"Wowee!" shouted Herbie. "When do we start?"

"Soon enough, Mr. Shackman. Fine restaurants. Hot dog stands. Exquisite boutiques. Dime stores. Drunken soldiers. Rich businessmen. Stripteasers. Belly dancers. Bar girls. Telephone clubs."

Neon flashed about them, bouncing off the flanks of the bus, illuminating the windows. Red, yellows, blues, greens—preternaturally bright, full of faked life. There were hints of Broadway, the Ginza, Oxford Street. Yet it remained stolidly German.

"Just beyond, ladies and gentlemen," Virgil said, "the Soviet Victory Monument. It is in the Western Sector, a Russian enclave. There are always two Red Army soldiers on duty—one to watch the other in case he decides to defect, as one once did."

J. P. Huggins saw the distant mountains and spoke to the cab driver. "Mountains? With snow?"

"Yes, sir. Just beyond the Zurich See."

"Beautiful."

"September gives nice weather in Zurich. But we are getting troubles like you have—smog, dirty water. We were once the cleanest city in Europe."

The lawyer liked what he saw—masculine buildings, spotless streets, well-dressed people. Shops filled with everything, prices not exorbitant. Some memories of a literature course at Fordham flickered at his mind. Did not he and Buck Sweeney once sit through a course on James Joyce? And had not that grand Irishman made his home in Zurich? He asked the cab driver.

"Yes, sir. I have never read the books, but I know about him. There is a statue of Mr. Joyce in the cemetery. And you should dine at the Pfauen where he wrote *Ulysses*."

Huggins was sorry he did not know more about Joyce.

"Once I saw Mr. Joyce when I was a little boy," the driver said. "A strange man. Almost blind. Thick glasses. Red face from the wine. He admired Zurich, even though he said our weather was as uncertain as a baby's bottom."

Only in Europe, Huggins thought. A cabbie who could quote Joyce. Was it merely a *shtick* for tourists? For Russians, he would remember where Lenin hid out in Zurich.

"He was a great writer," Huggins said. "What kind of a weatherman was he?"

"You will see. Clear today. Maybe rain tomorrow."

Rain suited J.P. fine. Under heavy clouds, in alpine mists and rain, he would make his criminal rounds.

"Gad, it's a Richard Burton movie," Rose-Anne Wicker said. In her slip, she was standing at the hotel window. Distantly she could see the Brandenburg Gate and part of the wall. Zither music filtered over the hotel speaker. The room, furnished with cheap chairs, beds, desk, lit with plastic lamps, seemed to be a stage set. The reality was in the city outside, a place that had nurtured awful savageries.

"Quite a sight," the dentist said.

"If Michael Caine knocks at the door and wants refuge, what do we do?"

"Send for Bettenhausen. Movie people are his department." In droopy underwear, the dentist sat at the edge of the bed and thumbed through the West Berlin directory. He was looking for a man who had invented a new tooth positioner.

"That wall," his wife said. "Hideous. I can see the barbed wire and those tank traps. Lucky us. We get to cross over and come back tomorrow. We've made a tourist site out of the whole darn world. There are even tours to Auschwitz."

"We learn from the past, Rosie. Nothing wrong with that. Who said that?"

She walked away from the window, a long-limbed woman, a tireless skier, expert with salad spoons and garlic presses. Her competence, her involvement endowed her with a mild sense of guilt, like a low-grade fever. Millions of people were less fortunate than she was, unhappier, poorer, unfulfilled. Did Americans understand their blessings? Were the bounties that inundated them, in the long run, burdens?

Wicker wandered to the window and looked at the city. Everything on the ride from Tempelhof seemed normal. A place full of prosperous people. Looking down at the wall, he sensed how fragile these evidences of placidity were. He thought of his letter to Borkin.

In the bierstube that night, complete with oompah band and fräuleins to serve heady pale beer, he would be a new man. Rosie may have been kidding about Burton and Michael Caine and all that spy stuff. Little did she suspect . . . Stretched out on the bed, he nourished the new image of himself.

The German band, with its Tyrolean hats, lederhosen, and cloppy shoes, gave Bettenhausen a headache. Twice he changed his seat, to escape the belching tubas, soupy trombones, flatulent trumpets.

A. T. Gunthorpe, the Memphis man, had gone out of his way to sit next to the Grants. Virgil was always delighted to discover that Americans did not run true to stereotype.

"Watch'all lak to heah?" Gunthorpe shouted across the table—as if Dr. Grant were hard of hearing.

"Whatever suits you, Mr. Gunthorpe."

"How 'bout you, Miz Grant?"

"How about 'The Tennessee Waltz'? Tribute to your home state."

"Don't that beat all. Yoah wife a mighty smart gal, Doctor. Pepi!"

"Yes, sir?"

"Ast that fellah with the violin ovah yondah does he know 'The Tennesse Waltz,' hyeah? Give him this." He wadded a five-dollar bill into Virgil's hand.

"I am sure he knows it, Mr. Gunthorpe." The musicians had a repertory of state favorites. In his service to Planet Tours, Virgil had learned such songs as "Sidewalks of New York," "The Eyes of Texas," "Missouri Waltz," "California, Here I Come," and in the past few years, since statehood, the delightful "Aloha Oe." Was there an Alaskan song?

"Got us some mighty fine colored people in Memphis," Gunthorpe blurted out.

"We have some mighty fine whites in Minneapolis," Ibith said.

"All a matter of education. Got nothin' 'gainst anybody so long as they got manners."

Dr. Grant was ashamed of his overeager denunciation, the day before, of street crime and the revelation that he carried a gun. What he had said was the truth; he merely regretted that he had come on so strongly. There seemed to be no way of handling these matters any longer. Old Gunthorpe, with his booze-stained face, white hair, belly, calloused hands—the man must have been wealthy, for he talked about his rice plantation and the hundreds of mallards he shot—was

107

not a bad man. He wanted to be loved. If you did not love him, he would kill you. Or was that an ungenerous simplification?

"A doctor and a teacher," Gunthorpe announced to Herbie and his party, who were seated a few seats away. "We got us some smart people on this trip."

Herbie hooted. "Don't look at me, Gunthorpe. I flunked out of *yeshiva.*"

"Herbie, they don't understand," Flo said. "Stop with the Yiddish."

Across the smoky table, laden with Hasenpfeffer, Schnitzel à la Holstein, mounds of red cabbage and dumplings, Dr. Grant was clanking steins with Gunthorpe.

"I wonder," Rosie said. "Henderson Grant may be enjoying the camaraderie as much as that dealer in Purina Chows."

Herbie was staring at Mrs. Legrand. "You remind me of someone. I can't remember who."

"Harvey, you're teasing me."

Herbie leaned forward. "I mean it. Like a teacher I had once? A movie actor?"

"Your mother, Harvey?"

Leaning closer, studying her wrinkled face, Herbie sniffed alcohol. *Stoned!* The old broad was stoned! No wonder she was impervious to fatigue, cold, crowding!

Father Konay tried to divert Barbara Huggins. Once established that she was a Catholic, with a convent education—"Oh, the Ursulines are wonderful, just wonderful"—he hoped they would find common ground. But nothing he said cheered her up.

"Your husband will be back tomorrow or the day after," Father Konay said.

"Yeah, its rotten being alone. I mean, without him."

Father Konay lit her cigarette. She might as well be alone, seated with him and Mr. Wattle at a remote table. The priest regretted that he had no small talk, no charm. A lifetime in a coal town, baptizing, marrying, burying. Hard-working people who knew nothing of the "new Church," all those windows Pope John had opened, those flashy nuns in their short skirts, and bearded young priests—*troublemakers!*—like Father Folker. Everything was going too fast.

Gunthorpe, returning from the men's room, weaving his way through the diners, now swaying in time to *"Ich Hat Einen Kameraden,"* grabbed one of the waitresses by the arm. The girl was homely and big-busted, with a mop of yellow hair falling over her eyes. Virgil moved toward them.

"Hey, sweetie," Gunthorpe said, "evah been on top a real Tennessee walkin' horse?"

The waitress pulled her arm away. She was not offended, merely bored. "Get lost, Papa. I haff a boy friend from Texas. He knows more about horses than you."

"Come on visit me at mah hotel, we find out."

"My boy friend is a big black dude. He cut you as soon as he talk mit you, *versteh?*"

"*Yahoo!*" Gunthorpe hooted. "Tha's what Ah lak to hear!"

Several of the party turned to look at the Tennessean. Mrs. Legrand whispered in her husband's ear. The old man did not budge. Was he in pain? Semiconscious? Forever sedated?

Another waitress walked by. Gunthorpe, stumbling, made a grab for her. She dodged, spilling beer on Si Shapiro.

Virgil took Gunthorpe's arm. The man was not drunk, merely enthusiastic.

"I think we should sit down, sir," Pepi said. "Apple strudel is coming. German coffee."

"Ole Peppy. Ole Peppy always theah. Dang, Ah was just gettin' somewhere with that lil gal. My wife been a sick abed the last six years. Mama ain't got a thing to offer me 'cept tears. Tha's why my children sent me on this. Ain't gonna live forever."

"Nobody does, Mr. Gunthorpe."

"Ah want me poontang. Nothin' fancy. Just a lil gal to be nice to ole A.T."

"That is not part of our service, sir."

"Ah lak to die from bein' lonely, Peppy. Just point me in the right direction, ole A.T. can manage."

The man's sincerity stirred Virgil. At least there was nothing hypocritical about Gunthorpe. Pepi could not leave him without hope. "Berlin can be dangerous, sir. Perhaps tomorrow. A secret between us."

Gunthorpe ran the back of his hand across his mouth. "Ah hold you to it, Peppy. Didn't come on this trip jus' for churches and pictures. Man got to git his ashes hauled."

"Indeed he does."

The waitress, breasts bobbing, eluding Gunthorpe's reach, brought a tray of pastries to the table.

"*Napfkuchen, Streuselkuchen, Bienenstich, oder Apfelstrudel,*" she called out.

"One of each!" Herbie shouted.

"Ice cream," Mr. Wattle cried. "Vanilla and chocolate."

The cry went up from his followers. He had created an ice cream crusade. A few adventurous souls opted for the pastries. The band was marching around the restaurant, blaring *Tannenbaum;* patrons beat time with knives and forks.

Virgil retired to a beamed archway, losing himself in the smoke, the dark wood, the noise. He never came to Germany without a bow to the gods who had rendered his jailers fat, prosperous, rather comical. A bit torpid, they seemed, freed of old blood lusts. A reasonable man, Virgil appreciated the harmless pleasures of tourism, of which the Germans were a vital part. Better tours, restaurants, hotels, faked entertainments, than all those icy floodlights and screaming people! And the voice of destruction. Gone, thank goodness. Under their peasant dirndls the waitresses wore panty hose manufactured in Israel.

"No pastries," Bettenhausen grumbled. "They look plastic, fabricated in a Japanese toy factory. I'll finish the Limburger. I'd advise you to do the same, Corny."

"I'm for the strudel. A big piece."

"You will be up all night with indigestion."

"So what?" Cornelia asked. "I want my money's worth."

Her husband mumbled slyly: "Hmmph. Last year it was kill Japs. This year it's make money."

The laden fork paused halfway to Mrs. Bettenhausen's opened mouth. "Wait a minute . . ."

"Eat your strudel, dear. Frederic March in *The Best Years of Our Lives.*" Bettenhausen drained his stein. Foam clung to his beard like sea spume. Memories of old movies were sometimes more real than life.

"You call that mush ice cream?" Mr. Wattle cried.

Day 6: Berlin, East and West. A day of comparisons. Three Worlds visits its first Communist country, the city beyond the wall, East Berlin. Before that, a tour of the wonders of West Berlin—Charlottenburg, the Olympic Stadium, the Brandenburg Gate, the John F. Kennedy Memorial, the Kurfürstendamm. Following a relaxed lunch at one of West Berlin's sidewalk cafés, we pass through Checkpoint Charlie and into East Berlin, along the Leipziger Strasse to the Russian Memorial. Then via Karl Marx Allee to Unter den Linden and the Wilhelmstrasse, site of the old chancellery. Our return route is through the wall again, and into the French Sector.

Come evening, a taste of Berlin's naughty night life!

In each city a local guide took over from Virgil. In Berlin, the guide was a blond youth named Helmuth, with the bearing of a Luftwaffe cadet. Yet he wore a peace symbol in his lapel, and his hair was long. With much charm, he combined German orderliness with the new freedom.

"Charlottenburg Castle," Helmuth said, "was begun as a plain country house in the seventeenth century. Why Charlotten? It was built by the wife of the Emperor Frederick I, whose name was Sophie Charlotte. Please, are we ready to go in?"

Across the street Dr. Wicker was clicking off photographs of the castle. The day was cloudy and warm, with a sticky haze. He kept changing f-stops, doubting his exposure meter under such conditions.

A few paces behind the dentist, Murray Yasuda was also taking pictures. That morning, before boarding the bus, Yasuda had bought a $150 lens in a shop near the hotel. Herbie had gone along and had been astounded to see his Japanese friend plunk down the money, writing traveler's checks without attempting to bargain.

"You don't *hondle?*" Herbie asked. "You coulda knocked that Kraut's price down fifty bucks." "Nah, nah," Murray said impatiently. "Life is too short. Easy come, easy go." Herbie shrugged: "Restaurant business must be good in California."

Rose-Anne and Flo Shackman were calling to their husbands. The party was entering the castle. Herbie, moving lightly—gliding and sashaying, he resembled a redheaded Zero Mostel—sidled up to the dentist. "Somethin' botherin' us, Doc," Herbie murmured. "Me and Si and the rest."

"Can I help?"

"A small thing. Don't take it personal."

"I never do."

"Herbie, move your ass," Murray shouted. "You're blocking the whole castle."

"Sorry. Doc, are you Joosh?"

"Joo—? Oh. Jewish. Yes. Is anything wrong?"

"The missus?"

"Rosie's a Protestant. Unitarian, I guess."

Herbie's lips protruded—wisdom, approval, inside dope. "That's nice, terrific. Like to see that."

"What?" Wicker was grinning.

"Intelligent people, handling these matters correctly. I mean, all of us admire you and the missus. High-class educated people. Not snooty. Not like my son. A full scholarship to Yale, *du herst?* But has he ever got a kind word for his parents?"

"That's a shame. A lot of kids are like that."

Near the parking area in front of the castle, a husky man in a gray suit got out of a black Opel sedan, talked briefly to the driver, and walked toward Wicker.

Herbie nodded gravely. It seemed to Wicker that there were pools of doubt and fear in the fat man. Nor was he quite the clown he pretended to be. Rosie had remarked how shrewd he was, how interested in paintings, history, foreign places. "Yeah, well, with you and your wife maybe it makes a difference. I mean, being educated. Your kids might respect you. Anyway it's a pleasure to have people like you along."

"We enjoy *your* company, Herbie. You're a million laughs."

Herbie trotted toward Flo's irate figure. She was tapping a shoe, pointing toward the castle portal. "Yeh, yeh, a million laughs."

Wicker stopped for a last photo with the wide-angle lens. He shouted to Rosie that he would meet her inside.

The man in the gray suit waited until Wicker took his picture.

"Are you with this tour, sir?" he asked.

"Yep."

"I'm with the Defense Intelligence Agency. Here's my ID." He showed the dentist a card in a plastic holder. It was similar to Leland's but with a different designation, and the overprinting seemed dissimilar.

"Gosh . . ." Wicker recalled Leland's admonition about the identification of football and baseball teams. Baseball first. Then football. The contact to make the first move with the name of a city . . .

"You're Dr. Wicker?"

"That's right."

"Do you have a minute?"

Wicker, a trusting man, was nevertheless on guard. Whom was he to believe? Whom could he trust? He waited for "Kansas City"—or "Oakland"—or "Los Angeles." The man, shave-headed, small-featured, seemed decently American. "I'm late for the tour. My wife just went in. I don't want to miss Gertz's mausoleum."

"It looks like any other. Were you approached by someone at Kennedy a few days ago?"

"Hmmm." Dr. Wicker was the world's worst liar. In dealing with his patients, that army of terrified children, he found that truth was the greatest weapon. Now, waiting for the name of a baseball city, and hearing none, he decided that lying was required. "By a Planet Tour man. An old friend."

"Someone who said he was a U. S. Government intelligence agent?"

"No."

"You're positive?"

"Yes."

"Carrying a letter for anyone? A package?"

"I am hoping to visit some orthodonists in Europe, for a paper I want to write. Dental schools, so forth."

"A message whose contents you don't know?"

"I'm a patriotic citizen but you're wasting my time." Wicker wished the man would give him the name of a city. New York, please. San Diego. Montreal.

"All right."

"Thanks." Wicker hurried to the castle. The man returned to the Opel and got in.

"Can't believe a guy like that would lie," he said. "Scoutmaster, PTA president. I never knew an orthodontist who told a lie."

The man at the wheel began to study notes he had made in a small pad. "It might have been a feint. What do we know? It's supposed to be a man who left New York on a packaged tour five days ago. It could be one of a thousand guys."

"New York says there are two hundred and fifty-four possibilities. You check out this crowd from the manifest?"

"As best as I could. It's quite a mob. Lemme see the list again."

"I checked it against the group. The fat guy, Bettenhausen, never. The colored doctor, maybe. The little Japanese fellah. The joker with the red mustache. Do we have time to talk to all of them, Clyde?"

113

Clyde rubbed his nose. "I'm afraid to. If the guy is witting, he'll get wise and make a different move. Even if he's unwitting, he might try something crazy. I wish New York had narrowed it down."

"They screen them carefully. A lot of them are too shrewd to get suckered into something like this." He studied the list. "Hold it. One of them was missing."

"Who?"

"Huggins. New York lawyer. I saw his wife, the broad with the black hair and the big bazooms."

"You would."

"But no Papa Bear."

"He could have finessed the sight-seeing. Maybe resting up for a run into East Berlin. Talk about covers. They don't check those tour buses for anyone."

"Or nursing a hangover in his hotel room."

The husky man chewed his Titralac, savoring its minty flavor. People in his line of work tended to develop tender stomachs. It came from operating in ignorance all the time.

"You know, this thing might be a fake?" Clyde asked. "They could have planted a dud on some tour and leaked it to us, and then sent it through channels."

The driver yawned. "They've been known to do it."

Twenty minutes later the party emerged from the castle. Virgil had advised Helmuth to hurry. The tombs were of interest, and the Rembrandts and Dürers, and that was about it. Virgil saw a few people suffering severe cases of museum feet. Mr. Bettenhausen, burdened with his bulk, seemed to be puffing more than usual. Mrs. Flemington had cut short her walking and had sat down in the waiting room.

Clyde crossed in front of Herbie and Mrs. Legrand and approached Pepi. He showed him the ID card. Virgil stepped aside. "All aboard, ladies and gentlemen. We are behind schedule."

"Please?" Virgil asked. He had no strong feelings about spies, agents, *apparatchiki*. Berlin was a stew of them. Once he had been detained for two hours by Britain's MI 5 and accused of being an agent of the Shin-Bet, the Israeli Military Intelligence. It was a case of mistaken identity.

"There's a man named Huggins on this tour?" Clyde asked.

"Yes."

"Where is he?"

"Zurich." Virgil's eyes darted to the bus. Mrs. Huggins was inside talking to the priest.

114

"When did he leave?"

"Yesterday, sir."

"He say why?"

"A business trip."

Clyde looked toward the stragglers. What an assignment! Nothing to go on. No leads. No specifics. Just someone on a packaged tour that left Kennedy five days ago. . . . The Jap? Never. The fat clown who was shrieking after being goosed by one of his pals? The old dame in the bedroom slippers?

"Do you know where he's staying?"

"I am afraid not. He said he would find a hotel. He is only going to be gone a day or two. He intends to meet us in Vienna tomorrow. We will be at the Pacher Hotel on the Ring."

"Hey, Pepi!" A. T. Gunthorpe roared. "Time's a-wastin'!"

"We paid for this trip, we're entitled to a maximum of sight-seeing," Mr. Wattle announced. "And these bus windows are filthy."

"Who's the dude Pepi's yakking with?" Murray asked. "Looks like a Yank."

"Secret agent," Herbie muttered to Mrs. Legrand. "He's got the plans to Bloomingdale's carved on his *tochis*. Trying to sell it to the Syndic."

"Harvey, I don't believe one word you say."

Herbie squinted at her face, trying to read the wrinkles. "I almost had it. Who you really are."

Outside the bus Pepi asked if he could leave.

"You Swiss?" the agent asked.

"I applied once for Swiss citizenship but the delay was too long. I was a student at the Ecole Hôtelier in Lausanne. Gentlemen, I am sure you have a dossier on me. Planet Tours will vouch for me. Also the International Association of Certified Travel Guides. I am a British subject. If you insist on my pedigree it will take all morning. May I go?"

"Don't say anything to Huggins. Or anyone else. Some of our people may contact you in Vienna."

"At your service." Pepi leaped aboard.

"Ladies and gentlemen," Helmuth said, "we proceed to the Victory Monument. The Siegesäule. And we are lucky. The weather is clearing and we will get a good view of the city."

Arnold Wicker had observed the colloquy between Virgil and the man who had questioned him. An unsettling sensation seized him. Who was the fellow? Why didn't he know Leland's code? He drew his long-legged figure out of the seat, excused himself as he stepped over the Flemingtons' carry-on bags, and walked to Virgil.

115

"Hey, Doc," Ed Hutzler called, "ask him to have the driver wash the windows at the next stop."

"And clean them well," Mr. Wattle shrilled.

"Yeah, we can't see anything," a woman complained.

Wicker, normally attentive to requests, did not hear them. He bent to Virgil, trying to make himself heard over Helmuth's narration over the microphone: ". . . when President Kennedy honored us with a visit and said he was a Berliner . . ."

"That fellow you were talking to," Wicker said. "I thought I knew him. . . ."

"A man I had on a trip a few years ago. He wanted some advice on hotels in Düsseldorf."

When the bus departed, Clyde and his driver took off for their office. "My money's on Huggins," Clyde said. "Get Zurich on the phone."

The driver reached for the car phone under the dashboard. "What about the guide?"

"Might as well. Ask London to check Virgil out. I never trust these friggin' men without countries."

Huggins, refreshed after a deep dreamless sleep induced by a pill given him by the concierge, strolled about Zurich and felt better. The Swiss would rescue him. The Swiss, in their efficient way, would take his money, invest it, launder it for the Malfis. He and Barbara could spend the rest of the tour relaxing, sight-seeing, making love. In Rome, the last stop before home, he would treat himself to some custom-tailored suits and take Barbara to one of the fancy couturiers.

James Joyce and the cab driver were right. A fine misty rain fell over the city. The solid buildings, shops, the lake, the distant mountains were softly outlined, pleasantly gray. Huggins felt at peace in his olive Abercrombie & Fitch raincoat, his English umbrella, the camera case (would anyone wonder about it on a rainy day?) on his shoulder.

The concierge had told him to go to the Investors' Club on the Bahnhofstrasse, have coffee, await the opening of the banks, and ask for advice.

"You mean I just walk in? I don't have to be a member?"

"Open to all, sir. It is run by the Union Bank. Pretty waitresses. Stock quotations. Newspapers."

Switzerland was his kind of place. Everything seemed in order. Huggins loved New York, but nothing seemed to be running properly any more. No one was in charge.

Huggins found the Investors' Club with no trouble. It was a splendid building, with that lasting look he so admired in the city. He shook the water out of his Borsalino and sat at a table. In front of him yesterday's stock market prices flashed on a screen. A waitress— not quite as pretty as the concierge had promised but passable— brought him coffee and a cinnamon bun. A few dark-suited types, quiet, cigar-puffing men, studied their morning papers. The aroma was intoxicating, almost sensual—tobacco, strong coffee, wet wool, perfumed soap.

"You are an American?" someone was asking him.

A man with a pale bony head and gold-rimmed eyeglasses was talking to him. He sat a table away.

"Yes. But I feel more Swiss every minute."

The man lit a cigar and chuckled. "I appreciate that. We are tired of all the jokes. You know, a thousand years of democracy and what have we achieved? The cuckoo clock."

Huggins waved his hand. "You people got a lot going for you. It's called civilization."

"You are a tourist? On business?"

J.P. hesitated. Who knew for sure—about any of these nice customers? He had heard about the international grapevine of illegal currency dealers. It was not impossible that Moussac had tipped someone. Two hundred thousand dollars was not petty cash.

"Business," the lawyer said. "I'm looking to exchange a fortune in box tops."

"Beg pardon?"

"Box tops. From old cereal boxes. They have a steady value in the United States. Rice Krispies. All-Bran. I have some rare ones, too— Cap'n Crunch, Froot Loops, Sugar Smacks. They tell me they're convertible."

The bony face struggled to smile. "You are right to be wary. Actually you have nothing to fear from me. I'm with the Independent Bankers' Association. My job is to spend the day here and help people. If you don't want my assistance that is all right."

"I want a bank that will sell me gold."

"They all sell gold."

"All?"

"To anyone with money."

J.P. sipped the potent coffee. It was the best he had tasted since leaving New York. If the banks were as reliable as the coffee, he was home free. He'd drop his load of treasury bills, get a receipt, and present it to the Malfis: "Here it is, *walyones*, give me my ten grand."

"I just walk in?"

117

"A calling card will help. But, of course, you need not be hasty. There are good buys in tungsten and platinum. Molybdenum has become popular. Or perhaps you want to open a neutral account."

The man ticked off the possibilities like the shopping editor on station WINS who recommended "good buys in broccoli today, prices on cauliflower down again." It amused Huggins. There was no danger. No one could possibly take any of this seriously. He gulped the coffee and put on his coat.

"A bit of advice," the man said. "I assume you will be making a hand payment."

"That's the only kind I ever make."

"You should keep your purchase of gold to no more than ten thousand per bank."

"Well, that shouldn't take too long. I mean, my box tops don't amount to that much. Thanks anyway."

Huggins left the warmth of the club. On the flashing board he was glad to see that Ciba had gone up a fourth of a point and Montecatini was unchanged.

Over the bus loudspeaker, the German guide said: "The name of this street, ladies and gentlemen, is Strasse des 17 Juni."

"Seventeenth of June," Rose-Anne said. "When?"

"In 1953, madame. The day on which Russian tanks shot down German workers in East Berlin. Now, look at the big area at the center of the street. Grosse Stern—Great Star. It is like the Étoile in Paris."

In the center of the immense traffic circle rose the Siegesäule. The party began to leave the bus for the ascent up the tower. Only Mr. Legrand did not stir. Half asleep, he rested his head against the window. "Are you all right, Weston?" Mrs. Legrand asked. Herbie stopped to see if anything was wrong.

"Fine, fine, Liz. You go ahead."

Mrs. Legrand smiled at Herbie. "Poor sweetie. He gets tired."

"Rest, rest, Pop," Herbie said. "You can see it from the window. Big deal, a tower."

"You want me to stay with you?" Mrs. Legrand asked.

Herbie, leaning over the seat, trying to think of something useful to say, noticed the neck of a Four Roses bottle peeking out of the bag.

"No, dearest." The old man's voice sounded distant, coming to them through malfunctioning switchboards.

"Maybe he needs a doctor," Herbie said. "Ask Doc Grant to look him over. Pills or something."

"That's all right. Sweetie will take his own pills and have a nice rest." Mr. Legrand shut his eyes. Herbie helped guide Mrs. Legrand

118

toward the door. "We moved to Bisbee because it cost less," she said. "It worked wonderfully. We travel all the time and, with our pensions, we manage nicely."

"Maybe he's too sick to travel."

"Sweetie? Every minute is valuable to him. I told you, he's been on heavy sedation for twenty years."

"Pain?"

"It comes and it goes. We are of hardy pioneer stock, Harvey."

Father Konay shaded his eyes and looked to the top of the tower. He had heard the guide say that the Victory Monument was formerly in front of the Reichstag Building. The Nazis, looking for an excuse to seize power, burned it, blaming the deed on the Communists. *All so complicated!*

Father Konay was of Hungarian ancestry. He had been seven when his parents took him to America. His father had gone into the mines and died early, and his mother had worked in a bakery to send him to the seminary. They were misty memories. They used to talk about Hungary. But he had become a flag-flying American, equating his country with his faith, his God, his cross.

Father Konay blinked. He hardly knew what to say. The priest tried to recall—how did Hungary stand? They were allies of Hitler, weren't they? And they seemed to have killed a lot of Jews. But with the Communists breathing down their neck, who could blame them? After all, the faith had to survive, and Stalin was the enemy. Still, it was a shame all those innocent people had to get gassed and shot. One thing, he decided, had nothing to do with the other. He had heard that many priests saved Jews. And wasn't it just the Hungarian *government* that had been Hitler's ally? In a way, he was glad he knew little about history.

Once more the bus rode past the Russian War Memorial, with its immobilized tanks and the Red Army sentries watching one another.

Helmuth resumed. "Please note, ladies and gentlemen, the golden horses on top of the Brandenburg Gate. Who knows what such a team of four is called?"

"A quadriga," Theresa called out.

"Say, that is admirable," Mr. Wattle said. "Good work, Mrs. Carrell."

"Us teachers," Terry laughed. "Heads full of random information."

"Correct, madame," the guide said. "A quadriga. A two-wheeled chariot and four horses. You know, when the Red Army fought its way into Berlin, the original horses were ruined and a red flag was flown above the gate. Then a miracle occurred. In West Berlin, they lo-

119

cated the original molds. They made a new one, covered it with gold —and look! East-West co-operation over four horses."

"Should have filled it with dynamite and blown them all to kingdom come," Mr. Wattle shouted.

Huggins entered the Nord-Helvetia Bank midway down the Bahnhofstrasse. The street breathed money, wealth, success. J.P. was feeling sure of himself. He now saw himself as an adventurer. Was it any different from passing college courses with textbooks hidden in the john, notes secreted in his jockey shorts?

He was directed to a glass partition at the rear of the bank. Amid white marble pillars, under a high ceiling, sat a vice-president in charge of foreign transactions. His name was Baumeister—a stout man with eunuchoid cheeks. Huggins introduced himself and gave him his card.

"An attorney, so. How may we help?"

"I want to buy gold."

"You understand that it is illegal for an American to purchase gold."

"I've been told."

"The law requires me to tell you that before we transact business."

"But the law doesn't forbid you to sell it to me, right?"

"Quite so. Many of your countrymen buy gold. The dollar has lost its attractiveness. There will be other devaluations. I am afraid your dollar, sir, is no longer cock of the walk." Like Moussac, Baumeister seemed pleased by the dollar's fall from grace.

"It's not my personal dollar."

"Very good, Mr. Huggins. Are you buying gold for yourself or for a client?"

"Does it matter?"

"I shall have to know. We will sell gold to anyone. And you can buy it in a great many places—Canada, Mexico, Luxembourg, Lebanon, Hong Kong, Abu Dhabi, Dubai—"

"What? Where?"

"The Arab states on the Persian Gulf. Most larger buyers go to South Africa, the source of gold. For smaller amounts, Switzerland is preferred. We give fair rates and our banking services are reliable."

"You're so reliable you help American citizens break the laws of their own country."

Baumeister was not offended. "We perform a service. We warn the buyer that he runs a small risk."

"How small?"

"Should you be convicted of a crime in the United States, or should you be indicted, or be under investigation for a *major* crime, we are obliged to divulge the details of your transactions."

J.P.'s mind ran over the possibilities: a distant risk. It would be better to keep the account in his name. The in-laws would be more likely to get in trouble.

"What do I do with the gold after I buy it?"

"We register your purchase. But we do not report it to any authority. You may, if you choose, keep it in the bank's common pool. Or you may rent a safety deposit box. Or we will be happy to give it to you before you leave today."

"Give it to me? What do I do with gold?"

"That is for you to decide." The banker smiled humorlessly. "Once, some years ago, two gentlemen bought a great deal of ten-tola bars, about twenty thousand dollars' worth, with the idea of selling them in India at twice what they paid. So they had designed special vests with slots on the inside for these bars. They intended to go directly to New Delhi from Zurich. Time was of the essence. Their flight was canceled, and they decided to go the other way—back to New York. Gold has no smell, but it is heavy, and when these two fellows walked off at Kennedy Airport, both of them bent double at the waist, they were uncovered."

Huggins did not enjoy the story. "What'd they get?"

"A fine. They had influential friends."

"I don't intend to carry samples with me. How else can I keep my gold here?"

"If you intend to buy and sell frequently, the safe deposit box is not recommended. You cannot open it between Friday afternoon and Monday morning. Since devaluations are announced after the Friday closings, the authorities quickly order the boxes sealed, to be opened only in the presence of an official. It can be burdensome."

"I imagine it is."

"The Liechtenstein Anhalt is another possibility."

"Really? How does that work?"

"The Anhalt is a semicorporate organization. It will cost you five hundred dollars to open it and three hundred dollars annually to operate it. A Swiss or a Liechtenstein attorney can help you establish. It pays no taxes. It can own gold and other precious metals and currencies. There are no inheritance problems since the names of beneficiaries are secret."

A mental image of Mario's five furtive brats and Ralphie's dull-eyed twin girls flitted through his mind. *Beneficiaries. Heirs.* The Liechtenstein Anhalt, whatever it was, was too good for them.

"I think I'll go for the—what'd you call it?—common pool."

121

"A wise choice."

"Or is it dirty pool?"

Baumeister sucked at his teeth. "Beg pardon?"

"Just a joke."

"In what amount?"

"Ah . . . ten thousand dollars?"

Baumeister scrawled on a pad. "You have been given good advice. You have a bank check, or funds . . . ?"

"I got the horse right here." J.P. hefted the camera case onto Baumeister's desk. He took out the Pentax, the Rollei, two lenses. Then, as Mario had demonstrated to him in the basement that day, he carefully snapped off the stiff leather lining the bottom of the case. Beneath it was a large yellow envelope. He slid it out.

The bank official watched the procedure with casual interest. He was used to this sort of thing. Once an elderly American lady, an international society figure, had gone to the ladies' room—and she had told him so with great pride—rolled down her corset, and extracted thirty thousand dollars in bearer bonds.

Huggins reached inside the envelope, riffled the papers, and deftly detached one document. "No fair peeking," he said to Baumeister. "They all look alike anyway."

"But with different numbers."

"Cash on the barrelhead." Huggins placed a United States Government treasury bill, value ten thousand dollars, on the desk.

"Treasury bills."

"Bill. You only get one."

"We see a great deal of these." He held it at its edges, studying the engraved face. "There is a considerable black market in treasury bills. Because they are negotiable they are stolen frequently. And counterfeited."

Huggins shifted the case to the floor. He had no idea how Mario had gotten the two hundred thousand dollars in U.S. treasury bills. He had heard something about the Bahamas.

"We shall have to run a routine check."

"Oh, it's legitimate. The ink is wet."

Baumeister slid forms across the desk. "These forms must be filled out. They are for bank records."

"I'll buy it." J.P. glanced at the papers—identification, date, storage fees, commissions, all in three languages. The official forms seemed to legitimize the dirty business, the money born of stolen hi-fis and heisted cameras. "How long to check out this piece of paper?"

"Two hours or so. We will use the telex."

"To New York?"

"The central bank in Switzerland."

Huggins kept the pen poised. "Every bank I go to, they'll have to do this?"

"I am afraid so."

J.P. signed his name in five places. He was required to show his passport and two other identifying items—his New York driver's license and an American Express card. He slid the envelope back into the false bottom of the bag, thanked Baumeister, and resolved to go down the line, hitting as many banks as he could.

Outside Huggins walked to a kiosk and bought a *Herald Tribune.*

"Did you get the free market price or the commercial rate?" the pale bespectacled man asked him.

"Hah?" Huggins felt a shiver in his bowels.

"Did you get a good rate?" the man persisted.

"I decided not to buy gold." Huggins' hand shook slightly as he took change from the news dealer.

"So?"

"I bought tax-free bonds. City of Tacoma Power & Light Company."

The man did not smile. "One need not come to Zurich for that."

"I like the food here." He waved to the man. "Thanks for every-thing."

"If you want a good meal, try the grillroom at the Carlton. The sole meunière is superb."

Waiting for the man to leave, Huggins walked some distance down the street, crossed, then returned to the bank. He walked in, circumnavigating a mob of Japanese in dark gray suits, and returned to Herr Baumeister. The single U.S. treasury bill was still on his desk. He was on the telephone.

"I changed my mind," Huggins said. "I think I'll buy real estate in-stead. They say it's the best investment."

The Swiss covered the phone. "Yes?"

"As Will Rogers said, they aren't going to make any more land."

The banker spoke in German, hung up. "I have not expedited the papers. This is irregular, but—"

"That shouldn't bother a Swiss bank."

"Indeed not. Sit down, Mr. Huggins. You are joking of course about real estate. Can I help you in any other way?"

"How do I get to the cemetery?"

"Sir?"

"The cemetery. I want to see the James Joyce statue."

"Ah, the cemetery. It is called Fluntern. Near the zoo. Whose statue did you say?"

123

"It wouldn't matter to you. He never could afford a Liechtenstein Anhalt."

Later that day, the pale man telephoned Clyde in West Berlin. "I followed orders, sir," he said. "No attempt at interrogation. Huggins claimed he wanted to buy gold, made a purchase, then changed his mind. Then he took a walk to the cemetery, possibly for a rendezvous, but he met no one. He spent some time near a statue but he did not pick up a note or leave any. He is spending the night at the Carlton and is leaving on Swissair 2344 tomorrow, arriving Vienna at thirteen-ten hours."

"He contacted no one?"

"Only the bank official. It was strange the way he changed his mind."

In a green-walled air-conditioned office in West Berlin—the sign on the door read INTERNATIONAL COMPUTER ELEMENTS, INC.—Clyde hung up and turned to his aide. "This guy Huggins is either witting or he's a nut."

The aide shook his head. "Or stupid. What kind of a cover was that —buying gold?"

Clyde picked up the phone. "There's four more tours in today. How can we check them all out? And no more information from New York. Let's kick this to Vienna."

"What about Huggins? He had a ten-thousand-dollar treasury bill. It's got to be dirty. Maybe he's got a load of them for laundering. Want me to call Interpol? Or the Treasury people?"

Clyde made a weary gesture. "I suppose so. Do they ever do as much for us?"

The bus rolled down the Unter den Linden. It was a street made for monsters, Pepi Virgil thought. Too wide. Too huge. Man was rendered futile. It was designed by Germans, but it suited Russians also. He never once made the trip to East Berlin that he did not touch his British passport, a talisman, an amulet. Thank God for the British! The bucket-hatted East Berlin police, the Vopos, and the baggy-trousered Red Army men no longer filled him with fears. He had learned to regard them as victims as much as persecutors.

"Looks modern, new," Herbie said. He was less boisterous in East Berlin. Virgil had heard Flo Shackman telling one of the other girls— Shirl? Sylvia?—that Herbie had lost relatives in the Nazi years. They had this *thing* about Germany, and they had seriously considered another tour because of the two days in Berlin. Virgil could sympathize.

124

"*Alles in Ordnung,*" the border guard had said at Checkpoint Charlie, with a nod at the stack of passports, a few words with Virgil. The guards knew him. One guard had stuck his face into the bus, glanced blankly at the members of Three Worlds, and departed.

"*Gevald,* I thought he came for me," Herbie muttered. "Murray, was he looking at me?"

"Do you realize," Mr. Wattle cried out, "that East Germany is the fourth most productive nation in the world? That this country ranks third in precision instruments, fourth in lenses, and in the top ten in milling and shaping tools?"

They rode by the television tower, the Soviet Embassy, St. Hedwig's Cathedral, the National Gallery. There was much comment about the shops, the well-dressed—if somber—East Berliners.

"What can you buy here?" Flo shouted.

"Very little, madame," Virgil said. "Banners with Lenin and Marx and Herr Ulbricht."

"They look satisfied," Dr. Wicker said. "Don't you think so, Rosie?"

Rose-Anne looked pained, weighing some unpleasant notion. "Arn, I get the feeling people don't care about freedom all that much."

"After an hour of riding in East Berlin?"

"I think they want their refrigerators full and a new suit and a car. Freedom comes after that."

"Awful lot of these people escaped to the West. Some got killed. That's why the Russians built that wall."

"I know. I don't fault them. But were they running to freedom and all that stuff we admire—free press, free speech, freedom of religion— or were they running away from rotten diets and bad shoes and no automobiles? You read me, Arn?"

"I do, but I'm not sure."

Bettenhausen leaned toward the Wickers. "Rose-Anne is right. It's only a handful want freedom, only a small group of cranks. Almost everyone else will settle for meat on the table and a Volkswagen."

"Scary, isn't it?" Rosie said to Bettenhausen. "It could happen to the best of us. Who needs the New York *Times* or Harvard or the Unitarian Church? So long as they got the color TV and the new Pontiac."

"Never, never," Dr. Wicker said. "Look at those people out there." He pointed to a crowd of East Berliners, lined up for tickets outside the opera. "Can't tell me decent notions haven't touched 'em. They want to be able to speak, and write, and get together same as anyone else."

"Hey, Herbie!" Yasuda yelled. "How do you get four elephants into a Volkswagen?"

125

"Tell me, tell me, Father! How do you get four elephants into a Volkswagen?"

"Two inna front and two inna back!"

For the visit to the Berlin night club, there was an extra charge of eight dollars per person, entitling the tourist to a floor show, running from 11 P.M. to half past midnight, and one drink. Tips were included. These "extras" were painful to Virgil, but the company had discovered that many elderly tourists preferred to forgo entertainments. It was thus wiser to make these excursions optional. (There would be several others: the belly-dancing exhibition in Istanbul, the ballet in Moscow, and the last two nights in Rome, for which no dinner provision was included.)

"Eight dollars?" Mr. Wattle cried. "Eight dollars to see some slut take her clothes off?" He refused to go. The Legrands also declined to attend. A. T. Gunthorpe did not want to go either. He had other plans.

The grain dealer did, however, accept a ride in the tour bus to La Petite Chaumière, the striptease establishment which had the contract with Planet Tours.

The party debarked into the misty Berlin night. They were dreadfully tired. Already Virgil could see advanced cases of tour fatigue setting in. He wondered how they accumulated all that energy. Among the Midwesterners—the Kuchtenbergs? the Forces?—was a couple almost as old as the Legrands. But they plugged on, in and out of the bus, upstairs, downstairs, eager, expectant, full of American optimism, that eternal hope for something exciting, different.

"All arranged, ladies and gentlemen," he said. "The show starts in ten minutes. This way, please."

Dutifully they followed.

"We may regret this," Dr. Wicker said, taking his wife's arm.

"Not me," Rosie said. "For years I've watched these NBC documentaries about sinful Berlin, with the naked girl on the horse. At last."

"No horse, Mrs. Wicker," Virgil said. "But I think they do a cowboy and Indian number."

La Petite Chaumière was lodged in a subbasement. Descending, Flemington at once sensed the change in temperature, and he began to worry about Lulu. She walked slowly, leaning on his arm. It was cold and damp. But she did not complain. He had permitted her a double scotch after dinner. That afternoon, after returning from East Berlin, she had bought a half dozen Meissen pieces in a shop in Keithstrasse. She had spent only several hundred dollars and had supervised the wrapping and packaging of the items. "Madame is cer-

126

tain she wants to carry these with her? We cannot be responsible for breakage."

The owner stared at the Gucci bag Harry was holding.

"Do as I say," Lulu commanded. "You're saving money, aren't you?" Flemington was grateful. The Meissen pieces had kept her content all evening. She had barely noticed Theresa.

Outside, Mr. Gunthorpe watched two girls, booted, swinging leather bags, vanish around a corner. He said nothing and, with a speed belying his years, skittered after them.

Down in the depths of the club, the group huddled for warmth at midget-sized tables. They were the only clients.

A three-piece band appeared. The drummer, a long-haired youth, tested the traps, hit the high hat once, clonked the cowbell. A waitress in black tights, unsteady on high heels, materialized. Orders for the single drink to which members were entitled were taken—Cokes, brandies, scotch, beer. These were brought immediately. (A second drink, or a third—beyond the package—would cost them two dollars each.)

The lights dimmed. "Cold as a tomb," Bettenhausen said in a clipped voice. "It's cold down here. *Cold as a tomb.*"

Cornelia talked out of the side of her mouth, as the band struck up "Buttons and Bows." "*Winterset.* Eduardo Ciannelli."

Bettenhausen twisted his mustache. A spotlight painted a white circle on the green curtain. There was a fanfare from the band, and from the center of the curtain a girl of no more than twenty, stunningly beautiful, with creamy skin and a fall of auburn hair, emerged. She was dressed as the Girl of the Golden West—boots, fringed buckskin skirt, matching buckskin blouse, white sombrero. To the lilting tune of "Home on the Range," she began to undo the buttons of her blouse.

"Take it off, baby!" Herbie boomed. "It's cold in here!"

Back in Memphis Mr. Gunthorpe had been a steady patron of a respectable black brothel. A vigorous man needed release, and with Sally Sue bedridden all these years he had gotten into a routine—a Wednesday night visit to a frame house on the south side of town, where he was treated courteously.

"Colored people got the right idea," he said. "No fuss, no tricks."

As to why he did not patronize white prostitutes, his answer was truthful. "Ain't as purty and ain't got decent manners. Mountain grills and lint-heads. Gimme a nice-mannered black gal any day. The gals at Barrison's bathe reg'lar and use perfume."

Mr. Gunthorpe considered himself a liberal where Negroes were

127

concerned. He liked them. He had employed many in his store. Not behind the counter or in the office, but in the warehouse, as drivers, loaders, messengers. His gifts were frequent—Christmas, birthdays. And at the farm, in northern Mississippi, where he hunted mallard ducks, he kept two wonderful black couples. The women were artful cooks, adept at creating tasty rabbit stews and venison roasts, or performing culinary wonders with the green-headed ducks, basting them in a beer sauce. As for the men, no one in the world could pluck a mallard the way a Mississippi black man could.

"Ah ain't no KKK'er, and Ah ain't no racist, Ah lak colored people, an' Ah always have. Don't hold with these agitators and radicals, but the colored people roun' hyeah know A.T., and Ah know them. We git along."

A.T. pretty much let his sons-in-law run the business (Gunthorpe's: Hay, Grain, Seed, Feed, Coal & Coke). But for all his free time, he had no contact with the real world. "Martin Junior" dying of Ray's bullet; the garbage collectors' strike; boycotts; busing battles. He paid little heed to these, preferring to spend days at the farm outside of Sardis, waiting for the sky to turn black with undulating ribbons of mallards. "Got me more ducks than any man alive," A.T. would tell his guests. "But Ah only let a few friends kill 'em, and then they got to observe A.T.'s limit."

Turning the corner into a street illuminated by flashing neon, Gunthorpe felt his heartbeat quicken. The two girls had stopped beyond a street light. *Hot damn!* Just like in them old movies. They turned and he saw that one was white. Thin and blonde, in a dark slack suit. The other was a black girl, medium brown, wearing a yellow plastic outfit—a beanie hat, a jacket, a short skirt, and yellow boots to match. She had thick thighs, a flat face, and soft eyes. Mr. Gunthorpe knew where to go for value. He headed toward the girl in the plastic suit. The girl in the slacks walked away.

"Howdy, sugar," Gunthorpe said. "How yew tonight?"

"You vant to come mit me?"

"Yeah, boy. Wheah you git that Kraut accent? You look lak a Memphis gal."

"Cost fifty dollars, Papa."

"Fifty dollars? That's robbery."

"You Texas big shot, hah?"

"Memphis, honey, Memphis." Gunthorpe was intrigued. She was as dark and as broad-nosed as Eltheria, one of his favorites at Barrison's. But she sounded like the desk clerk at the Berlin hotel.

"You vant, or you don't vant?"

"Ain't you purty. Yo' pappy musta been one of them colored GIs. Bet yew think Ah'm some redneck nigger-hater. No, ma'am."

"Enuff bullshit. Fifty bucks."

"Dollahs, traveler's checks, or Deutsche marks?"

"Marks iss besser." She took his arm. The feel of her dark body rustling next to his in its crinkly plastic coverings, her perfume, filled him with joy. "Your dollar iss no pick deal, huh, Papa? Serve you right."

"What's yoah name, honey?" Gunthorpe walked on air.

"Ingrid."

"You 'n' me gonna git along fahn." Let those innocents stare at stripteasers, Gunthorpe thought. Let the men nurse their aches, the women feign shock. It was all a fake. You had to go after the real thing. Colored people understood that. They began to screw when they could walk. He admired them for it. Gunthorpe's daughter Lillian, who had once taught in a South Side elementary school, had them guffawing one Christmas with tales of her ten-year-olds fornicating in the supply closet.

Ingrid squeezed his arm. "You no kid, Papa. You be all right? I don't vant trouble mit police."

"Honey, I am the man from Temple, Texas."

"You say Memphis before." She steered him down an alley. There were a dozen signs advertising hole-in-the-wall hotels. Nachtigal Hotel, Die Lorelei, Freudliche Haus.

"It's a joke, honey. The man from Temple, Texas, went to bed with three sisters, an acrobatic team from the circus. You know? Acrobats? He was so good he had one gal on the bed and two in the air all night."

"In here," Ingrid said. She pushed Gunthorpe into a lobby. A gray-haired woman in an apron, dangling keys, appeared. "Giff her ten dollars for room and key, Papa," the girl said.

"On toppa the fifty?"

"Fifty is for me. *Und* also a tip for her. Two dollars. *Und* your passport."

"Passport?"

"In case it happens something. Don't vorry. No sveat. Tvelve dollars. Upstairs, now."

The concierge handed Ingrid a key attached to a wooden disk and a towel. Gunthorpe studied the lilt of the girl's plastic-skirted hips, the enormous muscles of thigh and calf, and was filled with gratitude. Her father must have been some buck!

Less than half an hour later, returning to the tour hotel alone—

those at the night club were yawning their way through a girl in dirndl and wooden clogs—he waited for the elevator. The lobby was empty.

"Not ole A.T.," Gunthorpe said as the elevator approached. "Ain't never too late for A.T., not for poontang." So saying, he consulted his wristwatch and found it missing. He patted his pockets—topcoat, jacket, shirt. Gone. Lost. Maybe in his room?

He searched the room, his luggage, the bathroom. It was not like him to lose anything. And certainly not a $400 watch, a gift from his daughters on his sixty-fifth birthday. It was a beauty—gold, with a calendar, a sweep second hand, and a stop watch which he used at the dog track in Jacksonville.

Gunthorpe sat in his baggy undershorts on the edge of the hard hotel bed. He began to laugh. "Dang. Bust my britches, if lil ole Ingrid didn't git herself a dividend." Momentary anger caused him to curse, to mull the possibilities. Virgil? No good. The police? And be humiliated? A return to the street of joy? And get whomped by Ingrid's fancy man?

Falling on the bed, he decided he had gotten his money's worth. "Yeah, hit was worth hit. Git me a watch at the duty-free shop when we take off tomorra." He snorted, cleared his head, and turned over. "Watch is a watch. A woman lak that there is somethin' special. Let 'er have it."

Day 7: Berlin–Vienna. A short flight takes us into the magic land of Strauss, Habsburg monuments, and the most toothsome pastries this side of heaven: Vienna! In the morning, a look at the city's major sites—the Hofburg, the Schönbrunn Palace, the National Library, and the magnificent streets, Kärntnerstrasse-Rotenturmstrasse, with their elegant shops.

Try a leisurely lunch at one of Vienna's thousand cafés, where perhaps Mozart or Beethoven once hummed his tunes. In the afternoon, a ride up to the hills of Kahlenberg for a breath-taking view of the city and the Blue Danube. We return through the Vienna woods, with a stop for coffee and pastry. In the evening, opera or theater. Will it be The Bartered Bride? Das Rheingold? *Or light opera at the Volksoper?*

Henderson Grant, M.D., did some fast calculations. He was averaging about three hours' sleep per night. At home, he needed seven or eight to do a day's work. Now, battling jet lag, irregular hours, strange food, and inhospitable beds, he found himself, at two or three in the morning, staring at the ceiling. A hesitant dispenser of drugs, Dr. Grant did not like barbiturates or tranquilizers. A sleeping pill would give him one hard night's sleep, then leave him hung over and beset with pains in his temples for two days. So he suffered his insomnia and did not complain to Ibith, who slept, as she put it, like an "ole cotton picker in harvest time."

Waking at 3:15 A.M. on the morning of the flight to Vienna, Grant felt less miserable than usual about his rising. They were scheduled to leave the hotel for the airport at 6 A.M. Virgil, who made a fetish of being well ahead of any departure, wanted them at the airport at seven-thirty. This meant a call at 5 A.M. The guide allowed an hour and a half for dressing, breakfast, packing, and travel. Several of the tourists, notably Herbie and Murray, had complained that the amount of time was unreasonable. They accused the Flemingtons, with their baggage train, of being responsible. "Not so, gentlemen," Pepi said. "I am allowing the specified time for an international flight. Company regulations, and I am a company man."

Dr. Grant, staring at the play of car headlights on his second-floor hotel room ceiling, awaiting the ring of the night clerk, heard the people next door arguing about the bathroom. He had difficulty placing them, but suspected they were the couple named Hutzler

131

from Vandalia, Illinois. The man was partially deaf, extremely good-natured, with a fixed openmouthed smile and a ducklike walk. ("Got a cob up his ass," Herbie confided to Henderson. "Holler in his earpiece and he'll pop kernels all over the joint.") Mrs. Hutzler was younger, fat and sexy in tight dresses and boots. They did not speak to one another on the bus, or while sight-seeing, or dining. But at some unearthly hour, usually four-thirty or five, Dr. Grant could hear them squabbling over the bathroom.

"You goin' in?" Mr. Hutzler would shout. "Another hour in there? And I gotta wait?"

"You were first yesterday. Only forty minutes. What in blazes are you doin' there?"

Water running; toilets flushing; barrages of phlegmy coughing; sneezes; throats being cleared. Dr. Grant, eyes glued to the ceiling, listened and was filled with compassion. Mr. Hutzler was past sixty and his cough sounded dismal. A possible lung condition. On other mornings, lying awake, eyes seeming to him more wide open than normal, his brain swarming with images, worries, Dr. Grant heard the sounds of love-making from other couples—creaking bed, gasps, shuddering exhalations. He felt like a voyeur and did not attempt to guess who was so full of passion at 3:22 A.M.

The insomnia now became bothersome. It would render him weak-kneed during the long day. He would have been happy to skip the stripteasers. But Ibith wanted her fling. Still it had had its educational points. Odd, the physician thought, Americans were supposed to believe that every black man wanted nothing more than to ravish white women. Yet when they had watched the parade of fräuleins removing bras and panties and stockings, no one had cast an arch glance at him. No one had peeked to see whether Sambo was drooling. Indeed, a few of the Midwesterners had joked with him as an equal—Ed, Al, Vernon—winking, asking his medical opinion on a girl with protruding buttocks.

"It looks to me like a mild lordosis," Dr. Grant said. "It can give a woman that nice round silhouette."

"Doc, you are a pistol."

They seemed to like him. After the first few days, people vied to sit with the Grants at lunch or when they stopped for coffee. The physician decided that the reactions of the other tourists were not keeping him awake. At first he felt that it was the terrible wrenching of time. Dr. Grant was an early-to-bed man, often snoozing heartily at 9:30 P.M., up at six, brewing coffee, scanning the morning paper, studying his schedule. Late hours were bad for his system. Above all he was a man of regular habits, temperate, organized, concentrated. That was how he had struggled through the U. of M.—scholarships, meal jobs, night work, averaging four hours of sleep per night. Medical school was even rougher. Henderson Grant had learned that if he functioned without a schedule the machinery of life went hopelessly out of whack. Thrown into a new routine—packings and unpackings, early morning staggering in darkened hotel rooms, climbing on and off buses, on and off planes—he could not relax. Under the best of conditions, as his wife knew, Grant was a secretive man. Never raising his voice, he paid for it with migraine, a pinpoint ulcer, pains in his legs. (Unlike the stereotype of blacks, Dr. Grant was not especially muscular, strong, or co-ordinated. He had never been a good athlete and he found sports boring. Efforts by Ed and Al to engage him in conversations about the Minnesota Vikings and their Negro linemen filled him with sadness. He appreciated their attempt at kindness, but he had only a vague idea who Carl Eller and Alan Page were.)

Other matters were keeping him awake. One had to do with a problem he had left behind. Dr. Grant, associate chief of medicine at High Ridge City Hospital, was given the job of negotiating with the Inner City Committee, a black group who were determined to block the hospital's acquisition of old buildings for a maternity wing. It was an old story. He had discovered that he was not emotionally fit for the work. He did not like being called an Oreo, an Uncle Tom, a stooge for Whitey. He was none of these things. He was a weary man, aware of the problems of the poor, but convinced that their salvation did not lie in attacking the institutions that existed to help them—universities, hospitals, social agencies.

The meetings had been protracted and venomous. He had been told by Dr. Calman, the hospital director—who noticed the frown deepening—that he would relieve him of the job. "Hen," Calman said, "I get the feeling they're taking advantage of you. I can take over the negotiations." But Dr. Grant declined the offer. He'd stick it out. Finally, he had rotten eggs thrown at him by some kids with a paramilitary group of some kind. (*"Power to the People!"* they shouted. Grant, wiping eggs from his lapel, wondered: Do they really understand what power to the people will mean for them? What makes them think they are the only people? The people may vote to round them up and ship them to concentration camps in Alaska.)

When Dr. Grant suffered his fourth migraine in one week, Dr. Calman ordered him to take time off. Ibith, comparing notes with Theresa Carrell, discovered Three Worlds. That would be it. Europe. A new life. New vistas. Different impulses. Stimulation. His decision

133

was given impetus by a telephoned threat. *"White man ass-kisser, you gonna die."* In a way, Dr. Grant's problem was analogous to Father Konay's, although neither of them—they had exchanged only greetings, since both were reticent men—realized it. Standing in the middle, both were under assault from extremes—Father Konay from the angry Ospreys, Dr. Grant from inner-city militants.

In these dawn ruminations, Henderson Grant found that his mind was commingling recent events at the hospital with the new places he was visiting. He could not quite get a fix on what disturbed him. London . . . Paris . . . Berlin . . . What in the world, he found himself wondering, was he doing in Berlin? Or Vienna? What was Beethoven to him, or he to Beethoven? ("Smile, Hen," Ibith taunted, "you can look at Freud's house, maybe lie down on his couch.")

In the room next door, Mr. Hutzler coughed as if part of a lung were about to come up. Emphysema? Virus bronchitis? It had a raw sound. Grant found his medical curiosity piqued. "Make it a short stay, willya?" Mrs. Hutzler's voice came through the hotel wall loud and clear. "God a-mighty, half hour in the toilet." Did the Hutzlers have more right to gawk at the treasures of Europe than did he? The black *philosophes,* the Afro-haired girls and dashiki-wearing boys would agree; and would grant them their churches, paintings, cities, bridges, hospitals, orchestras. *On to Africa! Benin bronzes and Swahili! The bride dowry of the Nuer! Lion hunting with the Masai!* To Henderson Grant, who had made it the hard way in a white man's world, this was nonsense of a high order. It was fine to be interested in Africa, in black art, in tribal folkways. But dammit to hell, for better or worse, he was an *American.*

And yet the agitators had done something to him. "Gonna Europe, Doc?" Harry Mokaka had sneered. "Look at all them honky churches? They ain't for us. You make yourself more of a Tom than you are now. What we got to do with Paris or Rome? It's where all these oppressors come from. Europe their bag. Africa ours, man."

Wrong, wrong, Mokaka, Henderson Grant told himself. The wonders of the world, the great works of art and science, belonged to everyone. If white Americans and Europeans could become lovers of African and Asian art, why could not Henderson Grant stand in awe of Michelangelo's David or the Parthenon?

Four forty-five. Soon the phone would ring. They would stumble around the room, yawning, blinking, facing another trip, another day of looking at the works of man's ingenuity and imagination and industry, the places that gave birth to white America. I'll try harder today.

An hour later, walking through the halls of the Berlin hotel, the valises placed outside each door—there was a mountain outside the Flemingtons'—Dr. Grant felt better. Everyone he passed on the way to the elevator looked half asleep. Herbie Shackman, leaning against a wall, his finger jammed in the elevator button, eyed him with half-closed orbs. "Oi, Doc, it hurts me everywhere," Herbie moaned. "Whaddya got for total collapse?"

"Go to bed early," Dr. Grant said. "Eat less."

"What? After paying for all this?" Herbie straightened up and patted his gut. "Put on four pounds awready."

The Yasudas, bouncy and alert (Grant was convinced it was their metabolism—they went forever on rice and vegetables), came down the hall. It might have been midday. They were beautifully groomed. "Hey, Herbie!" Murray shouted. "How do you make an elephant float?"

Herbie moaned and leaned against the wall again. Quaveringly, he muttered, "Tell me, tell me, Father, how do you make an elephant float?"

"Two scoops of ice cream, soda, and some elephant! Waaaaaah!"

Dr. Grant began to feel better. The merriment of minorities in the morning.

"Our guide for the tour of Vienna, ladies and gentlemen," Pepi said, "is Doktor Gunter, who is a scholar on Viennese history, and I am sure he will make this trip most enjoyable."

"Let's hear it for Doc!" Herbie shouted.

Murray Yasuda whistled between his fingers.

The Viennese guide tipped his homburg. He was a gray old man with a clipped mustache, the most elegant guide yet encountered.

"Welcome, my friends, to our beautiful city, the city of Beethoven, Mozart, Strauss, Franz Josef, Maria Theresa, and Sigmund Freud. We are today, Austria, a small country of eight million, but once we were the heart of the mighty Austro-Hungarian Empire. And who made this empire? It was the genius of one family, the great Habsburgs, who are no longer here, who ruled from 1273 to 1918."

"This guy sounds like Sid Caesar's German professor," Herbie muttered. "But I got to admit, he tells it like it is."

The bus moved down the Opern Ring, passed the Staatsoper, and crept on to the Kärntner Ring. Proceeding toward the Danube Canal, the tourists saw the belfry of St. Stephen's Cathedral.

"More churches," Huggins moaned. "I need less religion and more contacts."

"What? What'd you say?" Barbara asked.

"Nothing." Huggins yawned. It seemed his mouth would never

close. He had arrived in Vienna that morning, waited at the airport for the Austrian Airlines flight bearing his wife and the Three Worlds party. Surly, he could barely talk to her. And inside the camera case, stowed above him in the rack, there nested the Malfis' two hundred thousand dollars. Where? To whom?

"Stefansdom, our cathedral," Doktor Gunter said, "is a miracle. Built, destroyed, built, destroyed, so many times. By the Turks in 1683, worse by the Russians in 1945."

"And Germans," Bettenhausen grumbled. "Dammit, they both bombed it."

"Easy, Betts," Cornelia warned. Bettenhausen looked bilious. He had imbibed too much beer. Normally, his system absorbed food and drink with ease. It was the 5 a.m. call, she decided, that had ruined his digestion. Indeed, most of the tourists, even the hardy Midwesterners, Ed, Al, Vernon and their wives, appeared de-energized.

The bus halted at the Hofburg and the party was asked to debark for a tour. Mrs. Legrand was seated near the rear. Sliding by Herbie and Murray (Weston, her husband, remained, his eyes closed), she greeted Shackman with a grin and skipped out the back door.

Herbie grabbed Murray's arm. "I got it."

"Got what, buddy?"

"I know who that old broad reminds me of."

"Tell me, tell me, Father," Yasuda cried. "Who does the old broad remind you of?"

"Ma Barker."

"You're nuts."

"Look, she's Ma Barker. She's got a Thompson submachine gun inside the tote."

The group, moving lethargically in the chill air, gathered around Pepi and Doktor Gunter at the entrance to the Hofburg. The semicircular façade of the Michaeler Platz embraced them. Rushing waters played in the fountains. Beyond the façade rose the domed roof of the Hofburg.

Am I getting enough out of all this? Dr. Grant wondered. Should I feel guilty in the heart of the Habsburg monarchy? Would I be a better man were I touring the grasslands of Zulu country, in the steps of Chaka and Cetswayo?

"So, ladies and gentlemen," the Austrian guide said, "you will follow me into the great square called In Den Burg, beyond the rotunda, where we will stop to look at the statue of Emperor Francis II. The Hofburg is a city inside a city. The first buildings are from 1220, even before the Habsburgs."

Dr. Grant found himself closing his mind to the guide's oration. He hid behind smoked glasses, trying to blot Europe and that most European of boulevards, the Ringstrasse, from his mind. How had these Austrians accomplished so much? He and Ibith had been stunned with the beauty of the Ringstrasse, that majestic encircling boulevard. The wide street seemed built by talented giants—pedestrian malls, bridle paths, park benches, pollarded trees, and the flow of traffic, not too fast, not too slow, buses, trams, cars. It hummed with life, the essence of a city. And yet he had always had a low opinion of Austrians—bush-league Germans, leather shorts and funny hats, slapping their thighs and kicking wooden heels. And this magnificence was *theirs?* Not his. Not the work of black men. Back to your Benin bronzes, Oreo!

"Pay attention, Hen," Ibith said. "You'll miss the history lesson."

"I'm asking questions later," Theresa Carrell said. She had just jotted down in her guidebook: *visit Natl Library later, also Albertina, graphics collecn.*

"It's getting too rich for me," Grant said. "I always thought the Habsburgs were losers. How did they accomplish this?"

The group, chivvied by Virgil, hurried past the Habsburg regalia. They goggled at the tenth-century crown of the Holy Roman Empire, the imperial crown of Austria, the cradle of the King of Rome.

"I think the Austrians are the English of the Continent," Bettenhausen said. "They acquired their empire, all those lands and peoples, by default, hardly aware of what they were doing."

Virgil laughed. "I agree. My parents lived under the Austro-Hungarian Empire. They said the same thing. One barely knew they were around. We were Croats, Serbs, Jews, Italians, Hungarians, but we never thought of ourselves as Austrians, and I dare say we rarely saw an Austrian. Still, it was an empire."

Father Konay stood in front of the sacred treasure in the Schwarzkammer. The vestments and reliquaries, to his surprise, did not move him. They were too magnificent for his humble soul. Like Notre Dame, they spoke of a church far removed from homely Sacred Heart with its smoke-stained red brick façade and the chancery, covered with yellow brick siding. Why did these old European cities speak of such grandeur? Oh, he knew about St. Patrick's in New York, and other American cathedrals. But they weren't the same thing. It bothered him. Was Father Folker, that troublemaker, right? Were the old churches and the treasure "irrelevant"?

"The Holy Lance, Father," Pepi said to the priest. "And there, a bit of the True Cross."

The other members of the group had wandered off amid the glories of the Habsburgs. Father Konay looked at the artifacts. Father

137

Folker would laugh at them. But did he, old shepherd, whose parents lived under the Habsburgs (and not too long ago), did he *really* believe?

"They claim that seventy-three per cent of all these relics are fakes," Mr. Wattle cried to his roommate. "No offense, padre. But it's all salesmanship. If you add them up, John the Baptist would have had two hundred fingers."

"Is that so?" the priest asked.

"Afraid so, padre. That lance in there, I don't think it any more pierced Christ's side than did my penknife."

"But people like to believe. It helps them."

"So it does," Pepi said. He took Father Konay's arm. Old debts, old memories. He would never forget the priest he had talked to in Latin the day he left Buchenwald. "In fact, if St. John had as many fingers as Mr. Wattle says, that makes it even more of a miracle."

Flemington found he was jealous of the group to which Theresa had attached herself. After a tour of the Hofburg that included the Schwarzkammer, the porcelain and silver collection (Flo Shackman and the girls were disappointed that none of it was on sale), the imperial apartments, and the Kaisergruft, Virgil took the party to Demel's for morning coffee and pastry.

Harry and Lulu sat with the Hutzlers. Lulu objected to them the least since Mr. Hutzler was deaf, said little, and smiled a great deal, and Mrs. Hutzler was cheery and knew a lot about art. Across the marble-topped tables, Flemington saw Theresa and the Grants, Bettenhausens, and Wickers.

"They call it *Schlamperei*." Harry heard Bettenhausen's rising voice. "An Austrian quality—inefficiency, indifference. The waitress will come when she is ready. Ah, I see they have the Obers omelet on the menu. Anyone for an Obers omelet?"

"What's in it?" Dr. Wicker asked.

"As I recall, it's a large crepe, sugared, folded over whipped cream."

"*Yech*," Rosie said.

"The Turks again," Bettenhausen huffed. "Sweet tooth. Characteristic of many warlike peoples. Some kind of formula there for Lévi-Strauss, but I'll leave it to him."

Theresa's laughter rippled across to Flemington. He stirred his coffee and smiled at Lulu. They were going to look at antique crystal in the afternoon. Lulu had heard about a shop where it was possible to bargain. Most Viennese establishments dealt in fixed prices.

"*Mamenu*," Herbie said, staring at his chocolate layer cake. "Blacker

138

than a *schwarzjahr.*" He chewed on it. Bits of dark brown crumbs dribbled onto his orange mustache. "Oi, what chocolate. That Nazis should be able to cook like this."

"They weren't all Nazis," Flo said.

"Don't kid me, they all got murder in their heart."

"Not so loud," Si warned him.

"Who cares? We're paying the bills." Herbie looked around the café, the air pungent with sugar, almonds, honey, spices. Could these people have been what they were supposed to have been? "Yeah, I'm wise to it. Fancy cakes. Whipped cream on the coffee. And in the back room, look out. The screws and the whips." He shoved his chocolate cake away. "I lost my appetite."

"Nudnik," his wife said. "Your size, you had to order rich cake?"

"Shove it here, Flo," Yasuda said. "Got to sample all the merchandise."

"And that religious stuff is getting me down," Herbie said. "I can't take it on so little sleep. Lance, shmance. A piece of the Cross, yet. I'm supposed to believe that?" He bent over the table, jostling everyone's coffee. "Even the priest didn't look so sure of himself in front of it."

"Harvey, you look dreadful," Mrs. Legrand said. "You and poor Weston. He hasn't budged from the bus all morning."

"Good, good. Lissen, Ma, there's a hock shop down the street, full of cameras. Me and the boys could knock it off, if you got some rods."

"Why does he keep calling me Ma?" the old lady asked.

J. P. Huggins, watching Barbara nibbling at tiny cream puffs, read the card on the table:

OUR FAMOUS SACHER TORTE

SHIPPED ANYWHERE

IN THE WORLD

Huggins studied the case on his lap. It was getting scuffed. The leather was too fine, too soft for rough handling. He had not gotten rid of a single treasury bill. A mad idea seized him—the kind of thing he and Buck Sweeney would have dreamed up in the old days. He would order two hundred thousand dollars' worth of Sacher tortes and ship them to Mario and Ralphie. *Dear* walyones, *I invested your loot in Austrian cakes. . . .*

His charges checked into the Pacher Hotel, a modular structure near Vienna's west station, Virgil settled down to his midday meal. It was a bit late, half past one. He would have to rush to make the three o'clock departure of the tour and he would probably be deprived of his nap. No matter. He was alone, happy with a *Wiener Kurier* in a café run by refugee Hungarians, who prepared a respectable fish gulyas and a satisfying pork cutlet.

No sooner had he ordered his meal from Frau Halasz than an American in a checked brown suit, carrying an attaché case, approached. *Not again,* Virgil thought. He was certain that it involved Huggins. Huggins was up to something. The trip to Zurich should have warned Virgil. In his years as a guide he had never had a tourist arrested, interrogated, under suspicion. He would regard it as a personal affront if Huggins were in trouble.

"Mr. Virgil?" the man—he was thickset, pasty-faced, and his accent was southern.

"Yes."

"Hunterden. My ID." He flashed the card.

"I am sorry, sir, but I cannot talk to you until I finish my luncheon. It is a rule with me. I dine privately. If you will wait in the café outside, under the grape arbor, I will join you in one hour and fifteen minutes."

"Just a question or two . . ."

"Impossible. As you know, I am a British subject and am under no obligation to talk to you."

"We know. We called Planet in London. They said you'd cooperate."

"I said I would. When I finish eating."

Americans, of course, would never understand the necessity of eating as much as one could, *when* one could, preferably in broad daylight, when it was less likely one would be arrested. Virgil worked his way through fish gulyas, stewed pork, potato dumplings, cold pickled paprika, and a *Palatschinken,* a sugared crepe stuffed with plum jam and topped with cream. He lit a Gitane, complimented the proprietor on the Riesling, and walked out to the sidewalk tables. The restaurant was in a modern quarter. Buses and cars whizzed by. Across the street a record store blared Brahms's Academic Festival Overture.

"Buy you a drink, Mr. Virgil?"

"A slivovitz, please."

The American drank beer. He spoke too loudly for an agent. Americans were no good at hiding things. Secrecy and deviousness were European traits.

"The day your tour left New York," Hunterden began, "a—"

"I was not there."

"Someone, an agent, or a private party, or a nut, gave an object or a message to be delivered to someone in an East European country. Our guess is the Soviet Union, but it might be Hungary or Czechoslovakia."

"Three Worlds does not go to Czechoslovakia."

"Anyway, our side would like to know just what it is that's being taken in, who is carrying it, and what it means. They pull this now and then."

"So do you, Mr. Hunterden."

The American agent's face beamed. "Yes, we do. But there's *us* and there's *them*."

Virgil smiled back. "Good guys and bad guys."

"We'd expect you, of all people, to know the difference."

"I know which side I am on. Are you familiar with the novelist Joseph Conrad?"

"No."

"You should be. He wrote, among other great works, a novel called *The Secret Agent*. He was a Pole who learned to write English, served as an English merchant marine officer, and adopted Britain as his country. But he retained a hatred for the two nations that had persecuted his homeland for so long—Russia and Germany. Really, sir, you are a college graduate and you have never read *Lord Jim?*"

"I, ah, I think I saw the movie."

"In a modest way I am a modern Conrad. I have no talent except for survival, and assisting tourists in seeing our wonderful world. But I do know good guys from bad guys. I have been in both Nazi and Soviet prisons and have been beaten and starved by Russians and Germans. Of course I shall assist you."

"Good. We have a couple of options. Your party is under surveillance. We've interrogated several members. The dentist and the lawyer. They seem okay."

"And me."

"We eliminated you. You're too smart to carry stuff into Eastern Europe. But there's Mr. Bettenhausen."

Virgil's eyes flicked open. "Mr. Bettenhausen? At his age?"

"In 1968 a group of Russian film directors and actors toured the States—New York, Hollywood. Guess who was appointed their escort."

"Mr. Bettenhausen. I can see why. He is a man of culture. He knows a great deal about the arts."

"He was sleeping with Russkies for three weeks. Had them to the White House. Corresponded. He doesn't speak Russian, but he knows a lot of guys in touch with the high echelons. We've rechecked your tourists and there's a rising vote in favor of him."

Virgil was chuckling.

"What's so funny?"

"No, no. Not Mr. Bettenhausen. Not in a million years. Anyone trying to enlist him as a courier—he would laugh in their face."

Hunterden drained his beer. "You'd be surprised what suckers people can be. Besides, whoever commissioned this didn't come on as a Russian. He played it cute. So cute we can't crack his password, or whatever he did to keep his patsy quiet."

Virgil lit another Gitane. "We will be in Budapest the day after tomorrow. The day after that, the Soviet Union for four days. You had better hurry, Mr. Hunterden."

"That's where you come in."

"Indeed?"

"Sometime tomorrow we'd like you to make a speech about Communist countries."

"I always give such a speech."

"Add something. Warn them about trying to smuggle anything— currency, gems, anything they think they can sell. Then tell 'em not to bring any messages, no matter what kind of favor they think they're doing the people on the other side."

Virgil listened to the Brahms come to its mighty conclusion. Even over the clank of trams, the music survived, shimmering with beauty, full of eternity. A new record was played. Mozart: the opening bars of *Don Giovanni*. Wryly he thought of himself as Leporello, a cunning servant doing the Don's dirty work. But Hunterden was hardly Don Giovanni.

Mangiar mal e mal dormir . . .

Leporello's complaint drifted across to him. "If it is really Mr. Bettenhausen who is carrying a message," Pepi said, "no warnings from me will stop him. He will be convinced he is doing the right thing. I know what kind of man he is."

Non voglio più servir . . .

Leporello didn't want to serve any longer. But Virgil reflected that there was nothing in the world he would rather do than guide Planet Tours. For the most tiresome of tourists, he nursed an affection that went beyond checking them in and out of hotels, sending them to discount shops for perfume. He could never satisfactorily explain it, not even to himself.

"You spoke of options," Pepi said.

"Our people will handle that."

"Yes. You will let whoever is the courier take his message into the Soviet Union and try to make some advantage out of it there. Find out who is the recipient and why he is so important. All this at great risk to the bearer."

"Virgil, not a word about this. Make your little speech about Russia, and then forget it."

"At your service."

O che caro gentiluomo . . .

J. P. Huggins, in a bleak mood, tried to soothe himself with beer. He, Barbara, Father Konay, Mr. Wattle, and a few of the Midwesterners found themselves in a dark restaurant near the hotel. A large sign over the small bar advertised that beer was served *direkt vom Fass*—right from the cask. Huggins sparked to the notion. He was a hard drinker but a good drinker, and had learned his limits. He felt the need for something to smooth the rough spots, make him forget the camera case.

"Out of the barrel," he marveled. "Like in Sweeney's father's gin mill on Rose Hill." Buck Sweeney's father, a cultivated gent who had attended Trinity College in Dublin, had for years "served up the gargle," as Buck put it, to generations of Fordham men. Huggins had pleasant memories of the wiry little man, expert at bung starting, drawing off the foam.

"Jimmy, go easy, that's your third stein," Barbara said.

"Curse of the Irish," J.P. said. The beer was heavier than he had anticipated and he suspected artificial coloring—molasses or caramel. It made his head buzz, and he enjoyed the snack of *Schweinshaxe*—a slice of roast ham.

"They use an ounce of hops per gallon of beer," Mr. Wattle said, watching Huggins drain his stein. "The water should have a temperature of 104 degrees Fahrenheit."

"How do you know so much?" Father Konay asked. That morning the rubber manufacturer had fixed his wristwatch with his pocket tools.

"It's the way to success," Mr. Wattle said. "That's why the Europeans are behind us."

All watched him with awe. Huggins, his eyes half closed, stifled a belch. Barbara glared at him. "Jimmy, maybe you better skip the tour in the afternoon. Take a nap. Coming down from Zurich and all."

"Nah. Got to use my cameras."

At Schönbrunn Palace, high in the hills southwest of the city, the party debarked. Doktor Gunter was back with them, jaunty in a green Tyrolean hat with a spiffy "bart." The formal homburg was evidently for city tours.

"Emperor Josef I wanted another Versailles," the guide said. "But even the Habsburgs ran out of money sometimes. So Schönbrunn is not Versailles, but is a beautiful palace. Maria Theresa made it a summer residence. Mozart played for her, right in here, you will see the room, when he was six. Also was performed here *Don Giovanni*. And later it was Napoleon's headquarters."

Murray Yasuda had raced back to the Neptune fountain—Der Neptunbrunnen—and was clicking away with two cameras. Herbie lumbered after him. Dr. Wicker joined them for photographs of the green and yellow façade. The Midwesterners were posing in groups.

"The color is characteristic," Doktor Gunter said. "Ocher, you would call it. We say Maria Theresa yellow. All over the old Empire you find it, especially beautiful against our blue skies, white clouds."

"Heavenly," Rosie Wicker said.

"Who knows the name of Napoleon's little son," the guide asked, "who lived here for many years, after Napoleon fell?"

"The King of Rome," Bettenhausen said. "Also called L'Aiglon, the eaglet."

"Bravo!" Doktor Gunter said.

"Played on the stage by Eva Le Gallienne," Bettenhausen added.

The haze seemed to be burning a hole into Huggins' head. The beer was giving him the staggers. It had been a long walk around the Schönbrunn Palace grounds, and the hedges and trees and monumental building swarmed in front of him, the colors too bright, the forms overwhelming. He saw his fellow tourists in noxious hues and irregular forms as if under water. Bettenhausen appeared a purplish gray, Mr. Wattle snot green, Herbie Shackman a vomitous orange. "Steady, Jimmy baby," he told himself. It was that Austrian beer— *direkt vom Fass*—curdling in his gut. The strap of the camera case was eating a groove into his shoulder.

"Show 'em. Show 'em ole Jimmy can take pictures too." He felt left out of things. The kid on the block nobody wants for the stickball game.

Huggins fell to one knee, opened the case, and took out his Pentax. He barely knew how to work it. Ungifted mechanically, he had not even read the booklet. Well, there was a lens on it. And the little button on the top. And you turned the lens to get focus.

"So, ladies and gentlemen, follow me, please, we go in to look at the apartments," the guide said. "There are forty-five rooms open to the public, but we will see only the most beautiful."

"Jimmy, come on," Barbara pleaded.

"G'wan, beat it. I'm takin' pictures. Anyone can. If that Jap and Herbie can, J. P. Huggins can."

He stumbled into the park, an expanse of formal flower beds, ponds, statues. Once Huggins stepped into a pool. Once he trampled over a bed of pansies. Barbara looked helplessly at Rosie Wicker.

"Is he all right?" the dentist's wife asked.

"Oh yeah. Jimmy's fine. He does this now and then." Tears gleamed in her eyes.

Without a glance over her shoulder—she would have seen her husband climbing the pedestal of a stone nymph—Barbara followed the group in. Her stomach trembled. There was something wrong with Jimmy. She knew about the old days, his wild bacherlorhood, the drying-out sessions, the all-night binges with Buck Sweeney.

Fifteen minutes later J.P., bluffing his way past the uniformed attendant—he refused to pay the seven shillings, arguing that he was part of a tour—rejoined the party in the Old Lacquer Room. His chest was heaving. His face was scarlet. The tour was bunched behind the velvet rope, studying the walls covered with rococo miniatures.

"Get your pictures?" Barbara asked.

"Call me Flash," he gasped.

Doktor Gunter led them on. "This they call the Room of the Million. It cost one million florins to decorate, and is paneled with Chinese rosewood."

Barbara was squinting at her husband. He had the Pentax and an exposure meter draped around his heaving chest. But she did not see the camera case.

"Where's the bag?" Barbara asked.

". . . move on to the Great Gallery, where we will look at the frescoes. This way, please."

With an involuntary cry, Huggins burst through the crowd of tourists, propelled by a terror that pumped adrenalin through his sodden frame. He spun A. T. Gunthorpe around, slammed Ibith Grant to the wall, scattered Midwesterners, and fled through half of the forty-five rooms of the Schönbrunn Palace.

Down the staircases he flew, swirling around balustrades, tripping, once tumbling in a drunken heap at the foot of a statue of Josef I, and then burst from the main entrance. Distantly, his tortured eyes saw the gallery of the summerhouse. Did he leave it there? At the Neptunbrunnen? At any of a half dozen spots, where, with sublime ineptitude, he had clicked off a roll of 35-mm. Kodacolor?

In a frenzy he began to race around the gardens of the Schönbrunn, his tie undone, his fitted jacket flying, his loafers impeding his progress. Like a caged hawk, his heart battered his ribs. His throat scorched. The camera banged against his chest and his eyes wept beer.

145

"Jesus, Jesus," Huggins moaned. "Two hundred grand. In the bag. They'll kill me. Kill me."

It was not at the summerhouse, where a stone imperial eagle mocked him. Nor at the Neptune fountain. Nor the Naiad fountains. Exhausted, trembling, he slowed to a walk, through baroque, rococo, and fake classical settings. Under arbors and in flower beds he looked for his camera case. But it was gone. Vanished. Surely stolen, picked up by one of the tourists or employees wandering through the Schön-brunn. A sign read: *Romische Ruine.* He had not photographed it, but he jogged to it, looked, saw nothing. Roman ruins. An appropriate place for J. P. Huggins. Ruins. Ruined by Romans, *walyones,* swag-men. *You see, Mario, it wasn't off me more than ten minutes—and wham, gone! How could I go to the cops? Or should I have?*

An attendant in a blue uniform walked by. Huggins raced for him, grabbed his arm. "A bag? Camera bag? Like so? So big?"

The man, a gray-haired retainer, probably an old Austro-Hungarian corporal, shook Huggins' hand off. *"Nein, nein. Versteh gar-nicht."*

The beer formed a clot in his stomach. He was sweating beer. Out of the barrel and into Huggins. Into the mouth and out of the armpit. What else was there to do? He would have to tell whoever ran the dump to look for it. Lost and Found? Place an ad somewhere. *Camera case, tan, pigskin, answers to the name of Mario.* He'd organize a search party. Comb the park, every bench, every pansy, every clump of grass, every rock, for his loot. But to what purpose, if some pipe-smoking Austrian peasant had hidden it under his *loden-mantel?*

Tears trickled down Huggins' nose. He yanked his tie down, un-loosened his belt. His feet were not responding. Gravel accumulated in the loafers. Bench-made, forty-eight bucks a pair, and they couldn't keep out Maria Theresa's pebbles. . . .

In front of the entrance to the yellow and green palace, he saw the members of his party awaiting him. They looked like a jury. To one side, Herbie and his *landsmen,* at the other Wattle, Gunthorpe, and the Midwesterners. And in the middle Virgil. Virgil was smiling. And holding something aloft.

"The case," Huggins muttered. "He got it. Good old Virgil."

"Dumdum," Barbara yelled at him. "You left it right here."

"And what a pity to lose so beautiful a bag," Pepi added. "The custodian was kind enough to hold it for you."

"He doesn't know how kind he is," Huggins croaked. He was tempted to feel the bottom, to make sure no fink had undone it and found the notes.

"We have fifteen minutes," Virgil said. "Some of you may wish to walk in the park, or rest, or visit the Wagenburg and see the collection of royal coaches."

Lulu Flemington filled a small suitcase that afternoon. She had been directed to an antique shop off the Graben, just beyond the monument to the lifting of the plague. There, after some bargaining, she settled on two matching pitchers of black and white underglaze, reputed to be genuine Powolny designs. Each bore the mark of the Wiener Keramik. Harry thought them to be rather ponderous but Lulu liked them, and her knowledge, as always, astounded him. No less affected was the proprietor, a stout Viennese named Pfeiffer, who tried vainly to sell her a Kolo Moser tea service, priced at three thousand dollars. Like poor I. Kleinerman in the silver vaults, he surrendered to Lulu's aristocratic manner.

"Two thousand is my limit," she said. "I want them wrapped, and I shall take them with me."

Back at the Pacher Hotel, Lulu went to have her hair done. In Grosse Pointe she had it set three times a week *and* combed every day. The hairdresser, Mr. Fred, came to their mansion in his Porsche, stayed an hour or so, took tea, cheered Lulu up with dirty stories, and left. It bothered Harry, for some vague reason. He had no strong feelings against homosexuals, but it disturbed him that his wife, stingy with laughter, should be so joyful in Mr. Fred's presence.

The *friseur* at the Pacher Hotel was run by efficient busty Viennese women. Born servitors, they bowed to Lulu. Harry left and strolled into the street. As he did the tour bus pulled up.

Herbie burst from the door, struggling to pry himself loose. He seemed to have added several inches of girth. Moreover, his impedimenta appeared to grow by fission. Where yesterday Flemington noted he had two purple Planet Tour flite bags on his person, he now struggled with four. Somewhere he had acquired a straw basket crammed with towels and blankets, and a plastic sack.

"Hey, Harry, you missed a great show!" Herbie shouted. "Kahlenberg, Wienerwald, palaces. *Ver vays.*" He nestled close to him. "I don't trust any of them. Stick you in a gas chamber as soon as look at you." Herbie had divined that Harry was a man you could kibitz.

"Maybe we'll do it tomorrow," Harry said.

Flo Shackman, laboring with nearly as many bags as Herbie, walked up to Flemington. "Wadja buy?"

"Oh, odds and ends," Flemington said.

"Ya kiddin'," Mrs. Shackman said. "I betcha Mrs. F. knows where to find bargains."

Herbie leaned his abdomen against Flemington. "You know what's a *metsieh?*"

"Anything like a *mitzvah?*"

"I love this guy," Herbie said. "Nah, nah, a *metsieh* is a bargain, but a *real* bargain. The group here, me and Flo, and Si and Sid, we decided your wife, God love her, is the queen of *metsiehs*. By her it ain't just bargains, it's a whole national financing scheme."

In pained steps, the tourists drifted into the hotel. They looked exhausted. Mrs. Legrand seemed to be shoving her husband.

Herbie said out of the side of his mouth: "I saw her ditch the dead soldier. Stuck it in a wastebasket when we were on the Kahlenberg. I hope they don't charge her too much for a fifth of Old Crow. They watch every cent."

"She'll manage," Harry said.

"Why don't we chip in and buy her a bottle?" Si asked.

"Nah, nah," Herbie said. "They got pride. Don't sell them short."

The Bettenhausens and the Wickers and a few others had stopped Virgil in the lobby and were asking about opera tickets. It was a free evening. Tomorrow night would be spent at a *Heuriger* in the village of Grinzing—peasant music, dancing, new wine.

Flemington saw Theresa at the edge of the group. Of course she would go to the opera if Virgil would wangle tickets. He longed to go with her. Perhaps she would wear a long skirt, a dark dress, low-necked. Some arch perfume. Strands of pearls. His knees and his ankles assumed that watery feeling again. Years lost, opportunities wasted, pleasures denied. How could any man of discernment and intelligence have been such a self-destructive fool?

"I shall try, Mr. Bettenhausen, I shall try," Pepi was saying.

"I insist," Bettenhausen huffed. "The travel literature of your company says we can attend the opera."

"I am aware of that, sir. I shall make every attempt to get you opera tickets. How many?"

"Seven in our party," Rose-Anne Wicker said.

"And there may be others," Theresa added. "I think the Hutzlers and the Zuflachts wanted to go."

Virgil excused himself. He seemed—for the first time—harassed.

Cornelia clucked. "You provoked him, Betts."

"I don't provoke."

"I think you had a right to say what you did," Dr. Wicker said.

"I don't pro*woke*," Bettenhausen growled at his wife.

The Wickers, the Grants, and Theresa were silent. None of them knew one another well enough to witness husband-wife squabbles.

148

"Oh, he doesn't mean anything," Cornelia said. "He's playing his game again. It's a movie line."

"Akim Tamiroff," Bettenhausen said. *"For Whom the Bell Tolls."*

Flemington pretended to be reading the opera posters on the side of a kiosk. They were giving *Tosca* that night. It was not one of his favorites. But he would have been willing to sit through a poor performance of *Parsifal* to be with Terry.

"Do you want to be included in the opera group?" she was asking him.

Flemington turned from the poster. The others had gone into the hotel. "I don't think so," he said. "It would be too long a day for Lu."

"Maybe you could wangle seats some distance from us. From me."

"My wife isn't an opera fan."

"And I suppose she's worn out from shopping."

"That's not like you, Theresa. You were never short on compassion."

"Lulu makes it difficult. There's a guessing game going on. What she buys and how much she spends. Herbie Shackman wants to start a pool. Five dollars each, all of it to whoever comes closest to her customs declaration."

He saw she had two guidebooks in her tote—the green Michelin and her Blue guide. "I'm doing a little rubbernecking," she said. "Want to join me?"

Flemington glanced toward the hotel. Lulu was in the hairdresser. She would be there at least an hour, resting, reflecting on her Wiener Keramik. "Well, I'd like to . . ."

"But?"

"I don't have to spell things out. Whatever you may think of my wife, she's a sick woman. I took her on this trip on a doctor's advice. When she saw you, I thought we'd blown the whole thing. I've convinced her you don't mean anything to me. I'm honor bound not to look at you, talk to you, sit near you."

"I'm an unperson."

"As far as Lulu is concerned, yes."

"And as far as Harry Flemington is concerned?"

He took her hand. "Why should I lie? I'm still in love with you."

She drew her hand away. "Really? And if you're so in love, so consumed with passion, you're afraid of a stroll in Vienna?"

"Okay," Flemington said. "Christ, you know me too well."

"Yes, I know you. Main Chance Flemington."

"Terry, I'm in agony. If you start recriminating, I'll . . ."

"What? Run back to Mama and her millions? Or is it billions by now?"

Flemington's face was splotched with ruddy marks. He had hyper-

149

tension (although his lethargic manner belied it) and under stress his blood pumped too quickly. He said nothing, walking alongside her. There was no Vienna; no tour; no Lulu. Only Theresa's presence. His. For anything he wanted. At any hour. A long time ago. Now, pensioned, he had forsworn sex. It tired Lulu. It did not interest her. Once lean and supple, Lulu's starved body filled him with pity. Indeed the cold marriage bed in the great house had, in some curious way, reduced his sexual needs altogether. Less and less he found himself staring at a trim butt, a ripe breast, a pretty face.

"There's an interesting area just south of here," she said.

"I never knew anyone to get so much out of a guidebook."

"I'm insatiable."

"In many ways."

"Quiet, Harry. That's a closed subject. Now let's see. If we keep walking south on Währingerstrasse we should come to it."

"I'll play tourist. What's so great there, Mother? You see one church, you see 'em all, as Mr. Wattle would say."

"Mr. Wattle would, but you never would." Theresa adjusted her glasses. They walked at a leisurely pace. Flemington began to feel the old excitation. He had never been able to wait when he was alone with her. His hands would shake. His voice strangled.

Strolling in the clouded city, he felt as if he were alone in a hotel room with her. Once he glanced guiltily over his shoulder. Could Lulu be far behind?

"Harry, cut that out. She isn't following you."

"Sorry, Terry. Tell me what we're going to see."

"Just south of here is something called the Dreimäderl Haus."

"Who were the three girls?"

"It doesn't say what their name was, but Schubert was supposed to have courted the three young ladies, all from the same family."

"How in blazes do you remember things like that?"

"Oh, you know me, Harry. Let's see. We can also see the Molkerbastei, if I'm pronouncing it right. Part of Vienna's ramparts. Number eight is where Beethoven lived. On the way down there's Roosevelt Platz. We ought to visit the Votive Church. Those two spires yonder."

Flemington looked at her with affection. Part of everything she touched. A romantic, he liked to believe that most women possessed these qualities. They were quite simply *better* than men. They felt more, understood more, reacted to beauty, art, the past, the mysteries of the human condition, with more understanding than men.

"I'm glad you're enjoying the tour, Terry."

"It was a little rough at first." She squinted at the map in the Michelin. "Oh, gosh. It isn't as far as I thought. Look, Harry." She stopped to show him the map. Their heads were close. A lock of brown curls brushed his cheek. He caught a scent of Detchema—her perfume.

"See?" she asked. "There's the Votivkirche and beyond is that long street that leads to the Hofburg, where we were this morning. I adore maps. Half the fun is figuring a city out—where we are, where we're going."

Flemington touched her cheek with his lips. What lunacy! Twenty-five years of a postponed love? And knowing all the time he loved her? He marveled at his weakness, his stupid ambition. In high school, he had played for a football coach whose only critique of a missed tackle, a bad punt, were the words "you goddamn dumb dope." Looking at Theresa's smiling face (forty-four? had any woman ever looked better at forty-four?), he realized the words were meant for him. *You goddamn dumb dope.*

"They'll arrest you for that in Vienna," she said.

"I doubt it. I carry my old press card. Privileges of the fourth estate."

"Well. We're too old for doing this in public. Move on, Harry."

"I want to sleep with you."

"No, Harry."

"You have a room to yourself. I'll visit you when Lulu corks out to-night."

She took his hand. "Three times is out, Harry. What am I supposed to do? Roll over whenever our paths cross?"

"You came looking for me five years ago. After Wade died."

"Don't remind me." She moaned. "God almighty, thank goodness only you and I know about that. One week widowed, and I was back asking if you'd divorce Lulu."

"I couldn't. She's a sick woman. And with Robbie on her mind."

There was a shaded park in the Roosevelt Platz, near the Votive Church. They sat on a bench in the checkered shade. It was late afternoon. City noises were muted. Young men looking like students walked by. They must be near the university, he thought.

"I don't feel like going into a church," Flemington said. His calves were torn with pain. Was he ready for support hose? A man's girdle? He had always been vain about his figure, his good looks. Newspaper-men usually did not lean to self-adoration. At the paper he took some razzing about it.

"Robbie isn't on her mind," Theresa said. He edged close to her and she did not draw away. "Harry, face up to it, your wife is a miserable woman. You're kidding yourself thinking she cares about your son. Or anything except what she can buy next."

151

"She does that to forget Robbie."

"I wonder. Aren't you embarrassed lugging those valises of loot around the world?"

"Don't be cruel."

"I shouldn't dig the needle into you. After all, it's given our fellow tourists something to talk about. That's the number one subject of discussion—next to who's going to make out with me."

Flemington smiled. Terry had a talent for putting things into context. Unlike most women, she saw the absurd in daily life.

He stared at her neck. Incredible. No sag. No double chin. Her face was only faintly lined—at the cheeks, around the mouth. Flemington found it made her even more desirable. Strange how she always camouflaged her attractiveness—minimal cosmetics, glasses, hair a bit undone. With the barest artifice—hair set, a dab of lipstick, the glasses removed—she drew longing stares from men.

"Then you shouldn't invite me on these walking trips," he said. "Maybe you should see the house where Schubert wooed his ladies without me."

It had turned cool. A gust blew leaves from the trees in Roosevelt Platz. It would be fine, Flemington thought, if it were 1946 again. Back from his wartime service with the Armed Forces Network, a new start at his career, Theresa in Minneapolis.

"I'm told a lot of free-lancing goes on in Grosse Pointe. But then, you never were much of a swinger."

"Give me credit for that. I have no lovers. No executive's wife, no college girls. I'm not part of the scene. The corporate wives call me for recommended reading, or inside dope on the lecturer at the Presbyterian Church."

"And old Harry knows."

"It doesn't take much to be the village explainer in Grosse Pointe. Hell, if you read *Time* once a week you're ahead of most of them."

"Do you try to write? At all?"

"Had an article in the *Detroit Athletic Club News* two years ago."

Theresa looked at Flemington's somber face. It was hard to feel pity for a man who wore custom-tailored suits and bench-made shoes and did not have to work. Harry had craved security, a life free of financial uncertainty, so that he could "write," sit in a paneled study and set down original ideas on paper. But he was lacking in self-knowledge. He was an easy-way-out man, addicted to the line of least resistance. Years ago, he told her, that had been his strength—and his weakness— as an editor. He moved too quickly. His rewrites were perfect, full of verve. And too quickly done for his own good. Marrying Louise Deaver and her fortune, a short cut to fame, he found that he did not have to work at all. The article once a year; meetings, reunions with old newspaper friends; an occasional lecture at Wayne or Michigan. ("Like the float in a toilet tank," he had written many years ago to Theresa. "I reached my level. The water got as high as it had to and Float Flemington came to rest. No higher, or I flood the bathroom floor.")

"I wish it were different," she said.

"Crazy. We've been wishing that for over twenty years."

"Maybe if I hadn't made up my mind to marry Jack. Harry, I damned near got on my knees. Did any woman ever debase herself in front of a man? I tried to set traps. Almost dragged you to the license office. When I told you I was getting married, you acted insulted. *You* were the injured party."

"Let's go," he said hoarsely. "I can only stand this immersion in guilt so long."

They got up. Theresa buttoned the top of her coat. "Should have learned my lesson," she said.

"What lesson?"

"What a damned fool I am. Let's go into the Votivkirche. This has to be in the nature of a confession."

"What the hell . . . ?"

"I came after you."

"On the tour?"

"It was no coincidence. I have spies in Detroit. I get reports about you. I have ever since we separated. I know just about everything about you, and Lulu, and Robbie. I keep praying it'll fall apart and I'll catch you."

"How . . . ?"

"It was easy. Lulu going on a tour was a subject for conversation in Grosse Pointe. People were wondering how you'd keep her sober for twenty days."

"Don't be cruel."

"I can't help it, Harry. She won you. I have to hate her. Anyway, an old friend of mine, Sarah Wyzanski—she's a school principal in Detroit—got word of it. She says you speak once a year to the creative writing classes. She heard about your trip. We correspond."

Flemington knew the woman—gray, strait-laced, the same age as Terry, but looking ten years older. Odd that she should be working as a love spy in her free time. "An informant? Dr. Wyzanski? I may have to say no next time she asks me to lecture."

They walked into the Gothic building. It was cold and gloomy. The afternoon light was suffused, absorbed by the stone, the stained glass. A few old women knelt in the pews.

"So this was a plot. You sought me out."

153

"I did. How much of an idiot can a middle-aged woman be?"

"You're not. I'm more ashamed of myself than ever."

"I've kept track of you. I know about Lulu's breakdowns. The last one was the worst, wasn't it, Harry?"

"Extreme insult to the liver. She's pretty good about her drinking so long as she can keep buying things."

They made a brief tour of the church.

"I don't know whether to pity you or be angry with you," she said. "It's absurd. You—and your heiress—and the widow spurned."

"I could never spurn you. We'll make love tonight."

"And then?"

"We'll talk. We'll work something out."

"In motel rooms near the Detroit airport?"

"Something better."

"It has to be all or nothing," Theresa said. "I think it's going to have to be nothing. If you left her—she wouldn't last a year. Let's go. This church isn't what the guidebooks say it is. It's depressing."

Outside leaves swirled in the early autumn wind. Students passed by. Flemington envied them their open-ended existence.

"So you worked out this plot," Harry said. "And now you're chickening out. There's an old Elizabethan comedy called *A Trick to Catch the Old One*. The Old One was the Devil."

"You're no devil, Harry. And it wasn't much of a trick."

"Let's give it a try. I might . . . might . . ."

"What? Have your flings with me? Play back the old tunes? And then what? I knew it the moment I saw you with her in London. Don't make me feel any worse than I do. This was my fault. I don't usually make these rash moves, but when I do, they're disasters."

Flemington said nothing. The burden of her love was too much for him. Women never seemed to get over these things. He loved her but he had managed. Evidently she had not.

"So we end up with nothing," he said. "Terry, you can't spring this on me all at once. Lulu may improve as a result of this trip. She looks better already. Maybe in a month or so she'll be well enough so that I can talk to her about a divorce. I mean it."

"It doesn't work any which way. I can't be a home-wrecker, even if it's the Deaver mansion on five acres. Maybe I'd better cut the trip short. Virgil may be able to sneak me onto another Planet Tour for the same price."

Flemington lingered on the steps of the Votivkirche. She walked away from him, a confident, smartly dressed woman, not the kind to weep in public. He ran after her.

"Look, this is ridiculous. We're together, we're here. I'll lose my mind if I don't sleep with you."

"I, I, I. Forget the whole thing. Besides, I'm behind in my sightseeing. It's a short walk to the bastions."

"Am I still invited?"

Her voice quavered; there was a tearful wrench to her words. "Suit yourself. You always have."

Flemington thought about following her. But the pain of watching her cry would be unbearable. Once, years ago, she had wept in bed, and he had so convinced her of *his* misery that she had never done it again. He could never be so convincing again. Checking his watch, he realized Lulu would soon be finishing at the hairdresser.

The people attending the opera gathered early in the lobby of the Pacher. From the informal garb of the daily grind in the bus, they had changed into evening wear. The women wore long gowns. The men were dapper in dark suits. Two men wore dinner jackets—Murray Yasuda and Mr. Wattle.

"It don't look like the same mob of shleppers," Herbie said to Dr. Wicker. "I never seen so many beautiful broads. Your wife is a knockout, Doc."

"Rosie likes to get gussied up every now and then."

"Hi, Herbie," Rose-Anne said. "You're pretty sharp yourself. I like the mod suit with the stitches showing."

"My son says I'm a phony," Herbie said jovially. "Send the kid to Yale, he wants to wear dirty pants and a *shmatte* for a shirt. I worked for every dollar I got, and if me and the missus wanna doll up, we'll doll up."

Flo Shackman and her friends were magnificent in low-backed gowns, strands of pearls, piles of lacquered hair. Shirl had festooned her beehive of golden hair with small red velvet bows. "If you can't look like this for the opera in Vienna, when can you?"

"That's right, Shirl," Rosie Wicker said. "It's good for the soul to get out of those suits and sweaters. Am I underdressed in this knit?"

"Hoo-hah, listen to her!" Shirl shouted. "Some knit. I know class when I see it." From the moment the dentist's wife entered the lobby, Shirl and Flo had studied her lean figure in a blue and white knitted two-piece affair. It was so simple, so perfect, so full of style, that they wanted to applaud. Only Sandra Yasuda in a powder-blue silk cheongsam was a match for Rosie.

"This group gets A for appearance, A for decorum, and C minus for knowledge of opera," Herbie shouted. "Except for Mr. Bettenhausen here. The professor. I watch every move he makes."

155

"I think opera is overrated," Mr. Wattle said. He spun about, spied Theresa Carrell in a long gray dress, stared, decided he would be her escort, and whirled to face the Wickers and the Bettenhausens. "Of course, they claim Verdi is the greatest."

"*Tosca* was written by Puccini," Bettenhausen said icily.

"Same thing."

"No, not the same thing at all." He rumbled to his wife: "I'll throttle that rubber tycoon before I'm through."

"Now, Betts. He means well."

"Let's get the show on the road," Yasuda said. "We lose Pepi, this whole thing falls apart." He was resplendent in a mauve dinner jacket, ruffled pink shirt, paisley bow tie. "He's takin' the night off, so we got to do this on our own. Everyone on the bus! Anyone missing?"

"The Hugginses," Rosie Wicker said. "They were late entries for *Tosca.*"

J.P. and Barbara came out of the elevator. After the incident of the misplaced camera case, the lawyer decided he had to relax. He liked opera.

"Move it, Jimmy," Yasuda called. "Curtain goin' up. Wow, dig the missus."

In a low-cut black chiffon, Barbara's breasts seemed to have inflated. The cleft, Herbie Shackman observed sotto voce to Si, went all the way down to her *pupik*. "That's some little *tsatske* Huggins has there," he muttered to his brother-in-law.

"Don't look too hard," Si said. "It's bad for your heart."

"That ain't all it's bad for."

"Move it, willya, Herbie?" Murray shouted. "When I run a tour, everybody shapes up or ships out."

Mr. Wattle, bouncing, preening—he wore a single-breasted tuxedo with a silk vest from which depended a gold watch—approached Theresa. "Mrs. Carrell, may I? We appear to be the singles on this expedition."

"Of course, Mr. Wattle."

He took her arm. "I'm harmless," he crowed. "Seventy-one and interested only in a little companionship."

"A bit ornate, the interior," Bettenhausen said at the intermission. "But acoustically superb. And what a performance."

"Say, this is some place," Dr. Wicker said, studying the white and gold décor. "I don't know how to express it, but it's just right. The people belong. The music was great. And the price was right. What was it? Less than half of what we pay in the States?"

"All true," Bettenhausen said. "Europeans understand these things.

When you attend the opera or a concert or theater in Europe, the experience seems to be part of your existence. In America, the theater arts are just that—artifice. Even our realistic works are fake. When that fellow sang *E buona la mia Tosca,* I had the feeling he was living it."

"It's only opera, Betts," Cornelia said.

"It's more than that. It's part of their lives."

He sounded morose, despairing for all the bad plays and boring movies and inept operas he had seen. Walking toward the ladies' room with Rose-Anne, Cornelia shook her frizzed hair. "Poor Betts. He never got over those Hollywood conferences. It makes him bitter."

"But he's right."

The older woman waved her hand. "Oh, pooh. I wish he'd stop rubbing the scar."

At the bar Mr. Wattle was elbowing his way forward to purchase champagne for Theresa and himself. "Do you realize that this is entirely rebuilt?" he called over his shoulder to J.P. "Destroyed in 1945, put together like new, and opened in 1956. You wonder how they did it."

"Marshall Plan," Huggins said. He was alone. Barbara, drowsy, did not want to parade about the lobby during intermission.

"No, sir. Two champagnes, please. Nothing good came out of that boondoggle."

Mr. Wattle, with feints and darts, got to the bar ahead of three people in front of him, grabbed two champagne glasses intended for someone else, and shoved a twenty-shilling note at the bartender.

"Wrong change," he shouted. "Try again."

While patrons cried their orders and eyed him malevolently, he awaited additional coins. "More like it," he cried. "Don't try to slip one past H. T. Wattle."

Huggins, balancing a glass of beer, jostled his way back, joining Theresa Carrell and Wattle. "He taking good care of you?" J.P. asked her.

"Better than I deserve."

"Impossible, Terry," Huggins said. He found himself using her first name easily. What was she? Five years older than he was? A widowed schoolteacher from Minneapolis? The old fire stirrred in Huggins. She was not merely a pretty woman. She had some rare quality. Grace? Manners? Compassion? Or maybe a little bit of all. Not once had she raised her voice on the trip. Not once had she yelled orders to Pepi. (*Hey, Pepi, it's hot! Now it's too cold! Hey, can't we stop for pictures?*)

157

"May I say the honor is all mine," the Washingtonian said, bowing. "Mrs. Carrell is my notion of a lady."

Henderson and Ibith Grant, standing at the rear of the opera lobby, saw Mr. Wattle bowing, sneaking a pat of Theresa's arm. "Terry's got herself a conquest," Dr. Grant said. "She won't be able to shake him for the rest of the trip."

"Too bad," Ibith said. "It's not the conquest she wants."

A buzzer sounded, summoning the audience to the second act of *Tosca*. Amid candlelight, Tosca would plunge the knife into Baron Scarpia.

Sipping beer, Huggins lingered at the bar. He enjoyed being alone for a few minutes. He had not thought of his camera case all evening.

"Mr. Huggins?"

A stout man with coal-black hair parted in the middle, sideburns, and a black mustache was at his side. The man wore a dinner jacket. He was rounder than he was tall. The front of the jacket seemed to be hiding a basketball.

"Yeah."

"I am an associate of M'sieu Moussac."

"I don't want any stamps."

"You did not want them when you saw him in Paris."

"Sorry, Jack."

The buzzer sounded again. The fat man—his face was moist and Levantine—followed J.P.

"Please, sir, my card," he said. "I have an investment program. It might interest someone with your problem. I will be at my office all day tomorrow."

In the fading light—they entered the orchestra as the house lights dimmed—Huggins squinted at the card.

BEIRUT, DUBAI & SHARJA
TRADING COMPANY
Schwarzenberg Platz, 15
Wien

"It doesn't have your name on it," J.P. said.

"On the back. Thank you, sir."

The man vanished, whether out of the theater or into an aisle, Huggins was not certain. Rotund, oiled, he might have simply rolled away. Just before the lights went out Huggins read the name on the back: *M. Sulman Chahoub.*

"What kept you?" Barbara whimpered. "Leaving me all alone like that."

Huggins suppressed a beery burp. He ran his hand under the black chiffon skirt, squeezing the thigh, searching for the naked flesh above the stocking. "Business contacts, Barbs. Jimmy works every minute."

"Liar," she whispered. "Looking for broads."

"Nah, I got the best broad here."

Bettenhausen, seated behind them, shushed them into silence. Huggins turned and winked. He felt good again. He would make love to Barbara with all her clothes on. Fetishistic variations delighted him. And the mysterious Chahoub would straighten everything out tomorrow.

Day 8: Vienna. An entire day to fall in love with this most romantic of European cities. In the morning, we return to the art
treasures of Vienna for a longer look. Half of the morning is
given to a tour of the Art History Museum, housing some of
Europe's greatest works—Titians, Tintorettos, Caravaggios.
Then, a visit to the National Bibliothek in the Hofburg, or
alternately, if a performance is scheduled, to the Spanish Riding
School.

Take your choice of sidewalk cafés for lunch. Then, a free
afternoon for exploring side streets, homes of the composers,
little shops, and charming alleys. In the evening, a visit to the
nearby village of Grinzing, for a country dinner, new wine, and
dancing!

Virgil let the smoke from his Gitane drift into his eyes. He was trying
to be patient, listening, nodding. But he was tired of Horace T.
Wattle's badgering.

"Those bus windows are filthy dirty," Mr. Wattle said. "They were
filthy in Berlin and they are filthy here. I don't intend to ride around
all day not being able to see Vienna."

"It is not the same bus," Virgil said.

"Well, your company hires dirty buses everywhere. Order the
driver to clean them."

"I shall *ask* him to clean them at our first stop. We cannot delay,
sir. It is only a short ride to the art museum."

"They are pretty *shmutzig*," Herbie said to Flo.

"Butt out," she whispered. "Let Pepi work it out."

"Ole Peppy," A. T. Gunthorpe said. He waddled toward the guide.
Wattle had not let up. "Ole Peppy gon' git 'em cleaned. Come on,
Horace, time's a-wastin'."

"I assure you they will be cleaned when we stop at the museum,"
Virgil said politely.

"Not good enough." Suddenly, with one of his darting moves,
Wattle leaped on the bus and fished inside his Planet Tour bag. He
took out a wad of cleaning tissues. He slid his window back, to the
annoyance of Sandra Yasuda, who caught a gust of morning air,
and began rubbing the dirt from his window. "Do it myself," he
shrilled. "That's how to get things done." He handed the wadded

160

tissue to Ed Hutzler, seated in back of him. "Pass it on. Everyone do their own."

Hutzler, with a prod from his wife, opened the window and, in arthritic strokes, began cleaning his. There was a rising murmur of rebellion in the bus. They were being forced to clean their own windows. A few uncomplimentary remarks were made about Pepi, about the driver, about Doktor Gunter, who was back for their morning tour.

Virgil settled into his seat, cradling the microphone. Best to let the mutiny run its course. It was the eighth day, about time for the first signs of surliness. Mr. Wattle had a point. The windows were rather cloudy. Austrian *Schlamperei.*

"The natives are restless," Cornelia said.

"Yes," Bettenhausen snorted. "For years I have been trying to get Mohammed Khan to come out of those hills."

"Oh no. Not this early."

"Montagu Love. *Gunga Din.*"

Virgil noticed that there were more dropouts from the sight-seeing, from late evening festivities. Mr. Legrand had remained in his hotel room. Insisting that he was merely tired, the old man refused to let Dr. Grant examine him. ("Nothing personal, Mr. Virgil," Mrs. Legrand told Pepi, "we have absolutely nothing against black people, it's just that Weston doesn't believe in doctors of any coloration. Not since they gave him six months to live.") The Flemingtons were also absent from the museum tour. Virgil ruminated: something to do with the Carrell woman?

"You are well, Mrs. Legrand?" Virgil asked, as he helped the old woman off the bus. They were parked in the Maria Theresien Platz, opposite the art museum.

"Oh, I'm fine, Pepi. Weston is too, just tired." As she stepped down, he sniffed her breath. A new aroma. She had run out of bourbon yesterday. He had seen her, with a fretful mien, asking the Pacher concierge where she could find a liquor store. But evidently she found no bourbon or could not afford it. Virgil, whose nose was acute, smelled Steinhager, a fruity liquor.

Herbie too had noticed. As they trudged into the Kunsthistorisches Museum, he approached Virgil. "Ma Barker changed brands."

"Indeed?"

"What is that stuff? I saw the bottle in her bag. No color. Like vodka? Only it smells."

"Steinhager. It is similar to Aquavit."

"Ma gets enough of that stuff in her, she may wanna give me and Murray the rods to knock off the bank."

161

Virgil smiled. "I hope she doesn't mind your little jokes at her expense."

"Ma Barker? She loves it. How else could she get such attention?"

The Flemingtons used the morning for some desultory shopping. Lulu went back to her antique shop off the Graben, and with fore-knowledge of her adversary's moves, was now able to relieve him of an eighteenth-century red and black bonbon dish, the work of Jacob Helchis. The proprietor had asked nine hundred dollars. Lulu beat him down to five hundred and forty.

"Your wife is a woman of great intelligence, sir," the man said. "Please take my card. I shall take the liberty of sending you notice of any exceptional items that come my way. Only a woman like Mrs. Flemington can appreciate antiquities."

Flemington was glad she had made the shop owner happy. All over Europe were small gray men in small gray shops who benefited from Lulu's largesse. They were her true children.

In the mild morning air she became expansive. The Helchis dish was cocooned in felt and paper. Harry carried it in his flite-pak. It nested there like an amulet. Every few minutes Lulu glanced at it. *Mine! All mine! I own it!* Despair gnawed at Flemington's vitals. How could a human live in bondage to the thingness of things? Was she happier than Terry Carrell, writing notes in a Blue guide, trying to figure out why guards at Buckingham Palace marched to Mozart? Or old Bettenhausen, that master of trivia, commenting on the powerful feet of Piero della Francesca's saints?

"Harry dear," Lulu said, "I feel good. Are you pleased with me?"

"Of course, darling."

"I've been an awful witch."

"Not at all. This trip was a challenge to you. I felt a little guilty forcing you into it. You're a trooper, Lu."

"I feel so good, I'm in the mood for a lavish lunch. Something elegant."

"That can be arranged, dear." Flemington was elated. He had not seen her looking so well, sounding so cheerful, in months. Part of it was due to the restrictions he had placed on her drinking. He and Virgil had been watering her scotch, warning waiters to go easy with the wine. Beyond that it was the sustained buying that was buoying her spirits. Spending more, accumulating more, she felt secure. The bulging suitcases were an assurance: she lived, she had power, she counted for something.

Harry had consulted the concierge that morning. He recommended a restaurant called Am Franziskaner Platz as the ultimate in high cuisine and service. They took a cab to the restaurant. It proved to be a magnificent six-hundred-year-old building in a picturesque square.

"It's adorable," Lulu said. "So charming."

Again the employees knew at once—how did they divine these things?—that she was American blood royal. The captain ushered them to a prize table. Flowers appeared. The sommelier lingered, beaming, fingering his wine list. Delicacies were suggested. Lulu made little jokes, complimented the captain on the décor.

Flemington uttered a silent prayer of thanks to Dr. Crichton in Detroit. The man was right. It would be a hard haul but Lulu needed to get away. To be in different settings. Different people.

"I think a half bottle of wine will do," Flemington said.

"If you say so, Harry. It *is* rather early in the day."

They were the only patrons, arriving as soon as the doors had opened. It was like a private club. Just the two of them, a secluded corner, the hovering waiters.

"Let's see," Harry said, "we're having crayfish salad and pike perch *à la Viennois*. That calls for a good white wine. I'm in your hands, sommelier."

The man bowed. He had just the thing, something from a local vineyard owned by the proprietor.

"I feel very gay today," Lulu said.

"You look marvelous."

She cocked her head. The hairdresser had done a splendid job. (While he, villain, was pursuing Theresa in the Roosevelt Platz.) In the subdued light of the restaurant, the lines in her face softened. The aristocratic outline—sharp nose, pointed chin, long neck—was improved by the dimness.

"I'll let you in on a secret," she said, stroking his hand.

"We don't have many left, do we, Lu?"

"It's because of that woman."

Lulu was filled with odd mental movements, faked starts, thoughts and words that came out of nowhere. For a moment he had no idea what she was talking about. His frown was precisely the reaction she sought. Puzzle him, give dependable Harry something to sweat over.

"Your old flame."

"What about her?"

"You don't know me as well as you imagine you do, Harry. When I saw her, when I laid eyes on that frumpy teacher, when I saw this creature out of your past, I realized I had a fight on my hands. I may not act it, but I'm a fighter."

Flemington winced. He mulled the irony: the Jewish members of the tour, Herbie, Flo, Shirl, Si, Sid, Sylvia were amateurs compared to Lulu. She was the greatest haggler of them all.

"Don't look so glum. Oh, the wine is here. Isn't it a beautiful color, Harry?"

"Viennese gold. Go on, dear. Tell me about your reaction to Mrs. Carrell."

"I knew when I laid eyes on her that I had to fight her for you."

"If you want to think that, fine. You've got to believe she's out of my mind and my range of interests. I was unnerved when I saw her. But I got over it."

Lulu rotated the stem of the crystal glass. "I *made* you get over it. Harry, you are behaving yourself. You don't even look in her direction. Just as I warned you. You don't moon after her and you've been good at avoiding those people around her, that fat man from Hollywood, and that dentist, and the colored people . . ."

"Of course. I wouldn't want to upset you."

"I'm not upset. I have her just where I want her."

"Terry didn't come on this trip in search of me, Lu. This was a coincidence. Planet Tours is an active Midwestern outfit, with offices in Detroit and Minneapolis, and this is one of their best tours . . ."

"I'm not so sure."

Flemington shook his head. Woman's intuition? Lulu was hinting that Theresa had booked on Three Worlds on a hunting expedition. And it was the truth. Only he would have to lie, keep Terry's plot secret. And what did it matter? Theresa had seen him, had not liked what she had seen, and had changed her mind. Ironies on top of ironies.

"She came after you. But I handled her. You're a good boy, Harry. I love you, you know. I'm grateful for the way you took care of me those first few days. I feel good now."

"I'm delighted."

Four waiters hovered about them. Flemington had never seen a seafood salad displayed so artistically. It was like a pop art piece. His pike perch from the Danube swam in a pinkish sauce of piquant herbs. Nothing was overspiced, overdone. Textures and tastes were choreographed.

"I'm going to write a card to Robbie this afternoon."

"He'll love it, Lu. I sent a card to the school from London. You know, he understands a great deal."

"I'm getting him one of those Lanz sweaters this afternoon, maybe several of them."

"Wonderful." He had not seen her so happy in a long time. "Robbie would love that. We should visit him when we get back."

"Yes. If I keep feeling this good, I intend to."

You won a few, you lost a few, Flemington thought. He was a better nurse than he imagined, and the Detroit physician was a better diagnostician than he suspected. For Lulu to admit to a desire to visit her son, that twenty-year-old waif in a football helmet, attended by a male nurse, was damned near unbelievable. He brimmed with sorrow. Lulu had no family to speak of. She had been an only child. Both parents were dead. The old millionaire had given up the ghost in Palm Beach ten years ago, alone in his mansion, not having exchanged more than a score of words with his son-in-law, and only a few more with his daughter, since her marriage. There were a few aging uncles, some marginal cousins. None had been cut in on the Deaver fortune. All detested Lulu.

"I've made my mind up, Harry. I am going to spend a day with Robbie."

"We'll see when we get back, dear."

She leaned over and kissed him. She was fragrant, fragile. But nothing sparked in Flemington. He hoped—he prayed—she would not ask for sex.

"I have a brief announcement, ladies and gentlemen," Pepi said when the bus stopped at the Pacher Hotel. "And then you are on your own until seven this evening, when we meet in the lobby for our trip to Grinzing."

"Always instructions," Shirl said to Flo.

"It cuts into shopping time. You remember where the linens are? That embroidered stuff we saw?"

"May I have your attention, please?" Virgil asked for the third time. The buying frenzy intensified whenever free time was imminent. They would gulp a brief lunch, then, heavy with pastry, *Schlag*, and beer, would stumble about spending the weakened dollar.

"Speak, speak, leader!" Herbie shouted. "Ma and me got a caper to pull, right, Ma?"

"Tomorrow you will be awakened at six-thirty in the morning. Bags outside the door at seven. We leave at eight by bus for our four-hour ride to Budapest. We want to start early, because there is much to see in Budapest."

"Hoo boy!" Herbie yelled. "Hungarians! You got a Hungarian for a friend, you don't need an enemy!"

"An old joke, Mr. Shackman. Passports, please, to me, since I must

165

check visas. Now a word of advice. We will be spending six days behind the so-called Iron Curtain—Hungary and the Soviet Union. You will find people friendly and courteous. But they are strict on certain matters and I mention them now as a matter of company policy."

"They shoot you soon's look at you," A. T. Gunthorpe confided to one of the Midwestern women.

"Ladies and gentlemen," Virgil said, "some advice. Do not exchange any money before you go into Hungary or the Soviet Union. People may approach you in Vienna to buy Hungarian forints at a high rate. It is illegal to do so. It is illegal to take Hungarian money into Hungary. In Budapest do not exchange much more than you will actually need for odds and ends, since the tour is paying for almost all your needs. There is little worth buying in these countries."

"Nuts," Flo said.

Shirl agreed. "So why we goin' there?"

"That'll kill Countess Flemington," Herbie muttered to Murray.

"How do you stop a herd of elephants from charging?" Yasuda asked.

"Tell me, tell me, Father, how do you stop a herd of elephants from charging?"

"T-t-t-take away their credit cards!"

"Gentlemen in the back of the bus, I would appreciate your attention," Virgil pleaded. He was vaguely upset. He did not appreciate the visit from Hunterden. He did not relish the notion of one of his clients serving as a time bomb, bearing illegal goods or a dangerous message. It could make for messiness, a crimp in their schedule. One did not go looking for trouble in those places. He scanned his people. Bettenhausen? Impossible. Dr. Wicker? Maybe. Huggins? A possibility—but too jumpy, given to dark moods, sudden elation.

"Further, do not, even if you think you are doing a favor, attempt to bring in any messages of any kind, no matter how harmless you may think they are."

Dr. Wicker felt color rising on his neck—scarlet, purple. Did Rosie sneak a look at him? Had she seen the envelope?

"Some Americans have friends or relatives in these countries. They think they are doing favors. The letter may be nothing more than a greeting. But it can make trouble for its recipient. So, no written messages, letters, anything of that kind."

"Dang," A. T. Gunthorpe said. "He makes it sound like a dang prison."

"It is," Mr. Wattle said. "But they keep everyone in their place.

166

We won't find any hippies or gangsters there, that's one thing I'm sure of."

Huggins had to get rid of the loot. He was beginning to panic. Mr. Chahoub's card was burning inside his wallet. All morning, gawking at paintings, trying to eradicate the Malfi family from his mind with Rembrandt and Holbein, he had mulled his options: come home with it, lose it, sell it, buy gold. The next six days would be a loss. Communist countries were no place to unload two hundred thousand dollars in treasury bills.

The misplacement of the camera case at the Schönbrunn had filled him with wild fear. Was it a Freudian error? A desire to lose Mario's loot? What would they do to him if he failed anyway? They loved Barbara. She was dumb and a woman, but she was *family*. The brothers were not real killers. As far as he knew, they had never let a contract in spite of their boasts of having rubbed out a black checker at Newark Airport. They were liars. They were schemers. They were accomplished thieves. But they worked on a system of pay-offs, bribes, commissions. Everyone got greased and everyone co-operated. Would they not accept, with scowls and snarls, a loss of two hundred thousand dollars? And J.P. was no common hood. He was a Wall Street lawyer. He went to opening shows at the Guggenheim and to Park Avenue parties.

Virgil's speech distressed him. He sat with Barbara, Father Konay, and A. T. Gunthorpe in the hotel restaurant, his stomach quivering at the sight of the priest eating *Kaiserschmarrn*—a sweet omelet laced with raisins—and Gunthorpe, that ridge-runner with his raw-sirloin face and meat-hook hands, staring at Barbara's boobs and shoveling *Weisswurst* into his maw. Both sipped from mugs of coffee crowned with a half pound of *Schlag*.

"I know, it's almost sinful," the priest said to J.P.

"Anyway, a small sin," Barbara said. She now went out of her way to seek out Father Konay. He was uncomplicated. He reminded her of the Ursulines.

Huggins liked the padre. He'd been smacked across the knuckles too often in his parochial school days to nourish affection for all clergy—of his own church or any other—but he appreciated Father Konay's quiet manners. He was no blowhard coming on strong with handshakes and off-color jokes and Notre Dame football.

Barbara's *Salzburger Nockerl* arrived—a creamy yellow-white pillow, heavily sugared, giving off a sweet aroma.

"Ooh. It's too much. Jimmy, help me."

167

Huggins' stomach was ravaging him. He got up. "Listen, Barbs, I got errands to run. I don't feel so hot anyway. I'll meet you in the room in an hour or two."

"Gotta eat, son," A.T. said. He ogled Barbara's bosom. "Man got hisself a beauty lak you' lil Eye-talian gal, he got to be in tiptop shape. Right, padre?"

Huggins slung the case over his shoulder. It had become a curse, a hunchback's deformity. The doorman told him where Schwarz-kammer Platz was located and hailed a cab.

Virgil had just ordered his six-course lunch when the man who said his name was Hunterden reappeared. The guide did not invite him to sit down.

"You told them?" the man asked.

"I did."

"Any reaction?"

"None. I think you have the wrong tour."

"It's possible. Anyway, keep your eyes open. Try to keep tabs on three people—Bettenhausen, Huggins, and Wicker. They all seem likely."

"Dr. Grant?" Virgil did not know why he asked. It seemed a prankish idea.

"Who?"

"The physician from Minneapolis."

"Oh. The dinge. No. They never pick anyone obvious. Besides, those people are unreliable."

"What do I do, sir," Virgil asked, sipping his wine, "if I find Mr. Bettenhausen attempting to sell photographs of American missile sites to Mr. Brezhnev?"

Hunterden's face was impassive. "Get in touch with the U. S. Embassy and ask for the legal officer. Someone'll see you."

Virgil smiled at his *Leberknödlsuppe*. "You will please let me finish my lunch. I intend to take a long nap."

"You should also know we've decided to let this sucker make his run. We want to find out the terminal. Maybe the whole apparatus."

Pepi said nothing. The man left. The liver dumplings went taste-less. Letting an unwitting agent make his run in order to divulge contacts was nasty business. Oh, it would be bad, very bad for the company—and he was a company man—if there were violence or an arrest or an expulsion.

Huggins entered a frosted glass door with the same title he had seen on the card given him by Mr. Chahoub.

A huge blonde girl in a mini-dress sat at a desk typing. Her thighs were like stone pillars.

"Mr. Sulman Chahoub, please."

"Who is calling?"

Huggins gave her his card. She got up and lumbered into a rear room.

"Mr. Chahoub can see you right away, please."

Huggins was surprised by the elegance of the interior office. It was not large, but it was handsomely paneled. There were green velvet drapes and the furniture had a rich look. Mr. Chahoub, looking rounder and oilier, was seated behind a rococo table—curving legs, curlicues on the corners, a Florentine marble top. He waddled to his feet to squeeze Huggins' hand.

"My associate, Sheikh Sabari."

The lawyer, faintly giddy, was confronted by a slender young Arab in a black robe and a black and white kaffiyeh. He was gorgeous—beige face, sparkling teeth, mournful black eyes. A thin mustache and beard outlined his soft mouth. He took Huggins' hand in both of his. J.P. heard the tinkling of beads. What Chahoub's business was, he was not certain. But his associates were clearly more exotic than Moussac's stamp merchants or Herr Baumeister's Zurichers.

"Pleasure," Huggins said. "Mind if I smoke?"

"Please do," Sheikh Sabari said.

Huggins sat in a wing-backed chair and lit up. There seemed to be some subtle arrangement between the businesslike Chahoub and the young Arab in the robe. The sheikh, Huggins guessed, was the boss.

"Mr. Huggins, there is no point in delaying matters," Chahoub said. "I understand you are leaving Vienna tomorrow morning."

"For Budapest."

"And six days in the Eastern Bloc."

"You know my itinerary. I have no secrets any more."

"Money, dear Mr. Huggins, has no morality, no patriotism, and keeps no secrets."

"I've known that since I was a kid in New York. I keep hearing it all over Europe."

"I am sure you do."

The Arab in the robe and kaffiyeh retired to a chair. He seemed to slither into its contours. His eyes were shut. Occasionally Huggins would hear the *clack-clack* of a string of amber beads which the sheikh fondled. J.P. was enjoying himself. Even if he did not unload a dollar the séance with these brigands was exhilarating.

"You are carrying two hundred thousand dollars in United States treasury bills." Chahoub said it as a flat statement.

"Someone's got a big mouth."

"We accommodate."

The beads *clack-clacked* a bit louder. Huggins offered his boyish smile to the Arab.

"Mr. Huggins, my company is in a position to offer you an interesting investment program, on which you are virtually guaranteed a return of twenty-five per cent, and the possibility of unlimited reinvestments at twenty-five per cent."

"That's better than tax-free bonds."

"Much better."

"But not that safe. Or legal."

"You have not heard what it is." Chahoub laughed noiselessly. Then he chattered in Arabic to the sheikh.

"Gentlemen, I get nervous," Huggins said, turning to face the Arab. "May I make a request?"

"Please do," Sheikh Sabari said.

"Keep it all in English, huh? No spikka da Arabic."

"Of course, sir," Chahoub said. "I was merely telling the sheikh, who is my partner, that you are a young man of intelligence, which we appreciate. You are not, sir, the normal type of *passeur* or *cambiste*."

"Moussac said the same thing. I guess class will tell."

"Indeed it will. Sir, we are a trading company. We trade in gold and precious metals. We buy gold in Europe at the current rate. From our headquarters in Dubai we ship it to countries where it can be sold at a generous profit. Hence your guaranteed twenty-five per cent."

"Where the hell is Dubai?"

"Be careful, Mr. Huggins, Sheikh Sabari is Dubai royalty. He is a prince."

The sheikh clanked his beads.

"Sorry, Prince," Huggins said. "I make lousy jokes. I won't any more."

"Please do."

Chahoub got up and pointed to a large map of the Middle East on the wall. "I am speaking of the Persian Gulf states. They are small countries, unified now as the Union of Arab Emirates."

"Dubai, huh?" Huggins turned to the man in the flowing robes. Beneath the black outer garment, he was draped in white.

"We are a tiny country, sir," Sabari said.

"Like to visit you."

"Please do."

"Okay," Huggins said to Chahoub. "What am I supposed to do? Take your word like that? Fork over two hundred thousand dollars?"

"Mr. Huggins, the Arab principality of Dubai is one of the great world centers for the shipment of gold to India and Pakistan. It is their main business in fact. Our company is one of five syndicates engaged in the Persian Gulf gold trade. You may read our prospectus. It is in English, French, and German."

He gave J.P. a lavish brochure. The border was designed to resemble the etched crosshatching on stock certificates. The titles were in dark blue bordered with gold. *The small, progressive country of Dubai, ruled by hereditary desert princes, is today the world's third largest exporter and importer of gold . . .*

"I don't get it," Huggins said. "You got this piece of sand on the Persian Gulf." He glanced at the pamphlet. "What the hell? Is this legit? Twenty-five tons a month shipped in by plane, and out by boat?"

"Quite so," Chahoub said. "At this very moment, a ship of our fleet, or one of our competitors', is loading ten-tola bars for Bombay, or Karachi, or Madras."

"So I invest. I help you buy gold."

"Precisely. We buy half our gold in London, the rest in Switzerland, France, or the Low Countries. All quite open and aboveboard."

"And for this I get twenty-five per cent?"

"Give or take a few points."

"That isn't bad. You ship it to India or Pakistan . . ."

"Or Ceylon," the sheikh broke in cheerfully. "Or some of the Arab brothers."

"It's just sold? Like that? To the government? To banks?"

"Ah. Ah, hah, hah." Chahoub's laugh was like olive oil glugging out of a narrow-necked bottle. "Mr. Huggins must know more about this than he allows. After all, a man who has been to Moussac, who has tried to buy gold in Zurich, who carries around a fortune in treasury bills . . ."

"I get it. It's smuggling."

This convulsed the sheikh. He tossed his bearded head back and laughed, as happy as if his favorite falcon had just scored a mid-air hit on a dove. Chahoub clapped his hands in joy. "Oh, Mr. Huggins! Now you understand!"

"Goddamn smugglers." Huggins laughed. "Gold smugglers!"

"But of course, sir." Chahoub was pushing a form toward the lawyer. It read:

BEIRUT, DUBAI & SHARJA TRADING COMPANY
Letter of Agreement

"Mind if I read it?" Huggins asked. "Lawyer, you know."

The sheikh, flashing ivory teeth, giggled: "Please do. Please do."

J.P.'s eyes scanned the contract. A simple agreement. He was a limited partner in the company. He assumed all the risks that the general partners did. He had the right to be paid off in any currency he desired, but not gold.

"These risks," he said. "What kind? A man doesn't get back twenty-five per cent just for supplying capital."

"We run a slight risk." Chahoub rubbed his chin. "The Pakistani and Indian navies may intercept one of our ships. Once on land we are safe. On rare occasions customs can be a problem. But the civil servants are accommodating."

"Intercept? How often?"

"I should guess less than once a year. I shall ask the sheikh." He spoke Arabic to him. The Arab prince responded.

"Once last year. Twice the year before. Not a grave risk."

Huggins opened his camera case. Removing the cameras and the exposure meter, J.P. lifted the snap-off leather bottom and drew out the envelope. He placed it on Chahoub's desk.

"You are willing to become a limited partner?"

"Looks that way. What can I lose? I mean, besides two hundred grand."

This drew hearty laughter from both men. Chahoub pressed a button. The blonde appeared. He ordered coffee—*weiss ohne,* milk but no whipped cream.

Huggins felt free, abandoned to some wild fate. How could the Malfis complain? It was foolproof. Investing two hundred thousand dollars, he would get back two hundred and fifty. He could reinvest it again and again, keeping the money in circulation, letting Chahoub buy gold and sell it at an enormous markup in India or wherever.

"How do I find out about my profits?" he asked.

"Follow the shipping news in the English newspapers," Chahoub said. "Your investment will be in a shipment aboard the S.S. *Lautaro,* sailing under Chilean registry from Dubai."

"To where?"

"We are not certain. Again, within the next week, you should read of its sailing. Possibly to Bombay. Or Karachi."

Chahoub was counting the treasury bills. He did so with a dexterity denoting long experience with money. "As agreed, Mr. Huggins. Two hundred thousand dollars. You are wise to be rid of them. They can only decrease in value. Buy gold, sell gold. The Indians are paying record prices."

"So your profit could be a hundred per cent. Or more."

"My dear sir, we are the syndicate. We rent the ships. We have offices in twelve cities. Our overhead is considerable."

"I bet it is. You like the color of those bills, Chahoub?"

The Lebanese lowered the sheaf of notes. "Ah, hah, hah, Mr. Huggins. Lovely color. Here is our coffee. Thank you, Inga."

"Mr. Huggins has not said how he wishes to get paid," Sheikh Sabari said. He flounced toward the desk, drawing a chair up.

"Can I get in touch with you people?"

"Everywhere but in the Communist countries. You will be in Istanbul, Rome, yes?"

"Israel also."

"Ah, hah, hah," the sheikh said.

"My associate is laughing because we have contacts there too. It sounds odd, does it not? But money knows no religion. A reliable bank in East Jerusalem. Not the bank itself but one of its officers. We shall give you a list."

"Dollars, Mr. Huggins?" the sheikh asked. "Swiss marks? Or credits for reinvestment? Many of our partners find the association so profitable, they stay on for another shipment, and another. The price of gold, Mr. Huggins, can only go up."

"And the dollar down."

"As Allah wills it."

J.P. sipped the coffee. Relaxed, he felt as if he had just had a thundering orgasm or a thorough bowel movement. How good to be rid of the stuff! He would have to cable Mario at once.

"How long before I get paid?"

Chahoub consulted a calendar. "Ten days. Or less."

"Sir, to your health." Sheikh Sabari held up his coffee cup.

"You people realize I represent some hard customers in the States. They don't like to be cheated or fooled."

"I understand, sir," Chahoub said. "One does not acquire two hundred thousand dollars in treasury bills, and send them about the world in a camera case, without a degree of bad manners."

"So long as you understand. You mind if I run a few checks on you people?"

"Is it not rather late, sir," Chahoub asked, "now that you have signed your contract and given me the funds?"

"Yeah, it is after the fact. But better safe than sorry." He grinned boyishly. "I want to know who to sue in case this is a racket."

"Oh, it is no racket, Mr. Huggins," Chahoub said.

"Be that as it may, I'll put out a few inquiries on your organization." Sheikh Sabari flashed his teeth as if he wanted to bite Huggins' cheek. "Please do," he whispered.

Herbie Shackman, his cheeks purple, his forehead coated with droplets of sweat, his breasts jigging, his gut heaving, pounded around the floor of Die Blaue Gans in Grinzing, grabbing fräuleins in dirndls, locking arms with village louts in lederhosen.

A *Schrammel* orchestra—accordion, zither, violin—played folk tunes and selections from Strauss. Herbie was astonishingly light on his feet for a huge man. His feet were small and pointed, and his legs moved nimbly, as if trying to free themselves from the bloated torso.

"*Ayn, tvai, ut a zay!*" Herbie boomed out in time with the music.

Si shook his head. "With his Yiddish, they'll mob us here."

"*Forvitz, Tageblatt, hooray!*"

"Y'all know," A. T. Gunthorpe observed to the Bettenhausens, "Ah ain't never seen no one like ole Herbie in mah life. Ole Herbie sure a pistol."

Shackman fell into a wooden chair. "*Gevald,* enough awready," he gasped. "Seltzer, seltzer. Murray, be a good boy and get Herbie some seltzer."

"I do declare," Gunthorpe said. "You a pistol, Herbie. They ain't another like you in a flock of mallard ducks. You the biggest red-ass coon hound in the pack."

"What the hell's he talkin' about?" Herbie moaned. "Is that a compliment?"

Dr. Wicker, bouncing and turning with his wife, looked distracted. Bumping into the Grants, and again into Theresa and Mr. Wattle, he was unable to exchange dance-floor banter. Ever since Virgil's lecture that afternoon about Iron Curtain countries, he was upset. Why had not Leland's coworkers, those sharp fellows who knew the sports code, contacted him? And why had the man named Clyde who had accosted him in West Berlin been ignorant of it?

"You look thoughtful, Arn."

"Thinking about Mark Abrams' bite plate. That kid is bound to lose it while I'm away."

"He'll survive."

Barbara Huggins stroked J.P.'s arm. "Wanna dance?"

"You know me, Barbs. I'm strictly a Lindy man. When I was a kid I did a great Peabody."

She drew him to his feet. Her perfume, her pneumatic breasts, the pressure of her cushioned thighs hardened him. Huggins felt marvelous. He drew his wife close and let his hand wander down her back, tweaking her buttocks.

"Not in public."

"Nobody saw."

"Love me, Jimmy?"

"More than ever, Barbs. I apologize for all the lousy jokes I made about your family."

"Forgiven." She stood tiptoe, offering her lips. As he kissed her, she slid her tongue into his mouth. It seemed indecent to J.P. that married people with children, a couple with little in common, the woman given to sulks and the man to insults, could so enjoy the union of their bodies.

"I did my errands for Mario and the clients," he said.

"Look, look, a distinguished couple!" Herbie shouted from his chair. Murray was fanning him with a wine list. "You see, Moishe, what high-class people on this trip? Mr. Huggins is a famous lawyer. And his sexy wife! *Gevald*, what a spumoni she is!"

Barbara smiled at Herbie. Jimmy gave him the upright finger. He was loose, able to enjoy himself for the rest of the tour. Arab smugglers had his money. The deal had been made—an open-end operation. His advice to the Malfis would be to keep it going. Money into gold into money into gold . . .

Airs from *The Gypsy Baron* kept them in motion—gliding, stepping, whirling.

"Enough of this Mickey Mouse," Murray Yasuda shouted to the *Schrammel* leader. "Play 'Exodus' for my friend Herbie."

> *Day 9: Vienna–Budapest. An early rise for a four-hour bus trip to historic Hungary and its jewel city Budapest astride the Danube. We pass through Danubian countryside on the way and arrive in time for orientation: St. Gellért's Hill, with its stirring view of the river, the Soviet Memorial, the fortress.*
>
> *On to Castle Hill with its charming old quarter, the Fisherman's Bastion, Matyas' Church, the palace, and baroque homes, not to mention the oldest pastry shop in Eastern Europe!*
>
> *In the afternoon, a boat trip up and down the beautiful blue Danube, beneath some of the most intriguing bridges in the world.*
>
> *Evening—gypsy music and robust Hungarian wines, and some of that superb Hungarian cooking.*

A bad start. Virgil was annoyed. The mood had been good in Grinzing. But they had stayed too late. His tourists had indulged too liberally in dancing and raw wine. *Heurigen* wine, he had warned them, went down smoothly and then had a tendency to irritate the lining of the alimentary canal. But they had been having fun, the best evening since the tour started. Mrs. Flemington had smiled at Herbie when he invited her to Lindy. (She refused, but she was not offended.) Later, Ed Hutzler had fallen flat on his face, and Mr. Wattle had to carry him outside to regurgitate, give him first aid, and walk him through a pine grove to restore him. ("It always helps," Mr. Wattle consoled Mavis Hutzler. "A little fresh air, a little vegetation. Most inebriation is in the mind, anyway.")

On the way back to the Pacher Hotel—it was now past midnight and the call was for 6 A.M.—Murray Yasuda, who had left ten dollars in tips at the inn—decided he was hungry. He wanted a seafood dinner. Reluctantly, Virgil dropped Murray, Herbie, Si, Sid and some wives near an all-night restaurant on the outer ring. They did not get back to the hotel until 2:30 A.M., which meant they had had less than four hours' sleep.

Now, approaching the Hungarian border at Hegyeshalom—they had whizzed through the Austrian frontier at Nickelsdorf with a wave of the guard's hand—Virgil saw that half of his people were asleep or, if awake, looking poorly. Herbie was snoring on the back seat. Yasuda was doubled up, fetuslike, below Herbie's bulk.

The looming barbed-wire fences, the sinister watchtowers, the no man's land marked off with cyclone fencing, these stigmata of the people's democracy, heightened the somber mood aboard the bus.

"Quite a contrast," Flemington said to Pepi. "The border stations."

"It was worse some years ago. They worry about people leaving. Ever since 1956. What the Hungarians call 'The Regrettable Events of October.'"

The bus waited for a red and white barrier to be raised. It went up slowly, permitting a half dozen cars, an East German bus, a Polish bus, and finally the Planet Tours bus—owned by Ibusz, the Hungarian tourist bureau—to proceed.

"They get many Eastern Europeans," Pepi explained. "Budapest swarms with East Germans, Czechs, Poles. And many Russians, who are not very popular."

There were at least four different uniforms, Flemington noticed. Customs men, border police, military, and so forth. He had read that Eastern European countries, like all totalitarians, favored a variety of uniformed forces. It kept unemployable people busy and more ambitious citizens out of trouble.

"They're well policed," Mr. Wattle said. "They don't stand for any nonsense."

"I thought he hated Communists," Ibith Grant said to Theresa.

"Oh, he hates them. He's just envious of the way they suppress everybody. He'd like to see it that way in the States, but with *him* deciding who policed *what*." The black woman smiled at Theresa. "Your new suitor."

"Ibith, you and Hen may have to save me from a fate worse than death. He's asked me to call him Horace and he pinched my arm twice at Die Blaue Gans."

"You could do worse, Terry. He's loaded."

Theresa laughed. "I took a vow I'd never be a three-time loser."

"But all that rubber. You'd never have to send a kid to the principal's office again. Never have to stop fights in the lunchroom. Never have to mark exam papers." She saw Terry's face change— somberness replacing the smile. "Sorry, Terry."

"He keeps showing me color photographs of his estate outside Seattle. A forty-four-foot swimming pool and a tennis court. I'm being tempted."

"Come on, Terry."

177

"Joking, of course. Still, when you've gone through two husbands, and you zip past forty, you get desperate."

Virgil returned to the bus. "Will the following people please come outside for customs inspection?" He consulted his list. "Mr. Shapiro, Mr. Hutzler, and Mr. Huggins."

"What the hell is this?" Herbie shouted at Si Shapiro. "You smuggling gold, *shmuck?*"

J.P. shuddered. *Luck!* How lucky could he be? He thanked any available saint (did *passeurs* have a patron?) for directing him to Mr. Chahoub and the Beirut, Dubai & Sharja Trading Company.

"Knew you were in some racket, Ed," one of the Midwesterners taunted Mr. Hutzler. "They gotcha now."

"Ed looks the part."

"Mavis, give him an alibi. Probably got a valise full of marijuana."

Mr. Hutzler, in his stiff gait, walked off the bus, following Shapiro and Huggins.

"What I do?" J.P. asked Virgil.

"Spot check," the guide explained. "They are liberal about customs in Eastern Europe, especially big tours. So they made a check of only two or three valises."

Virgil spoke in Hungarian to two customs men in dun-colored uniforms with red epaulets. They motioned the three tourists toward a bench under the customs shed.

Huggins discovered that it was Barbara's bulging valise that had been opened. He was required to poke around a fluffy mountain of bras, girdles, garter belts, panties, slips. Barbara never traveled light. A fiery bed bikini, trimmed with black lace, got locked in his fingers. The customs man chuckled and winked at J.P.—as if to acknowledge the charm of such garments—and ordered the valise closed. Si Shapiro's was looked at even less carefully. Shapiro, a member of Herbie's party, was a meticulous, well-organized builder, and his suitcase was beyond reproach.

Mr. Hutzler, however, presented a problem. As soon as the guards opened the valise they were confronted with a half dozen magazines with titles like *Stud, Dude,* and *Big Daddy.* On the cover of each was a photograph of a girl. The blonde girl on *Stud* had enormous pointed breasts. The high yaller on *Dude* showed protruding tan buttocks and endless legs. The lady on *Big Daddy* reclined on a couch, cupping her bosom.

"A little light reading," Mr. Hutzler said.

"Charming," Virgil commented.

One of the customs guards, with a leisurely pace, began turning the pages in *Stud.* The other started to leaf through *Dude.* Breasts, legs, thighs, butts paraded in front of them. A soldier carrying an automatic rifle joined to study capitalist decadence. Two men in navy-blue uniforms with gold stripes also appeared. Soon a dozen members of the border security force were looking on.

"Mr. Hutzler, I am sorry," Virgil said, "but apparently such publications are not allowed in the People's Republic of Hungary."

"Why not?" the Vandalia man asked. "It's all in fun."

"Socialist states are strict on these matters."

"Well, gosh, what are they gonna do? Arrest me?"

"Oh no. They will confiscate the magazines." Virgil spoke sharply to the guards. They grinned. They had taken the magazines out and slammed Mr. Hutzler's valise shut.

"I want a receipt," Mr. Hutzler said. "I paid for those magazines."

"Do you really, sir?" Pepi asked. "We will delay the entire group."

"Oh, heck. Nuts to them. Tell 'em I'm going to protest."

Virgil conveyed Mr. Hutzler's sentiments, but the customs men, the security police, the soldiers were not interested. A group had gathered around each magazine, turning pages, rolling eyes. In back of the Three Worlds bus, a score of cars, trucks, and buses were backed up, honking, grinding gears. Drivers cursed. People got out to see what was causing the holdup.

Virgil ushered Mr. Hutzler aboard.

"Darned nerve they have," he said. "Taking my magazines."

His wife Mavis offered him a mocking laugh. "Huh. Maybe you'll spend less time in the bathroom in the morning now. Don't have your dirty books to look at."

He fussed with his hearing aid. "Good thing in a way."

"What is?"

"Those fellahs got so innarested in my magazines. I bought four hundred dollars' worth of Hungarian money in Vienna. Get double what they give in Budapest. It was all in the envelope right under *Big Daddy*."

Contrary to the tour literature, the ride across northern Hungary to Budapest was not inspiring. The villages were primitive but hardly picturesque.

Virgil did a little lecturing as they rode. "A country of ten million, with more than a tenth of them living in Budapest. They speak a language unlike any in Europe. It is perhaps why they remain proud of their heritage, their writers, musicians, scientists, soldiers, theatrical people, and so on. Surrounded by Slavs, they have kept a unique culture, good cuisine, and excellent wines—"

"What's there to buy?" Flo shouted.

"Are the stores open today?"

"The city of Budapest is actually two cities," Virgil said, ignoring the women. "Pest is the modern section and is flat, part of the Danubian plain. Buda is across the river and is hilly, more charming, with old sections we will visit later."

"Hey, look, Murray, soldiers," Herbie said.

"Oh boy. Let me get that. Pepi, can't you stop the bus? There's a big army camp there."

"I am afraid not, Mr. Yasuda. You know the rules on stopping for photographs. Schedules and all that."

"Ah, chicken."

Virgil turned around. "Those are Russian soldiers. That is one of their biggest camps in Hungary. They are not happy having their pictures taken."

"Russians?" Mr. Wattle yelled. "Still here?"

"Yes, sir," Virgil said. "You will see many of them in Budapest, but you will not recognize them. They wear civilian clothes."

"Why don't they throw 'em out?"

"Oh, the Hungarians tried that in 1956," Virgil said warily. "Ah, lovely vineyards on the right. Beautiful red grapes. For *bikavér*, bull's blood, a fine wine."

"I hate grapes," Mr. Wattle said.

The guide did little speaking, apart from answering an occasional question. As always, he was of two minds in Communist countries. He tended to like the people of Eastern Europe and dislike the governments. From time to time he met with Communist officials— usually men in the Ministry of Tourism—and he had found them to be the most nervous of Europeans. They lived in perpetual fear of being found out. Virgil knew why. Nobody was responsible for anything under Communism. They made a great show of efficiency and production, but they had trouble running an inn or serving a meal or making a pair of shoes. Oh, they managed, but usually when the Marxist rules were thrown out and some enterprising fellow decided to go it alone. *Responsibility. Competition.* But most of all—*rewards, little extras for the job well done.* The Communists had not learned this. And so they suffered. Nobody was in charge because it was not worth while to be in charge.

On Castle Hill the bus stopped and the party was met by their Hungarian guide, an attractive young woman in a severe blue suit, open-collared white shirt, and low-heeled black shoes. She was short, shapely, and moved like a ballerina. Her name was Eva, she told them, she was a student, and she spoke seven languages.

"A requirement here in Hungary," she said. "Mmmmmmmmm. You know, nobody else in the world speaks Hungarian. Mmmmmmmmmm."

"Say, she's a looker," A. T. Gunthorpe said. "Ah like these heah Hongarian women."

"They can be dangerous," Pepi whispered to him. "Like the paprika they put on their food. Tastes wonderful, troublesome later."

"Yeah boy," Gunthorpe said. "Ah settle for some of that indigestion."

"Mmmmmm. This is heart of Buda, old section of Budapest," Eva said. "Mmmmmmmm. Almost all houses here have been restored to original shape and style, because Germans made it here fortress in 1944 and 1945. Royal palace down there, was German headquarters."

"Why does she keep saying *mmmmmm* like that?" Mr. Wattle asked Pepi—in a voice loud enough for Eva to hear.

Pepi answered. "She is not sure of some English words, sir. So rather than use bad English, or ask anyone, she says *mmmmmm*. It helps her remember or find another word. She wishes to be as precise as possible."

"We stay outside first," Eva said, "and, mmmmmmmm, I tell a little about famous church, most famous in Buda."

"Churches, churches," Herbie Shackman muttered to Pepi. "There's no synagogue anywhere?"

"In Budapest, several, sir. But you know, of course, most of the Jews . . ."

"Yeh, yeh. I know the story. Could we go later?"

Pepi looked at the fat man. Traveling was exacting its toll. Overweight people fared poorly. Herbie's flesh was dragging him down. His cavorting in Grinzing had taken the fight out of him. Beneath his small eyes, great brown gouges had been dug. His orange mustache seemed to have assumed a rotting brownish tinge. And he was sweating unnaturally, as if coming out of a fever.

"So, ladies and gentlemen," Eva was saying. "First built by Bela IV in thirteenth century, rebuilt by King Matthias 1470, but for a long time church was occupied by Turks and was, mmmmmmmm, mosque. Then, many restorations. We go inside and you will see more decorations, beautiful colors."

It was dark and cold in the church. In Bettenhausen's mind, fierce mounted warriors of Central Europe thundered across the Danubian plain—Magyars, Huns, Avars, Slavs, Mongols, Turks. One bloodier than the other. Thousands impaled on wooden spears jammed into their anuses. Thousands cut down by cutlass and broadsword. Blood oaths, bloody crusades, pogroms, mass murders, right down to 1956 when Red Army tanks shot workers in the streets. Yet what charm! What style! What blithe self-confidence these people had! Bettenhausen decided it was their jaw-breaking language, incomprehensible to the surrounding Slavs.

"American?"

A white-haired priest, chubby, scarlet-faced, stopped Father Konay as they left the Matyas Church.

"Yes, I am."

"You look Hungarian. *Servus*." He extended his hand.

"*Servus*," Father Konay said. "Very nice to meet you. Are you with the Matthias Church?"

"No, I am just parish priest from Csepel Island. Where the factories are. You speak Hungarian?"

"Badly. Some German."

They chatted, switching from English to German to Hungarian. Father Konay learned the man's name—Father Havas. He had taken a morning off to visit some friends at the Matthias Church. His own parish was a working-class section.

The two prelates walked out of the church and followed the group to look at the equestrian statue of St. Stephen and the baroque eighteenth-century column to the Trinity.

"It's beautiful here," Father Konay said. "You are proud of your city."

Father Havas smiled. His Magyar eyes became slits as his ruddy cheekbones rose. "Yes, yes. For the tourists up here, great beauty. In the city . . . in the working sections, where I am . . ."

"Is it getting better?"

"You have heard the joke?" the Hungarian priest asked. "We are still very poor. All we have is our high standard of living."

"But the religion?"

Father Havas made a *comme ci, comme ça* gesture with his right hand. It was crazy, Father Konay thought, but he had once seen a great Hungarian, the late Ernie Kovacs, make the identical gesture in a movie.

"The churches are filled," the priest said. "Filled. More than ever. Come on Sunday, you'll see. And we have mass, sermons. Of course, we can only criticize up to a point."

"But things are better since 1956?"

"So long ago, hard to believe. Look, you are falling behind your group." Father Havas took the American priest's arm and directed him toward Andras Hess Square—more charming homes, an air of medieval intimacy, rough stones, a sense of orderly communities.

"So, Andras Hess Tér. Tér means Square or Plaza." Eva brushed her hair back. She darted a look at Father Havas, who had joined the Three Worlds tour, spoke to him in a friendly way, then resumed her English. "We will enter the House of Red Hedgehog, and in courtyard, mmmmmmmm, please look at Gothic vaults, stone stairs from Middle Ages, Gothic doors. You are back in Middle Ages."

"What did she say to you?" Father Konay asked in German.

"Oh, joking. I know her. All Budapest people know each other. She is a Party member. She knows me from way back. Her husband was a foreman in the steel factory in Csepel, where my church is. In 1956 he helped organize the revolt in the streets. She has to watch her step."

"She is a Catholic?" Father Konay watched Eva's shapely figure as she led them to another medieval building which housed a de luxe restaurant. Father Konay had to believe she was a good Catholic girl, with her sedate blue suit, low-heeled shoes, unadorned face.

"Of course she is."

"And a Communist?" the American asked incredulously.

"You are so American, Father Konay. In our country many Communists are Catholics. Eva's two children have been baptized. She was married in a church. She does not go to confession, and her husband makes fun of us, she knows what she is."

"But . . . but . . . Communists?"

"It's that kind of country," Father Havas said. He lowered his voice and spoke English. "It's better than in 1956, and better than in 1966, but . . ."

"Not as good as it could be?"

"And now, ladies and gentlemen, you must act like Hungarians," Eva said, "and, mmmmmmmmm, take time out for coffee and pastry."

"*Gottenu,*" Herbie moaned, "not again. My gall bladder."

"But this is treat, sir," Eva said. "The oldest pastry shop in Hungary, Ruszwurm. The building is from Middle Ages, and from 1500 it has been a bakery."

"I believe you, I believe you," Herbie said. "Only his doughnuts shouldn't be that old."

"A congenial group," Father Havas said. "I must leave you." He pumped Father Konay's hand. "A pleasure meeting a Hungarian priest from America. How is it there?"

"Oh, we manage." How could he possibly begin to tell this man about his problems with the Ospreys, with Father Folker, with the aroused citizens of Ash Valley? How could he explain the manner in which he had been denounced as guilty of "conduct unbecoming a Brother Osprey"? How explain all that to a man who had seen Russian tanks shoot down the steelworkers of Csepel?

"You are a rich country with many wonderful people," Father Havas said sadly. "We admire America. And we like to see Americans—all

183

kinds—black, white, Jews, Catholics, Protestants, and from all parts of America. You are such lucky people. Such kind people."

"Oh, Hungarians are nice also."

"And so gifted. Has any nation of ten million ever produced seventeen Olympic medals? And our writers, Nobel prize scientists, musicians. I am afraid we are only a shadow now."

The two shook hands. "*Servus*," Father Havas said. He tipped his hat and walked away.

"*Servus*."

Father Konay walked into the shop. Yes, very Hungarian. History and faith around them, the life-or-death struggles of political and religious systems—and all had to stop for a chocolate trifle.

"All we seem to do is sit and eat on this trip," Dr. Grant said to Dr. Wicker.

"And all of it cholesterol."

"They don't know about it," Henderson Grant said. "They all look healthy. You see those sculls on the Danube? How come so many people are off on a weekday, rowing on the river?"

"And half the population," Ibith said, "are in sweat suits. They spend all their time jogging."

"Hungarians are marvelous athletes," Theresa said. "They always seem to be winning something. Olympic medals of all sorts."

Eva, the guide, cradling a cup of coffee, walked over. She heard Theresa's remark. "Oh, we are a gifted people. Musicians, composers, so many. Szell, Ormandy, Reiner, Kodaly, Bartok. Incredible for such a small country." Eva's chin was pointed upward. She seemed determined to sell Hungary. "And in the theater, Molnar, Korda, Dery, others."

"I like that," Bettenhausen said. "I like that very much." He turned away from a powdered cruller. "You know the story about Molnar, their great playwright," he said to his retinue. They all were quiet—his wife, the Wickers, the Grants, Theresa. Even Harry and Lulu Flemington leaned forward.

"Molnar was a late-night carouser and café sitter. He usually went to bed at dawn and did not rise until late afternoon." Bettenhausen harumphed and sipped his coffee. "On one occasion he was called as a witness at a trial. He was required to rise at some unearthly hour like eight in the morning, dress, and proceed to the courthouse. As he rode to court in a taxi, he noticed that the streets were swarming with people. 'My God,' Molnar cried, 'can all these people be witnesses?'"

Everyone roared. Herbie coarsely boomed out a mocking laugh. It was gratuitous rudeness, as if he resented Bettenhausen's capture of the audience. A few people looked at him critically. Si Shapiro shook his head. "Herbie, that was not nice. Apologize to Mr. Bettenhausen."

"Yeah, you should," Shirl added. "So he told a funny story? You're the only one allowed to *tummel* around here, hah?"

"Perhaps Mr. Shackman has some funnier stories," Pepi said.

People began to walk out. They had eaten too much sweet stuff. Lunch would be an effort. As yet they had not checked into the Gellért Hotel. Pepi assured them their rooms would be ready and there would be time for lunch and a swim before boarding the boat for the Danube cruise.

"Nah, I got nothing but *tsuris*," Herbie said moodily.

"Ole Herbie got himself the croup. Look lak he swaller a hoptoad." A. T. Gunthorpe waddled off.

"Hey, Pepi," Herbie said. "No hard feelings. I go bananas sometimes. I'll apologize to the professor."

They were the only ones left in the pastry shop. Herbie paid his bill. The rows of creamy confections, the trays of rich cakes and tarts, filled him with nausea. As a boy, the poorest on their street in Brooklyn, his widowed father, a tinsmith-roofer, had cooked *mamaliga* for him—corn meal mush with a piece of herring. He could taste it now. Better than all that sweet glop.

"Pepi, I got the urge to see a synagogue. You said there was one near here?"

"The synagogue in Obuda. It is not far. A bus or five minutes in a taxi."

"I won't miss nothin'? Flo raises hell when we miss something. If we paid, she figures we got to see it. I wish I could be like Murray and Sandra. They do what they want. Not the Shackmans. Everything is GI."

"No problem, sir. A cab can take you from Obuda to the Gellért. We leave at two-thirty."

Stale air wheezed from Herbie's mammoth figure. His scarlet sports jacket was rumpled and stained. Lavender slacks drooped in seat and crotch, as if, huge as he was, he had lost weight during the exhausting travels.

"Who's comin'?" he asked. "Si? Sid?"

"What's he up to?" Shirl asked.

"He wants to go to a synagogue, my husband," Flo said. "*Nu*, what's to lose?"

"But I thought we'd have an hour free to shop?"

"Pepi says there's nothing worth buying."

"So why'd we come here?"

Herbie paused in the cobbled square, watching the others walk toward the bus. They were to ride up the Gellért Hill to see the Soviet War Memorial, then check in at the hotel.

"So? Find us a taxicab, Mr. Tour Director," Flo said.

Herbie's group found two creaking cabs. The driver of one spoke German; Herbie's Yiddish was common ground. Soon they were bouncing through cobbled streets, to the northwest bank of the Danube. Everything seemed covered with pale yellow dust. Sid, a builder, saw that a great deal of construction was taking place. Modern apartments were rising throughout the area. The dust was a result of the excavating.

Houses were old, flaking, bricks showing beneath the exterior plaster. Pastel shades lent a certain charm—oranges, ochers, Maria Theresa yellow. Intermingled with the old houses and dilapidated shops were modern factories, new housing developments.

The cab stopped in front of a tall colonnaded building in neo-classical style. It stood by itself in a field of weeds and detritus, surrounded by a ruined wire fence. On the gates a wrought-iron Star of David hung limply.

"*Shul, shul,*" the driver said.

"That?" Herbie asked. "That wreck?"

The travelers got out. A few workmen in dusty blue coveralls walked by. In the shade of a tree across the street, a woman in a babushka fed cherries to a small boy.

"*Ja, ja, Judische Shul.*"

They approached the building slowly. It must have been magnificent at one time. It was of white limestone and it was badly chipped. The fluted columns soared to handsome capitals. The roof was vast and sloping. To one side was a small wing. Everything suggested ruination. Some attempt was being made to repair the old synagogue. There were wheelbarrows and mixing bins in the yard, a stack of bricks, blocks of limestone.

The tall wooden doors were locked. Herbie tugged at them. They would not budge. "Closed," he said. "I guess they only open on Friday night and Saturday. I wonder if there's a *shammes?*"

"You have to go inside?" Flo asked.

"Why not?" asked Si. "Churches, crosses, the whole thing we've been getting. Why not some of ours?"

"So wait till Israel," Shirl said. "There at least it'll look good. This dump . . . I can imagine what the Nazis did to these people. Maybe no one is allowed."

"Pepi said it's open," Herbie said. "Hoy! Hoy, anyone home?"

Before he had begun to shout, a gangling unshaven man in a bagging brown suit and brown fedora turned the corner. He could have been anywhere between fifty-five and sixty-five. He had a cross-hatched face and his eyes were merry. Seeing Herbie tugging at the doors, he called to him in Yiddish.

"So wait, so wait, *Yankele*," the man said. "You can get to *shul* five minutes late. The rabbi won't be angry." He jingled a key ring.

They exchanged greetings. He introduced himself as Mr. Fisch, *shammes* (sexton) of the synagogue. Opening the door, he led them into an enormous marble vestibule running the width of the building. Daylight flooded through the opened doors and the high cracked windows.

On the wall of the vestibule was a long marble plaque. On it were engraved hundreds of names. A single candle burned from a lantern above the huge slab.

"That's what I thought I'd see," Herbie said. "The jokes stop here."

"Killed by the Nazis," Mr. Fisch said. "All dead, taken away."

"From all of Budapest?"

"No, no. Just from this synagogue."

Flo began to weep. Shirl sniffled.

"What the Germans didn't do, the Szálasi people did. They were the Hungarian Fascists, may God curse them forever. Worse than the Nazis." Mr. Fisch squinted at the endless names as if he had never seen them before. "All my friends. Schoolmates. *Chaverim. Yeshiva buchers.* Would you believe that I am eighty-four years old?"

The names on the marble plaque hypnotized them. The Americans stared, read names, noted the reappearance of many. There were Weisses, Roths, Cohens, Goldbergers.

"I can't stand it," Flo said. "I want to go away."

"Listen, *ketzeleh*," Herbie said, "you can never get away from it. It's our dues."

Mr. Fisch nodded. "Three hundred thousand dead. No one helped. Nothing. A few prayers from the churches, a few apologies. First they would pray, 'Don't kill Jews, because they might be converts, Christians.' Then they would apologize, 'Excuse us, Herr Eichmann, excuse us, Herr Heydrich, excuse us, Herr Szálasi, we didn't mean to be critical. It's all right to kill Jews, but don't make such a fuss over it. Do it quietly, do it so nobody will write about it. And don't bother us.'"

The man's guttural Yiddish, delivered in an oldster's singsong, drifted in and out of Herbie Shackman's ears. Ah, the names, the names. How lucky he and his friends were! He glanced at his friends—well fed, well housed, safe, children at Yale and Brandeis and Ohio State, futures, incomes, swimming pools, vacations in the Caribbean. Did those kids understand what American meant? Did they know how lucky they were that some grandparent, some old Jewish *zayde* or *bubbe* in a Romanian town, decided to go to America? And those kids went into the streets to curse that great country? What did they know about Europe and what happened to Jews there?

"Szálasi, *feh!*" Mr. Fisch said. "When the Russians surrounded Budapest and it was all over, the last thing he and his gangsters did was kill another twenty thousand Jews. Left them to die in the streets. Bodies frozen. I saw Szálasi's soldiers—hah, what soldiers, lousy cowards, murdering women and children!—throwing old Jews into the Danube, they should drown. *Nu*, that was Szálasi."

The inside of the synagogue was in semi-ruinous state. Some repairs seemed to be in progress.

"We are a national monument now," the *shammes* said. "But work is slow, no money, better they should build apartments. But we are still here."

"It must have been gorgeous once," Flo said. "Look at the beautiful benches and the carvings on the balcony."

The ark remained. It appeared to have been regilded. The cabalistic sign of the touching hands, the decalogue, the six-pointed star, had a shiny look. On the lectern, where once the rabbis of Obuda had sermonized, was a red cloth, embroidered in gold. It showed a rampant lion. The figure seemed more out of medieval heraldry than any Judaic tradition. The lettering on the cloth was in Hebrew and Latin characters.

"Goldberger again," Si said. "Who was he?"

Mr. Fisch's eyes rolled upward. He rubbed thumb and forefinger together: the sign of wealth. "The Goldberger family owned the biggest textile factory in Hungary. It is right down the street from here. They gave money to the *shul*. Everyone in Hungary knew Goldberger textiles."

"Are they . . . ?" Herbie asked.

"Dead. Gone. Mauthausen. Auschwitz."

The sexton led them back to the vestibule with the plaque with its incised names. Vanished. Eaten up. Devoured by the fires of the Third Reich. Herbie wondered: was the whole story known? Were there secrets? He was not an educated man, or a reflective one, but he was not stupid. A life dedicated to making out other people's tax returns; a nice home; two cars; vacations whenever he wanted. Why kick? But there had to be something else to know. Too many people, he felt, too many who weren't Germans or Nazis or anything at all, but ordinary people, people like the ones on the Three Worlds tours, did nothing, nothing at all—or *applauded*—when all those Weisses and Roths and Goldbergers were packed off to Mauthausen.

Ah, what could one man do? How much was one man supposed to mourn?

They walked through the weed-choked plot in front of the synagogue, through the gate ripped from its hinges. "There's still a few people around who don't like us," Mr. Fisch said, pointing to the gate. "After the Six Day War, the Russians ordered everyone to be against Israel. Never mind, I heard plenty of *goyim* say how brave they thought the Jews in Israel were. So maybe it'll get better someday."

They followed Mr. Fisch down a cobbled street, past another high-rise in construction. Factory workers in stained clothing walked by. One greeted Mr. Fisch. A tailor poked his head from a minuscule shop with windows decorated with fashion plates from what looked like 1946 magazines and called to him.

They entered a four-story brownstone building. Were those shell holes on the outside? Herbie wondered. The hallway stank of ammonia, cat's urine, garbage. The sexton led them up a flight of canted stairs, turned a corner, knocked on a door. There was a small sign on the panel in Hungarian.

A stout elderly woman—she did not look Jewish, but had the slanted eyes of a Magyar—let them in. They walked down a hallway lit by a dim bulb into a room that seemed a combination of a hospital ward, community kitchen, and parlor.

"Oh, my God," Flo cried. "An old people's home."

A dozen old people were in the room. Several were propped up in hospital beds. One white-haired woman wearing gold-rimmed glasses sat in an easy chair and read. Another, with slow determined movements, was washing dishes at a sink. At a white-covered table, apparently used for services, an old man with handsome white earlocks was reading a Hebrew book. An unlit candelabrum and a silver plate were on the table.

As Herbie, Flo, and the others entered, there was movement in the room, a sense of excitement, the routine being broken. The old man at the table closed his book and shuffled toward them. He wore a frazzled gray bathrobe, tattered slippers. He spoke a Yiddish which Herbie could barely understand.

"Says he's glad to see you," Mr. Fisch says. "Nobody ever visits them. That's why I brought you."

"Who is he? What is this?" Shirl asked.

"The old people's home. The city helps out. These are the ones who were left behind. No families. No money. Too old for Israel. No place to go. But they're still Jews. Friday night, you should see them get dressed up, right, *zayde?*"

The ancient nodded his head. "Ninety-two years," he said, pointing to his chest. "Ninety-two years. Mauthausen. Auschwitz. God let me live."

Herbie thought: Yeh, but he let six million others die. Figure that one. Give me a joke to go with that, something that'll make everyone on the bus laugh.

The old people moved slowly toward Herbie and his friends. They talked. They touched their hands. They asked about America.

"Yes, we are American Jews," Si said in halting Yiddish. "We are traveling in Europe. There are lots of Jews in America, and they are good citizens, and their sons go to colleges, and they are doctors and lawyers."

"And we're going to Israel at the end of this trip," Shirl said, "tell them."

Herbie tried to. Mr. Fisch helped out. But it seemed to Herbie that the old people did not want information. They were content to look at the visitors, touch them, make contact with Jews whom they knew to be secure and wealthy and happy and living in a free country. One toothless woman, her eyes hidden behind smoked lenses, was trying to say something to Shirl. Her voice was thin and lost, veiled with decades of sorrow.

"She is blind," Mr. Fisch said. "She lost her sight after she came out of Mauthausen. They all have stories, they could keep you here all day."

"Are they well taken care of?" Herbie asked. The words choked in his throat. *Fat dope. Full of salami and steaks and prune danish.*

"So-so," Mr. Fisch responded. "A little here, a little there. They are old people and some are sick. At least here is a warm place, three meals a day, and a little nursing care. Mrs. Szabo over there, the city sends her around. She's a nurse."

The woman in the uniform was administering a hypodermic needle to one of the women in bed. It seemed like trying to pump life into a corpse.

"The one there in bed," Mr. Fisch said casually. "Ninety-eight. You hear? Ninety-eight years old. Lost everyone in the camps or to Szálasi's people. She hid in a cellar."

Flo, beyond tears, unable to resist, walked toward the bed. On a small end table was a photograph of a bearded husky man in a work shirt, arms folded, wearing a kibbutz hat. Pinned to the cardboard frame was an Israeli flag.

"Her grandson?" Flo asked.

The sexton shrugged. "She doesn't know who he is. But it's a reminder to her there are other Jews in the world."

In the street, Herbie took up a collection.

"Everybody cough up," Herbie said. "Come on, Si, Sid, all of you. Leave enough for cab fare and lunch."

"I don't want to eat," Flo said. "Not now."

Shirl was weeping. "And I don't want to go shopping."

Father Konay found himself a celebrity. His knowledge of Hungarian made him useful for information, translating menus, chatting with people. The tour—except for the group that had gone to Obuda to see the synagogue—were ordering lunch on the terrace of the Gellért Hotel. It was warm, the sky grittily hazed. Pepi explained that below the city were the Csepel steelworks. Whenever there was no breeze Budapest suffered from smog.

"It's a sign of progress," Mr. Wattle said. "If you want progress, you pay the price. Even the Communists understood that. Ecologists are a bunch of cranks and fakes."

Was it possible, Rosie wondered, that the commissars and certain businessmen were sisters under the skin?

Father Konay had crossed the trolley tracks in front of the hotel to a square with a monument in it. Someone had asked about it, and since Virgil was enjoying his usual solitary lunch, and the tourists understood he was never to be disturbed, the priest volunteered to find out what it was.

"It's a liberation monument," the priest said.

"Who was liberating who?" Dr. Grant asked.

"Oh, the Russians liberating the Hungarians. And something about the workers' army."

"There're monuments all over this place," Cornelia said. "Everything is commemorated."

"That's very Hungarian," Bettenhausen said, studying a dish the waiter placed before him. "Ah, *gansenleber*. I have a feeling the signs on them can be changed. You know that statue of Lenin we saw on the boulevard earlier? That great metal monstrosity?"

"What in the devil have you ordered?" Mr. Wattle said, staring at the fatty brownish lumps surrounded by jellied consommé on Bettenhausen's plate.

"Goose livers. Not adulterated pâté but goose livers, as only Hungarians can prepare them." He tasted one. "Sublime."

"What about Lenin?" Rose-Anne Wicker asked.

"The Hungarians say the statue has no coat because he won't be around when winter comes."

"But he was. And is."

Bettenhausen shrugged. "The *gansenleber* is heavenly. Pepi recommended a bottle of *bikavér* to accompany it." He waved to the waiter.

"The food is great," Arnold Wicker said. "This omelet is crazy—mushrooms and herbs. Why were we told Communist countries have such lousy food?"

"It isn't Communism—it's the Hungarian in them," Father Konay said timidly. He looked out with tired eyes at the crowds of midday pedestrians. They looked sturdy enough but few were smiling. Their clothes were drab and homemade. There was not enough noise, not enough gaiety. He had always heard what a lively and handsome city Budapest was. His mother had talked about it, how when she was a little girl her parents would bring her to Budapest from the Balaton. He wondered. It was surely beautiful—if run down—with the great river winding its way, the palaces, the Parliament, the parks and squares, the old quarter around Castle Hill where they had spent the morning. But lively? He found the people gloomy and silent. Not at all like the Hungarian-Americans he knew in Ash Valley.

"This country has the highest rate of suicide in the world," Mr. Wattle said as he tasted his chicken soup. "Twenty-six point eight per cent per hundred thousand. Austria is second, 21.7. Then Czechoslovakia, followed by Finland, West Germany, and Sweden."

"What do you make of those figures?" Father Konay asked. "Isn't it possible that it's because some countries keep records?"

"Not that well up on it," Mr. Wattle said. "I don't give suicide a thought. My life is too full and rich and active to contemplate ending it." He grinned at Theresa. "I may live forever."

Dr. Wicker, touring the Gellért, came back to the luncheon table bright with enthusiasm. "Say, they've got the darnedest thing in back —a mineral-water pool that makes waves."

"Waves?" Rosie asked.

"There's a mob of people in there and every few minutes some machine throws waves over them. And there are smaller pools with people squatting, taking the salts. Guys reading, writing letters, making business deals, lovers. All in mineral water."

"It's an old Hungarian tradition," Bettenhausen said. "The country is a crust on top of a lake of yeasty waters. It helps explain the Hungarian character."

Mr. Wattle, his arm draped around Theresa's chair, but never touching her, leaned back. "I've done some research on it. Exactly a hundred and twenty-three mineral springs are located in Budapest, supplying fifteen million gallons a day."

"They say it's good for the bones," Cornelia said.

192

"I hate mineral baths," Mr. Wattle countered. "They give me diarrhea."

"I think I'll try it," the dentist said. "All that riding in the bus and no exercise. I want to get hit by one of those fake waves. Anyone for the pool?" Bettenhausen lumbered to his feet. He detested exercise but Mr. Wattle's presence was ruining the *gansenleber*. What had gone down smooth as velvet had turned to a sodden divot in his stomach. "I'll go along," he said. "I always wanted to see a pool full of Hungarians."

Huggins enjoyed a laugh over the incident at border customs. Those Hunkies leafing through Ed Hutzler's porno magazines! And the old farmer with a valise full of Hungarian forints bought illegally in Vienna! He was thankful he had met those Arabs in Vienna. Now all he had to do was keep an eye out for the shipping news in the *Herald Tribune*. But in the lobby of the Gellért the desk informed him that they received only four copies, and that these vanished in minutes.

The gold of Dubai danced before him. Smuggler's gold! What did those *walyones* back in the Bronx know of his ten-tola bars? Two hundred grand in solid bullion, to be sold at top black market price in Karachi or Bombay!

He recalled that he had failed to send a cable to Mario. Illiterate, unschooled, stupid even in the details of crime, they would be sitting nervously in Pelham awaiting word.

Crossing the lobby, J.P. saw Herbie barreling toward him. The comic looked appalling. His gut seemed to droop a foot lower than it had nine days ago. Lugging that lard around, Huggins thought, was no fun.

"Feel better, Herb?" J.P. asked him. "You look like death warmed over on a bad Monday morning."

"Death, don't talk to me about death."

"What's bugging you?"

"Jimmy, you wouldn't believe what we saw today. We went to the old synagogue."

"Oh. Pray?"

"Who could pray in that misery?" He told J.P. about the ruinous building, the empty pews, the marble plaque with its roster of the dead, the old people, the sick, the blind, the remnants of the Jewish community. "It was hard to take, Jimmy, I tell you. I ain't recovered yet."

Huggins was touched. Years ago in the Bronx, his pal Buck Sweeney, had worked as a *Shabbes goy*. Huggins, who used to torment Mr. and Mrs. Lieberman in their candy store with pranks, had always harbored a little guilt over his dumb anti-Semitic tricks.

Sweeney was different; Sweeney was all heart and liked everyone, even spades. "A bad scene, huh, Herbie?"

"I tell you, it broke me up. I started to cry."

"What can you do, Herbie? It's the past."

"I know, I know, Jimmy. But to see those old people . . . the names on the wall. Ah, I'm sorry."

"It's okay, Herb."

"Don't get insulted. I can talk to you. It's like I had to tell a Christian about it. I can't explain it. Somebody who would understand."

"I understand, Herb."

Sid and Si, from a rear arcade in the vast lobby, came walking toward them. Each man carried four cigar boxes.

"Herbie, look what we found," Sid said.

Herbie sniffed the boxes. "Havana?"

Si nodded. "They got a humidor the size of Grand Central Station. The Cubans can't sell any of their stuff to America. So they ship all the surplus to Budapest. And the prices! Five bucks for twenny-five Julio Mendezes. Six bucks for Felipe Reyes. Hoyo de Monterey. El Sols."

"You can't take 'em to the States," J.P. said. He regarded himself as an expert on contraband. Was he not a limited partner in the Beirut, Dubai & Sharja Trading Company?

"No?" Si looked wounded.

"Well, we'll have to smoke 'em in the next ten days," Sid said. "I'll suffer. Herbie, go. You'll go crazy there. It's like being turned loose in a whorehouse with a credit card."

Herbie examined the cigar boxes. Real Havana. Names he had not seen in years. Si opened one box. The aroma was like the scent of gold—rich, earthy, sunny. The blunt, rough-coated, dark brown cigars lay redolent in their wooden chest.

"Ah, later," he said wearily. "Maybe later. I got cards to write."

"First time I ever saw Herbie run from a cigar," Si said.

Whenever he came to the Gellért, Virgil tried to lunch with a fellow alumnus of Mauthausen. He was a man named Imre Veg, six years older than Virgil, an official of the National Tourist Board, who spent a great deal of time in hotel lobbies. Veg, like Virgil, was stocky and dark and spoke, in addition to his native Hungarian, seven languages, which put him on a par with the tour escort. They were capable of switching from German to English to French to Italian, and to a generalized Slavic, which they called "Russo-Croat."

They sat at the last table of the long dining room, affording them a view of the tree-lined street and a corner of the pool with its artificial waves.

Veg, as a government functionary, got special attention from the headwaiter, and he advised his friend to order eggs Esterhazy with a side dish of asparagus Széchényi.

"A bit of Habsburg elegance," Veg said. "And of course you are not permitted to pay, so we will have the best Olasz Riesling from Lake Balaton."

"Olasz Riesling," Virgil said reflectively. "From grapes picked by Hungarian virgins. Is it true, Imre, that they extract the juice by pressing the grapes against the insides of their thighs?"

"If you wish to believe that, Josip, do so."

Veterans of beatings, thin soup, isolation cells, work gangs, they utilized not only several languages but a variety of names. Virgil, as a boy in the camps, was known as Josip Barmak, or Joseph Barmash, or Janos Baramatz. The name Pepi Virgil—on his passport Joseph Francis Virgil—had been adopted much later.

"One survives by wishing to believe," Virgil said. "Once on the BBC I saw a marvelous American play by Eugene O'Neill. The BBC is my first love, Imre. The theme struck me as a truth I had known ever since I was arrested in Rijeka selling newspapers, but never understood. It took O'Neill to dramatize it for me."

"And what was it?"

Virgil sipped his Budvar beer. Truly, there was no beer in the world like it. "We live by illusions," the tour guide said. "We are sustained by them. When we lose them, we cannot survive."

"You and I have survived," Veg said. His face was rather unlined for a man who had experienced such misery. "But was it our illusions —or our intelligence, our resources?"

"Some of both." Virgil looked at the eggs Esterhazy. They were magnificent—simmering in a brown sauce in a ramekin, ringed with mushrooms, rivulets of a herb-scented gravy running across the yellow yolks. "Yes, both," Virgil said. "No eggs like this at the camp, eh, Imre?"

"But we were good at stealing bread."

Virgil sipped his beer. He ate slowly. The eggs were only a first course. Imre Veg suggested the Danube carp Petöfi as a main course. "I am not much on psychiatry. Luck. Courage. Good health. We were young and had strong bodies."

Veg was shaking his head. "You are still an uncomplicated man,

Josip. An optimist. It comes from these associations with Americans. The most innocent people in the world. Such innocence should be painful to a professional European like yourself."

"On the contrary. I find it refreshing. Because it is innocence—and something else. What? Power? A sense of being able to change the world? Hold the future? They have not lost that, Imre."

"Oh, they are losing it every day. The whores in front of the hotel are refusing American dollars. Last night I heard Juditka demand Deutsche marks or francs suisses."

"But no Hungarian forints?" Virgil asked, winking. "Or rubles? Not yet anyway?"

"Dear Josip, when the forint becomes a hard currency, that is the day I resign from the Party. It will mean we have been reborn as capitalist pigs, thank goodness."

Virgil looked at Veg's patient face, a face that told you little, and recalled how they always would volunteer for outdoor duty—the camp farm, the construction site. You ate better when you worked. On the farm one could steal a turnip. Hide your eyeglasses and speak ungrammatically, camp old-timers warned them. They had. Veg in his early twenties, Pepi in his teens—two shrewd young prisoners who always managed to get the extra slice of bread, avoid the "transport" lists . . .

"You have a Dr. Wicker in your group." Veg was sampling a pancake stuffed with sugared cheese and topped with chocolate sauce.

"You are still doing business on the side." Virgil let the smoke from his cigarette form a veil between them.

"I merely asked about Dr. Wicker. I saw him when your tour checked in. Arnold Wicker, a dentist of Riverford, Connecticut. His wife is a blonde woman with excellent legs."

"You know all you need to know."

"Ah, the honor of these tour escorts."

"Believe me, *caro,* I could not care less about these police jobs you are required to perform from time to time. That is your affair."

Veg lit a blunt Cuban cigar. The aroma was intoxicating. They were the same cigars that Si and Sid had just purchased. Under Hungarian law they were to be sold only to tourists. Veg, as a part-time member of the secret police, got them at the same price as foreigners.

"I may have to talk to Dr. Wicker. You will not object?"

"How can I?" Virgil asked. "Knowing you, Imre, you will be a model of courtesy."

Although the rich food, the liter of golden beer, the cigarettes, had relaxed him, cocooning him in comfort, Virgil did not feel at peace.

196

He was bothered by the recurrence of questioners, of probers, of agents and quasi agents. There had been the American chaps in Berlin, Hunterden in Austria, asking him to make a statement about bringing messages into Communist countries, and now Imre Veg.

Until Veg mentioned the dentist, the affable man, always concerned about teeth, taking endless photos, had seemed, the least likely man to be on a mission, a secret run. Yet Veg must have been working on information. A tour company could have its image soiled by being involved—however innocently—in dirty dealing.

"Why not interrogate him right now?" Virgil asked.

"He's enjoying the baths. I'll wait till later."

"We will be sailing the Danube this afternoon."

"I know. On the *Voros Csillag*. I have to go aboard also. We've had some complaints from German tourists about the cleanliness."

Lulu Flemington had found nothing worth buying in the "hard currency" shop at the hotel. She complained bitterly to the manager. Where were the antiques? Where was the embroidered work she had heard about? The man, all bows and smiles, assured Madame he would give her the names of stores that sold Herend china, old silver, and anything else she wanted. She would have all of tomorrow morning before the flight to the Soviet Union.

Harry began to get edgy. A Lulu prevented from spending money, a Lulu unable to fill another valise with treasure, was a dangerous Lulu. She demanded a drink (after a lunch at which she had eaten nothing, finished a liter of Pilsen beer, and refused to write to Robbie) and to make matters worse, when Harry refused, she stormed from the shop, bumping into Murray Yasuda and Mr. Hutzler, the two of them puffing cigars and beclouding her in thick smoke.

"They taste like candy," the Japanese said cheerfully. "I'm buyin' the whole stock."

"How you goin' to get 'em into the States?" Mr. Hutzler asked.

"Same way you got your porno magazines into Hungary."

Mr. Hutzler chuckled. "Won't work, Yasuda. They were confiscated."

By the time they boarded the *Voros Csillag* (*Red Star*) for the afternoon ride along the brownish Danube, Lulu was coughing, covering the lower part of her face with a pink scarf and settling into a deck chair for a long sulk.

"Wife under the weather?" J. P. Huggins asked. Relieved of his burden, he now found it pleasant to be interested in other people's troubles. The Flemington woman fascinated him.

"Lulu's tired."

197

"I'll send Barbara to hold her hand. Barbs is good at that. A big Italian heart."

Huggins made the offer generously. Flemington struggled to find some way out. In these bouts of pouting and self-pity, Lulu was best left alone.

The two men were standing off the bow of the slow-moving boat. Across from them, as the *Voros Csillag* sailed north, rose the spires of the Parliament Building, a neo-Gothic monster dominating the Pest side of the river.

Eva, the guide, approached Huggins and Flemington.

"Mmmmm . . . façade of Parliament is in other side. You saw in morning. Statues of Kossuth and Rákóczy, you remember?"

Flemington looked puzzled. "Rakosi? Didn't they kick him out in 1956?"

Eva laughed, covering her mouth. "No, no, not that man. That is Rakosi Matyas. Statue is Rákóczy Ferenc, fighter against Habsburgs in . . . mmmmmmmmm . . . seventeenth and eighteenth centuries. You see?" The girl moved on to describe the Parliament to Dr. and Mrs. Grant and the Bettenhausens.

"That takes care of my knowledge of Hungarian history," Flemington said. "I was only a century and a half off."

"I didn't know either of them," Huggins said. "You're well informed. Newspaperman, right?"

"Oh, a little free lancing."

Huggins nodded. Two racing sculls bearing young men in blue sweat suits skimmed past them. The *Voros Csillag* edged to the right as it approached the bridge where the Danube divided on either side of Margit Island.

"Why am I trying to con you?" Flemington asked.

Halfway down the deck, Lulu dozed in a canvas chair, her face absorbing the thin September sunlight.

"I'm a hard man to con," Huggins said. "I'm usually the conner, not the connee."

"So you must know that I don't write a bloody thing. I'm just married. To money."

"That's nothing to be ashamed of. I have a related problem but it's too complicated to discuss."

Flemington pushed his suede hat back, a move suggesting the old film notion of the ace reporter. But his face was too aristocratic, his clothing too fancy. "You have a lovely wife, Jim. Kids, a career. I envy you."

"I'll never make it to Grosse Pointe. But what the hell, I could never root for the Tigers. And most of the motor industry crowd give me the creeps. Handicap golfers and gin drinkers."

On the bow deck below Theresa Carrell and the Wickers appeared. Theresa walked to the point of the bow and began to take pictures. The wind blew her dark brown hair, and she arched her neck and threw her head back: a bowsprit goddess.

"Good-looking woman," Huggins said.

"Mrs. Carrell?"

"Yeah. The class shows. She never makes a bad move. I mean, physically or in conversation. Some people have that talent."

"That's well put," Flemington said. He took his hat off, as if saluting Huggins' tribute to his old mistress.

"You . . . ah . . . you and your wife knew her before."

Harry turned his tweedy back to the wind blowing from the Danubian plain and lit his pipe. He was a careful man; he put the burned matches in his leather pocket. "Well, I did. Some years back. Before I was married."

"When you were a newspaperman?"

"Ah, yes. More or less. Even before then. We met when we were at the University of Minnesota."

Flemington's voice had gone husky as if a muscle in his throat had tightened. J.P. was sorry he had begun to ask about Theresa. Yet he could not help feeling that Flemington wanted to talk.

"Crazy world. All the people who go on tours, and you meet up again like this."

Huggins looked at the modern buildings on the Pest side. The afternoon sun painted them orange-gold. On the hills of Buda where they had spent the morning, shadows were darkening old alleys and narrow streets.

"Don't mention this to anyone, will you?" Flemington asked. "I just feel the need to tell someone. Preferably someone I don't know very well."

"Safe here. A lawyer, remember?"

"And I won't get billed?"

"You could afford it, Harry. I'm sure Mrs. Flemington's handled a helluva lot bigger law fees than anything that would come from Jabloner & Kuraskin."

"Quite true, Jim." Flemington stared at Theresa. He saw her face in profile. She was talking to Rosie Wicker. The dentist was loping around the deck photographing everything he could get into his view finder.

"Never think she's the far side of forty," Huggins said. "I guess it's the spirit that keeps some women going." With a dose of self-pity, he realized that Barbara's breasts, as huge and satisfying as they were now, were beginning to droop menacingly. Tires were forming in her middle regions.

"Terry's got some gift of youth," Flemington said. "She's always had it."

"So you've seen her, on and off?"

"I am hopelessly in love with her. I'll be in love with her the day I die in my twenty-seven-room house, surrounded by my grieving wife and seven in help."

Huggins brushed his hair back. "You got to grab for the brass ring, Harry."

Flemington shook his head. He had told Huggins—a man with an Irishman's capacity for barside confessions—more than he wanted to. But it would be too complicated to go into detail. Robbie in his football helmet. Lulu and the booze, the buying, the collapses. His cowardice and failed career. And how would he make a living, with nothing published in years and no confidence in his ability, if indeed he ever had any talent beyond that of being the fastest rewrite man in Minneapolis?

"You draw your own conclusions, Jim," Harry said. "I'm dying a little each day looking at her."

"And Mrs. Flemington? How is she taking it?"

"Lulu's fine." Harry turned from the railing. Theresa was meeting his gaze but making no sign of encounter. Then he looked down the deck at Lulu. She waved a gloved hand at him. "She knows she's got me, Jim. She raised a little fuss at first."

"I remember in the pub in London."

"She tried to get Virgil to throw Theresa off the tour."

"No kidding?"

"Pepi wouldn't hear of it. I'm behaving myself. It's all working out. I suppose it is."

"Must be painful to look at her every day."

"It is." Flemington studied Huggins' face, the face of a deceiver, someone you would be wary of trusting with money, but in whom you would confide precisely because he seemed to have no scruples. In his very shiftiness he could be sympathetic to someone trying to walk the straight and narrow. "I hope you don't mind. I'm in agony. I was managing until about an hour ago. I don't know how I'm going to get through this trip."

Huggins winked, talked out of the side of his mouth. "Try a replay."

He left Flemington, appreciating the man's misery. Huggins knew what it was to ache for something you could not have, so badly that you could not think clearly about anything else, could not sleep, could not put your life in order.

The Detroit man's unhappiness assured him he was a fortunate fellow—money invested, possibilities opening, ten more days of travel. He would try to latch onto the Bettenhausens and the Wickers now that he was free of his loot.

A Hungarian family—a young couple in ill-fitted holiday clothing and two neat little children—were standing in front of Bettenhausen. The youngsters, a boy and a girl, were hypnotized by Bettenhausen's beard. The father was trying to explain something to Bettenhausen in halting German.

"I think he says the boy likes your beard. He wants to touch it." Cornelia was struggling to recall her college German. "Go on, be a sport, Betts."

The father shoved the boy forward. As his hand reached out, Bettenhausen's beard seemed to bristle. "Boy," he said, "I know you boys, and you are a bad lot of fellows."

The child retreated.

"Oh, Betts, you scared him," Cornelia said.

Warren Bettenhausen looked contrite. "I did not mean to frighten the tot. I was testing you."

Cornelia narrowed her eyes. "Once more, with feeling."

"I know you boys and you are a bad lot of fellows."

"*Oliver Twist?*"

"Close."

"*David Copperfield?*"

The Grants studied them with astonishment, much in the same way Mr. Hutzler stared at Herbie from time to time.

Bettenhausen cleared his throat. "*Great Expectations.* The scene—"

"Yes, darn you. I remember it. Lawyer Jagger to Pip on the stairs. 'A bad lot of fellows.' How could you, Betts?"

"Lawyer Jagger was played by that marvelous actor, Francis Sullivan."

Henderson Grant studied Bettenhausen's face with wonder. "Your memory. Incredible. How do you do it? Have you ever forgotten anything?"

"All the important things," Bettenhausen said. "I have retained only the trivia."

Imre Veg, the functionary of the Ministry of Tourism, sat in the interior cabin for a while, sipping Tokaji Aszu and waiting for a chance to catch Dr. Wicker alone. He had decided against asking Virgil to introduce him to the dentist. There was no point in involving

Pepi. Pepi was a friend. As far as Veg knew, he had never worked as a courier, never done any espionage, black or white, witting or unwitting. The important thing, he had learned, was non-involvement, a skill that could be practiced—this was a true Hungarian skill—*even when one was involved.* That was how Veg had survived Mauthausen, Szálasi, the Red Army, Rakosi, 1956, Kadar, and the great socialist experiment. *Non-involvement even when involved.*

Veg had identified Arnold Wicker. He had wandered out to the Gellért pool after lunching with Virgil and had seen the long-limbed, long-jawed man yelling joyfully as the machine-made waves washed over him. The dentist had convinced some members of the Planet Tour to join him in the water—a middle-aged Negro couple, their dark bodies glistening in the mass of white skin, a deaf gentleman with a younger wife, splashing one another playfully, like a couple he had once read about in an Aldous Huxley novel.

At the town of Szentendre, the *Voros Csillag* turned and began the trip back to Budapest. Dr. Wicker had gone to the topmost deck to get a panoramic shot of the village spires. Veg, warmed by two glasses of wine, watched him climb the steps—a chilly wind was now blowing —and followed him. They were alone.

"A lovely place," Veg said.

Wicker was bracing himself against the rail, using a long lens, balancing it with professional skill.

"Sure is," he said.

"Szentendre. St. Andrew. Artists live there. Beautiful baroque and rococo houses. A shame you cannot visit it."

"You can't do everything."

Veg stood alongside the dentist. "Dr. Wicker?"

"Yes?"

"Detroit."

"Oh, thank goodness. I thought you'd never show up. Oh, wait a minute. Tigers. Ah . . . Green Bay."

"Packers."

"Boy, am I glad to see you."

"You have the message for Dr. Borkin?"

"In my pocket."

"No one knows?"

"Nobody. I have to hand it to you people and to Mr. Leland. This thing has worked like a charm. All kinds of nutty things have been happening. Strange people quizzing me. Our tour escort—you know Mr. Virgil?"

Veg nodded.

"He made a speech before we left Austria. I could swear he made it for my benefit. About not bringing in stuff to sell, or messages. Is that possible?"

"Most certainly. Mr. Virgil was merely following someone's orders."

"Someone on *their* side?"

Veg put a finger to his lips.

"But you . . . you're . . . I mean, one of us. But a Hungarian. It must be dangerous." Things were hopelessly jumbled in Wicker's mind.

Veg smiled. "Now, please, not a word about this meeting. You are satisfied I am the contact, are you not? I had a devil of a time memorizing all those teams and cities. They change so often. Imagine my surprise to find there is a baseball team called Texas now. What happened to Washington? And a football team in New England?"

"The Patriots. They used to be called Boston."

"Very confusing. I am much indebted to the USIA Library in the American Embassy."

"Isn't it dangerous for you to hang around there?" Wicker asked. "Working for us and being Hungarian, wouldn't you want to avoid such places?"

"Not at all. My work permits me to consult American newspapers and magazines regularly. I'm with the Ministry of Tourism."

"I'll know who to ask for a hotel room." Dr. Wicker grinned. "One that's properly bugged, for sure."

Veg did not smile. Was he in something he did not quite understand? Was this silly dentist on to things that he did *not* know? And why in heaven's name was the man staring at his mouth?

"You've got a bad situation on your left side," Dr. Wicker said. "Someone did a terrible job on your teeth. They botched the cross bite of your left incisors and then ruined it with that steel prosthesis. I could take care of you in two weeks. If you come to the States . . ."

Ah, he was too good, too simple. Veg was satisfied.

"You have the message and you will find Dr. Borkin, and you will tell no one. They may make further attempts to intercept you. But only the password is acceptable. The same system—baseball, then football. All right?"

"Sure. Can't wait to meet Dr. Borkin."

"And in that connection, you were told to contact him at . . . ?"

"The Lenin Institute."

"That has been changed."

"Oh? Why?"

"I have not the faintest idea, Dr. Wicker, I only transmit information."

"Sure, sure."

"Four days from now, you are scheduled to spend the entire morning touring the Kremlin. Consult your itinerary. During the first hour of that tour you will find yourself in Cathedrals Square. Dr. Borkin will meet you at the Queen of Bells."

"Pardon?"

"The Queen of Bells. It is a bell mounted on a pedestal. The heaviest bell in the world. You cannot miss it."

"How will I know Dr. Borkin?"

"He has a description of you. He will be wearing a light brown cap and a matching topcoat. He is of medium height, has brown hair, and a small scar on his chin, the result of laboratory burns."

"A keloid," Dr. Wicker said.

"Give him the envelope and leave. No words will be exchanged."

"That's all?"

"Those are my instructions. You are to attract no attention and rejoin your tour."

The Parliament building on the Pest side was shadowed. The Gothic arches and spires assumed a morose air. Veg wished they would remove the Red Star from the top. A traitorous thought for a Communist, but he felt it did not sit well atop the corbels and pinnacles.

"And that's it?" Wicker asked.

"I have discharged my duty. I am sure you will do yours."

"And Dr. Borkin will do his, whatever it is."

"Whatever it is. I assure you I have not the faintest idea what any of this involves."

"I wish I did. Anything for the good old CIA and good old Mr. Leland."

Herbie and Murray came lumbering up to the top deck. Veg quickly turned away and left Wicker.

"Now ain't that a purty sight?" A. T. Gunthorpe asked J. P. Huggins.

The group was on the terrace of the Citadella, the restaurant on Gellért Hill in the walls of the Habsburg fortress. Beneath them, the city sparkled by night. The Danube glowed.

"It's better from up here," Huggins said. "You don't see all the cracks and shell holes."

Mr. Wattle pivoted away from Theresa Carrell and came to a snappy halt alongside Gunthorpe. "Lenin once wrote that Communism is socialism plus electricity."

"Ole Wattle," Gunthorpe said appreciatively. "Ole Wattle he know jes' about everythin'. Whut he don' know ole Bettenhausen knows.

'Tween the two of them we got us a passel of brains on this tour, raht, Jimboy?"

Huggins studied Gunthorpe narrowly. Old faker! Old con man! He was as shrewd as a raccoon. He played the ridge-runner marvelously. Full of corn pone and moonshine. But count your change.

"Yes, that's what Lenin said," Mr. Wattle went on. "Hah! Their per capita wattage is the lowest in Europe! Which means, if you follow me, that they'll *never* have Communism!"

"You should tell the Minister of Power," Huggins said.

"They wouldn't listen. The people would, though. Say, I talked to some of their kids. They want cars. They want money. They want clothing. They're dying for capitalism. Can't wait. Do you know, these Eastern Europeans admire us more than the French or English or West Germans? What I wouldn't give to have a General Motors franchise here! They wanted to know why Buick discontinued the Skylark."

Virgil called to them. The Three Worlds table at the restaurant within the fortress was ready. It was too chilly to dine out of doors. Mr. Wattle saw Theresa walking away with the Bettenhausens and the Wickers, and went into a two-step after her.

"Gon' git me some poontang tonight," Gunthorpe confided to Huggins as they left the terrace.

"Be careful, Pops."

"Always am, Jimboy."

"They say these Hungarian women can kill a man."

A.T. grabbed Huggins' arm as they entered the cavernlike restaurant. The air was smoky. Gypsy music came at them from every corner. "Had me a little ole mulatta gal in Berlin. The night you folks went to the night club. Reckon I had me a better time than y'all did."

"Dark meat, huh, Pops?"

"You know it." Gunthorpe licked his lips. He said nothing about the four-hundred-dollar watch that had been lifted from his wrist. Huggins, with his sharp New York way, would regard him as a dumb hill-billy. Like many self-made men, Gunthorpe took care to keep his image in trim. It was all right to play the rube but one did not want to be taken for a fall guy. Not this old catfish. Not this buck alligator.

"After dinner, watch ole A.T.," Gunthorpe said. "Got me some addresses. Ah hear it's expensive, but worth hit."

Strolling gypsy violinists in silk shirts, flowing ties, pantaloons and boots surrounded the Grants, who were seated with Theresa Carrell and Father Konay.

The black couple looked pained. Dr. Grant was trying to smile. His

205

eyes were secretive behind dark glasses. Ibith laughed and said something to Theresa.

> "Ve shell hovercome,
> Ve shell hovercome,
> Ve shell hovercome, someday, hay-hay-hay-hay. . . ."

"I'll be dipped in blackstrap molasses," Gunthorpe said to Huggins. "They playin' ole Martin Luther's song."

"Tribute to our black Americans," Huggins said. He began to sing lustily. He admired the marvelous nonsense of the moment.

"I'm touched," Henderson Grant said to Theresa and Father Konay. "Only two weeks ago, one of our black militants called me an Uncle Tom, an Oreo, and a member of a pseudo class created by the white bourgeoisie."

"And he said when Mr. Charley went we'd go too," Ibith added.

Father Konay blinked. "I would like to talk to you about this thing . . . this problem. . . ."

They could not hear him over the violins. "What say, Father?" Dr. Grant asked.

"Tell you later." The Ospreys were pecking at him again. He wondered if he would be better off in a little parish church in Budapest. No, that was a mean thought. His future, what was left of it, was in Ash Valley.

Herbie, seated at the head of a long table, a father figure to Si, Sid, Murray, all blowing clouds of smoke from their Havanas, did not sing. He sipped mineral water. Salty, fizzy, good for his liver. But no help for his frame of mind.

The violins ended their homage to civil rights with a flourish.

"How do they happen to know that song?" Mrs. Hutzler asked Pepi.

"It is very popular with their young people."

"Sort of sympathy?" she asked. "With our colored?"

"Rather more than that. They sing it when they demonstrate—for jobs, free speech, whatever."

"I'll be darned."

Virgil circulated in the smoky gloom of the Citadella. Father Konay was moving around tables helping with the menu. He was enjoying the attention. Up to now he had retired, melted into churches and museums. With his chair vacant, Mr. Wattle attempted to take it.

"May I?" he asked Theresa.

"I'm afraid Father Konay is sitting there. He's helping Herbie and Murray order." Theresa smiled.

"I'll ask him to change."

"I wish you wouldn't," Ibith said. "He asked to sit with us."

Wattle saluted. He was uninsultable. "Those liberation songs, that civil rights stuff, wasn't that something?" The man was made of plastic, Theresa thought. "Virgil says they demonstrate in the streets and sing them. But I haven't seen anyone doing that. The police are tough. Don't find much of that trash rioting in a country like this."

Dr. Grant was trying to formulate an answer, something hinting that Mr. Wattle was possibly a pinko or some kind of left-wing nut, but he desisted. To what purpose?

"Let's see," Father Konay was saying, as he adjusted his glasses and leaned over Herbie's shoulder. "*Magyaros izelito*, that's tasty bits, a little bit of everything. *Fatányéros* is a stew. *Fogas* is a fish. They fry it whole. And lots of paprika in everything."

"No *mamaliga?*" Herbie asked.

"Come on, Herbie," Father Konay said. "I heard you the other day. That's Romanian, not Hungarian."

The gypsies struck up a slow waltz. The Wickers were the first on the dance floor. Mr. Wattle, spotting his chance, dodged deftly around waiters and dancers to reach Theresa and ask her for a dance.

Huggins, free as air, divested of the Malfi loot, felt freed of his wife also. Moreover, he was feeling the old wild hair beckoning him to adventure. For a long time he had admired Theresa—her bearing, her good manners. Now, having heard Flemington's confession—the poor bastard! in love with her, forced to see her every day and play nursemaid to a drunken wife!—he was aroused. Why not? She was alone. A room of her own. At an age where she would welcome attention.

"This is my dance," J.P. said. He faked Wattle out of position. Into the cheap seats, as Buck Sweeney would have said. "Terry promised me a dance way back. In Paris. Or London. Or maybe it was Southampton five years ago."

"I'd love to dance, Jim."

Mr. Wattle cracked his palms together. "Darn. Horace T. Wattle loses again. I never lose for long, I tell you." He was about to ask Ibith Grant to dance. But the Grants were getting to their feet and walking away.

"Don't tell me," the rubber manufacturer said. "Is Wattle turned down again?"

"Mr. Legrand is ill," Ibith said. "His wife called and wants Henderson to look at him."

"Can I help? I'm a handy fellow."

"Thank you," Dr. Grant said. "I think I can manage."

The black couple followed Virgil through the tavern out to the terrace.

Huggins pressed Terry close. A strong woman. "Everyone's getting to know everyone a little better," J.P. said. "Like a small town. Doc Grant's got a practice. Father Konay's the official translator. Herbie and Murray have the entertainment concession. Bettenhausen gives art lectures."

"And what do you contribute, Jim?"

"Love."

"Really? Your wife looks happy. She's an adorable girl. You should encourage her more."

"She gets enough encouragement." The wine made him glib. "I'm in the market."

"That a fact?"

"It's a long tour. Ten more days. Don't you get lonely in that room? Especially between five and seven in the evening?"

"I write postcards."

"It's no substitute."

Theresa hummed the gypsy air. "I've known that a long time."

Day 10: Budapest–Leningrad. A free morning in Budapest to shop or sight-see. The Fine Arts Museum awaits, or a morning on the charming Váci Utca, Budapest's Fifth Avenue. A leisurely lunch, perhaps at the chic Vörösmarty café, then on to the airport for our flight into the great northern metropolis of the Soviet Union, Leningrad! Our Russian guide meets us at the airport and we get our first look at the superb city, the architectural gem of the U.S.S.R. that combines the glory of czarist times and modern Communism. Marvel at Leningrad's famed arched bridges, the canals, the Neva River Embankment, the Nevsky Prospekt.

Dinnertime—and what better way to become a true Russian than vodka and caviar?

"You are quite sure you are well enough to make the flight?" Virgil asked Mr. Legrand.

Morning sunlight flooded the hotel room. The art deco furnishings seemed to have been frozen in time. Was Admiral Horthy occupying his three-room suite on the first floor? Virgil had the odd notion that it was 1936, that the Legrands had been in the room for over thirty years. Their bags were packed. Only a few toilet articles and some pill bottles were in evidence. Mrs. Legrand's flite-pak rested on the dressing table. From its opened zippered top peeked a bottle containing yellowish liquid. Pepi had seen her in the dollar shop that morning. Evidently the Steinhager had given out. She was on *barack* now—apricot brandy.

"Yes, yes, I'm all right," the old man said. His voice seemed to be coming from another room.

"What do you think, Dr. Grant?" Pepi asked.

"If I were Mr. Legrand's physician, I'd advise against that flight. What is it? Five hours? Maybe he should rest here a day then catch up with us tomorrow."

"What do you think, Weston?" Mrs. Legrand asked.

The old man brushed aside their doubts with a shake of his feathery head. "I'm going."

"If my sweetie says he's going, he's going," Mrs. Legrand said. "My sweetie knows his mind, don't you, Weston?"

There was no reaction from the old man. He was sitting up in bed, propped on four pillows, fully clothed, including his long coat and homburg. His eyes were angry.

"Doctor?" Pepi asked.

"If Mr. Legrand insists. But he'd better stay in the hotel room until we're ready to go to the airport. I suggest you stay with him, Mrs. Legrand."

"My sweetie and I are always together. We have rarely been apart for more than a day in sixty years of happy married life. Isn't that right, Weston?"

Mr. Legrand did not second her tribute to marital bliss. Yet he did not seem wroth with her.

"If he can manage," Dr. Grant said, nodding his head at the dressing table, "I'd stay off the tranquilizers for a day. The vitamins are okay. He should try to eat more than he does."

"I manage on damned little," Mr. Legrand said. "Got no insides, so I don't need to fill 'em."

"Something nourishing, soup and toast perhaps," the physician said.

"My sweetie will be fine. Thank you, Doctor. And do we owe you anything for the visit last night and this morning?"

Henderson Grant held up his pink palms. "Of course not, Mrs. Legrand."

"We're grateful. We don't have much and we count pennies. Weston and I have it figured out to the last cent. We can travel, we can see places, enrich our lives. All on our pensions and our Social Security and a little savings, provided we watch every cent."

"You do a marvelous job, Mrs. Legrand," Virgil said.

"It comes from experience. Ever since they told Weston twenty-five years ago he wasn't going to live, we've fooled them."

In the hallway the tour escort asked the doctor what he had found last night. Was the old man seriously ill? Was it a good idea for him to travel?

"Near as I could find out, it was just a synergistic reaction to too many pills. And he hardly ever eats. She doesn't eat much either, but she gets her nourishment another way."

"But nothing serious with the old man? Heart?"

"She told me he fibrillates when he's tired. He's eighty-five, you know. And he seems to have chronic stomach trouble. That's what most of the pills are for. I think with a day's rest he'll be in good shape. If you ask me, I think they're both loony for taking a trip like this. It's exhausting even for younger people. My wife and I are about ready to collapse."

Dr. Grant saw his wife waiting at the door of the Gellért. Bettenhausen was about to lead a morning tour of the art museum.

The museum party had grown. Pepi was glad to see the Wickers, the Grants, Mrs. Carrell, Father Konay, Mr. Wattle, and even Huggins and his wife.

Halfway across the lobby, Imre Veg signaled to Virgil. Veg wanted to know whether the scheduled departure via Aeroflot from Budapest to Leningrad, with a stop at Warsaw, was still in effect. Virgil, somewhat piqued, assured him it was. They would be in Leningrad that night at the Baltiiskaya Hotel.

Dr. Wicker observed the conversation. He excused himself from the group around Bettenhausen and walked toward Virgil. "Excuse me, Pepi," the dentist said. "Who is that fellow you just spoke to?" Veg disappeared into the hotel office.

"An old friend. Why?"

"He looked familiar."

"He was on the boat ride yesterday. He is an official of the Ministry of Tourism. It's natural for him to be around tourists."

"Ah . . . he's with the government?" the dentist asked.

"Everyone is with the government in these countries."

Virgil was disturbed also. He had seen Veg talking to Dr. Wicker on the *Voros Csillag*. Veg had admitted to an interest in the dentist. The tour escort did not care which Americans were chosen to run errands, or what Veg, paying off debts to the Communists, was required to do to keep a cushy job. But he did not want any scandal, any arrest, any run-in with officialdom to occur on one of *his* tours. Back in London, the Planet office regarded him as the most reliable of guides. Distraught women, jealous wives, aged men, lecherous husbands, hysteria, fear, greed, stupidity—all of these were problems that Virgil handled with calm efficiency. But espionage, especially in a Communist country, was something else. He had to stay aloof. He was sensitive himself. The Russians had a file on him. Once a KGB lout in Moscow, after a night of winebibbing at the Aragvi Restaurant, had promised to show it to him. "A small file, Virgil, or Barmash, or Barmatz, whatever you wish," the Russian joked. "After all, you were young and spent only a year in Vorkuta. You are British subject now. We like you, bring tourists with dollars."

Dr. Wicker loped across the lobby to join the museum tour. He could not set his mind at ease. The man who had talked to him in Berlin at the Charlottenburg was so darn American, so completely a cop! And Veg? Veg was a Hungarian, a minor functionary. But Veg had the code. Veg knew the football and baseball cities. The man in West Berlin knew nothing. It was baffling.

Wicker, a communicative man, was bursting to ask someone's advice. He dared not worry Rosie. She was having a marvelous time

211

absorbing paintings and history and architecture, luxuriating in the company of people like the Bettenhausens and the Grants and Mrs. Carrell. Normally they were frank with one another. (In mixed doubles Arnie never hesitated to criticize her hesitancy to come to net; Rose-Anne often reminded him of his habit of running around his backhand.)

But this was no mixed doubles match. Virgil had indicated, with his evasive responses about Veg, that he did not wish to be involved. True, the guide was a sort of Everyman, an all-purpose European, to whom one came for information, comfort, direction. But to reveal to him the mission, the letter to Borkin, the changed orders—Queen of Bells?—seemed inappropriate and perhaps perilous.

"Anything wrong?" Rosie asked as her husband climbed into the taxi. "What were you after Pepi about?"

"Getting rid of those forints I cashed."

"Let's see," Rosie said, looking at Mr. Bettenhausen's scrawled note. "*Szépmüvészeti Múzeum*. On Hösök Tére? Okay, driver?"

"Yes, madame. Fine Arts Museum." His English was good.

"Got to watch those Hungarians every minute," Dr. Grant said. "Step ahead of the tourist."

The driver waved his hand in appreciation. "Live in Pittsburgh two years. Drive cab. You like Budapest? I like."

In midmorning, while his friends and his wife visited the shops on Váci Utca, Herbie settled his hulk into a chair in the Gellért lobby and began to write a letter to his son at Yale. "Go, go, spend my money," he said to Flo, with a wave of his hand. "*Hondle*. Get bargains. I've had enough *hondling* to last me the rest of my life."

He watched them board a bus for the Váci Utca—noting that the Flemingtons, bound in the same direction, took a cab but did not offer to share it. Herbie remained fascinated with them. Money on top of money. Real *gelt*. And traveling with a bunch of *shnorrers*. Flemington appealed to him. A gent. *But the wife!* That *farbisseneh*, with her gloves and umbrella and skinny legs. She must have been a knockout before the booze put those lines in her face and gave her a baritone like Robert Merrill.

"No shopping, Herbie?" Flemington had asked before departing.

"Nah, I got correspondence to catch up on."

"All morning? You must write long letters. Or have a lot of friends."

"I got friends I haven't used yet. Have a nice day." He gestured to the interior of the cab where Lulu sat in silence. "The missus looks great. If she finds any bargains in diamonds, I'm available. Like between five and ten grand."

"Harry," Lulu ordered. Unsaid, but hinted at, was the rest of the thought: "Stop talking to that obnoxious fat man and get in here."

Alone in the lobby, Herbie set a sheet of hotel stationery on the writing table, dated the letter and began.

My dear son Sanford,

Your mother and I are well and are enjoying this trip, although I wish I could keep your mother from *hondling* and buying everything she sees, making more of a *shlepper* of me than usual. Already, four extra bags. I look like a peddler from the old country, you should excuse the reference.

You will forgive me, Sanford, for writing this letter. We have hardly talked to each other these last two years, since you won the scholarship to Yale, and I know I am a perpetual embarrassment to you, with my Yiddish jokes and fat belly and the house in Westbury to which you refuse to bring your friends ever since we put in the swimming pool. Did your mother and I ever say we did not want your black friends to swim in it? Did we ever hint that Roosevelt Davis and Luana Harrison were not welcome, even though they both, on their first visit, informed me, a UJA vice-chairman for Westbury, that Israel was a fascist state and should be destroyed, and they stood with their brother Arabs (hah-hah!) against the Zionist imperialists? No, not a word from your mother or me.

Anyway, that is not what this letter is about, although it is a related subject. You do not have to answer this, because we will no doubt be home before it reaches you, considering the mail service in Communist countries. But I would like this in writing. Yesterday, your mother and I and Uncle Si and Aunt Shirl and the others visited an old synagogue in Budapest. It must have been a beautiful building once. But it is a ruin now and used only by a handful of old people. In the lobby of this synagogue, my son, is a marble plaque, almost a whole wall of names. With your intelligent mind, you are no doubt ahead of me. Yes, these are the names of Jews from this *shul* who were murdered by the Nazis and the Hungarian fascists. Later we went to an old people's home, to see some old Jews, and they kissed us and welcomed us.

Why do I tell you all this? I tell you this so that perhaps you and your friends will think a little better of the United States of America, where my father and your mother's father, and many of your friends' grandparents found refuge and safety and prosperity and a good life. I can see you already laughing at my dumb patriotism. No, I am not a flag-waving foolish professional American. I know all about what Negroes are suffering in the United States and I appreciate your concern. The Vietnam war was a disgrace and there are many things that can be criticized and fought in the USA. But

213

the United States is fascist? The United States commits genocide against the black people? My boy, come to Europe, come to the synagogue in Budapest, and I will show you what genocide is.

You will argue that of course the Nazis were terrible people, and of course you know what happened to the Jews, but that America, and you will spell it Amerika, like your friends Roosevelt and Lu-ana (and, believe me, I sympathize with their plight), is just as bad. No, no, my son, it is not as bad. Not nearly as bad. And I am no conservative right-wing bigot. I know all about our faults. But what about what America has meant to us Jews? To plain poor people who came from Europe, from ghettos and czars and commissars and Nazis? Has that ever occurred to you, that maybe once a month you and your young friends could think a little gratefully of what our country has meant to you? Believe me, my boy, a scholarship to Yale and a ten-room house in Westbury with a swimming pool, and yes, the right of you and your associates to condemn the USA all day long, that is somewhat different from Mauthausen and Auschwitz and that marble wall of names I saw yesterday. . . .

Herbie stopped writing. His eyes were moist. He thought of Sanford in New Haven, in his filthy apartment, a madhouse of empty wine bottles, black power posters, the kitchen piled with crusted greasy dishes (Flo almost threw up the last time she was there, and spent two hours scouring), and he realized the letter was a waste of time. The boy was too bright. Too hostile. He would read the letter aloud to his friends and they would mock him.

Slowly his huge hand surrounded the thin air mail paper. He crumpled the sheets into a wad and tossed them into a wastepaper basket. Then he lumbered across the lobby.

"You look tired, Harvey," Mrs. Legrand said. "Weston is resting today. Maybe you should also."

"I'm great, Ma. Pa Barker need anything?"

"No, he's fine. My sweetie never complains."

"Wish I could say the same." He walked past Mrs. Hutzler. She was writing postcards. "You look terrific, Mavis. I might even make a pass at you. Where's Ed?"

"Pooped out. Herbie, he just doesn't have it any more."

"Go to my room and lie down."

Mavis giggled. A cute little Midwestern *tsatske*. Smart, too. Never underestimate an American woman, Herbie knew. But the men were unraveling. Mr. Legrand was near collapse. Ed Hutzler was flat on his back. Bettenhausen, the professor, was beginning to sag. The bags under his eyes were the size of used teabags. Herbie bought postcards at the kiosk. Bones protesting, his gut forcing him to bend low, his

214

feet shrieking, he returned to the writing table. This time he wrote a card.

Dear Sanford,
Mother and I are having a terrific time with a lot of wonderful people, although I wish she would stop buying everything in sight, *hondling* with merchants, and making me the greatest *shlepper* in Europe.

Love,
Dad

"A fitting will take at least three days, madame."

The Flemingtons were in Klara Rothschild's establishment on the Váci Utca. The woman speaking to them was gray-haired, ivory-skinned, wearing a smart pale blue suit and a double strand of pearls. She was not young, but she possessed a beauty and a bearing that staggered Flemington. She spoke English to them, Hungarian to the seamstresses, French to a young man who was her aide.

"That is ridiculous," Lulu said. "A few adjustments, and you can mail the dress to me at one of our stops."

"Madame Rothschild will not permit anything to be made without three fittings. Particularly so beautiful a gown."

Lulu's eyes had gone to an apple-green long-skirted affair, perfect for cocktail parties at the club. Flemington's mind boggled. *Communism? High fashion under Lenin?* (His picture was not in sight; Madame Rothschild's establishment was far too bourgeois.)

"I wish to speak to her," Lulu said. The old command power colored her voice. The woman was not impressed.

"Madame is not in today. She has gone to Paris to purchase fabrics." She smiled, displaying teeth, Flemington thought, that even the fastidious Dr. Wicker would have found commendable. "We use only French fabrics in our creations."

Bad, bad, Flemington thought. Lulu's nostrils widened. The flesh around them turned white. She inhaled, dug her umbrella into the carpeted floor, and glared at Harry. "I won't accept this. I want you to complain to someone. In the government. At the hotel."

The Flemingtons walked into the Váci Utca. It was closed to traffic. Pedestrians strolled in the late morning sunlight. Again the irritating haze hung in the mild air. The steelworks at Csepel, Flemington remembered.

"The nerve of them," Lulu said. "The absolute nerve of that woman."

"They do things differently, Lu. After all, she did have a point. Isn't there a New York store that says they won't let you wear it unless it fits?"

"But I wanted it."

Flemington said nothing. *She wanted it.* Poor Lu! She was like a patient getting intravenous feeding. Her system demanded the continual infusion of things. Otherwise the emotional metabolism went haywire. It amused him that the Midwesterners made remarks about Herbie and his friends and their buying. But it was Louise Deaver Flemington, an American princess, the purest product of Midwestern wealth, who was the most frenzied buyer. Herbie, Flo and the others were pikers compared to Lu.

Flemington studied the citizens of Budapest (did not Mr. Wattle say they had the highest suicide rate in the world?) strolling the narrow street with its shoddy shops. A Communist notion of Fifth Avenue. The people seemed alert and intelligent. The personnel at the Gellért, the waiters, chambermaids, desk people, had impressed Flemington. Indeed, there appeared little difference between Hungarians and Parisians. Europe was one country. It was the hard luck of the Hungarians to have gotten a raw deal. His single lasting impression of the city was of a frustrated people, waiting for some miracle that would bring them a new car, a new apartment, new clothes, a raise in salary. But would they be happier? Was there any limit to human wants?

"Take me back to the hotel," she said.

Her voice was tremulous. Flemington sighed. They had the flight to Leningrad that afternoon. Baggage problems, check-ins, customs, delays in airports . . .

"I thought we might look at some porcelain, Lu." Flemington recalled an espresso machine they had seen the day before in the elegant pastry shop, the Vörösmarty. It was of Herend, fine porcelain, a beautiful apparatus, pink and gold and white. Virgil told him that Queen Elizabeth had a copy of it at Buckingham Palace. Wouldn't that be something for Lulu to order? To install in their den in Grosse Pointe? Appropriate for a queen of shims, gaskets, and valves. Of course they could not pack it in their luggage (unless there was a portable one-cup model) but it would be worth waiting for.

"Remember the espresso machine yesterday, Lu?" he asked hopefully. "We might try to find one."

"My feet are killing me. I need a drink."

"Sure, Lu. Whatever you say."

They found a cab. He was going to suggest it would be a good time—they had hours to kill at the hotel—to write to Robbie. But the lines had set around Lulu's mouth and her chin was quivering.

At Ferihegy Airport in late afternoon the members of the group were delighted to find a duty-free shop, well stocked with more

216

Havana cigars, liquors, French perfumes and cosmetics. The prices, Flo and Shirl told everyone, were lower than at Vienna or Paris or London. A wave of buying was touched off at once.

"But no *drehdels*," Herbie bellowed from the restaurant. "No more folklore carvings, for Chrissake. I got a sore back from shlepping extra bags already." He nudged Murray Yasuda, nodding toward the corner of the terminal where Pepi was counting the Flemingtons' bags. "See, if you and me were rich we could buy all we want, shlep, shlep, shlep all over the world."

Murray yawned prodigiously. He was wearing an embroidered peasant jacket he had bought in the dollar shop of the hotel. Sandra, dozing on his shoulder, wore a matching peasant dress. They looked like bisque figurines.

"I hear we get all the caviar we can eat on this Rooshian flight," Murray said. "Man, that's for me."

"I hate caviar," Mr. Wattle cried.

"I'll eat yours," Yasuda said. "Don't you ever get tired of chicken soup and well-done steaks?"

"Wouldn't trust any of their food if it came wrapped in sanitized cellophane, with a guarantee from the Ministry of Health. I stick to what's simple and well cooked and what I can recognize."

"Jee-sus," the Japanese moaned. "Don't come to my place in Victorville."

"Never touch Asiatic food."

Herbie looked moodily into Mr. Wattle's hard eyes. With his egg-bald head, his stiff white collar, he seemed to be concocted of plastics and metals, hard, shiny materials. Ai, there was a beauty, Herbie mused, rich, smart, successful, but what . . . ?

Inside the duty-free shop, Mrs. Legrand was comparing Polish and Russian vodkas. Her puckered face studied the labels. She opted for the Polish brand. Weston Legrand, breathing heavily, sat like an outpatient in a city clinic.

"Thank God," Herbie muttered to Huggins, who had just come out of the shop, cradling a liter of scotch.

"For what?" Huggins asked.

"Ma Barker is changing brands. That apricot brandy she was breathing gave me asthma. At least the vodka won't smell."

"Sensitive, Herb?" Huggins asked.

The fat man's eyes vanished in a smile. He enjoyed bantering with Huggins. They understood one another. They fought each other with rocks and bricks and curse words when they were kids, but they grew up understanding one another, made deals, ended up in the same advertising agencies, law firms, insurance companies. Jewish merchant princes gave money to the cardinal. His Eminence put in a good word for Israel.

"Sensitive like a baby, Jim."

"Not you, Herb. Not the old Brooklyn street fighter."

"Fight? Would you believe I was skinny when I was a kid? I was the fastest kid on the block. I won four PAL medals in Prospect Park."

"You look like a fighter to me, Herb."

Shackman tugged at his orange mustache. "Only against people I figured I could beat up. You, you're the fighter."

Huggins spoke out of the side of his mouth. "Don't believe that crap. There's as many yellah Irishmen as there are dumb Jews."

Bonds affirmed, Huggins and Herbie studied their fellow travelers. A. T. Gunthorpe was holding court amid a group of Midwesterners— the Kuchtenbergs, the Forces, the Hutzlers. He was telling a long story about getting "froze up to my belly button" in a duck blind.

"He wasn't after ducks last night," Huggins said slyly. "Pepi talked him out of it. The Hunky cops have been arresting hookers all week, and sometimes the studs who pick 'em up. Something to do with currency speculation."

The talk of lechery stirred Huggins. He was as bad as Gunthorpe. The trouble was that if he cheated he'd always come back to Barbara because no woman could do to him what she could, with that sluggish pink body. He heard Theresa Carrell's musical voice and wondered again about her. When they danced last night, he had marked her as a possibility. A hard woman to con.

"It's all with hand signals," he heard her saying to Ibith Grant. "The Kodály system for teaching music. I'm so glad I found the book. And in English, too."

J.P. turned in his seat. Theresa and the black woman were studying an illustrated booklet. With their hands they imitated the various signals for notes. It intrigued the lawyer. A book that cost a few bucks, some simple gestures, and teaching kids to sing. Worth-while small things in a world full of big-money deals and frauds.

"Who'd you say invented that?" he asked Theresa.

"Kodály," she said. "K, o, d, a, l, y. You don't pronounce the l."

Huggins nodded. He'd heard the name. Maybe at a party at Manny Jabloner's. Ibith Grant made a fist, the signal for do. "Oh, brother," she said. "Will I catch a chorus of 'Right ons' with this one."

"Ah, Mr. Huggins," Virgil said, "may I see you a moment?" He gestured to the lawyer to follow him.

J.P. unlimbered his legs and spoke to Herbie. "Watch the bags, Herbie. Never know the kind of people who turn up in these package tours."

Virgil stopped. "Could you please bring your camera case along, sir?"

The shivering began in Huggins' knees, spread to his crotch, circled his gut a few times, and settled in his chest. "We going to take pictures?"

"A routine customs matter."

"One of those spot checks?" His voice rose hopefully. "Like when they found Hutzler's girlie magazines?"

"Rather like that."

What was he afraid of? It was gone, *gone*, invested in a sure-fire scheme. Gold purchase. Smuggling, actually. But who knew? And who could stop it? As he shouldered the pigskin case, following Pepi's blue-coated figure, he realized that it had to happen.

Huggins said nothing to Virgil, winked at Ed Hutzler and A. T. Gunthorpe, waved at Mrs. Legrand, who was bending low over her dozing husband, whispering in his transparent ear. What would *they* have done with two hundred thou?

Virgil led him behind the Malev Airlines counter. In an ill-lit rear room—dowdy girls in blue uniforms manned phones under the gaze of V. I. Lenin—the escort pointed to a small office enclosed in frosted glass.

"In there?" Huggins asked. "Who? Cops?"

"No, no. An American gentleman. Mr. Ross."

"I don't know any Ross."

"He will explain."

"I won't miss the plane, will I?"

"It will be held for you. Mr. Ross is with the embassy."

The guide walked out—neutral, non-committed. The creep knew everything, Huggins thought. From the kickoff. The game plan. Stole the signals. J.P. knocked on the door. An American accent told him to come in.

A lean man in a gray tweed suit got up from a desk. The scruffy room was part of Malev's socialist operation. Mr. Ross's trim figure and Brooks Brothers neatness put it to shame. The high gloss on the American's cordovan shoes, the alarming white teeth and tanned face, the college ring—all these signs of status unnerved Huggins.

"Mr. Huggins?" he asked.

"That's me."

"John Ross. I'm with the embassy."

They shook hands. Two slender knowledgeable gentlemen. Ross gestured to a chair.

"What's wrong?"

"May I see your passport?"

Huggins reached into his inner pocket, then hesitated. "I'd appreciate knowing what this is about before I consent to even admitting we're in Hungary." He flashed his gin-mill grin. There was no reaction from Ross. J.P. cautioned himself: Amherst or Wesleyan. "I'm a lawyer, you know," J.P. added.

"My apologies, Mr. Huggins. I'm sure nothing is wrong. But we have an inquiry from Interpol and it may concern you."

J.P. made a tent of his fingers and touched the apex to his lips. "Really?"

"I'm sure there's a rational explanation, but it's part of my job to follow up on these things." He indicated a yellow telex in his manicured hands. "Interpol doesn't have offices in the Communist countries, so whenever any query comes about an American citizen, it gets routed to us. In a way it's a protective measure. We feel Americans would prefer us handling these matters than *them*."

"Include me, Mr. Ross."

The functionary stared at the telex. Huggins fished his passport out and moved it across the desk. Almost as if reluctant to check up on such an estimable tourist, Ross compared the passport information to the yellow sheet.

"Wrong man?" J.P. asked.

"I'm not sure. They seem to have the right information. Name, date of birth, passport number. But that doesn't mean anything. They can be wrong. They work out of a big barn near Paris. They're only a clearinghouse. Forget all that James Bond stuff. Most Interpol men don't even carry guns. They're clerks."

"Golly, I was scared for a minute."

"No point in beating around the bush." Ross stared at the yellow sheet. "Mr. Huggins, according to this memo, the Interpol office in Zurich reported that two days ago you tried to make a transaction with a U.S. treasury bill in the amount of ten thousand dollars."

James Patrick said nothing. It was supposed to be secret. The dependable Swiss bank. He pondered his move. The interview with Ross would have no legal force. He was not under oath. He doubted they were recording him—not for anything so trivial. Vagueness was in order. "Oh, that," Huggins said. "What's wrong with that? I was making inquiries at one of their banks. I'm told Americans do that all the time."

"The number on the bill was checked out by Interpol."

"The man I dealt with at the bank said that was routine. Not by Interpol, but by some clearinghouse."

Ross looked gloomy. It was as if Huggins, like Lord Jim, was "one of us"—and had betrayed every well-dressed, well-groomed, successful young American on the rise. "Apparently, after you left Zurich, new information came through, and the matter was referred to Interpol."

"What kind of information?"

"It seems that bill was stolen. There's a tremendous illegal trade in stolen treasury bills, you know."

"I don't know."

"Interpol believes that it's part of a much larger theft. About half a million dollars altogether, in ten-thousand-dollar denominations."

Lenin's metal face over the doorway melted. It became Mario Malfi, low forehead, thick lips, blunt nose, a tribal god born in a cave on Mount Etna. Huggins crossed his legs. He was surprised by his poise.

"Mr. Ross, I will not confirm or deny that I was engaged in a minor currency transaction in Zurich," J.P. said. "But I have no knowledge of stolen treasury bills, or anything approaching the amount you indicated. I'm as shocked as you are."

"I'd imagine you would be. Mr. Huggins, I'm sorry to do this, but they've asked me to ask you where you got that bill and if you're carrying any others with you. They've transmitted the serial numbers to me for checking."

Huggins laughed. "I told you. I don't have nearly that kind of money. In stolen treasury bills or Hungarian forints."

"But you did have a ten-thousand-dollar note? The one you showed to the bank in Zurich?"

J.P. leaned back. A problem there. Baumeister the banker had seen it and kept a record of it. Of course it was long gone, invested in Chahoub's gold-smuggling operation. "I don't have it," J.P. said. "It doesn't matter what I did or did not do with it—"

"How did you get it, Mr. Huggins?" A note of authority crept into Mr. Ross's polite voice. Huggins wondered: what job at the embassy? In a Communist country probably half the staff were in intelligence. Someone had told him that every legal counselor at every embassy was an FBI man.

"Through legitimate channels. Actually, it was a gift. A going-away present."

"From whom?"

Sooner or later someone, somewhere, would establish his relationship to the Malfis. But he was not required to reveal it. With the money gone, not just the note he had shown in Zurich, but the entire load, he was safe. Without the evidence, they could not lay a finger on him. Ah, his lovable in-laws. *Stolen bills!* He wondered how they had gotten them. Probably by mistake; rifling shipments, opening packages. Or had Ralphie picked them up in the Bahamas at a discounted price? Ralphie, the younger brother, always seemed to be running off for "vacations" in obscure islands.

"I'm not required to say. I'm not under oath. I'm an attorney and I know what I have to answer and what I don't have to answer."

"In certain circumstances, Mr. Huggins, diplomatic personnel can assume police duties. I suspect this may be such a circumstance."

"If you only *suspect*, you haven't done your homework. I have a plane to catch. I have ten more days of touring coming to me and I don't like having it upset by this third degree. May I go?"

Ross looked aggrieved. "I'm sorry, Mr. Huggins. I can't force you to do anything. But when you return to the States, you can be assured that Treasury agents will meet you at the airport. The first thing they'll ask is where you got that note."

Huggins got up. "They'll probably know by then. Save me a lot of trouble."

Ross also rose. "You can say no to this too," he said. "But Interpol asked me to look at that." He pointed to the case.

"The camera bag?"

"They seem to think you were carrying the bills in it."

"Be my guest, Mr. Ross." J.P. hefted the tan case from his shoulder and set it on the desk. "Go ahead. Look."

"You don't mind?"

"Not at all. Be careful with the lenses."

The diplomat unzipped the case and removed Huggins' lenses, cameras, the rolls of unused film, the metal containers of exposed film. Then he ran his fingers around the bottom.

"Snap, it's open, snap, it's closed," J.P. said, using the intonations of a commercial announcer.

The interior bottom of the case came loose. Ross lifted it up gingerly.

Huggins, exhilarated by the emptiness of the false lining, went on: "Nothing up my sleeve, nothing in my coat, and nothing in the bottom of the camera case."

"So I see." The man snapped the buttons closed. "I apologize again, Mr. Huggins. I'll have to file a report to Interpol and to the Treasury Department."

"Sure. Want to check my luggage?"

"It won't be necessary. I'll take your word. After all, the only evidence I have is that you tried to pass ten thousand dollars."

"That's no crime."

"It is if you try to buy gold."

"The Swiss don't tell."

"Or if the money is stolen."

"I told you already, it was a present. I have no idea where it came from."

"Mr. Huggins, you are a man of intelligence. I would hate to see you get in trouble. I'll take your word that you had no knowledge of the origin of those notes. If so, you'd do well to turn them over to me, whether you have one, or ten, or twenty, or all fifty. Straighten it out when you get home."

J.P. found it hard to tell the truth. "I don't have them. I don't have any bills."

"Did you have them when you left New York ten days ago? Or did you have them for any period during this tour?"

"I don't have to respond. But the answer is negative." He paused. Which way to jump? Admit to the one note that someone saw? But what about what he had told Moussac? That he had two hundred thousand dollars to unload? How much did they know about him? Damned little, he imagined. All they had done was trace the number on a single bill and learn that it was part of a stolen batch. It could have gone through a half dozen parties before reaching him. Treasury bills were negotiable.

"You had no bills at all?"

"The one I showed to the bank in Zurich."

"Those are usually handled by banks, aren't they? It seems rather odd to be carrying a bill of such denomination in one's hand luggage."

"I've never trusted banks since my father was cleaned out during the depression when the Saloonkeepers and Trolley Car Conductors Bank of the Bronx failed. 'Thank God for Roosevelt,' my old man used to say."

The glibness was lost on Mr. John Ross. But he smiled charitably. "I've done my job. I assume you know that penalties are involved. On the other hand, I'm willing to believe you, and I suggest you look into who gave you that stolen bill and ask him how *he* got it."

They shook hands again. Huggins slung the camera bag over his shoulder.

"If it were only a single bill," Ross said, accompanying him to the door and opening it, "why that fake bottom in the case?"

"Contracts, letters. I don't carry an attaché case."

"Of course."

Virgil was standing some distance from the door. "Flight has been called, Mr. Huggins," he said. His eyes were invisible behind a screen of cigarette smoke. "Everyone is on board."

Two legs of the Three Worlds tour always demanded an extra effort from Virgil. One was the Budapest–Leningrad flight with the stop at

223

Warsaw, the other was the non-stop Moscow–Istanbul flight. The former was over nine hundred miles, the latter over a thousand miles. Neither was an extraordinary distance, but he had learned years earlier, when the Eastern European business began to expand, that the Communist airlines were less than efficient. The planes were safe enough and the crews experienced, the service polite. But no one seemed to be in charge. No one ever had answers. Delays were the rule, not the exception. Departures were late; stopovers prolonged; red tape incessant; and no one seemed to know why. For a precise man like Virgil, these impediments to a smooth tour were maddening. But he usually found himself forgiving the Russians.

"It is difficult to lose one's temper with people who suffered twenty-five million dead fighting Hitler," the guide said to Harry Flemington as the four-engined TU-114 bore them through darkening skies toward Warsaw.

"Twenty-five million?" Flemington asked. Next to him, Lulu slept, deep in seconal. Her frail chest rose and fell under a powder-blue cashmere she had bought in London. Incessantly concerned about her, worried lest she frown, or get a headache, or refuse dinner, he found it hard to envision twenty-five million people dying.

"In Leningrad alone, they now think that as many as a million and a half people died during the siege."

"A million and a half?"

"The two cemeteries are filled with mass graves. Piskarevsky is all mass grave, eight hundred thousand corpses. And three hundred thousand more at Serafimov. Then you must add the military dead. Who knows? Two hundred thousand? More?"

"Aren't there official statistics?"

"No. The Russians are reluctant to relive these disasters. They don't report plane crashes or earthquakes in their press. They are like your Christian Scientists. They think, by not recognizing a catastrophe, perhaps one will come to think it did not occur."

"I thought they were realists. At least, that Communists were."

"Ah, you have put your finger on the difference, Mr. Flemington. The Communists? Yes, they are realists, or think of themselves as such. But the Russian, that brooding Slavic soul? He is still a mystic. Those millions who died—did they die for Marx and Lenin? Or did they die to defend Mother Russia?"

"What do you think?"

"I feel that the Russians fought and died so courageously in spite of Marxism. I could be wrong. Marxists are, after all, well organized. At least they were when the struggle was going on—the Revolution, the war with Hitler. But, as you shall see, they have atrophied. Perhaps they endowed the Russian resistance with a framework. But something else impelled those people to defend Stalingrad and Leningrad and to die in such numbers. It is rather outside the European experience. When one thinks of refined France, and how the French fawned on the Germans, how they collapsed, one must give these Slavs high marks. But! How much of it was political and how much racial? This observer cannot say, except that my prejudice leans toward the racial."

Dr. Wicker joined them. "Are they loosening things up over there?"

"I don't know, Doctor," Virgil said. "There was a writer who was jailed recently, who intimated in a smuggled essay that the political system had triumphed."

"That's awful," Cornelia said. "With all that money we spend on the Voice of America?"

"What the man meant was that this acceptance of the status quo, this day-by-day existence without freedom, was being bred into the bones of the Russian people and that it will take a miracle to change the system."

"Rather depressing," Bettenhausen said.

"And too pessimistic," Arnold Wicker added. "Look, I read all the time in the newspapers about opposition groups—writers, scientists, intellectuals—who are agitating for free speech, free press, the right to strike and dissent and leave the country."

"Oh, they exist, Dr. Wicker," Virgil said. "But they are under constant surveillance. The regime regards them as a freakish group of intellectuals with no base among the masses. And the regime is probably right. You see, Doctor, totalitarian regimes have learned that they stay in power to the extent that they supply material needs. Hence the emphasis on food, apartments, cars, cosmetics, clothing. They feel that so long as they improve goods they can get away with anything."

Dr. Wicker shook his head. "It won't stop people like the ones I was reading about, Professor Marmaladov and the others. I forget what their group is called."

Virgil responded: "I have read about them too. But I am a European. I have been in and out of too many jails. Without the bombs and planes of America, and the twenty-five million Russians who died, Hitler would be in control of Europe. It would shock you to learn of the support he had, the enthusiasm that greeted him, and not only in Germany. We walk on thin ice, sir."

The dentist frowned, loosened his tie. As a man who lived in perpetual hope of things getting better, he was irritated by Virgil's misanthropy. "But don't ordinary people get sick and tired of living in a cage?"

"Not if they are well fed," Virgil said.

The stewardess came down the aisle with second servings of caviar. She was a huge woman with a coy smile and thick make-up.

"Vill be lending Varsaw vun hour," she said cheerfully. "Lest chence caviar."

Virgil spoke to her in Russian. The girl laughed loudly.

"What did you say?" Bettenhausen asked.

"I told her that as soon as our discussion got political she came with caviar and vodka, a Russian trick."

"But the people I read about," Wicker said, "those scientists and writers. They meet, and they publish, and they're still protesting."

"Up to a point, Dr. Wicker, only up to a point. Their lives are limited. They are under threat at all times. There is a difference."

Russian crackled over the loudspeaker. Bettenhausen had the feeling he was on some ancient passenger train. The appointments in the cabin were old-fashioned—plush upholstery, small carriage lamps for reading, wobbly chandeliers.

"Fasten seat belts," the guide translated. "We are landing in Warsaw."

As Virgil had feared, there was an unexplained two-hour delay at the Warsaw airport. His people began to fret. Fatigue was rampant. A few looked dreadful, notably Mr. Legrand, Herbie Shackman, and two violet-haired Midwestern wives, neither of whose names he could remember.

"What's the holdup?" Herbie asked as they settled into chairs in the waiting room.

"I am afraid I don't know," Pepi said.

Virgil sensed growing anxieties, the result of too much traveling, too much information, too many changes of venue, food, and water. A tour escort had to be alert to these. They would not get to Leningrad until dark, which was just as well. He would skip the bus tour, get them to the hotel for dinner and a night's rest. No night-clubbing, no dancing.

He checked again on an estimated departure, was told by the Aeroflot girl that she wasn't certain (no one ever was) that it would be no less than two hours, and retired to the drab restaurant for a cup of tea.

From his vantage point, he could see Flo and Shirl emerge from the duty-free shop clutching Polish peasant dolls. It was not a total loss.

After the delay over the Flemingtons' baggage—Virgil got his exhausted people aboard a new Intourist bus at Leningrad airport. It was ten-thirty at night. They were three hours behind schedule.

"What are those domes out there?" Mr. Wattle called out.

"That is an observatory, sir," Virgil said.

"What kind of an observatory?"

"Murray, go stuff an egg roll into his mouth, willya?" Herbie muttered.

"Wouldn't stop him."

"Astronomical, sir," Virgil said. He chatted in Russian with the driver. The highway was dark. Fields, factories, a sense of open space. And beyond, stretching all the way to the Pacific, the enigmatic country. Who could understand them? By comparison, Americans were as simple as the drip-dry shirts they wore.

"What kind of astronomical?" Mr. Wattle persisted.

"It is called Pulkova Observatory," Pepi said. "The area is Pulkova Heights. It is where the German artillery was stationed to bombard Leningrad. I believe the instruments are used to track Russian satellites today."

"Hah!" Mr. Wattle shouted. "Wouldn't take their word for anything! They're spying on us from those domes! Spying all the time!"

"Shaddap," Herbie yelled. "Give yourself parade rest, *shmuck.*"

Mr. Wattle did not hear him. He was peering out his window, apparently looking for the telescope that was trained on him personally.

In the lobby of the Baltiiskaya Hotel on Nevsky Prospekt, there was another delay while Virgil roused porters to bring in the luggage and then engaged in a dispute over room keys with a surly woman behind the desk.

There was a heavy gloom in the lobby. To Theresa Carrell, it seemed mystical, something out of one of those plays or movies where everyone discovers he is dead, bound for a distant shore. Fatigue, she told herself, weariness resulting from the long enervating day. Her eyes sought Harry. He was seated in an overstuffed chair, looking gentlemanly, as he always did. Lulu, frigid with disdain, was seated opposite him. Dark glasses hid her misery.

"Stop looking at him," Ibith whispered.

"Can't help it. He sort of sticks out in these surroundings, don't you think? With the suede hat and the two-hundred-dollar jacket?"

"You're hopeless. You keep talking like that, I'll arrange for Horace T. Wattle to batter down your door tonight."

"I might be civil to him."

Flo and Shirl were drifting toward a shop in the lobby—it was closed for the night, but a display window showed a collection of

227

lacquerware, copperwork, ivory carvings—when Virgil, tinkling a handful of keys, turned from the desk.

"There is a snack bar open till midnight, ladies and gentlemen, and also buffet on each floor," he said. "Now for our room keys. Mr. Hutzler. Mr. Kuchtenberg. Mr. Shackman . . ."

Halfway through his labors, a short man, wearing a tan topcoat two sizes too big, and a tan cap that hid the upper part of his face, emerged from the cavernous lobby and approached Pepi. He spoke in Russian. The guide responded. He seemed annoyed. The colloquy lasted only a few moments. Then the man, floating inside the tentlike coat, vanished.

Dr. Wicker, waiting for his room key, thought he heard something familiar in the conversation. A name? word? Suddenly he remembered Veg's words—Dr. Borkin would wear a light brown cap and coat. As he took his key, he asked Virgil: "What did that fellow want?"

"Mr. Wattle. Father Konay . . ."

"That fellow who spoke to you . . ."

Virgil halted his distribution of keys. "Some local character. A money-changer, some such thing. Russian hotels are filled with them, working a little private enterprise. Some will buy the clothes off your back."

"But . . . did he ask for someone?"

"He wanted to know if there was someone on the tour who knew a Dr. Borkin. It's a trick they use to get access to Americans."

"Oh." Wicker was stunned. He dared not admit to Virgil his mission. He recalled the system of passwords. Only Imre Veg had known it. "What did you tell him?"

"I told him to get out before I report him."

"But . . . do you know him?"

"No. Just one of these hotel hangers-on. Mr. Yasuda. Mr. Bettenhausen. Ah . . . Mr. Huggins? Where is he?"

"I'll take it," Barbara said.

Across the lobby, J.P. had found a copy of the *Herald Tribune*. It was three days old, the same paper he had seen in Vienna. No luck there. He would probably have to wait until they got to Turkey to find out about the passage of the S.S. *Lautaro*.

228

Day 11: Leningrad. An entire day to absorb the magnificence of the Soviet Union's "window on the West." In the morning, a bus tour of the major sites—the Admiralty, the Bronze Horseman, St. Isaac's Cathedral, the Neva River, the Kazan Cathedral, the Winter Palace and Palace Square, the Hermitage, Decembrist Square, the Peter and Paul Fortress, the cruiser Aurora, the Yussupof Palace.

In the afternoon, Three Worlds offers several options—a boat trip along the Neva, or a visit to the Peterhof Palace, or a return to the Hermitage, for a look at one of the world's most treasured collections of art! In the evening—ballet or opera at the Kirov Theater.

"Towards west is Gulf of Finland, Kotlin Island, and town of Kronstadt. In Russian Revolution sailors from Kronstadt were fighters for revolutionary victory."

The Three Worlds group was in the top of the dome of St. Isaac of Kiev. The air was clear and tangy. They could see for miles around. The guide was a chubby, thick-legged woman with scrubbed features and a wide smile. Her name was Irina.

"Say, I want a picture of that," Murray Yasuda said. He raised his Nikon, turned the focus.

"Please, no photographs," the guide said. "Is signs all over, no photographs."

"Hey, that's chicken," the Japanese protested.

"*Shah, boychik,*" Herbie said. "She thinks you're Chou En-lai."

"Hah, very funny, sir," the woman laughed. "He is not but still no pictures."

"Look, please, out there," the guide went on. "Is whole of Neva River delta. Beautiful. Is Leningrad's river."

The Americans absorbed the view, then followed the girl along the railing inside the church dome. Virgil was pleased to see that most had recovered from last night's trip. Only Mr. Legrand was missing. Mr. Shackman and Mr. Hutzler still complained of diarrhea, and Mrs. Grant told him the bed was unsleepable—narrow, too soft, and with a hole in the middle. The black woman did so little complaining that Virgil made it a point to have a new bed moved in. Dr. Wicker looked out of sorts. His camera dangled unused from his neck, and he showed little interest in the surroundings.

"Ladies and gentlemen," the guide said, "long street going other way is Nevsky Prospekt, biggest street in Leningrad. Later you will see beautiful shops, restaurants, buildings."

"So what's to buy?" Flo asked.

"Caviar and vodka," Shirl said. "They can keep it."

"Squares below are St. Isaac's and Decembrist Square, where is beautiful Admiralty Building, with steeple and golden roof. Admiralty was built in 1704 by Peter the Great, who is builder St. Petersburg."

"He used Italian architects," Bettenhausen announced.

"Yes, is true," Irina said. "But Russian workmen, best workmen in world."

"What was the fellow's name?" Bettenhausen asked. "Rossi?"

"Yes," the guide said. She was mildly annoyed. "We have in Leningrad street for him. Architect Rossi Street."

"And another fellow. Rastrelli." Bettenhausen managed to look vaguely Italian. He seemed to enjoy extolling the talents of Latins at the expense of Slavs.

"Gentleman knows much about Leningrad history," Irina said. "Is professor?"

"He's from Hollywood," Mr. Wattle yelled.

"Gollywood!" the guide cried. "You know Gumphrey Bogart?"

"What are the other steeples?" Rosie Wicker asked.

"Admiralty. Peter Paul Fortress. Engineer's Castle. Look after Admiralty. Winter Palace, which is where Germitage Art Gallery is, then Smolny Monastery, headquarters for Revolution in 1917. Inside is Lenin's room, museum today."

"No room for Trotsky?" Bettenhausen asked. "He lived there too."

"Trotsky never live there."

"Oh, but he did," Bettenhausen said. "No matter. He's an unperson." He shook his head. "Why is it that all I can think of in Leningrad is Trotsky?"

"Maybe it's because they neglect him," Dr. Wicker said.

"Perhaps. I almost feel we owe him a bit of homage. One of history's grand inexplicable figures. Woke up one morning, this bespectacled, pamphleteering, superintellectualized son of Jewish farmers, and decided that, in addition to everything else, he was a general, a war commissar. And what does he proceed to do? Whip the tar out of all those czarist officers."

Dr. Wicker was silent. If Trotsky had become a military leader overnight, as Bettenhausen contended, what was to prevent Arnold Wicker, D.D.S., orthodontist, from turning into a master spy? The letter in his inner pocket was burning. In two days he was supposed to find Dr. Borkin at the Queen of Bells. And who was the man in the topcoat and cap in the lobby of the Baltiiskaya Hotel? Was it Borkin? Or a confederate of the scientist?

"Leningrad is young city," Irina said as the group stood in the thin sunlight admiring Peter the Great. "Was founded only in 1703 by Peter the Great. Is most beautiful city in Soviet Union. Is also one of five Geroic Cities—"

"What did she say?" Mrs. Hutzler asked.

"Can't hear a word," her husband answered. He fiddled with his hearing aid.

"Heroic, *Heroic*," Mrs. Legrand said. Fortified with a bottle of vodka purchased in Warsaw, she tingled with energy. "They have trouble with the letter *h*. It comes out *g*. Didn't you hear her say Gollywood?"

"Yes, excuse me, Heroic City." Irina brushed her blonde hair back. "In addition Leningrad, are also Heroic Cities Odessa, Kiev, Sebastopol, and Volgograd—"

Flemington whispered to his wife: "I hate to ask her. But was it Heroic when it was Stalingrad?"

Lulu made no response. She rested on her furled umbrella. Harry had the feeling she would not last the day, perhaps not even the morning. He would have to huddle with Virgil. Surely there were items of great value worth buying in Leningrad. Was Fabergé available?

"People in Leningrad showed bravery in nine-hundred-day siege," Irina said. She had raised her voice. "Die here more than million Russian people, all ages, all kinds, civilian and military. Starvation, bombardment, disease, cold. And Nazis surround city. More than hundred fifty thousand shells fall on Leningrad from big German guns, and from planes more than hundred thousand bombs. But Leningrad does not surrender. City received Order of Lenin. In Piskarev is carving on wall of cemetery—'*Let no one forget, let nothing be forgotten.*'"

Two tears trickled from the girl's eyes. They came so unexpectedly that most of the tourists did not notice.

"You believe what she said about the siege?" Flemington asked Mr. Wattle.

"These people have a custom of killing each other in great numbers. Nothing new to them. They die like flies."

Harry sighed. "It's not quite like that. I'm sure they didn't enjoy starving and being bombed and dying. I'll bet that girl lost some of her family during the siege."

"I suppose they suffered terribly. But they brought it on themselves."

Harry turned his head. There was a time when he would have pursued the argument, nailed the likes of Horace T. Wattle to a drying board with facts. But he was weary of disputation. Increasingly he avoided confrontation.

"Feel okay, darling?" he asked Lulu.

"I'm a little headachy."

"Want an aspirin? Or a BC?"

"Nothing, dear," Lulu said. "Just open the window. I need air."

Flemington obliged. He glanced to the back of the bus. Herbie and Murray had lit up cigars. They were far enough away, he hoped, so as not to offend Lulu. But the Hutzlers got up and moved several seats forward.

"We go now to cross Palace Bridge and visit Peter and Paul Fortress," Irina said. Her eyes were dry. "Big fort, also beginning 1703 by . . ."

"Peter the Great!" a chorus led by Herbie, Murray, and Si shouted.

The bus moved through St. Peter's Gate. They could see the soaring gilt spire of the basilica. Atop it was a statue of an angel holding a cross.

"Look, please, gentleman from Gollywood," Irina said. "Statue of Angel."

"I see," Bettenhausen said. "It is quite beautiful."

"By another of gentleman's Italians. You know name?"

"Rastrelli?"

"Almost correct. Rinaldi. Easy to remember, architects all with R. Rossi, Rinaldi, Rastrelli."

Huggins nudged his wife to rise and start for the exit of the bus. "See what your relatives accomplished? Take a bow, Barbs. They built the city of Leningrad." He tweaked her girdled rear as they inched down the aisle.

"I saw that," Herbie said. "I'm jealous."

"Be my guest," J.P. said. He felt liberated. Now all he needed was a *Herald Tribune* with news of the S.S. *Lautaro's* departure. Luck was with him: how else explain his shedding of the stolen bills a step ahead of the sheriff?

"Building there, opposite entrance, is *Monetny Dvor*," the girl said. She spoke in Russian to Virgil, then apologized to the tourists. "Always forget English word. Mint."

232

"Yeah!" Herbie yelled. "Where the *gelt* is! How about free samples?"

"No, sir, is no gifts of rubles permitted," she said. "Please, no exchanging money except in official places. People come to you on street or in hotel, bad people, do not give dollars for rubles. Is serious crime against people of Soviet Union. Very bad for people who do this."

Dr. Wicker, trailing the party—he had begun to take a photograph of the Winter Palace, then lost interest because the light was poor—thought about the man in the oversized coat who wanted to know about Borkin. A money-changer, Virgil had said. He had said it too offhandedly, and the dentist suddenly felt that Virgil had lied to him. But why?

The group returned to the hotel for lunch and a rest before resuming the tour.

Flemington was unable to absorb any more information, any more dates, any more history. The bloody past of Russia interested him less than the recent past of Harry Flemington. BC powders. The overnight desk. His recurrent headaches. And coming to Terry in the morning . . . How did his contemptible ambition and his fear of economic deprivation drive him away from Theresa and into the arms of Louise Deaver, who, when he met her was already a veteran of drying-out sessions in expensive sanitaria?

Lulu was in the bathroom, running both faucets so that her discreet tinkling could not be heard—not even by her husband. The gloomy room with its drab trappings filled him with despair. The area near the curtained window was piled high with their loot—cashmere, perfume, silver, pewter, porcelain, antique brass, silk ties, Lulu's accumulated treasure. For a moment Harry was grateful to Communism for producing so few things worth buying. Poor bastards! Lives of perpetual frustration. And a million and a half dead in the nine hundred days of Leningrad.

Lulu was stretched on the bed. She asked for a drink. He convinced her mineral water would be better. It was warm, salty and fizzy, in a dark green bottle with a re-usable hinged top, such as Flemington had not seen since his boyhood in Minneapolis: the type Swedish farmers used for cider.

"It's full of vitamins, Lu," Flemington said. "Anything that tastes that strong must be."

"What are we doing this afternoon?"

"There's a boat ride on the Neva. Some folks are going to the

233

Hermitage to see the paintings. They rushed us in and out this morning."

"No paintings. That woman will be there with that bore from the movies and that awful dentist."

"And there's a bus trip to a palace outside of town."

"This is the worst country I've ever seen. There's nothing to buy."

"I asked Virgil. He said there isn't any more Fabergé available in Russia. It's all gone."

Her slender hands went to her temple: a severe blow. "Ask him again. Ask about ikons. Or old silver."

"Yes, dear." Flemington slumped deep in a prickling chair. It was mud-brown, matching the heavy drapes. "Will you be feeling like some lunch later?"

"No. Ask the concierge about shopping. Call the American Consulate if necessary. I'm going to write a letter about that man Virgil. He has been no help to me at all."

"It isn't worth fretting over. I'm told that Moscow has excellent shops. Virgil says there are special places where people bring antiques. Why don't we take a trip this afternoon and save the shopping for Moscow?"

Flemington heard footsteps in the corridor. Loud, laughing voices. People joking, teasing, flirting. Herbie was kibitzing Dr. Grant. "You hear about the Polish surgeon who won the Nobel prize, Doc?" And Ibith and Henderson laughing before Herbie's punch line: "*He made the first hemorrhoid transplant.*"

"May I join some of our party for lunch?" Flemington asked Lulu.

"Yes. But do not sit with you-know-who."

"I won't, dear. I haven't even thought about her."

"And bring me some tea and toast."

Flemington brushed his hair and stepped into the corridor. It smelled of disinfectant, a powerful sinus-clearing Russian brand. Ahead of him, he saw his fellow tourists walking toward the elevator. Theresa was walking with the Bettenhausens.

"I kissed a Polish lancer, too, before he died," Bettenhausen growled.

"Betts, you're digging." Cornelia shook her head. "Garbo to Mel Douglas in *Ninotchka.*"

Flemington's chest heaved. He had gone as far as he could, denied himself too much. He was going to make love to Theresa. He was going to surprise her in her room. It would be the way it was twenty-five years ago in the old house on Tenth Street near the university. Passion would free him. Had not Terry come looking for him? She thought—or so she claimed—that seeing him, chained to Lulu, had changed her mind. No longer pursuing, she would be pursued. Their bodies joined again, he would be encouraged to break the news to Lulu. (When they got back to Detroit, of course.) He would leave her. He intended to marry Theresa.

"How do you make a statue of an elephant?" Yasuda shouted at Herbie.

"Tell me, tell me, Father, how do you make a statue of an elephant?"

"Get a great big stone and carve away everything that don't look like an elephant!"

Flemington, walking slowly after them, felt like Murray's elephant emerging from stone. The true Harry Flemington was ready to appear. The surrounding stone would be chipped away. At forty-eight, he was ready to be reborn.

Lunch in the hotel proved a disaster. All that seemed to be available was a rubbery veal cutlet. It came cold, surrounded by a wilted salad with a suspicious odor. There was caviar for a first course and black bread and red Georgian wine, rather like a Burgundy, according to Bettenhausen. But the inedible cutlet ended lunch.

Bettenhausen rumbled. "These meals are like F. Scott Fitzgerald's life after Princeton. It's all anticlimax after the first course. One must live on caviar and brown bread."

The menu was stained. The women explored it for a dessert, and decided on ice cream. Finding the waiter was an exercise in frustration. Virgil had warned them about disappearing waiters and advised them to be patient. The guide himself was not in sight. He apparently knew of a better place to lunch; his tourists were trained not to disturb his privacy.

"I give up," Dr. Wicker said after a circuit of the dining room. "The secret police probably picked him up. Nobody else will take our order, not even the captain. It's like Pepi said. No one's in charge."

"I want ice cream, and I stay here till I get ice cream," Rosie said. "I get it, or I go out and put holes in the cruiser *Aurora* this afternoon."

The dentist draped two cameras over his neck. "I've had enough. The caviar and bread will hold me. I want to take some pictures on the Nevsky Prospekt. Warren, care to join me?"

"Excellent idea," Bettenhausen said. "Ladies. We will meet you in the lobby in what . . . ?"

"Oh, twenty minutes," Wicker said.

Rose-Anne looked questioningly at her husband. A model of pa-

235

tience, Arnie seemed a bit unstrung or, as their son would have said, spaced out. Was it possible that he was bothered by all those sets of teeth in Connecticut? Before lunch he had sent three more postcards to his more serious cases of open bite and malocclusion.

The broad busy avenue, Leningrad's main street, swarmed with people. Bettenhausen shaded his eyes. "Amazing. One-thirty in the afternoon, and all of Russia seems to be out window shopping."

"I guess it's the fine weather. Europeans just spend more time in the streets than we do. These poor buggers have that endless winter to contend with. I guess they get the sun while they can."

Bettenhausen consulted his guidebook. "Let's walk this way. Toward Herzen Street. There are supposed to be some interesting neo-classical buildings here."

Dr. Wicker began to take photographs, changing lenses, switching a filter, studying his exposure meter with grave concentration. Bettenhausen admired the younger man. He liked his efficiency, his willingness to learn. And he and his pretty wife were, Bettenhausen admitted to Cornelia, the best audience he had ever played to.

"Ah, this must be the Stroganov Palace," Bettenhausen said. "Baroque. Rastrelli again. Gilded sculptures and white colonnades overlooking the banks of the Moika."

They crossed the street. Dr. Wicker affixed a wide angle lens to his camera and took several photos of the Stroganov Palace. "Looks like we can walk in. There's a garden inside."

A crumbling sarcophagus stood in the garden; two hideous sphinxes. Bettenhausen read: "Garden of the former Festival Court . . . hmmmm . . . not much worth seeing here. Shall we move on?"

Wicker hesitated. Ever since the incident in the hotel lobby, the man inquiring about Borkin, he felt the need to confide in someone. Was Bettenhausen the right man? In two days he would be meeting Borkin and delivering the letter. A routine matter, Leland had assured him. Done all the time. Co-operative citizens helping their government.

Puffing, Bettenhausen sat on a stone bench in the garden. "Can't say I have a fix on this city. The architecture bothers me."

"It's quite beautiful," the dentist said.

"But it isn't Russian. It's . . . what, French, Italian. All that neo-classical show. Façades, columns, plinths. It isn't Russian. It isn't anything. They are not a visual people. Russians have no sense of form."

Wicker sat next to him. "Warren, how in blazes have you remembered so much?"

Bettenhausen shrugged. "Cursed with recall. Did you know that Eleonora Duse died in Pittsburgh?"

"I don't even know who she was."

"No matter. Ask me someday to tell you how I know she died in Pittsburgh."

"Look . . . I have to take you into my confidence," Wicker said suddenly.

"Oh?" The white eyebrows bristled.

"I shouldn't do this, but I've got to talk to someone about it."

"Go on, my boy. Maury Fallsberg invited me to board meetings because he liked the way I listened."

"You do more than that, Warren. And did more for him, I'm sure."

"What is it? Some personal crisis?"

"I'm not sure. What I tell you has to be kept secret."

"Of course, Arnold." Bettenhausen yawned enormously. As his jaw widened, Arnie Wicker peered into his mouth.

"By golly, you've got one of those new implants in back. I never noticed it."

Bettenhausen shook his head. "Good God, Arnold, you start by saying you have some dark secret to reveal to me and end up by studying my dental work."

"Can't help it. But it is a beauty. I bet your dentist anchored the whole bridge on that implant. Is it the kind with the claw foot that they drive right into the jawbone? You remember what the X rays looked like?"

Bettenhausen stared at the younger man in disbelief. Was he kidding? How serious could his problem be if he found time to talk about corrective dentistry? "I don't recall. If it truly interests you, I'll put you in touch with Dr. Yarosh in Sherman Oaks. He is almost as intoxicated with his profession as you are."

"Sorry."

A uniformed guard, an old man in a shapeless suit, ambled by and nodded at them. He had one arm. Veteran of the siege of Leningrad? Bettenhausen hoped the old retainer would not open his mouth and reveal rotting stumps. Wicker might start working on them.

"Do you remember that speech Virgil made in Vienna about not smuggling letters into Communist countries?" the dentist asked. "It was for my benefit."

"I don't follow you."

"Warren, the CIA has asked me to deliver a letter to a scientist in Moscow. But I don't know whether I should. It's all screwed up."

Bettenhausen's eyes became horizontal slits. He rubbed them with

237

his knuckles. "Just a moment. You say you are acting as a courier for our intelligence? You do this regularly?"

"No, no. It started when this guy Leland got hold of me at JFK before we left. He said they do it all the time, find reliable citizens like me to deliver messages. Scientific data, he said."

"That's all he said?"

"Yes. He said it was no big deal. I wasn't supposed to tell a soul."

Bettenhausen scratched his beard. "Something's happened to give you second thoughts?"

"Not exactly." Dr. Wicker's lips tightened. He rotated his head, as if trying to get his thoughts in orderly fashion. "People have been sort of sidling up to me since then. Maybe it's my imagination."

"You think you may be in danger?"

"I doubt it. But maybe this fellow Borkin is. Or will be."

"Start at the beginning, Arnold."

Speaking in a low voice, Wicker told Bettenhausen about the meeting with Leland, the article in the *Herald Tribune* that had started him wondering whether Borkin might be associated with the Humanists, the attempt by the agent in West Berlin to draw information from him, Virgil's warning on the bus, and the contact with Imre Veg in Budapest—the only person who knew the sports code.

"Then there was Virgil last night, shooing away this guy in a coat that didn't fit and a big cap, before I could talk to him," the dentist said.

"What did our *cicerone* say?"

"The man had asked if anybody on the tour knew Dr. Borkin, or was related to him."

"You didn't pursue it?"

"He was gone. Virgil chased him, said he was a pest who wanted to change currency." The dentist looked at his shoes. "I have some doubts about Virgil, let me tell you. A great guy, but boy, if ever there was a natural for a spy."

"Unlikely, Arnold. Our guide is too happy in his work to ruin it with errand-running for an intelligence operation. He's had his share of European danger. I think he knows nothing about Borkin or your message."

They walked through the garden, through the Stroganov Palace, and back onto the Nevsky Prospekt. An ice cream vendor was in business. The two men stopped for vanilla cones and strolled toward the hotel. Bettenhausen suggested they walk a bit farther and look at Our Lady of Kazan, which housed the Anti-Religious Museum.

"Leland, Leland," Bettenhausen said. "Name means nothing.

238

Mankiewicz and Welles had a character named Jed Leland in *Citizen Kane*. Played by Joseph Cotten."

"Who knows if it was his name? But I did see it on his card."

"He could have been a fake."

"He told me to call the FBI office in New York and that they would vouch for him."

"Did you?"

"No. I believed him. There was this letter asking me to help the government . . ."

"And what bothers you are these apparent attempts to abort your mission?"

The dentist laughed. "Yes, like they've got their signals crossed. The guy in West Berlin also had an ID card. I don't recall his name. Clyde? Claude? Maybe we should go to the American Embassy in Moscow."

"Embassy," Bettenhausen said reflectively. "That would be an obvious move. They would have to contact Washington. The intelligence branches don't always let the diplomats know what they're up to, you know. You might get stuck in Moscow and have to do some explaining while the tour went on."

"No way. I paid for this tour and I won't miss a thing."

"This whole affair may be in your imagination, Arnold. You did get a confirmation on the mission from that Hungarian?"

"A shifty character, that Veg." They walked into the cathedral. It was dark and mysterious. Four rows of columns supported the dome. The walls and pillars were hung with trophies of the Napoleonic wars. Ikons abounded, glittering, gleaming, bursting with reds and blues and purples, colors too passionate for faith.

"Shifty?" Bettenhausen asked.

"I don't know. A friend of Virgil's. He's the one who told me that the meeting place with Borkin had been changed. From the Lenin Institute to the Queen of Bells."

"Let's go down to the crypt," the Hollywood man said. "The book says that's where they keep the exhibits. I'm in an iconoclastic mood today."

In the basement the two men paused before a group of life-sized models of monks torturing victims. One was in the stock. Another sat on a chair spiked with nails. A third was being crushed under weights. In a fireplace, branding irons glowed.

Headquarters of the Inquisition of the 16th Century.

"I guess they take this seriously," Wicker said.

"Religion is the opium of the people. You know what Hemingway said about Marx's dictum."

239

"Don't recall."

"He always thought marijuana was the opium of the people."

They walked past paintings of leering priests. "Shabby stuff," Bettenhausen said. "I'm no Christer, but this Madame Tussaud gimcrackery doesn't change the world for the better. You replace one group with another."

They walked out of the church. "My neck was getting itchy in there," Wicker said. "I have a wife, three kids, a mortgage, and a lot of expenses. They still jug foreigners in this country, Warren. Sure, I'm just running an errand. But whose? And why? And suppose they want to make a case out of it?"

They walked toward the Baltiiskaya Hotel. The broad avenue was more crowded than ever. Buses lumbered in file, motorized elephants.

"Permit an old Hollywood hand to take over," Bettenhausen said. "You are in no danger. Borkin may be. We don't know. I don't believe this ridiculous story about scientific information. But there are enough warning buzzers sounding to make us proceed cautiously."

"Maybe we should just open the letter and read it."

"No, no, Arnold. You may be under surveillance. That's why it is good that you enlisted me. Now listen to me. In my early days in Hollywood I developed a reputation as what they call a *constructionist*. I always fancied that the title meant I wore paint-spattered coveralls, a white Johns-Manville cap, and carried brushes, rules, T-square, and trowel in my outsized pockets. But no. It meant merely that I was skilled at developing plots. I shall bring my talents as constructionist to bear on this matter."

"I came to the right man."

"Let me mull these facts overnight. Tomorrow we'll be in Moscow. I have contacts there. We will eschew the American Embassy for the time being. We shall have a day to unravel this before your rendezvous with Borkin, correct?"

"You sound a little like Tom Sawyer trying to arrange Jim's escape."

"That is not especially flattering, Arnold."

Wicker began to wonder. Had he done the right thing in telling Bettenhausen? What did he know about the bearded man, except that he was erudite, full of movie trivia, an expert on cheese, and a frustrated director?

"Cheer up, Arnold," Bettenhausen said.

"Oh, I'm cheerful."

"Your long face betrays you. There are only two possibilities. Either Mr. Leland was a legitimate American agent and what he told you

240

was the truth: a message for Borkin. Or he is a Soviet agent trying to get Borkin into trouble. We can find out by some nosing about in Moscow tomorrow."

"Who's this contact of yours?"

Bettenhausen explained. Four years ago a group of Russian film personalities—directors, writers, actors—had visited Hollywood. Bettenhausen, by far the most cultured man on the Fallsberg lot, was assigned the job of liaison man. He loved the chore. The Russians loved him.

"You aren't going to ask one of those Russian movie people?" Wicker was aghast.

"No. I have an ace in the hole. Ah, Virgil summons us. I'll explain later."

Pepi had set up an efficient program. Those who wanted to take the boat ride on the Neva had been dispatched earlier. Those wishing to tour the Hermitage under the guidance of Bettenhausen and Mavis Hutzler would be dropped at Palace Square. The remaining members—people who did not choose to rest or shop—would be bused to the Peterhof, twenty-five miles from the city.

Huddled in Palace Square as if to protect each other from the enormity of Russia, they listened to Irina talk about the Revolutions of 1905 and 1917. When the girl mentioned Father Gapon ("was bad priest, traitor, lie to people") who had led the marchers in 1905, a few tourists looked at Father Konay, expecting a comment. But the priest had never heard of Gapon and admitted his ignorance.

"They should stay out of politics," Mr. Wattle shouted. "I hate these young ones with their beards, picketing and stirring colored people up. It's the clergy keep telling them they're as good as us."

Everyone found it important to crane their necks and stare at Alexander's column and avoid looking at Dr. and Mrs. Grant. The black people said nothing. Strolling around the endless square, in a strange city, they felt isolated. A rude joke from Herbie would have helped at the moment. Sometimes, the physician reflected, it paid to be a funky, bad-ass, illiterate nigger, one who would have responded to the Washington man in appropriate terms.

"Peterhof was biggest summer residence of Czar," the local guide said. He was a young, lank-haired student. "All nobles do is build more palaces, people get poorer and hungrier. We go in palace soon, but first walk in park."

They drove past a pond in which rested jewel-like islands, each bearing ornate pavilions. Late summer flowers were still in bloom.

241

"First villa is copy of Pompeii in Italy," the guide said. "No time to visit today, but is decorated with tiles and statues from Pompeii."

"They treated themselves good," A. T. Gunthorpe said. "Yeah, ole Czar he knew where it was at."

"They shot him when they were ready," Mr. Wattle said. "Neither of them were worth a hoot in hell—Czar or Bolsheviks."

The park was cool, the lawns soft and green. There were more fountains, more pavilions. Once, Dr. Grant recalled, he had seen a documentary film of the Czar and his family at play—possibly right here in this park. He recalled men in white jackets, girls in flowing white dresses, people playing croquet, tag, boating on a small lake. The images had remained frozen in his mind.

"Façade of Great Palace," the guide said, "is three hundred meters long. Plenty room for Czar and relatives, friends, nobles."

Huggins, moving away from Barbara—she was whining again about her feet—came abreast of the Grants. "You wonder why in hell people accepted this garbage for so long."

"Gets bred in them," the doctor said. "Need a geneticist to answer that one."

"I dunno," J.P. said. "I'm not surprised they had a revolution. I'm just surprised it took 'em that long."

"Well, what did it get them?" Herbie boomed. "A *toit in bankas*."

"That sounds bad," Ibith laughed.

"It is. Look. Lousy food. No money. Shoes that wear out. No life in these people. No sex."

"Don't be too sure," Huggins said. "I read somewhere they go at it like minks."

"How do you know so much?" Barbara whined. "And what kinda way is that to talk?"

"Read it in John Gunther," J.P. said. "He says sex is rampant in the U.S.S.R."

"Sounds like a song," Herbie shouted. "'Oh, sex is rampant in the U.S.S.R.! If you like to *kitzel*, you will surely go far!'" He went into a buck and wing in front of the statues of Adam and Eve.

"Please, mister," the guide said. "Is *ne kulturny* to dance in public place, not nice."

"If she says stop, I stop," Herbie said. "They catch you dancing, it's off to Siberia. You don't believe me, Ibith? That's what got Trotsky in trouble. He was a peachy dancer, but he couldn't run fast."

At mealtimes a vigorous competition took place to see who sat with the Grants. Virgil was not quite sure how it started, but everyone appeared to be striving to dine with the black couple. As a result, Dr. Grant and Ibith tried to arrive early and sit at a long table so that they could accommodate a group of their companions.

"We're the prize packages," Ibith said in a low voice. She and Henderson had taken seats at an eight-place table in a corner of the dining room. "It's only fair we spread it around."

"I hope Gunthorpe doesn't win us tonight. The redneck's in love with me. Found him a nigger who carries a gun to keep off muggers."

Ibith poured mineral water. "You brought it on yourself. Bragging about how awful it was in the streets, what a big law man you were."

The frown lengthened on Dr. Grant's forehead. "I guess I was uptight. Problem is people aren't mean to us, they're too *nice*."

Across the lobby, Herbie, in a navy jacket, and Flo, in a floor-length emerald dress—it was Kirov ballet night—appeared. Behind them were the Yasudas. Murray wore a ruffled shirt and a pale blue dinner jacket and Sandra was in a scarlet *ao dai*.

"I'll settle for Herbie and his crowd," Dr. Grant said. "Holy smoke, aren't they duded up? I feel like a straight in my gray suit. And you in a wool dress."

"We're conservatives, Hen."

To the disappointment of the Grants, Murray and Herbie, followed by Herbie's friends from Westbury, did not see the doctor and his wife and took a table at the other end of the restaurant. The Grants liked the Shackmans and the Yasudas. They were easy to talk to, kidded a great deal, and their appreciation of Henderson's medical eminence was sincere. Herbie, a tax accountant, knew a great deal about medicine—costs, hospitalization plans. Behind the coarse exterior, Dr. Grant divined, was a hard intelligence.

The Hutzlers—Mavis in a long white dress and a brown mink cape—appeared, accompanying Father Konay. They saw the Grants, waved to them, and came over.

"May we?" Mavis asked. Her Midwestern twang made Ibith Grant think of Minneapolis.

"Of course, Mavis," she said. "And Father Konay too."

"Say, that's fine," the priest said. He held a chair for Mavis, then sat next to Dr. Grant and across from Ibith. "I haven't had much of a chance to talk to you folks. I get so tired, I can't be sociable."

"Try the mineral water, Father," Dr. Grant said. "They claim it cures everything from migraine to ulcers."

"I don't have either, but I'll try. Excuse me." The priest bowed his head, and in a low voice, so as not to offend any of the others, said grace.

"Amen," Dr. Grant said.

"I always worry about bothering people with that," Father Konay said. "It's sort of an intrusion."

"Not at all," Ibith said. On the tip of her tongue was some comment about intrusions she regarded as more serious—anti-abortion laws, anti-contraception laws, anti-divorce laws. But she made no comment; indifference and neutrality were well advised. And the priest was the most gentle of men. Why bug him?

"Are you enjoying the trip?" Ibith asked him.

"Oh yes. But it's too much to digest. I could have spent a week or two in each place we visited. Your mind gets cluttered. You have to be like Mr. Bettenhausen and have a photographic memory, or like Mrs. Carrell, who keeps notes all the time.

"A lovely woman," Father Konay said. His gray eyes were enigmatic, asking for information, yet not quite sure he wanted it. Ibith Grant, with her finely honed intuitions, caught the nuance. She had sensed this quality in clergy: a sly interest in other people's secrets.

"Theresa is a close friend," Ibith said.

"Yes, I know," Father Konay said. "You wonder how come a pretty woman like that and so intelligent isn't married."

"Oh, she's been that route," the black woman said. "One divorce and one death. Maybe she's happier single."

Father Konay sipped his Narzan. The party had gotten used to heavy infusions of mineral water and wine. Waiters appeared infrequently, vanished, forgot orders. Virgil had warned those attending the Kirov ballet to order sparingly, and not to be disappointed if they had to leave before getting fed. He advised them that there was an acceptable buffet at the theater. Besides, the tour escort said, sitting through *Swan Lake* on a stomach full of fried veal and potatoes could be an ordeal.

"But it isn't a natural state," Father Konay said—and then let his mouth stay open, as if shocked by his own statement.

"Better to marry than burn, Father?" Ibith asked.

A waitress appeared. She gave off a ripe odor and Dr. Grant found himself averting his head as they ordered. It had become a routine—caviar to start, veal for a main course. The woman walked away, scratching her head.

"What are the odds on getting fed?" Dr. Grant asked.

"I'll stay here all night," Father Konay said. "I'm skipping the ballet. I don't understand it."

"Oh, come on, be a sport, Father," Mavis said. "Gosh, if I could get old Stick-in-the-Mud here to go, you could."

Mr. Hutzler fiddled with his earpiece. Dr. Grant, recalling morning noises from the Hutzlers' rooms, told himself that Ed was not that much of a stick-in-the-mud. A stick-in-the-john, maybe.

"This country kind of sets me on edge," Father Konay said. "That Anti-Religious Museum made me sick. I was sorry I went in."

"But people go to church," Ibith said.

"Yes, in spite of it all. I wish some of those radicals I have to contend with would see what goes on here."

"They're not in favor of this kind of government, are they?" Dr. Grant asked.

"What they want leads to it. Free love. No traditions." He thought moodily of Father Folker in his beard and blue jeans, antagonizing his parishioners. "I have this young hot shot on my hands now, and let me tell you, he's made problems for me." He fixed his gray eyes on the Grants. "Let me ask you folks. Do colored people really want to be in on everything whites do?"

The question was so unexpected, so out of character, that Dr. Grant removed his eyeglasses and studied them. Ibith, less in awe of the white world, answered. "They want the same opportunities and the same consideration."

"But I mean, like joining clubs, and that sort of thing, private affairs. This young fellow I have got the community stirred up and got me in trouble. All over letting colored—"

"Black," Mavis Hutzler corrected.

"Sorry. Black. It was a private social club. We don't pay taxes, so Father Folker decided we had no right to keep black people out. But there are only a few black families in Ash Valley and they live on the other side of town. Let me tell you, it was a battle. What do you and Dr. Grant think of something like that? I mean, I'm going to have to face it when I get back home, and I have no idea what colored—black—people want."

Theresa Carrell, flanked by A. T. Gunthorpe and Mr. Wattle, entered the dining room. She was wearing a floor-length black dress. It was daringly slit at one side. She walked toward the table where the Grants were sitting. A seat for her alongside Father Konay had been saved.

"Dang," said A. T. Gunthorpe, "look lak Miz Carrell done faked us out again, Horace." He was the only one who called Mr. Wattle by his first name.

"Okay," Mr. Wattle said. "Okay, if that's the way it has to be. But I've arranged to sit next to the lady at the ballet. Don't anyone try to do me out of that pleasure."

He pirouetted and danced off to where the Flemingtons were seated. A. T. Gunthorpe shuffled after him.

245

"May we?" Mr. Wattle asked.

Lulu did not respond.

"Of course," Harry said.

"Nice afternoon?" Mr. Wattle asked Lulu. "Find anything worth buying?"

"We took the boat ride. It was deadly dull."

Flemington studied the wilted menu. It was in four languages. The English was generously misspelled. An old desk man with an eye for errors, he found *veel stew* and *chucken liver and pepers* upsetting. The menu had an elaborate red and gold cover. It reminded him of himself. Stylish Harry, tweed and suede and gold cuff links on the outside—misspellings and errata within.

Harry pretended to be searching for the waiter. In scanning the restaurant, he managed to stare at Theresa—animated, laughing, incredibly attractive. He thought of all the misery he had caused her, the way she had loved him, given herself so unselfishly, and, after two bad marriages, come in search of him. It was not easy, Harry wanted to tell someone, to turn down great wealth. And did he not love Lulu once? When she was young and supple, and responded to him in bed?

"Stop looking over there," Lulu said.

"Sorry, dear. Trying to find the waiter."

"You folks goin' to the ballet tonight?" A. T. Gunthorpe asked.

"Yes, we plan to go," Harry said.

"I don't think so," Lulu said huskily. "Harry, I don't want to go."

"You do look a bit pale, Mrs. Flemington," Mr. Wattle said. "That traipsing around gets most people down, but not me. I can go forever."

Flemington, nursing a desire to throttle the man, took Lulu's hand. She drew it away. Perhaps it was just as well. By now, most of the members of Three Worlds knew that there was something between Theresa and himself. They would gossip. He would stare at her, unable to deny himself the reminders of an irretrievable joy. And Lulu would get furious. Once Flemington had been regarded as a whip at making quick decisions. At the newspaper, executives relied on his intuition of what was right and newsworthy. Where had that talent gone? And if he still had it, why was it not applicable to his tattered personal life?

Mrs. Legrand walked briskly through the disinfectant-scented corridor, carrying Weston's dinner. Odors in Russia, she noticed, were powerful, unidentifiable. But at least the pot of hot tea and the two slices of buttered black bread had a healthful aroma. They reminded her of her childhood—how long ago!—in rural Nebraska. Her mother baked her own bread.

The floor clerk smiled at the old woman. "Meester still not fill gud?" the woman asked.

"He is better, thank you. He needs a little food."

"Gud. Please, leave key next time."

"But I only went to the food shop."

"No matter. Leave key, please."

How like them! Mrs. Legrand thought. Polite, friendly—but sticklers for rules. Elevator operators made people get out if they were one over the limit. Waiters refused to make substitutions. At the Hermitage their party had been detained while a check was made to make sure the exact amount of tickets had been handed in. Rules, rules, rules. Mrs. Legrand believed in rules, of course, but at age eighty-one she was something of a free spirit. Little did Herbie know that she reveled in being called Ma Barker.

She balanced the tray, opened the door, and turned on a light. It was a sickly light, badly placed, and as soon as she could get to the bed and switch on a bed lamp she turned it off. Weston was sitting up in bed. He had taken his pills and he was drowsy.

"Some nice strong tea and some nutritious bread," Mrs. Legrand said. She set the tray on the night table.

"Thank you, dearest."

"You feel a bit stronger?"

"Well, sleepy."

"Maybe I could get Dr. Grant to look at you again."

"No, I hate to bother him. I'll be okay in the morning. I think I'll just stay in the hotel a few days in Moscow."

"Poor Weston. You'll miss the Kremlin and Lenin's tomb and Red Square. I'm so sorry you got sick. It's all my fault."

"Certainly not, Elizabeth, and I don't want you to talk that way. Aren't you eating?"

"I had a bite downstairs. I sat with Mr. Huggins and his wife."

Mr. Legrand winced. For so long he had suffered so much pain, such diverse dolors and aches, that they were almost old friends. There was one that started deep in his bowels and radiated up the sides of his abdomen. There was another on his left side, under the rib cage. An intermittent jabbing often twinged in the small of his back. Now, it seemed, all were at work, competing for his attention. But the demerol was doing its work. He was fuzzy, drowsy; he would sleep well. A bit of bread a half cup of tea and he would manage the flight to Moscow.

"They brew good tea," he said.

"Indeed they do. These people just need a chance to branch out and they could be as great as America." From a plastic bathroom

247

glass, Mrs. Legrand sipped at her Stolichnaya vodka. It was not as cheap as she had thought it would be, but it would be advisable to buy an extra bottle. After Moscow they went to Istanbul, and who knew what would be available there and at what price?

Mr. Legrand's eyes closed and he turned on his side, snoring apologetically. For a while, Mrs. Legrand sat by the window looking out on the Nevsky Prospekt. Below she could see her fellow tourists boarding the bus for the evening at the Kirov Ballet. She supposed she could have gone. The tickets were extra, about five dollars, and she could have afforded it, but she disliked leaving Weston when he was ill.

The truth of the matter was she was unhappy away from him. They had been together so long! They were like part of one another's bodies, a familiar piece of clothing, like a worn raincoat or the dependable bedroom slippers in which Mrs. Legrand shuffled around the world or Weston's homburg. And they had moved about a great deal. Both had been born in Nebraska, met at the state college, gone on to a variety of jobs. But rarely in the same place. Weston had been a bookkeeper, later an accountant, and toward the end of his career, as assistant manager of a factoring company, had earned the title of comptroller. Elizabeth taught home economics in elementary schools.

They had raised three children but rarely saw them. Parents and children had been constantly in motion. Urbana, Illinois; Zanesville, Ohio; Charlotte, North Carolina; Oneonta, New York; Shawnee, Oklahoma—wherever the jobs looked better, or the climate or the medical care. They owned almost nothing and Elizabeth was an indifferent housekeeper. The mobile home they now rented in Bisbee, Arizona, was the best place in which they had ever lived—compact, neat, no trouble to maintain. And it kept them close together. They were with each other continually, holding hands, touching knees, reminders of each other's existence. They read little but watched a lot of television. Elizabeth did needlepoint. Their children and grandchildren, like the old folks, seemed to have made all of America their home. San Diego, Houston, Phoenix, Huntsville, Orlando . . . The children had become names on postcards, wanderers on the face of the earth. In their mobile home they did not even keep photographs of the children and they had lost track of how many grandchildren they had. When one died at the age of four, hit by a motorcycle while playing in the street in Jacksonville, Weston and Elizabeth did not learn about it for four months.

And yet Mrs. Legrand felt close to her family. They were hers. If the children chose to wander, to pull up stakes every few years, to be less than faithful correspondents, that was acceptable to her. She had

Weston. He had her. They saved no money, but they had so meticu-
lously calculated their income—Social Security, pensions, interest on
bonds—that they did everything they wanted, and managed a trip
every year.

"Aren't they beautiful?" Mrs. Legrand said. She was looking at the
tourists entering the bus. The women wore gowns. Mrs. Carrell and
the ladies from Westbury were especially dolled up. Her friend
"Harvey" was in a dark jacket that made him look thinner. And there
was that thoughtful Mr. Virgil, counting heads, distributing tickets.
The world, Mrs. Legrand thought, was filled with decent people.
How good people had been to them all these years! Maybe it was because as nomads (their longest stay had been six years in Modesto,
California, where Weston kept books for an aluminum extruder) they
had no ties to anyone and strangers felt obliged to be courteous.
They didn't even have any relatives, apart from the children. Weston
had had a brother—long dead. She had a younger sister who had always disliked her, mocked Elizabeth's footloose freedom, her refusal
to take root. "When I die," Mrs. Legrand had told Dr. Grant, who listened with a sympathetic scowl, "she won't care a bit, she told me so,
would serve me right for gallivanting around the world at my age."

"That wasn't nice," the physician had said.

"I don't care a whit. My sweetie and I go our way. We have each
other and would you believe that's always been enough?"

"I do indeed, Mrs. Legrand. You take good care of him, you hear?"

"I always have and he knows it."

The bus departed, moving under the dim street lights of the Nevsky
Prospekt. She did not mind missing the ballet. A few of the tourists
chose to spend a quiet night at the hotel or take a walk. The Kuchtenbergs, she recalled, were going to stroll around Palace Square after
dinner. Full of strength, Mrs. Legrand thought of joining them, then
decided not to. It was very peaceful, very pleasant sitting by the
window, watching the traffic. Sipping her vodka, she listened to
Weston's labored breathing. He was old and ill and exhausted, but he
was hers, and his very presence was a source of happiness to her.

"You are enjoying it, Mrs. Wicker?" Virgil asked. They were in the
Kirov lobby at intermission. Dr. Wicker and Bettenhausen were
standing patiently at the crowded bar trying to buy splits of
Georgian champagne.

"I'm intoxicated, Pepi," Rosie said. "It's beautiful. Unbelievable.
You know, every afternoon I get my usual case of museum feet.
They're like two hot stones. Then the evening's entertainment beckons
and I'm ready for action again."

"Mind over matter."

"Over crippled feet," said Cornelia. "It's a great show. Even the audience. Look at the kids. Soldiers. Sailors. People who look like they just came from a collective farm."

"And probably have," Virgil said. "The Russians love their artists. In Moscow, you will see how they honor Gorky, Tolstoy."

"Excuse my ignorance," Theresa said, "but who was Kirov? I see the name everywhere. Was he a ballet master? Like Fokine or Massine?"

"Hardly, Mrs. Carrell." Virgil let his eyes linger on her splendid figure. It was a shame he was bound by company rules. Tourists were off limits. A few guides got involved. Eventually they were found out and fired. Pepi's job meant a great deal to him. Far more than a night of passion. "Sergei Kirov was Communist boss of Leningrad."

Rose-Anne turned her ear. Virgil was incredible. He was dropping the definite article, in the manner of Russians.

"But why was he so famous?" Cornelia asked.

"Kirov was assassinated. I think 1934. It was a *cause célèbre*. At first, the murder was blamed on reactionaries, anti-Bolsheviks. Then Stalin accused Trotsky. Kirov's murder was used by Stalin as an excuse to kill thousands of people. It was the start of the terror."

"Who did kill Kirov?" Theresa asked.

"No one knows. Maybe Stalin's police. To give him an excuse. But not Trotsky or the ones who were blamed."

Rose-Anne shivered. "And they name this beautiful theater for him?"

"All over Russia Kirov is remembered. There is a district, a city, theaters, museums, parks, stadiums, factories, swimming pools. Stalin was grateful to have an excuse to shoot people."

Theresa shuddered. "That lovely dancing—the music—the orchestra in white tie—the way the audience loves them. And here we get these stories of murder."

"I am only a messenger, Mrs. Carrell. I did not indicate my approval of these atrocious things."

From across the lobby, packed with Russians promenading arm in arm, staring at one another and at tourists—there were a dozen Africans in colorful robes, Chinese in Mao suits, and many Americans —Theresa saw Horace T. Wattle prancing toward her. She could not bear to be rude but the man was upsetting.

"I'm for some fresh air," Theresa said. "Anyone joining me?"

Wicker and Bettenhausen volunteered. Each took an arm and escorted her toward the stairs, fighting their way through what seemed half of the Red Navy's Baltic fleet. Cornelia and Rose-Anne decided to stay.

The air was mild, the Theater Square illuminated. For all the crush of bodies inside the Kirov Theater, the streets seemed deserted. An occasional taxi scooted by. Even the omnipresent ice cream carts had packed up for the night.

Bettenhausen fluffed his beard. He was feeling a bit czarist, an old retainer. Ballet was not his dish of tea, but Cornelia liked it. And the side show of audience, orchestra, the intermission mob . . . He felt fulfilled. The afternoon at the Hermitage had imprinted itself in his mind. The colors and forms and images would last forever—Rembrandts, Rubenses, Titians, Veroneses, Van Dycks, Tiepolos, Renoirs, Picassos . . .

"There he is, Warren," Dr. Wicker said.

"Who? Where?"

"The man in the topcoat and the cap. Across the square."

Bettenhausen squinted into the dark street. Under a street light opposite them was a short man. The tan cap seemed to fall over his ears. He looked to either side, then came toward the Americans.

"A friend of yours?" Theresa asked.

"I don't know."

The man appeared to be frightened. He looked to his right, then his left. A taxi cruised by. He stepped around it quickly.

"Who is Mr. Vicker?" he asked. "Please, is Mr. Vicker?"

"Me," the dentist called. "Right here."

As if borne on the flying coat, the man floated toward Wicker. He had a pinched face and dark concentrated eyes. "Please, Mr. Vicker . . ." The cap wobbled as his head moved from side to side. From the crowd in front of the Kirov, two men in dark suits stepped out and moved toward him.

"Not by bell," the man said. "Not by bell. Museum with bread. Bread in museum."

"What is he saying?" Wicker asked Bettenhausen.

The Americans stepped into the street and walked toward the man in the cap. "What's that about bread?" Bettenhausen called. "What are you saying?"

But the men in dark suits had grabbed him, each one taking an arm, moving him backward, his feet flopping on the pavement, into the gloom.

"Hey," Dr. Wicker shouted. "Let him go! He's got a right to talk to me."

"*Spekulyanti*," one of the men shouted back. "No good. No good for tourist. *Spekulyanti*."

The figures vanished in the darkness. Wicker heard someone saying in English that the streets were full of drunks. Another voice com-

251

mented, with a British accent, that the Russian police were to be complimented—no one was allowed to raise a disturbance.

"He wasn't drunk," the dentist said, impelled to defend the man in the cap. "He wanted to talk."

The voice responded: "Absolutely pickled, old boy."

Bettenhausen looked at Wicker and Theresa. "What was he saying? What was that about bread?"

"Something about a museum and bread," she said. "It doesn't make any sense."

The interior lights of the theater flickered. A bell sounded. Intermission was over.

In the lobby, pushing their way through, the dentist spoke quietly to Bettenhausen, so that the teacher could not hear. "He wasn't drunk, or a nut, or a speckled bird or whatever that hoodlum shouted. What do we do now?"

Bettenhausen cleared his throat. "Leave it to the constructionist. I'll work something out tomorrow. It's becoming clearer. The images are focusing."

Wicker said nothing. Once again he felt like Huck Finn letting Tom Sawyer sucker him into a lunatic escape plan. But who was their Jim?

Day 12: Leningrad–Moscow. A short flight whisks us across 400 miles of the Soviet Union to Moscow, capital of the incredible country that is one sixth of the earth! On arriving, we visit Red Square, St. Basil's Cathedral, the Bolshoi Theater, the Kremlin walls. A free afternoon for shopping and mingling with our Russian hosts. (Be sure to ask about people-to-people contacts!) What to buy? Lacquerware, semiprecious stones, hand embroidery, unusual toys. Try to get to the "Commission Store" and rummage around for antiques. After dinner, a drive around the illuminated city, a never-to-be-forgotten experience!

"I got a medical rarity, Doc," Herbie called across the aisle of the Aeroflot TU-104. "The only man in the world ever to have diarrhea and constipation at the same time."

"Don't eat for a day," Dr. Grant called back.

"It was the caviar," Herbie shouted. "All that black bread. They kill you with it."

Virgil walked the aisle of the Soviet plane bearing them to Moscow. The group seemed in good shape, except for Mr. Legrand, whose face was the color of gesso, and Herbie. The fat man grabbed Virgil's arm as he walked by. "Listen, I got to have some *mamaliga* to settle my stomach. Like my mother used to cook."

"I cannot promise, Mr. Shackman, but perhaps we can find a Romanian restaurant in Moscow."

"Oi, I'm getting the pains again."

Mavis Hutzler leaned across and touched Herbie's arm. "It's the chicken Kiev. Ed tried to cut it and it squirted half a pound of melted butter on his seven-dollar tie."

"Serves him right for showing off, Mavis."

"Now, Harvey, be nice to Mavis." Mrs. Legrand was piqued. Lately Herbie had been paying more attention to Mrs. Hutzler.

"Ma! How you doin', Ma? Pa okay today?"

"We're wonderful, Harvey."

"Know how to stuff a Russian chicken, Ma?"

"Now I know that's going to be dirty, but I'm dumb enough to ask."

"Stuff it up—"

Flo clapped a hand over her husband's mouth. "That's enough!

253

You're so sick, be *sick!* In fact, take the outside seat." She looked across the aisle at Shirl. "Can you believe him? I can't believe him."

The early morning raillery—*so loud! so vulgar!*—exploded on Lulu Flemington's ears. Before checking out of the Baltiiskaya that morning, she had demanded a double scotch. Harry, observing her shaky state, had given it to her. Flemington cursed the economics of Communist countries that made it impossible for his wife to buy anything. It dawned on him, although he was reluctant to admit it, that he was as material-minded as Lulu. But being mannerly Harry, he was quiet about it. How else explain the way he reveled in the good *things* that marriage had brought him?

"Madame wishes anything?" Virgil asked. He was standing alongside the Flemingtons. Lulu had her black eye shield on. She managed a greeting.

"We're fine, Pepi."

Virgil sat on the arm of Flemington's seat and bent low. Obviously confidential stuff, only for their refined tastes. "I can recommend some shops in Moscow."

Like an outfielder snapping up sunglasses, Lulu's hand flew to the black shield and lifted it. She was smiling. "I knew you'd come through," she said.

"Semiprecious stones are a good buy," the tour escort said. "There is a store for that. Topaz, malachite. The prices are reasonable. A gentleman from Pasadena some months ago had a topaz appraised when he got home, and it was six times the price he paid in Moscow."

"Really?" Lulu asked. "Can we go today?"

"I can arrange a car and driver for this afternoon if Madame wishes. You should also visit the Commission Shop, which is sort of an antique store. It takes some looking, but there are good buys—old silver and gold, china, quartz."

"Fabergé?" Lulu asked. She adjusted her seat so that it was upright.

"I am afraid not. Fabergé is long gone. In all my visits to Soviet Union, I have never once known of a tourist who found a Fabergé piece."

"I'll pay."

"Price is not the problem."

"Darling," Harry said to her, "if there's a piece of Fabergé left in Moscow, we'll find it. Right?"

Bettenhausen was anxious to talk to Dr. Wicker. Both had agreed that their wives were not to be told about their mission. All night long Bettenhausen had tossed in bed, coughing, making frequent trips to the bathroom for meditation, drinking liters of salty Narzan water. He

254

found it sharpened his thought processes. By now he had worked up what he felt was a credible scenario, but he needed the dentist's compliance. The problem was getting to Wicker without crowds of people around. That was the trouble with tours—one was rump to rump most of the time. He decided that he would reveal his plan to the dentist in bits and pieces during the morning tour. Meanwhile, a few loose ends needed tying. Invigorated, he started to make notes on the back of a postcard.

"Writing to someone, Betts?" Cornelia asked.

"No. Just some chores that have to be done when we get home."

"Gad, aren't we thorough."

"The pool needs a new filter system. The cactus garden is in shameful condition."

"And I don't feel so good myself."

Bettenhausen grunted. All night long he had been aware of the accuracy of Dr. Wicker's perception: Tom Sawyer concocting plots to liberate Jim. But it was more than that. It was the chance he had never been given in Hollywood. His own creation! *Produced and Directed by Warren Bettenhausen!*

"Pepi, my boy!" he called.

"Sir?"

"What the devil is a *speckle auntie?*"

"Ah. *Spekulyanti.* Black market person. Illegal buying and selling of goods or money. Don't do business with any of them."

The Hollywood man scratched his beard. Another plot twist? A case of mistaken identity?

"Is strange church, no?" the Russian guide asked.

"Strange?" Herbie bellowed. "It looks like Disneyland."

"Haw, very funny, sir. Yes, like Valt Disney. Something from Gollywood."

It was late morning. The group stood in Red Square outside the Cathedral of St. Basil. Their new guide had met them at Sheremetyevo Airport. Her name was Marika, and she was dark, with braided black hair wound around her head. Her eyes were slanted and her nose short: a suggestion of Tatar or Chuvash or Buryat. Around them Red Square stretched endlessly. Four football fields in length, J. P. Huggins remarked, a meadow of paving blocks. In its great emptiness it was awesome—the Lenin tomb, the Kremlin wall with its battlements and towers, the candy-striped St. Basil, and the façade of the GUM department store.

"Has been restored many times," Marika said. "Last in 1954. In 1812

255

Napoleon gives orders to burn to ground, but very lucky, French general refuses to burn."

St. Basil was unlike anything in the world, Rose-Anne Wicker decided. Like a cluster of Christmas tree ornaments—striped pine cones, pineapples, onions, bulbs. The colors dazzled, amused. The architects must have had a sense of humor. A style rarely imitated. Perhaps it needed the vastness of Red Square, a lot of space and air around it. In an enclosed Florentine square of piazza in Seville it would cause vertigo. But Russia was huge, flat and somber: the dab of brightness that St. Basil offered was beguiling.

"We take time for photographs," Marika said. "Is good view of St. Basil over by corner of GUM."

"That's for me, baby," Yasuda said. Herbie shambled after him.

Dr. Wicker started for the corner also, waiting for taxis to pass. Bettenhausen, who regarded photography as a waste of time, waddled after the dentist.

"Arnold, I'll give you a hand."

The dentist winked at him. They had not had an opportunity to discuss the message from the *spekulyanti* in front of the Kirov Theater.

Wicker turned his light meter away from St. Basil, holding his hand in front of the eye. "Lots of light," he said. "These hazy skies fool you." He raised the Pentax. "Boy, what a sight. I have the Kremlin wall and everything. I wish Rosie would wave."

"Arnold my boy, I've worked this out—more or less."

"I'm listening." They moved into Red Square, away from Murray and Herbie.

"I told you I have a contact here in Moscow. He's a television journalist with United Broadcasting. Bright young fellow we can trust. I met him when those film people toured Hollywood. He speaks Russian and he can give us guidance."

The dentist sucked in his breath. He turned his camera, focused with telephoto lens, and framed Lenin's mausoleum. Outside the truncated pyramid a line of people had already formed, frozen in time and space for the opening of the tomb. "Is that a good idea, Warren? That means three people will know about this deal."

"Actually it's an advantage. Whoever Leland is, whoever his sponsors, they won't know that you have a good right hand. Me. I'll go to see this fellow and ask him to clear up a few things."

"Such as?"

"Information on Borkin. Who is he? Why should the CIA want to reach him?"

"Is this guy reliable?" Wicker asked.

"His name is Sparling, a bright lad. He'll keep a confidence."

Cornelia was waving at them. They were being hurried into the bus. There was more sight-seeing ahead, then check-in at the Ukraina Hotel. Bettenhausen planned to visit his friend Sparling in the afternoon.

"What about the guy in the cap?" Wicker asked. "What did Pepi say?"

"The word means a speculator, a black market operator. Russian cities are full of them. Every time they see a foreigner, they try to do business, or *hondle,* as Herbie would say."

"He was no black market guy. What would he want with me? First he shows up at the airport asking about Borkin, then last night he knows my name, so he's got a contact somewhere. And he had on a tan cap and coat, like Veg said. What was he shouting about bread? And a museum?"

"We shall ask Mr. Sparling."

A. T. Gunthorpe leaned from the bus window. "Shake it but don't break it, Bettsy boy. All these people waitin' on them dang photographers. Come on, git on board, lil chillun."

Bettenhausen labored up the bus steps. Wicker followed. Herbie and Murray ran across Red Square.

"*Gevald,*" Shackman huffed. "Like the Cossacks were after me. I can't believe it. The line goes all the way around the corner. You follow it to the end, you'll end up in Siberia."

The bus stopped in Sverdlov Square so that they could see the Bolshoi Theater. Gardens and fountains abounded. It was a gay and lively place. A brooding head of Karl Marx, embedded in an enormous chunk of granite, glowered.

"No time for photos?" Yasuda yelled.

"We are on strict schedule," Marika said. The guides in the Soviet Union seemed to assume many of Pepi's prerogatives. It was their country; their schedule; their show. "Ukraina wants we should be by check-in by half past noon."

Virgil whispered in her ear. She smiled. "All right, special for Mr. Virgil, who is old friend Intourist and Soviet Union. Five minutes."

The camera buffs hustled down the aisle. This time J. P. Huggins went along. At last he had gotten around to using his cameras.

"Hey, I don't believe it," Herbie cried. "Jimmy's takin' pictures! Look!" Stepping down, he boomed after him: "The way you were shlepping that fancy case, Jim, I figured it was full of money!"

J.P. flashed his teeth. "It was, Herbie. I got rid of it in Budapest. Invested it in a paprika farm."

"Don't mention paprika," Herbie winced. "I'm still tasting that last meal in Budapest. Those Hungarians had it in for me." Herbie raised

257

his camera, thinking: But not the way they had it in for my people twenty-eight years ago.

"It looks like Moscow University," Theresa said. They were crossing the bridge over the Moskva River, approaching the towers of the Ukraina Hotel.

"Same architect, lady," the guide said.

"Hideous," Bettenhausen said to his wife. "Stalinist notions of architecture. The booby prize for form. I tell you these people are bereft of the visual sense. There is more harmony in a Kaffir kraal."

"That's a *hotel?*" Herbie asked as the bus parked in the square facing the soaring structure. "I think once we're in they'll never let us out."

As Virgil led them out, some of the tourists noticed an argument in front of the hotel. A man about to enter a car was getting a ticket from a policeman. He was protesting mildly, looking more pathetic than irate.

"What did he do?" Mr. Wattle asked. "Park in a no-parking zone?"

Marika shook her head. "No. Is getting ticket for driving dirty car."

"What?" the rubber manufacturer cried.

"Is law here," she said.

"Well, I'll be darned." He jabbed Gunthorpe in the side. "You know, there's something to be said for this system? They'll make a Red out of me yet."

The lobby of the Ukraina was thick with people. Virgil had difficulty battling his way to the desk. A convention of some kind was being held. There were Indian women in saris; Africans in dashikis; men in Castro-style fatigues; Arabs; Koreans in quasi-military uniforms, seated near the elevators.

In the midst of the lobby was a newsstand. J. P. Huggins made directly for it. But he found no *Herald Tribune,* no English newspapers.

"Nothing?" he asked plaintively. "*Times* of London? *Telegraph?*"

"No, mister," the woman said. "But is beautiful stamps of Soviet cosmonauts. Also photographs. Gagarin, Leonov, Belyaev. Please, nice to take home. Also teacup with Gagarin."

Half the vast display counter was covered with sets of stamps, small banners, colored photos of Russian space heroes. A dark man in a Nehru cap was buying a set of fold-out postcards illustrating the history of Soviet conquests in space.

"Sure you aren't saving one copy of an English paper?" Huggins begged. "For a friend of the Soviet Union?"

"Is one copy London *Telegraph,* but is for regular customer," the woman said. "You cannot buy, but I lend you for a few minutes."

258

Unbelievable, Huggins thought. A country of over two hundred million people where you couldn't get anything to read from outside. He tried to be generous. Pepi had said that the Ukraina was used mainly by Russians and was not popular with tourists. He turned to the back of the paper, the flimsy air mail edition sticking to his fingers. There was nothing under shipping news; only sailings from British ports. He turned to the financial news.

A headline stared at him.

PRICE OF GOLD REACHES RECORD HIGH:
EUROPEAN EXCHANGES GETTING $167

If the price was $167 in Europe, Huggins wondered, what would it be in Bombay? It sounded like the title of a song. J.P.'s Song. His Arab friends knew what they were doing. With a little help from Allah, they'd sneak the S.S. *Lautaro* into port. Chahoub had promised him a twenty-five per cent return, maybe more. On two hundred thousand, that would be fifty thousand dollars. He'd reinvest it. Hit me again, dealer.

Huggins, returning the newspaper to the woman, wandered around the lobby, nudging two black men in purple robes, admiring an Indian woman in a golden sari, winking at the Cubans. He had some money of his own at home. Or he could borrow from Dan Kuraskin, who always had an eye open for an investment. Better than letting the Malfis into it, he'd run up a fortune of his own. He'd make frequent trips to Europe, contacting Chahoub and the Beirut, Dubai & Sharja Trading Company. . . .

"Mr. Huggins, your key, please," Virgil was saying. "And everyone be patient about elevators. The Ukraina is famous for slow lifts, but the attendants are the prettiest in Moscow. Lunch is available in the restaurant and we meet at two-thirty in the lobby."

Bettenhausen spoke to his wife: "My dear, I feel the need of a stroll. Could you please see the bags to the room?"

"I don't trust you."

Bettenhausen moved his leonine head forward. "Don't be too sure I'm as crooked as I'm supposed to be," he said, barely moving his lips.

Cornelia patted his cheek. "There, there, poor Betts must be tired. To try to fool me with *The Maltese Falcon*. Bogie to Mary Astor."

The Hollywood man looked for Dr. Wicker. The dentist was at the concierge's desk.

"Arnold, the letter."

"Hunh?" Wicker was studying a telegram.

"Quickly, my boy, the letter. I'm about to track down my friend Sparling."

259

Wicker did not seem to hear him. His eyes were affixed to the telegram. "This is terrible. Oh, my God, this is just awful."

A Buryat woman in native costume jostled both men away from the
desk. "What is, Arnold? What's happened?"

"Mark Abrams got hit in the mouth with a baseball."

"Indeed?" Bettenhausen began to quiver.

"The poor kid. With all his tooth problems. His gums are swollen
and the retainer was broken. And to think of the work I put into the
boy's teeth and how good he's been about it."

"Arnold, I am brimming with sympathy for Mark Abrams' teeth,
but please give me the letter. I am about to make my run."

"What? Oh, the letter. God, this is the worst thing that could have
happened. Mrs. Abrams will be furious."

"The letter."

Wicker reached for a telegram pad on the desk, stopped and, without looking at Bettenhausen, handed him the long manila envelope
he had carried in his jacket since John T. Leland had given it to him.
"Can I send a cable here?" he asked the concierge.

"Please, yes. Fill out."

"Arnold. I shall have information for us shortly."

Wicker barely heard him. He was, with a concerned look in his long
face, composing a message.

MARK ABRAMS
MALLARD CIRCLE
RIVERFORD CONNECTICUT USA
PLEASE CONTACT DOCTOR TUROFF AT ONCE ASK IF DUPLICATE RE-
TAINER POSSIBLE FROM FRAGMENTS OLD STOP ESSENTIAL YOU KEEP
USING AS SOON AS GUMS LESS SWOLLEN TERRIBLE SHAME LOSE ALL
THIS GROUND STOP TEETH MUST BE PUSHED INTO CORRECT POSITION
NO MATTER WHAT STOP WHEN NEW RETAINER AVAILABLE USE IT
UNTIL PAIN TOO MUCH PERHAPS TEN MINUTES EVERY HOUR AND
KEEP IN GLASS WATER WHEN NOT IN USE . . .

"Trouble?" Rose-Anne asked him. She had gotten their key from
Virgil but the mob around the elevators indicated a long wait.

"Disaster. Mark Abrams got hit in the mouth. I feel personally responsible."

"What did you just give to Warren?"

"What? Nothing."

"You gave him an envelope."

"Did I? I guess it was something to mail."

There was a long room off the lobby where young ladies who spoke
foreign languages provided information, theater tickets, reservations,

and other services for tourists. Bettenhausen walked in and tried the first desk.

"Please?" asked the girl. She grinned at his tam-o'-shanter.

"Can you help me look up someone's name in the phone book?"

"Yes, please." The woman reached under her desk and dragged out a ragged directory. "Who is, please?"

"He's an American journalist. He might be listed under his bureau, the United Broadcasting Company, or his name, Eliot Sparling."

"Meester Sparlink?"

"Yes. You know him?"

The girl's chunky face beamed. "He is here in hotel. We dun't need directory."

"You mean . . . he's here *today*? Covering a story?"

"No, no, Meester Sparlink lives in hotel. Also bureau here. Room 1212. I see him already this morning."

"Thank you very much, my dear."

"Very nice man. Always makes jokes."

Virgil was right about the elevators. The waits were endless. Luckily, most of the Three Worlds people had already gone up, or, tiring of the delay, had straggled into the restaurant. A few lingered in the enormous lobby—Huggins reading a paper, Flo, Sylvia and Shirl studying lacquerware in a glass showcase, Mavis Hutzler buying cosmonaut postcards.

Two Ugandans in robes shoved Bettenhausen into the elevator. It was lucky they did. The attractive operator held out a strong arm and barred entry to a party of irate Finns. The rules were strict. So many, no more.

"Is there a conference here of some kind?" Bettenhausen asked one of the Africans. "Conference?"

"Oh yes. Oh yes. People's Congress on Literary Criticism."

Fair enough, Bettenhausen thought. He felt honored to share a cramped elevator with the Ugandan equivalents of Lionel Trilling and Granville Hicks.

At the twelfth floor, Bettenhausen got out and saw the Russian floor clerk, a middle-aged woman, seated behind a desk. They'd gone Napoleon's system of spy-concierges one better. He at least kept them on the ground floor. In the worker's fatherland every floor had its policeman.

"Room 1212?"

"Yes. Broadcasting?"

"No. Just visiting."

Did she pick up a phone as he walked off?

Some twenty feet from the opened door of the United Broadcasting Company office, Bettenhausen heard Eliot Sparling's booming voice.

"Fa Chrissake tell 'em that's an outrage!" the voice reverberated. "One lousy refrigerator and they want one hundred and thirteen bucks for a month's electric bill? *Tell him to shove it!*"

"I cahn't veddy well, Eliot," a woman's Oxonian-accented voice said.

Bettenhausen entered the room. It was a suite, it appeared, but the precise outlines of the office were hard to discern, since every inch of surface space—chairs, beds, desks, tables, floor—was littered with the impedimenta of Sparling's calling. Rolls of audio tape teetered in precarious stacks; cans of film rose nervously toward the ceiling; stationery, old newspapers, manila folders, books, office equipment—staplers, adding machines, paper cutters—lay about in junkyard arrangements.

The woman with the U-accent, a thin gray-haired person, was on the telephone, covering the mouthpiece, looking at Sparling with terrorized eyes. Inexplicably, the correspondent, a tall ungainly man with a mild long-nosed face and close-cropped brown hair, was holding a pink toilet seat in his hands, as he stood in the midst of the debris, barking orders at her.

"Tell that bastard," Sparling shouted, waving the toilet seat, "that he's trying to rob us. They hate it when we bring in appliances from Stockmann's store in Finland, so they try to cheat us. The dopes can't make a decent refrigerator of their own."

The woman spoke in Russian on the phone, then to Sparling in English. "Mr. Korolenko says perhaps they did overestimate the bill. He wants to know what an American public utilities company would charge for a month's use of a refrigerator."

"Jesus. How in hell do I know?"

The woman's eyes widened. Then she nodded toward Bettenhausen, who was watching from the doorway. Sparling turned around and looked at him.

"About twelve dollars," Bettenhausen said.

"Yeah," the correspondent said. "Tell him twelve dollars."

The secretary spoke again in Russian. She seemed to be thanking Mr. Korolenko, then hung up. "He says that's fine, Eliot. If we send him twelve dollars—in *dollars*, not rubles—he'll mark the bill paid."

Sparling spun away and raised the toilet seat over his head. To Bettenhausen he suggested the Soviet Victory Monument on Gellért Hill.

"UBC comes through again!" he shouted at the Hollywood man. "Got him down from a hundred and thirteen bucks to twelve! Socialism plus electricity equals Communism!" He fiddled with his eyeglasses, staring at the caller. Bettenhausen noticed they were held together at the bridge by a piece of Band-Aid. Five years ago, when he met Sparling, he had been wearing the same mended spectacles. "Can I help? You looking for someone?"

"For you, Eliot."

"Who . . . ? Whah?" Sparling squinted at his visitor. "Betts! Warren Bettenhausen! Holy smoke! What a pleasure! You visiting? Making a movie?"

The men shook hands and laughed. In many ways they were kindred spirits: iconoclasts, disbelievers. "A mere tourist. Here for a few days with one of those packaged affairs."

Sparling introduced him to his secretary. Mrs. Frome was the wife of the British commercial attaché. Her Russian was flawless (Eliot's was excellent but he tended to lose his temper) and she was expert at handling outrageous electric bills.

"That business with the refrigerator," Sparling said, leading Bettenhausen into the inner room of the suite. "Typical of the idiots. They'll charge anything. No rules. He took twelve bucks rather than argue. Boy, isn't it a beauty?" Sparling pointed to a gleaming white refrigerator.

"A work of art," Bettenhausen said.

"Got it last week on the relief train from Helsinki. There's a department store there, Stockmann's, where the foreign colony in Moscow goes to buy stuff. They'll order you anything from a Cadillac to a pencil sharpener."

The young man was still holding the toilet seat. Bettenhausen pointed to it. "That too? A bit of Finlandia?"

"Oh. I was unwrapping it when you walked in. Can't get a decent toilet seat in the whole Soviet Union. I got to get our cameraman to install it this afternoon."

He tossed it onto what appeared to be a bed. If possible, the interior room where Bettenhausen assumed his friend slept—there was a bathroom in one corner—was more anarchic than the outer office, where Mrs. Frome was now on the phone, arguing about a film shipment. Bettenhausen recognized parts of and accessories for three different kinds of 16-mm. cameras—an Arriflex, an Auricon, and a Filmo. Lenses, magazines, tripods, reflectors, batteries lay about in disarray. If Sparling slept in the bed, it surely took him hours to prepare it. On the pillow rested a Nagra tape recorder and, beside it, two smaller Sony recorders. Even the broad window sills were in use—piles of yellow film boxes, both 100- and 400-foot rolls, were stacked there, as well as pads, shipping labels, odd bits of stationery,

263

and several opened boxes of American cookies such as Lorna Doones, Fig Newtons, and Mallomars.

"Eliot, how in God's name do you find anything?"

"Don't knock, it Betts. The finks search the place every week. I make it a little harder for them. One of their cops even complained to me about my lousy filing system. 'Stay the hell out of it for a month,' I told him, 'and I might straighten it out.'"

"Tea, Mr. Sparling?" Mrs. Frome asked.

"Yeah, yeah. You Betts?"

"I'd love some."

The correspondent's reference to the searches of his office disturbed Bettenhausen. Over strong tea—it was Earl Grey, Bettenhausen noticed, no doubt brought from the British Embassy by the likable secretary—the two men reminisced. When Bettenhausen met Sparling, during the Soviet directors' tour, the young man had been a Los Angeles correspondent for UBC. A few years later he got his chance, through perseverance and a Berlitz course in Russian, to head the bureau in Moscow. It had wrecked his personal life, Sparling told his visitor casually, but made his professional career. His fiancée had come to Moscow shortly after his assignment. It was December— dark, icy cold, gloomy, lonely. She cried every day and they broke off their engagement. Eliot settled into his bachelor suite in the Ukraina, worked fifteen hours a day, and became a well-known face on American television.

"You like it, then?" Bettenhausen asked.

"Yeah, sure. It's frustrating. It's a loony bin. I'm watched. I'm censored. They can drive you nuts. But something's always going on. And it beats covering landslides in Pacific Palisades."

Bettenhausen edged closer to Sparling. They were seated on what appeared to be a metal trunk, amid piles of mimeographed press releases. "Is . . . ah . . . this room bugged?" he whispered.

"I dunno. It was for a long time. Who cares? I holler loud to make it easy for them."

"Would you care to take a stroll with me?" Bettenhausen was glorying in his role. It was a shame Dr. Wicker would not witness his mastery of the situation.

"Huh? You wanna see Moscow? It's pretty dull around here. But I could spin you around in my new Pontiac. From Finland."

"Eliot," Bettenhausen whispered, "some personal matters. A walk might be easier."

"Oh, sure, sure." Sparling, always helpful—friends of network executives came to Moscow regularly and he was required to take them on tours—lumbered to his feet, scattering envelopes and carbon paper.

There was the usual delay for the elevator. Sparling joked in Russian with the woman at the desk. He said to Bettenhausen: "Been here close to four years and I haven't found the stairs yet."

"In a twenty-nine-floor building?"

"It's a fact. Once I was late for a broadcast—the communications center is about a ten-minute ride—and I got nervous. So I raised hell with the manager. 'Your elevators stink,' I said, 'they never come, show me where the stairs are.' It was against hotel rules, he said. 'What if there's a fire?' I asked. The guy shakes his head. 'If we ever *have* to,' he says, 'we'll show you stairs, but you can't see them.' I once took an afternoon off and looked all over my floor. No stairs. I think the architect forgot them and they're afraid to admit it."

Sparling suggested they walk along Kutuzov Avenue, a broad street of high-rises and stores. It was a depressing place, Bettenhausen thought, but sufficiently noisy so that anyone stalking them would have trouble eavesdropping.

"They can't build," Sparling said. "The buildings don't come out right. They can't connect them to the ground. Somebody screws up the measurements. They're always a few inches off, so they start to crack. Look at the foundations. Full of cracks and holes."

On the broad pavement, near a bus stop, Bettenhausen noticed that women in babushkas had set up stalls. One sold eggs, another apples, a third beets.

"Private enterprise," Eliot said. "You can't kill it. The old ladies come in from the farms at dawn. But if you think they're selling bargains guess again."

"Eliot, I must take you into my confidence," Bettenhausen said. "I can't give all the details of this matter, but I need information. Perhaps before I'm finished I can tell you what it's about. The problem is, I'm not sure myself."

"Anything for Warren Bettenhausen. The man who knew the line 'I'll sue you as soon as my lawyer graduates from law school.'"

For once Bettenhausen was reluctant to play movie trivia. But he smiled to acknowledge the tribute. "You weren't too bad yourself, Eliot. Groucho in *Duck Soup*."

"What can I do?"

"Translate this letter for me."

Under the awning of a Gastronom store, in front of a window stocked with toxic-looking sausage and tins of sardines, Bettenhausen gave the typewritten sheet to Sparling. The correspondent adjusted his eyeglasses, squinted at the letter, and began to translate.

"Hmmm. No date. It says, 'Dear friend.' No name. What is this?"

"I can't tell you, but go on."

"Okay. Hmmm. Hmmm. Something . . . let's see. 'The proposal . . . offer we are making is for . . . for . . . hmmmm . . . the amount agreed upon and can . . . even be greater.'" Sparling looked at Bettenhausen. "Excuse my curiosity, but what the hell is this all about?"

"I don't know. If I did, I might not tell you." He looked around apprehensively. Two women in drab coats were looking into the Gastronom window. One was pointing at a fat sausage.

"'The money can be paid any way you wish . . . hmmm . . . in any currency in any country or . . .' Word I'm not sure of. 'Given,' or 'marked for.' Ah, 'your family.' No, 'heirs. Marked for your heirs.' Let's see. 'In exchange, you will give us all the material you possess, to be delivered within one month of your acceptance of this agreement.'"

Bettenhausen was scowling. Two small boys had stopped to stare at his tam-o'-shanter. He barked at them and they scuttered away. "Anything else?" he asked Sparling.

"One sentence. Ah, 'The bearer of this letter knows nothing of its contents or meaning, but you may give him a one-word answer—yes or no.' Something about protecting the properties and giving them wide . . . mmm . . . distribution, I guess."

"What's the name at the bottom?"

"Begins with an L. . . . Let's see. . . . Lel . . . ?"

"Leland."

"That's right. You needling me, Betts? Can you read Russian?"

"No, it was a hunch. I'll take the letter, Eliot. And not a word to anyone."

Sparling gave the sheet to Bettenhausen, who replaced it in his coat pocket. So. An offer was being made to Borkin. A great deal of money, evidently. For "materials." What kind? Scientific? Related to defense?

A small truck—a metal bin mounted on a motorcycle—pulled up to the curb. Immediately a crowd gathered. A teen-age boy climbed on top of the tank and began lifting eels from the tank. Women jostled one another to buy them. A second boy wrapped them in sheets of *Pravda*.

"More private enterprise," Eliot said. "These kids play hooky and catch eels in the Moskva. Then they go into business. The whole country is looking to make a ruble one way or the other. Including your friend who got that letter from Mr. Leland."

The two men stared at the mobile fish store. The eels looked splendid to Bettenhausen—fat, dark, perfect for stewing or smoking.

They crossed the street and walked on. "What do you know about a man named Anatoly Borkin?" Bettenhausen asked.

Sparling's eyes were crafty. "That's who the letter is for."

"Damn you, I didn't say that."

"You're in deep, Betts."

"I asked you about Borkin."

Sparling looked over his shoulder. "Reputed to be the head guy in the intellectual resistance."

"Humanist Society? Marmaladov?"

"Maybe. The police tolerate them—sometimes. Brave guys. I did a radio piece on them last month."

"But what about Borkin?"

"Only rumors. Guy at our embassy told me a few days ago— Warren, for Chrissake, this is off the record—that he's the head of the whole thing."

"What whole thing?"

"Who knows what to call it? To change the country around. Free speech. Free press. Unions. Freedom of worship. Freedom to emigrate, and that includes the poor shnooks who can't get to Israel. They claim Borkin heads up the apparatus, or at least could if he wanted to."

"Why doesn't he come out into the open?" Bettenhausen asked. "Like Marmaladov and the others I read about. That general who keeps getting arrested at demonstrations. And Solzhenitsyn."

The correspondent frowned. He bobbed his head, gesturing to Bettenhausen to turn around and walk back to the Ukraina. "I think he's safer under wraps. The KGB lets him talk to people, write papers, make contacts. They know what he's up to. But they don't want him to get any publicity. It would look bad."

"Why?"

"Borkin was on their team. Director of the Lenin Institute. Top job at Moscow University. Order of Karl Marx. Every honor they have and maybe a Nobel prize one of these years. It's esoteric stuff he's into. Genetic code. You know—RNA, DNA, amino acids, creating a living virus out of a drop of oatmeal. If a guy like that started sounding off against the cops and how they intimidate everyone it would look bad. They'd have a tough time sticking him in a laughing academy."

"Suppose he defected?"

"It's unlikely. You got to understand these guys. They're Russians.

267

They love this miserable place. And they have guts. It takes something to hang on here, trying to change things."

They turned the corner on Kutuzov and headed toward the Ukraina. The Westbury people and the Yasudas were standing on the steps, ready for *hondling*. If the U.S.S.R. would sell, they would buy. Herbie was talking to a thick-necked man with a crimson face and short curly hair, shaved high up the back of his head.

"Money speculator," Eliot said. "Patenko. Also pimp. There's rackets here also. You can't keep good men down."

Bettenhausen told him about the man in the oversized cap and topcoat who had tried to intercept Wicker once, then had appeared again in front of the theater in Leningrad. "Our guide insisted he was one of these *spekulyanti*, but I doubt it."

"Could be. It's a mania here. Money, gold, clothing, transistor radios. They'll try to buy the shoes off your feet."

"Eliot, would the words 'museum and bread' mean anything to you?"

"Museum and bread?"

"Yes, something like that."

"They got lots of both in Moscow."

"It doesn't strike you?"

"Let me check my files."

"My boy, if the information is in *your* files, you will not find it until Easter. I do wish you'd clean your office up."

"Don't knock it. It discourages the KGB."

Murray Yasuda took a picture of Bettenhausen and his friend ascending the steps of the Ukraina. "Smile, you're on Candid Camera," the Japanese said.

"Friends of yours?" Sparling asked.

"Fellow tourists."

"Hey, hey!" Herbie shouted. "I know that guy. I seen him on television. Hey, that's the guy on UBC, in the fur hat. Flo, what's his name?"

"Sparling," Si said. "Foreign correspondent."

Bettenhausen was required to make quick introductions. Eliot did not seem to mind. He autographed Sandra Yasuda's guidebook.

"The professor goes first class," Herbie said. "See the kinds of friends he has? And what are we doing? Looking for bargains." He pointed to the money-changer-procurer, the bullish Patenko. "Mr. Sparling, tell this creep to get lost. I got no dollars to change."

Sparling shouted in Russian at the man. It had no effect. He grinned, displaying steel incisors.

In the lobby Sparling asked Bettenhausen where he could find him. The Hollywood man invited him for dinner, but Eliot declined. "Listen, I'm horny as a rhinoceros. I lined up this Swedish airline hostess. Tonight's the night. But I'll meet you for a drink here at six o'clock. Okay?"

"Good. Remember. *Bread and museum.*"

Sparling hesitated by the elevator. He was being pointed out to members of Three Worlds as a famous person and he enjoyed the notoriety. Mavis Hutzler was chattering about how much she liked him—especially when he wore his fur hat in front of the Kremlin. Mr. Wattle was informing Gunthorpe that most of "those fellows in the media" were not to be trusted. "Don't know anything about that one there," he shrilled, "but most of 'em are pinkos. The media are ruining the country."

Sparling pulled Bettenhausen close. "If that letter I translated for you is for Borkin, forget it. Don't deliver it." He battled his way into the lift.

Bettenhausen, bereft of appetite, found his wife and the Wickers in the dining room. Most of the tourists had forsaken heavy lunches. Rest and tea were better advised at midday. Soviet cuisine was hardly an inducement.

"Ah, caviar, black bread, and tea," Bettenhausen said. "For me, nothing but tea."

"Take some of mine," his wife said. "We'll never get the waiter back. It's this conference. They can't handle it."

"Imagine, Warren," Rose-Anne said, "two hundred literary critics from Communist and neutral nations. That man in the robe and the funny hat over there is the Mongolian People's Republic's leading authority on verse. Can you tie that?"

Bettenhausen scowled at a red and black lacquered box at his wife's elbow. "Did you purchase that, Cornelia?"

"Now don't carry on, Betts. It was only thirty-two dollars."

"Good God," Bettenhausen said. "Isn't it amazing the things some people would rather have instead of money?"

Wicker did not laugh. He was bursting to know what Bettenhausen had learned. An orderly man, he had taken care of Mark Abrams' gums and was now ready to handle the Borkin matter—with an assist from the Hollywood man. But the tilt of Bettenhausen's beard, the look in his eyes told him: *not in front of the women.*

"Let me tell you what they're behind in," Mr. Wattle said. "Oil drilling. Automated machine tools. Food packing. Road-building equipment. Name it. They need it."

"Feed 'n' grain ain't much neither," Gunthorpe said. "Seen me some scrawny critters on the way in from the airport."

The two men were strolling down Kutuzov Avenue in mild afternoon sunlight. They had been stopped four times by money-changers. Father Konay, walking with them, was silent. Wattle and Gunthorpe seemed to know so much more than he did. And both were so sure of themselves.

Father Konay admired Mr. Wattle but he could not fathom how a man could reap such joy from making rubber. Oh, it was important work, he was certain. Modern society functioned in terms of machines. But to be so in *love* with them? To be intrigued with every aspect of them? Father Folker, with his hippie friends in beads and Indian shirts, would hate Mr. Wattle, denounce him. Wasn't there some place in between? the priest mused. Where you could take the comforts Mr. Wattle's machines provided, yet not let them strangle you?

"The Italians are building a thousand cars a day here," Mr. Wattle said. "I thought they were traitors at first, doing business with Bolsheviks, but I've come around. Something's got to civilize them, and it might as well be capitalism."

"Maybe religion?" Father Konay asked.

"Oh, that's all right also. But greed comes before faith."

"And faith triumphs."

There was an explosion of honking and shouts from the street. Mr. Wattle and his companions turned around. Near the boulevard curb, a crowd was gathering. A small truck was attempting to push a passenger car to get it to start. A policeman was hurrying toward the vehicles, blowing his whistle. The truck tried once more, bumping the sedan, but the engine failed to respond. It came to rest defeated, with its wheels against the curb.

"Don't take much to draw a crowd in Rooshia," Gunthorpe marveled. "They doin' better than the ballet."

"It's because they don't know a thing about automobiles, and have so few of them," Mr. Wattle said. "Say, let's watch. This is going to be good."

The policeman, tooting frantically, moving traffic around the vehicles, ordered the passengers out. A sad middle-aged man and a terrified woman got out of the car. It was an older Russian make, looking like a converted taxi. The truck driver shouted at the officer, backed his truck away, and sped off. The policeman took his license number.

The policeman, robbed of one victim, turned his wrath on the couple. The woman wept, her face turning red, her body shaking.

The man, explaining the failure of his car, kept repeating what sounded to the Americans like "battery."

"It's not the battery," Mr. Wattle said.

"How can you tell?" Father Konay asked—awed by his roommate's knowledge.

"It's the electrical systems. There was a heavy rain last night."

The policeman was writing a ticket. The woman reacted as if she had just been assigned to a work camp in the Crimea.

"They go hard on 'em hyeah," Gunthorpe said. "Car gits stalled, they lock a man up. Ain't fair."

"I'll handle this," Mr. Wattle said.

The priest was distressed. "Please, Mr. Wattle, remember what Pepi said. We're guests here."

"Nonsense. If they're too dumb to solve this, it's the least I can do." He bounced on invisible springs through the crowd of passers-by, smiled at the policeman, smacked the rusty blue hood of the car. "Open. Open up, young man."

They looked at him with bemused eyes. The policeman, less angered than confused, made a motion to Wattle to leave. The industrialist made a gesture of raising the hood.

"Aaaaah," the driver said. "Aaaah . . ." He yanked vigorously at the hood. It creaked and sprang open. Mr. Wattle looked at the corroded innards of the Russian car with distaste. "Good heavens, what a mess. Say, look at the way they hang the carburetor on there. We haven't done that since the 1929 Essex."

Opening his immaculate jacket, he reached into his shirt pocket and took out his multipurpose tool—screwdriver, pliers, hammer, file, cold chisel, and wrench.

"*Amerikanski?*" a well-dressed man in the crowd asked Gunthorpe.

"You damn said it, boy."

"Aaaaaah." The murmur spread through the crowd—*an American was at work on the engine.* Even the policeman drew closer.

"It has to be the distributor cap," Mr. Wattle pronounced. "It always is. Except where did they hide it?" Clouds of rust rose from the motor as he poked around. Orange flakes dropped from the cylinder block, the air filter, the generator. "Ah, there she is. Now. How in blazes do I get the top off?"

He removed his jacket and gave it to Father Konay. He rolled up one sleeve and bent his head deep into the engine. "Yup. Yup. I've taken many an engine apart but I've never seen one rigged as badly as this."

It seemed to Gunthorpe, who knew a little about cars himself, that the distributor cap could not be reached from the angle at which

Mr. Wattle had positioned himself. Nor, as far as the grain merchant could ascertain, did it seem a normal sort of cap, with a detachable head.

"Gunthorpe, hold my left leg, and you, Father, grab my right leg, so's I can get my hands in there." The men obliged. Mr. Wattle crawled into the engine. The Russians broke into applause. The policeman was smiling. "Now, ask that driver if he's got a big screwdriver. I can't reach it with my gimmick."

"Russian ain't that good, Horace."

"Yell loud at him."

"Screwdriver!" A.T. bellowed.

"Tool," Father Konay tried, feeling Mr. Wattle's leg slipping from his grasp. "Like so." He made a twisting movement with his hand, as if working on a bolt.

"Aaaaah. Aaaaaaah." The driver rummaged under his front seat and gave Gunthorpe a rusted screwdriver.

"Say, that's fine," Mr. Wattle said from the gloom of the engine. "I can get this into the two hooks on either side. I see how they release. Now you know what we'll find? I'll tell you what we'll find. We'll find a film of moisture inside that cap. I'm never wrong. I know these foreign systems. They are not waterproof. A film of moisture, and neither hell nor high water, nor a hundred pushes, nor two hundred battery jumps will make that engine kick over until she's dried out."

There was a snapping noise inside the engine. Mr. Wattle reached in carefully, jiggled something—a few parts fell to the street from the ruined motor—and then asked that he be retrieved.

Standing on the street, his white shirt streaked with grease and rust stains, he showed the driver, his wife, the policeman, and his friends the disconnected cap. "Now then, what do we see?"

Father Konay peered into the cuplike object. "It's moisture all right. I can see the drops."

"Now all I need is something to dry it with. Anyone have a cigarette lighter?"

Gunthorpe offered his. It was a TWA souvenir and threw a lusty flame.

The Russian spectators gathered close. An awed silence attended Mr. Wattle's ministrations, as if he were installing a plastic valve in a damaged heart. He moved the lighter flame around the damp interior of the distributor cap.

"Dry 'er out and she'll turn right over," he said briskly. "They all do this, all these foreign vehicles." He held the cap to his face. His glinting eyes studied the interior. "Almost dry. Once over lightly."

Again he rotated the darting flame inside the part. "Dry now. Boys, give me a hand again."

Once more Mr. Wattle climbed into the decrepit motor. With the screwdriver he affixed the cap. A few more bits of hardware tinkled to the pavement.

"Start 'er up," the rubber manufacturer ordered.

The man's vacant face was filled with dumb worship. The policeman, mollified, ordered him into the car.

"Give it the floor," Mr. Wattle snapped. He mimed turning the ignition, then stamped his foot to the sidewalk vigorously. "Let 'er have it."

The crowd moved back in hushed wonder. Suddenly the engine exploded with earsplitting vigor. The driver grinned. The policeman waved him on. The woman threw a kiss to Mr. Wattle. And to the amazement of Father Konay and A. T. Gunthorpe, the audience of Russian citizens broke into rhythmic applause, in the manner of spectators at the ballet.

"They givin' you the big hand, Horace," Gunthorpe said.

"And you deserve it," the priest said.

The policeman came over and pumped Mr. Wattle's hands and delivered a short speech of gratitude. The car blasted off in a discharge of black fumes.

People would not stop applauding. Mr. Wattle had not seen so many grateful smiles since the last Christmas bonus was announced to his 312 employees, four years ago.

The man from Bay Landing wiped his hands on a newspaper and looked unhappy as the ancient car chugged away. "I'll bet his cylinder head is warped or maybe even cracked," he said. "That's another thing with these European engineers. They never seem to get a decent fit between the block and the head." He looked accusingly at the policeman, who understood not a word. "It splits the gasket after a while."

The tourists strolled away. People were humming about the American who, with nothing more than a cigarette lighter, had magically made an old Moskvich start.

"Ole Horace," A.T. said admiringly. "Ole Horace. Turn him loose in Rooshia, he'd make a dang capitalist out of ever'body in a week."

On the steps of the Pushkin Museum Bettenhausen had a chance to talk to Dr. Wicker. Their wives and Theresa Carrell had lingered at the souvenir counter, buying postcards and reproductions. Terry had seen the original of Degas's *Blue Dancers* in the exhibit. The clerk was searching the folders for a print of it.

"I'll have to make this fast," Bettenhausen said. "Sparling is meeting us for a drink in a few hours. Borkin is believed to be the head of the intellectual underground. There's a conspiracy on the part of the foreign press not to mention his name. Top scientist, future Nobel laureate, so on. They'd be hard put to declare him insane or expel him. So he treads a fine line."

"Leland never told me this."

"Your Mr. Leland may be the biggest fraud since the late Stephen Weinberg, posing as Commander Stephen Weyman of the United States Navy, presented Princess Fatima to President Harding."

The dentist looked disconsolate. That nice fellow Leland! "Who is he?" Wicker asked.

"I can't say. Sparling translated the letter for me. It's an offer for material Borkin has. It sounds like a large financial offer for scientific data."

"He could still be a CIA man. Don't they do a lot of work in that line?"

"They do," the Hollywood man said. "But Leland may be gambling with Borkin's life even if he's working for us. Sparling says if a letter like this was found on Borkin, particularly if he were caught getting it from you, there'd be hell to pay."

"For who?" asked Dr. Wicker.

"For Borkin. All those honors wouldn't mean a damn. And the bearer of the letter might catch a bit of jail himself."

Wicker swallowed. He was frightened. But his generous view of people would not admit to dread possibilities. Who was he, after all? An innocent man engaged by a spy. It occurred to him that had he not told Bettenhausen, and had not Bettenhausen involved his journalist friend, he could have pleaded ignorance of everything. Now he had no excuse. He knew about Borkin. He knew what was in the letter. He knew what he was letting himself in for.

"Warren . . . what the heck?" Wicker asked. "What do we do now?"

"Sparling is checking that phrase about museum and bread, uttered by our friend in the cap. After he meets with us this afternoon we'll decide."

The women emerged from the museum. They looked animated and happy. Theresa Carrell held a rolled-up cylinder. She'd found her Degas. Rosie was laughing at something Cornelia Bettenhausen had said. A terrifying notion seized Wicker. Suppose he went to jail? He would be an accomplice. Who would pay the mortgage back in Riverford? Or his son's tuition? And what would happen to Mark Abrams' teeth? What would Rosie do for a doubles partner?

274

"So . . . so . . . this may be a trap for Borkin?" the dentist asked.

"A possibility. Leland may be a Soviet agent, ordered to, as the underworld says, set Borkin up."

"And set me up."

"You are an unwitting agent, Arnold. They understand these things."

Wicker began to get angry. "Not any more I'm not. I have a pretty good idea what this is about. Thanks to you."

"You missed the Picassos," Rose-Anne Wicker called. "A whole room of them. Arnie, they were incredible."

He did not hear her.

"Deny everything," Bettenhausen said. "If they arrest you, plead ignorance. Tell them about Leland. He's probably one of their own. Our intelligence people can get a line on him."

"While I spend the rest of this tour in jail?" Wicker did not want to hurt his friend's feelings. But Bettenhausen could see the accusing look on his face.

"Cheer up, Arnold," Bettenhausen said. "If you wish, you can use Hardy's line to Laurel. I can see you feel that way."

"Holy smoke, Warren, this is insane."

"'A fine mess you've gotten us into,'" Cornelia said. "That's the line, isn't it, Betts?"

"What mess?" Rose-Anne asked. "Who got who into what?"

"Oh, we're just kidding, Rosie," the dentist said. "Deciding where to eat tonight—that awful hotel grub or the Georgian restaurant Pepi told us about."

Her pretty face, turning slightly away, told Wicker that she did not believe him. Was there a poorer liar in the world?

"But these are *not* precious stones," Lulu Flemington said. "They are semiprecious."

Virgil had agreed—reluctantly, because he needed an afternoon to himself—to accompany the Flemingtons to the shop he had recommended. "Quite right, madame. It is a bit of a misnomer. They sell semiprecious stones here. But there are some lovely things to buy."

"I don't see anything worth buying."

"Look at these clear topazes," Flemington said. "I always thought a topaz was yellow."

"Russian topaz is clear," Lulu said huskily.

"Madame is right. But that makes it more valuable."

"I doubt that," Lulu said. Harry was surprised by her conciliatory tone. Virgil remained an unknown quantity to her. He was not a serf, not a climber. Defying categorizing, always obliging, he pleased her and puzzled her. The tour escort would be worthy of a generous tip.

"What is this thing here? It says crystal topaz." Lulu, at one of the counters, was pointing to the English sign over a tray of earrings, brooches, and cuff links. "And why is it so cheap?"

"It is cut glass, Mrs. Flemington. Do not bother with it."

"I don't like any of them," Lulu said. "And they have no right to call this a precious stones store." She steadied herself on her umbrella.

"The clear topaz is a good buy," Virgil said. "Perhaps Mr. Flemington would like a pair of cuff links. Or Madame some earrings? You can buy the stones and have them set when you get home."

Lulu's head was moving in short negative strokes from side to side and her mouth was a line. Flemington looked appealingly to the guide.

"The specialty here is malachite," Virgil said. He spoke in Russian to a woman behind the counter. "And the best items are not displayed." He spoke in Russian and pointed to the back of the store.

Lulu removed her dark glasses. The woman came out of a rear room bearing a malachite casket the size of a cigar box. It was quite beautiful, Harry could see, an exceptional piece. The green was unearthly, veined, smooth, full of secrets of the Russian earth. Lulu was hooked.

"The price?" she asked.

Virgil spoke to the saleswoman. "She says fifteen hundred dollars. Special sale. It is marked down from seventeen hundred."

"I don't believe a word she is saying. I'll give her a thousand, take it or leave it."

"That is impossible, Mrs. Flemington. The stores are run by the state and the prices are fixed."

"Rigged would be more like it. What's it in rubles?"

"In rubles fifteen thousand, Mrs. Flemington, but they will not accept rubles in this store. It can be paid for only in dollars or pounds, or Swiss francs. Or any other hard currency."

"I've seen enough," Lulu said. "I want it, but if she won't cut the price, I am not interested." She stroked the surface of the green malachite casket. It was a remarkable piece, and Lulu, whose taste was impeccable, desired it. But to buy it without hacking away at the price was against her principles.

"Let's go," Lulu said. "I don't want it."

Flemington knew she did. He whispered to the guide: "Take her to another shop. I'll be with you in a minute. Didn't you say there was a place down the street that sold peasant blouses? She may want some for our servants. Suggest it. I'll stay here a few minutes."

Pepi bowed his head slightly. He walked after Lulu, following her into the Stoleshnikov Preoluk, guiding her to the store selling Ukrainian blouses.

Flemington whipped out his traveler's checks and pointed to the malachite casket. After much explaining and arguing, he paid the price and got them to write both a true receipt, which he hid in his wallet, and a faked receipt for a thousand dollars.

While he waited, he bought, with some dollars he had left, a clear topaz necklace set in antique gold, for a hundred and seventy-five dollars. He had gone to it unwaveringly, and bought it as fast as he could count out the money. Before the tour was over, in a darkened hotel room, he would place it around Theresa Carrell's neck, and let it remain there after he had removed all her clothing and made love to her. In his mind were visions of Rubens goddesses, Rembrandt's women of the Bible—nude and unashamed, wearing only a string of pearls, a pendant of jewels.

To Bettenhausen's horror, Mr. Wattle spotted Eliot Sparling as the young man emerged from the Ukraina elevator.

"Say, I do know your face," Mr. Wattle said. "I see you on Channel 6 all the time back in Bay Landing, state of Washington."

"Hi," Sparling said. "Welcome to the U.S.S.R."

"I enjoy your reports," Mr. Wattle said. "You tell things with a great deal of fairness, which is more than I can say for most of your colleagues. The media are ruining our country."

Pleasure at being recognized curdled in the correspondent's stomach. A True Believer. Still, a fan was a fan. "Well, nice seein' you, buddy."

"Horace T. Wattle, Bay Landing, Washington. My friends—Father Konay and Mr. Gunthorpe. He's a Memphis man."

"Yeah, I know the face but not the name," Gunthorpe said. "Sure enjoy you fellahs with the news. Y'all bring us the world raht in our home. We grateful."

"Yes indeed," said Father Konay. "We enjoy you very much, Mr. Sparling."

"Thanks," the correspondent said. He saw Bettenhausen's white beard glowing in the darkness. A long-jawed man with a shock of curly brown hair was seated with him.

"Are you aware," Mr. Wattle crowed, grasping Sparling's lapel, "that sixty-two per cent of the American people don't trust anything that's said on television?"

Sparling's eyes narrowed; his skin prickled. The bald-headed tourist was attacking his church. "Inaccurate figures. The new survey shows that seventy-seven per cent of all Americans would vote for

David Brinkley for President, sixty-five per cent like Garrick Utley's haircut, and eighty-one per cent would go to the ends of the earth for Barbara Walters. Excuse me, I got an appointment."

"Nice young man," Mr. Wattle said.

Bettenhausen, seething over the interception of Sparling, introduced Dr. Wicker to the broadcaster but did not elaborate on the dentist's role. They ordered mineral water—Sparling claimed it was the best in the world and that he, a shivering hypochondriac, had not had a cold or a headache in years thanks to the salubrious effects of Narzan—and the correspondent produced a clipping which he had been using as a marker in a red-jacketed book.

"Found out something about your friend Borkin," he said.

"Is it safe to talk here?" Bettenhausen asked.

"Yeah. I get lots of visitors. No sweat. They don't keep guys like me under surveillance. A phone tap, a mail check, that about does it."

Dr. Wicker's mouth opened, as if he wanted to say: "But what about me?" After the twists and turns and false starts of his mission to Borkin, who was not to say that he was being watched every minute? Bettenhausen had the same thought; but he was brimming with excitement, his new life as impresario of espionage. Was it not possible that he could sell the idea to a producer and shoot the film on a low budget? He himself would direct, of course, shoot most of it through a telephoto lens, creating artistic distortions much in favor with the hot young directors. Also freeze frames, slow motion, and lots of out-of-focus sequences. This would make up for any gaps in narrative. Behind scenes of unutterable violence, they would play Mozart, preferably concerti for wind instruments. This, too, was in vogue with the young directors who mattered.

"I dug this out of the files," Sparling said. "It's from *Pravda* two months ago. I'll give you a fast translation."

"I'm impressed," Dr. Wicker said. "You read and write Russian."

"Anyway, there was this protest meeting for the Odessa Eleven," Sparling said. "Two hundred people—hooligans, the article says—gathered in Pushkinskaya Street and attacked the police to protest the jailing of the Odessa Eleven."

"Who are they?" Dr. Wicker asked. "Like the Catonsville Nine?"

"Same idea. Ukrainian nationalists. All the guys want is a chance to write, and read, and make a speech now and then. Anyway, they're still in jail, awaiting trial. They could have a long wait."

"And what was Borkin's involvement in this?" asked Bettenhausen. "Did he participate?"

"No. But his name showed up on this a few weeks later." Sparling—

with a glance around the crowded lobby—took from the book a thin sheet of paper. There was a heading, a text, and a list of names on the bottom.

"A circular protesting the arrest of the Odessa Eleven?" Bettenhausen asked.

"With a list of signers. That's pretty gutsy in this country. Usually these protests are anonymous. Nobody wants to get hit. And they hit, they *hit*. They may not shoot you the way Stalin did, but they fix you good. Anyway, they got a bunch of writers and intellectuals to sign it, and it included an A. Borkin, otherwise unidentified."

"Go on," Bettenhausen said.

"This list was impressive. If there's one thing the Russkies hate it's nationalities getting their dander up. Ukrainians, Tatars, Lithuanians, Jews. It gives them fits. They must have sat hard on those Odessa people. This flyer must have given them double fits—with Borkin's name on it. He's a favorite, one of their stars. I told Warren about that Nobel prize he may land if he ever separates the DNA from the RNA, or whatever it is he does."

"So Borkin may be in serious trouble?" Bettenhausen queried.

"He's dropped out of sight, at least out of the press reports. I tried calling someone at the Lenin Institute—I used a cover, asked about some stuff I'd read in *Time* about the genetic code, and they said he couldn't be contacted. No reason. They never have to give you one."

Bettenhausen rubbed his hands. He was enjoying the chase too much, Dr. Wicker thought, reveling in the scheming, the subterfuges. What chance did they stand against the secret police?

"Warren, why don't we just go to the embassy?" Wicker asked. "No offense to Mr. Sparling here, but why pursue this? Borkin's in trouble. Why involve him?"

"You got a point," Sparling said. "But you might do him more harm than good, telling the embassy. The KGB goes to lots of trouble to build cases against people. Borkin is important, but so were Pasternak and the Medvedev brothers. I don't know what to tell you."

"We still have time to construct a plan," Bettenhausen said. "What about 'bread and the museum'?"

"I found it in here." The correspondent showed them his *Travel Guide to Russia*. "This is where you find things. It's Irving R. Levine's guide to the Soviet Union, and it's the best. Levine's a journalist, and he knew this country the way no travel writer ever could."

"It's that easy?" Dr. Wicker asked. "In a guidebook?"

"It can't be anything else," Sparling said. "Levine says there's something called the Museum of Secret Communist Meetings. Bolshevits-

279

kaya Ulitsa 4 in the Presnya District. I've never been there. Anyway, it's got all kinds of mementos of the Revolution, including a hunk of preserved brown bread."

"So," Bettenhausen said with satisfaction, "your friend in the over-sized cap was not talking gibberish."

"Evidently not," the dentist said.

Sparling's distorted eyes went from the stout man to Wicker. "I don't know what you guys are up to, but take it easy. You know it's against the law to bring in a message to a Soviet citizen? This isn't Raritan, New Jersey."

"Go on, Eliot," Bettenhausen said. "What about this bread?"

"Here's what Levine says. 'One morning in 1917 a mother gave a son a piece of bread as he left home. For this poor family during the revolution period of food shortage this half-pound of bread was the boy's ration for the day. The lad was a sixteen-year-old Communist Party member named N. V. Khodyakov. After he had gone, his mother discovered that he had hidden the bread on a table for her. He was killed that day by a bullet while fighting with Czarist soldiers near the Metropole Hotel. His mother kept the bread in a small glass container for forty years as a precious memento of her son's bravery and generosity, and finally she gave it to a neighborhood museum where it is being preserved with chemicals.'"

"I think I got the rest of that loaf with my caviar at lunch," Wicker said.

"The name of the museum again?" Bettenhausen asked.

Sparling scrawled it on a memo pad. "Forget the name, you'll never get it in Russian. The district is Krasnopresnaya and the address is Bolshevitskaya Ulitsa, 4. That should get you there."

Wicker started to say something about the meeting. It had been understood, according to Veg, that the meeting would take place in midmorning during the tour of the Kremlin, at the Queen of Bells. The man in the cap had said nothing about a time for the rendezvous. They would have to assume that the time of the meeting with Borkin was unchanged. But why had it been changed twice? Leland had specified the Lenin Institute; Veg had changed it to the huge bell; the little man, to the Museum of Secret Communist Meetings. These ruminations distressed the dentist.

"Tomorrow is Thursday," Bettenhausen said. "We shall be there at ten."

"Who?" Sparling asked. "Both of you?"

"I'm not sure." Bettenhausen shut his eyes. He tugged at his beard, as if trying to draw inspiration from it.

The elevator doors opened and some of the Three Worlds people emerged—J. P. Huggins, with a bourbon flush on his face, Barbara Huggins, wobbly on spike heels, wearing a low-cut crimson dress, a group of amiable Midwesterners.

"The letter, please, Arnold," Bettenhausen said.

The dentist reached into his pocket and gave his friend the manila envelope with its single sheet of paper. They had not resealed it.

"Man, look at the lungs on that one," Sparling said admiringly as Barbara Huggins walked by. "Fellow tourists?"

"Nice couple," Wicker said, waving to J.P. and his wife. "New York lawyer. Lovely Italian girl."

"Mama mia, atsa some spicy meat ball."

A sudden flaming startled both the dentist and the correspondent. They turned from their surveillance of Barbara Huggins' chest and saw Bettenhausen holding the twisted tip of Leland's letter over a large ash tray. The rest of it flamed brightly. Soon it was reduced to a flaky black ash. The Hollywood man shoved it into the tray, poked it into a mound of cinders, and looked up defiantly.

"So much for Mr. Leland's letter. Whoever he is, he will not entrap Dr. Borkin."

"Warren . . . what the heck?" Wicker asked.

"My plan is complete. It does not matter what side he's on or where Dr. Borkin stands, we are launching our counterattack this moment."

"But the message," the dentist protested.

"Eliot, can you recall the gist of the letter?" asked Bettenhausen.

"Sure. The amount as negotiated stands. It can be even more. Payable to him or his heirs in any kind of currency. Ah . . . for all the materials discussed. The bearer of the message does not know its contents and should be given a mere yes or no. That was it, roughly."

"Good. All three of us know it now. We shall get it to Anatoly Borkin, with harm to no man."

"But he'll be expecting an envelope tomorrow," Wicker said.

Bettenhausen got up, wheezing. Cornelia and Rose-Anne had come out of the elevator. Another dinner of rubbery veal loomed—unless they could find one of the Georgian or Armenian restaurants that Pepi had recommended—and already his gut was queasy.

"We shall not disappoint him, Arnold. Ah, the ladies are here. Eliot, you must meet our wives. Cornelia is a great admirer of your fur hats."

Day 13: Moscow. The day begins inside the Kremlin walls, amid the golden-domed Cathedrals of Holy Russia, dating from the 15th century. Among the sights—Ivan the Great's Belfry, the great Bell, the Czar's Cannon. A visit to the Armory Museum and its collection of costumes, armor, weapons, carriages, and royal mementos. No end of stirring sights—the Kremlin Palace, the Congress Buildings, the Imperial Apartments, the Arsenal!

In the afternoon, we drive to the Lenin Hills for a grand panorama of Moscow. And we spend some time at the skyscraper University—32 stories and 30,000 students. At night, a chance to visit the Bolshoi Theater for opera or ballet, the high art of Russia at its best!

Father Konay was always the first down for breakfast. More and more he found himself retiring early, rising earlier, nurturing what little energy he had left. Luckily he was a sound sleeper. His roommate Mr. Wattle, capable of long evenings of dancing, eating, sight-seeing, would return to the room after midnight and proceed to spend a half hour in the bathroom, in ablutions, messages, dowsings, and once, to the priest's surprise, in energetic exercises. He heard these dimly, as if dreaming. Indeed, Mr. Wattle and Mr. Gunthorpe and the other people of the tour (not to mention the exotic places) were assuming the texture of a dream. Not a nightmare by any means nor a satisfying dream—but a dream of oddness, of puzzling places and inexplicable people. A bit guiltily, he imagined that his state was something like that achieved by marijuana smokers. Of course he frowned on such vices, but Father Folker admitted freely—*the gall of the man!* —to having "blown grass" while in college and even at the seminary (hard to believe) and to have enjoyed the dreamlike state.

At 7 A.M., seated by himself in the cavernous dining room, sipping tea and munching black bread, his thoughts about Father Folker were reinforced.

One of the chubby girls who worked behind the desk at the Ukraina was coming toward him with a letter in her hand. "For you, Fodder. You are Fodder Konay, no?"

"Yes, I am." He took the letter and recognized the letterhead of the parish. Folker's name was scrawled above it.

"Is nice day today, Fodder."

Father Konay thanked her. How polite and helpful these people were! It was difficult to think of them as godless atheists dedicated to the crushing of religion. The rulers, perhaps. False dogma. Blasphemies of Party members. But it did not seem to have affected the Russians. Indeed, they seemed overfriendly to him, as if going out of their way to assure him that, although they knew he was a priest, they liked him. It would be impossible for him, he knew, to think ill of Russians as *people* ever again.

He opened the letter. It had taken eight days to reach the hotel. Even before reading it, he sensed trouble—some development in the matter of the Ospreys, and the battle over taking in black members. Why did Folker have to keep bothering him?

Dear Steve,

The enclosed clipping from the Ash Valley *Tribune* is self-explanatory and should be of great interest to you. I know I found it fascinating, considering our recent go-rounds with the Ospreys. It seems friend Ed Marciniek, First Nester, doubles as a strong-arm man at their initiation ceremonies, and some of the fledglings don't like it. No wonder they kept you out of the Swoop at those secret rites!

Whether this will help us or hinder us in getting them to change policies, I don't know. Otherwise, all is quiet in the parish. Sacred Heart looks to have the best football team in Coal County now that Coach Kupzinski is recruiting our black brothers in Christ from Railtown. The starting "eleven" will feature the Johnson twins, Enoch and Enos, Claude Wilson, Willie Jackson, Washington Boyd, and Roosevelt Harper.

I hope your trip is enjoyable, and enlightening, and that the Holy Land and Mother Rome fulfill all your hopes.

Yours in Christ,
Bertram Folker, S.J.

Father Konay sipped the hot tea from the glass and began to read the clipping.

ASH VALLEY MAN CHARGES OSPREYS WITH BRUTALITY

Joseph Ptacek, of 119 S. Watkins Drive, Ash Valley, charged today he was severely beaten and suffered injuries at the hands of Edward Marciniek, 356 Munsey Avenue, Ash Valley, in initiation ceremonies at the clubhouse of the United Order of Ospreys last Saturday night.

Mr. Ptacek, 38, a bricklayer, said that Mr. Marciniek, 56, owner of Marchy's Bar & Grill, 378 Munsey Avenue, and "First Nester" of the Ospreys, punched and kicked him repeatedly when Mr. Ptacek, a "fledgling" undergoing initiation, objected to aspects of the ceremony.

"This big guy dressed up in a bird suit, feathers and all," Mr. Ptacek told police, "told me to get on the floor on all fours and lick up what he said was a puddle of rat's blood. He said Ospreys had to prove they weren't afraid of the rats and snakes that infested America."

Mr. Ptacek, in his complaint, said he refused to do so, and also kicked aside a live snake brought into the room, refusing to strangle it with his bare hands. When he tried to leave, Mr. Ptacek said, Mr. Marciniek punched him about the head, the arms, and the stomach, then kicked him when he was on the floor. Other members, including a man dressed as a priest, looked on.

"It was no priest," Mr. Ptacek said. "It was one of those goofy guys dressed in a collar. I know Father Konay and Father Folker and it was neither of them."

Mr. Marciniek and members of the "Swoop," or governing board, had no comment on Mr. Ptacek's charges, other than to say through their attorney, Horace Cohen, of Cohen, O'Connor and Cassiano, 212 West Main Street, that they were innocent of all charges.

"The Ospreys are a private secret organization," Mr. Cohen said, "and Mr. Ptacek's accusations are a violation of a sacred trust."

Mr. Ptacek is five feet two inches tall and weighs 132 pounds, and Mr. Marciniek is six feet three inches tall and weighs 275 pounds, and is a former all-county defensive end, who played at Mary Our Mother High School and at Scranton Tech.

Father Konay ordered another cup of tea. Thank God, praise Christ, hail Mary, that he was out of town when all this went on! Now he knew why the Ospreys never allowed him—or any other priest—to attend their rites of passage. *Rat's blood! A live snake!* How could they? What kind of nonsense was all that? And who was the man posing as a priest, pretending to be part of that lunacy?

But above all Father Konay was a shepherd. He knew about wayward sheep. He knew who needed love and affection. And in his sly way, he realized that Ed Marciniek and his brother birds would be needing every friend they could lay their hands on. There might be a trial. The priest knew Ptacek and his family. They were not quitters. They were hard-nosed. Slovaks, a match for Marciniek.

He must have been smiling when Mrs. Legrand glided into the dining room in search of a pot of tea for her husband.

"You look happy, Father," she said.

"Letter from home."

"Say, isn't that nice? No one ever writes to Weston or me. I guess we're sort of left out."

"Oh, this isn't important. Just parish matters." He felt sorry for the old couple. A few nights ago Mrs. Legrand had told him their story—

the wanderings, the dispersed uncaring relatives. He decided to visit Mr. Legrand that morning, joke with him, give him a little confidence. That was his trouble; he had been thinking about himself too much, worrying about Ash Valley and Father Folker and the Ospreys, and failing to inform his mind and his heart, and worse, failing to minister to his fellow tourists.

"Let me help you with the tray, Mrs. Legrand," Father Konay said. "There, I'll take it."

"That isn't necessary, Father."

"I'm feeling particularly Christian today. Maybe I can cheer Mr. Legrand a little. I promise, no praying and no attempt to convert either of you."

En route to the Kremlin for the morning tour, Pepi took the empty seat next to Mrs. Carrell.

"Just for the short ride," Mr. Wattle warned him. "That's my girl you're sitting next to."

"I am sorry, Mr. Wattle," Virgil said. "But even a poor guide should be allowed to share Mrs. Carrell's company. You cannot monopolize her. It is a company rule."

"I see I'm being joshed," the industrialist said. "But she's my date for the opera tonight."

"Really, Mr. Wattle," Terry said. "You're *too* attentive. I feel guilty."

"Faint heart never won fair lady. And none but the brave deserve the fair. Say, look at that line in front of the food store. It's even bigger than yesterday. I have to photograph that."

Theresa whispered to Virgil: "I think I won him in a raffle."

"I am sorry. There's little I can do. You must discourage him yourself. Perhaps a few stratagems . . ."

Theresa said nothing. Virgil was being kind. The man seemed to know everything. She was certain he knew of her friendship with Harry and the strains involved in avoiding one another. Three rows back, across the aisle of the bus, she could almost feel Lulu's eye hot on her back. And Harry! Looking the other way, always seeking a table where neither she nor any of her friends, the Grants, or the Wickers or the Bettenhausens were seated.

"Are people happy here?" she asked Pepi.

"One learns to accept." Virgil bent his head to his cupped hands and lit his Gitane. "They have a dreadful time making love. It is so cold most of the year. The parks are frequently used, because apartments are small and scarce. There aren't many automobiles."

"There are hotels."

"Russians cannot afford them. It is unheard of to take a hotel room for an affair. There are those concierges on each floor, a scrutiny of identity cards when one checks in, other forms of surveillance."

The bus stopped in Red Square.

"But we haven't been under surveillance," Theresa said. "At least I haven't noticed it."

"We are a tour, under control. We are seeing what the Russians want us to see, doing what they want us to do. Try traveling independently here, in a car of your own. You will be stopped, interrogated, forced to fill out forms, inspected. It is a police state run by policemen."

Dr. Wicker, seated behind the guide, who now rose to assemble his tourists in the street, had listened. *A police state run by policemen.*

"Where's the professor?" Herbie asked Cornelia when the party gathered at the Borovitsky Gate. Virgil was counting heads. Only two truants—Mr. Legrand and Mr. Bettenhausen. The Flemingtons were at the edge of the group, much too elegant for a Planet Tours party. They had been late that morning. No breakfast. Long cold silences.

"Something called the Central House of Film Directors invited my husband to speak," Cornelia said to Herbie. "They have these clubs here for professions. Warren knew some of their people."

"I'm impressed," Herbie said. "I couldn't get into the Central House of Shnorrers. Excuse me, I wanna stay next to Murray so I don't miss anything."

Dr. Wicker was silent. He could think only of Bettenhausen and what he was up to that morning. Should he have tried to stop him?

"So, ladies and gentlemen," Marika said. "Is here Palace of Arms, one of oldest museums in Europe, with collection starting with Ivan the Terrible. But to assure ladies, is not only arms, but beautiful decorative arts museum."

For the first time since the tour had begun, Rose-Anne Wicker noticed, Arnold looked unhappy. "I'll finesse this one," he said. "I've seen enough porcelain and pewter to hold me. I'll meander around and take a few exterior shots."

"Want me along?" Rosie asked.

The dentist shook his head. "No, Rosie, you go in." Wicker sighted through his long lens. An awful lot to photograph inside the Kremlin. And what if someone did show up at the Queen of Bells? Bettenhausen was producing, directing, and writing, and Wicker, reduced to a supporting role, had to go along with the script.

He consulted the fold-out map they had given him at the Ukraina Hotel. If he walked down the street in back of the Great Kremlin Palace, then turned left into a street behind the Cathedral of the

Annunciation, he would find himself in Cathedral Square. Across the square would be Ivan the Great's belfry, and in front of it the giant bell.

The silver collection of the Palace of Arms piqued Lulu's interest. When Marika said it was one of the most important silver collections in the world, she had scoffed. Now, inspecting the treasure in the glass cases, she was forced to lift her sunglasses and register her approval— short, affirmative jerks of her head. A connoisseur's smile played around her lips.

"Now there is something," Lulu said to Virgil. He, noting her interest, made a point to be at her side. "The panthers."

"Exquisite, Mrs. Flemington. A gift from Elizabeth I to Boris Goudonov."

"Why aren't there any of these for sale in the stores?" Lulu asked.

"Madame, antiques are rare in the Soviet Union. After the Revolution, most of the good things were shipped out. The noble families were forced to sell them to eat."

Lulu's eyes glistened. Was she, Harry wondered, musing over missed chances? What a treat it would have been to meet the trains from St. Petersburg and Moscow and Kiev, in Paris or Berlin, and haggle with Grand Dukes over candelabra and salt cellars!

In the Gallery of Gobelins, Marika pointed out the tapestries depicting the story of Don Quixote. "Russians much love Don Quixote," she said. "Is great hero in opera, ballet, films. Great art speaks in all languages, is it not so?"

"It surely is," Rosie Wicker said. For some reason, her eyes were misty. I am a hopeless romantic, she thought.

"One tapestry, there," Marika said, "is by man named Audran. Who knows who is Audran?"

No one did.

"We miss Betts," Cornelia said. "He'd have known."

Outside the Hall of Facets Palace, Marika pointed out the cupolaed roof. "Here is a real jewel of Kremlin," she said. "Look, please, small cupolas, with decorations on bases. Sky is very clear today, and is one of most beautiful pictures in all of Kremlin, if you want to take photographs."

Flemington moved back toward one of the cathedrals and focused on the roof of the Facets Palace. It was a magnificent sight. A few yards behind him, he could hear Theresa talking to Ibith Grant and the doctor as she, too, took a picture of the cupolas. Lulu was not looking. He stole a glance at his old mistress. Her head was turned upward, her eyes obscured by the camera, but he could see her long neck. In his pocket the topaz necklace was burning.

"There's Arn," Rosie said. "By that bell."

Dr. Wicker had been lingering in Cathedrals Square, on the chance that the scientist would make his appearance. No one had approached him. No one noticed him, save for a Danish tourist who, for some odd reason, thought he was a compatriot and had asked instructions for getting to Stalin's tomb.

He saw Rose-Anne and Cornelia wave to him. He waved back and busied himself with the Pentax. There was so much to shoot in Cathedrals Square, so many angles, compositions, combinations of forms and colors—whites, golds, reds, blacks, and a clear blue sky. But he was working poorly, failing once to adjust his exposure meter for film speed, jiggling the camera, forgetting his ultraviolet filter, using the sunshade at the wrong time. He would never make a spy.

"Hey, join the party," Rosie called.

"A few more pictures," the dentist called back. Pictures, indeed. He craned his neck, towering over the crowds of dumpy Russian sightseers. A thickset people, not given to smiling or laughter or even raising their voices, but goodness knows, friendly. Wicker decided he liked them, in spite of what their rulers did to people like Marmaladov and Borkin. He looked again for a sign of recognition in the crowd—someone with a scholarly face, a harassed manner, a man with a scar on his chin. Or the pinched little man with burning eyes, wearing the oversized cap and the floppy coat. Nothing. Only a swarm of Russians, moving noiselessly from church to church—the great belfry of Ivan the Great, the Cathedral of the Annunciation, the Cathedral of the Assumption, the Cathedral of the Archangel Michael, the Church of the Deposition of the Virgin's Dress. He walked outside the square to take his vigil at the site of the Queen of Bells.

"The heaviest bell in the world," Dr. Wicker read from his guidebook. "Nineteen feet high and weighs 465,000 pounds."

"Is big bell, no?" a grinning man in uniform asked Dr. Wicker.

No, not Borkin. The uniform was unpressed, without visible rank. A low-level functionary who spoke a little English.

"Very big."

"In America is also big bell?"

"Yes, in Philadelphia. Liberty Bell. It's also cracked."

The man bobbed his head—understanding not a word—and drifted off herding a woman and a small boy. His day was made, the dentist felt; he had spoken a few words of English to an American. How little people needed to feel good! Wicker did not hold with the new breed

288

of anthropological popularizers who wrote about the bone-wielding ape from whom man was descended, a fellow eager to bash his neighbor's cranium and eat his brains. How would anything ever get done if that were the case?

Bending low, Dr. Wicker began to try to discern the carvings on the black bell.

"Looking for someone?"

Dr. Wicker's weedy figure straightened up, and he turned, expecting Borkin. But it was only Henderson Grant, enigmatic behind dark glasses, looking at his own guidebook, and beckoning to his wife and Theresa to join them at the bell.

The taxicab let Bettenhausen off on Krasnopresnaya Quay on the Moskva. It was a dreary working-class district. But the streets were spotless and an attractive park bordered the river. Wandering in narrow streets and crooked alleys, he was saddened by the shabbiness of the houses. Communism bred cleanliness, he supposed, but not the decorative arts. He yearned for a window box of flowers, a graceful arch, a courtyard.

Two old women in babushkas, sweeping the gutters with twig brooms, stared at him. He was a rare sight—tam-o'-shanter perched on his large head, aristocratic beard, nubby Irish tweed jacket and cavalry twill slacks. On soft space shoes he padded toward his destination.

On Bolshevitskaya Ulitsa he saw the sidewalk water pump which Levine's book had mentioned. Across from it was the frame building in which now resided the Museum of Secret Communist Meetings.

Bettenhausen looked up and down the street. There was no one in sight. It was five minutes past ten. A one-armed man in a blue uniform lolled outside the doors of the museum. He wore two medals on his rumpled jacket. A hero of Stalingrad? Or perhaps even more ancient—an old Kronstadt sailor. There was a stubborn bravery in these people. Courage. Resignation. Slavic acceptance of life.

The Hollywood man realized he was on the edge of some discovery —a revelation, an epiphany. A vision of Borkin rising in glory on the road to Damascus? He crossed the street, nodded at the old fellow leaning against the museum, and studied a plaque on the wall of the building. Levine's guide had a translation:

Here in October 1917 the District Committee of the Russian Social Democratic Workers Party of Bolsheviks and the Revolutionary Committee of the Presnyansky District were housed.

The guard held the door open and bowed.

"Good morning," the Hollywood man said. He took off his tam-o'-

shanter. The museum, after all, was something of a church, and although Bettenhausen had no affection for True Believers, he was a polite man.

The museum was small. Large photographs showing the miserable conditions of the workers before the Revolution were displayed. A diagrammatic drawing illustrated the pyramid of the social order—the Czar and his family at the pinnacle, then the clergy, the army, the capitalists and landowners, and at the base, supporting all, the exploited working classes. There were copies of *Iskra,* the underground Bolshevik newspaper, photographs of clandestine printing shops.

On a table was a diorama of the 1905 Revolution: mounted czarist soldiers charging the workers' barricades. It was an interesting work. Bettenhausen wondered idly—whatever happened to Father Gapon, the Orthodox priest who led the march on the Winter Palace? Wasn't he a secret agent of the czarist police? Didn't the Reds eventually assassinate him?

There was a small room with a single window, a wall telephone, a table and stools, the room in which the committee met in 1917. There are workers and workers, Bettenhausen thought. One could hardly imagine a party of American hard-hats meeting in such a hole, conniving against the established order. In human affairs things never quite went the way the prophets predicted.

In glass cases he studied a huge metal whistle. According to the book, it was used to signal the start of the strike that touched off the 1905 Revolution. A non-political man, he was nevertheless touched by these shoddy relics. These had been oppressed people, victims of the lunacies of the Romanovs. Nearby he saw the preserved chunk of brown bread. It was not alone in the case. An old pistol lay alongside of it. And a photograph of the martyr Khodyakov.

He patted the envelope inside his jacket. Now all he needed was Professor Anatoly Borkin. The guide shuffled in, tried a few Russian words on Bettenhausen, saw that he was not being understood, and walked out. The Hollywood man was alone in the musty room. It smelled of potent disinfectant. All Russia, particularly indoor Russia, was a mélange of penetrating odors. They were not quite the odors of decay or unsanitary conditions, but rather of chemical cleanliness, pungent antidotes for germs and garbage and dirt. Bettenhausen's sinuses began to protest. He sneezed with thunderous satisfaction, sniffed his nasal inhalant, and toured the room again.

At the door leading from the vestibule a man in a dark blue suit approached him. He was in his fifties, Bettenhausen gauged, with a mild face and gentle brown eyes behind gold-rimmed glasses. On the left side of his chin was a small round scar. Leland knew a great deal. His shirt had the look of home laundering and his dark red tie was carelessly knotted. A resigned gaze greeted Bettenhausen's eyes.

"Boston," he said.

"Red Sox." Bettenhausen paused, as Wicker had instructed him. "Chicago."

"Bears."

Bettenhausen extended his hand. "Anatoly Borkin?"

"Yes."

The Hollywood man studied him. So this was what courage looked like! An undistinguished man, average height, average weight. A bespectacled man, a bit broad in the chest, a pale face, short nose, firm chin, weary eyes.

"My name is—"

Borkin raised his hand. "Do not tell. You have for me?"

"This." Bettenhausen reached into his pocket and took out the envelope.

A second man appeared in the doorway. It was dim in the vestibule. No lights were turned on and the darkened walls did not reflect much daylight.

As soon as Bettenhausen handed the envelope to Borkin, he recognized the onlooker. It was the thin man in the oversized tan cap and coat. The cap was in his hand, the coat was open. He watched the transaction with hurting eyes.

"Him . . . ?" Bettenhausen asked. It was the man who had changed the place of rendezvous—from the bell in the Kremlin to the museum. An aide of Borkin's? A relative? A coworker in the Humanist Society?

Borkin turned around and stared at the man, who now put on the ridiculous cap. It half covered his ears and the brim formed a bill over his forehead.

"Too late," Borkin said. "I am sorry, sir. Too late."

Bettenhausen's rubbery feet, soft in space shoes, froze to the floor boards. His mind raced ahead. The old "constructionist" tried to outline the next scene—police station? embassy? Lubianka?

The man in the cap spoke to Borkin. The professor nodded—slow nods of resignation. They exchanged a few words and then the man in the cap held out his hand and took the tan envelope from the scientist.

"What? Who?" Bettenhausen huffed. "Who is he? You have no right to turn that over!"

"You come," the man in the cap said. He gestured toward the street.

"I come and I go," Bettenhausen said angrily. "I don't know your game, sir, but I am a free American citizen. Let me pass."

Bettenhausen stepped out the door into Bolshevitskaya Ulitsa. Later he would decide that he would have staged it differently. The police car was too close to the curb. The door should not have been open. The man in uniform at the wheel was a mistake. Too much was given away. And the second man in the green raincoat, standing at the opened door of the limousine, was too obvious. He would have made it casual, an everyday affair, perhaps a taxicab and a woman.

The man holding the door open was burly, with a high forehead and lank blond hair brushed far back on his round head, touching his collar. Bettenhausen could not be certain, but he might have been one of the policemen who, two nights ago, had roughhoused the man in the cap in front of the theater. He was glad he had not let Arnold Wicker go through with the business. They—the KGB, or whatever—were a step ahead of the poor dentist all the time. The man in the cap, asking for Borkin, changing the meeting place, was one of *them*.

"Passport, please," the blond man holding the door said.

"Why?" asked Bettenhausen.

"You under arrest. Passport, please. Visa. Airplane ticket. All papers."

"I object. I am an American citizen. I was visiting a museum when this fool in the cap interfered with my sight-seeing."

The man in the cap did not react. He spoke harshly in Russian to the blond man, then pointed to Bettenhausen, as if ordering his colleague to translate.

"You are under arrest, sir. You are under arrest for illegal transactions with Soviet citizen. Is illegal for you to bring in letter for Soviet citizen and is illegal for Soviet citizen to receive letter from foreigner."

"I am not aware of your barbaric laws. I am a freeborn American, a citizen of a republic where democracy is practiced."

"Passport. I not want force from you."

Bettenhausen reached into his pocket and took out his passport and the separate Soviet visa. Odd how they never stamped your passport but kept the information on detachable sheets. In effect, you could never produce evidence in your passport that you had been to Russia; tourists were a variety of unpersons.

"Airline ticket. Health card, please. Travel papers. You have international driver's license?"

"I do not. Here, take it all, blast you. Including my membership card in the Screen Directors' Guild, the Sherman Oaks Conservationists, and the San Fernando Valley Democratic Caucus."

"Good. Is better co-operate."

"Thank you. And now I take my leave of you." Bettenhausen slapped the tam-o'-shanter on his head, and started off. There was a Metro stop nearby. Once around the corner he would consult the guidebook and make his way back to the Ukrainia. And poor Borkin . . . ?

He had gone three steps when the uniformed policeman who had been at the wheel of the car and the long-haired blond man barred his way.

"Sorry, please, you are under arrest," the man said. He was polite. "Is crime to give letter. Professor Borkin is commit crime, both are prisoners. In car, please."

"I wish to be taken to the American Embassy at once."

"Later, please."

The man in the cap shouted at them. The blond man and the police officer each took one of Bettenhausen's tweedy arms and led him to the car. He got into the rear next to Borkin. The scientist looked strangely relaxed. A smile turned his lips. A good touch, Bettenhausen thought.

The man in the cap jumped into the front seat and barked an order to the uniformed driver. The car sped away from the Museum of Secret Communist Meetings.

Bettenhausen was about to offer an apology to Borkin, then thought better of it. There was no point in giving them ammunition.

"Where am I being taken?" he protested. "I demand an explanation."

"Soon," the heavy man said. He rubbed his nose. "Will explain to you all, soon."

The tan cap turned around. It seemed that the cap was the motivating force, the motor, on the agent's head. The pained eyes looked at Anatoly Borkin. He spoke Russian rapidly to him.

"I am a tourist here," Bettenhausen said angrily. "I expect to be treated like one." They were riding toward the center of Moscow. "I say, be a good chap and give me my bearings. Is that the Conservatory of Music over there?" He peered at the map in Levine's guide.

"Please, no talk any more, sir," the husky man said. "I take book also."

"That is a guidebook."

"Please, give."

"This is a violation of every known human right," Bettenhausen said. "I shall make this a *cause célèbre,* and you will be tried and found guilty in the courts of public opinion."

Borkin turned his face to Bettenhausen. Gently he touched a finger to his lips.

"Where the hell's the professor?" Herbie boomed. "It ain't an official tour without him."

The party was in the bus, returning to the Ukraina for lunch. It had been a tiring morning—in and out of the Kremlin cathedrals, gawking at ikons, tramping up and down palaces and fortifications.

"We needed Warren," Theresa said. "He's got a way of putting everything into focus. I don't mean to downgrade Pepi, or that sweet girl, but Warren is something special."

"Yeah, that's what I was sayin', Terry," Herbie shouted. He had lumbered down the aisle, planting himself like a trained elephant opposite Theresa and Ibith Grant. "It's an education listening to him. Boy, when they started on Ivan the Great, Ivan the Terrible, I needed the professor. You hear why they built that big bell tower? It was a famine, so it was a public works program. A regular WPA. Famine, pogroms, jails, murders. And the kids made fun of America. Listen, Doc"—Herbie bent toward Henderson Grant—"I know we got plenty of *tsuris* in America, but it has to be better than this."

"You are right, Herbert."

"I like Harvey better." He looked toward the rear of the bus. "Everything okay, Ma?"

Mrs. Legrand wiggled her fingers at him. She did not mind the clouds of cigar smoke in back.

"Pa okay, Ma?"

Mr. Legrand was sitting in the haze of Murray's and Si's cigars, as if preserved in gas.

"Weston is fine, Harvey. He had a nice morning."

Herbie clasped both hands like a fighter and shook them in Mr. Legrand's direction. "Hang in there, Pa. They ain't laid a glove on you. You're in better shape than any of us."

"Gut still bothering you, Herbie?" Dr. Grant asked solicitously. He had treated Mr. Hutzler for an ingrown toenail the night before and had prescribed an anti-histamine for Barbara Huggins, who had been afflicted with sneezing. Grant did not mind. He enjoyed the practice of medicine and, he admitted to Ibith, the power it gave him over people. ("Old Godlike Henderson," she'd teased him. "Black God come to save White Heathen from Naughty Virus." His silence—accompanied by a lifting of the frown—told her she had reached him with a sly truth.)

"*Mamenu*," Herbie moaned. "I haven't had a full meal in four

294

days. You know the funny thing? I ain't lost a pound. At least a man should get skinny with my troubles."

"Takes time, Herbie. The system has to lose water."

"And that's another thing. Every night, up four and five times to make pee-pee. Why is that?"

In the dining room Father Konay and Theresa Carrell joined the Grants at the rear of the high-ceilinged hall. Cornelia Bettenhausen, concerned about Warren, had asked Pepi if he could contact the Central House of Film Directors, to which Bettenhausen had been invited. Warren was a meticulous man, and it was not like him to fail to call, or leave a message, or indicate that he would be late.

"He said he'd meet me back here at twelve-thirty at the latest," Mrs. Bettenhausen said. "I'm not worried, but it is a strange city, and he doesn't know a word of Russian."

"It is not to worry, Mrs. Bettenhausen," Virgil said. "I am sure his colleagues started toasting each other with vodka and they are now opening the caviar, but I shall call."

The Wickers decided they would now skip lunch every day. They were feeling logy, stuffed, their tennis-trim arms and legs turning soft. Instead of the midday meal they would walk, jog, do simple exercises. They had gone into the park opposite the hotel, and the last Theresa saw of them, they were trotting happily, to the amusement of the Russians.

"There was too much to absorb this morning," Theresa said to the priest and to the Grants. "I took notes, but I got lost after the third cathedral. I'll have to study the book tonight. It's no fair if I can't keep the Assumption, the Annunciation, the Archangel, the Deposition, and Ivan's belfry separate. I'm sorry, Father. I didn't mean to be disrespectful."

"Not at all," Father Konay said. He was feeling confident, sure of himself. It was the letter from Father Folker. The whole pattern was changing in Ash Valley. Mr. Ptacek, that chicken yearning to become an osprey, would change everything. Ed Marciniek, all two hundred and seventy-five pounds of him, would be needing Father Konay. A scheme began to unfold in the old priest's mind.

"You look preoccupied, Father," Ibith said.

"I get that way every now and then. Funny, I'm not tired any more. I don't even mind Mr. Wattle's setting-up exercises in the morning."

"Or his comments?" the physician asked. Across the vast room Mr. Wattle was arguing with a headwaiter. "I said chicken soup, not

295

cabbage soup. . . ." The man was chicken-souping his way around the world, Ibith thought, searching for the perfect bowl.

"The strangest thing is, he's a nice person," the priest said. "He's so helpful. He can fix anything. He wants to help people." He paused, searching for the proper words. "And he's very fond of both of *you*, he admires you."

"Hard to figure some people," Dr. Grant said. An appropriate noncommittal remark.

"I've had my problems back home with people who aren't too tolerant," Father Konay said.

Terry was half listening. Old music was echoing in her head, Ibith knew. How did she manage, alone in her hotel rooms at night, with Flemington down the hall? Cold beds and cold comfort. Terry had stopped talking about him, but the darted glances, the rueful comments, told the black woman that her friend was not happy. A strong woman, but there were limits. It was inconceivable to Ibith that a woman, so attractive, so bright, could have experienced so unrewarding a love life. There was always an undercurrent of regret in her casual manner.

"What sort of problems?" Dr. Grant asked.

"Oh, the matter of integrating the local service club, the Ospreys."

"Ah," the physician said. "No cages for blackbirds?"

"This young priest, the kind who wears jeans and has a beard, he talked me into demanding a change in the bylaws so some colored— black people could join."

Dr. Grant rolled a piece of bread into a dry ball. "Guess you caught some flak on that one."

"They censored me."

"It will take time," the physician said solemnly. "I have had a similar problem, from the other end."

"Did you? Did you?" Father Konay asked. "I'd like to know. How do you handle it? When I get back, it may start all over. . . ."

The waitress appeared with armloads of steaming soup plates. An odor that reminded Theresa of the school cafeteria emanated from the bowls. With her head, the waitress was gesturing to two ebony men in green robes and caracul caps to take seats at the table. They exchanged somber glances and then sat at the end of the table, next to the Grants.

"*Jambo,*" Dr. Grant said, smiling.

"*Ha jambo, keena bwana,*" Ibith said. "But I'm afraid that's all the Swahili we know."

"It is more than we know," one of the Africans said haughtily. "We are West Africans and do not speak it."

296

Theresa smiled at them. "Nigeria?"

"West African," the man said. "Let it rest at that."

Dr. Grant nudged his wife's knee under the table. Clearly, there was no communication with these Ashanti dudes.

"Are you here for the conference of literary critics?" Father Konay asked.

"Ah, ah, ah, hah, hah," one of the men laughed. "Literary critics, literary critics. Ah, hah, hah, hah."

Dr. Grant wondered: Am I supposed to be insulted?

"Seems we have us a cultural gap here," Ibith whispered.

The physician sighed: no easy solutions to anything. Everyone began to eat hastily, conversation ceased. At the entrance to the dining hall, Theresa could see Cornelia talking to Virgil. It was the first time Pepi had permitted anyone to interrupt his lunch.

The black Zis limousine made a brief trip through central Moscow. Bettenhausen had no idea where they were. He tried to get his bearings, looking for the towers of the Ukraina or of Moscow University, but to no avail. The car parked in front of a gray stone building. Sparling was right. They didn't know how to make the bottoms of their buildings join the sidewalk. There were cracks and lumps of crumbled mortar at the base. And an ungainly exterior drainpipe. Two uniformed men cradling machine guns were on duty outside the building.

The man in the cap and the chunky blond man who spoke English got out and escorted Borkin and the American up the stairs. Inside the lobby smelled of potent disinfectant. It seemed an old prewar building, with frosted glass doors reinforced with wiring. And it was strangely chilly in spite of the mild weather. It was as if the building, full of secret nocturnal business, had retained the icy cold of Moscow winters, a warning to miscreants, a reminder of the terrors behind the massive doors.

The man in the cap opened a door. It seemed to be an ordinary suite of offices—desks, chairs, filing cabinets, a squat woman at a reception table. She spoke to the man in the cap as she helped him off with his coat. Divested of the oversized headgear and the coat, he shrank—a starved fellow, all of his energy concentrated in his hot eyes.

The thickset man, clearly the accommodater, held a door open and said to the prisoners: "Please."

They entered the small man's office and were seated in wooden chairs. The hot-eyed man sat behind the desk, the blond man to one side.

"I demand to know where I am and who you people are," Betten-hausen said. "I am an American citizen and you have violated every precept of international good will by these procedures. I demand to speak to the American Embassy at once and I have to go to the bathroom."

The heavy man—Bettenhausen was certain that he was one of the ruffians who had manhandled his own boss, Big Cap, at the Kirov—studied the tourist's passport and visa, the papers he had taken from him in the limousine.

"Please telephone my wife at the Ukraina Hotel," Bettenhausen said. "I am a client of Planet Tours and we are scheduled to ride to the Lenin Hills for a panorama of Moscow and a visit to Moscow University."

"Meester Bettengausen?" the heavy man asked.

"I am."

"You in trouble, Mr. Bettengausen. You break law of Soviet Union."

"I did no such thing."

The thin man whispered to his aide. Borkin, looking drained—but not afraid—seemed to lean forward.

Bettenhausen whispered in English to the scientist. "What are they saying? Who are they?"

"Internal security," Borkin said huskily. He pointed to the man in the cap. "Varvansky, boss." Then he nodded at the stocky man. "Butko, number two."

Varvansky, hearing his name whispered, leveled a finger at Borkin, advising him not to talk. But he spoke politely. No matter what crimes Borkin was guilty of, he was still a man to be respected. There had been no force used, and apart from Varvansky's truculent manner, they had been treated rather well.

"Mr. Bettengausen, you are work for CIA?" Butko asked.

"No. I am a tourist, and you may call my tour escort, Mr. Virgil, at the Ukraina, to confirm this."

Butko grinned. Dr. Wicker would have appreciated the steel-capped incisors. "We know you are tourist. Very nice cover."

Yes, this was fine, Bettenhausen thought, a Hitchcockian touch. A friendly interrogator with steel teeth. Smiles and compliments. And Varvansky, an undersized heavy, playing ally, then victim, and emerging as a chief of secret police.

"It is not a cover."

Varvansky held up the envelope. It had gotten a bit wrinkled and soiled in its passage. And having been steamed open once and re-glued, it had a disreputable look about it. The police boss spoke—somewhat more menacingly—to Borkin.

"*Nyet*," the scientist said.

"Who give you letter?" Butko asked Bettenhausen.

Another nice script turn occurred to the Hollywood man. *Why not tell the truth?* He was not at all nervous. Nothing would happen to him. He was an American. Besides, this was a scenario he had invented. Toying with his tam-o'-shanter, tugging at his beard, he had the notion that in a half hour he would be in Fallsberg's office outlining the plot. He would suggest Martin Kosleck as the sinister Varvansky. Butko could be a comic Russian, perhaps Leonid Kinsky or Vladimir Sokoloff. Borkin? Borkin would be difficult. Oscar Homolka —too strong. Paul Henreid? Maybe George Voskovec.

"Who give you letter?" Butko asked. "Please answer, sir."

"Mr. Leland."

"Ah, yes." Butko spoke to Varvansky. They bobbed their heads. They knew all about Leland. They were approving his veracity.

"Mr. Leland work for Central Intelligence Agency." Butko folded thick hands on the rise of his gut. It was a stomach that spoke to Bettenhausen not of sloth but of strength.

"Perhaps he does."

"You know he work for CIA. You make errand for him. You, Mr. Bettengausen, are courier. We think you know what you do."

Borkin leaned forward. He seemed to be troubled not by his arrest but by the involvement of an American. In a few short Russian words, he appeared to be dressing down both Varvansky and Butko.

"I tell them you are innocent of this," Borkin said to the American. "You know nothing. You bring letter is all."

Varvansky lit a cigarette and studied the smoke, then turned to Butko, ordering him to resume the interrogation.

"So, Mr. Bettengausen, you once meet group of Russian motion picture directors in Gollywood?"

"I was on the Directors' Guild Committee of Fraternal Welcome."

"You remember Zetkin?"

"Of course. Gleb Zetkin is one of the greatest of the new wave of Soviet film directors, a wonderful talent."

"Last month Mr. Zetkin is declared insane by state committee on psychological problems of artists and is now confined to mental hospital. You have message for him also?"

The game had its limits, Bettenhausen realized. And how would the constructionist handle this plot turn? A dryness afflicted Bettenhausen's throat.

"I knew Mr. Zetkin slightly," he said. "He is a young man of extraordinary talent. If he has run afoul of your blind obedience to dogma, the worse for you. A nation that stifles its artists can make no claim to nationhood but is a prison run by criminals. Mr. Zetkin will be vindicated, as will Solzhenitsyn, Sinyavsky, Daniel, Ginsberg, Litvinov, Amalrik, and all the other voices of freedom. Yes, and Professor Marmaladov, and this good man seated here. Someday the poets and artists will be heard all over Russia and the policemen will be forgotten."

Butko translated swiftly. He seemed to enjoy the challenge of Bettenhausen's oratory. Varvansky scowled.

"Major Varvansky says pretty speech, but lies, because you glorify fascists, hooligans, reactionaries, and Zionist imperialists. Besides, he says, he does not think you are Warren Bettengausen at all, but are Dr. Wicker, who is real agent."

"Nonsense. Dr. Wicker has nothing to do with this. He is a fellow tourist."

"Major say it is Dr. Wicker who is contact of CIA agent Leland."

"Your intelligence is faulty." Bettenhausen's mind tried to put sequences together. *Leland.* Surely this was proof that he was a Soviet plant, a double agent with the mission of incriminating Borkin.

"No, sir. We are correct. You are Dr. Wicker. Or acting for him. It does not matter. Your plot is discovered."

Varvansky whispered something in Butko's ear. The translator nodded.

"Major Varvansky says enough of fooling around. We have treat you very good. We do not intend to search you. We are good people, treat tourists all right. But if you are agent is another matter."

"I am not an agent of any kind. I delivered an envelope for a man named Leland, as a favor."

Butko smacked the desk. "Please show us badge."

"What badge?"

"Badge, badge. CIA badge, which you carry. ID card. Is not secret any more. You are real agent. Only real agent be so smart to take job from Wicker, who is amateur."

Varvansky leveled a finger at the stout man. "Bedge. Give bedge."

In an inept Mexican accent, Bettenhausen replied: "I don' have to show you any steenkin' badge."

Butko sat up. "What means this? You making jokes?"

"I have quoted you a line from the film *Treasure of Sierra Madre.* Uttered by Carlos Bedoya to Walter Huston and most appropriate at this moment. 'I don' have to show you any steenkin' badge.' You see, he was a bandit pretending to be a Mexican policeman and he—"

Varvansky slammed the desk. Then he picked up the telephone and barked orders.

"Major is nice to you, Mr. Bettengausen, and you make jokes about American movies," Butko said. "Is *ne kulturny.*"

There was a knock at the door. Butko shouted a command. The woman Bettenhausen had seen in the outer office entered. She carried a large camera, which looked to Bettenhausen like an ancient Speed Graphic. Varvansky gave her orders.

The woman positioned herself in front of the prisoners and took several pictures. Bettenhausen preened his beard for the second shot, held his head high, glared at the lens.

After she had taken four photographs of the two men, Varvansky got up.

"Now is proof," Butko said. "Major Varvansky open letter from Leland in presence of both gentlemen. You are seen giving letter to Borkin. You do not deny. We now open to show evidence of reactionary plot against people of Soviet Union."

With nervous fingers, Varvansky undid the sealed flap. It came apart easily, having been already opened. He took out the single white sheet of paper and unfolded it.

Bettenhausen could not control a wicked smile. Luckily, the beard camouflaged it. An old cartoon in the magazine *Ballyhoo* flitted through his mind. *Man with enormous black beard having his picture taken. Photographer: "Smile." Bearded man: "I am smiling."*

"Is joke?" Butko asked.

Varvansky turned the paper over, held it up to the light, examined its edges.

"You make joke, Mr. Bettengausen?"

How perfect! The *obligatory scene,* as the writers would have said at one of Fallsberg's meetings. Not an *offstage circumstance* but a *revelation in filmic terms.*

"Is nothing on letter," Butko said.

Major Varvansky was running a match under the blank paper.

"We can see that," Bettenhausen said. "May we be released?"

"Why you give Professor Borkin this?" Butko asked.

"I have no idea. You must ask Mr. Leland."

"Mr. Leland in America. CIA agent."

"The first part of your statement may be true. The second part is not." Bettenhausen rumbled to his feet and steadied himself on his space shoes. "I charge you both with a plot to incriminate this innocent man and to involve me, an American tourist, paying a visit of good will to the land of Chekhov and Turgenev and Gogol."

"Please, sit, Mr. Bettengausen."

The girl with the camera was edging toward the door. She looked frightened. Varvansky kept manipulating the sheet of white bond, inspecting the interior of the wrinkled envelope.

"I charge further that Mr. Leland, whatever his real name, is an agent of the KGB, given the mission of discrediting Professor Borkin, and depriving him of the right of free speech, free opinions, and every known freedom given to intellectuals in civilized countries. Rest assured, gentlemen, the world will know of your perfidy."

Varvansky hissed some questions at Butko. What was this fat man saying? Butko's response seemed to Bettenhausen unexpectedly mild.

"May we leave?" the Hollywood man asked. "I wish to report this incident to the American Embassy."

"Please sit, sir."

"I demand that I be set free. I will not leave until Professor Borkin is free. If he is detained or harmed in any way, representations will be made at the highest level."

Varvansky called the woman over. He folded the white sheet and put it in the envelope. Then he gave it to her. Bowing, she left.

"Your law states, I believe," the Hollywood man said, "that it is illegal to bring in letters to citizens of the Soviet Union. Is that not so?"

"Is so." Butko smoothed his lank hair.

"But I have done no such thing. Nor has Professor Borkin received any letter. You witnessed our meeting in the museum. No words were exchanged. Since I transmitted no letter, since your spy, Mr. Leland, sent a blank sheet of paper, no crime has been committed. Were I the KGB I would look into Mr. Leland's background and review his dossier. My own guess is that he has sold out. Any day he will be writing his confessions for *True* magazine, to be published in book form by Covici, Friede."

Varvansky, hands clasped behind his back, was pacing the office, pausing at the window, stroking his neck. Bettenhausen liked him better in his cap. He whispered into Butko's ear.

"Major say you wait little while."

"How long? This is outrageous."

"Until laboratory look at paper."

"I shall give you fifteen minutes to examine the paper. If your lab technicians are anything like your waiters, it will take the rest of the day. Gentlemen, the longer you hold us, the worse it will be for you."

Butko smiled. The steel-capped teeth looked like costume jewelry. "You like glass of tea, sir? Maybe cigarette?"

Bettenhausen turned to the scientist. "I want only my freedom. And Professor Borkin's."

"They have no recollection of his being there this morning?" Cornelia asked Pepi. Her voice was thin. Across the lobby, Arnold

302

Wicker, watching the woman's face, cursed himself. He never should have allowed Bettenhausen to go through with his scheme.

"The lady I spoke to says no," Virgil said. "You are sure it was the Central House of Film Directors?"

"That's what Warren said."

"She is only a secretary. Russians are not noted for efficiency. Very possible Mr. Bettenhausen was there, met with his friends, and they are at lunch."

"He would have called, don't you think? It's two o'clock already. And we leave in half an hour."

"Telephone service is not efficient either, madame. It is not to worry. His old friends are maybe taking him to the country to a good restaurant."

"Let's hope so."

"Anything wrong?" Rose-Anne asked her.

"Oh, Warren. Probably sassed a cop and got picked up by the police."

Dr. Wicker turned pale. Bursting, he wanted to tell Virgil about Bettenhausen's search for Borkin at the museum. But he was sworn to secrecy. If Bettenhausen did not return by three that afternoon he would ask Virgil to take him to the American Embassy and disclose everything.

Cornelia decided to wait in the hotel for Warren. Dr. Wicker, assuring her that everything was in order, remained with her, sending Rose-Anne along for the trip to the Lenin Hills.

"It's not like Warren," Cornelia said. "And it's not like me to be worried. I'm sorry, Arnold."

"Don't apologize. But I'm sure there's an explanation. Pepi explained about the telephone service."

"Warren didn't say he was having lunch with them."

"Oh, they probably made a last-minute decision."

"If only I knew the names of some of the people he went to see. There was a Mr. Zetkin, but the girl at the Central House told Pepi they'd never heard of him."

Dr. Wicker was silent. He was worried now, nursing a mounting guilt. He never should have let Bettenhausen pursue his crazy game. Sparling should have been left to handle the details.

"I have a feeling Warren is up to something," Cornelia said probingly.

"Why do you say that?"

"I don't know. He's been secretive lately. You know, Arnold, we've never kept anything from one another. We've been married over forty years and we've never played games."

"It's your imagination." But the dentist was an unconvincing liar. She had looked at him questioningly—as if to hint that she suspected him of being involved. Why those private strolls? Why those meetings without wives?

A cold film covered Wicker. Some years ago, Rosie had read to him a harrowing chapter from a Solzhenitsyn novel, a sequence in which a Communist official falls under suspicion and is jailed, deprived of his rights, his access to the outside, and put in a solitary cell, perhaps forever. "It's a nightmare," Rosie said. "Of course it's about Stalin's era. It can't be like that any more. No one would put up with it."

Wicker looked around the lobby and inhaled its laminated odors—potatoes, unwashed bodies, disinfectant. Virgil had said the odor was of unlaundered socks. But Virgil could joke. He was a survivor, a proud Briton after a life of deprivation in Europe.

"There he is," Cornelia said. She walked across the lobby. Wicker watched them kiss. Bettenhausen appeared fine, if a bit out of breath.

The dentist made his way through a party of Arab literary critics, including two men in camouflage suits and kaffiyehs. He felt vastly relieved.

"They insisted I see their new film laboratory," Bettenhausen said. "I couldn't say no. It's about five years behind our automated system, but they thought it was the last word. Their editing facilities are deplorable."

"We called the Central House of Film Directors," Cornelia said. "Pepi said they had no record of you coming there."

Wicker was searching his friend's face for a clue.

"I didn't stay long. They whisked me out to the sound stage. They were doing a Pushkin story. *The Captain's Daughter*. Quite spectacular. Then an endless lunch and then their laboratory. I gave them a few hints on improving the timing of color prints."

"Shall we try to join the tour?" Dr. Wicker asked. "We could take a cab up to the university."

Bettenhausen fluttered his eyes. Cornelia took his arm. "Warren, what's wrong?"

"Just a bit weary, love. I think I'll forgo sight-seeing. Moscow University is the ugliest building in Europe, with this cursed hotel running it a close second. I would like some tea and a long period of relaxation. Those directors ran me ragged."

"I bet they did," the dentist said.

"Arnold, would you mind phoning our friend Sparling? Tell him his contacts at the Central House were excellent and that I had a successful meeting."

Deprived of a fling in Budapest—the girls wanted fifty dollars and none of them could match the women at Mrs. Barrison's—A. T. Gunthorpe decided to prowl as soon as it turned dark. He had had his share of opera. The majority of the tourists were off to see something about Three Oranges.

"I must warn you," Virgil said as he waited with Gunthorpe for a taxi outside the Ukraina. "The girls are hardly Parisian, and the circumstances are not pleasant. They will demand Western currency, and they are often under surveillance."

"Ole Peppy." Gunthorpe beamed. "Ole Peppy sure look after his chicks. Ah ain't after nothin' fancy. But a man got to git his valves ground. Ah damn near bustin' at the seams."

Virgil gave the cab driver instructions: the Moskva Hotel. The taxi dropped Gunthorpe at the entrance to the looming red granite building. He gave the driver a fistful of rubles.

"Got it dollar?"

"Sorry, buddy. Need mah dollars for poontang."

Within five minutes, as Gunthorpe strolled the street fronting the hotel, another cab pulled up. Dimly, through dirty windows, he saw a woman beckoning to him. The door opened. A staring crowd of Russians, perhaps a dozen or so, looked on as the American hauled his big-boned frame inside the taxi. It lurched off and began to ride around the streets behind the hotel.

"Hi, honey," he said.

"Hallo. Forty dollar. Five for taxi."

"Now wait a damn minute. You gals got a union or somethin'? What is this? A dang monopoly? That gal in Budapest ast me forty dollar. And that nigger gal in Berlin. Who sets them prices? The OP and A?"

"Forty dollar."

"Hunh? Wheah we go? You got an apartment? Hotel?"

"No hotel. In taxi."

"In hyeah?"

"Only place. We go by park. In taxi."

"Heeeeell, no."

Gunthorpe looked at the girl. She had a wide face and a blunt nose, poorly covered with cosmetics. She seemed to be wearing an irregular blonde wig. Her skirt was hiked over her heavy thighs and the tops of her stockings were rolled in a manner that Gunthorpe had not seen since his boyhood in Memphis.

"Give you thirty dollars," he said.

"Forty."

"That's a gyp. Thirty is 'bout right."

305

"You got Swiss francs? French francs? Is better than dollar. Deutsche marks is best. Dollar not good."

The taxi was tooling down a tree-shaded street. Gunthorpe noticed two parked taxis with shadowy figures in the rear. The drivers seemed to have absented themselves.

"Dollar not good?"

"Gold best. You got gold for me?"

"Just a heart of gold, honey."

The cab parked at the end of the street. The quietness of Russia disturbed Gunthorpe. The people appeared to have quietly died or vanished. Lights in apartments were few, street lights low, silences oppressive.

"Might as well git hit over with," Gunthorpe said. He was losing passion. At his age? Acrobatics in the back seat of a cramped taxi? Damn Communists! They didn't know how to do anything right— from growing wheat to letting a man get his ashes hauled.

"Money, mister."

"Yeah, yeah. Shoot. Forty bucks for this?"

"Money."

"What about him?" Gunthorpe pointed to the driver. "Ah ain't doin' no side show. Ole A.T. never did lak these pony and dog acts. Git him outa hyeah."

The girl spoke to the driver. He held out a hand.

"Money," she said. "Forty for me. Five for driver."

"Dang, y'all know how to hurt a man." The Memphis man reached into his pocket and took out a wad of rubles, traveler's checks, dollars, Deutsche marks, and French francs.

He began to count out the money, placing the bills in the girl's hand. The driver watched closely. A.T. had the feeling they worked as a team but did not trust one another.

At the opposite end of the street there was the sound of a motor starting, gears shifting, an old car groaning into creaky movements. The girl turned her head and said something to the driver. He opened the door and looked out. Then he slapped both hands to his head. *"Boje moi!"* he moaned. *"Militsianer."*

Another car started its engine and drove off.

"We in trouble?" A.T. asked.

The girl was shoving dollars back at him. In her frenzy, bills fluttered to the floor. The driver tried to start the taxi. It coughed and died.

"You done flooded it, son. Ram the accelerator to the floor one time and try again."

A motorcycle with a sidecar pulled alongside. A policeman, beaming a huge flashlight at the taxi, loomed outside. He yanked the door open and played the cone of light on the floor. Alexander Hamilton's sharp features looked back at the officer from the face of a ten-dollar bill.

"*Spekulyanti*," the policeman said.

The girl began to protest. Tears rimmed her mascaraed eyes. Gunthorpe's heart went out to her. Twin rills trickled down her cheeks.

"You go," the officer said to Gunthorpe. He shouted orders at the driver, who this time managed to start the engine. Then he yanked the girl from the rear seat. To the American he said: "Bad lady. Go hotel. No give dollars lady."

"You damn said it. Gimme mah money."

But the dollars, Gunthorpe realized, were *evidence*. Oh, how money mattered in the socialist fatherland! The policeman gathered the fallen leaves.

"Hey, she ain't done nothin'," Gunthorpe said gallantly. "Let the gal go. She ain't hurt no one. We was just talkin', havin' a little chat."

"*Nyet*," the policeman said. "*Spekulyanti*. Bad."

"Yeah, but Ah never had a chancet to find out *how* bad."

Day 14: Moscow–Istanbul. A few hours remain in Moscow for our Three Worlds argonauts—perhaps to buy that mink hat, or that malachite pin, or to visit the State Literary Museum and pay homage to Russia's giants, Tolstoy, Gorky, Sholokov. Aeroflot becomes our Magic Carpet for a non-stop flight to Istanbul, former seat of the Sublime Porte of Turkey, city of Mosques, Mystery, and Magic.

Our ride in from the airport gives us our first views of the fantastic 2,700-year-old port on the Bosporus, astride Europe and Asia. A tantalizing glimpse of the Blue Mosque and Santa Sophia, a hint of the treasures to be seen tomorrow!

At night, Turkish delicacies, exotic and piquant!

Room service having proven incapable of delivering anything except mineral water, Flemington went to the "buffet" on his floor for Lulu's morning tea. In the corridor he passed Murray Yasuda and his wife. They were dressed like matching dolls in embroidered Cossack blouses.

"Lovely," Harry said. "How do you two look so great at eight in the morning?"

"Sandra does it, Harry," the Japanese said. "What a great broad. I get spaced out but she keeps me smiling."

Flemington envied them. The restaurant owner's tribute to his wife was accurate. Flemington had never seen the miniature woman cross, or pouting, or out of temper. A wise smile played about her babyish mouth. Her voice was low and tinkly. But did she pay for all this oriental equanimity? In ulcers? Headaches?

Balancing the tray, he walked past Theresa's door. Ah, memory, memory. He had seen her last night at the opera wearing the same long dark dress, looking more desirable than any woman in the Bolshoi. A Russian in a bemedaled uniform, some high-ranking air force officer, had demanded an introduction from Pepi. Harry had seen him chatting and laughing with Terry. Lulu had stayed in her seat during the intermissions of *Love of Three Oranges*. Her feet were bothering her. In the lobby, Flemington kidded with Herbie and Si and the Westbury people, avoiding Theresa, listening while Shackman bemoaned his son's ingratitude. "Let him come here,"

Herbie said, "let those snot-noses see what Communism is, they'll wise up."

What if he knocked on Theresa's door? Surprised her, half dressed? In his tweed jacket, in the buttoned flap pocket, nested the topaz necklace he had purchased. To stand behind her—her flesh, her body in a nylon slip . . . the click of the gold catch symbolizing a joining to come. . . .

Lulu was, to his surprise, sitting up in bed, cradling the malachite box in her lap. He brought the tea to her, relieved to see she was smiling.

"You are a dear man," she said. "And so innocent."

"I wouldn't say that. I can be cagey."

"You paid the full fifteen hundred dollars for this, Harry." She was laughing, waving a finger at him.

"How do you know?"

"I know everything in the world about shopping."

"But how . . ."

"Those stores will not discount anything." She mocked him with a smile. This was Lulu at her endearing best, flirting with the bartender at the club, conditioning him to her signal for a refill, a *tak-tak-tak* of her twenty-carat diamond against her glass. "If they won't discount it for *me*, they won't for anyone in the world, least of all a babe in the woods like you, Harry."

Flemington was touched. By denigrating his talents as a haggler, she was at least including him in her world of goods received and bargains made. "It is a beautiful box," Harry said. "You must admit that."

"It certainly is. I've never seen malachite with such luster. It'll be good to keep bills in. I might have compartments made for it—paid, unpaid, pending."

"Marvelous idea, Lu." She paid all the bills, kept strict books, always knew the bottom line in the checking accounts. Sometimes he wondered, had it not been for Robbie and had she not become an alcoholic, whether she might have made a business career for herself.

"I'd expected to have heard from the school by now," he said, sitting on the bed. "Some word about Robbie."

A glaze settled over her eyes. There was no hardness in her now, no greed. Just lost hopes, a sense of having been eternally cheated. She had enjoyed sex before they had learned about Robbie.

"I'll write to him today," she said. "Harry, get me some stationery."

Huggins was up early, prowling the newstand in the lobby for a newspaper. It was true about these flea-bitten countries, he told

Barbara the night before (in the midst of making love, a circumstance that always made her giggle), you were in jail all the time—no information, no newspapers, no radio reports. "And me, the original compulsive newspaper reader," Jimmy had said, pausing in his labors. "I'm going crazy for a Paris *Trib*. The back of a cereal box. A laundry bill."

The girl at the newsstand told him that foreign papers were due momentarily. He went into the restaurant and ordered coffee. Every few minutes he would rise, walk through the "dollar shop"—stale Havana cigars and sealskin hats were in heavy supply—and look at the newsstand.

A. T. Gunthorpe spotted him. "Hey, Jim boy," he called. "Y'all up early."

"Got to look out you ridge-runners don't get the jump on me."

The feed merchant beamed. He liked Huggins. A good ole boy. Like ole Herbie. And ole Peppy. There were people in the world—white, black, rich, poor—to whom Gunthorpe could relate. They met him halfway; they were not snooty; they talked straight.

"Heeell, we ain't that slick, Jim boy. We a buncha suckers, and these hyeah Rooshians know it."

Huggins tried to move around him. There was some activity at the newsstand. But Gunthorpe had grabbed his lapel. The Memphis man began to relate his misadventure.

"I declare, there ain't nothin' harder for a man to do in these places than git his valves ground. Ah jes' hope them cops went easy on that gal."

Huggins left Gunthorpe. The girl at the newsstand was untying a stack of newspapers. The lawyer saw a *Figaro*, a *France Soir*, a *Neuer Zeitung*, a *Messaggero*, several English papers. As the girl shuffled them, arranging them next to the *Pravdas*, he saw a single copy of the Paris *Herald Tribune*.

He reached for it. A brown hand got to it just as his did. Huggins looked up to see one of the African literary critics who had sat with the Grants grasping one end of the newspaper.

"Excuse me, I think I got to this first."

Teeth flashed in the black face. "Oh no. Oh no, no."

"Do you have another one?" J.P. asked the girl. He did not let go.

"No. Is only one *Tribune*."

Huggins glanced at the date. Three days old. After his visit to Chahoub in Vienna. The S.S. *Lautaro*. Sailing from Dubai . . . when?

"Let go of my newspaper, sah."

"I do believe I was ahead of you," Huggins said.

"You wish to make an issue of it?"

Huggins' eyes popped. His mouth opened, as if unhinged. "Kwame!" he shouted. "It's my old pal Kwame Nkrumah!" A cheap Bronx trick, but he needed the newspaper more than the Nigerian. His free arm flew forward. *"There!"*

"Where?" the African asked. His long head swiveled. Huggins yanked the *Tribune* out of his hand. All the black saw was a white man with a red face—Gunthorpe—waddling out of the restaurant, puffing a cigar.

"Ah, a trick," the Nigerian said. "Sah, give me back my paper." He advanced a few steps on Huggins.

"No spikka da Swahili, pal. Get lost." It pained the lawyer to be mean to the man. But life was filled with morbid decisions—to behave rattily or to behave decently?

Turning pages, Huggins drifted across the Ukraina lobby. Rose-Anne Wicker greeted him. He nodded, too preoccupied to even enjoy the sight of her well-bred legs. She was chatting with Cornelia Bettenhausen. He caught a sentence: something about Mr. Legrand being out of sorts again. Who told people that age to go floating around the world?

His victory over the Nigerian critic turned sour. There was not a word about any sailing from Dubai, by the S.S. *Lautaro* or any Chilean ship. There was not even anything close to Dubai. Sailings from Southampton, Marseilles, Le Havre, Genoa, Naples, Piraeus, Messina, and Haifa.

"Win a few, lose a few," Huggins said. At least in Istanbul he would be in touch with the world again. Chahoub's firm had an office there. He'd camp on their doorstep until he had word of his gold.

"You look grim, Jimmy," Rose-Anne Wicker said. "The usual bad news from home?"

"Yeah. The Mets blew a double-header."

"My boys are probably miserable. Where are they in the standing?"

His mind skipped from his fortune in gold to Rosie's long body. He wondered: Would I ever make it with that kind of woman? A pretty WASP married to an Americanized Jew. Suburban people, tennis players, conservationists. "Tied for second," he said. "But we never say die, do we, Rosie?"

"Never. Remember 1969."

The dentist and Bettenhausen, conversing with Virgil, stopped at the revolving door. They were off to something called the State Literary Museum.

"I have a feeling Warren is trying to get rid of me these last few days," Cornelia said.

"I get that sensation also," Rosie said as their husbands vanished through the door.

"I'm supposed to spend the morning looking for an embroidered Cossack blouse, size 48, like the one Yasuda was wearing. Can you see Warren as a Cossack?"

"Fascinating," Eliot Sparling said. "Tolstoy's eyeglasses."

"And his walking stick," Bettenhausen said.

Dr. Wicker bent low, squinting into the vitrine in the State Literary Museum. A family of oriental-looking people, Buryats according to Sparling, were the only others in the house honoring Russia's literary geniuses, on Dimitrova Ulitsa, 38. "A manuscript page. Which book?" the dentist asked.

"Ah . . . let's see. *Anna Karenina*." The correspondent lifted his glasses and read a sentence. "The real McCoy. I like Chekhov the best. There's a manuscript of one of the plays, *Uncle Vanya*, and some of his medical gear. You know he was a doctor?"

Bettenhausen had laid down the rules: a chance meeting in the Literary Museum to discuss strategies. They were to act as if they had never seen one another. It was possible Bettenhausen was under surveillance; but it was also possible that a resident American journalist would be visiting the museum for a feature story.

"Where you boys from?" Sparling asked.

"Sherman Oaks, California," Bettenhausen said. "Dr. Wicker is a native of Riverford, Connecticut."

"California, say," the TV correspondent boomed, so loud that the Buryats studying a photograph of Mayakovsky jumped. "I worked for UBC there a long time ago. TV reporter. Covered the Los Angeles area."

They wandered through the rooms—dark, musty, rarely visited.

"Ah, Mayakovsky," Bettenhausen said.

"Posters from his lecture tour of America," Sparling commented. "What brings you boys to a place like this? It's off the beaten track."

"I am a writer," Bettenhausen said. "And you, sir?"

"I'm bureau chief for UBC."

The two tourists made a show of excitement, acknowledged that they recognized the young man. Bettenhausen looked around the room. Gogol's face peered at them with shrewd eyes. *Dead Souls*. Oh, he was prescient. A quintessential novelist, seeing it all long before the historians and sociologists came around, Bettenhausen thought.

In a low voice the fat man spoke: "I gave the paper to Borkin. We were arrested by a man named Varvansky, a major in the KGB, and his aide, Butko. We were interrogated for over an hour, threatened but

312

treated well until their laboratory confirmed what I knew all the time—it was a blank sheet of 16-pound white bond."

"And Borkin?" Sparling whispered.

"We were both let go. I threatened to call a news conference in Istanbul if they so much as touched a hair on Borkin's head. Eliot, he is quite a man. Courage, dignity, intelligence. All you said about him."

"So what now?" Sparling asked.

"You are our ace in the hole, Eliot," Bettenhausen said. "You cannot let the scenario down."

The correspondent blinked a few times at Gogol. "Yeah, I'll figure something. Borkin still teaches twice a week at Moscow University. I might be able to get a pass."

"But nothing in writing," Wicker said. "Goodness, we got the poor man arrested already."

Pushkin—sensitive, a man patently condemned to die in a senseless duel—looked over their heads.

Bettenhausen said: "We have given them a lot to worry about. I have a feeling they will be concentrating on Leland now."

"Leland?" asked the dentist.

"I am reasonably certain he is one of theirs, a Soviet agent working the New York area. They knew his name. They knew a great deal about him. And about you, Arnold. The letter was planted on you to discredit Borkin and send him to prison or one of those mental hospitals. But what Mr. Leland and his masters did not count on were my years of experience in movieland. We have, in a manner of speaking, set them up."

"For what?" Wicker asked.

"I'm not sure," Bettenhausen said.

"Jesus," Sparling said. "You get me kicked out of Russia, there goes my career."

"No fear of that," Bettenhausen said. "We have shaken their eye-teeth, as the governor says. I accused Leland of being one of theirs, and Varvansky's face turned the color of a collective farm parsnip."

They paused in tribute to Gorky.

"I'll get to Borkin," Eliot said.

"You must. You have the itinerary. Cable us when the message is delivered."

The tourists left Sparling wandering amid the memorabilia of Russian writers and took a cab to the hotel.

"One thing I don't get," Wicker said. "If Leland is a Russian agent and the message was aimed at incriminating Borkin, and we've prevented it, why are you so determined to get the message to him now?"

Bettenhausen looked offended. He scratched his neck, below his beard. "I haven't satisfied my own mind on that score. You have to understand the way script meetings work. Ideas are thrown out, tested, discussed. I'm trying out a plot twist. I have no idea, frankly, why we must get the message to Borkin. But it surely is worth trying."

"Why? Why? He's gotten away by the skin of his teeth. Why keep pushing it?"

"Arnold, I'm not certain." Bettenhausen grunted and looked at his watch. "That took less time than I thought. Shall we have a look at the Tolstoy Home? Does the Museum of Safety at Work appeal to you? No, no, I have it. The Donskoy Monastery. Driver, Donskoya Square, understand? *Don-skoy-ya.*"

To Virgil's relief, the flight from Moscow to Istanbul was not delayed. Intourist employees whisked the Three Worlds people through passport control, handled tickets, lifted the detachable visas. Nothing would be left in anyone's passport to prove he had ever been in the Soviet Union. And always the soldiers on the runway, the sense of restriction, of being watched. When would they learn to relax? Not for a long time, he decided. That celebrated Russian soul accepted too much. It took abuse gratefully. The hard-eyed men who ruled knew this and so they abused their people needlessly.

The TU-114 rose, circled Sheremetyevo Airport, gaining altitude, turning south for the nine-hundred-mile flight by way of Orel, Kiev, and Odessa. In spite of all the intervening years of freedom, the British passport, the apartment in London and the small circle of friends (unmarried, Virgil saw several women on an alternating schedule), the escort always felt relieved to depart the U.S.S.R.

"You look worried, Pepi," Theresa Carrell said.

"Not at all. Everything is in order."

"No trouble with the Flemington luggage?"

"Mr. Flemington and I have worked out a system. The Russians were decent about it. We don't unload everything. I convinced them to let me check half the bags at the airport when we arrived."

"Brilliant."

Pepi shook his head. "I should hate to have to pay the duty on what they have purchased."

Across the aisle of the plane, Herbie Shackman proclaimed: "Gin. You're still on the schneid."

"What? How . . . ?" Sid studied his cards. "What did you pick? Queen of diamonds?"

314

"Yeh, yeh. Whore of diamonds."

"I thought it was out," Sid said. He had been playing gin rummy with Herbie for twenty years and had beaten him less than half a dozen times. The fat man had an adding machine for a brain. Amazing, Sid thought, for a guy who had never gone beyond the eighth grade.

"What's that game you're playing?" Mr. Wattle shouted.

"*Gevald,* someone throw him a fish," Herbie muttered.

Sid smiled over the seat. "Gin rummy."

"Say, that's a stupid game," Mr. Wattle said. "Why don't we play bridge? Who plays bridge? Where's Terry?"

"Hide me," Theresa said to Virgil. "I can't play, but he'll insist on teaching me."

"Pretend you are dozing."

"Oh, to heck with it. I'll refuse. Pepi, you should warn widows about these tours."

"Mrs. Carrell, no amount of warnings would keep suitors from you. You are an eminently attractive woman."

Theresa brushed back a strand of curling hair and smiled at him. "I'm overwhelmed."

A hostess bustled through the aisle, distributing—inexplicably—sour orange juice and sweet cookies. Behind them, Pepi and Theresa could hear Mrs. Legrand mumbling as she searched for her vodka bottle and spiked her husband's drink. "There's a good boy," she said, "you drink every bit of it. It will help you sleep."

Easing back in his chair, Virgil asked: "You knew the Flemingtons before?"

Theresa raised her eyebrows. "That's not like the old Pepi I've come to love."

"If you have come to love me, Mrs. Carrell, you will confess everything. I have these moments when I become curious about clients."

"I'm an old lady teacher."

"But full of mystery." Virgil let the smoke drift into his eyes. Over the years they had become inured to irritation. "Forgive me, and do not think I am being forward, but you are an intriguing woman."

"It must be that orange juice. Are you sure Mrs. Legrand hasn't slipped you some of her Stolichnaya vodka?"

"You see, there is an example. You gave it the correct Russian pronunciation. After five days in the Soviet Union."

Theresa looked saddened by her good ear for languages. "It proves I'm a nit-picking pedant. Making notes about Mozart in my guidebook and imitating your Russian. I'm a sedulous ape, as someone said."

"I have tried to analyze your charm, and I know now. Your face is quite pretty. A bit reserved—forgive me—almost schoolmarmish. But the sort of schoolteacher every boy yearns to impress, to love, to marry someday. But beyond the clear brow and the fine nose, the brown eyes, all of them rather proper, there is a well of passion."

"Oh, you presume too much."

"Your figure betrays a geat deal of emotion, almost mocking the decorum of the face. It is as if we are twelve-year-old boys, wary of your reprimands, wondering about your lovers, and yearning, in the tormented manner of young boys, for—I shall say it—your body."

"Well," Theresa said. "*Well.* I sound like Jack Benny. What am I to say? That I'm sorry I made you feel twelve years old? I think I'll send you to the blackboard. Pepi Virgil, you will write one hundred times, 'I will not say naughty things about Mrs. Carrell.'"

"I would do it with joy. So would many of the men on this tour. And most of all Mr. Flemington."

"Off limits, Pepi."

"Perhaps you want to talk about him? They are in the front of the plane. Mrs. Flemington has paid the extra charge for first-class seats."

"Do you do this with all tourists?"

"Only those for whom I feel a message from the heart. I know a little about you. Once divorced, once widowed. A grown son. Traveling with the Grants. A woman of intelligence. And perhaps a secret."

She gestured toward the first-class section. "Would you believe me if I told you I booked this trip to see if I still had a chance? If he still wanted me?"

An expression of profound understanding suffused the guide's face. Other people's problems rarely moved him. This room was too hot, that waiter was rude, this charge for drinks excessive, that shop had cheated. . . . He took them in stride, mediated, accommodated.

"I am saddened to hear that," Virgil said. "It is so hard for a woman . . ."

"He says he wants me. But I know *how* he wants me." She took a Kleenex from her bag and blew her nose. "An afternoon, an evening. Am I embarrassing you?"

"No, my dear."

"And then back to her. Seeing him at close range . . . I've lost interest. I don't care any more. It's too long to be in love. I sometimes think that the fact that I couldn't have Harry, that he kept running away, made me more determined to get him. I admit it. I've failed. I'm almost convinced I'm better off."

"Has it been painful for you to see him?"

"It was agony at first."

"And now?"

316

"Less than agony. But no fun. I've always been good at constructing compartments in my mind. I think I've assigned him to one—airtight, watertight."

"An oubliette?"

She wrinkled her nose, querying him. Yes, Virgil thought, a fine woman—full of curiosity.

"Now there's a word I've come across for years. I still don't know what it means."

"I shall tell you if you promise not to jot it down. An oubliette is a round prison tower with no opening except from above. Prisoners were lowered in—and forgotten."

"Ah, yes. From *oublier*—to forget." She stared out the window. It was a cloudless day. The tawny earth of Russia carpeted the world below. "Question is—who's in the oubliette and who's outside?"

Virgil said no more. It was hard to console her. An enormous sympathy for women overcame him: it was so hard waiting to be asked, called, pursued, wanted, taken. Men did not have those problems.

Theresa closed her eyes. She had welcomed the guide's attentions. But now she was sorry she had told him so much. His compliments, the hints, the interpretations of her character were disturbing. Desire was aroused again; she wanted to be loved, stroked by a man's hands, overpowered, joined, punished. The needs ran deep and no one had ever loved her as Flemington had. Be of strong will, she told herself; you can live without it, and you might be better off.

The bus ride from Yeşilköy Airport went quickly until the walls of Istanbul were in sight. Then the traffic clotted, amid clouds of dust, shouts, honking horns. The tourists grew uneasy. It was early evening and they were hungry and exhausted. And the crush of vehicles had a senseless air—new Mercedes, gleaming Cadillacs, shabby buses, wagons and flat-beds drawn by horses, flatulent motorcycles, motor bikes. Worst of all were the swarms of noisy taxicabs, stopping jerkily, blasting off, weaving in and out of lanes, passing on either side, driven by wild Turks who seemed gripped in the miseries of bridging Asia and Europe.

"I'd walk it, if I knew where to go," J. P. Huggins said to Barbara. It was after five. He wondered what hours the offices worked. He had an address for the Beirut, Dubai & Sharja Trading Company, Istiklal Caddesi, 78.

"A fantastic history," Pepi was saying. "First Byzantium, rival to Rome. It was named for a Greek sailor, Byzas, in the seventh

317

century B.C. Appropriate, for the Greeks have left their imprint here—in business, commerce, politics, religion. Yes, it is indeed Turkey, but for centuries the word Byzantine meant one thing—*Greek*. In the fourth century A.D. Constantine made it his capital, center of the Roman Empire. The Emperor Arcadius named it Constantinople. Persians and Arabs attacked her over the years. The Eastern Church spread north into Russia from Constantinople. Then the Turkish invasions, religious schisms, and the Italian republics, Amalfi, Genoa, Venice."

"What was worth so much?" Mavis Hutzler asked. "It looks pretty run down to me."

"A dump," Ed said.

"'Take me back,'" Ibith Grant sang to her husband, "'to Constantinople, no, you can't go back to Constantinople . . .'"

Herbie, rumbling up and down the aisle, looking for good places to take pictures (Murray Yasuda always seemed to beat him to the best points), joined in the singing.

> "Now it's Istanbul, not Constantinople.
> Why did Constantinople get the works?
> That's nobody's business but the Turks'!"

The bus started across the Ataturk Bridge.

"On your left, ladies and gentlemen," Pepi said, "the Golden Horn, a small river called Halic. We cross the Golden Horn and go to new Istanbul. That part is called Beyoglu. If you took a boat under the other bridge on our right, the Galata, you would come to the Bosporus, which goes south to the Sea of Marmara and north to the Black Sea."

In Beyoglu the streets were newer and wider. The traffic thinned. There were Ford agencies, Electrolux dealers, Coca-Cola signs.

"When do you think we'll hear from Sparling?" asked Dr. Wicker.

"I have no idea," Bettenhausen said. "I set up a code with him. Perhaps by the time we get to Israel."

"I still don't get it," the dentist said. "You're convinced Borkin was trapped by Leland and that Leland is a Soviet agent. Why insist on getting the message across?"

"I'm working on that. We have to give Borkin every option."

"The Bosporus is famous in legend," Pepi said. "Who would like to hear a romantic story before we get to the hotel? Perhaps to get you all in the mood for romance?"

"Hoo-hah!" Herbie howled. "In this collection of *kockers?*"

Yes, Flemington thought, a romantic story—full of sighs and blushes and moans, hot hands, sweet breath. All he had run from. Fear of a split-level house in a Minneapolis suburb; an aborted career; a rewrite man at forty-eight earning fifteen thousand dollars a year. Nothing for extras. No tailored jackets and bench-made shoes. A fair trade. He had his heiress and his millions (not his, but available to him) and he could dream about Theresa.

"On the Bosporus—or the Hellespont as it was then known—is a small island with a lighthouse," Virgil said. "In ancient times a beautiful girl named Hero was put there by her father. Her lover was Leander and he was a great swimmer. Every night Leander would swim across the river so that they could spend the night together, and when the lark sang in the morning, he would swim to shore. But finally there was a terrible storm, and Hero waited and waited for him—only to see Leander's body washed up on the beach. She died of a broken heart."

"I'm all choked up," Herbie said.

"You told that beautifully, Pepi," Cornelia said. "Tell us another."

"No, Mrs. Bettenhausen, I do not wish to destroy the romantic mood."

"Herbie, what's red and white on the outside and gray on the inside?" Murray shouted.

"Tell me, tell me, Father, what is red and white on the outside and gray on the inside?"

"An inside-out elephant."

"Why do they keep talking about elephants?" Mr. Legrand asked his wife.

"It's Harvey and the Japanese, dear. A joke they have."

"But there are no elephants in Turkey."

"Of course not, dear. Are you well rested?"

"I'm cold," Mr. Legrand said. "I wish I were in Arizona."

The party was quartered at the Seljuk Hotel on the Cumhuriyet Caddesi in the new part of the city. It was a broad boulevard full of automobile agencies, travel offices, a Hilton Hotel dominating all. The Seljuk was a smaller version of the Hilton—modular, stark, clean, with an outdoor dining area and a swimming pool.

As they awaited Virgil's distribution of keys, Herbie, Si, and a few others studied a placard in front of the hotel night club, the Sultan's Delight. On it were mounted photographs of belly dancers.

"Man, that's for me," Herbie said. "When is belly dancing—tonight?"

"Pepi said tomorrow," Ed Hutzler said. He fiddled with his hearing aid, as if better ears were needed—an addition to good eyes—to admire the protruding abdomens, lavish thighs, bulging breasts of the dancers.

Murray's eyes popped. "Yow. Look at that one, Herbo. Sarita the Slave Girl. Boy, I'd like to be her master."

"She'd crush you like a fortune cookie. Me, me, someone my size, that's what she needs. *Mamenu,* I can't wait."

"See?" Flo asked Shirl. "See the kind of culture my husband goes for? This makes the whole trip worth while for him."

Ed Hutzler read the information on the gold-flecked placard with solemn interest.

A NIGHT IN THE HAREM AT

THE SULTAN'S DELIGHT

10 BELLY DANCING GIRLS 10

☆ ☆ ☆

Each different, Each original,
Showing the Ancient Art of the Court!

"Nothing like that back in Illinois, hey, Ed?" Herbie leered.

"Not hardly."

"You look out. You might get so excited Mavis won't recognize you."

Unoffended, Ed's eyes blinked at Herbie. What was Herbie? Where did he come from? How could he be so funny all the time? "Oh, Mavis and me manage, we always have."

Nodding sorrowfully, Herbie plodded away. True. True enough. You didn't come as far as Ed Hutzler did, make the money he did, grow apples and pears, go on tours—*and be so calm, sure, and satisfied* —without "managing."

"He's a better man than I am, Gunga Din," Herbie said to Dr. Grant.

"How so?" asked the black man.

"You and me, we got our hang-ups, our *mishegoss.* Ole Ed Hutzler and ole A. T. Gunthorpe, it's their America."

Henderson Grant, who had studied the belly-dancing photos from a distance, shook his head. "Don't believe it, Herbert. They have their problems. Ed and Mavis fight over bathroom rights every morning. They are not as steady on their feet as one would believe."

"Glad to hear it, Doc. Listen, I got these pains in my *kishka.*"

"Don't eat for a day."

"Me? Not eat? Some doctor. Henderson, I have to have a talk with you. Ibith looks like she isn't getting enough."

There was an air mail special delivery letter for the Flemingtons. Harry saw the return address—Robbie's boarding school—and he wondered about showing it to Lulu. She was weak again. There had been an argument with the officials at the Istanbul airport, some business about their refusing to pass the luggage without inspection. Virgil did some fast talking about the ten valises which the American tourists did not want to take to the hotel.

320

"They are worried about terrorists," Virgil explained. "Anything out of the ordinary upsets them."

"Do we look like terrorists?" Lulu asked, the color rising in her cheeks.

"Of course not, madame. But the number of bags . . . and leaving them here . . ."

"You will handle it for us," she said.

Harry read the letter. The old dread. Sons were supposed to play Little League baseball, root for the Red Wings with their fathers, go to Princeton or Michigan or Williams and edit the school newspaper. Tall and straight and intelligent and American. "A better writer than his old man ever was," Flemington imagined himself telling some of the rich boobs at the country club. . . . "Random House is taking his book. . . ."

> Dear Mr. & Mrs. Flemington:
> I do hope you are having a pleasant vacation on your tour. It sounds exciting, all those interesting places. Your cards to Robbie have been coming regularly, and I have read them all to him. He seems to respond slightly and he studies the pictures on the cards, but I cannot honestly say whether he makes a connection between them and you. . . .

Flemington looked around the lobby for his wife.

"Your key, sir," Virgil said. "Mrs. Flemington is in the shop looking at rugs."

Harry took the key. With the letter in his hand, he walked across the lobby, smiling at Barbara Huggins, asking Mr. Legrand how he felt, joking with Herbie about the belly dancers. His heart was a block of cement.

He stood in the doorway of the carpet shop. The proprietor had spread rugs on the floor—bloody reds, unearthly blues.

"Genuine antiques, madame," the man said. "Hand-woven eighteenth-century prayer rugs. We are the only shop in Istanbul that specializes in them."

Harry held up the letter. "From the school, dear. News about Robbie."

She did not look at him but waved him away with a small motion of her gloved hand. "Don't bother me," Lulu said. "Can't you see I'm busy?"

Huggins found an edition of the Paris *Tribune* a day old, and two English newspapers—the *Telegraph* and the *Mail*. None of them had any news about ships leaving Dubai. And why should they? Monsieur Chahoub had lied to him, he concluded.

321

In the small hotel room, he watched Barbara ungirdle herself and pad about in a thin slip and a brassiere. Normally it would be a good time to make love—seize her, down her. But Huggins was troubled. It was just past five. What hours did smuggling offices work in Istanbul? He asked the operator for the number of the Istanbul branch of the company on the list that Chahoub had given. There was no answer.

"I'm going out for a walk."

"So much energy?" Barbara asked.

"I'm restless."

He grabbed her bottom. She squealed. But it was a *pro forma* move on his part. During the six days behind the Iron Curtain, he had been out of touch, suspended. The money was gone. The gold purchased. A risk was being run, and he had no control over it. But by the same token, the grasping hands of the Malfi family were no longer on him. Back in the "free world" he was part of the apparatus again, the network of stolen shipments, hot treasury notes.

"I'll be in the bath, Jimmy," Barbara called. She seemed in a better frame of mind the last few days. Sensible shoes helped. Some of the other tourists had forced her to talk, to laugh. Mrs. Hutzler was good at reaching Barbara. So was "Ma Barker." Typical of Barbs, J.P. thought, as he left the room. She would be wary of any good-looking, poised woman—Rosie Wicker or Mrs. Carrell—but would find common ground with someone with a motherly image. What, Huggins mused, would Barbara retain from the twenty days?

A man couldn't have it all. Clod that she was, Barbara was a queen of the bed. He appreciated it. He was grateful for her attentions to the children, her dumb adoration of him. But . . . but . . . there had to be something else, some other kind of marriage. Again he wondered about Theresa Carrell. All alone in a hotel room. A long-thighed woman who held her head high and looked you in the eye. Notes in a guidebook. Enraptured by Mozart.

Huggins had seen her entering her room. No man to help her unpack, run the bath for her. J.P. walked the corridor in his crepe-soled Whitehouse & Hardy boots. The old James Patrick, all Celtic charm, with a bottle of scotch and two glasses (didn't William Holden pull a stunt like that in a movie?) Would have knocked at her door, walked in, made her happy. Would he dare?

Mulling his chances, he saw Harry Flemington, wearing dark glasses and walking quickly, approach him. The Detroit man, seeing the lawyer, slowed his pace. Huggins greeted him. Flemington responded with a weak "Hi" and walked on. J.P. suspected something. You rarely saw Flemington without his wife. She kept him on a short leash.

The lawyer turned the corner, walked toward the elevator, and then did a U-turn, peering around the wall of the hallway. Flemington was knocking at Theresa Carrell's door.

Good luck and God bless, the lawyer thought. A few days ago Flemington had confided to him—he loved her. And the torture of being close to her on the tour, under orders from his wife, that Gorgon with dollar bills for hair, not to go near the Carrell woman. Huggins had heard other gossip—that Lulu had demanded that the teacher be thrown off the tour. How right she had been! Old Flemington was on his way. J.P. was happy for him.

"Just a minute," Theresa called. The musical voice made Flemington shiver. He looked up and down the hallway. Huggins had seen him. But that meant nothing. He had not seen him at Theresa's door.

"Who is it?" she asked. Her voice was louder.

"Harry."

He waited. For a painful moment, he hoped she would refuse him. Chastised, he would crawl back to Lulu. Lulu had bought two thousand dollars' worth of prayer rugs. But they would not fit in any of their bags. The rug merchant was trying to package them in heavy canvas so they could be carried along as personal luggage for the rest of the trip. The decision had exhausted his wife. She was napping.

The door opened. Terry was in a blue satin robe. She held it at her throat.

"May I visit?" he asked.

"Why?"

"I have a present for you."

Theresa frowned. "Harry . . . I said this was over. Finished."

He forced his way into the room, shut the door behind him. She moved away.

"I don't want you here."

"Don't be cruel."

"I'm not being cruel. I'm being sensible. I know what you want. This is lunacy. Two middle-aged fools. Harry, you're supposed to do this sort of thing with a woman half your age."

"Impossible. Would you believe I've never been unfaithful to Lu? Except with you."

"I'm honored, but this has to be put to rest. Ten years from now, twenty, when we're old and cackling like the Legrands, will you expect me to remember moments of passion in the Seljuk Hotel?"

He put his arms around her. The feel of her body convulsed him for a moment. He tried to kiss her; when she turned her head, he pressed his face to her neck, her shoulder. Firm, firm flesh. A genetic marvel.

An eternal woman. She moaned, but she seemed determined not to encourage him. With strong hands, she pushed him away. Flemington turned off the overhead room light.

"Atmosphere won't help."

"I can't stand bright lights," he said.

"Oh, of course. You always had a sense of the dramatic. It's that old rewrite man's awareness of details."

"It made me a better lover." His voice cracked. He felt like a seventeen-year-old trying to seduce a thirty-year-old married woman— all gasps and mumbles and lies.

"Sit down and be quiet," she said. The classroom strictness returned to her voice. Was it a fake? Flemington had wondered all the years he had known her. A pose to bank the fires within?

Chastised, Harry sat in a creaking modern chair. Why were there not divans and poufs and thick carpets in the Seljuk Hotel? What had happened to the glories of the Sublime Porte? There was something to be said for the way decadent monarchs went about things. Ataturk's republic had ended up with plastic hotels, strips of paper across toilet seats, sterilized glasses, and coffee shoppes serving "Sultanburgers" and "Golden Horn Pizzas."

Terry sat on the edge of the bed. Was that a good sign? An invitation?

"You can only stay a few minutes," she said curtly. "And be careful leaving. There are no secrets on this tour. Someone will see you and word will get back to Mrs. Flemington."

"Someone's seen me already, I think."

She shook her head. "Oh, God. Who?"

"Huggins."

She arched her neck. "One of my suitors."

"That courthouse Irishman?"

"Don't think you're the only amorous swain in this collection of senior citizens. You know that Horace T. Wattle is hopelessly in love with me."

"I gathered. You could do worse."

"I doubt it." Theresa laughed. "A sweet man, full of nice ideas. He regards Sirhan and Oswald as benefactors of their country."

"And Huggins? Has he made a pass at you?"

"No, but I've gotten the message. When Irish eyes are ogling, sure they give themselves away."

"Anyone else I know?"

Theresa tilted her head. In an innocent way, she could be the most provocative of women. It was a combination he never quite under-

324

stood—an unruffled exterior, edged with hints of unashamed, damned near violent sexuality.

"I think Pepi has his eye on me."

"Our fearless leader?" Harry tried to joke; but there was a draining sorrow in him.

"We had a long talk on the plane this afternoon. When one of those dark Europeans starts consoling you, look out. He wants to console you into bed."

"And nothing so far?"

"Of course." She sat up straight on the edge of the low-budget bed. How did they furnish second-class hotels? With surplus stores from army PXs? "It isn't easy at my age. You get tired of being used. It's flattering, but it's the reason I swore off cruises and poolside vacations. Travel is all I can manage. There's always something new to see. Some notes to make for my classes."

Flemington tried to suppress the sympathy that welled in him: it was no use. What a thoughtless bastard he had been, a selfish, self-serving, conniving male animal. All for me. Money and status and a career. Would the *Detroit A.C. News* buy an article from him on packaged tours, some funny "do's and don'ts"?

"And all my fault," he said.

"I suppose so. But you didn't arrange for Wade to die in a car crash or my first marriage to fall apart. Maybe you had something to do with it. I have a feeling both of them knew I was thinking about you every time they made love to me."

"And were you?"

"Yes. I always will be. But I won't let it affect what life there is left to me. At least I won't succumb to mildewed memories. How long can this kind of idiocy go on? This plot of mine was a failure, Harry. So go to your room and forget everything."

"I'm drowning in misery for what I've done to you. You know all I can think of at the moment?"

"I can imagine."

"I'm wondering about all the men you've slept with. I want to know all about every man who's ever made love to you. Your husbands. Boy friends. Casual types. Were any of them better than me? Did they make you happier than I did? I'd like to kill them. What right had they?"

Theresa got up. She was wearing nothing under the dressing gown. She held it together at the neck and at the waist. "Not any more, Harry. This is quits. Please go."

He stood up, an elegant trim man, too well dressed for a tour in a second-class hotel. "I forgot my present for you."

"Surprise Lulu with it."

"There are no surprises left for her. Besides, she'll tell me she could have gotten it for half the price."

Flemington took the necklace from his pocket. "It's clear topaz. A Russian specialty. And an antique gold setting." He held it up.

"Why? To make up for things?"

"I suppose so. Maybe to get you to change your mind."

"A bribe?"

"Christ, Terry. Stop digging it in. Maybe just as a remembrance . . . something to recall what it was like twenty years ago. More than twenty years ago."

She looked at the beautiful piece of jewelry. The stones had a rare luster, as if aged in the earth, full of Slavic mysteries. Fables about woodchoppers and witches and gnomes lurked in them. The offering should have insulted her, she felt. But it was no use. Harry had always had that power over her—the power of a weak man, an appellant. Was it her destiny to attract such mates? Both her husbands had been cast in the same mold—leaners, takers. The irony of it, Theresa reflected, was that she was not quite the Earth Mother that they imagined her to be. It was all in her manner, her appearance—serenity, confidence. Under the smooth skin, she was weaker than they were, every bit as much a trembler and self-doubter.

And there stood old Harry Flemington, first and only love, holding up a trophy. A reward for being a good sport.

"Like the inscribed gold watch after thirty years of service to General Motors," Theresa said.

"Take it. Don't make fun of me."

"Too bad you can't have it engraved with something suitable. To Theresa, who was usually there when I needed her."

"Let me put it on you. Then I'll go."

"I don't think so, Harry."

She saw his eyes rimmed with tears. The gall of him, the bottomless wells of self-pity! And yet, looking at his gentle face, she understood that she was still in love with him.

"Please. A final act. This ends it."

"All right. Give it to me. Or leave it on the dressing table. As someone said, 'In the name of God, go.'"

"Let me put it on you."

Unwilling, she walked toward him, then turned her back. Flemington, his hands trembling, put the necklace around her. The catch proved tricky. It was a minuscule hasp, too small for his clumsy fingers. Her body, covered only by the pale blue gown, was so close to his that he fancied he felt the warmth of her skin, sniffed the tantalizing odor of powder or perfumed soap.

"Can't seem to manage it."

"Hurry," Theresa said. "Any minute Lulu will be at the door."

"There," Femington said. "It's closed. From Russia and Harry Flemington with all our love."

She started to turn, to move away, and he embraced her from behind, kissing the back of her neck, her cheek, pulling the loosely belted robe apart. His hands took her breasts and held them gently.

"No, no, enough, Harry."

"I will make love to you."

"Go back to your wife."

She resisted him less than he had suspected she would; then not at all. It often had occurred to Flemington, in the early years of their love-making, that Theresa was stronger than he was. In a knock-down brawl he could probably overcome her. But there was a force in her that filled him with a wondering fear.

"I've made my mind up," Flemington said.

"Really?"

"I am going to get a divorce from Lulu and I am going to marry you."

"Is that what this reprise did to you? Harry, I'm a middle-aged discard."

Flemington, clothed, unruffled, covered with a fine sweat, sat on the bed. His hands ran lightly over her hips, her legs. "The joking is over, Terry. I can't confront Lu now, but as soon as we get back to Grosse Pointe, I'm making my bid for freedom. She doesn't need me any more. When I tried to tell her about the letter from Robbie's school, she waved me away. She was too busy haggling over a carpet. She can find herself an antique dealer and live out her days buying stuff from him."

"You won't."

"I swear it. I mean it this time." He kissed her, touching her body again.

"Ouch. That expensive tweed tickles."

"This kind of frantic grabbing is over," he said. "I have the feeling I've never made love to you properly. Maybe because we were never married. They claim you have to know a woman intimately, all the habits, all the quirks and oddities, to love her. There's years and years of passion ahead of us, Terry. Not to mention just holding hands and going on tours."

"It has a nice sound."

"I intend to make love to you in every de luxe hotel in Europe,

327

to celebrate this renewal of our relationship. And not half clothed, with glances at the bolted door, but prolonged periods of amorous dalliance. We'll behave like newlyweds."

"It sounds marvelous, but I don't believe you for a minute."

"Don't be surprised if I call you a week after this is over."

She covered her face. "Harry, you manage to screw everything up. Why are you off on this high? You know you need her money. I couldn't even keep you in cuff links with my teacher's salary."

"I'll work."

"At what?"

"I'm a newspaperman. An editor. There are any number of things I can do. I have connections. I'll try my hand at public relations. It pays well."

He was standing in front of the mirror, adjusting the knot in his Sulka tie, tugging at his jacket, brushing back a few hairs. As he engaged in these acts of grooming (not without a hint of self-love) both of them realized he was summoning up fake courage, a locker room pep talk. Who would hire him now? Where were all those magazines that would buy his articles?

"I won't sit by the phone and wait," Terry said. "Age has hardened this gal." She got up—naked, unashamed. Her skin glowed in the darkened room.

"Are you angry with me?"

"No, darling. Seize the day and so forth. But it won't happen again."

"Until we are man and wife."

She kissed him lightly. He stroked her back—shoulders, spine, buttocks.

"'In the name of God, go,'" Flemington said. "That line you used."

"What about it? I'll be darned if I remember who said it."

"Cromwell. You just reminded me. It had something to do with the Rump Parliament."

They both giggled, then laughed raucously, helplessly. Theresa covered her mouth, still guffawing, as he left. Just like the old days. They had laughed a good deal in bed.

Day 15: Istanbul. An entire day given to the beauties and myster-
ies of this ancient crossroads! We board our Planet Tour bus
for a ride back into history—Greek, Roman, Byzantine, Cru-
sader, Turk! Some of the morning highlights—the Galata Bridge,
the Golden Horn, Santa Sophia, the Blue Mosque, the Sulei-
man Mosque, the Topkapi Museum, the old cisterns, the cov-
ered bazaar.

After a typical Turkish lunch—try kadin budu, *"woman's*
thigh," fried rice and meat balls, or a dugun corbasi, *"marriage*
soup"—we move on to the Dolmabahçe Palace and Taksim
Square. Then a ferry ride across the Bosporus to Usküdar, the
tip of Asia.

And do save a little energy for one of Three Worlds' high-
lights—a night with Turkish belly dancers!

"Why are you running off again?" Barbara Huggins asked. "This is
the first place I've liked and you have to go on some crazy business
call. Who do you know in Turkey?"

"Turks," J.P. said irritably.

They were outside the Blue Mosque. Barbara may have been
obtuse but she had certain insights. Istanbul was surely other-worldly.
The six minarets of the Blue Mosque soared into the cloudy sky. The
great round dome was like a woman's belly. Phallus and omphalos,
the architectural forms were full of secrets.

"The architect Mehmet Aga, and Sultan who ordered it Ahmed I.
Work begin 1616. Seven years to finish. Most beautiful."

The guide, a change from the succession of personable people the
tour had encountered, was a bald ball of a man, his figure forming a
sphere from the crown of his head to his feet. He spoke swiftly and
was hard to comprehend, but it did not seem to bother him. Swallow-
ing words, skipping others, mispronouncing many, his attitude seemed
to be: I'm a Turk, take me or leave me.

They had stopped outside the Blue Mosque and were being fitted
with stretch slippers over their shoes. A. T. Gunthorpe huffed and
wheezed trying to get his on. A shave-headed boy with sickly eyes
assisted him.

"Tha's a nice tad," Gunthorpe said. "Hyeah, son." He gave him a

329

dollar. In seconds a mob of howling boys surrounded the feed merchant, palms up, faces contorted.

Huggins followed Barbara into the mosque. He had wanted to leave, to take a cab to the office of his "trading company." Although the morning paper had no news of the S.S. *Lautaro*, or anything departing from the Persian Gulf, the price of gold on the world's free bullion markets had risen again. If they had bought it five days ago, when he was in Vienna, they had paid less; presumably the price in India or Pakistan had risen phenomenally higher. Greed began to nibble at him. Money on top of money. He would show his in-laws a few things.

"Oh, it's a dream," Cornelia said.

Rosie Wicker drew her breath in. "Unlike anything in the world. Arnie, it's too beautiful to believe."

Of all the sights the Three Worlds people had seen in their travels, none had the intoxicating effect of the interior of the Blue Mosque. Virgil had noticed this before. Surfeited with churches, palaces, boulevards, the mosque was a wonder so enchanting, so elusive, that the most bored of tourists were moved.

"Greatest all Turkish mosques," the fat guide mumbled. "Glaze tile. Glaze tile. All over blue glaze tile. Better than Santa Sophia. Pure Turkish art."

No one heard him. Ed Hutzler kept tuning up his hearing aid but got nothing. Around them, Moslem worshipers knelt on prayer rugs. Morning light streamed through the high windows and created a cool blue haze inside the room. It was as if, Bettenhausen reflected, the colors of the magnificent tiles—and what colors they were!—had life and movement and gave off sprays of blue light, aureoles and coronas in a thousand shades of blue.

"Are 260 windows here," the guide said. "Yes, 260 windows. So light all the time. Look at carpet on floor, very rich, very old, and also old prayer rugs."

"Mine look every bit as good," Lulu whispered to Harry. "I cut his price in half."

"Go nicely in our hallway," Flemington said. He glanced at Theresa. She was not writing in her book, but staring at the inner dome. Naked and all mine, Flemington thought: I will have her.

"Please, walk around," Murat said. "Not disturb prayers. We are nice religion, like guests to see us."

Huggins looked at his watch. It was not quite eleven. They had trudged through Santa Sophia but there were still the Suleiman Mosque, the cisterns, and the Topkapi Palace to go. He had delayed long enough. Fearful of calling the number given him by Chahoub and getting a frustrating response, he would go to the office on Istiklal Caddesi and demand information. Surely a man investing two hundred thousand dollars deserved an answer.

"I'm splitting, Barbs," he said. "See you at the hotel."

"When?"

"Lunch. Or after lunch. I'll be back in time for the afternoon sight-seeing. A.T., take care of the missus for me."

"Mah pleasure, Jim-boy."

Huggins padded around praying Moslems. A shame to leave. The Blue Mosque had captivated him also, but business was business. He could see Herbie looking at him with a shrewd New York squint, nudging Sid and Si and Murray, as if to say: "There goes Jimmy again, off on some hustle." It wasn't easy breaking the routine on these package things, J.P. realized. The people clung to every scrap of the itinerary, every monument, every bus ride, every bad meal, every shopping fraud, like drowning victims on floating wreckage. You dared to miss a dinner or take an afternoon off, it was a subject for prolonged debate. Hailing a taxi outside the Blue Mosque, Huggins decided he liked his mysterious departures. Herbie would bust a vein trying to figure out what he was after. Someday he would tell him.

"A small hustle, Herbie," he would inform the fat man, "only a quarter of a million bucks and I didn't even work up a sweat." It would be worth it to see the shock on Shackman's pink and orange face. It would be almost as much fun as telling the Malfi brothers how he had pyramided their stolen treasury notes into a gold machine.

The morning's sight-seeing had a sensual, erotic air. It was a warm overcast day, and the tourists moved from mosque to square to museum lethargically, looking at the forms and colors of the Moslem world, a place of jewels and rugs, domineering men and compliant women. Theresa Carrell found the atmosphere affecting her. The hour she had spent with Harry the night before remained vivid in her mind. A woman who doled out passion with careful contemplation of future damages as well as present joys, she found herself edgy, as if anticipating their next meeting.

But did he mean what he said in high passion? Was he telling the truth about leaving Lulu? Too many frustrations, too many false starts had left Terry a skeptic. Things did *not* work out. No pessimist, she had grown inured to men's lies and the cries of commitment uttered while straining for climax or beseeching a woman to

331

succumb. In Harry's case, she knew, it was impossible to tell whether his vow of last night was self-deception or an honest decision, one he would honor. She tried not to care. So they had had their middle-aged fling. And maybe they would again—a year, two years from now.

It was a source of amazement to her that she had survived the years of longing in such serviceable condition. (Using the adjective, as she reviewed the events of last night, she laughed to herself; *serviceable*—like a brood mare or a prize heifer. Still she had a right to be proud of her figure and her responses. Harry, she could not help noticing, was running to fat around the middle and his perform-ance, even making allowances for his terror of Lulu, had been dis-tinctly below his best.) But her frame of mind was rather healthy, she decided. She had not only come through the years of deprivation with spirits reasonably high, she had matured. Harry's promise was not to be taken as a certainty. By now she knew him. Would he leave Lulu? Splendid. They would summon up joys denied them since they were college students. Would Harry turn coward? Then she would manage anyway. At a certain point juices ran dry, limbs withered, desire was muted. . . .

"I have never seen such Ming in my entire life." Lulu Flemington's voice was loud. They were in the former kitchens of the Topkapi Palace.

"It is a fantastic collection," Rose-Anne said.

Lulu, who had avoided the women of the tour for fifteen days, honored the dentist's wife with a small smile. She had divined some-how that Rosie's credentials were in order—Bryn Mawr, tennis, *clubs*.

"I know Ming," Lulu said as the tour stood in front of the showcases filled with Chinese porcelain. "These are some of the finest in the world."

"Madame is quite right," Pepi said—pleased that the heiress was enthusiastic.

"How many pieces do they have here?" she asked.

"Over ten thousand, lady," Murat mumbled. "Ten thousand. All special for sultans."

"Priceless," Pepi commented.

"Don't be too sure," Lulu said. Her eyes gleamed. "Everything has a price."

"True enough, madame," Virgil said. "But there must also be a willingness for the owner to sell, price or no price."

A group had gathered around them. Inside the glass cases the Ming treasures, subtly hued greens and blues and reds, a parliament of bowls, plates, pitchers, vases, rested in silence, no longer spotted with the sultan's gravy, the grand vizier's lamb chop, an odalisque's spinach pie. . . .

"Those are T'angs over there," Lulu said. "That's tenth century, and even rarer and costs more. Try and buy some."

"She knows, she knows," Flo said to Shirl. Both were awed by the woman's knowledge.

"The cream-colored slip," Lulu said. "Perfect Sung. And the brown decorations. Dragon and forest. When you see that brown, it's got to be Sung."

"Sung me a song of the islands," Herbie crooned.

"Shaddap," Flo said. "Learn something."

"Madame's knowledge is astounding," Virgil said.

"There's some with the incised brown glaze. That's typical Sung also. Temmoku. I have a piece at home."

Herbie grabbed at his wife's rear end. "I got a piece at home also, lady."

"Pepi," Flemington said easily—he felt expansive, a man needed by two women—"do you think Mrs. Flemington would qualify as a tour escort for Planet?"

Lulu smiled coquettishly at her husband.

"She is overqualified, sir, far more intelligent than most of us. But we would be honored to hire her—if only to share her knowledge of porcelain."

Theresa, at the edge of the group in the Topkapi, trailing the Grants and the Bettenhausens, began to finger her neck. Tonight she would wear the topaz necklace.

At Istiklal Caddesi 78, Huggins found that there was no record of the Beirut, Dubai & Sharja Trading Company. It was a shabby office building. A sleepy porter lounged in the doorway on a Coca-Cola crate. He spoke no English. As Huggins kept showing him the address, he kept pointing to the brass plaques in the corridor. There was a doctor, a dentist, several companies.

No, Huggins did not want to see Osmin Cetkak, D.D.S., or the Golden Horn Casualty & Life Insurance Company, or the Istanbul branch of American Superba Bathroom Products. He wanted the Beirut, Dubai & Sharja Trading Company. Small fingers of panic probed his intestinal region again—the same fingers that had grabbed at him in the Schönbrunn gardens when he lost the case.

He walked out of the hallway, leaving the porter dozing on his crate. The notion that he had been swindled grew in him. There was still the phone number. The operation could have shifted addresses. They were the kind of people who had to stay a step ahead of the

333

law. He walked a short distance on Istiklal Caddesi. A few banks were open for business—the Osmanli Bank, the Bank of the Near East. Knees shaking, he wondered about going into one and inquiring whether they knew about the company in which he had a two-hundred-thousand-dollar investment.

It was a short walk to the Seljuk Hotel. The tour had not returned for lunch yet. They were still—how he envied them!—listening to Herbie's jokes and Pepi's lectures, unconcerned with being swindled. In the lobby he saw Mr. and Mrs. Legrand, seated on a sofa, holding hands.

"Is the bus back?" she asked him brightly.

"No. I came back early. How is Dad today?"

Mr. Legrand waved feebly at J.P. "I get by, son."

You sure do, Huggins marveled. Riding up in the elevator, he envied their equanimity. They lived on pensions, Social Security, made every dollar count, traveled, loved one another. He'd heard Mrs. Legrand regaling Herbie and Si one night about the way she and Weston, after a lifetime of hard work, were dependent on no one, needed no one, had no relatives, no friends. They managed on a limited budget, took a tour every year, never missed a good movie, read every best seller.

In his room, the lawyer asked for the Istanbul number of the shipping company. There was no answer. He told her to try again in fifteen minutes. After ordering a double scotch he got the operator again and asked for the Vienna number in the leaflet given him by Monsieur Chahoub.

It took barely ten minutes for the call to go through.

"This is Chahoub speaking."

J.P. heard the smooth voice. He expected oil to flow from the earpiece. "Chahoub? James Patrick Huggins here. In Istanbul."

"Ah, yes. Lovely city. Please, do not miss the underground cisterns. I assume you have seen Santa Sophia? And the Blue Mosque?"

"Not only that, I've been to your office on Istiklal Caddesi. Chahoub, it doesn't exist."

"Oh, my apologies, sir. The office moved. We neglected to change the address."

"You expect me to believe that? What's the new address?"

"We are represented by Mr. Karakoy. He is assistant manager for the Marmara and Black Sea Shipping Company."

"You are a lousy Ay-rab liar," Huggins said. "You have no office here. You are a gold smuggler and you stole my money."

"Ah, please, please, Mr. Huggins."

"Please, my ass. Chahoub, where is my money? Or would you like me to call Interpol?"

"Really sir, you should not make threats." There was a clicking noise, as if a phone had been picked up on the other end. Or had Chahoub activated a recording device?

"I want to know where my money is," J.P. persisted. Some of the snap had gone out of his voice. It was difficult enforcing your will on a shifty Lebanese six hundred miles away.

"Your money is safe."

"Has the ship sailed? It doesn't take that long to get across the Persian Gulf, does it?"

"Mr. Huggins, it is a perilous trip. The captain never knows the destination until he arrives. That is rather like life, is it not?"

"Not my life, pal."

"I am not so sure."

"What the hell does that mean?"

"Mr. Huggins, you are a naughty boy. Very naughty indeed."

Huggins listened to muffled chuckling. "Who the hell is on that line with you?" he shouted. "Is that the creep in the bed sheet? Sheikh, is that you?"

"Y-y-y-y-es, sir. Oh yes, Mr. Huggins."

"You taping me?"

"On no, sir," the sheikh responded. "Oh, you are a funny man, Mr. Huggins."

"And so naughty," Chahoub added.

"I might come back to Vienna," J.P. said. "Just to lean on you two."

"Please do," the sheikh simpered.

"Pull you out of that shroud and beat the piss out of you."

Both Arabs roared at this.

"Yes, yes, please do."

There were some exchanges of Arabic on the other end. Then a click. When Chahoub spoke he was all business. "Mr. Huggins, are you there? You gave me stolen treasury bills."

"You're kidding."

"Oh no, sir. You must have known it. Those treasury notes were stolen. When our agents attempted to buy gold, the day you entrusted them to us, he learned they were stolen. That made it impossible to deal with any reputable seller of gold. It made it very hard indeed."

"I had no idea they were stolen." In a sense, he was telling the truth. Huggins had only learned about the notes at the Budapest airport, from Ross, the man from the embassy.

335

"My dear Mr. Huggins. You are an eminent New York lawyer and I must take your word. The fact remains that your investment presented us with an entirely new problem."

"Maybe you better give me the money back. You can send it with a courier to Israel. Or Rome."

"That is impossible, sir. We have invested it, but in somewhat different fashion. We have used the funds as collateral to purchase platinum."

"*Platinum?*" Huggins' mind swiveled. It felt the way it did one July afternoon, ages ago, when Buck Sweeney, swinging a softball bat at raindrops falling from the roof of P.S. 188, had slammed the bat into his pal Jimmy's head. He had a lump the size of a medium egg for weeks.

"We were fortunate to locate a dealer who was less concerned with the origins of money. Actually, we have not turned the notes over to him but put them up as collateral on a loan. With the loan, we have bought platinum, and when the shipment is delivered to its destination, we redeem the loan."

"Just like that?"

"Not quite, Mr. Huggins. Since no one wants your notes we must keep using the collateral until the original loan is paid off, until sufficient profits have been realized from platinum shipments so that you can be repaid with your original notes and the profits. It may take some time."

"How long?"

"That is hard to say. The price of platinum is rising faster than that of gold. We may try to buy palladium and molybdenum, both of which also command high prices in the subcontinent. Platinum is now at more than three hundred dollars an ounce and sells for double that in India. It may be a month or so."

"A month?"

"Perhaps less. You have no choice, sir. The first consignment of platinum has been purchased and is in Dubai. An obliging first steward has placed it in a toilet tank in the officers' quarters."

"Chahoub, you are out of your mind."

"No, sir, we are just willing to take risks. I have drawn up a new contract for you. Where shall I send it?"

Huggins groaned. "United States Treasury Department, Enforcement Division. How does that sound?"

"You are joking with me again. The Vittorio Veneto Hotel in Rome, sir? Is that all right?"

"Yeah, yeah." He was going to ask Chahoub to repeat the financial finagling, the precise way in which his notes were used as collateral, to be reclaimed when profits from smuggling equaled the loan plus interest, when he heard the waiter knocking at the door with his scotch. He badly needed some of the disturbance, as Sweeney would have said.

Bettenhausen, invigorated by the Blue Mosque, was taking charge of lunch orders on the hotel patio. "Hmmm, something light?" he asked the Grants. "Try the *biber dolmasi.* Green peppers stuffed with rice and meat. Or a *hunkar begendi*—stewed lamb and eggplant."

A porter tinkling a bell and carrying a blackboard appeared on the patio. On the board, scrawled in chalk, was the name MR. BETNOSSEN. Herbie and his group, seated near the entrance, saw him first. Si pointed to Bettenhausen.

"The professor," Herbie said. "The fellah *dorten,* with the white whiskers. He's really a rabbi, so watch it."

"Does he ever stop?" Flo asked Shirl. "Does he ever stop?"

Si sucked at his pipe. "And he complains his feet hurt. I think the exhaustion goes from his mouth downward."

Flo sipped her Coke. "It's true, Herbie. You're *kvetching* for three days now. *This* hurts you, *that* hurts you. If you'd just sit quietly in the lobby like Mr. Legrand does, and rest up—"

"Hah! I'm in the same league with that *alter kocker,* Pa Barker, yet! Waiter! Bring on the kootchy dancers! I wanna dance!"

Shackman lumbered to his feet and began dancing among the tables, using the napkin as a veil, a brassiere, a scarf to flick teasingly at Ed Hutzler and A. T. Gunthorpe. "Yeah, I wanna dance. I wanna be the Sultan! I wanna lotta broads!"

Bettenhausen followed the bellhop into the lobby. There was a message at the desk. The man tried to explain to him that he had to sign for it. Why? Bettenhausen realized that it was a cable. He signed his name in a ledger and the concierge gave him the envelope. Bettenhausen adjusted his eyeglasses and walked toward the door to get maximum light.

HAVE LOCATED BOOK YOU REQUESTED TITLED UNDERSTANDING SOVIET SYSTEM BY IVAN TIGRANIAN HAVE ENGLISH EDITION SHALL EYE MAIL IT YOUR HOME OR WILL YOU TRY TO BUY STATES STOP HAVE FEELING OUT OF PRINT

SPARLING

Bettenhausen folded the letter. A sly smile curled his lips. He tugged at his beard. Any minute he expected Colonel Haki, the chief of the Turkish secret police, to appear in the doorway. How marvelously Welles had used the Eric Ambler character in his films!

337

He saw Wicker loping across the lobby. It was a problem keeping their adventure from their wives. Surely by now the women suspected some hugger-mugger. But now it was ended; the great construction-ist's plot had worked. What had been denied him all those years in Hollywood—*Produced and Directed by Warren Bettenhausen!*—was born with hair and teeth. And better than any fiction on Eastman Kodak stock! More exhilarating than any wide-screen nonsense with stereophonic sound!

"Anything wrong, Warren?"

"Mr. Sparling has delivered."

They strolled toward the patio restaurant. The Legrands were hav-ing tea in the lobby. They did not seem to eat much. Wicker saw the Planet Tour bag at Mrs. Legrand's feet. Was she on *raki* now?

"He met Borkin?" Wicker asked.

The Hollywood man showed him the cable. "Eliot and I set up a code before we parted. Book means Borkin."

The dentist read the cable. "Ingenious," he said. "You really are something."

"Read on."

"Is there such a book?"

"Of course. You don't think the KGB isn't going to check Sparling on this? Book means Borkin. The title means the message from Mr. Leland was delivered, with a warning that we are fairly certain Le-land is a Soviet agent. Sparling's comment about the book being out of print means that Borkin had nothing to say to him when the mes-sage was transmitted."

"Mission accomplished."

Bettenhausen frowned. "I hope so. We have done all we could have done."

"What now?" Wicker asked.

"I'm not certain." Bettenhausen doffed his tam-o'-shanter to Mrs. Legrand as she slid by in her scuffs. *There* was someone to include in a spy story. Herbie was wrong. She wasn't Ma Barker. She was on the payroll of the Defense Intelligence Agency.

"But Borkin . . . did we help him? Or what?" The dentist looked pained—as if the corrective work on Mark Abrams' overbite had failed.

"We surely didn't *hurt* him."

Virgil entered the lobby, returning from his long lunch at a superb restaurant known only to guides and Turkish businessmen.

"Ah. News from home?" He pointed to the telegram in Betten-hausen's hands.

338

"Yes. Good news."

"How nice," Pepi said.

"Warren, I have a feeling we didn't do Borkin any good," Wicker said. "That crazy game you played—the blank paper, baiting the Russian cops. Sending Sparling after him. How do you know he wasn't tailed?"

Bettenhausen tucked the message into his pocket. "This cable from Eliot confirms all went well. His plan was to accost Borkin in the lavatory near his classroom at the university."

"The police could have followed them there."

"Borkin has kidney trouble and must often relieve himself. Sparling seemed to feel that the KGB didn't go after him every time he felt the call. I rather liked that."

Wicker moaned. His friend was still plotting, sketching in characters, working on dialogue.

"I like to think they stood side by side at the urinals, and amidst the gleaming white vitreous enamel Eliot whispered our message to him."

"I still don't get it. We did what Leland wanted."

Bettenhausen's eyes were flinty. "Mr. Leland is being smoked out. If he is a Soviet agent, he will be in for a great deal of discomfort."

"But we sent his message."

"Ah, but without the evidence. Without any letter or any trace of contact with the West. Borkin is still free and uncompromised. It would please me no end to hear that the clever Mr. Leland is in residence in Lubianka, or assigned to kitchen chores in Vladivostok."

The tourists began to assemble in the lobby for the afternoon tour of the Dolmabahçe Palace and the ferry ride to Üsküdar across the Bosporus. It was a small group. People were running down. The Legrands were absent. So were the Flemingtons, and Father Konay, and the Hutzlers, and several of the Midwestern ladies. (But not the Yasudas or Herbie Shackman's party; Herbie still complained of diarrhea and abdominal cramps, but he led his party forward. Who knew where a bargain lurked? Where some *hondling* would produce a treasure?)

"I am tempted to send your Mr. Leland a message," Bettenhausen said.

"I'm ready. Go on."

The Hollywood man, in a fair imitation of Humphrey Bogart, said: "'This will put you in good with your boss.'"

"I'm no good at this. I give up."

"Bogart to Elisha Cook, Jr. *The Maltese Falcon.* I have the sensa-

339

tion that we have put Mr. Leland in the worst possible way with his superiors."

Half hearing Murat's mumbled comments, a party of travelers walked through the baroque excesses of the Dolmabahçe Palace.

"A remarkable place," Pepi said to Theresa. "There are 365 rooms."

"One for each day of the year?"

"Quite. And each in more dreadful taste than the next. In its enormity it is possibly the ugliest building of its kind extant. The motifs alone are enough to give a man vertigo. Hindu. Turkish. Italian. By the time the nineteenth century came around the Turks had lost any sense of identity. What were they? Europeans? Asians?"

Theresa stared at the crystal chandelier above them in the throne room. "And that monstrosity?"

"A gift from Queen Victoria."

Terry laughed. "The Sultan could hardly say no."

"Yes," Virgil said. "One has that problem often with gifts." His eyes were fixed on the topaz necklace.

"You aren't subtle, Pepi."

They strolled out of the throne room, following Murat down a winding staircase with crystal railings. Statues of eunuchoid blackamoors and overstuffed goddesses lurked in the corners.

"It was a shame that Abdul lifted the ban on representational art," Pepi said. "Look at the horrors that resulted. Some of the worst statuary in the world."

"Why are we brought here?" Terry asked.

"If you were not, Mrs. Carrell, you would complain. What we miss we mourn. Often when we have it, we wonder what all that yearning was about."

"Are you being subtle again?"

They walked through corridors and foyers, crammed with Victorian gimcrackery, useless furniture. The sunlight sparkling on the Bosporus outside was a relief.

"I am not paid to be tour psychologist," Virgil said.

It was a short bus ride to the ferry boat for the trip to Usküdar.

"You do very well."

"Who was that guy who swam the Hellespants?" Herbie shouted. "What was his name?"

"Leander," Rosie said.

"That's for me. Gimme one of them hootchy-kootchy girls on that lighthouse there. I'd be a regular Johnny Weismuller."

"That is a lovely necklace," Virgil said. He took the seat on the bus next to Theresa.

"I was admiring it too," Ibith Grant said. "Where'd you get it Terry?"

"Moscow."

"Of course," Virgil said. "In the shop for precious stones."

Flo Shackman leaned over the back of Theresa's seat. "Did you *hondle*, Terry? Did you get a deal?"

"I'm no good at haggling."

"Ah, come on. Shirl and I both spotted it on you. It's only gorgeous. It's better than the *shlock* we've been buying. Whadja pay, Terry?"

"You'd make fun of me. You'd say you could have gotten it for less."

Flo looked at Shirl. "She won't tell, so she won't tell. I'm busting to know what it cost."

Virgil looked archly at the teacher. "I am sure the price was right, Mrs. Carrell. On the other hand, you were correct not to tell anyone what it was. It is no one's business but your own."

Theresa touched his hand. "It isn't even the business of our Planet Tour escort, is it, Mr. Virgil?"

"Least of all." He winked at her. He knew, he knew.

The Istanbul touring was badly balanced, Virgil had thought for a long time, and he intended to make recommendations to New York. The morning was too rich, too rushed, too full of revelations—the mosques, Santa Sophia, the Topkapi, the Galata Bridge. And the afternoon, with the atrocious Dolmabahçe Palace and the pointless trip to Üsküdar—a dull port full of noxious trucks—was a letdown.

"Everyone please get a rest," Virgil told his wards in the hotel lobby. "Tonight, after dinner, we will be treated to belly dancers."

"For an extra eight dollars," Mr. Wattle yelled. "They get you coming and going."

"No one forces you to attend," Pepi said.

"That's not the point. The literature you people put out says there's a night to watch belly dancers. It doesn't say there's an extra charge. It was the same way in Berlin and Vienna. Always a little more graft." He turned to Gunthorpe. "You think he's pocketing some of it?"

"Not ole Peppy. Be reas'nable, Horace."

Arnold Wicker stopped at the concierge's desk to purchase postcards. The clerk looked at him a moment, then gave him a yellow envelope.

"For me?" the dentist asked.

"Yes, sir. Cable. Please sign in book."

Arnold opened the envelope. Borkin? Sparling? His fingers tear-

341

ing at the paper, he assumed it was from one of his young patients in Riverford.

He read quickly, unaware that Rose-Anne was approaching.

YOUR FAILURE CARRY OUT ASSIGNMENT EXTREMELY GRAVE BREACH
OF COMMITMENT TO US STOP THIS MATTER NOT ENDED EYE ASSURE
YOU STOP INVOLVEMENT THIRD PARTIES FURTHER BREACH OF AGREE-
MENT AND WE DO NOT INTEND LET REST STOP YOUR INSTRUCTIONS
ARE TO DO NOTHING FURTHER TELL NO ONE REVEAL NOT A WORD
STOP WE WILL CONTACT IMMEDIATELY YOUR RETURN UNISTATES

LELAND

Wicker was about to crumple the paper in a rare show of anger when Rosie took it from his hand.

"What's this?" she asked. "A cry for help from Mark Abrams?"

He grabbed it back; it ripped. "No. No. It's—ah—Jimmy Donohue. His kid brother banged his head into his mouth and knocked out two incisors. A big job."

Rosie cocked her head. "That happened in March. You mean to tell me the kid grew two front teeth so fast? And got them knocked loose again?"

"Uh . . . something like that." He reached for the half of the cable Rosie retained. She pulled her hand away.

"What is this?" his wife asked. "What is this breach of commitment? What are they not intending to let rest? What the devil does this mean? *Not a word?* About what? Arnold, what have you been up to?"

Wicker looked around for succor. Where was Bettenhausen now that he needed him? He took Rosie by the elbow. "I need some coffee. Rosie, let's sit down over there. I'll tell you everything."

Later, dressing for dinner, Wicker's wife remained confused by the events he had related. She confessed to him that she had been suspicious of Leland all along. "I did a lot of your correspondence for that Columbia fund-raising deal," she said, "and I didn't remember any Leland. I figured he was a hustler trying to get you to buy something for him in Europe."

"I guess he was. The only thing is, I'm in hot water now."

"Well, he took his chances. You're no spy, Arnold. You're too honest."

"That's why he picked me." He admired his wife's willowy figure. She was wearing a floor-length green sheath. It set off her tanned bare arms, her long hair, superbly. Somehow the fact that she now knew about his mission made him more comfortable. Women like

Rosie were dependable, optimistic, helpful, judicious. He should have told her rather than Bettenhausen.

"What bugs me is that Warren is wrong about Leland," the dentist said as he knotted his Columbia blue tie. "He keeps insisting the guy was a Soviet agent using me to get Borkin into trouble. But this proves he wasn't."

"Why?" asked Rosie.

"He knows that Bettenhausen and I faked him out. We lobbed one over his head when he charged the net. Okay, he loses. But why should he keep after me like this? He knows I'll go right to the CIA or the FBI when I hit New York. I'll tell them everything. His cover's blown. Now they can pin something on him."

Rosie turned from the vanity. "If he is working for the Russians, his people in Moscow told him all about Bettenhausen."

"What's that got to do with it?"

Rosie wagged a finger at her husband. "Leland is betting that Warren will keep you quiet and away from *our* agents. Warren wants the perfect plot—a couple of amateurs tracking down a Soviet spy."

"Hmmm. A possibility."

"Don't bet that when we land at JFK five days from now Mr. Leland isn't there to greet you with some cock-and-bull story."

The dentist applied after-shave lotion to his face. "He'll have to go some to top Warren. I love him, Rosie, but he's got me dizzy."

In the hotel bar Bettenhausen squinted at Leland's cable.

"Curious," he said. "The return address. A post office box in Glen Cove, Long Island. Why does that make me even more certain that this man is a Russian agent?"

"Beats me, Warren." Wicker sipped his *raki*.

"Of course," Bettenhausen said. "There is a mansion in Glen Cove that houses members of the Soviet UN mission. *Quod Erat Demonstrandum.*"

"But why is this guy still pursuing me?"

"He has to pretend we haven't blown his cover, Arnold."

"You think he knows what we pulled off?"

"At least part of it. You can bet Varvansky's boss got a report on their interrogation of me. That blank sheet of paper convinced them we were wise to their scheme."

"What if they followed Sparling into the men's room? Or interrogate Borkin again? Maybe torture him?"

"Most unlikely. Borkin is too important a figure. Even the Soviets have a smidgin of conscience with a man that eminent. Besides, he's kept his mouth shut up to now."

Herbie lumbered across the bar toward them. In a double-breasted scarlet jacket, he seemed to have changed his shape, the gut shifting upward into a fatty chest. "What are you two guys up to? How come you're always plotting? *Gevald*, I just saw Doc Grant upstairs. He says old man Legrand is barely making it. He's gonna recommend he stay here to rest and meet us in Rome for the flight back. Skip Israel."

The dentist and Bettenhausen looked concerned. All the tour members had come to regard Weston Legrand as their ward. Flo Shackman made him tea with her heating immerser. Horace T. Wattle had given him a bottle of superpotency therapeutic vitamin and mineral pills.

"What is wrong with him?" Wicker asked.

"Doc don't know where to begin. Heart, kidneys, asthma, prostate. As a matter of fact I feel pretty lousy myself."

Theresa entered the bar, followed by Mr. Wattle. His hairless head threw off winking lights in the dim room.

"Terry's being pursued again," Wicker said. "I thought she shook him."

Bettenhausen looked at him, in intimate conversation with Theresa, his hand touching her arm. She was the essence of politeness. "He is a *thing*. Our friend Wattle is a machine. He is run by gears and wheels and meters. He understands mechanical things because he has no heart, only a computer."

"That's intolerant, Warren."

"Shall we rescue Theresa?"

The dentist shook his head. Even the likes of Mr. Wattle deserved companionship. Widowed, he had confided to several people that he had been lonely much of the time since "Mrs. W." died.

"State of Washington isn't that far from Minnesota," Mr. Wattle said. He held his scotch on the rocks up to the light. "I think they cheat on this. This doesn't look to me like J & B. I don't drink much, but I make it my business to know scotch. I'm required to do a lot of entertaining."

"Try some *raki*. It's light and cool." Terry held the glass under his nose.

"God-awful. These people don't know anything. As I was saying, Washington isn't far from Minnesota. I have customers in Duluth. I could visit you. The symphony, the theater, whatever you'd like. You are an exceptionally attractive woman. I know I have a few years on you, but I'm in my prime."

"Mr. Wattle, you're very kind, but I'm spoken for."

The industrialist's eyes were blank, short-circuited. "Spoken? You

344

mean you're married? Or a boy friend? And he lets you go off on these jaunts?"

"I'm a free soul."

"Not that free. You are a most discreet woman. Are you quite sure all options are closed to me?"

In the foyer leading from the bar to the restaurant, Theresa saw the Flemingtons, followed by the Hugginses. As always, Harry looked like an *Esquire* advertisement. Lulu, she noticed, seemed to be dressing *down* for the evenings, as if asserting her superiority over the Flo Shackmans and the Mavis Hutzlers, who dolled up in gowns and wigs. Louise Flemington favored wools and short skirts, as if to advertise her contempt for their flamboyance. Theresa had to give her high marks. She watched the Flemingtons enter the dining room. How odd! Last night Harry and she had embraced, naked, joined in ultimate commitment. Secrecy had lent it zest. She recalled the times they had been together over the years: nothing in her consciousness was as brightly colored, as detailed. She knew, down to the color of a rug, the shape of a mirror, the words of endearment and submission, the private jokes, precisely what had occurred between them on every occasion. And he did too. He had admitted to her that he had forgotten how to count type for a headline or how to write a proper lead for a complex political story. But the shoes she once wore; what she had said when a chambermaid knocked at a hotel door as they lay together; the rituals they observed before coming to climax—all these he remembered, and would till the day he died.

"There's a bit of gossip going around," Mr. Wattle said.

"Really?"

"I heard tell Louise Flemington's husband is sweet on you."

"Isn't that remarkable? They should use me as an advertisement for Planet Tours. I could draw maiden ladies in droves."

"I shouldn't have opened my big mouth. I heard you knew each other before this got under way."

"We did. Slightly." Theresa sipped her *raki*. The perfumed taste was cloying in her mouth. "A long time ago."

"I heard more than that."

"If you think so highly of me, Horace, maybe you'd better keep it to yourself."

"Goodness, don't misunderstand me. It's just the kind of silly talk that makes the rounds. Just that you knew him better than slightly. They say Mrs. Flemington got wind of it and wanted to have you tossed off the tour."

Inwardly Theresa felt relief. Lulu's temper fits were long past. According to Harry, the buying had distracted her sufficiently so that

345

she did not notice her rival as much. But could Wattle have stopped short of saying all he knew? Nosy, sharp-eyed, was it possible he was guarding something? Had he pumped Virgil? And had not Harry said that Huggins had seen him outside her door?

"Horace, shall we go in? I see the Grants are beckoning. You said you wanted to talk to Henderson about your company's training program for minorities."

"I don't actually," Mr. Wattle said. "Most of them are lazy, shiftless, and ungrateful. But if it means I can sit next to you, I'll talk to Dr. Grant about anything he wants."

He took her arm, running his hard hand the length of it. "That's a gorgeous necklace, Theresa," Mr. Wattle said. "Buy it in the covered bazaar today?"

"In Moscow."

"Didn't know the Russkies had things like that. Evening, Mrs. Flemington. Harry. Mr. Huggins, and the beautiful Mrs. H." He pointed a finger at Dr. Grant as they approached the table. "If I can help with the old man, I'm good at massage and bone manipulation. Learned it when Mrs. W. was suffering arthritis."

"He's resting," the physician said. "But thank you anyway. I gave him a little sedation. He's had so much of it all his life you just let him sniff the pill and he's off."

"Hmmm. Sort of addicted." Mr. Wattle nudged his knee against Theresa's. She drew away. But she had to admit she was almost enjoying his attention. Harry had roused her. She needed companionship, a hand to touch, the comforting knowledge of a male who cared, a man to need her as badly as she needed him.

A headwaiter dressed like a chief eunuch but with the sullen features of a Turkish accountant appeared, making suggestions about the menu.

"I don't trust any of it," Mr. Wattle said. "I want a steak, you understand, a steak?"

"Yes, sir."

"I want it very, very, very well done. I want it split open." He made the gesture with his hands, as if miming the opening of a book. "Split open, and each half, very, very, very well done. I wouldn't touch the rest of this."

"Well, when in Rome," Ibith said. "I was raised on greens and red-eye gravy and my stomach takes anything. What's a real Turkish opener?"

"*Imam bayildi*, madame," the captain said.

"What's in it?" Dr. Grant asked.

346

"It is a cold dish, sir. Fried eggplant with onions and tomatoes and spices. Delicious served cold."

"I'm game," Dr. Grant said. "You, Ibbie? Terry?"

"Chicken consommé for me to start," Mr. Wattle shouted.

Dr. Grant cupped his ear and listened. There was no rising cry for chicken soup, no rush to follow Horace T. Wattle to the consommé. "You are losing your grip, Mr. Wattle," Dr. Grant said. "The group used to rush for the consommé when you spoke."

"The worse for them. They'll all get sick as dogs before the trip is through. I haven't had to take a pill or a drop of medicine, nor have I missed a night's sleep, or my Canadian Air Force exercises, or a bowel movement."

A small rock orchestra appeared obligatory in places catering to Americans, Huggins realized. There was an amplified guitar, a piano, a bass, drums, and a sax. Not a bad group, either. Except for the electric guitar, it might have been the kind of combo he and Buck Sweeney had Lindyed to years ago in the Bronx. The Pelham Manor. The Neck Inn. Weddings at Huberts and Mayer's. Ah, the easy life. Huggins and Sweeney were poor but dishonest. Now he had an apartment in the East Eighties and belonged to a classy law firm. And where was Sweeney?

"Wanna dance?" Barbara asked him.

"Sure, Barbs." She seemed gayer than usual. Forget all that jazz about lively, outgoing Italians. The Malfis (it was the Sicilian strain that did it) leaned toward morosity and silence. He would give them plenty to sulk about when he got home. What was happening to his loot? As nearly as he could understand Chahoub, the notes had been used as collateral and could not be reclaimed until the profits from successive shipments equaled the original amount. At that point, Huggins would be repaid with his own stolen bills.

"You're still a peachy dancer, Jimmy."

"Yeah. Old light-feet."

"I feel good. Know why?"

Henderson Grant, M.D., holding Mrs. Carrell lightly, bumped them. Oddly graceless for a spade, Huggins thought. That frown and that tight way of talking. But all brains, all ambition. He doffed the Stetson to Grant. And he doffed more than just a hat to Theresa Carrell. Lot of woman. And Flemington sneaking into her room? Good luck, buddy.

"Sorry, Jim," Dr. Grant said.

"Hit me with Terry next time," Huggins said. "You look great, Theresa."

347

"You're both rather elegant yourselves," Theresa said. "Barbara, I adore your hair down. You have a beautiful wife, Jim."

"I deserve one."

Barbara crinkled her white nose. Give her another ten days, J.P. thought, and she would lose her shyness.

"You didn't guess why I'm so happy," Barbara repeated.

"You're gonna belly-dance on the stage."

"No, dopey. It's because in five days we'll see the babies. Oh, the angels. I can't wait."

Huggins liked—*loved?*—his children. But they did not reach him. Nor could he see surrendering his existence to them. People who got something *else* out of the world—not money or possessions, necessarily —but impulses, sensations, revelations, such people impressed him. Old Bettenhausen for one. The dentist and his wife. And Theresa. He'd never be entirely that way, but he would try. He was enraged with the Malfis for forcing him to scoot after thieves and wrongos like Moussac and Chahoub, when all he had wanted to do was look at monuments and paintings. The Blue Mosque had gotten to him. That haze of unearthly blue light, the play of blue shades. What went through Matisse's mind the first time he painted a nude?

The lights dimmed. The combo sounded a mournful chord. The musicians retired and were replaced by a different group—turbaned chaps, two thumping tambours and the third playing something re-sembling an extended recorder.

"Get the show on the road!" Herbie shouted. "Where are the broads?"

The room went dark. Flo Shackman shrieked. Herbie had goosed her as she was about to sit down.

"No fair picking on wives," Yasuda taunted. "Tonight we go after other people's wives."

"Yeh, yeh, some chance in this crowd of *kolyikas.*"

Music started, a writhing melody in a minor key. A spotlight illumi-nated the stage.

"This is belly-dance music?" Herbie cried. "This is music for a snake to come out of a basket. I saw that once in India when I was in the Army. Ten rupees to see a cobra fight a mongoose. Would you believe it was a fixed fight? *Shmuck* that I am, I bet on the snake. It rolled over. The cobra took a dive. Good-by, Charlie."

"Herbie is funny but he doesn't know when to stop," Si said to his wife. "Tell him to can it." He puffed on his pipe.

Shackman was slamming his huge hands on the table. "Whoo boy! Where are the girls? Let's have it, *tuchis afn tish!*"

The undulant music grew louder, the drums more resonant. In the dark, Lulu took her husband's hand and stroked it. The best of both worlds, Harry thought. Last night, love with a desirable and good woman. And the company of an heiress who let him live the life of a gentleman. But the choice had been made. Soon after their return he would break the news to Lulu. She was only fifty. She would have to fight off suitors. A good deal of late marrying went on in the automotive Olympus—divorces, deaths, falls from grace. A younger man perhaps. Handsome, quiet, an executive on the rise at GM.

Over a loudspeaker a voice announced:

"Ladies and gentlemen, the first of the Seljuk's harem, the tantalizing—Izmira!"

Arms a-dangle with bracelets, a long black wig hiding her face, a girl appeared from the wings, arched her back, protruded her abdomen toward the audience, and began to gyrate. The basic dance movements were almost innocent. These served to get her from place to place on the stage so as to give each member of the audience a chance to admire her. (As at previous entertainments, like the strip club in Berlin and the *Heurigen* in Vienna, the Three Worlds people seemed to make up the entire audience. It was as if the acts were reserved for Planet Tours, perhaps owned and run by them.)

"Shake it in front of me, baby!" Herbie thundered. "Take it and shake it, you can't break it!"

The girl thrust her belly at Herbie's face. With convulsions originating in the pelvis, she threw her belly forward and back, then rocked it from side to side. Hidden muscles wiggled, activating ligaments, forcing her flesh into unexpected expansions and contractions.

"Say, that's jes' fine, jes' fine," A. T. Gunthorpe said. "That lil gal know how to throw it."

"It leaves me cold," Mr. Wattle said.

"I bet you'd like me to do that in the bathroom," Mavis Hutzler whispered to her husband.

"Fat chance," Ed said. Old fruit grower, he had his dreams. "All I get is a lot of back talk. Golly, look at what she just did. Thought she'd lose one of 'em."

There was applause for Izmira. The band played a faster tune and a second girl appeared. Apparently the Seljuk programed the girls in order of talent and beauty. The first dancer, Izmira, had been ugly and ungainly. The second was an improvement. Her name was Zenobia and she wore a long red wig. Her face was far from pretty, but it had a mocking quality—insolent green eyes, a mouth suggesting odd sexual appetites. She used her hands well.

"That's the stuff!" Herbie shouted. "Get rid of the veil right away! Start already moving it around!"

349

Zenobia danced gracefully. She had slim legs, well-padded buttocks and a belly that popped and bumped in outrageous rhythms. The music was livelier. She favored swift lateral movements of her hips and forward thrusts that threatened to hurl her navel into the audience.

"Nice set of abdominals," Dr. Grant said. "Poupart's ligaments are well developed, and I like the way she handles the costal cartilage."

A voice over the loudspeaker announced: "And now, Miss Zenobia will give free belly-dancing lessons to any man who wishes them!"

The music stopped. The drums beat out a tattoo.

"The amazing thing about this," Wicker said to his wife and the Bettenhausens, "is that it isn't sexy. Like they're kidding us."

"Get up, Herbie!" Dr. Grant was shouting at Shackman. "Show 'em, Herbie!"

"Yeah, ole Herbie gon' dance!" Gunthorpe hooted. *"Yah-hoooo!"*

"They seem to want you, Mr. Shackman," Virgil said, bending over the Westbury party's table. "A vote of confidence."

"Wahoo! Let's hear it for Herbie!" Murray Yasuda was standing on a chair and whistling with two fingers jammed into his mouth. He made an alarmingly loud noise for so small a person.

"For the honor of the block, Herbie," Si said. "Never let it be said that the biggest *bulvan* on Prospect Place wouldn't take a lesson in belly dancing."

Herbie, whose ruddy face had turned to tones of gray and brown the past few days, and whose bloated body sagged drearily, was resisting. He melted formlessly into the chair and sipped the bitter sediment in his cup of Turkish coffee. "Nah, nah, let one of the young guys go up. Murray, go on, or Jimmy Huggins, he's a fancy dan."

"Hah!" Mr. Wattle crowed. "Not the big shot he thought he was! A bad case of stage fright, I'd say."

Forceful hands clutched at Shackman. It was no easy job moving his bulk. The truth was, Herbie's alimentary canal, from esophagus to rectum, was driving him insane. Never, never, in his hard-working, hard-living life, had Herbert Shackman endured such miseries. Gas collected in secret passages of his colon. Bubbles ricocheted against his duodenum. In the morning, foul vapors rose from his stomach, and at night, when he strained at stool, blood oozed forth. Strange waters, strange food, strange air. There was a lot of him to work on, he conceded. But how far could a man of fifty-five, one hundred pounds overweight, go?

"Up you go," Si shouted. His friends raised Shackman to the stage. Everyone applauded. Ed Hutzler got up, adjusted his hearing aid, and stared, enchanted at the spectacle of Herbie being lofted to the apron.

350

Zenobia drew him toward her, her semi-nude breasts pressing against his scarlet blazer. She kissed him on the forehead.

"*Mamenu,* this'll kill me. I'm too old for this *narrishkeit.*"

"Show us your stuff!" Mr. Wattle cried. "You've been bragging all the time!"

Flo leaned toward Shirl. "I hate that guy. I don't like the way he's needling Herbie. From Sid or Si or Murray, it's a joke. Look at that rat. His face is like ice."

Zenobia began to undress Herbie. She began with his jacket, unbuttoned it, and tossed it into the audience.

"Hey, go easy. That's a Lorry's special. Cost me over a hundred bucks."

The belly dancer unbuttoned Herbie's candy-stripe drip-dry shirt. The tourists howled. Herbie put his hands on the rise of the girl's hips, his fingers on the elastic band that held up her bikini. She wiggled her behind in appreciation; purple tassels jumped.

"Hoo boy," Herbie said. "She tickles. Hey, dollink, go easy on the merchandise."

"They did this to him at Grossinger's last year," Flo said to Shirl. "At first Herbie wouldn't get up on the stage, but when he did, they wouldn't let him sit down. Wait, you'll see the way he takes over."

The shirt fluttered into the audience. Ibith Grant grabbed it.

"What am I offered?" she shouted.

"Don't take a buck less than a dollar forty-nine," Si yelled back. "I was with Herbie when he bought it in Korvette's."

Herbie's undershirt barely hid his enormous dugs and his great gut. He was quite hairy, his skin covered with wiry orange fuzz. Little prickly tufts erupted on his thick upper arms, peeked over the rim of the undershirt, blossomed around his navel. Zenobia began to roll the undershirt upward.

"I have seen enough," Lulu said to Harry. "This is obscene."

She got up and started to leave. Flemington left a five-dollar tip and followed her. For once, he could not fault Lulu's taste. There *was* something unseemly about undressing Herbie Shackman in public. There was simply too much of the man—too much flesh, hair, fat, muscle. Gross and overwhelming, a victim as much as an attacker (his jokes were often commentaries on his own size), there was something painful about watching him denuded.

"Listen to that, *tsatske!*" Herbie boomed. He slapped his stomach. The noise reverberated in the night club. "Beat it out in a minor key, boys," he howled to the band. "Oh, rock it for me!"

Zenobia began to lower his trousers. They were expensive slacks, with an expanding elastic waist, and the girl had trouble handling them. The idea, Flo explained to Shirl, was to get Herbie to look as much like her as possible. "The pants don't go down allaway," Flo explained. "Just like the way she wears the bikini and the tassels. You know, low on the hips?"

"So who can find Herbie's hips?"

The dancer rolled Herbie's trousers well below his navel. The tops of his plaid undershorts peeked above them. These, too, Zenobia rolled down.

"Hey, take it easy," Herbie said. "I don't wanna show the family jewels."

"It's a little hard to take," Theresa said to Ibith.

"I wonder if Herbie is enjoying it that much."

Dr. Grant frowned. "Herbie's got to be the star. He set it up that way, now everyone expects it."

One of the drummers tossed Zenobia a padded pink halter. She began to pin it on Herbie's shoulders, adjusting the fake boobies over his breasts. As she did, Herbie reached for the catches holding her bra and tried to unto them. She recoiled like a cobra. Fun was fun. But no one was going to expose *her* bosom.

"Come on, Zenobia," Herbie said. "Be a sport." He reached for the catch again. His fat fingers fumbled with the snap. This time she pulled away and slapped his hand.

"You see?" Theresa said to the Grants. "It *is* innocent. No dirty stuff allowed. It's a joke."

While Zenobia fastened the bra on Herbie, he tried to undo the catch on her tasseled slit skirt. This she resented even more, and her wide-mouthed face looked irked.

The music began—a thin, repetitious sound. The recorder slithered around Middle Eastern notes, scales invented by court musicians to the Grand Turk. Tambours took up the beat. Zenobia began to glide around Herbie, throwing her abdomen at him, gesturing with fluid hands.

"You do like me," she said.

"I do like you, I'll make a fortune in Greenwich Village."

"Dance, Herbie, dance!" Murray shouted.

Si cupped his hands: "Remember, Herbie! For the honor of the block! Remember who tied for fourth place in the Harvest Moon Ball in 1938!"

Herbie danced. He followed Zenobia's moves, shaking his girth from side to side, the sweat sprinkling from his body in a fine spray. He thrust his paunch forward and popped it in and out in imitation of her. He bent low with sideways wiggles, rose tippy-toe, his hands reaching for the ceiling.

"It's the darnedest thing," Arnold Wicker said. "I think he's a better dancer than she is."

"You're right," Rosie said. "Go on, Herbie! Show 'em!" She began to lead the applause. "He's terrific. Look at those moves!"

Incredibly Herbie was outdancing his teacher. First in mincing, stingy steps, he jigged alongside her, then with a toss of his head and a wild gesture with his arms, he shimmied away, shivering his belly, flipping the folds up and down, side to side, and often, to the amazement of Zenobia, gyrating the folds and muscles in circular tracks.

"Go, Herbie, go!" Yasuda shouted. "I got you on flash! This way, Herbie, right into Murray's camera!"

A drummer tossed a blue chiffon scarf to Zenobia. She held one end in her teeth and gave the other to Shackman. Herbie clamped his teeth on the cloth. Zenobia, in fitful jerks of her rear, lowered herself to a squatting position, then crawled backward, away from her partner. Herbie imitated her. It was remarkable how loose he was—a stuffed man, but full of grace. The scarf stretched taut between them, a gossamer blue line, and they rotated, counterclockwise, on their haunches.

"Enough already, Herb," Flo called to him.

"Nah, leave him be, Flo," Si said. "He's just getting hot."

Zenobia rose and released the scarf. The drummers smacked the tambours loudly, a rising series of beats. The dancer took Herbie's hand and led him forward to accept the plaudits of his fellow tourists.

"We ain't through yet, baby," Herbie said. "Maestro, a fast Lindy, please. Come on, ya chicken or something?"

Murray tossed a ten-dollar bill at the musicians. "Play, you guys. When my buddy Herbie says play, you play."

The flutist grinned, acknowledged the *baksheesh*, and struck up a tricky tune. Herbie took Zenobia around the waist. He handled her delicately: Astaire and Rogers. There was nothing boorish or erotic in his manner: he was a performer.

"It ain't exactly 'One o'Clock Jump,' but it'll do," he shouted. He was gasping. Sweat cascaded down his forehead, dripped from his nose, his armpits, his navel. He swung Zenobia away from him and back to him, crossed hands, tossed her lightly, executed the quick steps of the Lindy.

"Light-feet," Herbie groaned. "That's what I was known as in Brooklyn. Yeah, baby, show it all to Poppa." He began to sing:

> "Spread your legs, ya breakin' my glasses,
> Glasses are hard to get . . ."

Like a contestant at Loew's Pitkin, Herbie flung his legs out, shook his shoulders, changed hands. Turkish couples got onto the dance floor. They did the Lindy with stiff arthritic moves—as if they had no ankles, knees, or elbows.

"A little more with the belly," Herbie said. He stood side by side with Zenobia and began to shimmy. "Fool around with Herbie Shackman, I'll learn ya. Try this." His gut popped and retracted, a tangerine monster with a life of its own. Zenobia mimicked him.

"A true performer," Bettenhausen said. "His timing is fantastic. His moves are the moves of a professional."

"Enough awready," Flo called to her husband. She had stopped dancing with Si and was at the edge of the stage. "Your face is like a plate of borscht. Herbie, siddown. You did your share."

Herbie sang:

> "I wish I could shimmy like my sister Kate,
>   She shakes like jelly on a plate . . ."

Huggins squeezed his wife. "Good old Herbie. I haven't heard that since George Brunis used to sing it at Nick's in the Village."

The fat man shuddered, breathed heavily, sang again:

> "All the boys in the neighborhood
>   Knew she could shimmy, and it's understoooo-ooo-oooo . . ."

Like an old wind-up Victrola, Shackman ran down, his voice drooling into a gasping silence. Tottering, he looked around for something to lean on, rested an arm on Zenobia, then slowly, with much dignity, sank to his knees.

"Aaaaaagh," Herbie moaned. "Aaaaaaagh. I got something . . . aaaaaagh."

His elephantine body thundered against the boards. The entire room shuddered. Inert, Herbie lay on the splintery stage, his mouth sucking air, his eyes bright with pain, his hands clutching at the padded brassiere. His abdomen rose like Ayers Rock in the Australian outback, a natural wonder changing colors as the spotlights rotated above. Under blue, green, and red gels, his belly heaved clonically. Waves of intractable pain washed over him.

"Herbie!" Flo screamed. "Herbie! What is it?" She clambered onto the stage. Sid and Si were a step behind her.

"Doc!" Si shouted. "Is Doc Grant here?"

Henderson Grant made his way across the dance floor. The music stopped. Zenobia knelt next to her fallen partner. She began to mumble apologies.

"Please stay away from the stage," Virgil said. "Only Dr. Grant, please."

354

The physician got to his knees over Herbie. "What is it, Herb?" he asked. "Where?"

Shackman could not speak. One hand fluttered over his chest. His lips formed the words: *"Heart. Right here."*

Dr. Grant took his pulse. "What else?"

Herbie's lips responded: *"Pain."*

The physician saw the claylike pallor on the man's face, the way his right hand kept returning to his chest. Gently Dr. Grant removed the brassiere. He bent an ear to Herbie's heaving midsection. Then he looked out at the fearful faces of the tourists and found Virgil's calm eyes.

"An ambulance," he said. Flo was weeping, embracing her husband. "Alert any emergency service they have."

Day 16: Istanbul–Israel. A free morning for shopping for that pair of Turkish slippers, or a robe, or an antique. Then on to Israel, the Holy Land, the world's most unique new nation. We land the Mount of Olives, a trip around the walls, a look at some of the new archaeological work.

Dinner? Try typical Israeli specialties or spicy Arab dishes.

Perhaps a concert or theater in modern Jerusalem at night, or a ride to the summit of the Mount of Olives to see the lights of the sacred city. Unforgettable!

The day would be a long hard one. Virgil paced the lobby of the Seljuk Hotel, awaiting Dr. Grant. Herbie, suffering spasms of pain, had been taken to the American Hospital at Nisantasi last night. His wife and his brother-in-law Si had gone with him. Virgil had helped with the arrangements, and once Herbie was bedded down and Dr. Grant had consulted with a Turkish physician, the escort returned to the hotel.

He checked his watch. It was a little past eight in the morning. Already he had downed four cups of Turkish coffee and smoked three Gitanes. Yet he did not feel irritable or tired or downcast. The day would be a challenge, part of his job.

A cab pulled up under the porte-cochere. Dr. Grant got out, paid the driver, and walked in.

"Well?" Virgil asked.

"Not too bad," the black man said. "I'm almost positive it isn't his heart."

"Ah. What then?"

"I'm reasonably sure our friend suffered a hiatus hernia. The pain is severe and is damned near as bad as a heart attack."

"Hiatus hernia?" Virgil loved medical details.

"What we call hiatal hernia pain. From overeating. The stomach forms a protrusion and doubles up into the chest. It can be caused by acid running into the esophagus."

"How serious is it?"

"Hard to say. Mind if I sit down? I'm a little woozy myself, listening to Mrs. Shackman bawl all night. I never did have much tolerance for screaming wives."

"Of course. And please, have some coffee."

356

"Thanks." Dr. Grant blinked a few times. It was odd, Virgil thought, you could not see the fatigue on his dark frowning face; but he sounded exhausted. "One out of three adults have probably had a hiatus hernia at some time . . . unexplained chest pains, so on. Herbie had a severe one. The EKG was normal, but I ordered another one for later today. I also ordered a series of enzyme tests. Won't try to explain, but if they're normal it's pretty certain that he didn't have a cardiac seizure. We'll know this afternoon."

"Afternoon? We leave at one o'clock."

"Not Herbie or Flo."

"Ah. This shall require a report to the agency. Forgive me, Doctor, but I remain a company man."

"That's okay. Nothing wrong with routine. Herbie seems to be better—he goosed a nurse this morning—and he says he's raring to go. But I'll have to insist that he spend at least two more days here. Maybe he should fly to New York and forget the rest of the trip."

"I see. Arrangements will have to be made."

"On the other hand, he's kicking and screaming. He wants to go to Israel. Says it's the high point of the trip and he won't miss it."

"What do you think?"

"Frankly, I think he's in pretty good shape. I guessed it was a hiatus hernia when I listened to his chest while he was on the stage. There were bowel sounds in his chest, usually a symptom of the stomach backing up."

"Poor Mr. Shackman. He has been such an asset to this trip. Jokes, songs, laughter. To end this way."

Dr. Grant got up. "Don't count him out. When I left, he was daring his wife to get into bed with him. She was so furious, I thought she'd hit him with a bedpan. She said he's been stuffing himself on every kind of indigestible garbage and it's no wonder his stomach doubled up. She saw him eat fried doughnuts yesterday that some Turk was selling from a stall. Bubbling lard and raw dough and Herbie ate them like they were saltines."

"Dr. Grant, will you do me the favor of contacting the hospital later and seeing what his status is? I shall have to arrange hotels and transportation for them."

"No sweat, Pepi. I'm going back in an hour or so to look at the enzyme tests."

Having checked on Herbie's condition, Virgil next visited the Legrands. He found Mr. Legrand sitting in his bathrobe at the window, gazing at the Istiklal Caddesi. Mrs. Legrand was serving him a cup of tea made with Flo Shackman's immerser.

357

Mr. Legrand appeared a bit healthier. He smiled at the guide. "Fit as a fiddle," he said in that lost voice. "Elizabeth's tired, though."

"I am not. Don't you go worrying Pepi."

"I am not at all worried. I suggest you rest this morning. There is so much to see in Israel."

"It doesn't matter," Mr. Legrand said. "It's just the getting around that we like. Can take or leave the places."

"He adores traveling," Mrs. Legrand said. A whiff of *raki* emanated from her face. "That's what keeps us going. You know, Pepi, we have no family. We never get a letter or a card or a present. But we have each other."

"That is a great deal. I compliment you on your devotion to each other."

"Yes," the old man said, patting his wife's hand. "I think I'll keep her. You get used to the same model."

"And how is poor Harvey?"

Virgil, satisfied that half of his invalid list—Mr. Legrand—was fit for travel, started to leave. "He is fine, Dr. Grant says. Overeating and overexertion on the dance floor."

"Poor Harvey. I do hope he stays with the tour. I love it when he calls me 'Ma Barker.' "

"I'm gonna Israel," Herbie grumbled.

"Not if I have anything to say," Dr. Grant said.

A lace doily rested on Herbie's head. He had raised his belly under the sheet and was miming knitting, with a knife and fork. Every time the nurse walked by, she dissolved in hysteria. Even with his floppy red mustache, he managed to suggest a pregnant woman.

"Herbie, stop with the *tummeling*," Flo said. "You listen to Henderson and to Pepi."

"Planet Tours can assume no responsibility for anything that may happen to you," the guide said. "Dr. Grant feels you should spend two days here, then fly home."

"I'm gonna Israel."

"You'll go home," Flo said.

"I'm gonna Israel, I don't care if I drop dead in front of the Wailing Wall. Clown, joker, funny guy, life of the party. I've had enough."

"Who asks you to?" Flo asked tearfully. "Who holds a gun to your head and makes you carry on?"

"So what did I get? Like indigestion."

"You had a hiatus hernia. It could hit you again."

"Some friend you are, Henderson," Herbie sulked. "This hospital food. They got the same caterer like at Beth Moses in Mineola. Dietetic jello and tea."

"That's right," Flo said. "Think of your stomach."

"How can I help it? According to Doc, it's somewhere near my brains by now."

"I shall make arrangements for you to leave for New York. When, Dr. Grant . . . the day after tomorrow?"

"That would be wise," Dr. Grant said.

"We gotta pay the air fare home?" Herbie asked.

"You'll get a credit from what you've paid," Virgil said. "You realize, traveling as a group on a packaged tour, air fares are lower. There will be a difference."

"And I miss Israel? And Rome?" Herbie was beginning to get out of bed.

"Siddown, Herbie!" Flo yelled.

He was on his feet, a billowing tent of a man, doing a soft-shoe dance in his bare feet. "Try and stop me. Hoo boy! I paid for twenty days and I'm gonna Israel! I'm not gonna miss nothin'!"

Virgil looked appealingly at Dr. Grant.

"I won't approve it," the physician said. "But at least one day here. He can join us in Israel tomorrow. But no exertion, no late hours, and no rich food. In fact, tea and dry toast for three days."

"Good old Henderson! You're my idea of a doctor!" Herbie fell back on the bed. It protested with creaks and twangs. "Hey, Pepi!" he shouted at the guide. "Do we have to pay extra for the separate flights to Israel?"

But Virgil did not answer. Oh, the determination of Americans to see everything, absorb everything, miss nothing! They had yet to learn the joys of sitting aimlessly in a sidewalk café and sipping an aperitif. They paid and they wanted the goods. No, Herbie could not be faulted. He might collapse outside the Church of the Holy Sepulchre or be seized with vomiting on the Mount of Olives, but he would barge on. Virgil had seen men suffering with angina climb Masada, women afflicted with crippling arthritis ascend the Tower of Pisa.

The El Al plane was parked on a distant runway at Yeşilköy Airport. Several bus trips were necessary to load the passengers. Police vehicles—jeeps, station wagons—surrounded the plane. Turkish police armed with automatic weapons were stationed around the 707. In the overseas lounge, hand baggage had been inspected, and at the main check-in, major luggage had been opened.

359

"I was afraid of this," Flemington said to Bettenhausen, who was standing behind him. "And me with fourteen pieces."

"It's understandable. The Israelis tend to be sensitive about this sort of thing."

Flemington smiled. "It's a little embarrassing. There's my wife's set of silver being undone. I didn't want her to see this. She's in the duty-free shop. God, he's looking at that service as if it's loaded."

Bettenhausen was silent. Next came Mrs. Flemington's cashmeres, then her antique pewter, then the Herend china, then the porcelain from the Wiener Keramik . . .

The chief customs guard was speaking to Virgil, pointing to the Flemingtons' accumulation. Virgil appeared to be explaining something to him. The man looked skeptical, then walked away.

"Probably asked if you're a smuggler," Bettenhausen puffed.

"I'd be flattered. It's a living."

He knew what Flemington was referring to—the life of illusion, the missed career. Bettenhausen, however, had small sympathy for the Grosse Pointe man. He had often contemplated the joys of being wed to a woman of great wealth. He would have bought a fez and a quilted jacket, smoked a nargileh, and reclined on swansdown pillows, dictating essays on "The Essence of D. W. Griffith" or "Symbolism in Early Von Stroheim" for publication in *Cahiers du Cinema.*

Behind them, a customs guard had located the false bottom in J. P. Huggins' camera case. He fingered the snap buttons. Huggins obliged him, opening the flap to reveal the bottom of the bag. The man pointed at it. "For what?"

"Papers. Documents. Hey, Pepi. Tell him I'm a lawyer."

The guide spoke in Turkish. The man looked skeptical. Virgil wondered: Did this explain Huggins' frenzy when he misplaced the case in Vienna? And what had he been carrying there?

At the gangplank of the jet stood two bulky men in lumpy jackets, studying the faces of each passenger. One was blond, the other dark. They had impassive faces.

"Who are those guys?" Huggins asked Virgil.

"Israeli security guards. The new breed, Mr. Huggins. They will accompany us to Lod Airport."

The security was even more rigid at Lod. Bags were opened and inspected again. Soldiers in tan uniforms, solemn-faced men carrying machine guns and rifles, patrolled the airport. The two young men in civilian clothes—Huggins noticed that one sat up front, the other at the rear so that they could cover the entire plane—lingered at the passport desk, then followed the party into the terminal.

And yet, Dr. Wicker remarked to his wife and the Bettenhausens, there was a chaotic, vivacious atmosphere about the place, as if it were uncontrolled and uncontrollable, and as if the silent soldiers and grave policemen were from a different nation, possibly occupiers. People wept, shouted, kissed. A Mediterranean effusion of emotions dominated the scene. Shops were jammed. Taxis and buses arrived in herds and left honking minutes after parking. The loudspeaker never ceased bellowing information in English and Hebrew.

"You get any of it?" Shirl asked Si.

"A word here and there. Listen, it's forty years since I went to Hebrew school."

Shirl clucked. "What a pity Herbie's missing this. He'd go crazy."

"Give him time. He'll arrive in a chariot tomorrow."

"Is it always this frenzied?" Cornelia asked Virgil.

"Usually, Mrs. Bettenhausen. They live every second of their lives. People with their memories have to. And besides, it is tourist season. High holidays next week."

"Oh, I see. Yom Kippur and all?" Having spent years in Hollywood, often a guest at the homes of executives, Cornelia knew a little about Jewish observances.

"Height of the season. Impossible to get a hotel. I always try to get my people into East Jerusalem. I have nothing against Israeli hotels, but the Arab places are less frantic. Ah, there is our guide."

Through the crush of churning bodies—a long queue had formed at the money-changing booth and was impeding passage—a tall young man carrying a notebook approached Virgil.

"*Shalom*, Hanan," Pepi said.

"*Shalom*, Yosef."

"Ah, how nice of you to remember. What shall it be—English, German, or French this time, Hanan?"

The young man was hawk-nosed and hollow-cheeked. He had solemn black eyes and a shock of waving black hair. "You still didn't learn Hebrew, Yosef?" he asked bleakly.

"Forgive me. I am too old to start on a new language. Your Hebrew verb conjugations are too much for me. Perhaps someday."

"Okay, okay," Hanan said impatiently. "English, English. How many?"

"Thirty-four. One fellow got ill in Istanbul. He and his wife will join us tomorrow."

Virgil studied his party. Some had collapsed in chairs, others were at the newsstand, a few at the parking area searching for their bus. "They are exhausted but determined. One Catholic priest. Several

Jewish couples. A black doctor and his wife. What can I tell you? Americans."

"We get them under way at once. It is a madhouse at the hotels. I suggest we skip checking in and take them right to the Old City."

Virgil tilted his head. "A few are dead on their feet. There is one old man who does nothing but sleep."

"So? He can sleep on the air-conditioned bus."

Israeli guides, Virgil had learned, were marvelously trained, well informed, and opinionated to the point of arrogance—the younger ones anyway. But their judgment was sound, and if Hanan said sight-seeing first, hotel later, he had his reasons. It was 2:30 P.M. and the heat was insufferable, its effect heightened by a dry wind. Virgil agreed and walked toward his people, using Bettenhausen's beard as a rallying point. Abruptly the stout man waddled away from the midst of the group and fled—as if being chased—through the terminal doors. He shouted to Dr. Wicker as he ran out. The dentist sped after him. Virgil gathered the rest of the party and pointed to a blue and yellow Egged bus.

If the interior of the airport had been frantic, the parking area was even more maddening. And yet it all seemed organized. Pale tan taxis —Peugeots and Mercedes were favored—and black Checker cabs (the fabled Israeli *sheruts*, ferrying groups of people at cut rate) wove in and out of the ranks of buses.

Bettenhausen, puffing in the heat, sweating under the merciless sun, had run into the main traffic lane and was pointing at a black Mercedes sedan. "In there!" he shouted to Dr. Wicker. "I saw him! In there?"

Wicker approached the Hollywood man. "Who?"

"Borkin."

"You're sure?"

"Try to stop them. Arnold, you are more agile than I am. I know it was Borkin. I got a look at him inside. They were hustling him away before anyone could recog—"

The Mercedes, driven by a bald man with eyes like black olives, swerved past Bettenhausen, mounted a traffic island, and accelerated. It sped toward the airport exit.

"Damnation," Bettenhausen said. "I got another look at him. I know it's Borkin."

"What's he doing here?"

Bettenhausen's eyes were fierce with frustration. "I have no idea. Arnold, you and I are going to find out."

Aboard the Egged bus, the tourists complained about the absence of the dentist and Bettenhausen. They were eager to see Jerusalem.

Father Konay's hands trembled. He did not know what to expect or what was expected of him.

"So, ladies and gentlemen," Hanan began. "My name is Hanan Gilad, I am third-generation Israeli, student at law school of the Hebrew University. We welcome you to Israel. *Shalom.*"

He made his introductory remarks rather like a sergeant talking to a platoon of recruits. His *shalom* was less a greeting than an order.

"I feel proud already," Si said softly.

"Yeah, but why the delay?" Shirl asked.

Mr. Wattle got to his feet. "Yes, why the delay? Why are those two holding us up? Who are we waiting for, Moshe Dayan?"

Hanan Gilad's eyes fixed themselves on the bald man. "Mister," he said, "in this country is everybody Moshe Dayan."

On the black-top highway from Lod to Jerusalem, they saw many soldiers, young men and women, hitching rides. The entire youth of the nation seemed to be in uniform, rifles slung over their shoulders. Rosie Wicker worried about it but said nothing. Mr. Wattle found the compulsory service, as explained by Hanan Gilad, admirable. But he, too, was silent. The sabra guide did most of the talking; he was abrupt, severe, and explicit, a young man devoid of subtleties. In answer to Yasuda's query, he explained that the burned hulks of trucks and buses at the roadside were mementos of the 1948 war of liberation, when the road was under Jordanian guns. Now, Israel controlled the road, he said, and it would be forever free.

Once, after Hanan pointed out the Arab village of Abu Ghosh and remarked that it contained a beautiful Crusader church, a wail of protest over the lack of time to stop and inspect it went up from the photographers.

"Chicken," Murray Yasuda said. "You tell us all this stuff is here, then we don't have time to photograph it."

"Blame Planet Tours," Hanan said gruffly. "Complain to Mr. Virgil. Two days in Israel is a disgrace. And four days in Russia, to look at bloody Communism? In one small corner of our beautiful Israel is more history than all of Moscow." He sulked for a few minutes; no one said anything. The hills and terraces of the Judaean countryside, baking in the sun, sped by them. At last they saw the honey-gold towers of Jerusalem.

"Ah, our golden city," Hanan said.

Father Konay opened his breviary but discovered he could not read. Was it the fierce light or the brash young man's attitude that was keeping him from concentrating on his prayers?

"I'm suddenly exhausted," Cornelia said. "Can't move."

"I am too," Mavis Hutzler said. "My legs can't make it any more."

363

They were standing in the Citadel inside the walls of the Old City, sipping grapefruit juice from bottles. They had entered by the Jaffa Gate, where, in the shade of David's Tower, Hanan had lectured them on the history of the city.

"It is a Turkish minaret," he said, annoyed to have to disclose the information, "and has nothing to do with David. But beneath it are the remains of Herod's fortress and the three towers he built. You will sometimes see a big stone at the bottom. That is Herodian from the start of the Christian Era."

"For a fact?" Mavis asked.

"You believe what you wish to believe," Hanan said. "You see that round pool? A cistern. Probably Mameluke. But there is a tradition that it is the pool at which David saw Bath-sheba. A romantic notion and it does no harm to believe it. People believe even stranger things here."

Theresa walked toward the dry pool and peered into it.

"Hold it there, Terry," Dr. Wicker said. "I'll get a shot of Bath-sheba."

"Who knows Old Testament?" Hanan asked. "Who knows the story of David and Bath-sheba?"

"He didn't behave nicely," Father Konay said. "I mean, he sent her husband into battle to get killed, didn't he?"

"Good, Father. You and I must have some discussions on texts." Hanan smiled—flashing white teeth, the black eyes warm for the first time. Virgil folded his arms: the Israelis were especially cordial to Roman Catholics. "Second Samuel 11:2. 'David arose from off his bed and walked upon the roof of the king's house, and from the roof he saw a woman washing herself, and the woman was very beautiful to look upon . . .'"

Flemington saw Theresa hazily, as if surrounded by a golden corona. She was standing motionless at the pool. His Bath-sheba. *And she came in unto him and she lay with him.* Was his problem easier than David's? There was no Uriah the Hittite to get rid of. But what about Lulu? Was there some battle she would be sent into, where she might "be smitten and die"? He envied King David. Sunlight dazzled on the topaz necklace Theresa was wearing. Desire for her made him giddy. Bettenhausen saw him moving with Lulu toward the shade, under one of the arches in the old Citadel.

"You look a bit weary," Bettenhausen said.

"The heat," Flemington said. "It's like a burden."

The Hollywood man squinted at the sky. "And the light. Even more so the light. I have never seen anything as intense. I'm beginning to understand why these religions got their start here. People needed something to explain the light. Look at the stones. Look at the pavement. The color is burned out of them. I wonder how they manage color film here?"

Hanan was listening attentively to Bettenhausen. Like most Israelis, he was intrigued with argument. "I shall discuss that with you later. One of my teachers, Rabbi Glueck, had some interesting theories about intensities in the Holy Land."

The shaded alleys and arcades of the Arab market inside the Old City came as a relief. Although the streets were teeming, the surcease from the sunlight gave the tourists a chance to breathe, to rest at stores and stalls and the stations of the cross.

"Stay together," Hanan ordered. "It is safe here, but one can get lost. And if you want to buy, bargain. They expect you to."

"What's to buy?" Shirl shouted.

"Mostly junk, but buy anyway. Camelskin bags. Yemenite jewelry. Embroidered dresses. Some antiques. Maybe today you just should look, then come back tomorrow."

People flowed endlessly through the narrow streets, singly, in pairs, in groups, gawking, buying, absorbing the strangeness, the rich aroma of donkey droppings. There were hordes of cheerful American Jews; Germans in sandals and lederhosen; Arab merchants in jellabas and kaffiyehs; Arab boys with shaved heads hawking salted rolls, hardboiled eggs, chewing gum, soft drinks. Food stands dispensed the grapefruit juice (which Hanan recommended for dehydration) and pungent kebabs of lamb. Above all hovered a rich, rotting, fermenting odor.

"It stinks here," Mr. Wattle shrilled at the guide. "It smells godawful."

"Mister," Hanan said, "you should have smelled it before 1967."

The sabra led them past monasteries, antique shops, souvenir stands. Olivewood rosaries and glass beads from Hebron abounded on stalls, pushcarts. The crush of tourists was suddenly greater. Father Konay could not believe what he saw—mobs of people in summer clothing moving past stacks of cheap souvenirs toward an archway with a black and white sign over it: HOLY SEPULCHRE. A party of talkative German seminarians in red cassocks walked by him, then some white-clad French nuns. What would Father Folker say about this? He would probably bring his guitar and some of his young friends and sing folk songs outside the holiest shrine in Christendom!

"Stop here, please," Hanan said. He smiled at a Franciscan in a black beret and brown cassock, and spoke a few words of French.

"It is crowded inside. I will give you fifteen minutes." Hanan frowned at a display of spade-shaped candles, decorated with gold scrolls, for sale at a stall outside the gate.

"Fifteen minutes for Calvary?" Father Konay asked.

"You are right, Father, not enough time. But you deal in eternities, so a short visit to the Holy Sepulchre is maybe as good as a long one. Be sure to look at the unction stone when you enter, also the rotunda, which is all that is left of the Crusader church, aside from the portal."

"You aren't going in?" Dr. Grant asked.

"Some of us prefer not to. There are priests of many faiths, custodians, sextons to show you around—Catholic, Greek, Coptic, Armenian, and Syrian. Each has a part of the church. Look also for St. Helena's Chapel. After all, she was responsible for all of this. There are also Crusader tombs. And do not miss the Chapel of Adam, which is supposed to hold the skull of no less a person than Adam himself."

They walked into the sunlit courtyard. Work seemed to be in progress. Building materials littered the site—bricks, wheelbarrows, lumber. Hanan and Virgil walked as far as the Crusader façade.

Dr. Wicker, taking pictures with his wide-angle lens, stopped to talk to the guide. "How much of this do we believe?"

"As much as you find necessary."

"Suppose I don't want to believe any of it?"

"That is your privilege."

Rose-Anne Wicker cocked her head. "I have my doubts. I've read about St. Helena's perambulations, finding sites here and there."

Hanan smiled. "I must tell you, there is an alternate site of Calvary available."

"You're kidding," said Rose-Anne.

"I will take you there if you wish," the sabra said. "It is above the Damascus Gate, and it is called the Garden Tomb. General Charles Gordon, the Englishman they called 'Chinese,' found it. The British maintain it to this day. Many Protestants regard it as the site of the crucifixion. There is an English garden, some tombs of the Herodian period, and for all we know, it is where Christ was crucified and entombed."

"Not here?" Dr. Wicker asked, peering into the dark interior.

"Maybe not in either place," Hanan said. "You see, it is believed that people could not be executed within the city walls in that time. And evidence is coming to light that the walls of Jerusalem were much bigger than we thought. So . . ."

"Then where did it take place?"

"Who knows? Myself, I am an atheist. I was born and raised on

Kibbutz Gesher under Arab guns and I am a firm believer in *this* world."

Father Konay wandered through the church, dazed, unable to relate what he saw to all he had ever learned about Him. *Here? In this place?* In this peculiar church with its ornate chapels and lamps and confusion of faiths? Here was a Greek Orthodox corner—there an Armenian section—a Coptic—a place for Syrians . . . Where should he go? Who was the Catholic in charge?

A fat, bearded, soft-faced functionary in flowing robes was dragging him to the Chapel of the Sepulchre, pushing him through a crowd of Maronite Christian Arabs, veiled women and shave-headed boys.

"All here," the soft man said. "Catholic, Orthodox, Coptic, Syrian, Armenian. Inside is tomb. Tomb of Jesus."

Father Konay kneeled and crossed himself. A greater glory should have surged into his chest. But things were happening too fast. Would he swoon? Have a vision? Experience an epiphany? The chapel was tiny and dark. People were clamoring to get in. Germans in hiking shorts, blond muscular types, loomed in the doorway behind him.

"Not time to pray," the official said to Father Konay. "Pray outside."

The priest got to his feet. Had he done the wrong thing? A breach of etiquette?

"Back of tomb, Coptic," the man said, and pulled Father Konay to the rear. There was a curtained cubicle at the back of the holiest of tombs. The priest could not figure out the significance of the Coptic chapel. Was it the rear of the sepulchre?

A curtain parted and a dark hand clutched at him. The hand belonged to a Coptic priest, a dun-colored old man with a gray beard and an odd hat. He dragged Father Konay into a room smaller than the chapel of the Holy Sepulchre and pointed to the stone below. The back of the tomb he had seen on the other side?

"Stone rolled by angel," the fat man called from outside.

"Touch," the dark guardian said. "Hand."

Father Konay bent down, feeling his knees creak, and touched the stone. But what had he touched? It was irreverent to think it, but wouldn't Father Folker call it "a piece of the action"?

"Please," the Coptic priest said. His hand pointed to a display of wrinkled dollars, Israeli pounds, Deutsche marks, French francs, littering the paving around the holy place.

"Ah," Father Konay said. "A contribution. Well, why not?" He dared not admit it, but he was frightened. Whose church was it? Who was running things? The custodian of the Coptic chapel was a Christian, of course. But . . . ? Who? Why? And was this truly where the Lord . . . ? He halted before he indulged in blasphemous thoughts. From his trousers he extracted a wrinkled dollar bill and dropped it to the floor. The Copt kissed his hand.

Outside, the bearded man took him by the arm. "Syrian chapel here, beautiful, tombs of Joseph of Arimathea and Nicodemus."

"Where is the Roman Catholic section? That happens to be my church."

"Ah. Ah. You are Roman Catholic. Latin Church. Come."

Dutifully Father Konay followed his guide.

"Is nice in Holy Sepulchre. Is place for everyone. Roman Catholic here. Choir of Franciscans. Altar of Mary Magdalene. Very nice. I am Armenian, but Catholic nice also. I show you Christ's prison, come."

"Prison?"

"Where Jesus stay before crucifixion."

Down the narrow steps he followed his Armenian friend, looking over his shoulder at what he heard someone call "the arches of the Virgin."

On the way down, he passed A. T. Gunthorpe and Mr. Wattle, the latter striding energetically, the Memphis man puffing and holding the stone walls.

"Amazing, isn't it?" the priest asked.

"I don't believe a dime's worth of it," Mr. Wattle said. "It was all invented."

"Ole Horace a cynic." Gunthorpe winked at the priest. "Heck, it don't do no harm to believe. Don't hurt nobody, and hit might do some good."

On the way to the Western Wall, pausing to look at stations of the cross, to enter holy places (much too briefly, Theresa felt), the party, led by Hanan with Virgil bringing up the rear, they came to a jewelry store.

Shirl and her friends insisted on stopping. "Look. Those Yemenite necklaces and earrings. Like the rabbi's wife has back home. Si, I wanna *hondle*."

"Do it quickly," Pepi said. "There is a lot of ground to cover."

The shop was at a busy corner. A mini-caravan of donkeys bearing sacks of grain squeezed pedestrians against the shopwindows. Members of the Three Worlds party found themselves crushed into the store, beneath festoons of cheap jewelry, beads, crucifixes, pendants.

"How much? How much?" Shirl shouted.

"Ah, special for you, lady, ten dollars."

Shirl was holding a filigreed necklace. "I'll give you five."

"Oh, lady. It cost me five to buy."

"Final offer."

The proprietor, wearing pince-nez and a fez, prayed with delicate hands. "Oh, lady. Six."

"Five-fifty."

"I sell you two for eleven dollars."

Shirl's eyes widened. *Bargains!* "You got a deal. But throw in one of them pins. There."

"For twelve dollars. Please, lady."

"Okay, okay. Si, gimme twelve dollars."

Theresa and Pepi had watched with fascination. "How does she do it?" the teacher asked. "I'd have given him the full price."

"Flo is missing this," Shirl said. "I'll get her here as soon as the dope Herbie is better. She'll die when she sees these bargains."

Virgil winked at Theresa. "The proprietor lost no money on the transaction. The necklaces are lovely, but not in the same category as the one you are wearing."

Theresa's hand went to her throat.

Outside a fight had developed between a shopkeeper and two small boys. The man, a vendor of spices and sweetmeats, was holding one youth by the arm and shaking the other against a sack of saffron. Each time the child's shaved head struck it, yellow puffs exploded. No one intervened.

To escape the violent scene, Harry ushered Lulu into the shop. Shirl and Si, and now Dr. Grant and his wife, were haggling over pendants. Abruptly Lulu was face to face with Theresa, unable to move. Strands of beads—olivewood rosaries, glass rosaries, crucifixes on chains, Yemenite stringings—dangled over them. Lulu's eyes, behind dark lenses, betrayed no emotion. But hot jealousies boiled inside her. She saw the topaz necklace.

Virgil, with his instinct for crisis, noticed Mrs. Flemington, his special charge, and smiled at her. "A bit crowded, Mrs. Flemington? Not quite the silver vaults in Chancery Lane."

There was no response. The corners of Lulu's mouth formed little knots of skin. Her chin quivered. Flemington, idly studying prayer rugs, felt Lulu backing into him.

"Out," she said. "Take me out. I can't breathe."

"Of course, dear." He guided her to the door. A mob of Japanese, Munchkins in gray suits, white shirts, black ties, hurried by. Glancing

369

over his back, Harry saw Theresa look at him—almost challengingly—and finger the necklace.

They emerged from the Old City to the esplanade outside the Western Wall. It was late afternoon. Jews prayed at the foot of the immense stones. There were black-clad Orthodox, soldiers in khaki with guns slung on their shoulders, American tourists in sports coats and bell bottoms, Yemenites in bright garments, and a group of robust bearded men in striped caftans, boots, and round-brimmed fur-edged hats.

The high wall of the Temple Enclosure rose before them. It seemed rather anticlimactic and undramatic, except for the massive Herodian stones in the base. Hanan pointed out the archaeological excavations at the south corner. He explained that it was late in the day. Most of the digging took place in the cool of the morning. There were large square pits and some exposed boulders. Theresa asked him what they were.

"Shops, madame."

"Ooh," Shirl said. "I wish they were open."

"Not for what you want, lady," Hanan said irritably. "They sold sacrificial victims."

"People?" Mavis Hutzler asked.

"Now, lady, please," Hanan reprimanded her. "Animals, birds. It was one contribution to civilization of the Hebrews that they ended human sacrifice, which the Canaanites and the others practiced. You know about Abraham and Isaac?"

Ibith Grant nodded. "Yes, way back from Sunday school. The angel of the Lord stayed Abraham's hand. 'Touch not the lad.'"

"Quite right. It is symbolic of the end of human sacrifice in this part of the world."

Dr. Wicker stared through the terrifying light at the great wall. What drew people to it? What was the mystery? He had read that when the Israelis conquered the city in 1967 Dayan placed the first prayer on a chit of paper into a crack in the wall. It bore the single word *shalom*. But he felt nothing; no inspiration, no uplift. What he had read about Israel, what he had seen in a half day, had impressed him. But truth to tell, deep down, he was a *goy*, raised by atheist parents, never bar-mitzvahed, married out of the faith, never denying his Jewishness but making nothing of it, never hindered by it, never using it. He belonged to no temple; his friends were a mixed bag; he missed the point of Jewish jokes. What was he? Who was he?

Bettenhausen was shading his eyes. On surrounding rooftops, at the gates entering the area in the front of the Western Wall, were the omnipresent soldiers.

"Looking for something?" Wicker asked him.

"I half expect Borkin to turn up. I know I saw him at Lod."

"Well, he's a VIP. It would be in the papers."

Bettenhausen scratched his beard. "I'm not sure. It's a turn of plot that has me baffled. Damnation."

"But why is it so holy?" Dr. Grant asked. "Why do people make such a fuss over stones from an old temple? I always learned that Judaism was a religion of laws, of codes. The tangible aspects of religion are supposed to be less important."

Hanan nodded. "Very true, Doctor. The Wall . . . is the Wall. Call it what you will. Tradition, continuity, a symbol of the life of the Jewish people. As for myself, it is not the stones of Herod, beautiful as they are, that impress me. It is the *Shekhina*, the divine presence, that abides in the wall. That never dies and that transcends mere stones."

Two Arab guides, smiling men in pork-pie straw hats, wearing badges, approached the Three Worlds group as they entered the Haram es-Sharif, the "noble enclosure." Hanan spoke to them gently. Business was bad, one of them complained. Packaged tours were hurting their income.

"A nice chap," Hanan said to his party. "I captured him during the Six Day War. He was a lieutenant in the Arab Legion, and we met inside the Lion Gate. We have been friends ever since."

The Dome of the Rock's golden globe dominated the tree-lined enclosure, but the effect was harmonious. Inside the walls of the Haram es-Sharif it was peaceful, green, with space and air. Despite the smothering heat, it was pleasant to stroll in the Moslem sanctuary. Cypresses and pines bordered the stone walks. At one end was the small silver dome of the Aksa. Beyond rose the Dome of the Rock, covering the white promontory from which the Prophet ascended into heaven. A remnant of a Crusader arch formed tracery in front of the golden globe. Fountains, small flights of steps, smaller buildings, were comfortably spaced. Distantly the mosque on the site of the Antonia Tower hung in the bleaching light.

The party sat on a ledge under the cypresses, while Hanan reviewed the history of the Temple Area. All listened—weary, their bodies deadened by the heat, the inescapable light. In the Old City Lulu Flemington had bought a parasol. She handled it like a queen, holding it over one shoulder, twirling it occasionally. She knew how to use things, Harry thought. She could have been a hostess at a Southampton lawn party. A certain pride in his wife generated in Flemington. By God, *two* magnificent women in his life! When Lulu

371

had asked to be taken from the jewelry shop, he had imagined that it was the stifling air that had distressed her. He himself, his mind brimming with future joys—Theresa again? in the French Colony Hotel?—had not thought of the necklace.

Flemington relaxed. Things worked out. After the trip Lulu would be stronger. He would announce his plans. (He could not live any longer without Theresa's presence—the ageless body, that soft voice, that grasp of what was worth while in life. It was like an annuity, a stock come to maturity. All the years of deprivation would be worth it. In her forties, Terry was more desirable than when she was a college girl. There were rare women like that: their lives were rising curves. They offered more as they aged.) Lulu would cry and threaten him—and eventually agree. No problem. Looking at her shift her silken legs, move the parasol, as Hanan spoke, he had confidence in her.

"This is the site of Solomon's Temple," the sabra said. "No Orthodox Jew will walk here for fear his feet will tread upon the holy place. Destroyed by the Babylonians in 587. Before Christ. Then, the second temple, built by Herod and destroyed by the Romans under Titus, 70, Christian Era."

Murray Yasuda was standing in the sunlight, photographing the Dome of the Rock through the Crusader arch. "Boy, what a picture. Hey, Theresa, you and the Grants move in. That's it."

"She seems to get into everything," Lulu said.

"Hmmm?" Flemington, accustomed to the nuances in his wife's voice, caught the touch of spite. But there was more there: Lulu was fishing. "Mrs. Carrell? I haven't noticed. I've been a good boy."

"Have you?"

What did she know? For a chilling moment, he envisioned Lulu peeking through a keyhole, bribing a bellhop, a chambermaid. Naked with Theresa, he had felt exposed every minute. What if . . . ?

"Of course." His voice was clotted. "You know I have, Lu. I haven't exchanged five words with her since London."

"I noticed the necklace she's wearing."

"Necklace?"

"Clear topaz in antique gold. We saw it in the shop in Moscow, where you bought the malachite."

"Really?" He was a poor liar, the worst dissembler. He wished he were J. P. Huggins. That cold-eyed Irishman would have known how to handle himself.

"I wonder how she could afford it on a teacher's salary, and the way she counts pennies."

"Pepi may have gotten her a price. I can understand a woman being attracted to it. She must have gotten to the store sometime after we did."

"She went to museums that afternoon."

"I don't know what she did."

Hanan motioned to them. "Onward, friends," he said. "To the Mosque of Omar, as it is wrongly called. It is not built by anyone named Omar. After the fall of the Jewish temple, the Romans had a temple of Jupiter here. We skip some centuries and come to the Arab conquest in the seventh and eighth centuries."

"They've been here a long time," Ibith Grant said.

"Not as long as us," Hanan said.

"I don't want to argue," the black woman said. "I made a comment."

"It's all right, it's all right, lady," the Israeli said. "We love to argue. Inside you will see the rock. The Moslems say Mohammed, seated on his horse with the face of a woman, went up to heaven. Also, since they worship Abraham, they say it is the rock of Mount Moriah, where Abraham was ordered by God to sacrifice Isaac. But modern students do not believe that. It is too far from where Abraham pitched his tents and tended his flocks in the Negev. Too far to go for a sacrifice."

Rosie Wicker looked at the young man's hawkish face. He carried off these biblical references casually, as if he were one with the past. Abraham might have died a week ago, or lived around the corner. Yes, Moses. He was here. And Abraham? Not far away. The land of Benjamin. Down the road. David's city? You can see it from here.

"Please, look at the tiles on the face of the Dome of the Rock," Hanan said. "Nowhere in the world colors like that. Not even in the Blue Mosque in Istanbul. But the sun is too bright now. It is better at dawn or early evening. Blues and greens and yellows like none on earth. The secrets of the dyes have been lost. So look upon a glory that has vanished."

Inside, their feet were embraced by red carpeting. "Wow," Shirl said. "It's like the Huntington Manor. You ever see such carpeting?" She bent to feel the depth of the material, to finger the wool. "I can't believe. Boy, what a decorator would do to get this kind of thing."

Awed, they walked around the double row of pillars supporting the dome. Hanan explained that the soaring marble columns came from Hadrian's temple. The rock itself—"the Rock of Foundation"— rose whitish gray and scarred, in the center of the octagonal building.

"The prophet's footprint," Hanan said, with a smile. "And up on the

373

Mount of Olives, in the Chapel of the Ascension, they claim, is Jesus' footprint, but it is less celebrated. If you come with me to Kibbutz Sde Boker I will show you a lot of Ben-Gurion's footprints. Right in the peach orchard."

Harry noticed Lulu was walking several steps ahead of him. It was a habit of hers when she was annoyed with him. Ever since she had spied the necklace on Theresa, fury was simmering in her. Why, Flemington wondered, did Terry insist on flaunting the damn thing?

"Inside this box are kept the hairs of Mohammed, one of the holiest relics in Islam," Hanan said.

"All his hair?" Mr. Wattle called.

"No, just a few. It is like the bones of saints. A few here, a few there. But very holy."

Flemington hurried after his wife. She seemed to be wobbling again, supporting herself with the furled parasol.

"Here is an interesting thing," Hanan said. "One is permitted to put one's hand inside the rock through this hole. Then, a surprise. Go on, lady, you are nearest." He gestured to Theresa.

"In? In there?"

Flemington watched: *hand that had stroked him, caressed him.* He wanted her at once. As soon as they got to the hotel. No preliminaries. In a sealed hotel room.

Theresa put her hand in the aperture and drew it out.

"Now, smell," the guide said.

"Lovely. Jasmine." She extended her fingers to A. T. Gunthorpe, who was standing beside her. The Memphis man sniffed Terry's hand. "Dang. That smell purty. Whut they got in theah? A small Ay-rab squirtin' perfume?"

"The rock is anointed with oil. So that one's memory of the holy place will be a sweet one. It is a nice idea."

"Beautiful," Theresa said.

"Go on," Harry said, catching up with his wife. "Try it, Lu."

"Not after that bitch."

"Now, dearest."

"Go to hell. Get away from me."

Hanan summoned them. "We shall visit below the cave where the Arabs believe the souls of the dead hold their prayers—Bir el-Arwah. They believe that Elijah, David, and Abraham prayed in there."

The group started down the steps. Lulu stumbled, caught herself, and got a helping hand from Pepi and Father Konay. "One must be careful Mrs. Flemington," the guide said. "In this heat, one tires more quickly than one imagines."

"Are you all right, Lu?" Flemington asked.

"Stay away." The words were barely audible.

The remainder of the tour was on the air-conditioned bus. Only when the tourists got back into the icy interior did they realize how exhausted they were. In the dry heat they had pushed on—the Aksa Mosque, the Golden Gate, Solomon's Stables—motivated by new sights. At one point the Legrands gave up and sank under the roof of a soft-drink stand, holding hands, their faces blanched.

"So, ladies and gentlemen," Hanan said, "we stay on the bus until we take you to the hotel. Everyone rest. Drink liquids. It is so dry here that your sweat is barely visible. It evaporates from your skin as soon as it appears."

"How do you people do it?" Mr. Wattle shouted. "How do you work as hard as you do, and fight a war, and everything else?"

"We are a new breed, sir."

"You're human, like anyone else."

"Only more so."

They made a circuit of the Old City walls and looked at the church over the Tomb of the Virgin, the Garden of Gethsemane, the Church of All Nations, the rock-cut tombs of the Hasmonean era, and higher up on the Mount of Olives, the onion domes of the Russian church of Mary Magdalene.

"That is the *real* Garden of Gethsemane?" Ibith Grant asked. "That I learned about in Sunday school?"

The bus had stopped. They had a glimpse of ancient gnarled olive trees and a dazzling mosaic of flowers—roses, dahlias, huge daisies, iris. A bearded Franciscan was pruning a tree.

Ibith Grant was staring at the contorted olive trees. Memories of Sunday school in Atlanta, where she had been raised, haunted her. The church was the Mount of Olives Church. Her mother was a pillar of Bible study class and Ibith went not only on Sundays but twice a week at night to learn Old Testament. She had hated it. It had meant nothing to her. In college she had dropped it. What did all that Bible pounding mean to a black teacher and a black doctor, making their way in white society? But here it was: Mount of Olives, Gethsemane, Mary's Tomb, *Dominus Flevit*. To her, they evoked memories of poverty and ignominy. Bible bashing and shouts of "Amen" and fainting spells—substitutes for life.

The bus moved past the Old City walls again and turned into a street in East Jerusalem. The buildings looked Arabic. Huggins saw a sign:

375

"Hey, Hanan," he said to the guide, "any chance of stopping? I got to visit the bank there."

"For changing traveler's checks, sir? You will do as well at the hotel. Better at an Israeli bank."

"Personal business."

"Ah." The sabra looked at his watch. "They are closed for the day. Try tomorrow morning."

An iron grille had been lowered over the bank window. It looked closed not only for the day but forever. More and more Huggins' money seemed to be floating away, drifting into some misty world of grifters, swindlers, counterfeiters. Considering who it came from, it was only appropriate.

"Hanan," J.P. called. "What's the bit in the Bible about the man who fell among thieves?"

The French Colony Hotel was a refurnished old Turkish palace near the Mandelbaum Gate in northeast Jerusalem. It was a sleepy neighborhood of solid buildings constructed of honey-gold stones. Nearby was an ancient mausoleum, maintained for obscure reasons by the French government. It contained, Hanan said, as they debarked from the bus, the families of a certain Queen Helena of Mesopotamia, who came to Jerusalem about the year 45 (Hanan always said Christian Era, not Anno Domini)—and converted to Judaism. "Worth a visit," he told the Wickers and the Bettenhausens. "Fantastic rock-cut tombs. I have enjoyed this and I will see some of you tomorrow. *Shalom.*"

Bettenhausen followed him a few steps down the silent street. "My friend, a question."

"Sure."

"How can I find if a VIP is in town? A Russian scientist."

"You know him? A friend?"

"I thought I saw him at Lod. It's a long story, but how would one go about finding him?"

Hanan shrugged; he didn't seem to care one way or the other. "Call the Jerusalem *Post* and ask for Mendel Matzkin. He's a friend of mine. It's one family in this country."

In the lobby—it was faced with blue tile, had a lofty vaulted white plaster ceiling, and was not air-conditioned but was refreshingly cool—Bettenhausen went to a phone and asked for the Jerusalem *Post.*

Mendel Matzkin was located. What was he? Editor? An advertising solicitor? One got only so much information from these sabras.

"I am a friend of Hanan Gilad—"

"What do I care?"

Bettenhausen coughed, and held the receiver away. It took him a few seconds to decide that it was not rudeness; merely the desire to get the call over with. You want to talk, *talk*, never mind the references.

"I am an American newspaperman named Warren Bettenhausen and I am trying to find out if a Russian scientist named Anatoly Borkin is in Israel. He may have arrived today."

"Jewish?"

"I don't know. He is a geneticist at Moscow University. I thought I saw him at Lod."

"Hmmm. That already is interesting." There was a pause, as if Mendel were writing the information down. "No, no information on it. We check Lod every day for VIPs, and if he's a Russian, even more interest. But I don't see any Borkin. A hundred and twenty-two Georgian Jews arrived this morning, including the cantor of the Tiflis synagogue."

"What do I care?" Bettenhausen growled. "But thank you anyway."

"My pleasure."

Dr. Wicker crossed the lobby. "Any luck?"

"Either I was mistaken or they have a reason for keeping Borkin under wraps. I wish I knew someone in government."

"How did that woman get that necklace?" Lulu asked. She was prone on the bed. The room was lofty, with a multivaulted ceiling that gathered the warm air. The windows were shuttered. Despite the heat outside, it was cool inside the former Turkish palace. Flemington was intrigued with it: blue tiles in the walls, the irregular stones of the floor, the old bathtub on claw-and-ball feet.

"Bought it, I suppose."

"I'd like to believe that. She's probably been whoring for someone. I wouldn't put it past that guide."

"Virgil?" Harry was astonished—and overjoyed. He had a *beard*, someone to whom he could attribute his own transgressions.

"I've seen them having little tête-à-têtes."

"I don't know, Lu. Those fellows are under strict orders not to socialize with clients." He took off his jacket and hung it in a dark wood closet. The exterior was done in intarsia. Part of the pasha's collection? "If I had to guess," Harry said warily, "I'd vote for our friend from Washington."

"That boor Wattle?" Lulu was enjoying the game. The notion of Theresa sleeping around—with Virgil, with Wattle, with A. T. Gunthorpe—titillated her. "I could believe anything about her. As a matter of fact he's been at her elbow a good deal."

"Huggins overheard him asking if he could visit her in Minneapolis." It was working marvelously.

"And that shyster also," she cried triumphantly. "I'm wise to your old flame. Lady Round Heels. I wouldn't be surprised if they've all had a crack at her."

The game lost its savor. Flemington felt his mouth turn to ashes. In a way he and Lulu were a bit alike. She, of course, would think the worst of Theresa. It was Terry's grasp on life, her capacity to enjoy the world, as much as her past relationship to Harry, that infuriated her.

"Where are you off to?"

"I want to get some tour pamphlets at the desk downstairs. Would you like any ice water? Or a little drink?"

"Some ice water would be nice."

Outside the door Flemington began to tremble. He was being drawn to Theresa's room again—a micro-organism swimming toward the light, a tropism over which he had no control. He assured himself that Lulu did not suspect. She was having too good a time imagining every man on the trip making love to the teacher. Lulu had always been good at gossip, at guessing at affairs, at sensing who was sleeping with whom in Grosse Pointe.

Flemington's heart skipped in haphazard rhythms. He knew now that he loved Theresa more than anyone in the world. Love in your late forties was the best kind. It was full of old memories, full of experience, resigned to a few failings, exultant in its high moments. He walked through the pasha's corridors, up and down unexpected stairways, past a hall filled with glass cases displaying pottery, through a court of palms. Finally he went to the desk. Mrs. Carrell was in room 106. He retraced his steps, stuffing Egged Tour folders in his back pocket, and found Terry's room.

She came to the door wearing the pale blue dressing gown. Her face was slightly burned, and he sensed a weariness in her. Was it being alone in hotel rooms for so long? The waiting? The interminable flirtations?

"Hairbreadth Harry is here."

"Please, Harry. Not again."

"Of course again. And again, and again, as Churchill said." He took her in his arms. A pungent cologne emanated from her neck, her

378

breasts. Still young. Still resilient. Would she ever grow old and wrinkled, full of sagging flesh and short answers?

"Have you told her?" Terry asked.

"I promise. I'll be calling you in less than a week. I've made my mind up." He led her to the bed.

"Wrong, wrong. I swore never again this way. Stop. Stop."

Flemington dragged her down. "I'm a terrible voyeur," he whispered. "I want a full accounting. All the men you've slept with all your life and why I'm better than any of them."

"Oh, you haven't changed."

"Tell me. I've got to know."

She was crying discreetly. Flemington spent less than five minutes with her, another few minutes in the bathroom, and then, looking in both directions from a partially opened door, returned to Lulu, who had dozed off.

Day 17: Israel. Three Worlds tourists have a choice today. Either an excursion by bus to Masada, the fortress built by Herod and defended by Jewish freedom fighters against the Romans, with a return trip via Arad, Hebron and Bethlehem. Alternately tourists may spend the morning sight-seeing in modern Jerusalem—the Hebrew University, the Hadassah Hospital with the Chagall glass windows, the Israel Museum and the Dead Sea Scrolls, the Knesset, Mount Herzl, and the Yad Vashem, with a drive through the Orthodox quarter, Mea Shearim. In the afternoon, a visit to Bethlehem, scene of the Nativity.

In the evening, attendance at the "Sound and Light" Show in the Citadel of the Old City!

"I've come to say good-by to those few of you who are left," Bettenhausen said in an upper-class British accent. He surveyed the tourists who had opted for the Masada trip. "We take up with a strong heart."

"Oh, lawd-a-mercy, Betts," his wife wailed. "At 5:30 A.M. in the Holy Land? The sun isn't up, we haven't had our coffee, and this man is playing movie trivia."

Nine people were assembled outside the French Colony Hotel awaiting the Egged bus. The first streaks of light were peeking over the horizon, shedding a glow on a minaret, a row of handsome Arab homes, and a new high-rise.

"We give up, Warren," Rosie Wicker yawned. "Excuse me. I don't think I slept two hours. An Arab cur barked outside my window all night."

"*In Which We Serve,*" Bettenhausen said. "Noel Coward."

The Bettenhausens, the Wickers, the Hutzlers, one other Midwestern couple, and Theresa Carrell were the only ones who had decided on the Masada trip.

As the sun rose higher, spreading its liquid light, the tour bus loomed down the main street and then turned off to make a circle in front of the hotel.

"No escort today, Terry?" Rosie asked the teacher.

"Father Konay said he felt he owed it to the Israelis to see the modern city, the museums and the hospital, and so on. And Mr. Wattle was furious at the extra ten-dollar charge for the Masada trip. He convinced Mr. Gunthorpe not to go."

"And the court favorite?" Rosie's eyes twinkled.

"That's been closed a long time, Rosie." She lied easily. Their swift meetings—once in Istanbul, once here—had been so sudden, so unreal, that she was almost able to tell herself they had not happened.

"You look disgustingly perky for five-thirty in the morning," Cornelia said to Theresa as they settled into seats in the bus. It was filled with good-natured energetic Jews from Los Angeles.

"It's the dry heat," Terry said. "All those years I've been freezing in Minneapolis, I never realized how much I hated it."

"You like this oven? I get so I can't swallow."

"Thrive on it." Was it the desert or the passion in the desert that made her ready for adventure? Theresa wondered. Carrying a guilty secret; deceiving the innocent. Was sex better that way? Harry made her happier than any man she had ever known. Ah, but would it be the same if they shared toothpaste, argued over who was to put the garbage out, disputed over checking accounts?

"We will travel by way of Bethlehem and Hebron this morning, ladies and gentlemen," Hanan said. "But please don't start asking me to stop for photographs. We will want to get to Masada while it is still cool. On the way back will be plenty of time to take pictures and see Bethlehem and Hebron."

One of the Los Angeles tourists, a man in plaid Bermuda shorts, yellow knee socks, and a red kibbutz hat, shouted at him in Yiddish.

Hanan's eyes flashed. "I don't speak the ghetto language. Only Hebrew, English, and Arabic."

And how many languages, Bettenhausen wondered, did Anatoly Borkin speak? And which one did he use in Israel?

Herbie, ghostly pale, walking in unsteady steps, appeared in the tiled patio where the French Colony's guests ate breakfast. Flo was a step behind him, her tiny figure hidden by the bags of possessions they had bought during the tour. Two Planet flite-paks dangled from her shoulders. In one hand she clutched two camelskin bags purchased in Istanbul, in the other a denim tote and a plastic shopping bag from Vienna.

"They couldn't keep me down," Herbie said thinly. "Hiatus, shmiatus, Shackman will see Israel."

"Why, it's Harvey," Mrs. Legrand said. "Harvey, how nice to see you."

"Hiya, Ma. I got the layout of the museum with the Dead Sea Scrolls. We'll drill through the roof and pull the caper after it closes."

"He never stops," Flo moaned. "Never." She followed Herbie to where Jim and Barbara Huggins were seated, amid flower beds and soaring palms. It was a garden of delights. Huggins would have liked to spend a week there by himself.

"How goes it, Herb?" the lawyer asked. "Still in there swinging?"

"Don't ask. I forced them to release me. So what? A little stomach trouble. Boy, I'm starving. What's for breakfast?"

The headwaiter approached. He was a blue-eyed, brown-haired East Jerusalem Arab, a former pilot in the Jordanian Air Force. "Sir, anything you desire. The buffet is inside. Juice, cereal, fish, cheese, bread, vegetables. But if you wish, eggs, however you desire."

"Oi, I can't move after that plane flight. Right over the wheels."

"Shall I bring you something, sir? Tea?"

Herbie was studying the headwaiter warily. "*Bist a yid?*" he asked.

"Ah, hah, hah, no, sir. I am a Bedouin. I am a Jordanian."

"*Oi vay iz mir.*" Herbie held both hands to his sagging cheeks. "I made a bubu. Sorry, sorry. Listen, you're aces with me. Yeah, tea. And two fried eggs with ham on the side."

"No!" Flo shouted. "Tea and toast! That's all. He's a sick man."

The headwaiter left. Herbie looked at Huggins, at Mrs. Legrand, at the other members of the tour straggling into the patio. "So polite," he said. "He didn't want to kill me. Hey, Jim, you think they might slip something into the tea? Like a little poison?"

"He might not," J.P. said, "but look out for Doc Grant. He said he'd ride you hard if you left Istanbul too soon."

The Yasudas and the Grants appeared in the doorway. The physician shook an admonishing finger at Shackman. Murray spread his arms and flew to Herbie. He had been lonely ever since his friend had been hospitalized.

"Herbie baby, why do elephants have long toenails?"

"I'm starving and he asks me riddles. Doc Grant said a hiatus hernia can be the size of an egg and still make you feel like you're through. Oi, tea, tea, thanks, my friend. No offense."

Yasuda looked hurt. This was not his Herbie—cigars, jokes, crudities, goosing women, mocking guides. "Ah, come on, Herbie."

"All right, all right. Tell me, Father, why do elephants have long what . . . ?"

"Toenails," Sandra helped out.

"Toenails."

Murray fell against the tile walls, doubled over in giggles. "To . . . to . . . to . . . p-p-pick their *trunks!*"

"Yeh, yeh, very good. Pick their trunks. Flo, you're sure I can't have one fried egg?"

"Not while I'm around," Dr. Grant said.

"If I can't *fress*, I can't live."

"No, Herb," the black man said. "If you insist on gorging yourself, you won't live. You're in the land of your ancestors now—"

"Miami Beach?"

"Stop that!" Flo shouted at him. "Listen to Henderson!"

"—and one of their rules, I always thought, was temperance, no excesses. Try to live up to it."

"That's telling him, Doc," Si said. He and Shirl had emerged from the breakfast buffet, their plates heaped high.

"Can I help it if I am what I am?" Herbie mumbled.

J. P. Huggins excused himself once more. He'd skip the morning sight-seeing, although the prospect of the Chagall windows had tempted him. His law partner Kuraskin had a Chagall original, a brightly colored gouache, in his living room, and Huggins had seen the Chagalls at the opera house. But business called. Someday, someday, he would be rich enough to loll around museums, squire ballerinas, sponsor Off-Broadway plays.

Saladin Street proved to be a short walk from the hotel, through what was the wealthy Arab quarter of East Jerusalem. He passed shops, a police station surrounded by barbed wire, and some tempting Arab restaurants. A yeasty odor of newly baked bread hovered over the sunny street. Spirits rising, Huggins bought a Paris *Herald Tribune* and a Jerusalem *Post* and stopped at a sidewalk stand for a second cup of sweet black coffee. The *Post* had today's date on it. He turned to the financial pages. The S.S. *Lautaro* or, for that matter, any vessel sailing to or from the Union of Arab Emirates was not mentioned. But the price of gold was up again—a new record.

"If gold goes up," he murmured, "can platinum be far behind?"

With satisfying acidity, the coffee rimmed his stomach. Many of life's pleasures, Huggins had come to believe, were disguised pains. Scotch tasted dreadful and made you nauseous; sex could strain your back and dry your mouth; cigarettes killed you. But a man who could paint a face the way Raphael could, or write a poem like Keats, or design a building the way Palladio did . . . No pain there. At least not after the job was done.

The Old City & United Bank of Jerusalem was open. The heavy mesh shutter was raised. Inside a party of blond American youngsters were changing traveler's checks at the desk. J.P. read the sticker on a knapsack:

United Lutheran Bible Study Club
Crestline, Ohio

"Hi," a straw-haired young man said. "American?"

"Sure am," J.P. replied.

"Isn't it thrilling? I mean being where our Saviour walked?"

"You mean he was right in this bank?"

"Oh, you're kidding me. I bet you're from New York. All you New Yorkers kid about everything."

"Wrong. I'm a Medford, Oregon, man, myself." Huggins walked to the end of the counter and inquired of a clerk if he could speak to the representative of the Beirut, Dubai & Sharja Trading Company. The clerk peered over his glasses, as if assessing Huggins, decided he looked sufficiently corrupt, then gestured to him. Huggins followed him to the back of the bank. My twenty-day tour, the lawyer mused, is being spent in frosted glass partitions, talking to hustlers. . . .

"Mr. Huggins, I am expecting you," a short man in a gray suit said, rising to shake his hand. "I am Mr. Silwah."

"Colleague of Mr. Chahoub?"

"His representative."

"Good. You have any word for my investment in Beirut, Dubai & Sharja?"

"Good news. Your ship has come in. Last night I received a cable from Mr. Chahoub. I took the liberty of reading it because sometimes they require swift action on my part."

Huggins took the envelope and opened it. "In my business, we don't read other people's mail," he said.

"Mr. Huggins, this business is nothing at all like your business."

DELIGHTED INFORM YOU LAUTARO ARRIVED SAFELY DETAILS FOLLOW STOP ASSURED GOOD SALE BY AGENTS STOP MOST ANXIOUS REPORT THIS PERSONALLY TO YOU MAKE NEW ARRANGEMENTS WILL CONTACT YOU ROME KINDEST PERSONAL REGARDS

CHAHOUB

"That is dandy," Huggins said.

"We are so happy to be the bearers of good news, sir."

"What does he mean 'arrived safely'? Where? Bombay? Karachi?"

Mr. Silwah held a finger to his lips. "Mr. Chahoub must be discreet. The less mentioned the better. If he says he will meet you in Rome, he will."

"Why does he want to see me personally?"

Mr. Silwah opened his palms. "It is not for us to ask, sir. Be satisfied that all is well. I am sure he will have more good news for you."

Wary of good news from Lebanese smugglers but buoyed by the cable—at least his investment had not been intercepted by the Pakistani Coast Guard—he hailed a cab and rode to the Israel Museum, where Barbara and the others would be arriving in a little while.

For a gratifying half hour he wandered through the Billy Rose

384

Garden of the museum, appreciating the modern sculpture and elevated setting, the tourists and students strolling amid the Epsteins and the Lipschitzes. How lucky could he be?

"There it is," Hanan said. "It looks like what? The prow of a ship maybe."

"Carved right out of the mountain," Dr. Wicker said. "How in God's name did they do it?"

"Labor was cheap," Rosie said.

"What are the buildings on the end?" Cornelia asked.

"Herod's palaces," Hanan said. "On three different levels. He took good care of himself and his family. Colonnades, paintings, porches, bathhouses."

In the distance the Fortress of Masada hung suspended in the hazed air. The land was burned out. Rocks, boulders, sand, lifeless objects that had absorbed all the earthly heat they could. But instead of turning to black ash, they had by desert chemistry been transmuted to golds, beiges, pinks, and yellows. And the bleached-out colors blended into one shimmering backdrop—dead, hot, terrifying.

"I am at a loss," Bettenhausen sighed. "How did they *live* from day to day in the Judaean wilderness? Let alone fight wars, and farm and create a society."

"Determination," Dr. Wicker said. "It confounds me also. Look at the length of that thing. Hanan says it's six hundred meters long. And a wall around it. A double casemate wall."

"Maybe religion gave them their motivation," Cornelia said. "I couldn't do a day's work here."

Behind them on the winding blacktop an Israeli Army jeep had stopped. Three dark-skinned soldiers got out and began to change a tire. They wore dark uniforms, heavy paratroop boots, and put down their black weapons to work on the vehicle.

"That's what I mean," the dentist said. "I'd fall apart if I had to work in this heat."

Hanan had been listening. "You do what you must do. You see those boys? Moroccans, maybe Persians. Their fathers could not read or write and did not know a wheel from a hammer. Now look at them. They are among our best soldiers."

A black Mercedes, with an Israeli flag on its fender, whizzed past them, on its way to Masada.

Hanan squinted after it. "Hmmm. VIPs. We bring them here for a look. They are never the same after they see it."

Fifteen minutes later, after a pause for grapefruit juice at a shed (one of the Los Angeles men said it was the best juice he had ever

had, better than California's, and he would try to import it), they began the walk up the bank path on the northern side. No one took the
easy way up—the funicular.

"Walk slow," Hanan said. "And stop whenever you have to. There
are places cut into the rock for shade. It should take no more than
twenty minutes."

Theresa found the walking pleasurable, almost sensuous. The gentle fatigue in her limbs filled her with virtue: *a job done.* It was not
nearly as arduous as she had been led to believe. One managed with
an occasional rest, a bit of shade. Israeli children, not much bigger
than infants, scrambled past her. Once a middle-aged fat man suggesting a likely candidate for a coronary—chalky face, waddling in dark
pants and pointed black shoes—passed her on the pathway. "You're
in a hurry," Terry said. "Take it easy." He tipped his kibbutz hat to
her. "No time to waste. Masada's up there." She wanted to tell him
that it had been there a long time and would wait for him, but he
bustled by. Elderly Jewish ladies trudged upward, and a pair of
bearded elders in black caftans glided by as if airborne.

Like many challenges in life, Theresa decided, the threat, the advance worries, were greater than the obstacle itself. In college, in
graduate school, there were always horror stories about the impossibly
difficult final examinations. But they had never been that hard. And
the problems of teaching wild teen-agers in an inner-city high school.
Not easy; but not insurmountable. She wondered if the peace she now
sensed, the optimistic review of past difficulties (notions engendered
by the achievement of putting one foot after another on a desert
path), stemmed from Harry's promise. She thought of their love-
making: Harry the way he was years ago, fumbling and shaking. She
wondered whether after marriage he would calm down.

"What a sight," Wicker said. "I got to get this."

"What?" Terry asked.

"The Roman wall. What'd Hanan call it? Circumvallation. Look
at that thing. It runs for miles and miles around the fort." He held the
Pentax to his eye. "Incredible. Just incredible."

Theresa looked out at the bleached land and was saddened that in
a few days she would have to say good-by to the Bettenhausens and
the Wickers, all the members of the Three Worlds tour. But the dentist
and the Hollywood man and their wives were special people—happily
married, vigorous, interested, *alive.* She envied them. Neither of her
marriages had quite worked out. It always seemed that her husbands
were tired, preoccupied, worried. Was it the boredom of teaching, for
which neither man had been suited? Or was she the kind of woman
who in her very vigor was destined to draw losers, quitters? And was

386

she on the verge of another such commitment? Perhaps casual friend-
ships, like the one she shared with the two couples, were better for
her. And yet there was that damnable three o'clock in the morning
loneliness . . . empty bed . . . solitary breakfast in the tiny kitchen.
She moved upward again, enjoying the delicious pull of fatigue on her
muscles.

They spent more than an hour on Masada. Hanan was indefatiga-
ble. His curt manner left him. The monuments on Masada moved him
to smile, to flirt with the women, to talk at great length. A strange,
strange people, Bettenhausen mused: reaping pleasure from the
scorched site of an ancient massacre, a mass suicide. He had heard
quite enough about the Zealots and their intrepid leader Eleazer Ben-
Yair. They wandered through storehouses, palaces, swimming pools,
bathhouses, the palace with a mosaic floor, marveled at the ingenious
casemate—a double wall filled with earth, so that the Roman battering
rams impacted it and hardened the shield—and now paused in the
synagogue.
    "When you think of Masada," Hanan said, "do not think of Herod
but of the Jewish patriots who died here."
    Bettenhausen lumbered up from the stone bench of the synagogue.
History was bearing down too hard that morning. One needed days to
absorb Masada; a week of rereading Josephus; desert conditioning. It
was too much to ask of a fat old man.
    "I'll be damned," Bettenhausen said. "There he is."
    "Who?" Wicker asked.
    "Borkin."
    The dentist shaded his eyes. Bettenhausen was moving toward two
men, about a hundred feet away. One was stocky, bespectacled, in a
tan suit that melted into the surrounding coloration. The other was
slender and dark and wore an open-throated white shirt.
    "Where are they off to now?" Cornelia asked.
    Rose-Anne fanned herself with a broad-brimmed straw hat. "Plot-
ting." She knew by now: Arnold had told her. But she had no idea if
Bettenhausen had briefed his wife.
    A party of Baptist Sunday school teachers and students obstructed
the passage of the Hollywood man and the dentist. Bettenhausen
squinted at the distant Dead Sea. Full of salt and history.
    "To the Byzantine chapel," Bettenhausen gasped. "Watson, the
game's afoot."
    Several hundred feet south of the synagogue was a ruin that Hanan
had pointed out, but which they had not entered—a church built by

387

Byzantine monks, the last residents of Masada. Borkin and his companion turned a corner and vanished into the golden walls.

"After them, Arnold," Bettenhausen ordered.

The dentist broke into a run, but there was no need to. No attempt was made to hide Borkin. As Wicker hopped over the doorway of the chapel, he saw them, as casually as any tourists, studying the singular walls of the building. They were studded with bits of stones arranged in geometric patterns. The slender man was speaking softly, and the man in the tan suit listened.

Bettenhausen waddled into the chapel. The two men were standing in the apse.

"It's him," Bettenhausen said. "I shall demand an explanation." He tugged at his beard, pulled the tam-o'-shanter over his forehead, and approached the Russian. "Dr. Borkin, I presume?"

There was no doubt in Bettenhausen's mind. He saw the tolerant face, the calm eyes, the scarred chin, that he had seen at the Museum of Secret Communist Meetings.

"Mr. Bettengausen."

"The same."

The dark man looked annoyed. Bettenhausen studied him. A strange-looking fellow. Skin the color of saddle leather, sharp features, dark eyes. If Franz Kafka, Bettenhausen thought, had been healthy and aggressive, he might have looked like Borkin's companion. There was an extraordinary resemblance, even to the brushed-back black hair.

"Mr. Bettengausen, I cannot talk," Borkin said. The dark man spoke Russian to the scientist. Borkin began what seemed to be an explanation, pointed to Bettenhausen, miming the opening of an envelope.

"What the heck is this?" Dr. Wicker asked. "What's going on?"

Dr. Borkin smiled at Bettenhausen. "I explain to gentleman here, my host. You are brave man, courageous to do what you do. I am here because of what you do for me. I—"

The man in the open shirt made a silencing gesture, waving a hand from side to side. He and Borkin spoke in Russian again.

"I cannot explain. Can only thank you."

"Thank this gentleman also," Bettenhausen said. He pointed to Arnold Wicker. "It was he who got the letter from Mr. Leland. He had doubts about Leland's motives and asked me to assist. All of this led to our confrontation with Varvansky. But why are you here? Have you defected? Emigrated? Are you on a visit?"

Baptists surged into the tiny chapel. A mass of browned young limbs in hiking boots, knapsacks, tanned American faces, hemmed the

388

men in. The dark man—Kafka as athlete, Kafka as soldier—motioned to them, and they pushed their way into the next chamber.

The dark man bent his head at Bettenhausen and spoke in accented English. "Please do not ask further. Professor Borkin has explained your role. We are grateful. But it is so far secret. The word is not released. In a few days we will make an announcement. Until then I ask you and your friend to say nothing."

"How shall we find out?" Bettenhausen asked.

"It will be in the newspapers."

"You appear to be a man whose word can be taken," the Hollywood man said. "May I inquire to whom it is I have the honor to be speaking?"

"No matter."

There was something in the man's manner that suggested their guide Hanan, the same sabra brusqueness. But there was something else—*command presence.*

"I am jolly well fed up with mysteries," Bettenhausen said. "If you won't tell me who you are, then tell me who John T. Leland is."

Borkin laughed. Again they conversed in Russian.

"You shall have to find out for yourself. Now we wish to finish our tour of Masada."

Borkin and his guardian walked through the onrushing horde of Baptist youths, into the sun-scorched plateau of the fortress. Bettenhausen and Wicker followed them, then halted. The scientist and his companion walked toward the synagogue. As they did, they passed Hanan Gilad. The guide and the Israeli in the white shirt exchanged words.

"Hanan knows him," the dentist said. "Ask him."

"You saw the Byzantine chapel?" Hanan asked them.

"Fascinating. The mosaic floor is superb." Bettenhausen fell in step alongside the sabra. "The fellow in the white shirt, the one you greeted?"

"Who? Oh. Shlomo."

"Shlomo?"

"We were in the Army together. An old friend."

"What does he do now?"

Hanan squinted at the Dead Sea. "He is a colonel. Military intelligence. Colonel Shlomo Tal."

Bettenhausen cleared his throat. "He doesn't seem to go to any pains to conceal his identity. Just walks around the country in a white shirt? And is so easily identified?"

"It's a small country. We all know each other."

389

"How about the man with him?" Dr. Wicker asked. "You know him?" Hanan did not look back. "Don't know and don't care."

A persistent scent had been bothering Lulu Flemington all morning. She had a sensitive nose. In the dry desert heat, odors intensified, as if on a hot stove. Harry's after-shave lotion? Something one of the Westbury women was wearing?

The tour was rushed into the chapel of the Hadassah Hospital, under the guidance of a young girl. There was barely time to study the stained glass Chagall windows. It seemed to Virgil that the entire Jewish population of New York City was at the hospital that morning, and that Chagall's windows were the foci of attention. There was a crowd outside the chapel and an even bigger crowd inside, people jammed toe to toe, chin to chin. A crowd lingered at the exit doors, as if hopeful of being allowed in again to gaze at the master's impressions of the Twelve Tribes.

"Boy, they really are something," Herbie said. "I wonder what tribe I am."

"Whichever ate the most," Flo said.

"You all right, Herb?" Si asked.

"Yeah, yeah. Never felt better."

The girl was explaining the iconography of Chagall's work—doves, bulls, eagles, mystic signs and symbols. The Three Worlds people were jammed into one corner of the chapel and it was impossible to see more than three or four of the windows.

"I'm gypped," Herbie complained. "I came here for Twelve Tribes, and I'm getting only three. Naftali, Joseph, and Benjamin. I want to see the rest."

The long morning of walking up hills under the blinding sun, and particularly the visit to the Yad Vashem, where the six million victims of the Nazi era were memorialized, rendered the tourists silent. Even Mr. Wattle had made no comment when they walked through the stark building in which were kept the records of the holocaust, and down the tree-lined "Avenue of the Righteous Gentiles"—in tribute to Christians who had saved Jews. There was little to say. At one point, a family of red-faced Dutch Jews appeared and placed flowers at the foot of a tree. Flemington had asked what they were doing. Pepi read the name on the plaque in front of the tree: *Willem Kruis.* Then he spoke in Dutch to the family—an elderly couple with two sons in their teens. "They are from Amsterdam," he said. "This Dutchman saved their lives. He hid them in a cellar and arranged for them to escape from Holland." Flemington listened respectfully. "I see. Was he a government official of some kind?" Again Virgil spoke to the family. "No," he translated. "He was a waiter. He worked in the restaurant in the Amsterdam zoo."

The incident stuck to Flemington's mind. *A waiter in the Amsterdam zoo.* It had almost a comic ring. Yet there was nothing comic about Willem Kruis. One could spend one's life searching for a single noble deed, a single act of unselfishness. And where was Willem Kruis now? he had asked. Were the trees memorials to righteous Gentiles who had died? Oh no, the Dutchman told Hanan, Mynheer Kruis was living in Amsterdam.

A magazine article suggested itself to Flemington, as the bus descended Mount Scopus. "They Remember Willem Kruis." Doubtful that the *Detroit Athletic Club News* would be interested. He would need an agent, someone who knew the magazine field. It had all changed in the last ten years. Specialized periodicals. Different audiences. The generalized magazine was out. Another folded every day. But there had to be a market for his kind of writing—knowledgeable, brisk. No one could put a lead on a crime story the way he could. Nobody at the paper could reshape a routine interview with a visiting celebrity—actress, UN official—and make it a warm personalized account. He still had the touch.

Swift calculations took place in his mind as Lulu, exhausted, rested her head on his shoulder. He felt her frail skull, her hair with its hard veneer, against his Sulka sports shirt. The figures set themselves up in columns: Theresa's salary, about ten thousand dollars a year. If he could pick up another ten thousand by free-lancing—an advance on a book, magazine pieces, some TV documentary work for the local stations—they could manage. . . .

On the bus Lulu fell into a hard sleep on Harry's forearm. She slept dreamlessly, a habit brought on by long usage of alcohol and tranquilizers. Her doctor was puzzled. In most people drugs tended to produce detailed dreams. In Lulu it worked the other way. She was rendered inert. She snored delicately. But she slept fitfully, often awakening after an hour or less, staring at the ceiling, taking another pill, then falling into blackness once more.

She dozed no more than fifteen minutes. An odor awakened her. It was the same persistent scent she had noticed earlier in the day. Not once but several times. In the arid air it lingered—flitting about her nostrils. She had sniffed it first when they were in the statuary garden at the Israel Museum and had thought it was some perfume Mrs. Huggins was using. It would be like her, that overweight girl with her piled-up hair and pancake make-up. But it was not. Lulu walked in back of her and took a good sniff while they were pausing

391

to look at a Henry Moore. She was wearing Ma Griffe. Lulu knew them all.

Now, awakening, it filled her nostrils. It was on Harry's avocado silk shirt, his twenty-five-dollar shirt from Sulka. Silk retained odors. Lulu knew all about fabrics. And it was not his Agua Brava or his Floris. It was stronger, more feminine. But what? And how . . . ?"

The clear topaz necklace on Theresa Carrell's neck seemed to hang before her, suspended in the middle of the aisle, somewhere between Herbie Shackman's orange skull and J. P. Huggins' curly dark hair. A possibility—*monstrous! dreadful!*—began to formulate in Lulu's mind. Frenzy grabbed at her vitals. She wanted to shriek, to hit someone. But she had learned public self-control—at least while sober. Instead of shouting, or berating Harry or challenging him, she inhaled deeply again and tried to guess precisely what the fragrance was. She brushed her head against his shirt.

"Feels nice, doesn't it, Lu?"

"Yes. Beautiful." And I bought it for you, you cheating bastard, she thought. My money. My house. My everything. There was no need to panic. She could be mistaken. Her nose *could* deceive her. (Not likely, Lulu knew. She had sat long hours on high padded stools in the cosmetic department at Saks in Detroit, sniffing essences.)

"Had a little nap?"

"A shortie."

Flemington felt generous toward his wife, indebted to her in a decent way. She had been a sport about Theresa's presence on the tour. She smiled more often. Pepi had promised to take her to a leather shop in Tel Aviv tomorrow. They had two more expandable valises to be filled—one in Israel, the other in Rome. Sated with loot, they would fly home. Lulu, sorting out trophies, would be strong enough to confront the staggering news: he was leaving her.

Detchema, Lulu decided.

"You're *supposed* to buy Hebron glass," Cornelia said. "It isn't bad, Betts. I need a small pitcher anyway."

"Go ahead, my dear," the Hollywood man said. His mind was elsewhere. A jeepload of Israeli soldiers rolled by them slowly as they walked the path leading to the Machpelah—Abraham's Tomb. Any moment he expected to see Borkin and the mysterious Colonel Tal again. Military intelligence, Hanan had said. A small country. We all know each other.

"Hebron glass be damned," Bettenhausen said to Wicker. "There's something I really want for my study."

An Arab peddler, whose stall was an antipasto of rosaries, flags, postage stamps, postcards, and other trivia, displayed a row of curious soda bottles. On inspection, it developed that they were empty of soda but filled with varicolored sands. Inside the bottle, facing prospective purchasers, stared a small photograph of Moshe Dayan.

"Now what in Allah's name impelled an Arab entrepreneur to create that thing? And he has scores of them. Old Nehi bottles, a bit of dyed sand, and Dayan. I must have one."

"A lovely thing for the house, sir," the merchant said to Bettenhausen. "The sands were dyed by hand."

"I won't even haggle with the fellow," Bettenhausen said. "It's one of the most original items I've seen since we began this trip. A pity Mrs. Flemington isn't here. She could fill a valise with them. I could swear Dayan winked at me."

The dentist started after the rest of the party. Bettenhausen tugged at his sleeve. "Linger, Arnold. The tombs of Abraham, Isaac, and Jacob have been there a long time. I'm trying to sort things out." Bettenhausen shooed away a small boy and an old man hawking fold-out postcards. "What do you make of it?"

"For one thing, I'd have to assume Borkin's a Jew. That never came out in what we learned about him."

Bettenhausen wet his lips. He liked the furnacelike air. Like Sherman Oaks in a rainless September. The desert suggested simplicity, loneliness, an ability to make do with little. Husbanding rain water and thoughts, he reflected. Lawrence liked it because it was *clean.* Joseph Wood Krutch because it suggested the courage of desert creatures.

"It is possible," Bettenhausen said, "that Borkin is Jewish. Many eminent scientists and artists of Jewish origin, people long assimilated who regard themselves as pure Russians, are now under attack. The attacks are unexpected and vicious."

"But Borkin was never attacked on that score," Wicker said. "At least as far as we know. Heck, the guy was supposed to be their top geneticist. Why would they want to dump him? Or why would he want to go?"

"He was also alleged to be the head of the libertarian underground."

Bettenhausen coughed as they entered the Machpelah—it was a mosque, but also a Jewish shrine. Inside, the holy place was a garish affair, plaster walls painted maroon and pale blue, a sort of East Bronx bathhouse décor. The Hollywood man looked pained. "Arnold, we may have expedited a natural process."

"Helped get Borkin out?" Wicker felt a fragile kinship with the scientist.

"I think so," Bettenhausen said. "The parts aren't quite in line, but

I think I know what happened. I hope Tal was telling the truth about a press release about Borkin. If not, I may have to hold my own press conference."

"Oh, Warren, please."

They were shoved forward in a swarm of Moslem imams, Bible students, Chasidim, Frenchwomen in short skirts, Israeli soldiers. The mishmash of relics, graves, visitors, worshipers made Wicker light-headed. Outside the tomb of Abraham (the guide had said that it "did no harm" to so regard it) a Chasidic youth prayed. The tomb was a small barred room. Within was a stone covered with a blue cloth. The boy, sparsely bearded, earlocks spinning, bobbed and jerked in spiritual abandon, communing with the patriarch. An imam leading a party of Swedish tourists walked by; then the Three Worlds tour; then a group of fawn-eyed Jordanian children under the guidance of a German nun. The Chasid saw nothing, heard nothing. His passion was not of this world.

"I once heard the expression 'in Abraham's bosom,'" Wicker said to his wife. "Now I know what it means. Look at him."

Rosie did. Then she studied her husband's long innocent American face, the face of a reliable committee member, a doubles player, a PTA chairman. The same people? The same origins? Mysterious and inexplicable, she decided.

In Bethlehem the Three Worlds tour was reunited—the Masada party and the people who had spent the morning in Jerusalem. The rendezvous was in Manger Square opposite the Church of the Nativity.

Virgil checked his watch, saw an Egged bus approaching, and knew that Hanan was on time. Israeli guides usually were. Tourism was an enormous business, a huge earner of hard currencies. Efficiency was obligatory. "Almost like Germans we have become," Hanan once said sourly. "Everything on time. Everything in order."

Hanan bobbed his nose in Bettenhausen's direction. "That gentleman. In the Scottish hat. What is he?"

"Mr. Bettenhausen?" Virgil paused. "I'm not sure. Something in Hollywood at one time. He is retired."

"Interesting man."

"Extremely learned. Why do you ask about him?"

"He left the party on top of Masada and went after one of our military intelligence men. Then he pretended he did not know him and asked me who it was."

"Ah. Ah. And who was it?"

"No secrets between guides, eh, Yosef? It was Tal."

"The famous Colonel Tal? Of the Shin-Bet? I wonder what he wanted with him. Isn't Tal the fellow who got the French guidance systems out of Paris? Posed as a Jordanian agronomist, as I recall."

"Yes. No matter. We've had everything else on these tours, so why not CIA? I'll have to mention it to the ministry—that fellow running after Tal and then asking me. Do you mind?"

Weary, a bit frazzled, Virgil found a surge of energy—perhaps his one-eighth Jewish ancestry asserting itself. "I don't mind. Planet Tours is not responsible for Mr. Bettenhausen's extracurricular activities." His eyes scanned the group waiting at the entrance to the Nativity Church. The blockish building—Crusader with Mameluke additions— possessed a sturdy charm. In the dimmed light of late afternoon the gray square stones had a profound dignity. It was late; other tours had left. The Three Worlds group seemed unprotected in the shadows of the Church of the Nativity. Virgil had a rush of affection for his thirty-odd dependents. When they left, he would miss them. They had given him trouble, crises (who knew what was to come?), but also moments of laughter, of inspiration, and were always subjects for reflection.

For example: he was confounded by the manner in which all members—including the southerner Mr. Gunthorpe—battled to have the honor of sitting with Dr. and Mrs. Grant. How explain that? How make that clear to someone who would insist that Americans hated black people? And Mr. Shackman. Loud, rude, funny, overbearing, unafraid to intrude his personality, make his presence felt, indulge in ribald behavior (short of flirting with Mrs. Flemington), Shackman had been the life of the party. Yet how explain to an unknowing European that Mr. Shackman was *Jewish*, very much so, but these Americans did not object to his buffooneries, but found him comical, agreeable, and an asset to the tour?

"All present?" Hanan asked. Pepi was counting. They were all there, waiting patiently in the Manger Square, fending off souvenir vendors.

"To a man."

"Ah, counting heads again, Pepi?" Mrs. Hutzler asked.

"Oh no, Mrs. Hutzler. That is too easy. I count legs and divide by two."

"Goll-eeee," Mavis said. "He's as bad as Herbie."

Hanan gathered the group around him. "Ladies and gentlemen, this is Bethlehem, which means in Hebrew the House of Bread. I hope you are not too tired from Masada and from the tour of Jerusalem. Is it not a beautiful city? The most beautiful city in the world. A golden city."

395

"Never mind the commercial," Herbie said. "Where can I siddown?"

Hanan ignored him. "We are not permitted to take tours inside," he said. "This is occupied territory and we respect the local guides. Please tip your guide. Now, inasmuch as they are full of misinformation, I shall give you a little history. Fourth-century, original church built by Constantine. There are still mosaics from the first church. On top of it a sixth-century church built by Justinian. What you are looking at is a restoration from 1842, when the Turks ruled here. For Christians it is where the Saviour was born. You will see the Grotto of the Nativity."

"Nervous, Father?" Ibith asked Father Konay.

"Just awed. A man needs a week in these places to absorb them. I'll go back to Pennsylvania and I won't remember a darn thing."

"Incidentally," Hanan said, "Father will be interested to know this is a Roman Catholic basilica and is like the early Christian basilicas in Rome. So he can feel at home."

"Oh, I do," the priest said. "I feel very much at home in your country."

Hanan grinned. "So do we. Ah, your guide is here. Yes, we feel at home, because before Jesus was born here Bethlehem was the home of Boaz."

"Who?" Herbie asked. "What?"

"In the Old Testament. The story of Ruth and Naomi. Boaz married Ruth the Moabite. They were the ancestors of David."

The group walked under the windowless archway, past the ninth-century carved doors. The Arab guide halted them around the red marble columns and flashed a light on the Crusader paintings.

"Crusaders love this church," he said. "Very dear to Norman knights. Look. Paintings. St. Margaret. St. Leonard. King Canute."

"Did Hanan say that Boaz and Ruth were the ancestors of David?" Cornelia asked her husband. "What does that mean?"

Bettenhausen growled. "It gives the Israelis a genealogical claim. It also explains the tradition of Jesus' birth here. Boaz and Ruth—a union of desert tribes, Hebrew and Moabite. I think their son was Obed."

The guide overheard. "Yes, sir. Obed, father of Jesse. And Jesse, father of King David."

Flemington joined the colloquy. "Yes, of course, and the direct line to Jesus. There's something called the Tree of Jesse, a genealogical table showing Christ's ancestors."

Father Konay, his voice trembling, added: "'And there shall come forth a rod out of the stem of Jesse, and a branch shall grow out of his roots.' It was a prophecy about Jesus."

Whither thou goest I will go. Poetry of the old book, Flemington thought. It sent tremors down his back. Boaz lived in Bethlehem and Naomi had gone from there to Moab, then back to Bethlehem with her daughter-in-law Ruth. He would have to read the Old Testament again when he got home. But where would home be? He caught a glimpse of Theresa, chatting with Mrs. Huggins, as they descended the narrow stairs into the Grotto of the Nativity. Her place in Minneapolis? A bigger apartment? Room for his typewriter and books and papers?

"'Wither thou goest I will go,'" Flemington said under his breath.

"What's that?" Lulu asked, taking his arm.

"That line from the Book of Ruth. I was repeating it."

She teetered as they walked down the stairs into the murky grotto. The group assembled around the Arab. The doorways to the cave were of Gothic marble. Hangings in lurid reds and greens covered parts of the rough wall. Candlelight flickered on their faces. The guide pointed out the Crusader mosaic in the apse, then beckoned them to follow him to the site of Jesus' birth. Father Konay lingered. It was too hard to contemplate. Yet when he edged forward in the cave, shivering in the change from desert heat to cool darkness, he felt more confident. What was there to fear? The guide was pointing to a large gold star set into the stone of the floor.

"The star," the Arab said. "Where Christ was born."

"When was it put there?" Theresa asked.

"In 1717, madame."

"By the Turks?" she asked.

"Oh no, madame. By the Latins. The Roman Catholics."

In the crush of bodies around the holy place, Lulu found herself alongside Theresa.

"It was cause of Crimean War," the guide said.

Everyone looked blank. "War?" Bettenhausen asked. "Charge of the Light Brigade and so on?"

"Very complicated," the Arab said enigmatically. "Now, out, please, to see Well of Virgins, please move."

But only a few people moved. Theresa, her eyes dulled in the murky grotto, turned to Lulu—barely aware that it was she. "I don't understand what he was talking about. Did he say the Crimean War?"

Lulu did not reply. Theresa's face was less than a foot from hers. It was the closest they had been in the course of the trip. Flemington, behind his wife, supporting her frail waist, had a foreboding of disaster. But Lulu said nothing. Theresa sensed she had directed her query to a stone figure. She turned away.

As she did Lulu caught the aroma again. No mistaking it. On that

397

bitch. On that whore. That schoolteacher, with her fake smile. It was Detchema. Sloshed on her neck, her ears. And on Harry's avocado silk shirt. Her nose twitched. She could not be fooled by scents. She knew them. A sequence of events so appalling that she dared not consider them, at least not in one small bracket of time, formed in her mind. The clear topaz necklace Harry had admired in the Moscow store. His frequent absences—to get mineral water, to get ice, to send a postcard to Robbie. And now the scent of Detchema on the Carrell woman.

"Move, please, move, please," the guide said. "Other people wish to come in. Look, please, at ikons on the wall. From door at other end, leads to cave where St. Jerome translated Bible."

Lulu disengaged Harry's hands from her waist. He saw the splotches on her thin neck—a bad sign. What had he done?

"In far corner of grotto," the guide said, "is Well of Virgins. Only Virgins who stand there can see the star. Any ladies like to stand there and see?"

There was some giggling. "Hah!" Herbie shouted. "In this group? Virgins? Go ahead, Flo, you first."

"Herbie, shut up. This is a holy place."

"Oops, sorry. Didn't mean a word, Father."

Father Konay didn't hear him. He was looking at the gold star in the floor.

On the bus, riding back to Jerusalem in the fading light, Flemington tried to take his wife's hand. She yanked it away. She stared out the window at the arid countryside. Arab women squatted at road stops, hawking grapes, figs, vegetables. Hanan had said they were bargains. He and his wife often drove down to Bethlehem to buy produce—it was cheaper and tastier.

"Anything wrong, Lu?" Harry asked.

"You bastard."

"What have I done?"

"I'll settle with you at the hotel." Her voice was almost a baritone. All the soaked whiskey was asserting itself, a hard voice, a terror to headwaiters and caddy masters. Flemington wondered: The necklace? But he had lied effectively to cover that. Suddenly he was upset with Terry for flaunting the damned thing. She had that streak of recklessness in her—the need to show the world that she commanded Harry's love. She wanted to do a little crowing. Too many years of frustration impelled her to display the necklace. A token. A sign. So what if Lulu guessed at its origin? Flemington wondered whether she had done it in the full awareness that his wife, with her sixth sense, her capacity to smell out the essence of *things*, would make the connection.

Theresa was no weakling; no fool. Stronger than he was, Flemington decided. In bed, she often gave the orders, made the demands. He had always liked it that way. *There. Touch me. Again. Move, please.* Was she now—even before they were married, or he freed of Lulu—asserting her will? The notion terrified him and yet reassured him. It would have to happen. Or, as the Bible would put it, *And it came to pass . . .*

Hanan took command as they rode back to "his Jerusalem." Firmly, he forced Murray and Herbie to put out their cigars—something Virgil had been unable to do. Then, as a reward for good behavior, he explained how the star of Bethlehem was responsible for the start of the Crimean War—Russia backing the Greek Orthodox priests in Palestine, and France, England, and Turkey supporting the Catholic Church. His knowledge of history, dates, names, events, evoked admiration from Bettenhausen; he liked people with a historical sense.

"On the left-hand side," Hanan said, "the Tomb of Rachel, *Rahel Imenu*, our mother. Who knows how many sons she had?"

"One?" Mavis Hutzler asked timidly. "Joseph?"

"Close, lady. Two. People forget Benjamin, Jacob's youngest. Rachel died in childbirth and Jacob buried her here, 'in the way to Ephrath which is Bethlehem.'"

And Jacob had twelve sons altogether, Flemington thought. Wasn't a man supposed to have a son, plant a tree, and write a book in his lifetime? He had a son: a mindless creature. He had planted no trees, but Lulu's gardeners had done his bidding. The book was yet to come, he was certain, as soon as he began to live his new fruitful life.

Flemington sought his wife's face. But she kept it frozen against the window.

As soon as they were in the room, Lulu kicked off her shoes and fell on the bed.

"A drink, Lu? Some ice water?"

"Don't talk to me. You've been with that bitch."

"I swear, Lu, I haven't."

"Up to your old tricks. I know you bought her that necklace."

"I didn't."

"You've slept with her. I smelled her perfume on that shirt you're wearing. I'm never wrong about essences. You bastard."

"You're inventing this, Lu. You're tired."

"That whore. She came after you."

399

Flemington said nothing. It was enough trouble lying on his own behalf. To lie for Theresa, while advisable, would be painful.

"Lu, you're exhausted, and you are imagining things. We shouldn't have gone sight-seeing today. We should have taken the day off and gone shopping."

"Don't try to deter me. Don't pull that crap about shopping. You've been sneaking off with her. She's still after you. She always has been."

Flemington sat down across the room. The light was dim, the shutters closed, but two spears of sunlight cast yellow diagonals across the bed, gold bars on Lulu's thin figure. Parallel lines never meet, he thought. But Einstein said that they do. True or false? He and Lulu had led parallel lives—man and wife, sharing bed and board, but they had never met, never found a point of juncture, the oneness that was supposed to signify the good life. He thought of her as she had been twenty years ago—lithe, graceful, perceptive, good fun. Until Robbie. No, it was unfair to pin it on Robbie. But there were always omens of irresponsibility, of susceptibility to booze, of enslavement to things, to what was purchasable and of value. It seemed incredible to Flemington how little money did for some people. It afforded comfort, and indulgence, and pleasures, and a cushion against the pains and pressures of life. But did it, in the words of a losing football coach, "build character"? For that matter, was it supposed to?

There was something to be said for the tyrant kings and dukes and clerics, whose cruelties they had learned about during their tour. (Wasn't it Mrs. Wicker or some other decent-minded person who had asked, "Why did people put up with these lunatics?") At least these ancient oligarchs made no bones about their power and what it could do for them. The tendency today was for the rich to pose as benefactors, humanitarians. Just folks. His divagations became more cautionary: Lulu and her people were not bad people. Of course not. They created work. Kept the wheels running. Greased the machinery. Contributed to charities. Perhaps their sin was not against society and against their fellow men but against themselves.

Harry Flemington, former night editor, was worse than any of them. He was a rider of the rails, an educated hobo on the gravy train. "Git on board, lil chillun, there's room for many a more." But there wasn't. The train was overloaded. The youngsters understood this, so they copped out, went on drugs, vanished into the wilderness, lounged around communes, blindly seeking higher wisdom.

"We are going home," Lulu announced.

"Beg pardon, dear?" He was thinking of Theresa's body, the limbs

400

to embrace him, the soft mouth, the gasps and whispers and words that no one in the world knew about. The prim face and the pumping thighs.

"Home. Go see the guide right now. And see if you can stay away from her room."

There was a strength in Lulu that always astounded him. Not a physical strength, although she could stay on her feet for hours in search of an antique, but a strength of will. There was no quaver in her voice, no hesitancy.

"Are you sure, dear?"

"Don't try to weasel your way around me. I'll attend to you when we get back to Grosse Pointe."

Flemington swallowed, rested his head in one hand. Too much sun. What was the line from Danny Deever? He had recited it in high school. Kipling was his idol. *A touch of sun, a touch of sun, the color sergeant said.*

"It would be a shame to miss Rome."

"So you can sneak into her room again?"

"You have to believe me, Lu. I haven't been with Theresa."

"I know Detchema. She didn't buy that necklace. And don't give me any line about Wattle or the guide buying it for her." Lulu turned on her side and showed Flemington her narrow back, her pitiful buttocks. "She couldn't buy it for herself. Not on a teacher's salary, and besides, she doesn't know a decent piece of jewelry when she sees one."

But she asks about Mozart and Giotto, Flemington thought. The lying was getting stickier; he was no good at it. In the old days on the newspaper he had lied to cover for drunken reporters, stupid copy boys, desk men who botched headlines. The managing editor knew Flemington was lying to protect someone. Too tolerant for his own good, the managing editor told him.

"I can't argue with you. You're upset over nothing."

"Tell me how that perfume got on your shirt, that Sulka I bought you."

"You imagined it."

"Like hell I did. She wears it all the time. You were with her."

He would have to buttress the lie, insist she was mistaken, that in her fatigued state she was hallucinating, sniffing odors that weren't there, inventing fictions about Theresa's topaz necklace. He would be attentive, agree with her, get her home. In the quiet of the mansion he would tell her he was leaving. The divorce would be no problem. She would need nothing, would find a new husband. Applicants would be backed up in their circular driveway, clogging the port-cochere, parked on the lawn under the copper beeches.

"Are you sure you want to go home?"

"Tomorrow. I've had enough of this. We'll settle this at home."

A stab of dread touched Flemington's navel. Would Lulu throw him out? Get rid of him before he told her he was leaving? That would be hard to take. But it would solve a great deal.

"All right. I'll talk to Pepi about getting us on a flight tomorrow morning."

Flemington got up, gathered up his airline tickets, wallet, passport, and walked to the door. As soon as he was in the lofty corridor he heard her belly-deep sobs. She sounded as if she were in convulsion—the noises indecently loud and rhythmic. It's all pain, Flemington thought, the whole mess. Did anything work out any more? There was more to be endured than enjoyed in the general condition of human life, old Johnson had said. Flemington wondered: Is part of our problem that we refuse to accept this?

There was an ancient piano in one of the sitting rooms. Around it some of the tour members had gathered to listen to Ibith Grant. The doctor's wife played popular songs in a steady beat, as if she had taken proper middle-class lessons as a child in Atlanta.

Herbie was leading the singing. Everyone had a drink in his hand. The sun-seared day had come to a joyful close. More to be endured than enjoyed? Harry wondered. He should have been getting more out of the trip. Reacting to Bethlehem, and Santa Sophia and the Mattyas Church. But Theresa had ruined his powers of concentration. Craving her, he could not lose himself in the Schönbrunn Palace or the Louvre.

"Join the party, Harry," Herbie bellowed. "In ten minutes, my wife does a striptease. Flo, hang on the curtain and bump a few times for Mr. Flemington."

Dimly, through the fuzzed light, Flemington saw their smiling faces. Enduring or enjoying? Mr. Wattle was lifting a glass, beckoning to him. Mavis Hutzler was head to head with A. T. Gunthorpe and J. P. Huggins, trying to get them to harmonize. The perky wife of the fruit grower had a sweet voice. The Vandalia thrush?

"Fools rush in . . . where angels fear to tread . . .
And so I come to you, my love . . ."

Virgil walked toward Flemington. "Mr. Flemington. Will you and your wife be attending the sound and light show at the Citadel tonight?"

"No, we're tired. In fact, I have a rather urgent matter to discuss with you."

> ". . . so open up your heart and let
> This fool rush in!"

The men applauded. Herbie whistled. A waiter appeared with a new round of drinks. Mr. Gunthorpe was buying.

"We want to fly back tomorrow," Flemington said.

"Ah, I am sorry. Madame is . . ."

"Not feeling well. The heat was too much for her."

"Perhaps a day of rest tomorrow? You can skip Tel Aviv and meet us at the airport. Or fly to Rome a day later. . . ."

"No, thank you, Pepi. Any morning flight to New York. With a connection to Detroit. Two first-class seats. And if you could give our baggage your personal attention."

"Of course, Mr. Flemington."

Theresa appeared in the doorway of the lounge. She was wearing a soft white dress, white shoes. Her hair was done up in a pale blue turban. It was an old-fashioned style, but it was flattering to her— tufts of brown curls peeking from beneath the silk folds.

"Hey, Terry!" Dr. Grant cried. "We need one more soprano! Herbie keeps drowning out the women!"

"Good evening," Harry said.

"Hello." She smiled at both of them. "Pepi, this hotel is a dream. There's a hallway upstairs filled with cases of pottery from the digs at Jericho."

"I am glad you like it, Mrs. Carrell."

"You two look grim," she said. "Is the singing that bad?"

> "I left my heart at the stage door canteen . . .
> I left it there with a girl named Irene . . ."

"Mr. and Mrs. Flemington are flying back tomorrow," Virgil said. "I gather Mrs. Flemington is exhausted."

Theresa pursed her lips. "I'm sorry. It's nothing serious?"

"No. Fatigue. She'll be fine once we're home. Lu doesn't have too much staying power. It's a tribute to her courage that she held up as well as she did."

"It surely is, sir." Virgil bowed slightly. "If you will excuse me, I will call the airlines."

Flemington took Theresa's elbow—not before Flo Shackman and Shirl Shapiro noticed—and directed her outside the doorway of the lounge. In the corridor, he moved her toward a potted palm.

"Listen. She knows everything. Don't ask me how. Something about your perfume. Detchema."

"That's what I use."

"And the necklace. Terry, that was stupid to go around showing it off. Lulu has a nose for things. She knows where things come from, what they are worth, who buys them. I lied. I said she was imagining it all."

"Did she believe you?"

"No."

Theresa inhaled. Never, never had she seemed to Flemington more dignified, more excitingly the combination of aloofness and passion that had always intrigued him. She was a woman who always seemed to be saying, "I detest sex, I am untouchable," while her precise meaning was the opposite.

"So . . . you're going back to Detroit?" Her voice was unshaken.

"Look, this won't impede our plans. Once I get her home, and rested, and back into the country club, she'll calm down. I'll ask for the divorce. It shouldn't be a problem. I don't own a thing she wants and she can support an army of husbands, or lovers, or whatever."

Theresa pushed the curls back into the turban. "I have a feeling you won't. One more cop-out by the old rewrite man."

"I love you, Terry."

"I believe you. But I wonder if you want to carry that sentiment to its logical conclusion. Apart from seizing me in hotel rooms and throwing me onto a bed."

"You don't regret anything we've done, do you?"

"No, dammit. That's the tragedy of all this. I can't even try to get angry with you or lose patience. You're just there—a force of nature, an act of God—and I accept you."

He took her bare upper arms, kissed her softly on the cheek. "Oh, my love. It isn't late at all. For once in my life I'm going to make a decision. I promise, promise, promise. I'll be calling you every other day when I get back home."

"Will you really? Don't you think she'll know?"

"I'll sneak away. Keep a pocketful of change for long distance."

Mr. Wattle's bald head popped into view. He emerged from the lounge, amid strains of "Deep Purple," carrying a drink for Theresa.

"Ah, there we are. Terry, your scotch and soda. Evening, Flemington."

"Good evening." Flemington coughed, looked down, and mumbled to Theresa: "Yes, it's that small jewelry shop in the Old City. My wife says you'll find what you want there. Same sort of pin she was wearing."

404

Mr. Wattle stepped smartly toward them, as Flemington walked to his room. "Hear tell the Flemingtons are leaving us," he piped. "A pity. Fine people. Gave our humble group a touch of class."

From the singers, Flemington heard:

> "This love of mine goes on and on . . .
> Though life is empty, since you have gone . . ."

Day 18: Israel–Rome. We leave Jerusalem by motor coach to spend
a morning in Tel Aviv. A bus tour of Israel's modern metropolis
—Dizengoff Circle, Tel Aviv University, broad avenues and
teeming streets. A stop for shopping in late morning—leather
goods, antiques, and high fashion are worth a look.

Lunch in the charming old quarter of Jaffa, by the sea, look-
ing at Andromeda's Rocks. (A possibility for those interested:
lunch at a nearby kibbutz and a look at kibbutz life.)

In late afternoon we board our plane for the flight to Eternal
Rome. On the way to our hotel, some of the Italian capital's
monuments—the Colosseum, the Palatine, the Baths of Cara-
calla, the Piazza Venezia, the Victor Emmanuel Monument,
the Campidoglio. (Full bus tour tomorrow.) In the evening—
Aida in the Baths of Caracalla, or sitting in the Via Veneto,
sipping coffee, and watching the international set!

"*Mamenu,*" Herbie muttered. "She looks like a sick chicken."

With a dozen members of the party, waiting for the bus in front of
the hotel, he watched Lulu Flemington being helped into a Peugeot
taxi. The rack on the cab roof was stacked high with their luggage. So
was the trunk and the front seat. It had taken the driver a half hour
to arrange the valises to Flemington's satisfaction, before an audience
of the Shackmans, the Shapiros, and the Yasudas, who had awakened
at dawn and visited the Western Wall.

"Like to know what that haul is worth," Shirl whispered.

"She can afford it," Flo said.

"I hope she has enough dough left to keep that husband in line,"
Shirl muttered.

"Don't count on it."

"I heard, I heard. Him and Terry last night. Something was going
on. When we were singing, remember?"

Their two lacquered heads bobbed and chirped. *Oh, to know what
had happened!* The previous night at dinner, and after the sound and
light show at the Citadel, they had pumped Pepi, bought him a drink
at the French Colony Bar, probing the middle-aged triangle that had
become the talk of the trip. But the tour escort would divulge nothing.
"I am the soul of discretion, ladies," he said. "And besides, I am in ig-

norance of anything, except that Mrs. Flemington is exhausted and wishes to go home."

"Hah!" Flo laughed. "I'd like to believe that."

Huggins, seated at the bar, he and Barbara sipping Israeli beer, was tempted to tell what he knew. Flemington had confided in him. Why he would never be able to imagine. Lawyer? A sneakiness that suggested a confidant? Or perhaps because J.P. had simply been near at hand when Flemington could not contain his misery any longer.

"How about it, Jimmy?" Flo had asked, bending toward the attorney. "You know what happened? Ibith and Doc Grant told us Terry knew Harry a long time ago. Is it true?"

"Beats me, Flo."

"Ah, you're hiding somethin'," Flo said.

Huggins shook his head. Mixed feelings coursed through him. The Carrell woman: a lot of class. And maybe too much strength. Tall strong women were like that, full of character and sacrifice. They sometimes asked for trouble. Unless they lucked out on a first marriage, they often had a bad time of it. Rosie Wicker, she was in the same league with Theresa. But Rosie had found that long-legged dentist. A good marriage. Terry had selected losers, second-raters. Even Flemington—all surface, nothing inside. In a way, women like Barbara were more fortunate. They set limits on their world—husband, children, home, and such burning issues as whether the A & P or Finast was better for veal cutlets.

"I'm busting to *know,*" Flo said. "I'll die if I don't find out."

Herbie slumped deep in a low red plush chair. He appeared to be changing shape, his soft flesh melting into waxen puddles. "Finish ya drink, Florence. I'm gettin' up early to see the wall. I wanna wail a little."

"They don't wail any more," Si said. "Western Wall, Western Wall."

"Me they'll let wail."

Under the unabashed stares of the other tourists, the Flemingtons came out of the hotel. Virgil guided them to the Peugeot and spoke to the driver. Money changed hands. Lulu got into the taxi and vanished into a corner.

"Like the Queen of England," Herbie said to Si.

Flemington, as dapper as the first day they had seen him, suede hat on his handsome head, a shoulder bag draped over his seersucker jacket, looked toward the group—the Shackmans, the Shapiros, the Yasudas, several of the Midwesterners, the Hutzlers. Thank God, he thought, Terry isn't there.

407

"Good-by," Harry said. "Sorry we couldn't finish the trip with you."

"Likewise," Herbie said. "Hope the missus perks up."

"Thank you."

"You drive by Westbury, look us up," Flo said. "We're in the book."

"Thanks. Enjoy Rome." Flemington got into the taxi. Virgil leaned into the window for some final advice. Herbie and the others saw Flemington hand him something: *tip*.

"Wonder what he gave him?" Si said.

"That guy?" Herbie asked rhetorically. "The more they got, the more they hold onto it."

The cab sped off. Virgil watched it depart. He hated losing people before a tour ended. A report in triplicate would have to be filed. Already he had cabled New York, assuring them that nothing that Planet Tours had done had impelled the Flemingtons to leave. Trapani would meet the Flemingtons at JFK, expedite their baggage, arrange for the connection to Detroit. So occupied was he with the Flemington affair that he did not examine the bills until he was back in the lobby and had roused a few laggards at breakfast. "Mr. Wattle, please. Dr. Grant, we are ready. Mrs. Carrell. Mr. Kuchtenberg."

He glanced at his tip: *five hundred dollars*. It was a new record for him.

"What? No one gets paid? They work for nothing?" Mr. Wattle's voice soared. "That's inhuman. That can't work."

But there was a tremor in his voice; for once his cocksureness deserted him. Hanan Gilad had seen it happen before. Most Americans had trouble accepting the kibbutz formula. People worked for *nothing*? Doctors, school principals, factory foremen gave all their earnings over to the kibbutz? The members got only what they needed, and a bit more?

Over a heavy lunch, the feature of which was a chunk of fatty lamb in orange gravy, the sabra patiently explained the way Kfar Levin was set up. A new kibbutz; post-1948; non-religious; half orientals and half Ashkenazim with a few Americans. Mrs. Grant and Mrs. Carrell, teachers, had naturally been interested in communal child rearing. The Jewish couples wanted to know if there was a souvenir shop; if Kfar Levin had a resthouse to which they might return someday. But it was Horace T. Wattle who was most agitated by the dusty farm buildings on the outskirts of Tel Aviv.

"How many people live on these? Half the country? A third?" His eyes darted around the plain dining hall.

"A little over three per cent," Hanan said.

"Ahah! If it's so great—"

"We regard the kibbutzim as a cadre, an example for the rest of the country. Our Parliament members, army officers, a very high per cent come from the kibbutzim."

"Can't wait to get out!" Wattle said. "It can't work, no incentive. I heard you, young man. You were born on one and you left."

"We are not prisoners. People have a choice."

"And they leave. Nobody works without a reward, or a threat."

"That can't be true," Mrs. Grant said.

"Ask the man who pays the salaries," Mr. Wattle crowed. Still he was uneasy. Hanan had said that the kibbutzim made money, expanded from agriculture to manufacturing, raised children who ran the country, set an example. It was unnatural. It was unpatriotic. It was against everything in which he believed.

"You should stay here awhile," Hanan said, nodding in the direction of the kibbutz physician. "Like Dr. Rosenbloom, who gets no money, nothing, just lives here and takes care of them. He came from Brooklyn five years ago to look around. Listen, they assemble switchboards here, they'd make you a foreman."

"Not a chance," the Washington man shouted. "Nothing personal, but I give it ten years."

Gilad yawned. "So join the parade, mister. Kings, popes, dictators, they have been giving us ten years for a long, long time. We're still here."

On the bus, riding to Lod Airport, Hanan noted the soberness of the visitors. The kibbutz tended to do this to Americans. Turned their minds inside out. What? People work for nothing? But thank goodness only three per cent of them do!

Father Konay was seated across from the Grants. Several times he tried to say something to them, seeking the precise words. "This community business," he said, "raising the children together, working together. You wonder we haven't tried it. I mean, in the inner cities." He felt uncomfortable using the words; they were Father Folker's words.

"I wondered about that," Dr. Grant said. "Take the kids out of the bum homes, away from irresponsible parents. It might work."

"You couldn't help wondering. Away from drugs and bad influences." How far, the priest wondered, dare I go? What would Ed Marciniek think?

"You'd have to motivate them," Ibith said warily. "I don't think it would be easy. Henderson gets called an Oreo every time he tries to work on an interracial committee. If we suggested communal child rearing someone would holler genocide."

"It isn't easy, I guess," Father Konay said. What was any longer? "You wonder how these people did it, accomplished all this."

Herbie, eavesdropping, but refraining from offering opinions, shouted to Hanan: "Yeah, Hanan, how did you people do all this?"

Gilad turned around and adjusted his sunglasses. The bus turned into Lod Airport. It seemed even busier than the day they arrived—buses, cabs, *sheruts*, private cars.

"In five thousand years you learn a few things," he said.

Virgil, liberated from the Flemingtons' luggage—they had departed on a 10 A.M. flight to New York, escorted to the plane by a TWA public relations man—was able to move faster in getting people through check-in, baggage, customs, and the searches of Israeli security police.

"If it wasn't for Israel, I'd've screamed," Shirl said, coming out of the inspection booth. "Into the brassieres and girdle yet, looking for grenades."

"In yours they wouldn't fit," Herbie said. "Listen, that cop was in my *gotkes*. I said, 'Look, I'm a UJA member from Long Island, would I be carrying a gun?' Not a smile. I thought he was a proctologist."

Theresa, laughing with Ibith at the thoroughness of the search (the newspapers had carried stories of new threats by Palestinian guerrillas), came out of the curtained booth. "I would be wearing my tightest panty girdle," Ibith giggled. "It was an effort. The girl kept looking me over like I was Mrs. Eldridge Cleaver. She should know what a middle-class straight I am."

"Apologies are in order," Virgil said as he led them to the departure lounge. "They have no choice."

A hostess working for the airport, a girl in white blouse and blue skirt, came up to Virgil with an envelope.

The guide read the name: *Mrs. Carrell.* He looked around. Theresa had gone into the departure area. She and the Bettenhausens were walking toward the currency exchange counter. "A letter for you, Mrs. Carrell," Pepi said.

She recognized Harry's writing at once. A desk man's hand; readable, no problems for the typesetters.

"You go ahead," she said to Cornelia. "I only have some small bills. I'll buy souvenirs." She sat in a black chair, between two bearded elders in black suits. A taste of the ancestral land and back to Brooklyn? Their parchment faces appeared eternally peaceful. Arnie Wicker and she had talked about it after they had seen the Orthodox swaying in front of the Western Wall. Were these practitioners of an ancient faith the most serene men on earth? She tore open the letter. On a sheet of French Colony Hotel stationery she read:

Darling:
When you get this, Lu and I will be winging back home. She is in bad shape. Her radar is frightening. She knows everything about us—what happened on the tour. I denied it. I keep denying it. That seems to make her angrier. What can I tell you except that I am obligated to stay with her, calm her down, get her straightened out? This won't take more than a few weeks once we are back home, although I am worried about the bad influence her friends have on her. Once Lu is placid again, I'll try breaking my decision to her. By then she may be glad to be rid of me. We'll see. Meanwhile, I love you more than anyone in the world. The time we spent alone together on this trip—surely the best it ever was with us. Middle age has lent a certain tone to our relationship, and it is beyond my meager powers of description to do it justice. It's right and good and fine. Passion overlaid with reflection, reminiscences. I can't wait until we are together again. I'll put my ingenious mind to work and see what kind of arrangement I can rig for our next meeting.

All my love,
H.

"Letter from home?" Ibith asked.
"No. Just some local business."
"Hmmm. You look rough, Terry."
Theresa looked up. "I feel fine. Can't wait for Rome."
Across the lounge, the Westbury people had swarmed around a souvenir counter. Ibith and Theresa could hear Flo's voice: "Gimme two for five bucks? Hah? You know what it is to *hondle?*" And a salesgirl's firm response: "Not here, missus. Here is prices fixed." Flo was holding up a pair of woven neckties; she would not surrender.
They saw Herbie plodding away. He was talking to Dr. Wicker. "Not after the kibbutz. Not after what I saw this morning. That's the worst part of good people. They take the fun out of life. You worry you aren't any good any more, always buying, bargaining, grabbing. I'm through, finished. From now on I don't buy a postcard."
Theresa listened ruefully to Herbie's confessional. Years ago she had worked for a stiff-necked principal (was he a Mormon?) whose favorite lecture dealt with "wants and needs." Needs should be filled, he would advise the senior class, and no person need feel guilty about striving to meet his needs. But *wants* were another thing.

"More sorrow and more misery result," Mr. Brackthwaite intoned, "when we spend our lives trying to fill our *wants*. Boys and girls, learn to distinguish between *wants and needs*. . . ."

Mr. Brackthwaite loomed in her mind: cold comfort, a bleak prairie view of life, and the children would snicker and yawn. But was the man wrong? At this moment, sodden with goods, drowning in guilt because he had seen the self-denying people of the kibbutz, was not Herbie Shackman one of Mr. Brackthwaite's disciples?

And what about herself? She held Harry's letter lightly, as if it were a used Kleenex, a scrap to discard. *What kind of arrangement I can rig for our next meeting.* Between the assuring lines she read the bad news, the failure of nerve. No hero, Harry. Oh, he couldn't be blamed for worrying about Lulu, for getting her back to Grosse Pointe in one piece, dried out, the working parts in order. *We'll see.* Foolishly, a middle-aged woman weary of a lonely life, she'd come after her first and only love. A poor thing but her own. And then she had been unwilling to be victimized. Wants rather than needs. She did not *need* Harry Flemington. She *needed* a job, an apartment, food, some friends, and some security for her son in college. She *wanted* Harry. A rude business, she thought, and it would have been helpful to weep great gasping sobs, to fall into Ibith's arms, to bawl out the whole story. My strength is my weakness, Theresa thought. A woman of character, people always said about her. Calm brow, pensive dark eyes, soft voice. And inside the sense of loss. Missed chances, the great love gone forever. She tried to console herself: there was the possibility that, married to Harry, sleeping and rising with him, sharing arguments over breakfast, spats about the car, niggling disputes, her conception of him might change. Was it possible that his elegance and his style were dependent on subsidization—which she could hardly supply on a teacher's salary, even were it augmented with income from his "writing"? It was hell to be an economic determinist when thundering passions were involved but maybe it was best to let Harry play out his string. Feeble and trembling, like the Legrands, they might yet make it, if Lulu succumbed to cirrhosis of the liver or some other boozer's malady. At age seventy, they would find one another, too old for orgasm, holding hands in a St. Petersburg park. . . .

The last few days of a tour could be a trial, Pepi knew. Tempers frayed; bodies sagged; spirits flagged. Mr. Legrand had to be almost carried from the bus through passport control, security inspection. He was now stretched out on three black lounge chairs. But he did not appear to be asleep. His feverish eyes were open, staring at the souvenir stand.

"My sweetie is managing, Pepi," the old lady said. "Never complains. I'm so proud of him."

"If there is anything I can do, Mrs. Legrand."

"Need any medicine, Ma?" Herbie asked. "Flo got the first aid kit out. Anti-histamines, super-vitamins, decongestants, *vais vus*."

"Weston has everything, thank you, Harvey."

Herbie took her hand and squeezed it. "He got you, Ma, and that's everything. Flo and I should be so good to each other when we get as far as you have. *Seit gesundt*."

Bettenhausen, beckoning to Dr. Wicker with his leonine head, dialed the number of the Jerusalem *Post* from a pay phone and asked for Hanan's friend Mendel Matzkin.

"*Shalom*."

"*Shalom*. Mendel, this is Hanan Gilad's friend, the American journalist Mr. Bettenhausen."

"I don't care."

"I know you don't, my dear man. Do you have any further information on the arrival in Israel of Dr. Anatoly Borkin, the Russian scientist?"

"Oh. Oh. *That* fellow." There was a pause while Mendel sorted out his privy information. When he spoke again, there was a note of admiration in his voice. "Listen, mister, how come you knew before we did? Who are you with? New York *Times*? *Time*? I am impressed. That's very good to know about Borkin."

"Then he's here."

"Of course. But only a few people know."

"That should establish my credentials. Now can you tell me, sir, what are the circumstances of his arrival? Is he here for good? Why did the Russians let him out?"

"Ah, ah, ah, too much already you are asking."

"Why? Is it secret?"

"No. Is just nobody here knows. Listen, if the Jerusalem *Post* doesn't know, nobody knows."

"I knew."

"So? So maybe you're not a journalist. Maybe you're a CIA-nik."

"Maybe I am. You can't reveal anything else, except that Dr. Borkin is here?"

"He's having a press conference tonight. How come you weren't invited if you're such a big shot, hah? Six o'clock by the Ministry of Immigration."

"I shall be in Rome then."

"So, you'll read in the papers. All right?"

"All right. By the way, what is your job at the paper, in case I have to correspond with you?"

"Job? I run the cafeteria."

"Oh, of course," Bettenhausen said, raging. "That would explain your fund of accurate information."

"Don't joke, mister. Over a cup of tea, there are no secrets in Israel. We're a small country."

Bettenhausen hung up. He was livid. "An admirable people, your coreligionists, Arnold. But they are capable of driving a rational man up the wall."

Virgil appreciated the beautiful wide-eyed Alitalia hostesses. Italian women were his favorites. *La Favorita.* Bellini? No, Donizetti. Writing the daily report, the evaluation of the tour (the departure of the Flemingtons would require a separate letter), he hummed the overture to *La Favorita*.

A fair Italian girl with eyes like a Tintoretto madonna moved down the aisle, her limbs and back operating on ingenious ball bearings. Products of Italian art and engineering. Gratified, Virgil stared at the tight tan skirt. Superb. As aesthetically perfect as the Grand March from *Norma*.

Once, with a tour standing in spring sunlight outside the Quirinale Palace, he had heard the carabinieri band, in their black, white, and red uniforms, serenade visitors with a medley from *Norma*. Never had Bellini sounded better. It was before smog and dirt had begun to ruin Rome. A moment of absolute perfection hanging in the limpid Italian air. He had cried. Italy did that to him. All the beauty, all the grace, all the genius—and indeed all the cruelty, cunning, and meanness—of which men were capable, in one poor nation. Did he, mongrel European that he was, love Italy because he liked to think it was so much like himself?

"You're staring too long, Pepi," Theresa said to him.

"Beg pardon, Mrs. Carrell?"

"Back to your report. That stewardess is lovely, but she's vanished into first class."

"Ah, but she may return any minute."

"They don't always. Maybe she's on her way to a star."

"No, Mrs. Carrell. The Italian are earth-oriented people. They are part of this world. They will always be here."

"Are we supposed to take heart from that?"

"I think so. It is a shame you cannot spend a month in Italy. A year would be better."

He knew, he knew, Theresa thought. He knew everything. He

knew that she and Harry had been lovers—long ago and again on this tour. And he knew why Mrs. Flemington had ordered her husband to take her home. And this was Virgil's way of telling her to be hopeful.

"Therapy?" she asked. "A cure for unrequited love?"

Pepi shuffled the papers on the top of his battered attaché case. *Daily Log. Travel documentation. Expense Account.* "Perhaps."

"Eternal Rome, that sort of thing? I'm afraid the eternal verities aren't much help to a bruised ego and a battered heart."

"Eternal Rome may not be. One can take or leave the Christian monuments and the pagan stones. But, ah, the Italians themselves. They have learned the secret of holding on to what is valid. Not, I assure you, making the most of a bad thing, but getting the best out of everything. Even in their anger and despair, there is drama, color, a grasp of life."

"I guess I'm supposed to cheer up the first time one of those Roman Lotharios pats my rear end. Pepi, I'm in my middle forties."

"You shall indeed be patted. I assure you it will make you feel better."

Harry would never be hers. Oh, he'd come around in a year or so for his hour of shivering passion in a motel room. That was not what she wanted. In despair, she had come after him, connived, and reappeared, a vision from their panting past. But Lulu had been too strong, too clever by far, for either of them. She shut her eyes. They were beginning the descent to Rome.

"Hey, Pepi, what's that beach place down there?" Herbie shouted. "With the pine trees?"

"Fregene, sir. A beach resort."

"Wow," Murray Yasuda said. "Sophia Loren?"

"No longer. It was an exclusive place until the new airport was built. Now it is noisy and dirty and impossible to sleep. You can buy villas very cheap. No one wants to stay there any longer."

"I read somewhere that's happening all over Italy," Mavis said to Ed.

"Said what? Can't hear."

"Turn up your hearing aid."

"Oh. Sorry, Mave. Said what?"

"I said I heard that it's happening all over Italy."

"What's happening, hon?"

"Pollution. Industry. Airports. Ruining the beaches and the churches and the works of art. The statues in Venice are crumbling."

"You can't stop progress," Mr. Hutzler said.

"Amen," Mr. Wattle added. "That pollution thing is a racket. All those people complaining about industrial wastes and so on, they'd be the first to bellyache."

"Fasten seat belts," the girl said. "We are landing in Roma, Leonardo Da Vinci Airport, Fiumicino."

"Only the Italians," Rosie said. "Imagine—they name an airport after Leonardo."

"And," Bettenhausen said, "proceed to ravage the beaches and pine forests with it."

"So, ladies and gentlemen, that is San Giovanni in Laterano," Pepi said. "St. John in Lateran. The cathedral of Rome and of the world. Look, please, at the roof, with sixteen statues. Christ, the Apostles and saints. On the right, the big door is the Porta Santa, which is opened only in Holy Years."

Father Konay, invigorated, stared at the soaring two-storied façade of San Giovanni in Laterano. A bit different, he thought, than the fake red brick shingling of Sacred Heart in Ash Valley. It was the spirit that counted, not the externals. Why then all the magnificent palaces of Rome? No harm in them. Lasting beauty. Built for the ages. That Catholics might come and admire them. And non-believers be won over. Although from the casual comments of his fellow tourists, he wondered: Do these palaces and monuments bring in converts?

It was dusk, the sky charged with streaks of lavender and rose. The bus proceeded slowly in the late traffic. In a few minutes the tourists lapsed into silence. Rome, Virgil knew, worked its magic. It always did. It was, for all the noise and crowding and frenzy, a restful place. What was it? The ease with which the Italians contended with history? The fact that they lived—harassed, noisy, family-driven —among monuments of the classical world? Even the most obtuse of visitors was affected by the city and its people. Romans took their centuries of civilization with a cup of espresso, ate their *gelati* alongside Renaissance fountains, wheeled prams in the shadow of Farnese palaces, held hands and kissed under imperial arches.

"The Arch of Constantine, ladies and gentlemen," Virgil said to the silent passengers. "And beyond the Colosseum.

"And here is the Arch of Titus. For those of you of the Jewish faith, it will be interesting to look at the carvings inside which commemorate Titus' conquest of Jerusalem. There is inside the arch a carving of Titus' procession after conquering Jerusalem, with the soldiers carrying the candlesticks."

"The menorah?" Shirl asked.

"Yes, madame."

416

"Them too," Herbie said. "I always thought the Italians got along with us." He eased himself forward, puffing on one of the last of his Cuban cigars. "Hey, Barbara."

Barbara Huggins turned her face. "Whaddya want, Herbie?"

"See? See what your people did to our people? You gonna apologize? After the way we back each other in the elections?"

"What's he talkin' about?" Barbara asked her husband.

"Herbie's needling, Barbs. He thinks you're a descendant of the Roman emperors."

"Maybe I am."

"Arabs, more like it. All those southern *walyones* who came to America. Arabs and Greeks."

"That isn't funny."

"I know. It's terrible." Huggins was dreaming. He always knew Rome would do this to him. Up until several years ago he had corresponded with Buck Sweeney. Married to an Italian or French girl? Living in Rome, working for some foundation, some free-load? He would have to find Bernard Kevin Sweeney, old Buckie from Fordham.

The Forum, the Campidoglio, the Vittorio Emmanuel Monument. Huggins wondered: how had people like the Malfis blown this? They could have run America if they'd followed up on what the Romans had given them. But they (the Malfis anyway) had ended up drinking beer instead of wine, eating steak instead of pasta, unaware of the Emperor Trojan, or Brunelleschi's dome, or Giotto's "O." He tried to be charitable: the potential was there, but something had gone wrong.

"They blew it," he said.

"Who?" Barbara asked.

"Oh, the *walyones*. All this to work with. And they end up robbing airplanes at JFK."

The Hotel Vittorio Veneto was three blocks from the Via Veneto, on the Via Sicilia. It was a quiet neighborhood of office buildings and small shops, and the hotel, while attractive inside, had a severe look about it—the façade chipped and painted over in characteristic Roman tangerine.

"Another dump," Herbie said to Virgil.

"I do not think so, sir. You will find the rooms pleasant."

Virgil, despite the descending darkness, kept his sunglasses on. Better not to betray his impatience. He stood stolidly at the door helping people down.

417

"Opera tonight?" Rosie Wicker asked. "Is there a chance? In the Baths of Caracalla?"

"I shall check, Mrs. Wicker."

Sandra and Murray Yasuda, barely visible beneath their haul of purchases, were the last to get off the bus, except for the Legrands. The tiny Japanese woman looked frightened. "Pepi, Mr. Legrand is sick again," she said. "It looks like he passed out."

Virgil spoke in Italian to the doorman. (Crazy, Cornelia Bettenhausen thought: he had become an Italian now, gesturing, speaking in a staccato rhythmic manner.) The doorman responded: he would tell the concierge to look after room assignments.

Mounting the bus steps, Virgil's eyes sought Dr. Grant. He called to him. The physician deposited his handbag alongside the hotel entrance and followed the guide back to the bus.

The Legrands were alone. They were seated in the rear. Mr. Legrand's homburg was well forward on his head. He seemed to have lost control of his spine. His body looked as if it had been dumped into the bus seat. Mrs. Legrand was gently folding his hands in his lap. The day had been hot and dry, but he wore his black topcoat.

"My sweetie isn't well," Mrs. Legrand said.

"He has fainted again?" Virgil asked.

"I think so. I hate to trouble Dr. Grant. He has been so kind to us."

Beneath the down-tilted brim of the homburg, Mr. Legrand's mouth was frozen in a toothy smile.

Dr. Grant swallowed. The frown dug deep into his brow. He knew the look. He knew the smell. The attitudes of surrender. "May I get next to your husband, Mrs. Legrand?" he asked.

"Of course, Dr. Grant. He's so tired, the poor thing. Poor Weston."

Mrs. Legrand shuffled out of her seat. The bus was empty except for the old couple, the guide, and the doctor. On the sidewalk in front of the hotel, a Neapolitan whom Virgil had seen in the area for ten years was trying to peddle watches.

"So tired," the old woman said. "I sometimes think maybe this trip was a mistake."

Dr. Grant took his pulse, bent his head against the crumpled chest. It seemed to have been crushed inside the coat.

"Excuse me," the physician said. He put an arm under Mr. Legrand's shoulder and lifted him. When Virgil saw the old man's body flop, lax, boneless, in the doctor's arms, he knew at once. In Auschwitz. In Theresienstadt. The old people in the barracks. Taking them out in the morning after a cold night. He was twelve years old. Helping out. A strong boy.

Dr. Grant stretched Mr. Legrand on his back in the aisle of the bus.

418

Then he straddled him. He put his lips to the old man's and began to breathe into his mouth.

"Dr. Grant is so kind," the old woman said. "I can tell you, it won't help. Poor Weston has gone to his reward."

"Don't say that, Mrs. Legrand," Pepi said. His role as comforter, as the grownup who buoyed the courage of children, was sometimes a hard one to sustain.

Dr. Grant was massaging the man's chest. He had opened the coat, a jacket, a winter-weight shirt, yanked up the undershirt. He heard nothing.

"Dr. Grant, that isn't necessary." She was sitting on the arm of a bus seat, patting her white bangs. Virgil was astonished by her calm. On her creased face there was no tear. "Weston told me he was ready to move on. He said he had gone as far as he could, and that he was grateful he had me at his side all these years."

"I have great faith in Dr. Grant," Virgil said, with less conviction than he normally managed. His mind raced ahead: the night clerk at the American Embassy, the Questura, a man from the Health Department, the local office of Planet Tours, the New York office by telex. Perhaps the AP and UP men would want to know about the death.

Dr. Grant eased himself into a kneeling position. He had given up on mouth-to-mouth resuscitation, abandoned chest massage. The old man was finished, beyond help. He had simply run down. At age eighty-five, he had held on admirably, gone quietly and with dignity, bothering no one.

"I'm afraid, Mrs. Legrand . . ."

"I know, I know, Doctor. I knew it when Weston took my hand."

"I am terribly sorry, Mrs. Legrand," Dr. Grant said.

Herbie Shackman poked his bloated face into the bus. "Ma? You okay? Somethin' happen?" The fat man saw Legrand stretched out on the aisle, the feet pointing up, the doctor and guide with their heads huddled. "Pa fainted? He don't feel so hot?"

And outside Flo's shaking voice: "Herbie! Leave them be! Butt out!"

"I thought maybe I could help. Flo's got a whole drugstore . . ."

Virgil had to restrain himself from warning Mrs. Legrand not to say anything. It was a demeaning notion, but he had his job, and the old man was dead. The escort did not want news of the death disseminated until tomorrow. People took disasters better in the morning. And the tour was still in progress, people looking for fun, relaxation, their money's worth . . .

Mrs. Legrand was a step ahead of him. Admiration for the old

419

woman bloomed in Pepi. "Thank you, Harvey, but Weston is fine. He's tired, that's all."

"Only trying to help." His inflated figure retreated. Street lights had gone on. The neon sign outside the Vittorio Veneto Hotel blinked in frigid blue. Hardly the blue of the Virgin's robe in the Sistine Chapel, Pepi thought, but a sign of life, of movement, of beds and meals and tour reservations. . . . How delicious were the most mundane, trivial details, he reflected. The Italians had a marvelous word for detailed enlargements of works of art: *particolari*. The *particolari* of life were so important. No one knew this better than Italians.

"I'll help you with—" Dr. Grant stopped short.

"If you will stay with Mrs. Legrand, please," Virgil said. "I shall call the police and they will send an ambulance. The Italians are sympathetic and efficient in these matters." He bowed deeply and, to his own surprise, felt tears forming his eyes. "Mrs. Legrand, I extend my profound sympathies to you in your loss. Your husband was a gentle man, and he added much to this group. We shall miss him, and I shall do everything in my power to make this ordeal easier for you to bear."

"You're kind, Pepi."

"Would you care to come into the hotel and rest? Dr. Grant and I will stay with your husband."

"Oh no. We were together so long, you know. Never apart. I'm much happier being at his side. Weston looks peaceful, don't you think?"

"I do, madame. He died without pain and with the same dignity he manifested in life." Virgil bowed again. "Dr. Grant, if you will stay with Mrs. Legrand . . . ?"

"Of course." The physician put an arm around her shoulder. She was wearing her lavender suit. Gratefully, she patted his hand. "You don't have to. All the fun you'll have tonight . . ."

"No, no. I don't mind."

Virgil moved to the door. He wanted the driver to move the bus into an alley around the corner. No need to draw a crowd when the ambulance arrived.

In his hotel room, Virgil roused the Planet Tour office manager, a dour Milanese named Aldo Capelli, who arrived at the hotel in twenty minutes. Capelli took over the handling of the death of Mr. Legrand, while Pepi made arrangements for the night's entertainments.

"What's with Pa Barker?" Herbie insisted as the bus, divested of the corpse, fumigated, windows cleaned at Mr. Wattle's insistence, rode to the Baths of Caracalla. They were in luck: *Aida*. Elephants, camels, a cast of thousands in the outdoor amphitheater.

420

"I am not sure I know," Pepi said.

"He looked pretty *shvach* to me," Herbie said. "Stretched out on the floor like a herring. Where is he?"

"Hospital," Virgil said.

"You hidin' somethin', Pepi? Pa had a coronary, maybe?"

"I hope to know later. Dr. Grant is with him at Salvador Mundi Hospital. He is getting the best care." The very best, Virgil thought. A man from the embassy; a medical examiner; a lieutenant of the Rome police; Capelli.

And of course, the widow—calm, resigned, savoring the years together. But was it not possible she was stricken with terror? Virgil was full of pity for the woman. He had thought of asking Mrs. Grant, who seemed a sensible type, to stay at the hospital morgue with Mrs. Legrand. Mrs. Legrand wanted no one. Just the chance to be with her husband's body as long as possible.

Virgil checked his notebook as the bus maneuvered into the parking area outside the Baths of Caracalla. The huge lights of the emperor's ruined red brick pile loomed above them. Caracalla. One of history's less interesting monsters. Murdered his brother Geta. And twenty thousand of Geta's adherents, in order to claim the purple. Excesses and indulgences.

He led his people through gravelly paths toward the entrance. It was the middle of the week, late in the season. The crowd was smaller than usual, for which Virgil was grateful. He had his fill of problems. Losing the Flemingtons. Mr. Legrand's demise. Inconsiderate of the old man. He could have waited, spared Virgil and the tour much heartache. All around him, as they ascended the wooden steps to their seats in the floodlit outdoor theater, Virgil heard people talking about Mr. Legrand.

"The old guy looked awful," Herbie was saying.

"He'll never make it home," Si added. "Bet he has to stay here a week, if it's a coronary."

"I pity him," Herbie said. "When I had my hiatus in Turkey, I was more scared of being sick in a foreign place than of the disease. Believe me, when you think you're going, you wanna be home."

The beams of lights dimmed. It was a place full of mystery, of old sins, ancient crimes, ruins that might have been unbearable had they not been converted to an opera house. Verdi and Leoncavallo, Virgil thought: better Italians than Caracalla or Caligula or all those other lunatics. The first chords of the overture filled the theater.

"The orchestra has improved," Virgil said to Rose-Anne Wicker. "We shall perhaps see a good performance."

"I'll settle for the elephants," Dr. Wicker said. "I've heard about them for years."

"You may have to. They are often better than the tenors."

By the time the three-and-a-half-hour performance had ended, it was past midnight. Virgil felt as if he had been stretched on a rack. But most of his tourists were full of energy, buzzing with talk about Mr. Legrand, the vanished Flemingtons. A party of the adventurous wanted to have a late night drink on the Via Veneto, to look for movie stars, to taste Roman night life.

"I shall oblige you," Virgil yawned when they were on the bus, "but I assure you the Via Veneto has more Americans from Iowa than Italian actors."

"No *dolce vita?*" Dr. Wicker asked.

"Yeah. Anita Ekberg and them other broads." Herbie was full of fight, drawing strength from his fat. It was inconceivable that the man had suffered intractable pain three days ago. (It was the trip to Israel that did it, he told Pepi. All those silent young Jews carrying guns. It made him feel young.)

About a dozen people got out at the Via Veneto. Virgil directed them to the Café Roma. "There is a chance of seeing someone there," he said. "Perhaps some obscure American actor or a minor Italian starlet. But the ice cream is good and you will meet some fellow Americans."

The Bettenhausens, the Wickers, the Hutzlers, and a few of the Midwestern people were seated together under a flowered canopy. Mr. Wattle had maneuvered Theresa to an outside seat, so that only he was seated next to her. Bettenhausen, getting up to walk to the kiosk at the corner for a morning paper, noticed the way the industrialist had isolated her.

"Methinks our bald friend is about to make his move," Bettenhausen said to his wife.

"Not likely. He's determined but Theresa's smart. Besides, she can't abide him."

Mr. Wattle turned his back on Rosie Wicker, who was seated on his left, screening Theresa from the rest of the group. A whiff of his expensive cologne wafted toward the dentist's wife.

"He's got Terry nailed," Rosie whispered to her husband.

The dentist did not hear her. He and Bettenhausen were riveted to the early edition of the Rome *Daily American*. The Hollywood man was turning pages.

"What the devil is so fascinating?" Rosie asked.

"Ball scores," Arnold lied.

422

Bettenhausen was making subterranean noises. "Damnation," he rumbled. "Nothing. Ah, foreign news briefs. Riots in Manila. Earth tremor in Iran. The royal family is at Balmoral. Uruguay increasing its imports from the Soviet bloc. Nothing from Moscow."

"If the press conference was this evening . . . this is an early edition, Warren."

"Yes, yes, it's just that I'm getting itchy. I built this plot. I made this story. I helped create Borkin and get him where he is. It's like being kept out of the editing rooms by the producer after I've spent months directing the film."

"Betts, what are you muttering about?" his wife asked.

"Nothing, love. Cinecittà is for sale. Even the Italians have stopped making movies."

Mr. Wattle raised his glass of anisette. "To you, Theresa. The loveliest woman on this tour, and certainly the loveliest in the Minneapolis public school system."

"Mr. Wattle, honestly." Theresa was weary.

"It's the truth."

"Mr. Wattle, I wish you wouldn't shut me off from the others like this. It's embarrassing."

He took no hints. Instead he turned his back again, enclosing her. "I wish you would call me Horace."

"I will if you turn around."

"Ah, hah, hah. Theresa, my dear. I'm a tough bird. I never make deals unless I can approve of every detail, including the bottom line."

Theresa shuddered. What was coming? Good God . . . a proposition. A nocturnal visitor. Setting-up exercises and aerobics. "It's much too late for that sort of thing . . . Horace."

"There. That wasn't hard, was it?"

"I don't mind calling people by their first names."

"Theresa, I have come to a decision. Let me state first that I owe my success, and it's a considerable success, to energy, ingenuity, and courage. I make decisions. I know what I'm after, and I get it. I built my company by myself with no help from anyone. I designed our factories, and my house in Bay Landing outside Seattle. I developed our own accounting methods, a new way of merchandising, and the finest employee initiative program in the state. Never had a strike and never been unionized."

She could not be rude to him. Having suffered the rudeness of the one man she had loved, she found it degrading to hurt anyone.

"You are smiling at me, Theresa. I take that to be a sign of approval."

It was hardly that. She did not intend to smile. Impervious, isolated, energized, a driving force, but never driven, he could not be taken seriously. "I can't register approval when I don't know what it is you're going to say."

"Look, look, its Sylvia Manganese or somebody," Herbie shouted. "That broad in the short skirt and the big eyes. Isn't it, Flo?"

"Hodda I know? They all look alike."

"Nah, it's that new one. Sandra somebody? Sandy something?"

The Italian girl who sauntered by was an astronomically priced prostitute. She moved faster than usual. Two carabinieri, sloe-eyed men as beautiful as the emperor's catamites, followed her. "*Vai via, signorina! Non far' business qui!*"

"What a keester," Herbie said.

"The bazooms aren't bad either," Si commented.

"Italian women, *mama mia*," Herbie bellowed. "*Woi Marie, woi Marie . . .*"

"You think maybe we could arrange another hiatus hernia for him?" Flo asked Shirl. "Herbie, drink the anisette and *shaddap!*"

"As I was saying, Theresa," Mr. Wattle went on, "I have come to a decision. I wish Herbie would be quiet. I have nothing against his kind of people, but he never stops for a minute. You'd think that attack would have slowed him down."

But nothing slows you down, Theresa thought.

Mr. Wattle grasped her forearm firmly. "Theresa, I am asking for your hand in marriage."

"Oh, Mr. Wattle."

"Horace."

"Horace. This won't work. You're kind and generous, but I'm not looking for a husband."

"I've heard otherwise."

"You heard incorrectly."

He began to massage her arm. She tried to draw away, but his grip was firm and adhesive. In business he must have been the same way. A man who could not be discouraged or insulted. "There has been talk. It has been said that you were once sweet on Mr. Flemington. Old friends. That's why Louise Deaver left the tour. It explains her drinking and so forth."

"You know a great deal."

"I put two and two together. I'd heard about the fellow Louise Deaver married. I get to Detroit. Never met Flemington, but folks talk at the clubs and so on. No one could figure out how a woman like that would burden herself with a nonentity. . . ."

"Harry was a successful newspaperman." She was indignant. Her Harry. Witty. Erudite. A newsman's newsman.

424

"Ahah! I was right. The old flame burns. Got a rise out of you there. I knew the score. Of course it was painful for you. Wasting your time on a failure."

Theresa pulled her arm away. "Mr. Wattle, I hardly appreciate that."

"It's nothing to get offended at. Most everybody is a failure in this world. At something or other. You had this crush on Flemington. Understandable. Handsome fellow like that. And you were married twice. Not too successfully, I hear."

She tried to maneuver her head around him, to say something, anything, to Flo Shackman or Shirl Shapiro, but he was like a retaining wall. "Mr. Wattle, I'm exhausted. You've worn me out. I think I'll walk to the hotel."

"Theresa, I wish to marry you. You won't regret it. You won't live in the style Flemington does, supported by his wife's fortune, but I can offer you a great deal. Winters in Fort Lauderdale. I have a fifteen-room place down there, away from the New York trash. My own boat. Fishing camp in British Columbia. We can go to New York City for the shows two or three times a year. There's nothing I can't afford, and nothing I wouldn't give a lovely woman like yourself." The lights of the Café Roma winked on his head. "And I'm the youngest seventy-one you'll ever meet. I'll show those other fellows a few tricks they never even thought about." His tongue flicked at the corners of his lips.

"It's impossible. I can't consider it. I don't mean to be rude to you."

"You aren't, Theresa. Your presence alone makes me happy." His eyes were fixed on her breasts.

"But it is out of the question. You said it yourself. I've had two failed marriages and a romance that never got off the ground. Besides, I like it in Minneapolis."

"You'll change your mind," he called after her as she walked down the Via Veneto toward the Via Sicilia. "You'll come around."

Crossing the Via Veneto, a middle-aged Italian, bearded, sad-eyed, played the *mano morto* with her. Under the camouflage of the crowd, he placed a flat hand on her rump. Through dress, slip, and girdle, she felt the palm of love—and burst out laughing.

*Day 19: Rome. A truly imperial conclusion to Three Worlds' ad-
venture, our twenty-day romance with Europe and the Holy
Land. We give ourselves to Mother Rome, fount of the Christian religion, home of art and culture, and the classical civilization of antiquity.*

*Prepare yourself for an inspirational morning in the Vatican.
St. Peter's Square, the basilica with its treasures, and the
indescribable Vatican Museum. (If we are lucky, perhaps an
audience with the Pope!)*

*Lunch in Trastevere, the charming old quarter of Rome. In
the afternoon, we resume our bus tour—highlights include
Michelangelo's Moses, Castel Sant' Angelo, the Forum, and the
Trevi Fountain, where we toss our coins!*

*It's farewell time now for Three Worlds—and our last ban-
quet. Good-bys at La Locanda, a typical Roman inn—white
Frascati wine from vats, spaghetti carbonara, and roast suckling
pig!*

If only to avoid Mr. Wattle's noisy snortings while asleep and his
exercises in the morning, Father Konay took his breakfast in the
hotel restaurant. He could not get used to the sparkling china and
white napkins, the curls of butter and little foil packages of jam,
amid the rumpled bedclothing and opened valises. His roommate,
the priest recalled as he headed for the stairway, had come home
late, bursting with energy, awakening Father Konay to tell him he had
made his mind up to get married, that he had selected the lucky girl
and that it would be his first order of business on getting back to
Bay Landing, Washington. "The young lady will take a bit of per-
suasion," Mr. Wattle brayed, "but she'll come around."

Did he hear correctly? Father Konay wondered. He was half
asleep, drugged with one of the tablets Sister Luke had given him,
and he was not quite certain what Mr. Wattle had been talking
about, but it was surely marriage. Had he expected a comment from
his roommate? It hardly mattered, Father Konay thought. As much as
he envied (and feared) Mr. Wattle, he knew one thing about him—
he did not listen. It was a source of amazement to the pastor that a
man could be so rich, so successful, and yet never hear what others
said. He, poor shepherd that he was, had spent his life listening. But
no one seemed to listen to him any more.

There was another letter for him from Father Folker—air mail and special delivery. The white-coated waiter (how cheerful and polite these Italians were!) escorted him to the outdoor patio and brought him coffee and rolls.

He sipped the coffee—black, very sweet—and found it had an invigorating effect on him.

Dear Steve,

The latest chapter in the Matter of Joseph Ptacek, the man who has taken on the Ospreys. It is enough to waken the spirits, as Father O'Connor would have said, and set them to jigging around Von Steuben Square. The clipping is self-explanatory. They have got a tiger by the tail in friend Ptacek. He may weigh 132 pounds, but he's a killer, and he's got his teeth aimed at Marciniek's neck. Poor Ed! He called me last night asking if he could meet you in New York at the airport and drive you back. I didn't want to encourage him, so I said arrangements had been made. I'll meet you. Steve, this is the biggest break we have had in years. I'm working on a scenario, a quid pro quo, which envisions the UOO accepting some members from Railtown (perhaps Willie Jackson's father Franklin, who works for Penn Central) in exchange for some kind words from you to the bishop and the county prosecutor's office. You see, Steve, Mr. Ptacek is a Gift from Above, and we must seize the opportunity. What I'm looking forward to is seeing Marciniek in his Bird Suit, if what Ptacek says is true. . . .

There was some additional parish news. The youth group was to hold a teach-in on marijuana and discuss whether it should be legalized. Sister Luke was convinced the school would have to fire five more teachers unless state aid came through. The annual drive for Sacred Heart's Building Fund was lagging and Father Folker was honest enough to admit, in his cheery way, that the parishioners didn't like some of the newfangled things going on at the church. "Me, especially," the young priest wrote, "but we'll win 'em over."

He concluded with his usual wisecracks about Rome and the Holy Father. "What a joy if old John were still there and you could see that saintly man!" (But not a word about the incumbent Holy Father.)

The clipping from the Ash Valley *Tribune* was brief.

PTACEK CASE WILL BE PROBED BY DISTRICT ATTORNEY

Claimant Vows Civil Action Against Osprey Club

District Attorney Henry Schmalhaus said today he will begin an immediate investigation into charges by Joseph Ptacek that he was beaten, kicked, and abused during initiation ceremonies at the United Order of Ospreys of Ash Valley.

Mr. Ptacek, 38, a bricklayer, has accused Edward Marciniek, 56, Exalted First Nester, of hitting him and kicking him a week ago,

427

when Ptacek, a "fledgling" undergoing initiation for his "first flight," allegedly refused to strangle a live snake and lick up a puddle of rat's blood.

Mr. Marciniek, proprietor of Marchy's Bar & Grill, and a leader in last month's battle to keep Negroes out of the Ospreys, has denied the charges through his attorney, Horace Cohen.

DA Schmalhaus has taken depositions from Mr. Ptacek and Mr. Marciniek and intends to interrogate all persons present at the initiation, including an as yet unnamed member who was disguised as a priest.

"If I don't get any satisfaction from the DA, I am going to sue these people till it hurts," Mr. Ptacek told the *Tribune.* "They got no right to beat up on me or kick a man when he's down. I'll take on Marciniek or any of them in a fair fight in an alley or a bar, but I don't like getting ganged up on, even when it's supposed to be a ceremony."

Mr. Cohen said he has advised his client to remain silent until the District Attorney completes his investigation. "A key witness is not presently available," the lawyer said. "He is Father Konay, Chaplain of the Ospreys, who is due back from Europe this week."

He would be tolerant, polite, and forgiving. The truth was he had never been allowed to attend an initiation. Understandable. With snakes and rats, and Marchy disguised as a six-foot osprey. His simple answers would help no one, hurt no one. But if they wanted character references, a priest to go to bat for them, to talk about their kindly works (Did not Ospreys sponsor the picnic for crippled children? Had not Marchy's Bar & Grill donated the pop and potato chips?) he would be glad to do so: after a long, serious talk with the Exalted First Nester.

Mother Rome, give me strength! Father Konay prayed. How he had neglected his prayers on this trip! So much to see! So much to learn! He opened his breviary and began a morning prayer, something appropriate for the Eternal City, where motor bikes belched past him, boys of twelve in soiled white coats swept the sidewalk, and a woman with a face like the Madonna polished tomatoes before placing them in a pyramid on her pushcart. Holiness in everyday things, Father Konay thought. The sacred nature of daily duties. Mr. Bettenhausen, who knew so much, had said in Paris that an apple painted by Cézanne was as full of divine inspiration as a cathedral. A blasphemous thought, or at least a gnostic notion, but one with a certain truth.

Aldo Capelli took over for Virgil. Pepi had stayed up through the night with Mrs. Legrand. The old man's body had been removed to

Salvador Mundi Hospital, where Dr. Grant had conferred with the resident on duty. Cause of death was listed as a massive cerebral hemorrhage. An autopsy would be performed to confirm the diagnosis. Mrs. Legrand did not object when Virgil explained to her that it would expedite getting her husband's remains out of Italy and into the United States.

"You may have to stay perhaps a day or two," Virgil said.

"Oh no. I'll go home with the rest of you. I feel those people are my friends."

"Mr. Legrand's body—"

"I should like him cremated."

"Ah . . ."

"Will that be impossible?"

"This is a Catholic country, Mrs. Legrand. But perhaps. For non-Catholic foreigners."

"There must be some way. Weston always wanted to be cremated. He hated the idea of laying in the earth, moldering away, like John Brown's body."

They had sat for hours in the resident's office in Salvador Mundi, awakening officials, getting Planet Tour's local "fixer" out of bed—his mistress', it developed—and learning the procedure for cremation.

"*Che pensa, Pepi?*" Capelli asked him dolefully.

"*Se deva informar gli altri,*" Virgil replied. "We must tell the others of the misfortune. I would be glad to do it, but *la vecchia* wants to be present when the deceased is committed to the furnace. I cannot dissuade her and I honor her loyalty. I think I should stay with her."

"*Va bene.* I will tell them."

"*Ma, per favore, Aldo, con gentilezza.* We do not want to spoil their last day. Americans are resentful about death. They do not like to accept it. Not like us, eh, *caro?*"

"Americans, Swedes, Germans. *Sono tutti uguale con me.*"

Virgil lit a Gitane and tasted bronze. Mrs. Legrand sat upright in an easy chair across from him. The resident had offered her tea, coffee, a sandwich, a sleeping pill, a tranquilizer. She refused everything. "I'm fine, Doctor, just fine."

Virgil called for a cab for Dr. Grant. "Please, tell only your wife. This is a serious matter and the company feels obligated to tell all tourists at the same time. Signor Capelli will do so the first thing in the morning. My sincerest thanks."

Dr. Grant waved his hand. "Heck. After all you've done for us."

"I've only done my job."

"My wife and I think you've done more than that." Dr. Grant

429

looked at the terrazzo floor of the hospital. "I'm not very articulate. But you sort of . . . you were a civilizing influence."

"You give me too much credit."

In the shadows, Mrs. Legrand sat immobile. From a paper cup she sipped the last of her *raki*. "I agree. Pepi, you made Weston's last days on earth so pleasant."

Virgil felt humbled. He had done nothing beyond his job, perhaps a bit more.

"I have some sad news for you," Aldo Capelli said as soon as he had counted heads and the bus swung into the Rome traffic, inching toward the Angel Bridge.

"I bet I can guess," Flo Shackman said to Mavis Hutzler. "Poor Mr. Legrand had a heart attack. He looked awful last night."

"And how come Dr. Grant didn't show up for dinner or the opera?" Mavis pouted.

When anyone missed a meal, a tour, the worst had to be assumed. It was inconceivable that people would pay large sums of money and, barring a crippling accident, a high fever, or death, fail to take advantage of their due.

"Your fellow tourist Mr. Legrand died last night."

There were gasps and involuntary cries. Flo Shackman began to bawl. Father Konay crossed himself, took out his breviary, and found a reading. The Legrands were not Catholics, but he felt that the world was his parish, even if the thought had originated with the founder of Wesleyan Methodism.

"Pa?" Herbie cried. "Pa Barker is dead? Holy smoke, how . . . ? Pepi said he fainted last night."

"I have no details," Capelli said. "I am sorry that this sad event has occurred and I hope it will not mar your last day of the tour. Such things happen."

"God's will," Father Konay whispered.

"He looked awful these last five or six days," Shirl said to Flo. "Oh, that poor old lady."

"Yeah," Yasuda called. "How's Ma? I mean Mrs. Legrand. She okay? She took it all right?"

"She is bearing up well," Aldo Capelli said. He was distressed that there was so much discussion of the old man's death. Not that Capelli was hardhearted (a Milanese, he avoided emotional displays, lest people think him a southern Italian). He merely wanted them to get the most out of Rome. Already they had passed the Bernini fountain of Neptune and the Palazzo Barberini, and were into the Via Due Macelli, heading toward the Piazza d'Espagna, and he had not had an opportunity to describe a single place. Like Virgil, he revered monuments and he wanted these Americans to know about them. Death, after all, was a commonplace. A dreary business.

"On your right, ladies and gentlemen," Capelli said, trying to break into the sniffles and sobs of the women, the inquisitive buzzing conversation. "The famous Spanish Steps, or properly, the *Scalinata della Trinità dei Monti*, 137 beautiful steps built from 1721 to 1725. At the bottom, on the right, is the house of the English poet John Keats, where he died in February 23, 1821. On your left, ladies and gentlemen, the fountain *La Barcaccia*, a small boat, also by Bernini. And the streets leading away from the Piazza d'Espagna—"

"Maybe we should cancel the tour today," Mrs. Kuchtenberg said in a firm puritanical voice. "Out of respect to the Legrands."

"So what good will that do?" Si asked. "I mean, the guy's gone. Mrs. Legrand wouldn't want us to quit."

"Yeah, Ma, I mean Mrs. Legrand, was aces." Herbie wiped hot tears from the folds around his eyes. He felt dreadful. Worse than the hiatus hernia. He had joked with them, kidded with them in his crude way. But, dear God, Herbie prayed, he didn't mean it. Not a word. He knew they were old and lonely. He did it to make them feel important. Wasn't all his kidding designed to make the people he kibitzed feel good? And wasn't he the biggest clown of all, in his baggy red slacks and his plaid pork-pie hats?

"The tour goes on," Capelli said irritably. "Those who wish to take the day off may do so. The company has no choice but to give every tourist his full tour."

"What about those streets?" Flo asked. "You were saying . . ."

"Ah, on the left of the piazza," the guide went on. "Very famous shops, very good quality. Clothing, jewelry, luggage. Gucci's. But be prepared to write a great many traveler's checks."

"But what exactly did he die of?" Mr. Wattle shouted. "We have a right to know."

"I am not certain," Capelli said. "Dr. Grant was present."

Mr. Wattle spun around, his bald head like a polished piece of precision machinery. "How about it, Doctor? How about it? What was your diagnosis?"

"Tell him to go to hell," Ibith whispered.

"Heart," Dr. Grant said.

"That's all? No complications?" Mr. Wattle was on his feet, glaring at Grant.

Capelli sighed. "The Castel Sant' Angelo ahead of us, beyond the Angel Bridge. The angels are by Bernini. Look at the way the robes flow in the air, although we have not a breeze today. The Castello

431

was originally the tomb of Hadrian. In the Middle Ages it was a prison. It is now a museum."

"It was the rotten food and water that killed him," Mr. Wattle shouted. "He was poisoned. The wife should sue."

"Please, sir, I beg of you to be quiet," Capelli said. "The man is dead. Why ruin the tour for everyone? Look, ahead of us, Bernini's colonnade, and beyond that St. Peter's. If you are upset over the gentleman's death, go in and pray."

The sobering news of Mr. Legrand's death derailed Bettenhausen's outrage. He had bought what the man at the kiosk claimed was the late edition of the Rome *Daily American,* and thumbed through it as he, his wife, and the Wickers had their rolls and coffee in front of the hotel and, at first reading, found nothing. Then, in a late "roundup of international news" on the back page, he found a single paragraph:

SOVIET SCIENTIST DEFECTS TO ISRAEL

Jerusalem, Oct. 5—(Reuters)—Professor Anatoly Borkin, one of the Soviet Union's leading scientists, has been allowed to emigrate to Israel, the Israeli Foreign Ministry announced today.

"Damnation," Bettenhausen said. "A pox on them for cutting it short like that."

"It's probably all they had room for," Dr. Wicker said. "I bet the Italian newspapers have a fuller account."

"I have no Italian. And we are in strange hands this morning." He bobbed his head at the saturnine Capelli, directing people to the bus. "I like not the look of yon gloomy cicerone. We'll call the newspaper office later. Perhaps they have the rest of the item on file."

In St. Peter's Square Bettenhausen detached himself from the party and located a newsstand at the end of the Via della Conciliazione. "The latest paper, please," he asked. "*Nuovo?* New?"

The woman gave him a copy of *L'Osservatore Romano.* The act of buying it buoyed his spirits. An excellent touch, a winner on the screen, something the old constructionist would toss into a script meeting. He walked toward the group standing around Capelli.

"By God, there it is," Bettenhausen said.

On the fourth page was a photograph of Borkin in an open-throated shirt. The two-column headline read:

FAMOSO SCIENZATO EBREO E ARRIVATO IN ISRAEL

"I can understand that," Wicker said. "So Borkin *was* Jewish."

Bettenhausen quickened his pace, as if eager to grab Capelli

432

and force him, perhaps at gun point, to translate the article on Borkin.

"Curses," Bettenhausen said. "Something about emigration. Not part of the quota? Can't make head or tail of it."

Capelli was leading the tour across the Piazza San Pietro. No, he told them, His Holiness would not appear today. Nor would there be any possibility of an audience.

"More misinformation," Mr. Wattle said. "They promised us an audience. I hate being taken."

"The literature says if *possible*," Aldo said diffidently. He was slow to anger—a neutral Milanese who preferred saffron rice to spaghetti.

"The façade is baroque," Capelli said. "Some say it is too grandiose, too big, and harms the view of the dome from many places in the piazza."

Bettenhausen sidled up to the guide. Normally he would have been involved in the sight-seeing—offering information, summoning up bits and pieces from his prodigious memory. But all that concerned him at the moment was Borkin.

"When you have a minute, sir . . ." Bettenhausen asked. "A bit of translation . . ."

"Later, later."

Inside the basilica, the tourists were numbed into silence. It was too ornate, too rich, too overwhelming. Father Konay fell to his knees.

Again, the priest was having difficulty making connections. The Ospreys? Ed Marciniek, whose children he had baptized? And Joseph Ptacek, the bricklayer, refusing to be humiliated by a fat man dressed in feathers and wings? *His* children. Mother Church's children. Of course UOO was not a religious organization. Fraternal. Well-meaning.

The colossal statues soared above him—reprimands, monitors. Father Konay lagged. He felt his feet turn to stone, as hard as the porphyry pavement. Trailing some of the Midwestern ladies, following their bobbing blue heads, he felt giddy. Ahead of him was Bernini's baldacchino. In the background St. Peter's chair. On the right, the bronze statue of the Fisherman. Foot worn to a stump by kisses of the faithful. He wished he could bring all the aggrieved parties here, to kiss the metal foot of the saint: Father Folker, Marchy, Ptacek, and the black citizens of Railtown who wanted the benefit of cut-rate liquor served on Sundays. . . . A monstrous thought, he decided. Unworthy of him. Why even think of visiting his petty problems as chaplain of the Ospreys and pastor of Sacred Heart upon this eternal glory?

433

"Here, ladies and gentlemen," Aldo said, "the high altar, and the baldacchino of Bernini. The bronze came from the Roman Pantheon."

Bettenhausen approached Capelli. "I urgently need translation of a newspaper article. A short piece. Do you have a minute?"

"In the middle of a tour?"

"It is a vital matter. Why not let your lambs stroll around, and give them an appointed meeting place?"

Capelli saw the fire in Bettenhausen's eye; the man's beard seemed to be giving off electricity. "Ladies and gentlemen, proceed to the sacristy door, over there, after you have walked about the basilica. In ten minutes I shall meet you under the monument to Pope Pius VIII. I shall take you into the sacristy and we shall look at the Vatican Treasury."

Bettenhausen thrust the copy of *L'Osservatore Romano* at Capelli. "The article about the Russian scientist. I must have it translated."

The guide adjusted a pair of gold-rimmed spectacles on his nose. He led them toward a bench in front of the altars in the left transept.

The three men sat. A beam of light from a high window illuminated the cool space. Garish mosaics hung over each altar. Bettenhausen recalled that one was after a work of Guido Reni, one of his less favorite *seicento* painters.

"So?" Capelli asked. "This is about a Russian scientist. A Jew named Borkin, who is in Israel. It says he was told to leave the Soviet Union or face loss of his job with the Lenin Institute and go to work as a hospital attendant. Either that or leave Russia forever. It says his wife and his son are to follow in a few days."

"What else?" Wicker asked.

"Hmmmm. Interesting. This was a *conferenza di stampa*—press conference—in Jerusalem. He is said to be one of the Soviet Union's leading experts on *la genetica*."

"Genetics," the dentist said.

"*Sì*. It says, let me see. Ah, I understand. Borkin for many years . . . hmmm . . . *ha negato* . . . denied, yes, denied that he was Jewish. Recently, when he was suspected of being the *capo*, chief, of libertarian underground movement, he was attacked as a Zionist agent by Soviet officials of the Academy of Science. It says he kept denying the accusations until about a week ago—"

Bettenhausen's eyes stabbed Wicker, as if to say: "We did it."

"—when he was arrested and accused of having, hmmm, *affari*, business, traffic, with Western agents. There was not any truth to the charge, Borkin says, but the arrest so infuriated him that he admitted he was a Jew and said he would take the consequences."

"Which were?" Bettenhausen asked.

"According to this report, and *L'Osservatore Romano* is quite reliable," Capelli said, "he was given a choice. Go to Israel, since he had admitted his racial background, or lose his job." The guide folded the paper and gave it back to the Hollywood man.

Beneath the statue of Pius VIII, Wicker saw Si Shapiro, Herbie's brother-in-law, emerging.

"Herbie and Flo and my wife," Si called to Aldo. "They got in some kind of trouble. It'll be a bad mark against us forever."

"Excuse me," Capelli said. Ah, impatient Americans. He had told the group to wait for him *outside* the entrance. The rooms housing the Treasury, the Sala Capitolare, the sacristies, were not always open, and even if they were, it was advisable for tours to be accompanied.

"We need help," Si said.

"You were told to wait for me."

The Hutzlers, the Grants, Theresa Carrell, and Mr. Wattle, like good children, had waited for Capelli. They were now joined by Rosie and Cornelia, who had wandered around the pier of St. Andrew to study the Mosaic of the Transfiguration after Raphael.

"So?" Dr. Wicker asked.

"We were responsible, Arnold."

"I don't get it. . . . By faking that letter?"

"Precisely," Bettenhausen said. He set his jaw—Orson Welles as Citizen Kane—and tore out the article about Borkin's expulsion. "The Russians have pulled this trick a few times. They give an eminent figure the choice—get out and stay out or become a cipher. Borkin might have been faced with the dismal prospect or worse. Who knows? But you and I, Arnold, *we forced their hand.*"

"By delivering a blank sheet of paper?"

Cornelia was gesturing at them. She and Rosie wanted to see what had taken place in the sacristy to so upset Si.

"It was exactly the right touch," Bettenhausen whispered. "A bit of Hitchcockian perfection. The Master would have approved."

"You're overdramatizing, Warren."

"I am not." Bettenhausen let the glory of St. Peter's rise around him—high, eternal. But too ornate. His plots were artistically purer. He would compare his construction of the Borkin Affair to something clean and solid, perhaps a Romanesque church in the Périgord. "Had we given Borkin Leland's letter the Russians never would have allowed him to leave. They would have seized on the transaction—innocent through the geneticist may have been—and put him away to rot in a mental hospital."

"They could have done the same thing after you contacted him."

435

Bettenhausen halted at the tomb of St. Gregory the Great. "No, my boy. They have a crude Marxist sense of guilt and retribution. They knew something was afoot. They knew that you and I were aware of their plot to implicate Borkin. The white paper was a signal. In effect, I was acting the way our intelligence agencies often act—sending up a trial balloon, feeling them out. They accepted the challenge. Better to throw Borkin out of the country and denounce him than let his contacts with the West continue. The *next* letter might have been a real offer, not from some diabolical Leland. Who knows but that Borkin might have gotten his papers out?"

"So they tossed him out and now they'll try to discredit him?"

"They'll fail. Borkin is too respected in the scientific community. Besides, he's under the wing of that fellow Tal, that Israeli colonel. They are hard people to beat at this game."

"Happy ending, Warren?"

"One might call it that."

"Are you two announcing your engagement?" Cornelia asked.

"We are collaborating on a film script," Bettenhausen chuckled.

"In St. Peter's?" Rosie asked.

The Hollywood man rolled his eyes about, trying to encompass the vastness. "This is my Church," he said. "God is down here." They all looked dazed. "Karl Malden. *On the Waterfront.*"

Herbie and Si and their wives had wandered through the octagonal Sagrestia Comune, a handsome room with a cupola supported by yellow and gray marble pillars. A door on the left led to the Sagrestia dei Canonici, a smaller room with an altar and the usual cupboards and closets for priestly vestments. Normally the door was closed and permission was required to enter. But a service had been held earlier, a commemorative mass for an American benefactor, a supermarket owner from Batavia, Illinois. The sacristan had neglected to close the portal.

On an immense oaken table in the center of the room were heaped in disarray a variety of surplices, chasubles, cassocks, and assorted robes that had been used in the celebration of the funeral mass.

Except for Herbie, Si, and their wives, the room was empty.

"Hey, look at the stuff there," Flo said.

"Boy, what material," Shirl said. She walked up briskly and began to finger a chasuble of watered gold silk. "Wow. What a thing I could do to that sofa in the living room with this. You know the one I mean, Flo? The one Si got wholesale from his cousin?"

"Si gets everything wholesale," Flo said. "Herb, you like this thing in purple? Look at the design. I could make an evening coat out of it."

Si shook his head. "I dunno. What is all that stuff doing thrown out on the table like that? And nobody around?"

"Know what?" Herbie said. "They're for *sale*."

The women stared at him.

"Ya kiddin'," Flo said.

"Nah, I know how they work it," Herbie said. "After a while, these things get worn out so they sell 'em. Father Dolan at Holy Family, when I did the tax return for his sister, told me. They get rid of this stuff after a while. The new models come in, like the fall line."

"You like this on me?" Flo asked. She had picked up a lace-decorated chasuble, a garment in grass green and cream, and was holding it under her neck, tucking the waist in.

"I don't see no prices," Herbie said.

"Good," Flo said emphatically. "That means we can *hondle*."

Herbie looked around the sacristy. Not a soul in sight. Of course the merchandise was for sale. How else explain the helter-skelter manner in which they were displayed on the table? And they looked old, a bit frayed. A pity the Pope had to use such *shmattes*. It was good business to sell them cut rate and buy new ones.

"That don't look like a dress," Si said. He studied a white and red silk cloth that Shirl was unfolding, fingering, envisioning as a table-cloth. "It looks like, what? A flag or a banner or something."

"On our Castro, Si," Shirl said. "Perfect. It's just the right size."

"I ain't sure," Si said. "You think . . . ?"

"Of course!" Herbie cried. "We were lucky. We got here first. I'm all choked up. Ahah! There he is. Chaim Yankel. *Buon giorno*, comrade."

A hunched sacristan, his withered face clouded with confusion, shuffled into the Sagrestia dei Canonici. In a voice as hoarse as that of a Neopolitan fish vendor he reprimanded the couples. "*Eh, vai via. E chiuso, chiuso.*"

"Where's Capelli?" Herbie shouted. "I can't spikka da langweesh."

"Ask him what the prices are," Flo said.

"Tell him we wanna *hondle*," Shirl cried.

"Buy, buy," Herbie said loudly, under the assumption that volume would make him intelligible to the old man.

"*Chiuso, chiuso.*"

"What does he mean?" Herbie boomed. "Look, buy, we wanna *buy*. You see all them things, the clothing, the robes, the draperies? They gotta be for sale. Look, we're ready to do business. Name us a price."

437

"Price-a, price-a," Flo tried.

"*Non, non, per favore, parta.*"

"I don't think he wants us here, Herbie." Flo looked pained. She had already chosen the robes she wanted. "Ask him to get someone who speaks English."

"What English?" Herbie thundered. "It's the same in any language. They wanna do business, *I* wanna do business." He grabbed a white and crimson chasuble and held it up. "How much? How mucha you wanta, pal?"

"*Non, non, lascia stare, lascia.*" He pointed to the door leading to the octagon-shaped room.

"We ain't wanted," Shirl said.

An austere-looking priest in horn-rimmed glasses swept into the room. "Please, no one here. Private."

"The door was open," Flo said.

"You got this stuff out for sale?" Shirl asked.

"*Sale?*" His eyeglasses danced on his Roman nose.

"I better get Aldo," Si said.

Moments later, Si led Capelli into the Sagrestia. Ah, his brother and his sister and his wife, he reflected. Their lives (like Mrs. Flemington's) were bound round with buying, bargains, sales, the price of everything in the world. Herbie had not quit. He had both hands on a frazzled papal banner, white and gold, with papal crown and crossed keys. "If it ain't for sale, how come it's dumped out like this for everyone to see? Like Wholesale Harry's in the Bronx."

Capelli spoke in Italian to the priest. The cleric clapped a hand to his head.

"*Non posso crederlo,*" Capelli said. "Please, sir, you must take his word. These robes and banners are not for sale. This is the sacristy where the Church's vestments are kept. You have been trying to buy the robes and flags used in a funeral mass held this morning for Mr. Michael Terenzio of Batavia, Illinois."

"They ain't for sale?" Herbie was insulted.

"I am afraid not."

The other tour members peeked into the Sagrestia dei Canonici.

"Wait, please, outside, at the Treasury," Capelli called. "All right, sir, apologize to the sacristan and the father."

"Sure, sure," Herbie said. "I apologize. Only next time don't invite customers like that. I see stuff laid out like that, I'm gonna make you an offer."

The priest nodded his acceptance of Shackman's apology, then shouted at the assistant to start folding the robes.

"In twenty-seven years as a guide," Capelli said to Herbie and Si

438

and their wives as they moved through the rooms toward the Treasury, "I have never had a client offer to buy the Vatican robes."

"You just had one, buddy," Herbie said spunkily. "And if I had an extra ten minutes, I woulda been able to *hondle* with that guy." He grasped Capelli's lapel. "You know, they didn't get this layout just by saying prayers. They knew a little bit also about bookkeeping and mortgages."

Several times during the morning—during a break at St. Peter's, on their arrival at Santa Maria in Trastevere, where they were to lunch at Galeassi's—J. P. Huggins tried to reach Chahoub's Rome office. It was a failure. His last contact had been in Jerusalem, where the bank clerk, Silwah, had shown him the cable from Chahoub. The ship had come in. The platinum would be sold. He would realize an enormous profit. Chahoub would contact him in Rome. But thus far the Lebanese, the oily man whom he had met in Vienna, was hiding from him. It was understandable, J.P. told himself. In his kind of business, he couldn't be too careful.

"Ooh, I want the spaghetti with the little pieces of bacon and eggs in it," Barbara said. "Like we had last night, Jimmy. Isn't it gorgeous here?"

He was glad to see her vivacious and happy. Was some ancestral blood stirring in her? The Vatican, St. Peter's, the museums had not made much of an impression. Sore feet. Sore back. Pouting. Huggins felt a profound pity for Barbara. It welled up in him; he was sorry she did not have the capacity to appreciate her heritage. Leave it to the Jews to know how to do it: Herbie at the wall, Si and his wife walking around Israel as if they had invented it.

"Cold seafood salad, *signor*," the waiter said. Huggins sniffed it: the entire Mediterranean. A baby octopus' tentacle pointed at him.

"Beautiful," J.P. said. "Give the lady the rest."

"*Per la bella signora. Italo-Americana, signora?*"

"What's he sayin', Jimmy?"

"He guessed you're an Italian, Barbs."

"I am. Yes."

Ah, to hell with it, Huggins thought. She couldn't speak a word of the mother tongue. Language of Dante. Still, he had to love her. She was his, fat, juicy, better in the kip than any five women he had ever known. Maybe he could get her away from her "babies" long enough to take a course or two at the New School. *Renaissance Art and Architecture.*

"*Vino, signor?* White or red?"

"Anything you recommend."

439

Harmony. That was what Huggins sought. At that moment he had found it. A fountain bubbled in the center of the piazza. No big deal. No Trevi, nothing like the baroque monument with the river gods in the Piazza Navona, but an old, scarred, honest fountain. Kids ran around it. Italian mamas chased them. An old geezer came by selling balloons and pinwheels. Another peddled salted nuts. Flights of pigeons wheeled around the campanile. City life assumed pleasing, manageable proportions here.

"Meester Huggins, Meester Huggins."

J.P. looked up from his red wine. It was Chahoub. Sweat coated his round face. "Chahoub. I gave up on you."

"Sir, you do me an injustice. Mr. Silwah saw you in Jerusalem?"

"Yeah. With good news. This is my wife. Mrs. Huggins. Mr. Chahoub. We met in Vienna. Had a little business to contract."

Chahoub bent from the waist and seized Barbara's hand, kissing it wetly. She pulled it away. Creep. Unsanitary dope.

"May I . . . ?" The Arab hesitated.

"Join us for lunch. If we lucked out, the lunch is on me. If we didn't, you pay. Hey, waiter. A setting for my friend here."

"What is this thing supposed to be?" Mr. Wattle called from the next table. "What have you served me?"

"*Carciofo, signor. Carciofo freddo in oglio.*"

Theresa thumbed through her guidebook. In the rear were listed the names of common dishes. "It's an artichoke, Horace." Since turning him down, she had tried to be kinder to him. He did not realize it, but he needed love. Not the love of a single woman, a wife, a mistress; but the world's love.

"Take it away," Mr. Wattle cried. "I hate artichokes."

"You know, I sure wanted that white and gold bedspread," Shirl said sadly. "Si hadda go dragging Aldo in. If we coulda had those guys alone another five minutes, they'd've sold it."

Ibith and Henderson Grant, at the same table with the Westbury group, listened engrossed to their account of the attempt to buy the Vatican's garments. The Shackmans and the Shapiros told the story boldly, unembarrassed by what had happened, indignant that they had been deprived of a bout of *hondling*.

"It's a way we'll never be," Ibith whispered. "Hen, how I envy them."

"Cheer up, Ib. We got the inborn sense of rhythm."

Chahoub declined J. P. Huggins' offer to buy him lunch. He was extremely busy. Clients in Rome. A stop-off in Milan. Then on to Beirut to check on his bank.

"So we made out okay?" Huggins asked. He felt fulfilled. Their

440

ship had come in. But, awaiting Chahoub's report on the voyage of the S.S. *Lautaro,* he sensed his triumph change to ashes, destroy the piquancy of the mixed seafood salad. He stopped eating, doodling his fork in the cold squid and shrimp.

"*Yech,*" Barbara said. "Why you ordered *that.* I don't trust their Frigidaires. Prob'ly full of germs."

Huggins thought bitterly of the Malfis, stealing crates from airports. No wonder he was miserable. Chahoub would tell him about their ten-strike and what would it mean? More loot for Mario and Ralphie.

"You like Rome?" Barbara asked Chahoub. "You got an office here?"

"I love it. A city for all people. My home is Beirut but I consider Rome a second home."

"I think it's overrated," she said. "It's old and dirty and crowded. They think they're something."

Huggins could see that Chahoub was waiting for a signal. Was it permissible to talk in front of Mrs. Huggins? The Lebanese had handled enough of these matters to know that wives were better excluded. So they talked generally—the ship had docked at Karachi, the cargo had been sold, the operation was a success, the partners would be paid.

"What's that all about?" Barbara asked. "What ship?"

"One of Kuraskin's deals," J.P. lied. "He wanted me to buy drilling machinery in Austria. Mr. Chahoub handled it."

"I bet."

"Am I leveling, Chahoub?"

"Absolutely. Madame need not be suspicious. I am the agent for the shipping company."

Eventually Barbara excused herself to "spend a penny." As soon as her lush figure had entered Galeassi's, the Lebanese sprang forward. From a briefcase he took out an envelope. "A statement of profits, Mr. Huggins. Keep it in a safe place. The check will follow in a week. You have my name, my address, and of course you have a great deal more to keep me honest—the nature of our work."

"I wanted the dough."

"Alas, sir, your stolen treasury notes are a problem. But let me give you wonderful news. You are receiving twenty-five per cent on your investment, even after deductions for service charges, shipping, and the company's own profit. On your investment of $200,000, you have just earned $50,000 or, more exactly, $51,672.43. All tax free, since I am certain you do not intend to report this to any government. We had no idea that the price of platinum and precious metals had risen so swiftly."

"And my two hundred thousand?"

441

"I wish to talk to you about that, sir. The interest on the loan was forty-eight per cent compounded annually. The minimum they will accept is a month's interest, even though the loan was for less than two weeks."

"Four per cent?"

"A bargain, my dear Mr. Huggins."

"Okay. Pay 'em off. For eight thousand bucks, I can be a sport. I'm way ahead." He cursed Mario. Mario would sneeringly hand him his fee of ten thousand. And clear $33,000 without having moved off his behind.

"The association making the loan is fearful of sending your stolen notes out of their vault."

"Why?"

"They are . . . as you say, hot. They would like to reinvest them for you. Believe me, Mr. Huggins, such money is better kept in motion." Chahoub bent across the table. Pigeons wheeled in a flowing pattern over his head, over the campanile of Santa Maria.

"I got the feeling, Chahoub, that you and that bank are one and the same."

"A subsidiary of the shipping company. It is run by my brother."

Fair enough, J.P. thought. Everything in the family. All Mediterraneans were alike deep down. Trust no one but a brother or a son. He, poor Celt, poor shiftless Jimmy Huggins, was trapped between ancient races, the shrewd wisdom of the wine-dark sea.

"So I get nothing?"

"You invest your entire capital again. You will pay interest, of course, but only on your original loan. At four per cent per month, you surely can afford it. Especially if the price of platinum on the subcontinent continues to rise."

"And if we don't get robbed, or sunk by pirates, or intercepted by the Indian or Pakistani navies."

"Small chance, sir. The right people have been bribed. I admit our need for venture capital. Why not remain with us?"

Huggins saw Barbara, fussing with her hair (she had it in curlers and under a huge pink bandana), touching her hips as if to make sure they were there.

"I want a check for the forty-three grand."

"You shall receive it."

"Before I leave Rome."

"That is impossible, sir."

"You'll find a way, Chahoub. That sheikh, the guy in the blanket I met in Vienna, I have an idea he's stashing thousand-dollar bills in his sheets. Get it for me."

"Sir, I am hurt. You do not trust me."

J.P. pointed a fork at the Arab's necktie. "Listen, Chahoub, I'll go halfway. I want that check, a certified negotiable bank check in dollars for my net profit less the interest, delivered to my hotel this evening. Then I'll agree to keep my principal in your account, so you can invest it again."

"What's going on?" Barbara asked. "Still business? Over some machinery?"

"Details, Barbs." He spoke sternly to the Lebanese. "Our flight is at noon tomorrow. I'll give you part of the morning, but only part. Up to nine at our hotel, or 10 A.M. at the airport. That's it, Chahoub."

The Arab got up. "Mr. Huggins, I am afraid that cannot be done."

J.P. rose and put his arm around the man. He walked a few steps, out of earshot of the Three Worlds diners, across the piazza.

"But you *gotta* do it, Chahoub."

"I shall call you late this afternoon at your hotel."

"Beautiful."

"Between four and five?" the Arab asked.

"But not between five and five-thirty."

"Ah . . . ?"

"That's when I'll be placing an anonymous phone call to Interpol in Paris to tip them off on the operations of the Beirut, Dubai & Sharja Trading Company."

"Oh, Mr. Huggins, you would not—"

"Try me, Chahoub."

"A man dealing in stolen treasury notes?"

"They weren't mine. I was acting for someone."

The Lebanese smiled. A sad, understanding smile. "Ah yes, Mr. Huggins. And I know who."

"The spoils of Jerusalem," the Italian said. "Look how well preserved is the carving." They were under the Arch of Titus in the Forum.

"The menorah," Flo said. "So that's where it ended up."

"The candelabrum from the temple," Aldo said. "Also the altar from the temple, adorned with trumpets."

They strolled through the Forum, toward the shell of the Basilica of Constantine. On the Via Sacra Si drew alongside Capelli. "That business with Titus, I guess that's all forgotten. I mean, there isn't much anti-Semitism in Italy."

"Almost none," Capelli said. "An old and honored community, our Jews. Even under Mussolini, it was only when Hitler put pressure on him. It is a shame you will not have time to see the monument at the Fosse Ardeatine."

"More Roman stuff?"

"From after World War II. It is a mass grave with a single great stone over it, the place where the Nazis murdered 335 people in reprisal after the partisans killed German soldiers."

The party walked down the Via Sacra.

"In a way you can't blame them," Mr. Wattle said.

"Blame who?" Theresa asked.

"The Germans. They had a right to demand law and order. They were an occupying force. They couldn't allow their soldiers to be shot at. They were in charge and people were supposed to obey them."

"Good God, I can't listen to this. That's a horrid thought." The teacher walked quickly to the front of the group.

Si Shapiro, sucking an unlit pipe, also heard Mr. Wattle. The forms and colors of the Forum swam in front of him—old columns, chipped marble tablets, patches of green, broken roofs, cracked foundations. A lot of history. People should have been reverent. Mr. Wattle's defense of massacre infuriated him.

Mr. Wattle paused at the rear of the group. He was framing the Arch of Titus in his camera. "It was foolish to take the picture below," he announced to Si, seeing the Westbury man striding toward him. "Those people waste more film than they use properly. The light is good from just about here."

"Listen," Si said.

"In a minute. Stand aside."

Si knocked his hands, and the 35-mm. camera, from his face. "Listen for a change. It might do you good."

"What? Who do you . . . ? Guide! *Guide!*"

"Shut up. I heard that crack you made about the Nazis having the right to kill people."

"Oh, I understand. Yes, you and the others. Of course you'd be insulted. But it wasn't meant that way. Of course I'm against the murder of innocent people. But they were in *charge*. They were trying to impose some order on this country. Don't take it personally."

Si, a man toughened by golf and vitamin pills, twenty years younger than Mr. Wattle, grabbed the leather sling of the camera and pulled Wattle toward him, raising him to his toes. "You shut up from now on, you hear? We got one more day together, and if there's a peep out of you, I'll kill you. I'll beat the crap out of you."

"How would you like to be sued? How would you like to fight my lawyers in court?"

"How would you like my fist in your nose?"

They remained suspended, two angry Americans on the Via Sacra of the Roman Forum, the basilica's ruins rising behind them under a crystalline blue sky. Si released Wattle with a shove.

Si suppressed tears. He should have embraced the man, reasoned with him, asked him to be more humane. The truth was, he was sure that Mr. Wattle had not meant to be insulting or cruel. He merely liked things orderly and organized. No rioting in the streets, no threats to the authorities.

"What is your husband doing up there with that nut?" Flo asked Shirl.

"Si," Shirl yelled. "Get away from that jerk!"

Sid started after him, but Si had already moved away from Mr. Wattle, ashamed of his loss of temper, trying to invent a story to tell his wife.

"What was going on with you two?" Shirl cried. "What was he doing to you?"

Si blinked, wiped his tanned forearm against his eyes. "Ah, nothing. I told him I didn't like his attitude."

"Stay away from him," Shirl said.

By late afternoon they were at the Trevi Fountain.

"You know that song?" Herbie asked Theresa.

"'Three Coins in the Fountain'?"

"Yeah. But that wasn't the original title. It was written at Grossinger's. The title was 'Three Cohens in the Fountain.'"

"Herbie!" Theresa cried.

The fat man took her arm. "So what can you lose? Toss the coin in, make a wish."

"It says you'll come back to Rome," Flo said. She was looking intently into Theresa's eyes. They all suspected something had gone on between the teacher and Flemington, that the Flemingtons had left because of her. It intrigued Flo and Shirl and the other Westbury women: a *femme fatale* at age forty-four! A schoolteacher, twice married, still able to break up marriages!

"The fountain was built by Salvi," Capelli said wearily. He was dreadfully tired. The tour had upset his schedule. He was a bureau manager, graduated from conducting people from fountain to fountain. Only the untimely death of the old man had pressed him into service. He had forgotten how exhausting it was. Would he have the strength to visit his mistress for their usual seven-to-eight session? Even if he did he would be far from satisfactory. To go home directly to his morbid Milanese wife was more than he could bear.

445

Bettenhausen was pacing the crowded promenade in front of the chained posts that kept people out of the coin-studded pool. The sparkling *acqua vergine,* brought to Rome by Agrippa two centuries ago gushed in white torrents. Salvi? Bernini? Was there not some original work here by one of his heroes, Leon Battista Alberti?

"Already I threw fifteen coins," Herbie shouted. "For that much, I should spend a year in Rome."

"Terry?" Shirl asked. "No coin?"

"I'm out of lire. Gave my last to the guide at the Villa Giulia."

She wanted to add: "They don't grant you *any* wish, just the return to Rome."

"I'll lend you one," Dr. Grant said. He gave her a ten-lire piece.

The teacher tossed it over her shoulder. A foolish gesture, but no more foolish than her pursuit of Harry Flemington. She could laugh about it, taste the spice of lingering hope underneath the bitterness. She could hear Bettenhausen lecturing Mavis Hutzler about someone named Alberti, and walked over to catch a few words.

Lumbering like a wounded hippo, his feet shrieking with hot pains, Herbie, trailed by his wife, the Shapiros, and the Yasudas, turned a corner and walked into the second-floor bar of the hotel. It was dark and air-conditioned and it was a few moments before they noticed Mrs. Legrand sitting by herself in a corner. She was smoking a cigarette and sipping scotch.

"Oh, poor thing," Flo said. She and Shirl walked over and extended their sympathies to the old woman. Flo kissed her. Shirl embraced her. Sandra Yasuda wept. But none sat down. They felt alien, apart. Which of them knew Mrs. Legrand or understood her? Flo marveled at her. It was like Herbie said, they were *something else.* True Americans. Independent. Alone. Wanderers. From city to city, without family, without children, getting by with each other's companionship. No tumult, no strangling relatives. There was a lot to be admired in them, but Herbie and Flo and the Yasudas would not have had their life for a million bucks.

"Ma," Herbie muttered, "I'm real sorry, Ma. I mean Mrs. Legrand."

"Now, Harvey. You can still call me Ma."

"I, ah, it wasn't polite." Herbie's voice was buried in a stuffed derma. "Ma—Mrs. Legrand, I hope he didn't suffer. You were so close, you and Pa. I mean Mr. Legrand."

She drew on her cigarette and exhaled like a teen-age girl showing off with her first weed. "Harvey, I'll be angry with you if you keep muttering like that. Don't you know Weston and I could always take a

446

joke? We have a good sense of humor. We always did. Oh, we didn't show it, like you and Murray—"

Yasuda smiled weakly and bowed his head, chastised. Had his cigars and his lousy elephant jokes annoyed the old couple?

"—but we liked a good time. When you started calling me Ma Barker, it made the whole trip for us."

Flo sat down next to her. "Stop trying to make that dope of a husband of mine feel good. Are you all right? Can we help? What about . . . ?"

"Weston was cremated at three this afternoon. It was a beautiful ceremony. Pepi got the Protestant minister from the English church and he conducted a lovely service."

They were silent. Her courage was a reprimand.

"What about burial?" Shirl asked. "Here in Rome?"

"I suppose we'll have a small ceremony in Bisbee. It doesn't matter. Weston would be happy if I left his ashes in Rome. He was at home anywhere."

She looked up. Her eyes were bright, full of life and hope, unwilling to accept pity. "No one will be there from our families. Just me and Mr. Clay, our pastor, but I don't think Weston would mind. He and I are used to going it alone."

It was past six when Huggins and his wife got to their hotel room. Barbara groaned, shed clothing, fell naked on the bed, a Rubens nude, a woman full of folds and curves and quivering mounds of flesh.

"Jimmy. Relax me."

"Not right now."

"What did that Arab want? That creep with the mustache?"

"You, doll, you. Arabs like 'em fat."

"Nasty." She grabbed for his thigh as he sat on the edge of the bed. J.P. patted her hand. It didn't hurt to be nice to her. Poor broad. A world bounded by the A & P and Korvette's.

"No, Mr. Huggins," the concierge told him over the phone. "There has been no call for you. And there is no answer at the number you gave me."

On a chance, Huggins had looked up the Rome branch of the Arab bank in Jerusalem where Mr. Silwah had given him the good news. But it was a useless move—no bank would be open that late. By now Huggins was convinced he had a winning combination. He would brag to the Malfis how he had gotten the best deal with their stolen bills; curse them for saddling him with hot currency; demand a double

447

cut—twenty thousand dollars. Had he not led them to a new field of high profits?

He thought of Buck Sweeney. He had intended to find him. All he had to go by was a name remembered from a letter three years ago. The Wettlaufer Foundation. He asked the hotel operator to see if there was a number in Rome for them.

"Number is changed, sir," the girl said. "And it has a different name. I have for you someone on the line."

A woman's voice came through. *"Pronto. Chi parla?"*

"Mr. Sweeney?"

"Is not here. Is gone to beach for week."

"This is an old friend of his from New York. Mr. Huggins. Can you get in touch with him? Tell him I'm in Rome?"

"Sorry. Is away. Mr. Sweeney not want to be disturbed."

The woman did not want to be disturbed either. Before she hung up, Huggins succeeded in leaving the name of their hotel and the restaurant where the tour would be dining that night.

The waiters wore approximations of Renaissance costumes—doublets and hose, leather slippers. There was a vat of white wine in the center of the old square of apartments, which the American owners had purchased from the working families who had shared it for years. Overhead, lanterns and wreaths dangled. Musicians in checkered blouses and black hose strolled among the diners, none of whom were Romans. The mandolin player was the leader. He had shrewd eyes, and he made a point of picking out Italian-Americans, flattering them, but letting his contempt peek through with exaggerated grimaces and mocking renditions of "Oi Maria," "Faccem' Amore," and worst of all, "Sorrento," which he sang with inflated pathos.

"That fellow is making fun of the song," Bettenhausen said to the Grants and Wickers. "He should not do it."

"It isn't much of a song, Betts," Cornelia said.

"Quite true. But in mocking it he mocks people like Mrs. Huggins and others of Italian ancestry. I don't appreciate it."

"It's nothing to make a fuss over," his wife said.

"No, but he should be told off." The volcano began to rumble deep in Bettenhausen's abdomen. But this time he did not rise to reprimand the mandolin player, as he would have done three weeks ago. At the airport in New York, Cornelia recalled, he had chastised the waiter and the captain. Progress of a sort. The tour had done him a world of good. And that monkey business that he and Arnold Wicker had been engaged in. Betts had promised to reveal the matter in detail when

448

they were back in Sherman Oaks. He seemed slower to rage, a man no longer rubbing the old scar of frustration.

"It would be lost on the boor," Bettenhausen said, "but I wonder does he know that James Joyce once followed an organ grinder for a mile listening to him play 'Sorrento' over and over?"

"Now how did you know *that?*" Rosie asked.

"From the clutter in his big old head," Cornelia said.

"Wait a minute," Wicker said. "No loose ends here. Warren, two weeks ago you said something about Eleonora Duse dying in Pittsburgh. I forget how it came up. Is this the right time to tell us how you knew? And how come she died there?"

Bettenhausen studied the star-flecked sky. A cobalt-blue magnificence. The winds from the Tyrrhenian Sea blew away impurities. But how long would it last? He had seen the chipped and stained statuary; the churches turned into garages; the mosaics unrestored. He had read about the slow agony of Venice. Why was beauty so fragile, so unprotected? Why did men ignore the death of their grand achievements?

"The funeral director who made the arrangements for Eleonora Duse's body was my second cousin. He knew of my interest and told me the story." Bettenhausen sipped the white wine which La Locanda as claimed was from their farm in the Castelli Romani. Puckering, he said angrily: "Full of sulfur. Fake coloring. We are being treated to what the Italians call *sophisticati*—adulterated wine."

"What about Duse?" his wife asked.

"The great woman, in her late sixties, agreed to an American tour. In Pittsburgh she contracted a chill and died in April of 1924. It was her last desire to die in her beloved Italy. With her dying breath, she gave orders to pack, that she might catch the next boat. It was not to be. When her coffin was lowered to the deck of the battleship *Diulio*, humble Italian immigrants knelt on the quay and took off their hats in tribute to La Duse." Bettenhausen blew his nose. His eyes were damp. It was too much for him—Rome at night, the courtyard of an old palazzo, memories of Duse.

Across the courtyard Pepi, exhausted from handling the death of Mr. Legrand, was assisting the captain in taking the order.

"How many roast suckling pigs?" Virgil asked.

Hands shot up. Far more than in London at the start of the tour.

"Not here!" Mr. Wattle cried. "You're all crazy if you eat that poisonous stuff! Captain, captain!"

"Yes, sir?"

"A steak for me, you understand? A decent steak, if there is such a thing in Italy. Very, very, very, very well done. Split it open and cook it all the way through."

"Yes, sir, on the charcoal."

"No. In the stove. I don't want it contaminated. I don't trust any of this outdoor stuff."

"I think I'll have a steak too," Ed Hutzler said. Mr. Kuchtenberg was discussing it with his wife. He appeared steak-oriented. But he said nothing.

"The roast suckling pig is the specialty here," Virgil said.

"That's what they said in England," Mr. Wattle yelled.

"But you didn't try it," Pepi said.

"I'm warning all of you! You'll be sorry!"

Mavis Hutzler dug her husband in the ribs. "You stay with the pig, Ed. Don't you go following his lead. He doesn't know it all."

"Yes, pet," Ed said. He turned down his hearing aid.

"Any changes?" Pepi asked. A victory, he realized, a clear victory! Mr. Wattle and his well-done steak were isolated. If Three Worlds had done anything, it had opened up culinary horizons. Virgil prayed that the suckling pig would be tender, juicy, and free of trichinosis.

Herbie had expected gaiety at the farewell dinner. There was little. People kept looking at him to sing, to dance, to joke, but he could not. Not with Pa Barker gone. Not after his close shave in Istanbul. And especially not after what he had seen in the synagogue in Budapest.

"No jokes tonight, Herb?" Huggins asked him.

"Nah. I'm wore out."

"How's the gut?"

"Hurts. Flo says no suckling pig. Listen, waiter, you got maybe some nice *mamaliga*? A corn meal pudding with a baked herring on the side, like my *bubbe* used to cook?"

Virgil, in the midst of informing Mr. Gunthorpe that he would under no circumstances find a woman for him, heard Shackman's ragged voice and decided to do something for him. The fat man had been an asset to the tour. He had kept the party going. Even after his terrifying experience as a belly dancer, he had managed a few jokes.

"*Senti, Dino,*" Virgil called to the headwaiter, who was listening to Bettenhausen's complaint about the wine, "*un momento, per favore.*"

The escort huddled with the captain. They gave the impression of two *cinquecento condottieri* plotting against a duke.

Fifteen minutes later, led by musicians playing the grand march from *Aida,* the headwaiter appeared from the kitchen bearing a casserole. In step to the martial music they approached Herbie's table.

"Special for you, Mr. Shackman," Pepi said.

The captain set the white dish on the table. A warm homey aroma

450

arose as he lifted the lid. Under Herbie's twitching nose rested a mound of steamy yellow corn meal. In the center, swimming in a pool of earth-colored gravy, was a brown sausage.

"Italian *mamaliga*, Mr. Shackman," Virgil said. "They call it *polenta*. It is a northern specialty, but the captain had some made up. I am sorry we cannot provide the herring but perhaps a sausage will do."

"*Oi, gottenu*," Herbie sobbed. "I never believed I'd see it again." He sampled the yellow mush, letting a drop of the tangy gravy rim his spoon. "Here, everybody try."

The musicians struck up a Neapolitan song. Some of the waiters and waitresses stopped serving and began to dance a tarantella.

Struggling to his feet, Herbie pressed Virgil to his flabby breasts and kissed his forehead. "My buddy Pepi, my pal, my *yeshiva bucher*. Our last night on the tour and he brings me *mamaliga*."

"And it's only delicious," Shirl said.

"You see, people?" Herbie bellowed. "You see what service we get? Let's hear it for Pepi, everybody."

"*Wahoo!*" A. T. Gunthorpe yelled. "Le's have an old rebel yell fo' ole Peppy!" He shrieked like a Confederate infantryman charging at Second Manassas.

"Hey, Gunthorpe," Herbie called to him. "How about canning that ridge-runner stuff, huh? We're all civilized Americans here, you know what I mean? I heard enough of that cracker crap in the Army."

"*Wahoo!*" Gunthorpe repeated. "The South shall rise again! Ole Herbie is mah good buddy!"

Voices grew louder but bodies wearied. Several couples left early, taking taxis back to the hotel rather than wait for the bus. Ed Hutzler fell asleep sitting up.

"Did you enjoy the farewell party?" Virgil asked the remaining diners.

"I'm all choked up," Herbie said.

"*Herbie*," Flo said sharply.

"But I mean it this time. I *am* all choked up. When he brought me that *mamaliga*, it all came back to me."

"What did?" Si asked.

"How when I was a kid and was so poor," Herbie said.

"All that from corn meal mush?" asked Shirl.

"I can't explain it."

"Try," his wife said. The air was warm and soft. There was an indescribable tenderness in it, something that mellowed them (or was it the sulfurous wine? Bettenhausen wondered), made them succumb to a vague camaraderie. Virgil, sitting between Theresa and Dr. Grant, sensed it. It happened at the end of every tour. Proof of the brotherhood of man. Unlikely. But he knew what Herbie was trying to articulate. There had been hints of it in the refusal of people to join Mr. Wattle's well-done steak.

"It's like I love everybody," Herbie blurted out.

"A generous feeling," Pepi said.

"Even Wattle over there," Shackman went on. "Henderson and Ibith, and Terry, and Father Konay, and poor Ma Barker. Mavis and Ed."

"You're drunk," Flo said.

"Nah, I had hardly any. Besides, Professor Bettenhausen says this wine is cut with water and distilled from beans. And boy, isn't he something? If I had his brains I'd be a millionaire."

"Keep talking, genius," Flo said. "You'll put your foot in it."

A yawn turned Herbie's vermilion face into one cavernous mouth. A yawn grew on top of the yawn and his features vanished around the red wound. "Flo, dollink, take me home. I can't walk another inch. I can't look at another picture. I can't drink another glass seltzer. I just wanna go home."

"But you are in a good mood, sir?" Virgil asked.

"Yeah. If I don't fall on my face." He saw A. T. Gunthorpe waddling off, wandering into the street outside the block of apartments. "Hey, Gunthorpe! Before ya go, find out where the pro station is!"

A half hour after the bus had taken the lingerers at La Locanda to the hotel, Gunthorpe was still walking the streets in search of a woman. Those he saw appeared savage and terrifying. One had an odd rotting odor, another a set of huge white teeth that filled him with apprehension.

At length he found himself in a corner of the Piazza del Popolo, at the base of the steps leading up to the Viale d'Annunzio. Across the great square, opposite the obelisk with its lion fountains, lights shone in the sidewalk cafés. Taxis and private cars zoomed and skidded through the moon-flooded piazza, where (unknown to Gunthorpe) Communists and labor unions often held their rallies.

Walking slowly, his splay feet treading the stones of Rome, his big-boned, big-bellied body, unpained except for the yearning in his groin, Gunthorpe abruptly realized he had stumbled upon a swarm, a herd, an *army* of whores.

"Dang. Ain't never seen so many in one place in mah life." It reminded him of November over the rice fields—more mallard ducks than a man could imagine. So many with their green heads and bright eyes. And here also—in blonde wigs and black beehives, jiggling behinds, loaded breasts, wobbling in boots and high heels. Perfumes

452

clouded the air and clogged his nostrils. He hardly knew where to begin.

But there was something strange. The girls seemed to be milling around the base of the stairs as if gathering for some purpose other than solicitation. A squad of carabinieri in tan uniforms stood to one side. They seemed to be there to supervise, to keep order should trouble arise.

Gunthorpe touched a fat blonde's elbow, "Hi, baby."

"No, no. No tonight."

He tried an awesome tall woman with a winking gold tooth, breasts like twin puddings, in a tight green dress. "Hi, honey."

"*Via via, Americano.* Don' want."

For a third time, he approached a pale girl in a white mini-skirt; a bit young for the trade, but with a raunchy eye. "Sweetie, you workin' tonight?"

"No. No work."

Gunthorpe was puzzled. But his good humor never left him. There were clearly a hundred ladies strolling, chatting, arguing, not interested in customers.

On the stone steps, an authoritative-looking older woman in a startling long white wig, her face hidden behind a layer of cosmetics, was talking to a tieless man in a white shirt. The man was wearing a red armband. Behind them, bedizened girls were holding aloft hand-lettered placards.

"Whut in hell?" Gunthorpe asked. "Whut in hell is goin' on?"

The *grande dame* in the white wig began to speak. She had a potent voice. The crowd of whores at the base of the steps listened attentively. The combined aroma of their perfume, cologne, hair dressing rose in the warm night air, sweet laminated vapors of sin.

Gunthorpe walked toward the two policemen. "Y'all speak English?"

"Leetle bit."

"Whut's goin' on? Can't a man git hisse'f a woman hyeah? Nevah seen so much in one place. Ain't I good enough?"

"Is . . . *sindaco.*"

"Hunh?"

"Union meeting. Union, union. *Comunisti.* Is organizing ladies."

"Union? Like the dang CI and O?"

"Union. For girls, more money."

"Waaall, bust my britches." A.T.'s ruddy face beamed at the girls. He loved every one of them, their powerful odors, their fleshy rumps and bouncy boobies. But he also respected courage and initiative. "Ain't that a possum's ass," he said, full of wonder. "Onliest time in history a man been denied his poontang by a union meeting."

453

Day 20: Arrivederci Roma! Good-by to Europe and the marvels of Three Worlds! Planet Tours lets you sleep late, then on to a comfortable midday jet flight back to New York, full of memories, souvenirs, and new friends! Happy landing!

The hotel phone, stabbing the air-conditioned silence with a prolonged *brrrrring!*, caused Huggins to rise vertically from the narrow bed. One wine-swollen eye saw the time on his wristwatch: 8:05 A.M. Not too bad, considering the state of his head and his stomach. The official call was for eighty-thirty, with a 10 A.M. departure for the airport. Why so early?

"Hah? Whah?"

"Jimmy?"

"Yeah." He had been certain, once the fog cleared from his numbed head, that it was Chahoub. But this was a New York voice—gritty, knowing.

"Yeah. Who . . . ?"

"It's Buck. Buck Sweeney."

"Buck. Buckie? Bernard Kevin?"

"The same. Come on down. We'll have breakfast."

Barbara moaned and shifted her body under the sheet. It had been good last night—endless, varied, the two of them full of desire and invention. It had taken a long time to break Barbara of her prudish insistence on basics, but she had come around.

"Where are you goin'?" she yawned.

"It's Buck Sweeney. He's downstairs."

"Oh, him."

"Sweetie, will you finish the packing? You're better at it than me. I'll grab my personal stuff and the camera bag. I'll see you in the lobby."

Sweeney was seated across the shabby lobby, reading an Italian newspaper. If this linguistic talent impressed Huggins, he was less impressed with his old buddy's appearance. Buck wore a rumpled seersucker suit. His shoes were scuffed. The tumbling black curls that once suggested a Bronx Dylan Thomas or an Easter rebellion dynamiter were untrimmed and graying. Years ago Sweeney had been a thick-bodied, fleshy man who carried his weight well. Now he seemed

454

misproportioned. His limbs were thinner, his face sagged, and the fat had settled into a paunch that flopped over his belt.

"Jimmy. Old J.P."

"Buck, you old bastard. You old punchball player." The men embraced. Huggins was ashamed of his two-hundred-dollar suit and his Whitehouse & Hardy shoes. For a moment they studied one another. Both were thinking about the lost years. Parochial school. Fordham. The corner candy store. Playing dirty tricks on old man Lieberman. Sweeney's father's gin mill on Tremont Avenue. And the two of them, when they were twelve, in St. Nicholas of Tolentine uniforms, carrying a banner in the Paddy's Day parade: *England Get Out of Ireland.*

James Patrick felt his stomach flutter. The old days were not that great. But at least he and Buck had had a lot of laughs. One summer they worked as lifeguards at Rockaway. Did they once break into a brewery, cart off a dozen cases, and stay drunk for a week? They must have. And paid off the cops with a case.

Huggins, sipping San Pellegrino on his friend's advice—his aggrieved innards could not tolerate Italian coffee that early—filled Sweeney in on his career, his marriage, his family. He said nothing about the Malfis and their swag market.

"Stuffy old fart I am," Huggins said. "Getting on to forty, and still wearing Brooks Brothers clothes."

Sweeney's face was warm with admiration. "Glad you made it, Jim. You always had lots of smarts. I never knew anyone could get grades the way you did without cracking a book."

"I cheated."

"That takes brains also." Sweeney winked. Huggins saw it was a routine tribute. Buck did not mean it. He no longer respected a man who sneaked textbooks into the john or wrote answers on his cuffs.

"You're with some kind of charity? Some foundation?" J.P. asked.

Father Konay and Mr. Wattle emerged from the elevator. They greeted him. The industrialist went to the concierge's desk and began to argue about the price he had been charged for a bottle of mineral water.

"It's complicated." Sweeney paused. Huggins studied his face. The old drunken freeloader, the practical joker (nailed Solly Hymowitz's sneakers to the floor of the Young Men's Hebrew Association once) had vanished forever. This Buck Sweeney had something of the priest about him, a cautious, slow-moving priest, not the kind you could fake out.

"You been with them . . . how long? Seven years? All I could remember was the name. The Wettlaufer Foundation."

Sweeney smiled. "Yeah. The name was changed. We're called the

455

Committee for the Study of Freedom. Sounds like some Commie out-fit, huh? Or a buncha Birch nuts. Actually, it's in the honest middle."

"But what do you do?"

"I'm sort of administrative officer. Our headquarters are in Rome. We got a couple of sociologists and psychologists who handle the data."

"But what does the foundation do?" J.P. asked.

"Hard to say. We started about eight years ago. Arnie Wettlaufer was my CO in the Army. Loaded. Money on top of money. He hired me to start a survey of what he called Noble Christians."

"*You?*"

"I know, I know. My brother Leo used to sell *Social Justice,* and they were still reading the Protocols of the Elders of Zion on our block. Hey, how about the way old Fordham's changed? You dig those radical priests? And those crazy new nuns?"

"Oh, sure. But what about Noble Christians?"

"The idea was to conduct interviews with European Christians who had saved Jews from the Nazis. Ordinary people who had put it on the line, risked their lives. Some got killed. Tortured. Some sur-vived. Wettlaufer wanted to get their stories down before they were gone. It was a good idea. So I rattled around Europe on his dough—tape recorder, car, expense account." Sweeney smiled in self-depreca-tion. "I took the job because it looked like another freeload, and I was on my uppers. But you won't believe it, Jimmy, it made a man out of me."

"Why wouldn't I believe it?"

"You knew me way back, Jim. Was it you or me who pulled some old guy's beard on Arthur Avenue on Yom Kippur once?"

"Neither. It was that jerk Eddie Hanratty."

"Maybe, maybe. Anyway. I must have interviewed thirty of these people—Germans, Dutch, Belgians, Italians, Poles, Hungarians. All different. And all with some decent act, some courageous, unexpected thing they did once. A librarian in Belgium who hid Jewish kids on farms. An old lady in the Ukraine who saved a couple of families. A German engineer who faked the records at a concentration camp and kept a couple of hundred Jews from being murdered. An Italian editor who ran an underground railway. He died of starvation in a concentration camp."

"So you interviewed them for this Wettlaufer?" Huggins had diffi-culty seeing his old friend in this role. Vaguely he recalled Sweeney had once wanted a rich career in publishing, show biz. But basically Buck had been a sponger.

"Yeah. But I guess I blew it. I got drunk too much. I lost the tapes.

Meanwhile the foundation brought in some pros—sociologists, statisticians." He smiled at Huggins, and it was not that mocking street grin of Sweeney's: his eyes were frank and sorrowful. "Got me a wife out of it. I married an Italian girl. Her father was a carabinieri officer, a partisan."

"They say it's a good mix, Harps and Eye-talians. That makes two of us."

The two men looked at one another—Sweeney rumpled, scarred, carrying with him the look of a reformed drinker, a man who had been through some fiery furnace, and Huggins dapper, lean, sharp, moving upward.

"You like what you're doing?" J.P. asked.

"Sure. What else could I do? The foundation expanded some years ago. It's not just research on people who saved Jews. It's any kind of humanitarian effort. I know it sounds hokey and like a Christer's dream of the world, but I'm convinced. We do reports on guys in Communist countries who go to jail, or can't write, or get exiled for their ideas. Writers in Greece and Portugal. Dissenters in Russia and East Germany and Czechoslovakia. We did a project on the history of the civil rights movement. We've documented the Hungarian revolution."

"But you started it."

"Jimmy, that was a long time ago. Fact is I think Arnie—that's Wettlaufer—keeps me on because I once saved his ass from some ridge-runners when we were in the 997th Ordnance. I don't know. I'm something to him. Fact is, I'm sort of a paper shuffler at the office, which isn't to say I don't believe in the work."

It seemed incredible to Huggins. He did not lack sympathy for Sweeney's work, or an understanding of what the foundation was trying to do. To document and research the work of good people was hardly an undertaking at which one sneered. Humble people who saved Jews from the Nazis; workers in Czechoslovakia who demanded freedom; plain black people in America asking for a job and a home; Hungarian Freedom Fighters. Who could argue that there were some disputes to which there was no *other* side? But *Sweeney?* The old cop-taunter, the old pub-crawler? Years ago when they were undergraduates they would prowl the bars of the Bronx looking for weirdos, drunks, anyone at whom they could poke fun. They called them "stims"—short for *stimulation,* people who could be mocked, teased, made the butt of crude jokes. Maybe it was harmless, J.P. thought. But it was often cruel. Sweeney had led the chase. But now? Now he had had a vision.

457

"So. You make out all right? I mean, for your family . . . ?" Huggins asked.

"I get by. Rome isn't cheap. We got a little apartment up north. I got a boy. Five years old. That'll be it. Very Italian. Lots of birth control here despite you-know-who. Adriana says one's enough. Wettlaufer looks after me and I'm happy. What is happy anyway? I speak Italian. I know the storekeepers in the neighborhood. I ride a Vespa to work. I rent a dump up the coast in the summer. I got a great wife and a good kid, even though he's frail and sensitive—not a big dumb Mick like his old man. But most of all I believe in what we're doing."

He never saw any of the old Bronx crowd any more, J.P. thought, but if he did, and if he told them about Buck Sweeney, none would believe him. He damned near did not believe the story. Yet there sat Bernard Kevin, telling it calmly. Huggins was moved.

"Guy's looking for you," Sweeney said. He pointed across the lobby to the concierge's desk. Father Konay was studying the cover of *Time* magazine.

"The padre?" J.P. asked. "He's with us. On the tour."

"No. The dark guy at the other side."

It was Chahoub. With Lebanese politeness, he had been waiting for Huggins to finish his talk with Sweeney. The latter had seen him gesturing toward them and heard Huggins' name mentioned.

"Excuse me, Buck. A little business."

J.P. walked to the Arab. "Well?"

"I have it, Mr. Huggins. It took some doing, but I spent all of yesterday afternoon making the arrangements. Here it is."

He handed the lawyer a sealed envelope. Huggins opened it. There was a certified check, drawn on the Banco di Roma, for $46,187.42, payable to James Patrick Huggins.

"I hope your arithmetic is correct," J.P. said.

"To the last decimal, sir. Here is an accounting sheet, showing all costs, including postage and cables. The interest for the short loan was somewhat less than anticipated. I arranged it. For your good will."

"And the principal? My original investment?"

"Safe in a reliable branch of a Lichtenstein bank in Vienna. I understood you wished to make a second investment in our company."

"I'll authorize it."

"Good. I have the contract here. We will sustain our interest in platinum and other rare metals for the next few weeks. The market has never been better."

Huggins took the documents to the concierge's desk, scanned them and signed them. One more time. And maybe again. Chahoub wanted

458

more of his stolen money. Anything. So long as it was negotiable. He had over forty-six thousand dollars in his pocket for no work at all. Nothing. Some mad meetings and foolish interviews. And the Malfis would pocket it. He had led them into green pastures of which they had never dreamed.

J.P. gave Chahoub several of his cards. "All correspondence to my office. And no direct references to what we're doing, eh, Chahoub? My law partners aren't in this. The money comes from someone else." Did a career as a fancy *passeur*—as Moussac had called him—loom? A dapper *cambiste*, moving around the world and creating wealth as he traveled?

"Ah, thank you, sir. May all our endeavors be crowned with signal success." The Lebanese bowed and collected his copies of the new contract.

"One thing, Chahoub. Is this check negotiable?"

"Absolutely, sir. Because of its size, a letter from you may be necessary. But do with it as you will."

"Thanks. So long, Chahoub."

"Good-by, sir. I have enjoyed our transactions. And my regards to the charming Mrs. Huggins."

The lawyer lingered at the concierge's desk, studying the papers, staring at the check. Unfair, unfair. If only the mobs understood how easy it was to be crooked. Lacking confidence in their own dishonesty, thieves like his in-laws craved "legitimate businesses."

Huggins looked at Buck Sweeney. Then he turned the check over and endorsed it. He signed his own name with a flourish, and wrote beneath it:

In full payment to the Wettlaufer Foundation, Rome, Italy, Charitable contribution.

"Who was the Arab?" Sweeney asked as Huggins sat down. He had stuffed the papers into his jacket pocket.

"Some hustler. Listen. This foundation that supports your work. How is it fixed for money?"

"It's broke. It always is. Arnie feeds the kitty, but he's only one guy. We're always firing secretaries and canceling field trips. I was supposed to meet some Polish university people who were booted out last month. Couldn't afford the trip to Sweden to do the interviews."

Huggins gave him the check. "Don't ask questions, Buck. This is a fully deductible charitable contribution to you and your group. You can send me a letter later."

Sweeney stared at the check. "Come on, Jimmy. None of your schoolyard jokes."

"It's no joke, Bucky. It's for you. Get drunk on it if you want."

"I'm on the wagon."

"Give it to your boss."

"Holy horror. I'm stunned. Was this . . . ? Did you know . . . ? I mean . . . who . . . ?"

Sweeney's flustered red face, the popping eyes, made him burst into laughter. "An impulse, Bucky, an impulse." Huggins wiped tears of joy away. "The only good one I've had in years."

At his post at the entrance to the bus, Virgil checked his memo book. Baggage. Return air tickets. Contacts in New York for the people making connecting flights. Another cable about the Flemingtons: New York was upset. Mrs. Legrand.

The tourists came straggling out of the hotel early. They seemed eager to get to the airport. A peddler selling leather belts was being tormented by Flo, Shirl, and a few Midwestern ladies. But the fever was abating. There was no frenzy in their bargaining and they bought little from the man.

Theresa Carrell, in a beige traveling suit, came out of the hotel door. A superb woman, Virgil thought. Yet it was not unusual to find such attractive women leading lonely lives. As if men were unequal to them. Husbands and lovers could not measure up. Men probably had tried to make comparisons between her character, her bearing, and their own, and were rendered uneasy, self-doubting. Had she been born rich, Virgil mused, studying her splendid figure, the aristocratic line of head, neck, spine, and leg, she would have been better off. Perhaps a bit empty-headed and aimless, but more malleable, and less prone to make men feel inadequate.

"Feeling well, Mrs. Carrell?"

"A little sad, Pepi. I wish I could spend a month here. And a month in France, and England, and Russia, and Austria and all the places you took us."

"Someday you will."

"And thank you for being such a superb guide. No, that isn't fair. You were more than a *cicerone*. Did I pronounce that correctly?"

"Perfectly."

Gunthorpe and Mr. Wattle came out of the lobby. They looked subdued. The latter had been avoiding Mrs. Carrell. Had his galloping ego deserted him?

"Yes, more than a guide," Theresa said. "You were a part of every country you took us to. An Englishman, a Frenchman, an Italian. And making it all clear to us, easier to understand. I won't forget you."

"You are too kind."

Theresa gave him his tip: folded lire notes. He would not look at it. Perhaps never. He would let the money accumulate, and render judgments as to who had given him what. The five hundred dollars that Harry Flemington had shoved into his hand in Jerusalem would make this one of the most lucrative tours he had ever led. It would be nice not to know for a change who were the skinflints and who the sports. But he would have fun guessing. It was only money. He had enough for his needs. And as long as he had a supply of duty-free Gitanes, his apartment in Knightsbridge, and an occasional lady friend, he could be happy.

"He's counting heads again," one of the Midwestern ladies called out when most of the group was seated on the bus.

"No, no," another corrected. "Pepi counts legs and divides by two."

Murray yawned. "Hey, Herb. Why do elephants have white tusks?"

"Everyone is here," Pepi said to the Grants, who were seated up front, "but Mrs. Legrand."

"Saw her an hour ago. She seemed okay." Dr. Grant had assumed the job of looking after the widow.

"Tell me, tell me, Father," Herbie said huskily, "why do elephants have white tusks?"

"They use Ultra-Brite," Sandra Yasuda whispered.

"Hey, who asked you?" Murray protested—and kissed her. They were wearing matching green silk turtle-necks. Murray had bought them in the most expensive shop in Rome. At Gucci's he had ordered a specially constructed valise it would take two months to make, and would be shipped air freight to Victorville. Then he had cashed his remaining traveler's checks and given most of the money— two hundred dollars in lire—to Virgil.

"There she is," Ibith said. "Hen, give her a hand."

Dr. Grant got up and assisted Mrs. Legrand. She was carrying several travel bags. The physician offered to take them.

"No, Doctor. I can carry them. Independent folks, you know. You've done too much for me." She glanced at her bulging purple Planet Tours flite-pak. "And for poor Weston. You were so kind to him."

"Are you all right? Did you take the sleeping pill?"

"I didn't need it, thank you."

Aboard the bus, the old woman smiled at her fellow tourists. "As Harvey would say, Ma Barker is back."

"Attagirl, Ma," Herbie shouted. "You got lots of moxie."

"Yeah, Herbie right," A. T. Gunthorpe said. "They got lotsa heart. That ole man, that ole lady. Keepin' up with us. Heck, a man can cash in any time." There were secrets in the world, wisdom hidden, things unknown, Gunthorpe had learned. It wasn't all shooting mal-

461

lard ducks from a blind. Or golden retrievers breaking the ice for you in November. How did you account for a country where the hookers organized into unions?

"Would you like to sit next to Ibith?" Dr. Grant asked the old woman.

"Sit with me, Elizabeth," Flo Shackman said. "Come on, next to the window."

Others offered their companionship. But Mrs. Legrand, bearing her burdens, shuffled down the aisle in her slippers. What slippers! Dr. Wicker thought. They were tougher than any hiking boot. Waterproof, dirtproof, cushioned, braced with arch supports.

"I want two seats," she said.

"Of course, of course," Mavis Hutzler said. She and Ed had been separated, each with an empty seat next to one another. The battle over the bathroom had been unusually embittered that morning. "Honey, I'll move next to Ed," Mavis said.

"Thank you, Mavis dear."

Mrs. Legrand settled herself into the window seat.

"*Andiamo,*" Virgil said to the driver.

"There, that's fine," Mrs. Legrand said. From the purple travel bag she took out a burnished bronze urn. "There's Weston. Safe and happy."

"*Gevald,*" Herbie said. "I'm gonna be sick. The ashes."

"Whah? Whah?" Flo whispered.

"The old guy. Pa Barker. They had him cremated, didn't you hear? And he's traveling with her."

More than half the passengers turned to steal a glance at Mrs. Legrand. They whispered, marveled, shivered a little. She placed the bronze urn on the seat next to her. Virgil watched her closely.

"There you are, Weston," she said. "We're together all the time on this trip."

"Yeah," Herbie gasped. "I'm all choked up. I can't smoke this cigar. Air, air."

"Now, Harvey," Mrs. Legrand called over the back of her seat. "You stop that complaining at once. Weston paid for a seat and he's going to have one all the way home. And on the airplane also."

"Sure, Ma. Whatever you say."

"I think you are being put on, is the expression," Rosie Wicker said to Herbie.

"Don't I know it."

"Am I not entitled to a seat for Weston?" Mrs. Legrand called to Virgil.

"Most certainly, madame."

462

Virgil stared at the urn. Yes, a new experience for him, a totally new one.

In the departure lounge, Barbara Huggins became gay and talkative. She began to chatter at great length with Ibith Grant—a woman she had fearfully avoided during the tour. Hoity-toity colored woman. Thinks she's something because she went to college and got a doctor for a husband.

"Ooh, I can't wait to see my babies," Barbara said. "You have children?"

"Oh yes. Older than yours. One in college and one finishing high school. And Henderson's got a married son from his first marriage."

Prudence halted Barbara's friendliness. So. He was married before. You'd know it. Never expect anything from them, even the smart ones. But even as mean thoughts swirled in her head—a head full of sales, prices, upholstery fabrics, double-sized freezing compartments, shells of beef—she was rueful in a wasting way. They were black, and honest, and intelligent, and had wonderful manners. Why couldn't they *all* be like that? A deep hurt germinated in Barbara, self-pity at her own failures. It was better not to think about them, better to think of her beautiful babies, and the summer home she and Jimmy would build in Hampton Bays next year.

Virgil, who knew the Italian security people on a first-name basis, came to the departure lounge a few minutes before boarding time. He bade good-by to each member of the tour. He showed no great emotion, but his dark eyes were warm as he joked with the men and flattered the women.

Mrs. Legrand had taken the urn with her husband's ashes out of the flite-pak. Proudly she carried it under her arm—declining Si's offer to bear it—like a precious purchase, a bargain picked up in some shop on the Piazza Navona.

"I am so sorry," Virgil said. "I hope we were of help to you in your tragedy."

"You were wonderful, Pepi. You were all wonderful." Virgil kissed her cheek. He felt the strength in her old face; something peculiarly American—independent, footloose, wandering. Not like the old ladies of Europe who dressed in black and sat in kitchens. A faint whiff of scotch caressed his nose. Thank goodness, he thought, she had some sustenance to get her home.

"Good-by, Mrs. Hutzler."

"Good-by, Pepi. You are a dear man."

"Mr. Hutzler . . ."

"Thanks, young feller."

"Dr. Grant, it was an honor."

"Cut it out, Pepi. You made it happen."

"Mrs. Grant, good-by, and thank you for being so pleasant all the time."

Ibith winked. "Right on, brother."

And Virgil, grinning at the black woman's compliment, said to Horace T. Wattle: "Good-by, sir."

"No hard feelings, young man. I complain a lot, but only when I have a right to."

"Quite so, sir. Good-by, Father Konay. Mr. and Mrs. Zuflacht. Good-by, Mr. Gunthorpe."

"Ole Peppy. You the best dang guide in the world." A.T. pulled Virgil close. "'Cept you don't know nothin' 'bout poontang. Man could spend a year travelin' with you an' never git him an itty-bitty piece. Ah ended up in a union meetin' of Eye-talian hookers las' night—"

"Move it on, Gunthorpe!" Herbie shouted. "Stop tryin' to sell Pepi horse manure!"

"Ole Herbie sure gave us the laughs."

"Good-by, Mr. Shackman, a special good-by to you. I am grateful for your jokes and your good humor. I am sorry about the illness you suffered in Istanbul."

Laden with bags, cameras, sacks, Herbie managed to crush Virgil in a gorilla's embrace. He kissed the escort on both cheeks. "I'm all choked up. I love ya, Pepi. You're aces with me. Listen, me and Si and Sid and the whole crowd, we're goin' to California next year to visit Murray and Sandra, and eat him out of Kobe steak and tempura. You come along. Get Planet to assign you. We got to have you."

"I am sorry, Mr. Shackman, as much as I like Japanese food."

Murray inched forward. "So why doncha come, Pepi?"

"No *mamaliga*," Virgil said.

Herbie embraced him again; the fat man was weeping.

"Mr. Shapiro, Mrs. Shapiro. Mr. Huggins. I trust your camera case served you well. Mrs. Huggins, you beautiful dark lady of the sonnets."

"Oh, Pepi." Barbara's eyes widened. A European creep, she thought, but a wonderful creep. What was he anyway? A Greek, she decided. Some kind of slippery Greek.

"The camera case was great, Pepi," J.P. said.

"You made all your contacts?" A smile turned Virgil's mouth. Goddamn! Huggins thought. I've finally got him curious, turned on! "Zurich, Vienna, Jerusalem? All those business associates you had to visit? And Mr. Sweeney who called this morning? By the way, did he reach you?"

"Yeah. An old friend. Met 'em all, Pepi."

The tour escort learned forward. His lips barely moved. "A marvelous cover, eh, Mr. Huggins? But I beg of you, don't use Planet again for such transactions."

"You knew a lot."

"More than I will talk about."

The lawyer pumped his hand. "Good man, Pepi. Someday I'll give you the details. You got to believe one thing. It was for a good cause."

"Mr. Force, Mrs. Force, good-by. Mr. and Mrs. Kuchtenberg . . ."

The Midwesterners, exhausted, good-natured, full of plans, filed by. Virgil had a personal word for each. Patient. Undemanding. Decent tippers. And how they had swooned and vied for the favor of the Grants!

"Mrs. Wicker, you were a superb tourist," he said. "Your interest in everything is what a guide looks for. Happy voyage."

"You come visit us when you come to the States," Rosie said. "We love you, that's all."

"Oh dear, this is excessive. Please, Mrs. Wicker, before I cry, the way Mr. Shackman did."

Finally Theresa came by.

"Good-by, Mrs. Carrell. Was the tour satisfactory?"

"In every way."

Virgil took her hand and kissed it. Did his heels click? His eyes close? In that moment he seemed to Terry the distillation of all that was decent and civilized and resilient in Europe.

"I am sorry about the matter of the—" Pepi held his hands up.

"The Flemingtons. My fault."

"No, mine. I should have foreseen. I suspected. But it is not my business. I am not sorry that they left the tour early. Such things occur." Virgil shrugged.

"Let's go, Terry!" Rosie called from the entranceway. "The hostesses are getting anxious."

"What are you sorry about?" the teacher asked.

"That it did not work out. I hope you are not too disappointed."

"Learned a lesson, Pepi."

"I hope so. Good-by, Mrs. Carrell."

She waved a hand at him and left. The last of his group, in many ways the first. A shred of schoolboy yearning sparked in his chest: a woman he could have lived with, no doubt about it. But these things were better left unpursued. His life had settled into an acceptable groove. After the camps, one made accommodations, one halted ambition at a certain level. In a reflexive action, he patted his breast pocket to make sure that his British passport was there. Then he walked out of the departure area. Paperwork had multiplied in the last few days and he needed hours to catch up. He had a two-hour wait for his flight back to London. He would sit in the airport bar, sipping coffee, smoking and getting a leg up on his report on Three Worlds.

Aloft Mr. Wattle started an argument with the stewardess.

"Now look here," he said. "I chose to sit in the non-smoking section because I hate smoke. Now I discover that if you sit in non-smoking you get to see the children's movie, and that the adult movie is shown only in smoking. That is unfair."

"I'm sorry, sir. It seemed a fair way to break it down."

"Not to me. I hate smoke. I want to see the adult movie."

"We can arrange to get you a seat temporarily in the adult section, sir. Just for the movie."

"But they'll be smoking."

"I'm afraid so, sir. You see, the airline tries to satisfy a majority of people. Our surveys showed that less children smoke than adults."

"Are you being flippant with me, young lady?" Mr. Wattle's eyes sparkled. Father Konay tried to pull himself into his clerical collar. His eyes found some opposite words in his prayer book: *Vanity of vanities . . . as sounding brass . . .*

"Please fasten your seat belt," the girl said. "The sign isn't off."

"I intend to complain to one of your vice-presidents. He's a golfing friend."

"That's your privilege. Shall I give you the regular airline suggestion form?"

"No. I'll handle this my own way."

"Hey, Wattle!" Herbie shouted. "Leave her alone!"

"Yeah," Yasuda cried. "Lay off, buster! Boy, some guys never let it alone."

"That's the trouble with America," Mr. Wattle said. "Nobody complains."

Bettenhausen growled, shifted his belly, loosened the seat belt. "If I have to listen to that egomaniac all the way to New York, I shall be driven out of my senses." He leaned across the row of seats and touched Arnold Wicker's elbow. "Arnold, join me in the lounge. I have need of mineral water."

Cornelia and Rosie looked at one another.

"Now that the secret's out," Rosie said, "I mean, how those two heroes of ours accidentally got the scientist into Israel, you'd think they'd let us in on things."

Bettenhausen snorted as he rose. "The production is finished, but distribution and promotional problems remain. Like DeLaurentiis and Paramount, Arnold and I are about to divide up the world."

Wicker followed him to the rear of the plane. Actually he had wanted to check his list of patients, look over his progress charts. Mark Abrams' bite plate. Eddie McDowell's retainer. Harriet Miller's tooth positioner. Janet Rice's wisdom teeth. God, what a mess he'd have facing him. And the regional New England husband-and-wife doubles tournament. And the Riverford Ecology Movement battling to save Minnipack Forest, a fight to which he was committed. He needed a clear head and a responsive body. As much as he felt indebted to Bettenhausen for taking over the Borkin affair, the chase after the scientist, the crazy business initiated by the mysterious Leland, he wanted to obliterate such strange doings from his mind. A cluttered mind was an impediment, Dr. Wicker had long known. He needed memo pads, schedules, calendars, reminders. Borkin, Bettenhausen, and Leland were behind him, thank goodness, even though Warren kept insisting that the presumed KGB agent would be waiting for them at the airport.

"Look, Warren," the dentist said. "I'll buy you a drink, but I have to terminate the Borkin business. I have other things to think about."

"Of course, my boy." Bettenhausen scratched the short hairs under his throat. His beard needed a professional trim. Newly born as producer-director-writer—and *star!*—of a real spy story, he would allow himself the luxury of a visit to the homosexual stylist in Beverly Hills who specialized in beards.

"I mean it, Warren."

"Only the matter of Leland. I may need your help."

"If he's at the airport. And that's it. I'm a dull orthodontist, remember? I have a hundred kids with open bites and malocclusion waiting for me."

Bettenhausen was leaning forward, staring at a rack of reference books and guides at the lounge bar. Summoning the hostess, he asked: "Young lady, do you have a New York City telephone directory?"

"Regular or Yellow Pages?"

"Yellow Pages."

An intense look widened Bettenhausen's eyes. His hands gripped the sides of the lounge chair. The dentist wondered if he felt ill. "Warren! You okay?"

"I shall know in a moment."

"More notes in the Blue guide?" Ibith asked Theresa.

"I'm hopeless. It's the only way I'll remember anything."

"But you'll remember. I'm the total loss. I've forgotten already. Where did we see the Blue Mosque? Was the Schönbrunn in Vienna or Berlin? Who built the second temple, Solomon or Herod? My brain's a mess."

Father Konay leaned across the aisle. "You're not the only one, Mrs. Grant. I'm going to be mixed up for months. I'm grateful that the Lord let me live to have this experience, but my goodness, what did I see? And how can I possibly appreciate it? Just trying to understand the Sistine Chapel could keep me busy for a year. Mrs. Carrell has the right idea. She can go back and look at her books."

Theresa stroked her neck. *Her books.* Her folders, her notes, her projects, her teaching aids, her audio-visual gimmicks. Marvelous stuff. Voted "Most Popular" teacher every year. But no man in the house. No bed to share. A shivering recollection of Harry's smooth body, the coarse gray hair at his temples . . .

"Ah don' remember a dang thing," A. T. Gunthorpe said boastfully. "But, shoot, I was born stupid. Ah liked whut Ah saw, but don' ast me whut hit was."

"It doesn't matter, I guess," Dr. Grant said. "The young folks say you just have to dig it. Get a reaction. Okay for art, I suppose, but not for a lung operation."

Dig it. One of Father Folker's expressions. Used it all the time with his youth group, Father Konay recalled. Somehow he felt closer to the young priest, a bit more sympathetic to him. Father Konay could not explain it. Why? Was it the works of art, the monuments, the cathedrals he had looked at? Curious, the way the most impressive reminders of the faith's long, beautiful history were in paintings and statues and great buildings. And in some way Father Folker, with his childish advice to "dig" beauty, seemed closer to the Raphael madonnas and Bernini saints than he was. While a seminarian, Bert Folker had bummed around Europe. Maybe they would have something new to talk about, those long evenings in the cold parish house. Something besides Ed Marciniek and the Ospreys.

"It's a matter of circuitry," Dr. Grant said. "Electrical connections in the brain. You'll be surprised how much you'll remember. It's stored and someday you'll look at a picture, or read an article, and something you saw on this trip will come back. 'Hey,' you'll say, 'that's

468

the Dome of the Rock. That's the Ring in Vienna. I rode down that street.' Or, 'That's the statue of Moses in Rome.' And it will mean more to you then, maybe give you some insight."

"I hope so," Father Konay said.

"Ole Doc Grant," A. T. Gunthorpe said. "Ole Doc know what he talkin' about. If'n mah gut keeps botherin' me, Ah'm gittin' up to Minny-soda an' have Doc open me up."

"Oh, you're in great health, Mr. Gunthorpe."

"A.T.'s the name, Doc, A.T."

Circuits in the brain storing memories, Theresa thought: a boon and a curse. Peruginos and Dürers, basilicas and fountains. And a man's vanished face and body and voice.

"Mario's supposed to meet us at the airport," Barbara said. "I hope he remembers."

"He'll remember. When it comes to airports, Mario is always on time." Huggins wondered: Mario, and maybe Ralphie . . . and possibly the man from the Treasury Department? He had placed Chahoub's papers in the false bottom of the camera case. No one would ever know about the forty-six thousand dollar gift to Buck Sweeney. And the T-man—if indeed they bothered to meet the plane —would know only about a ten-thousand-dollar treasury bill he had flashed in Zurich. He would deny it. Mistaken identity. Nothing on him except some traveler's checks. Oh, there were traps and dangers ahead; but he felt refreshingly light on his feet, clear-headed. Everything could be explained to the Malfis later. They'd get their money after a few more of Chahoub's ships came in. The government would ask him a few questions and drop it.

"Wadja put in the bottom of the case?" Barbara asked.

"Papers."

"What kinda papers?"

"Dull stuff. For a client."

Huggins thought: My esteemed associates, swagmen and fences, selling air conditioners and ten-speed bicycles at less than cost. A fortune in hijacked transistor radios and hot tape decks. Could they find out he had stolen forty-six thousand dollars in profits, given it to an old friend who had seen a shining light? It was possible. The Malfis had connections. To hell with them.

"Look 'em right in the eye," J.P. said.

"Whah?" Barbara asked.

"Words to an old song." Across the aisle he saw Mrs. Legrand dozing in her seat. Her head was erect and proud. One arm was draped around the bronze urn with her husband's ashes. The urn sat on the seat next to her. She wanted no refund on Weston's ticket. They had been together a long time and they would come home from their last trip together. There, J.P. thought, was *courage* for you. If the old lady could handle herself that decently so could he.

Bettenhausen's hands trembled as he turned pages in the telephone directory. His breath came in short audible spurts. Dr. Wicker was concerned for him.

"You feel all right, Warren?"

Bettenhausen ignored him. He stopped under L and began to scan a list of names, hiding the yellow pages from the dentist's curious eye.

"Great God in heaven," Bettenhausen said. "The obligatory scene. An off-stage circumstance, but what a brilliant one. The last stone drops into place."

"Warren, what the devil are you talking about?"

The snowy eyebrows lofted. The Hollywood man's eyes were full of cunning. His voice approximated Sydney Greenstreet's. "My dear Arnold, the mystery of Mr. Leland is solved. His interest in Borkin. His subterfuge. His cunning. His resourcefulness."

"I'm lost."

"Mr. John Leland was indeed his real name. And he was indeed an agent."

"Ah. Like you figured. Soviet?"

"No."

"American?"

"No."

"British?"

"By no means."

"Heck, Warren, I can't keep this up all trip. Wait a minute. He was working for that fellow Tal. He was an Israeli agent."

"No."

"All right, I give up. What kind of agent was he?"

"A *literary* agent."

"A what?"

"A literary agent. The cleverest, most ruthless, most persistent of all. His ploy in enlisting you, the message, the contacts in Europe, the false trails. All were part of a scheme to secure Dr. Borkin's memoirs, the story of the suppression of freedom in the Soviet Union. For publication in the United States in hard-cover, soft-cover, book club, serialization, eventually television, motion pictures, and foreign rights. Arnold, there was a great deal at stake in this."

"How . . . ?"

"Something about the name rang a bell. Out of my Hollywood years. I don't know—a novel optioned, a letter about a short story. Look." He showed the opened directory to the dentist.

Wicker squinted at the small print. Bettenhausen had made a check mark against a name. The heading was *Literary Agents*—Wicker was amazed to learn there were so many in New York—and halfway down the list appeared:

Leland & Leland 580 Fifth Ave . . . . . CI 5-5500

"You're sure?" Wicker asked.

"Positive." A look of satisfaction settled over Bettenhausen's face. The beard seemed to give off sparks. "I shall call on Mr. Leland and negotiate in Dr. Borkin's behalf. I want nothing for myself, Arnold, nor, would I imagine, do you. But I intend to make sure that Borkin is rewarded. As my fellow conspirator do you agree?"

"Whatever you say, Warren." Wicker was dazed. It was too much for him, a world he did not know. He took out his address book.

"Warren," the dentist said, "Rosie and I want your address and phone number in California. How can we reach you?"

Bettenhausen's voice assumed a prairie twang. He leaned back in the seat. "Wherever there's a fight so hungry people can eat, I'll be there."

"What?"

"Wherever there's a cop beatin' up a guy I'll be there."

"Now cut that out, Warren," Wicker protested. "You know I'm no good at that game."

"Very well, my boy. It'll be my last until we meet again in Sherman Oaks."

"No offense, Warren. I've enjoyed listening to you."

"Good." He folded his hands on his paunch. "Henry Fonda as Tom Joad. *The Grapes of Wrath.*"

DATE DUE			
OCT 9			
DEC 17 '79			
OC 17 '83			